Henry Cary

Herodotus

Anatiposi

Henry Cary

Herodotus

Reprint of the original, first published in 1872.

1st Edition 2023 | ISBN: 978-3-38212-767-1

Anatiposi Verlag is an imprint of Outlook Verlagsgesellschaft mbH.

Verlag (Publisher): Outlook Verlag GmbH, Zeilweg 44, 60439 Frankfurt, Deutschland
Vertretungsberechtigt (Authorized to represent): E. Roepke, Zeilweg 44, 60439 Frankfurt, Deutschland
Druck (Print): Books on Demand GmbH, In de Tarpen 42, 22848 Norderstedt, Deutschland

HERODOTUS.

A NEW AND LITERAL VERSION

From the Text of Baehr.

WITH

A GEOGRAPHICAL AND GENERAL INDEX.

BY HENRY CARY, M.A.,
WORCESTER COLLEGE, OXFORD.

NEW YORK:
HARPER & BROTHERS, PUBLISHERS,
FRANKLIN SQUARE.
1872.

TRANSLATOR'S PREFACE.

WHOEVER wishes to become acquainted with the history of the times and countries of which Herodotus wrote, will read his writings either in the original, or some translation which may be found to represent his meaning with the greatest fidelity. Those who wish to acquire a knowledge of the author himself, other than that which they may glean from incidental remarks in his history, will have recourse to some one of the authors who have given an account of his life and writings. These are so numerous, and so easy of access, that it seems unnecessary, by adding to their number, to increase the bulk of the present volume.

It will be sufficient to inform the student in what respect the present translation professes to differ from those which have preceded it. Five have, at intervals, made their appearance. The first was that by Beloc, which, though flowing and easy in style, was rather a translation from an indifferent French version than from the original Greek. The second, by Littlebury, was a poor rendering from a bad Latin version. The third was a revision of Littlebury's translation, bearing the appearance of having been made by one who, though he understood his author, contented himself with merely removing Littlebury's grosser faults, without attempting to correct him uniformly and throughout. The fourth and most elegant version was that by Mr. Isaac Taylor; which, however, has met with less notice than its merit deserves, probably owing to the circumstance that the usually received division by chapters has been departed from, whereby the facility of reference has been much diminished, and also because, in too many instances, the translator has sacrificed the meaning of his author to purity of thought or elegance of diction. The last English version was that by Laurent, in making which the translator labored under the twofold disadvantage of being an inaccurate Greek scholar, and a far worse English one. Nor can the present translator hope to be free from some defect, equal perhaps in extent to those which he has pointed out in his predecessors. His object, however, has been to keep as closely to the sense of his author as the idioms of the two languages would allow. He has adopted throughout the readings of Baehr, and, except in some few instances, which are pointed out in the notes, his interpretation also. H. C.

Oxford, Nov. 10th, 1847.

HERODOTUS.

BOOK I. CLIO.

THIS is a publication of the researches of Herodotus of Halicarnassus, in order that the actions of men may not be effaced by time, nor the great and wondrous deeds displayed both by Greeks and barbarians[1] deprived of renown; and among the rest, for what cause they waged war upon each other.

1. The learned among the Persians assert that the Phœnicians were the original authors of the quarrel; for that they having migrated from that which is called the Red Sea to the Mediterranean,[2] and having settled in the country which they now inhabit, forthwith applied themselves to distant voyages; and that having exported Egyptian and Assyrian merchandise, they touched at other places, and also at Argos. Now Argos at that period in every respect surpassed all those states which are now comprehended under the general appellation of Greece.[3] *They say* that on their arrival at Argos, the Phœnicians exposed their merchandise to sale, and that on the fifth or sixth day after their arrival, and when

[1] By barbarians the Greeks meant all who were not sprung from themselves—all foreigners.

[2] The Phœnicians passed over land (see b. VII. c. 89) from the Red Sea to the Mediterranean, which in the text and in other Grecian writers is called "*this* sea."

[3] The region known by the name of Hellas or Greece in the time of Herodotus was, previous to the Trojan war, and indeed long afterward, only discriminated by the names of its different inhabitants. Homer speaks of the Danaans, Argives, Achaians, &c., but never gives these people the general name of Greeks.—*Larcher*.

they had almost disposed of their cargo, a great number of women came down to the sea-shore, and among them the king's daughter, whose name, as the Greeks also say, was Io, daughter of Inachus. *They add*, that while these women were standing near the stern of the vessel, and were bargaining for such things as most pleased them, the Phœnicians, having exhorted one another, made an attack upon them; and that most of the women escaped, but that Io, with some others, was seized; and that they, having hurried them on board, set sail for Egypt. 2. Thus the Persians say that Io went to Egypt, not agreeing *herein* with the Phœnicians; and that this was the beginning of wrongs. After this, that certain Grecians (for they are unable to tell their name), having touched at Tyre in Phœnicia, carried off the king's daughter Europa. These must have been Cretans. Thus far they say that they had only retaliated;[4] but that after this the Greeks were guilty of the second provocation; for that having sailed down in a vessel of war[5] to Æa, a city of Colchis on the river Phasis, when they had accomplished the more immediate object of their expedition, they carried off the king's daughter Medea; and that the king of Colchis, having dispatched a herald to Greece, demanded satisfaction for the rape, and the restitution of the princess; but the Greeks replied, that as they of Asia had not given any satisfaction for the rape of Io, neither would they give any to them. 3. They say, too, that in the second generation after this, Alexander, the son of Priam, having heard of these events, was desirous of obtaining a wife from Greece by means of violence, being fully persuaded that he should not have to give satisfaction, for that the Greeks had not done so. When, therefore, he had carried off Helen, *they say* that the Greeks immediately sent messengers to demand her back again, and require satisfaction for the rape; but that they, when they brought forward these demands, objected to them the rape of Medea; "that they who had not themselves given satisfaction, nor made it when demanded, now wished others to give it to themselves." 4. Thus far then *they say* that there had only been rapes from each other; but that after this the Greeks were greatly

[4] Literally, "had only done like for like."

[5] "In a long vessel." The long vessels were vessels of war; the round vessels, merchantmen and transports.

to blame, for that they levied war against Asia before the Asiatics did upon Europe. Now, to carry off women by violence the Persians think is the act of wicked men, but to trouble one's self about avenging them when so carried off is the act of foolish ones; and to pay no regard to them when carried off, of wise men: for that it is clear, that if they had not been willing, they could not have been carried off. Accordingly, the Persians say, that they of Asia made no account of women that were carried off; but that the Greeks for the sake of a Lacedæmonian woman assembled a mighty fleet, and then having come to Asia overthrew the empire of Priam. That from this event they had always considered the Greeks as their enemies: for the Persians claim Asia and the barbarous nations that inhabit it as their own, and consider Europe and the people of Greece as totally distinct.

5. Such is the Persian account; and to the capture of Troy they ascribe the commencement of their enmity to the Greeks. As relates to Io, the Phœnicians do not agree with this account of the Persians: for they affirm that they did not use violence to carry her into Egypt; but that she had connection at Argos with the master of a vessel, and when she found herself pregnant, she, through dread of her parents, voluntarily sailed away with the Phœnicians, to avoid detection. Such then are the accounts of the Persians and Phœnicians: I, however, am not going to inquire whether the facts were so or not; but having pointed out the person whom I myself know to have been the first guilty of injustice toward the Greeks, I will then proceed with my history, touching as well on the small as the great estates of men: for of those that were formerly powerful many have become weak, and some that were powerful in my time were formerly weak. Knowing therefore the precarious nature of human prosperity, I shall commemorate both alike.

6. Crœsus was a Lydian by birth, son of Alyattes, and sovereign of the nations on this side the river Halys. This river flowing from the south[6] between the Syrians[7] and Paphlagonians, empties itself northward into the Euxine Sea. This Crœsus was the first of the barbarians whom we

[6] The Halys had two branches, one flowing from the east, the other from the south: Herodotus speaks only of the southern one.

[7] Syria was at that time the name of Cappadocia. See I. 72.

know of that subjected some of the Greeks to the payment of tribute, and formed alliances with others. He subdued the Ionians and Æolians, and the Dorians settled in Asia, and he formed an alliance with the Lacedæmonians; but before the reign of Crœsus all the Greeks were free; for the incursion of the Cimmerians[8] into Ionia, which was before the time of Crœsus, was not for the purpose of subjecting states, but an irruption for plunder. 7. The government, which formerly belonged to the Heraclidæ, passed in the following manner to the family of Crœsus, who were called Mermnadæ. Candaules, whom the Greeks call Myrsilus, was tyrant of Sardis, and a descendant of Alcæus, son of Hercules. For Agron, son of Ninus, grandson of Belus, great-grandson of Alcæus, was the first of the Heraclidæ who became king of Sardis; and Candaules, son of Myrsus, was the last. They who ruled over this country before Agron were descendants of Lydus, sons of Atys, from whom this whole people, anciently called Mæonians, derived the name of Lydians. The Heraclidæ, descended from a female slave of Jardanus and Hercules, having been intrusted with the government by these princes, retained the supreme power in obedience to the declaration of an oracle: they reigned for twenty-two generations, a space of five hundred and five years, the son succeeding to the father to the time of Candaules, son of Myrsus. 8. This Candaules then was enamoured of his own wife, and being so, thought that she was by far the most beautiful of all women. Now being of this opinion — Gyges, son of Dascylus, one of his body-guard, happened to be his especial favorite, and to him Candaules confided his most important affairs, and moreover extolled the beauty of his wife in exaggerated terms. In lapse of time (for Candaules was fated to be miserable) he addressed Gyges as follows: "Gyges, as I think you do not believe me when I speak of my wife's beauty (for the ears of men are naturally more incredulous than their eyes), you must contrive to see her naked." But he, exclaiming loudly, answered, "Sire, what a shocking proposal do you make, bidding me behold my queen naked! With her clothes a woman puts off her modesty. Wise maxims have been of old laid down by men, from these it is our duty to learn: among them is the

[8] The incursion here spoken of occurred in the reign of the Lydian Ardys. See I. 15, and IV. 12.

following—'Let every man look to the things that concern himself.' I am persuaded that she is the most beautiful of her sex, but I entreat of you not to require what is wicked." 9. Saying thus, Gyges fought off the proposal, dreading lest some harm should befall himself; but the king answered, "Gyges, take courage, and be not afraid of me, as if I desired to make trial of you by speaking thus, nor of my wife, lest any harm should befall you from her. For from the outset I will so contrive that she shall not know she has been seen by you. I will place you behind the open door of the apartment in which we sleep; as soon as I enter, my wife will come to bed; there stands by the entrance a chair; on this she will lay her garments one by one as she takes them off, and then she will give you an opportunity to look at her at your leisure; but when she steps from the chair to the bed, and you are at her back, be careful that she does not see you as you are going out by the door." 10. Gyges therefore, finding he could not escape, prepared *to obey*. And Candaules, when it seemed to be time to go to bed, led him to the chamber, and the lady soon afterward appeared, and Gyges saw her enter and lay her clothes *on the chair:* when he was at her back, as the lady was going to the bed, he crept secretly out, but she saw him as he was going away. Perceiving what her husband had done, she neither cried out through modesty, nor appeared to notice it, purposing to take vengeance on Candaules; for among the Lydians and almost all the barbarians, it is deemed a great disgrace even for a man to be seen naked. 11. At the time, therefore, having shown no consciousness of what had occurred, she held her peace, and as soon as it was day, having prepared such of her domestics as she knew were most to be trusted, she sent for Gyges. He, supposing that she knew nothing of what had happened, came when he was sent for, for he had been before used to attend whenever the queen sent for him. When Gyges came, the lady thus addressed him: "Gyges, I submit two proposals to your choice: either kill Candaules and take possession of me and of the Lydian kingdom, or expect immediate death, so that you may not, from your obedience to Candaules in all things, again see what you ought not. It is necessary, however, that he who planned this, or that you who have seen me naked, and have done what is not decorous, should die. Gyges for a time was amazed at what he heard, but afterward he implored her not to compel him to make such a choice. He, however, could not persuade, but saw a necessity imposed on him either to kill his master Candaulès or die himself by the hands of others; he chose, therefore, to survive, and made the following inquiry: "Since you compel me to kill my master against my will, tell me how we shall lay hands on him." She answered, "The assault shall be made from the very spot whence he showed me naked; the attack shall be made on him while asleep." 12. When they had concerted their plan, on the approach of night he followed the lady to the chamber; then (for Gyges was not suffered to depart, nor was there any possibility of escape, but either he or Candaules must needs perish) she, having given him a dagger, concealed him behind the same door; and after this, when Candaules was asleep, Gyges having crept stealthily up and slain him, possessed himself both of the woman and the kingdom. Of this event, also, Archilochus[9] the Parian, who lived about the same time, has made mention in a trimeter Iambic poem. 13. Thus Gyges obtained the kingdom, and was confirmed in it by the oracle at Delphi. For when the Lydians resented the murder of Candaules, and were up in arms, the partisans of Gyges and the other Lydians came to the following agreement: that if the oracle should pronounce him king of the Lydians, he should reign; if not, he should restore the power to the Heraclidæ. The oracle, however, answered accordingly, and so Gyges became king. But the Pythian added this, "that the Heraclidæ should be avenged on the fifth descendant of Gyges."[1] Of this prediction neither the Lydians nor their kings took any notice until it was actually accomplished.

14. Thus the Mermnadæ, having deprived the Heraclidæ, possessed themselves of the supreme power. Gyges, having obtained the kingdom, sent many offerings to Delphi; for most of the silver offerings at Delphi are his; and besides the silver, he gave a vast quantity of gold; and among the rest, what is especially worthy of mention, the bowls of gold, six in number, were dedicated by him: these now stand in the

[9] Archilochus was one of the earliest writers of Iambics. All that remains of his is to be met with in Brunck's Analecta.

[1] See I. 91.

treasury of the Corinthians, and are thirty talents in weight; though, to say the truth, this treasury does not belong to the people of Corinth, but to Cypselus, son of Eetion. This Gyges is the first of the barbarians whom we know of that dedicated offerings at Delphi; except Midas, son of Gordius, king of Phrygia, for Midas dedicated the royal throne, on which he used to sit and administer justice, *a piece of workmanship* deserving of admiration. This throne stands in the same place as the bowls of Gyges. This gold and silver, which Gyges dedicated, is by the Delphians called Gygian, from the name of the donor. Now this prince, when he obtained the sovereignty, led an army against Miletus and Smyrna, and took the city of Colophon; but as he performed no other great action during his reign of eight-and-thirty years, we will pass him over, having made this mention of him. 15. I will proceed to mention Ardys, the son and successor of Gyges. He took Priene, and invaded Miletus. During the time that he reigned at Sardis, the Cimmerians, being driven from their seats by the Scythian nomades, passed into Asia, and possessed themselves of all Sardis except the citadel.

16. When Ardys had reigned forty-nine years, his son Sadyattes succeeded him, and reigned twelve years; and Alyattes succeeded Sadyattes. He made war upon Cyaxares, a descendant of Deioces, and upon the Medes. He drove the Cimmerians out of Asia; took Smyrna, which was founded from Colophon, and invaded Clazomenæ. From this place he departed, not as he could wish, but signally defeated. He also performed in the course of his reign the following actions worthy of mention. 17. He continued the war which his father had begun against the Milesians; and leading his army against Miletus, he invaded it in the following manner. When their fruits were ripe on the ground, he led his army into their territory, attended in his march with pipes, harps, and flutes, masculine and feminine. On his arrival in Milesia, he neither demolished nor burned their country houses, nor forced off the doors, but let them stand as they were; but when he had destroyed their trees and the fruits on the ground, he returned home; for the Milesians were masters of the sea, so that there was no use in the army's besieging it. And the Lydian king would not destroy their houses, for this reason, that the Milesians, having those habitations,

might come out to sow and cultivate the ground, and when they had cultivated it, he might have something to ravage when he should invade them with his army. 18. In this manner he carried on the war eleven years, during which the Milesians received two great blows, one in a battle at Limeneion in their own territory, the other in the plain of the Mæander. Six of these eleven years, Sadyattes, the son of Ardys, was still king of the Lydians, and during those he made incursions into the Milesian territory (for this Sadyattes was the person that began the war). But during the five years that succeeded the six, Alyattes, the son of Sadyattes, who (as I have before mentioned) received it from his father, earnestly applied himself to it. None of the Ionians, except the Chians, assisted the Milesians in bearing the burden of this war: they did it in requital for succor they had received; for formerly the Milesians had assisted the Chians in prosecuting the war against the Erythræans. 19. In the twelfth year, when the corn had been set on fire by the army, an accident of the following nature occurred. As soon as the corn had caught fire, the flames, carried by the wind, caught a temple of Minerva, called Assesian;[2] and the temple, thus set on fire, was burned to the ground. No notice was taken of this at the time; but afterward, when the army had returned to Sardis, Alyattes fell sick. When the disease continued a considerable time, he sent messengers to Delphi to consult the oracle, either from the advice of some friend, or because it appeared right to himself to send and make inquiries of the god concerning his disorder. The Pythian, however, refused to give any answer to the messengers when they arrived at Delphi, until they had rebuilt the temple of Minerva which they had burned at Assesus in the territory of Milesia. 20. This relation I had from the Delphians; but the Milesians add, that Periander, the son of Cypselus, who was a very intimate friend of Thrasybulus, at that time king of Miletus, having heard of the answer given to Alyattes, dispatched a messenger to inform him of it, in order that, being aware of it beforehand, he might form his plans according to present circumstances. This is the Milesian account. 21. Alyattes, when the above an-

[2] Assesus was a small town dependent on Miletus. Minerva had a temple there, and hence took the name of the Assesian Minerva.—*Larcher.*

swer was brought to him, immediately sent a herald to Miletus, desiring him to make a truce with Thrasybulus and the Milesians till such time as he should have rebuilt the temple. The herald accordingly went on this mission to Miletus. But Thrasybulus being accurately informed of the whole matter, and knowing the design of Alyattes, had recourse to the following artifice: having collected in the market-place all the corn that was in the city, both his own and what belonged to private persons, he made a proclamation, that when he gave the signal, all the inhabitants should feast together. 22. Thrasybulus contrived and ordered this, to the end that the Sardian herald, seeing so great a profusion of corn, and the people enjoying themselves, might report accordingly to Alyattes; and so it came to pass. For when the herald had seen these things, and delivered to Thrasybulus the message of the Lydian king, he returned to Sardis; and, as I am informed, a reconciliation was brought about for no other reason. For Alyattes expecting that there was a great scarcity of corn in Miletus, and that the people were reduced to extreme distress, received from the herald on his return from Miletus an account quite contrary to what he expected. Soon afterward a reconciliation took place between them, on terms of mutual friendship and alliance. And Alyattes built two temples to Minerva at Assesus instead of one, and himself recovered from sickness. Such were the circumstances of the war that Alyattes made against the Milesians and Thrasybulus.

23. Periander was the son of Cypselus—he it was who acquainted Thrasybulus with the answer of the oracle. Now Periander was king of Corinth, and the Corinthians say (and the Lesbians confirm their account) that a wonderful prodigy occurred in his life-time. *They say* that Arion of Methymna, who was second to none of his time in accompanying the harp, and who was the first, that we are acquainted with, who composed, named, and represented the dithyrambus at Corinth, was carried to Tænarus on the back of a dolphin. 24. They say that this Arion, having continued a long time with Periander, was desirous of making a voyage to Italy and Sicily; and that having acquired great wealth, he determined to return to Corinth: that he set out from Tarentum, and hired a ship of certain Corinthians, because he put

more confidence in them than in any other nation; but that these men, when they were in the open sea, conspired together to throw him overboard and seize his money, and he being aware of this, offered them his money, and entreated them to spare his life. However, he could not prevail on them; but the sailors ordered him either to kill himself, that he might be buried ashore, or to leap immediately into the sea. *They add* that Arion, reduced to this strait, entreated them, since such was their determination, to permit him to stand on the poop in his full dress and sing, and he promised when he had sung to make away with himself. The seamen, pleased that they should hear the best singer in the world, retired from the stern to the middle of the vessel. *They relate* that Arion, having put on all his robes, and taken his harp, stood on the rowing benches and went through the Orthian strain; that when the strain was ended he leaped into the sea as he was, in his full dress; and the sailors continued their voyage to Corinth: but they say that a dolphin received him on his back, and carried him to Tænarus; and that he, having landed, proceeded to Corinth in his full dress, and upon his arrival there, related all that had happened; but that Periander, giving no credit to his relation, put Arion under close confinement, and watched anxiously for the seamen: that when they appeared, he summoned them, and inquired if they could give any account of Arion; but when they answered that he was safe in Italy, and that they had left him flourishing at Tarentum, Arion in that instant appeared before them just as he was when he leaped into the sea; at which they were so astonished, that being fully convicted, they could no longer deny the fact. These things are reported by the Corinthians and Lesbians; and there is a small brazen statue of Arion at Tænarus, representing a man sitting on a dolphin.

25. Alyattes the Lydian, having waged this long war against the Milesians, afterward died, when he had reigned fifty-seven years. On his recovery from sickness, he was the second son of his family that dedicated at Delphi a large silver bowl, with a saucer of iron inlaid; an object that deserves attention above all the offerings at Delphi. It was made by Glaucus the Chian, who first invented the art of inlaying iron.

26. After the death of Alyattes, his son Crœsus, who was then thirty-five years of age, succeeded to the kingdom.

He attacked the Ephesians before any other Grecian people. The Ephesians then being besieged by him, consecrated their city to Diana, by fastening a rope from the temple to the wall. The distance between the old town, which was then besieged, and the temple, is seven stadia. Crœsus then attacked these the first, and afterward the several cities of the Ionians and Æolians one after another, alleging different pretenses against different states, imputing graver charges against those in whom he was able to discover greater causes of blame, and against some of them alleging frivolous pretenses. 27. After he had reduced the Grecians in Asia to the payment of tribute, he formed a design to build ships and attack the Islanders. But when all things were ready for the building of ships, Bias of Priene (or, as others say, Pittacus of Mitylene), arriving at Sardis, put a stop to his ship-building by making this reply, when Crœsus inquired if he had any news from Greece: "O king, the Islanders are enlisting a large body of cavalry, with intention to make war upon you and Sardis." Crœsus, thinking he had spoken the truth, said, "May the gods put such a thought into the Islanders, as to attack the sons of the Lydians with horse." The other answering said, "Sire, you appear to wish above all things to see the Islanders on horseback upon the continent; and not without reason. But what can you imagine the Islanders more earnestly desire, after having heard of your resolution to build a fleet in order to attack them, than to catch the Lydians at sea, that they may revenge on you the cause of those Greeks who dwell on the continent, whom you hold in subjection?" *It is related* that Crœsus was very much pleased with the conclusion, and that being convinced (for he appeared to speak to the purpose), he put a stop to the ship-building, and made an alliance with the Ionians that inhabit the islands.

28. In course of time, when nearly all the nations that dwell within the river Halys, except the Cilicians and Lycians, were subdued; for Crœsus held all the rest in subjection: and they were the following, the Lydians, Phrygians, Mysians, Mariandynians, Chalybians, Paphlagonians, Thracians, both the Thynians and Bithynians, Carians, Ionians, Dorians, Æolians, and Pamphylians. 29. When these nations were subdued, and Crœsus had added them to the Lydians, all the other wise men of that time, as each had oppor-

tunity, came from Greece to Sardis, which had then attained to the highest degree of prosperity; and among them Solon, an Athenian, who, having made laws for the Athenians at their request, absented himself for ten years, having sailed away under pretense of seeing the world, that he might not be compelled to abrogate any of the laws he had established; for the Athenians could not do it themselves, since they were bound by solemn oaths to observe for ten years whatever laws Solon should enact for them. 30. Solon therefore, having gone abroad for these reasons, and for the purposes of observation, arrived in Egypt at the court of Amasis, and afterward at that of Crœsus at Sardis. On his arrival he was hospitably entertained by Crœsus, and on the third or fourth day, by order of the king, the attendants conducted him round the treasury, and showed him all their grand and costly contents; and when he had seen and examined every thing sufficiently, Crœsus asked him this question: "My Athenian guest, your great fame has reached even to us, as well of your wisdom as of your travels, how that as a philosopher you have traveled through various countries for the purpose of observation; I am therefore desirous of asking you, who is the most happy man you have seen?" He asked this question, because he thought himself the most happy of men. But Solon, speaking the truth freely, without any flattery, answered, "Tellus the Athenian." Crœsus, astonished at his answer, eagerly[a] asked him, "On what account do you deem Tellus the happiest?" He replied, "Tellus, in the first place, lived in a well-governed commonwealth; had sons who were virtuous and good; and he saw children born to them all, and all surviving: in the next place, when he had lived as happily as the condition of human affairs will permit, he ended his life in a most glorious manner; for, coming to the assistance of the Athenians in a battle with their neighbors of Eleusis, he put the enemy to flight, and died nobly. The Athenians buried him at the public charge in the place where he fell, and honored him greatly."

31. When Solon had roused the attention of Crœsus by relating many and happy circumstances concerning Tellus, Crœsus, expecting at least to obtain the second place, asked

[a] Ἐπιστρεφέως. Baehr translates it *accuraté, diligenter.*

33. When he spoke thus to Crœsus, Crœsus did not confer any favor on him, and holding him in no account, dismissed him; since he considered him a very ignorant man, because he overlooked present prosperity, and bade men look to the end of every thing.

34. After the departure of Solon, the indignation of the gods fell heavy upon Crœsus, probably because he thought himself the most happy of all men. A dream soon after visited him while sleeping, which pointed out to him the truth of the misfortunes that were about to befall him in the person of one of his sons. For Crœsus had two sons, of whom one was grievously afflicted, for he was dumb; but the other, whose name was Atys, far surpassed all the young men of his age. Now the dream intimated to Crœsus that he would lose this Atys by a wound inflicted by the point of an iron weapon; he, when he awoke, and had considered the matter with himself, dreading the dream, provided a wife for his son; and though he was accustomed to command the Lydian troops, he did not ever after send him out on that business; and causing all spears, lances, and such other weapons as men use in war, to be removed from the men's apartments, he had them laid up in private chambers, that none of them, being suspended, might fall upon his son. 35. While Crœsus was engaged with the nuptials of his son, a man oppressed by misfortune, and whose hands were polluted, a Phrygian by birth, and of royal family, arrived at Sardis. This man, having come to the palace of Crœsus, sought permission to obtain purification according to the custom of the country. Crœsus purified him (now the manner of expiation is nearly the same among the Lydians and the Greeks); and when he had performed the usual ceremonies, Crœsus inquired whence he came, and who he was; speaking to him as follows: "Stranger, who art thou, and from what part of Phrygia hast thou come as a suppliant to my hearth? and what man or woman hast thou slain?" The stranger answered, "Sire, I am the son of Gordius, son of Midas, and am called Adrastus; having unwittingly slain my own brother, and being banished by my father and deprived of every thing, I am come hither." Crœsus answered as follows: "You are born of parents who are our friends, and you are come to friends among whom, if you will stay, you shall want nothing; and by bearing your misfortune as lightly as possi-

ble, you will be the greatest gainer." So Adrastus took up his abode in the palace of Crœsus.

36. At this same time a boar of enormous size appeared in Mysian Olympus, and rushing down from that mountain, ravaged the fields of the Mysians. The Mysians, though they often went out against him, could not hurt him, but suffered much from him. At last deputies from the Mysians having come to Crœsus, spoke as follows: "O king, a boar of enormous size has appeared in our country, and ravages our fields: though we have often endeavored to take him, we can not. We therefore earnestly beg that you would send with us your son, and some chosen youths with dogs, that we may drive him from the country." Such was their entreaty, but Crœsus, remembering the warning of his dream, answered, "Make no further mention of my son; for I shall not send him with you, because he is lately married, and that now occupies his attention; but I will send with you chosen Lydians, and the whole hunting train, and will order them to assist you with their best endeavors in driving the monster from your country." 37. Such was his answer; and when the Mysians were content with this, the son of Crœsus, who had heard of their request, came in; and when Crœsus refused to send him with them, the youth thus addressed him: "Father, in time past I was permitted to signalize myself in the two most noble and becoming exercises of war and hunting; but now you keep me excluded from both, without having observed in me either cowardice or want of spirit. How will men look on me when I go or return from the forum? What kind of man shall I appear to my fellow-citizens? What to my newly-married wife? What kind of man will she think she has for a partner? Either suffer me, then, to go to this hunt, or convince me that it is better for me to do as you would have me." 38. "My son," answered Crœsus, "I act thus, not because I have seen any cowardice, or any thing else unbecoming in you; but a vision in a dream appearing to me in my sleep warned me that you would be short-lived, and would die by the point of an iron weapon. On account of this vision, therefore, I hastened your marriage, and now refuse to send you on this expedition; taking care to preserve you, if by any means I can, as long as I live; for you are my only son; the other, who is deprived of his hearing, I consider as lost." 39. The youth answered, "You

are not to blame, my father, if after such a dream you take so much care of me; but it is right for me to explain that which you do not comprehend, and which has escaped your notice in the dream. You say the dream signified that I should die by the point of an iron weapon. But what hand, or what pointed iron weapon has a boar, to occasion such fears in you? Had it said I should lose my life by a tusk, or something of like nature, you ought then to have done as you now do; whereas *it said* by the point of a weapon; since, then, we have not to contend against men, let me go." 40. "You have surpassed me," replied Crœsus, "in explaining the import of the dream; therefore, being overcome by you, I change my resolution, and permit you to go to the chase."

41. Crœsus, having thus spoken, sent for the Phrygian Adrastus, and, when he came, addressed him as follows: "Adrastus, I purified you when smitten by a grievous misfortune, which I do not upbraid you with, and have received you into my house, and supplied you with every thing necessary. Now, therefore (for it is your duty to requite me with kindness, since I have first conferred a kindness on you), I beg you would be my son's guardian, when he goes to the chase, and take care that no skulking villains show themselves in the way to do him harm. Besides, you ought to go for your own sake, where you may signalize yourself by your exploits; for this was the glory of your ancestors, and you are, besides, in full vigor." 42. Adrastus answered, "On no other account, sire, would I have taken part in this enterprise; for it is not fitting that one in my unfortunate circumstances should join with his prosperous compeers, nor do I desire to do so; and, indeed, I have often restrained myself. Now, however, since you urge me, and I ought to oblige you, for I am bound to requite the benefits you have conferred on me, I am ready to do as you desire; and rest assured that your son, whom you bid me take care of, shall, as far as his guardian is concerned, return to you uninjured."

43. When Adrastus had made this answer to Crœsus, they went away, well provided with chosen youths and dogs: and, having arrived at Mount Olympus, they sought the wild beast, and having found him and encircled him around, they hurled their javelins at him. Among the rest, the stranger, the same that had been purified of murder, named Adrastus,

throwing his javelin at the boar, missed him, and struck the son of Crœsus: thus he being wounded by the point of the lance, fulfilled the warning of the dream. Upon this, some one ran off to tell Crœsus what had happened, and, having arrived at Sardis, gave him an account of the action, and of his son's fate. 44. Crœsus, exceedingly distressed by the death of his son, lamented it the more bitterly, because he fell by the hand of one whom he himself had purified from blood; and vehemently deploring his misfortune, he invoked Jove the Expiator, attesting what he had suffered by this stranger. He invoked, also, the same deity, by the name of the god of hospitality and private friendship: as the god of hospitality, because, by receiving a stranger into his house, he had unawares fostered the murderer of his son; as the god of private friendship, because, having sent him as a guardian, he found him his greatest enemy. 45. After this, the Lydians approached, bearing the corpse, and behind it followed the murderer. He, having advanced in front of the corpse, delivered himself up to Crœsus, stretching forth his hands and begging of him to kill him upon it; then relating his former misfortune, and how, in addition to that, he had destroyed his purifier, and that he ought to live no longer. When Crœsus heard this, though his own affliction was so great, he pitied Adrastus, and said to him, "You have made me full satisfaction by condemning yourself to die. But you are not the author of this misfortune, except as far as you were the involuntary agent; but that god, whoever he was, that long since foreshowed what was about to happen." Crœsus therefore buried his son as the dignity of his birth required; but Adrastus, son of Gordius, son of Midas, who had been the murderer of his own brother, and the murderer of his purifier, when all was silent round the tomb, judging himself the most heavily afflicted of all men, killed himself on the tomb. But Crœsus, bereaved of his son, continued disconsolate for two years.

46. Some time after, the overthrow of the kingdom of Astyages, son of Cyaxares, by Cyrus, son of Cambyses, and the growing power of the Persians, put an end to the grief of Crœsus; and it entered into his thoughts whether he could by any means check the growing power of the Persians before they became formidable. After he had formed this purpose, he determined to make trial as well of the oracles in

Greece as of that in Libya; and sent different persons to different places, some to Delphi, some to Abæ of Phocis, and some to Dodona; others were sent to Amphiaraus and Trophonius, and others to Branchidæ of Milesia: these were the Grecian oracles to which Crœsus sent to consult. He sent others also to consult that of Ammon in Libya. And he sent them different ways, designing to make trial of what the oracles knew; in order that if they should be found to know the truth, he might send a second time to inquire whether he should venture to make war on the Persians. 47. He dispatched them to make trial of the oracles with the following orders: that, computing the days from the time of their departure from Sardis, they should consult the oracles on the hundredth day, by asking what Crœsus, son of Alyattes and king of the Lydians, was then doing; and that they should bring him the answer of each oracle in writing. Now what were the answers given by the other oracles is mentioned by none; but no sooner had the Lydians entered the temple of Delphi to consult the god, and asked the question enjoined them, than the Pythian thus spoke in hexameter verse: "I know the number of the sands, and the measure of the sea; I understand the dumb, and hear him that does not speak; the savor of the hard-shelled tortoise boiled in brass with the flesh of lamb strikes on my senses; brass is laid beneath it, and brass is put over it." 48. The Lydians, having written down this answer of the Pythian, returned to Sardis. And when the rest, who had been sent to other places, arrived bringing the answers, Crœsus, having opened each of them, examined their contents; but none of them pleased him. When, however, he heard that from Delphi, he immediately adored it, and approved of it, being convinced that the oracle at Delphi alone was a real oracle, because it had discovered what he had done. For when he had sent persons to consult the different oracles, watching the appointed day, he had recourse to the following contrivance: having thought of what it was impossible to discover or guess at, he cut up a tortoise and a lamb, and boiled them himself together in a brazen caldron, and put on it a cover of brass. 49. Such, then, was the answer given to Crœsus from Delphi: as regards the answer of the oracle of Amphiaraus, I can not say what answer it gave to the Lydians, who performed the accustomed rites at the temple; for nothing else is related than that he considered this also to be a true oracle.

50. After this he endeavored to propitiate the god at Delphi by magnificent sacrifices; for he offered three thousand head of cattle of every kind fit for sacrifice, and having heaped up a great pile, he burned on it beds of gold and silver, vials of gold, and robes of purple and garments, hoping by that means more completely to conciliate the god; he also ordered all the Lydians to offer to the god whatever he was able. When the sacrifice was ended, having melted down a vast quantity of gold, he cast half-bricks from it; of which the longest were six palms in length, the shortest three, and in thickness one palm: their number was one hundred and seventeen: four of these, of pure gold, weighed each two talents and a half; the other half-bricks of pale gold weighed two talents each. He made also the figure of a lion of fine gold, weighing ten talents. This lion, when the temple of Delphi was burned down, fell from the half-bricks, for it had been placed on them, and it now lies in the treasury of the Corinthians, weighing six talents and a half; for three talents and a half were melted from it. 51. Crœsus, having finished these things, sent them to Delphi, and with them these following: two large bowls, one of gold, the other of silver: that of gold was placed on the right hand as one enters the temple, and that of silver on the left; but these also were removed when the temple was burned down; and the golden one, weighing eight talents and a half and twelve minæ, is placed in the treasury of Clazomenæ; the silver one, containing six hundred amphoræ, lies in a corner of the vestibule, and is used by the Delphians for mixing the wine on the Theophanian festival. The Delphians say it was the workmanship of Theodorus the Samian; and I think so too, for it appears to be no common work. He also sent four casks of silver, which stand in the treasury of the Corinthians; and he dedicated two lustral vases, one of gold, the other of silver: on the golden one is an inscription, OF THE LACEDÆMONIANS, who say that it was their offering, but wrongfully, for this also was given by Crœsus: a certain Delphian made the inscription, in order to please the Lacedæmonians; I know his name, but forbear to mention it. The boy, indeed, through whose hand the water flows, is their

gift; but neither of the lustral vases. At the same time Crœsus sent many other offerings without an inscription: among them some round silver covers; and, moreover, a statue of a woman in gold three cubits high, which the Delphians say is the image of Crœsus's baking-woman; and to all these things he added the necklaces and girdles of his wife.

52. These were the offerings he sent to Delphi; and to Amphiaraus, having ascertained his virtue and sufferings, he dedicated a shield all of gold, and a lance of solid gold, the shaft as well as the points being of gold; and these are at Thebes, in the temple of Ismenian Apollo.

53. To the Lydians appointed to convey these presents to the temples, Crœsus gave it in charge to inquire of the oracles whether he should make war on the Persians, and if he should unite any other nation as an ally. Accordingly, when the Lydians arrived at the places to which they were sent, and had dedicated the offerings, they consulted the oracles, saying, "Crœsus, king of the Lydians and of other nations, esteeming these to be the only oracles among men, sends these presents in acknowledgment of your discoveries; and now asks whether he should lead an army against the Persians, and whether he should join any auxiliary forces with his own." Such were their questions; and the opinions of both oracles concurred, foretelling "that if Crœsus should make war on the Persians, he would destroy a mighty empire;" and they advised him to engage the most powerful of the Grecians in his alliance. 54. When Crœsus heard the answers that were brought back, he was beyond measure delighted with the oracles; and fully expecting that he should destroy the kingdom of Cyrus, he again sent to Delphi, and having ascertained the number of the inhabitants, presented each of them with two staters of gold. In return for this, the Delphians gave Crœsus and the Lydians the right to consult the oracle before any others, and exemption from tribute, and the first seats in the temple, and the privilege of being made citizens of Delphi to as many as should desire it in all future time. 55. Crœsus, having made these presents to the Delphians, sent a third time to consult the oracle; for, after he had ascertained the veracity of the oracle, he had frequent recourse to it. His demand now was, whether he should long enjoy the king-

dom? to which the Pythian gave this answer: "When a mule shall become king of the Medes, then, tender-footed Lydian, flee over pebbly Hermus, nor tarry, nor blush to be a coward."
56. With this answer, when reported to him, Crœsus was more than ever delighted, thinking that a mule should never be king of the Medes instead of a man, and consequently that neither he nor his posterity should ever be deprived of the kingdom. In the next place, he began to inquire carefully who were the most powerful of the Greeks whom he might gain over as allies; and on inquiry, found that the Lacedæmonians and Athenians excelled the rest, the former being of Dorian, the latter of Ionic descent; for these were in ancient time the most distinguished, the latter being a Pelasgian, the other an Hellenic nation; the latter had never emigrated, but the former had very often changed their seat; for under the reign of Deucalion they inhabited the country of Phthiotis; and in the time of Dorus, the son of Hellen, the country at the foot of Ossa and Olympus, called Histiæotis: when they were driven out of Histiæotis by the Cadmæans, they settled on Mount Pydnus, at a place called Macednum; thence they again removed to Dryopis; and at length, coming into Peloponnesus, were called Dorians.

57. What language the Pelasgians used I can not with certainty affirm; but, if I may form a conjecture from those Pelasgians who now exist, and who now inhabit the town of Crestona above the Tyrrhenians, and who were formerly neighbors to those now called Dorians, and at that time occupied the country at present called Thessaliotis; and *if I may conjecture* from those Pelasgians settled at Placia and Scylace on the Hellespont, and who once dwelt with the Athenians,[5] and whatever other cities, which, though really Pelasgian, have changed their name; if, I say, I may be permitted to conjecture from these, the Pelasgians spoke a barbarous language. And if the whole Pelasgian body did so, the Attic race, being Pelasgic, must, at the time they changed into Hellenes, have altered their language; for neither do the Crestonians use the same language with any of their neighbors, nor do the people of Placia, but both use the same language; by which it appears they have taken care to pre-

[5] For the reason of their separation, see VI. 137.

serve the character of the language they brought with them into those places. 58. The Hellenic race, however, as appears to me, from the time they became a people, have used the same language; though, when separated from the Pelasgians, they were at first insignificant, yet from a small beginning they have increased to a multitude of nations, chiefly by a union with many other barbarous nations. Wherefore it appears to me that the Pelasgic race, being barbarous, never increased to any great extent.

59. Of these nations, then, Crœsus learned that the Attic was oppressed and distracted by Pisistratus, son of Hippocrates, then reigning in Athens: to this Hippocrates, who was at the time a private person, and a spectator at the Olympian games, a great prodigy occurred; for having killed a victim, the caldrons, which were full of flesh and water, bubbled up without any fire, and boiled over. Chilon the Lacedæmonian, who was accidentally there, and saw the prodigy, advised Hippocrates, first of all, not to marry any woman by whom he might have children; or, if he was already married, then to put away his wife; and if he happened to have a son, to disown him. However, Hippocrates, when Chilon gave this advice, would not be persuaded, and had afterward this same Pisistratus; who, when a quarrel happened between those who dwelt on the sea-coast and the Athenians, the former headed by Megacles, son of Alcmæon, the latter by Lycurgus, son of Aristolaides, aiming at the sovereign power, formed a third party; and having assembled his partisans under color of protecting those of the mountains, he contrived this stratagem. Having wounded himself and his mules, he drove his chariot into the public square, as if he had escaped from enemies that designed to murder him in his way to the country, and besought the people to grant him a guard, having before acquired renown in the expedition against Megara by taking Nisæa,[6] and displaying other illustrious deeds. The people of Athens, being deceived by this, gave him such of the citizens as he selected, who were not to be his javelin men, but club-bearers, for they attended him with clubs of wood. These men, therefore, joining in revolt with Pisistratus, seized the Acropolis, and thereupon Pisistratus assumed the government of the Atheni-

[6] Nisæa was the port of the Megarians, about two miles from the city.

ans, neither disturbing the existing magistracies, nor altering the laws; but he administered the government according to the established institutions, ordering it liberally and well. 60. Not long after, the partisans of Megacles and Lycurgus, being reconciled, drove him out. In this manner Pisistratus first made himself master of Athens, and, his power not being very firmly rooted, lost it. But those who expelled Pisistratus quarreled anew with one another; and Megacles, harassed by the sedition, sent a herald to Pisistratus to ask if he was willing to marry his daughter on condition of having the sovereignty. Pisistratus having accepted the proposal and agreed to his terms, in order to his restitution, they contrive the most ridiculous project that, I think, was ever imagined, especially *if we consider* that the Greeks have from old been distinguished from the barbarians as being more acute and free from all foolish simplicity, and more particularly as they played this trick upon the Athenians, who are esteemed among the wisest of the Grecians. In the Pæanean tribe was a woman named Phya, four cubits high, wanting three fingers, and in other respects handsome; having dressed this woman in a complete suit of armor, and placed her on a chariot, and having shown her beforehand how to assume the most becoming demeanor, they drove her to the city, having sent heralds before, who, on their arrival in the city, proclaimed what was ordered in these terms: "O Athenians, receive with kind wishes Pisistratus, whom Minerva herself, honoring above all men, now conducts back to her own citadel." Then they went about proclaiming this; and a report was presently spread among the people that Minerva was bringing back Pisistratus; and the people in the city, believing this woman to be the goddess, both adored a human being and received Pisistratus.

61. Pisistratus, having recovered the sovereignty in the manner above described, married the daughter of Megacles in accordance with his agreement. But as he already had grown-up sons, and as the Alcmæonidæ were said to be under a curse,[7] he, wishing not to have any children by his newly-married wife, had intercourse with her unnaturally. The woman at first kept the thing a secret, but afterward, whether ques-

[7] See the cause of this, B. V. 71.

tioned by her mother or not, she discovered it to her, and she to her husband. He felt highly indignant at being dishonored by Pisistratus, and in his rage instantly reconciled himself to those of the opposite faction;[8] but Pisistratus, hearing of the designs that were being formed against him, withdrew entirely out of the country, and arriving in Eretria,[9] consulted with his sons. The opinion of Hippias prevailing, to recover the kingdom, they immediately began to collect contributions from those cities which felt any gratitude to them for benefits received; and though many gave large sums, the Thebans surpassed the rest in liberality. At length (not to give a detailed account) time passed, and every thing was ready for their return, for Argive mercenaries arrived from Peloponnesus; and a man of Naxos, named Lygdamis, who had come as a volunteer, and brought both men and money, showed great zeal in the cause. 62. Having set out from Eretria, they came back in the eleventh year of their exile, and first of all possessed themselves of Marathon. While they lay encamped in this place, both their partisans from the city joined them, and others from the various districts, to whom a tyranny was more welcome than liberty, crowded to them; thus they were collected together. The Athenians of the city, on the other hand, had shown very little concern all the time Pisistratus was collecting money, or even when he took possession of Marathon. But when they heard that he was marching from Marathon against the city, they at length went out to resist him; so they marched with their whole force against the invaders. In the mean time Pisistratus's party, having set out from Marathon, advanced toward the city, and arrived in a body at the temple of the Pallenian[1] Minerva, and there took up their position. Here Amphilytus, a prophet of Acarnania, moved by divine impulse, approached Pisistratus, and pronounced this oracle in hexameter verse: "The cast is thrown, and the net is spread; by the moonlight the tunnies will rush in."

[8] Schweighæuser translates it "to his former partisans." See *Cary's Lexicon to Herodotus*.

[9] There were two places of this name, one in Thessaly and another in Eubœa. Pisistratus retired to this last.—*Larcher*.

[1] Pallene was the name of one of the boroughs of Attica, belonging to the tribe Antiochides, on the road from Marathon to Athens.

63. He, inspired by the god, uttered this prophecy; and Pisistratus, comprehending the oracle, and saying he accepted the omen, led on his army. The Athenians of the city were then engaged at their breakfast, and some of them, after breakfast, had betaken themselves to dice, others to sleep; so that the army of Pisistratus, falling upon them by surprise, soon put them to flight; and as they were flying, Pisistratus contrived a clever stratagem to prevent their rallying again, and that they might be thoroughly dispersed. He mounted his sons on horseback and sent them forward; and they, having overtaken the fugitives, spoke as they were ordered by Pisistratus, bidding them be of good cheer, and to depart every man to his own home. 64. The Athenians yielded a ready obedience, and thus Pisistratus, having a third time possessed himself of Athens, secured his power more firmly both by the aid of auxiliary forces, and by revenues partly collected at home and partly drawn from the river Strymon.[2] He also seized as hostages the sons of the Athenians who had held out against him, and had not immediately fled, and settled them at Naxos; which island Pisistratus had formerly subdued, and given in charge to Lygdamis: he, moreover, purified the island of Delos, in obedience to an oracle. And he purified it in the following manner: having dug up the dead bodies, as far as the prospect from the temple reached, he removed them to another part of Delos. Thus Pisistratus ruled despotically over the Athenians; but of them some had fallen in the battle, and others fled from their homes with the son of Alcmæon.[3]

65. Crœsus, therefore, was informed that such was, at that time, the condition of the Athenians; and that the Lacedæmonians, having extricated themselves out of great difficulties, had first gained the mastery over the Tegeans in war; for during the reign of Leo and Hegesicles, kings of Sparta, the Lacedæmonians were successful in all other wars, and were worsted by the Tegeans only. And long before their reign they had been governed by the worst laws of almost any people in Greece, both as regarded their dealings with one another, and in holding no intercourse with strangers.

[2] The country between the Strymon and the Nessus was celebrated for its mines.—*Larcher.*

[3] Megacles.

But they changed to a good government in the following manner: Lycurgus, a man much esteemed by the Spartans, having arrived at Delphi to consult the oracle, no sooner entered the temple, than the Pythian spoke as follows: "Thou art come, Lycurgus, to my wealthy temple, beloved by Jove and all that inhabit Olympian mansions: I doubt whether I shall pronounce thee god or man; but rather god, I think, Lycurgus." Some men say that, besides this, the Pythian also communicated to him that form of government now established among the Spartans. But, as the Lacedæmonians themselves affirm, Lycurgus, being appointed guardian to his nephew Leobotas,[4] king of Sparta, brought these institutions from Crete; for as soon as he had taken the guardianship, he altered all their customs, and took care that no one should transgress them. Afterward he established military regulations, the enomotiæ, the triecades, and the syssitia,[5] and besides these he instituted the ephori and senators. 66. Thus, having changed their laws, they established good institutions in their stead; and having erected a temple to Lycurgus after his death, they held him in the highest reverence. As they had a good soil and abundant population, they quickly sprang up and flourished. And now they were no longer content to live in peace; but proudly considering themselves superior to the Arcadians, they sent to consult the oracle at Delphi touching the conquest of the whole country of the Arcadians; and the Pythian gave them this answer: "Dost thou ask of me Arcadia? thou askest a great deal; I can not grant it thee. There are many acorn-eating men in Arcadia, who will hinder thee. But I do not grudge thee all; I will give thee Tegea to dance on with beating of the feet, and a fair plain to measure out by the rod." When the Lacedæmonians heard this answer reported, they laid aside their design against all Arcadia; and, relying on an equivocal oracle, led an army against Tegea only, carrying fetters with them, as if they would surely reduce the Tegeans to slavery. But being defeated in an engagement, as many of them as were taken alive were compelled to work, wearing the fetters they had brought,

[4] It is generally agreed that the name of Lycurgus's nephew was not Leobotas, but Charilaus.

[5] For an account of these several institutions, see Smith's Dictionary of Antiquities.

and measuring the lands of the Tegeans with a rod. Those fetters in which they were bound were, even in my time, preserved in Tegea, suspended around the temple of Alean Minerva.

67. In the first war, therefore, they had constantly fought against the Tegeans with ill success; but in the time of Crœsus, and during the reign of Anaxandrides and Ariston at Lacedæmon, they had at length become superior in the war, and they became so in the following manner: when they had always been worsted in battle by the Tegeans, they sent to inquire of the oracle at Delphi what god they should propitiate in order to become victorious over the Tegeans. The Pythian answered, *they should become so* when they had brought back the bones of Orestes, the son of Agamemnon. But as they were unable to find the sepulchre of Orestes, they sent again to inquire of the god in what spot Orestes lay interred, and the Pythian gave this answer to the inquiries of those who came to consult her: "In the level plain of Arcadia lies Tegea, where two winds by hard compulsion blow, and stroke answers to stroke, and woe lies on woe. There life-engendering earth contains Agamemnon's son; convey him home, and you will be victorious over Tegea." When the Lacedæmonians heard this, they were as far off the discovery as ever, though they searched every where; till Lichas, one of the Spartans who are called Agathoergi, found it. These Agathoergi consist of citizens who are discharged from serving in the cavalry, such as are senior, five in every year: it is their duty during the year in which they are discharged from the cavalry not to remain inactive, but go to different places where they are sent by the Spartan commonwealth. 68. Lichas, who was one of these persons, discovered it in Tegea, both meeting with good fortune and employing sagacity; for as the Lacedæmonians had at that time intercourse with the Tegeans, he, coming to a smithy, looked attentively at the iron being forged, and was struck with wonder when he saw what was done. The smith, perceiving his astonishment, desisted from his work, and said, "O Laconian stranger, you would certainly have been astonished had you seen what I saw, since you are so surprised at the working of iron; for as I was endeavoring to sink a well in this inclosure, in digging, I came to a coffin seven cubits long; and

because I did not believe that men were ever taller than they now are, I opened it, and saw that the body was equal to the coffin in length, and after I had measured it, I covered it up again. The man told him what he had seen, but Lichas, reflecting on what was said, conjectured from the words of the oracle that this must be the body of Orestes, forming his conjecture on the following reasons: seeing the smith's two bellows, he discerned in them the two winds, and in the anvil and hammer the stroke answering to strŏke, and in the iron that was being forged the woe that lay on woe; representing it in this way, that iron had been invented to the injury of man. Having made this conjecture, he returned to Sparta, and gave the Lacedæmonians an account of the whole matter; they, having brought a feigned charge against him, sent him into banishment. He then, going back to Tegea, related his misfortune to the smith, and wished to hire the inclosure from him, but he would not let it. But in time, when he had persuaded him, he took up his abode there; and having opened the sepulchre and collected the bones, he carried them away with him to Sparta. From that time, whenever they made trial of each other's strength, the Lacedæmonians were by far superior in war; and the greater part of Peloponnesus had been already subdued by them.

69. Crœsus being informed of all these things, sent embassadors to Sparta, with presents, and to request their alliance, having given them orders what to say; and when they were arrived they spoke as follows: "Crœsus, king of the Lydians and of other nations, has sent us with this message: 'O Lacedæmonians, since the deity has directed me by an oracle to unite myself to a Grecian friend, therefore (for I am informed that you are pre-eminent in Greece) I invite you, in obedience to the oracle, being desirous of becoming your friend and ally, without treachery or guile.'" Crœsus therefore made this proposal by his embassadors. But the Lacedæmonians, who had before heard of the answer given by the oracle to Crœsus, were gratified at the coming of the Lydians, and exchanged pledges of friendship and alliance; and indeed certain favors had been formerly conferred on them by Crœsus; for when the Lacedæmonians sent to Sardis to purchase gold, wishing to use it in erecting the statue of Apollo that now stands at Thornax in Laconia, Crœsus gave

it as a present to them when they were desirous of purchasing it. 70. For this reason, then, and because he had selected them from all the Greeks, and desired their friendship, the Lacedæmonians accepted his offer of alliance; and in the first place, they promised to be ready at his summons; and in the next, having made a brazen bowl, and covered it outside to the rim with various figures, and capable of containing three hundred amphoræ, they sent it to him, being desirous of making Crœsus a present in return. But this bowl never reached Sardis, for one of the two following reasons: the Lacedæmonians say that when this bowl, on its way to Sardis, was off Samos, the Samians, having heard of it, sailed out in long ships, and took it away by force. On the other hand, the Samians affirm, that when the Lacedæmonians who were conveying the bowl found they were too late, and heard that Sardis was taken, and Crœsus a prisoner, they sold the bowl in Samos, and that some private persons, who bought it, dedicated it in the temple of Juno. And perhaps they who sold it, when they returned to Sparta, might say that they had been robbed of it by the Samians. So it is, then, respecting this bowl.

71. Crœsus then, mistaking the oracle, prepared to invade Cappadocia, hoping to overthrow Cyrus and the power of the Persians. While Crœsus was preparing for his expedition against the Persians, a certain Lydian, who before that time was esteemed a wise man, and on this occasion acquired a very great name in Lydia, gave him advice in these words (the name of this person was Sandanis): "O king, you are preparing to make war against a people who wear leather trowsers, and the rest of their garments of leather; who inhabit a barren country, and feed not on such things as they choose, but such as they can get. Besides, they do not habitually use wine, but drink water; nor have they figs to eat, nor any thing that is good. In the first place, then, if you should conquer, what will you take from them, since they have nothing? On the other hand, if you should be conquered, consider what good things you will lose; for when they have tasted of our good things, they will become fond of them, nor will they be driven from them. As for me, I thank the gods that they have not put it into the thoughts of the Persians to make war on the Lydians." In saying this, he did not

persuade Crœsus. Now before they subdued the Lydians, the Persians possessed nothing either luxurious or good. 72. The Cappadocians are by the Greeks called Syrians; these Syrians, before the establishment of the Persian power, were subject to the Medes; but then to Cyrus; for the boundary of the Median empire and the Lydian was the river Halys, which flows from the mountains of Armenia through Cilicia; and afterward has the Matienians on the right and the Phrygians on the other side; then passing these and flowing up toward the north, it skirts the Syrian Cappadocians on one side, and the Paphlagonians on the left. Thus the river Halys divides almost the whole of lower Asia, from the sea opposite Cyprus to the Euxine: this is the isthmus of that whole country: as to the length of the journey, it takes five days for a well-girt man.[6]

73. Crœsus invaded Cappadocia for the following reasons; as well from a desire of adding it to his own dominions, as, especially, from his confidence in the oracle, and a wish to punish Cyrus on account of Astyages; for Cyrus son of Cambyses, had subjugated Astyages, son of Cyaxares, who was brother-in-law of Crœsus, and king of the Medes. He had become brother-in-law to Crœsus in the following manner: a band of Scythian nomades having risen in rebellion, withdrew into Media: at that time Cyaxares, son of Phraortes, grandson of Deioces, ruled over the Medes; he, at first, received these Scythians kindly, as being suppliants; so much so, that, esteeming them very highly, he intrusted some youths to them to learn their language and the use of the bow. In course of time, it happened that these Scythians, who were constantly going out to hunt, and who always brought home something, on one occasion took nothing. On their returning empty-handed, Cyaxares (for he was, as he proved, of a violent temper) treated them with most opprobrious language. The Scythians, having met with this treatment from Cyaxares, and considering it undeserved by them, determined to kill one of the youths that were being educated under their care; and having prepared the flesh as they used to dress the beasts taken in hunting, to serve it up to Cyaxares as if it were game, and then to make their escape immedi-

[6] The long flowing dresses of the ancients made it necessary to gird them up when they wished to move expeditiously.

ately to Alyattes, son of Sadyattes, at Sardis. This was accordingly done; and Cyaxares and his guests tasted of this flesh; and the Scythians, having done this, became suppliants to Alyattes. 74. After this (for Alyattes refused to deliver up the Scythians to Cyaxares when he demanded them), war lasted between the Lydians and the Medes for five years; during this period the Medes often defeated the Lydians, and often the Lydians *defeated* the Medes; and during this time they had a kind of nocturnal engagement. In the sixth year, when they were carrying on the war with nearly equal success, on occasion of an engagement, it happened that in the heat of the battle day was suddenly turned into night. This change of the day Thales the Milesian had foretold to the Ionians, fixing beforehand this year as the very period in which the change actually took place. The Lydians and Medes seeing night succeeding in the place of day, desisted from fighting, and both showed a great anxiety to make peace. Syennesis[7] the Cilician, and Labynetus[8] the Babylonian, were the mediators of their reconciliation; these were they who hestened the treaty between them, and made a matrimonial connection; for they persuaded Alyattes to give his daughter Aryenis in marriage to Astyages, son of Cyaxares; for without strong necessity, agreements are not wont to remain firm. These nations in their federal contracts observe the same ceremonies as the Greeks; and in addition, when they have cut their arms to the outer skin, they lick up one another's blood.

75. Cyrus had subdued this same Astyages, his grandfather by the mother's side, for reasons which I shall hereafter relate.[9] Crœsus, alleging this against him, sent to consult the oracle if he should make war on the Persians; and when an ambiguous answer came back, he, interpreting it to his own advantage, led his army against the territory of the Persians. When he arrived at the river Halys, Crœsus transported his forces, as I believe, by the bridges which are now there. But the common opinion of the Grecians is, that Thales the Milesian procured him a passage; for, while Crœsus was in

[7] Syennesis seems to have been a name common to the kings of Cilicia. In addition to the one here mentioned, we meet with another in the time of Darius (V. 118), and a third in the time of Xerxes (VII. 98).

[8] The same, says Prideaux, with the Nebuchadnezzar of Scripture.

[9] See ch. 121—130.

doubt how his army should pass over the river (for *they say* that these bridges were not at that time in existence), Thales, who was in the camp, caused the stream, which flowed along the left of the army, to flow likewise on the right; and he contrived it thus: having begun above the camp, he dug a deep trench, in the shape of a half moon, so that the river, being turned into this from its old channel, might pass in the rear of the camp pitched where it then was, and afterward, having passed by the camp, might fall into its former course; so that as soon as the river was divided into two streams, it became fordable in both. Some say that the ancient channel of the river was entirely dried up; but this I can not assent to; for how then could they have crossed it on their return? 76. However, Crœsus, having passed the river with his army, came to a place called Pteria, in Cappadocia. (Now Pteria is the strongest position of the whole of this country, and is situated over against Sinope, a city on the Euxine Sea.) Here he encamped, and ravaged the lands of the Syrians; and took the city of the Pterians, and enslaved the inhabitants; he also took all the adjacent places, and expelled the inhabitants, who had given him no cause for blame. But Cyrus, having assembled his own army, and having taken with him all who inhabited the intermediate country, went to meet Crœsus. But before he began to advance, he sent heralds to the Ionians, to persuade them to revolt from Crœsus: the Ionians, however, refused. When Cyrus had come up and encamped opposite Crœsus, they made trial of each other's strength on the plains of Pteria; but when an obstinate battle took place, and many fell on both sides, they at last parted on the approach of night, neither having been victorious. In this manner did the two armies engage.

77. But Crœsus laying the blame on his own army on account of the smallness of its numbers, for his forces that engaged were far fewer than those of Cyrus—laying the blame on this, when on the following day Cyrus did not attempt to attack him, he marched back to Sardis, designing to summon the Egyptians according to treaty, for he had made an alliance with Amasis, king of Egypt, before he had with the Lacedæmonians; and to send for the Babylonians (for he had made an alliance with them also, and Labynetus at this time reigned over the Babylonians), and to require the presence of

the Lacedæmonians at a fixed time: having collected these together, and assembled his own army, he purposed, when winter was over, to attack the Persians in the beginning of the spring. With this design, when he reached Sardis, he dispatched embassadors to his different allies, requiring them to meet at Sardis before the end of five months; but the army that was with him, and that had fought with the Persians, which was composed of mercenary troops, he entirely disbanded, not imagining that Cyrus, who had come off on such equal terms, would venture to advance upon Sardis. 78. While Crœsus was forming these plans, the whole suburbs were filled with serpents; and when they appeared, the horses, forsaking their pastures, came and devoured them. When Crœsus beheld this, he considered it to be, as it really was, a prodigy, and sent immediately to consult the interpreters at Telmessus; but the messengers having arrived there, and learned from the Telmessians what the prodigy portended, were unable to report it to Crœsus; for before they sailed back to Sardis, Crœsus had been taken prisoner. The Telmessians had pronounced as follows: "That Crœsus must expect a foreign army to invade his country, which, on its arrival, would subdue the natives; because, they said, the serpent is a son of the earth, but the horse is an enemy and a stranger." This answer the Telmessians gave to Crœsus when he had been already taken, yet without knowing what had happened with respect to Sardis or Crœsus himself.

79. But Cyrus, as soon as Crœsus had retreated after the battle at Pteria, having discovered that it was the intention of Crœsus to disband his army, found, upon deliberation, that it would be to his advantage to march with all possible expedition on Sardis, before the forces of the Lydians could be a second time assembled; and when he had thus determined, he put his plan into practice with all possible expedition; for having marched his army into Lydia, he brought this news of his own enterprise to Crœsus. Thereupon Crœsus, being thrown into great perplexity, seeing that matters had turned out contrary to his expectations, nevertheless drew out the Lydians to battle; and at that time no nation in Asia was more valiant and warlike than the Lydians. Their mode of fighting was from on horseback; they were armed with long lances, and managed their horses with admirable address.

80. The place where they met was the plain that lies before the city of Sardis, which is extensive and bare; several rivers, as well as the Hyllus, flowing through it, force a passage into the greatest, called the Hermus, which, flowing from the sacred mountain of mother Cybele, falls into the sea near the city of Phocæa. Here Cyrus, when he saw the Lydians drawn up in order of battle, alarmed at the cavalry, had recourse to the following stratagem, on the suggestion of Harpagus, a Mede. Having collected together all the camels that followed his army with provisions and baggage, and having caused their burdens to be taken off, he mounted men upon them equipped in cavalry accoutrements, and having furnished them, he ordered them to go in advance of the rest of his army against the Lydian horse; and he commanded his infantry to follow the camels, and he placed the whole of his cavalry behind the infantry. When all were drawn up in order, he charged them not to spare any of the Lydians, but to kill every one they met; but on no account to kill Crœsus, even if he should offer resistance when taken. Such were the orders he gave. He drew up the camels in the front of the cavalry for this reason; a horse is afraid of a camel, and can not endure either to see its form or to scent its smell: for this reason, then, he had recourse to this stratagem, that the cavalry might be useless to Crœsus, by which the Lydian expected to signalize himself. Accordingly, when they joined battle, the horses no sooner smelt the camels and saw them, than they wheeled round, and the hopes of Crœsus were destroyed. Nevertheless, the Lydians were not therefore discouraged, but when they perceived what had happened, leaped from their horses and engaged with the Persians on foot: at last, when many had fallen on both sides, the Lydians were put to flight, and being shut up within the walls, were besieged by the Persians.

81. Siege was then laid to them; but Crœsus, thinking it would last a long time, sent other messengers from the city to his allies; for those who were before sent requested them to assemble at Sardis on the fifth month, but he sent out these last to request them to succor him with all speed, as he was already besieged. 82. He sent, therefore, to the rest of his allies, and especially to the Lacedæmonians; but at that very time the Spartans themselves happened to have a

quarrel with the Argians about a tract called Thyrea; for this Thyrea, which properly belongs to the territory of Argos, the Spartans had seized; and, indeed, the country that lies westward as far as Malea, both on the continent and the island Cythera and the other islands, belongs to the Argians. The Argians having advanced to the defense of their country which had been thus seized upon, both parties, upon a conference, agreed that three hundred men on each side should engage, and that whichever party was victorious should be entitled to the disputed territory; but *it was stipulated* that the main body of each army should withdraw to their own country, and not remain while the engagement was going on, lest, if the armies were present, either side, seeing their countrymen in distress, should come in to their assistance. Having agreed to these terms, the armies withdrew, and the picked men on each side remaining behind engaged: they fought with such equal success that, of the six hundred, three men only were left alive; of the Argians, Alcenor and Chromius, and of the Lacedæmonians, Othryades; these survived when night came on. The two Argians, thinking themselves victorious, ran to Argos *with the news;* but Othryades, the Lacedæmonian, having stripped the corpses of the Argians, and carried their arms to his own camp, continued at his post. On the next day, both armies, being informed of the event, met again in the same place, and for a time both laid claim to the victory; the one side alleging that the greater number of their men survived, the other side urging that those survivors had fled, and that their countryman had kept the field and spoiled their dead. At length, from words they betook themselves to blows; and when many had fallen on both sides, the Lacedæmonians obtained the victory. From that time the Argians, cutting off their hair, which they had before been compelled to wear long, enacted a law, which was confirmed by a curse, that no Argian should suffer his hair to grow, nor any woman wear ornaments of gold, till they should recover Thyrea. On the other hand, the Lacedæmonians made a contrary law, enjoining all their people to wear long hair, which they had never done before. As to Othryades, who was the only one that survived of the three hundred, they say that, being ashamed to return to Sparta when all his fellow-soldiers had perished, he put an end to himself at Thyrea. 83. When the affairs of the Spartans were in this condition, the Sardian embassador arrived, and requested them to assist Crœsus, who was besieged in Sardis; they, however, no sooner heard the embassadors' report than they made preparations to succor him. But when they were now prepared to set out, and their ships were ready, another message reached them that the citadel of the Lydians was taken, and Crœsus made prisoner; they accordingly, deeming it a great misfortune, desisted from their enterprise.

84. Sardis was taken in the following manner. On the fourteenth day after Crœsus had been besieged, Cyrus sent horsemen throughout his army, and proclaimed that he would liberally reward the man who should first mount the wall: upon this, several attempts were made, and as often failed; till, after the rest had desisted, a Mardian, whose name was Hyrœades, endeavored to climb up on that part of the citadel where no guard was stationed, because there did not appear to be any danger that it would be taken on that part, for on that side the citadel was precipitous and impracticable. Round this part alone Meles, a former king of Sardis, had not brought the lion which his concubine bore to him, though the Telmessians had pronounced that if the lion were carried round the wall, Sardis would be impregnable; but Meles, having caused it to be carried round the rest of the wall, where the citadel was exposed to assault, neglected this, as altogether unassailable and precipitous. This is the quarter of the city that faces Mount Tmolus. Now this Hyrœades the Mardian, having seen a Lydian come down this precipice the day before for a helmet that was rolled down, and carry it up again, noticed it carefully, and reflected on it in his mind: he thereupon ascended the same way, followed by divers Persians; and when great numbers had gone up, Sardis was thus taken, and the whole town plundered.

85. The following incidents befell Crœsus himself. He had a son, of whom I have before made mention, who was in other respects proper enough, but dumb. Now, in the time of his former prosperity, Crœsus had done every thing he could for him, and among other expedients had sent to consult the oracle of Delphi concerning him; but the Pythian gave him this answer: "O Lydian born, king of many, very foolish Crœsus, wish not to hear the longed-for voice of thy son speaking within thy palace: it were better for thee that this

should be far off; for he will first speak in an unhappy day." When the city was taken, one of the Persians, not knowing Crœsus, was about to kill him. Crœsus, though he saw him approach, from his present misfortune, took no heed of him, nor did he care about dying by the blow; but this speechless son of his, when he saw the Persian advancing against him, through dread and anguish, burst into speech, and said, "Man, kill not Crœsus." These were the first words he ever uttered; but from that time he continued to speak during the remainder of his life. 86. So the Persians got possession of Sardis, and made Crœsus prisoner, after he had reigned fourteen years, been besieged fourteen days, and lost his great empire, as the oracle had predicted. The Persians, having taken him, conducted him to Cyrus; and he, having heaped up a great pile, placed Crœsus upon it, bound with fetters, and with him fourteen young Lydians, designing either to offer this sacrifice to some god as the first-fruits of his victory, or wishing to perform a vow; or perhaps, having heard that Crœsus was a religious person, he placed him on the pile for the purpose of discovering whether any deity would save him from being burned alive. He accordingly did what has been related: *it is added* that when Crœsus stood upon the pile, notwithstanding the weight of his misfortunes, the words of Solon recurred to him, as spoken by inspiration of the Deity, that "no living man could be justly called happy." When this occurred to him, *it is said* that, after a long silence, he recovered himself, and, uttering a groan, thrice pronounced the name of Solon; that when Cyrus heard him, he commanded his interpreters to ask Crœsus whom it was he called upon; that they drew near and asked him, but Crœsus for some time kept silence; but at last, being constrained to speak, said, "I named a man whose discourses I more desire all tyrants might hear, than to be possessor of the greatest riches." When he gave them this obscure answer, they again inquired what he said; and when they persisted in their inquiries, and were very importunate, he at length told them that Solon, an Athenian, formerly visited him, and having viewed all his treasures, made no account of them; telling, in a word, how every thing had befallen him as Solon had warned him, though his discourse related to all mankind as much as to himself, and especially to those who imagine themselves happy. *They say* that

Crœsus gave this explanation; and that the pile being now kindled, the outer parts began to burn; and that Cyrus, informed by the interpreters of what Crœsus had said, relented, and considering that being but a man, he was yet going to burn another man alive, who had been no way inferior to himself in prosperity; and, moreover, fearing retribution, and reflecting that nothing human is constant, commanded the fire to be instantly extinguished, and Crœsus, with those who were about him, to be taken down; and that they, with all their endeavors, were unable to master the fire. 87. It is related by the Lydians, that Crœsus, perceiving that Cyrus had altered his resolution, when he saw every man endeavoring to put out the fire, but unable to get the better of it, shouted aloud, invoking Apollo, and besought him, if ever any of his offerings had been agreeable to him, to protect and deliver him from the present danger: *they report* that he with tears invoked the god, and that on a sudden clouds were seen gathering in the air, which before was serene, and that a violent storm burst forth and vehement rain fell and extinguished the flames; by which Cyrus perceiving that Crœsus was beloved by the gods, and a good man, when he had had him taken down from the pile, asked him the following question: "Who persuaded you, Crœsus, to invade my territories, and to become my enemy instead of my friend?" He answered, "O king, I have done this for your good but my own evil fortune, and the god of the Greeks who encouraged me to make war is the cause of all. For no man is so void of understanding as to prefer war before peace; for in the latter children bury their fathers; in the former, fathers bury their children. But, I suppose, it pleased the gods that these things should be so."

88. He then thus spoke; but Cyrus, having set him at liberty, placed him by his own side, and showed him great respect; and both he and all those that were with him were astonished at what they saw. But Crœsus, absorbed in thought, remained silent; and presently turning round and beholding the Persians sacking the city of the Lydians, he said, "Does it become me, O king, to tell you what is passing through my mind, or to keep silent on the present occasion?" Cyrus bid him say with confidence whatever he wished; upon which Crœsus asked him, saying, "What

is this vast crowd so earnestly employed about?" He answered, "They are sacking your city and plundering your riches." "Not so," Crœsus replied; "they are neither sacking my city nor plundering my riches, for they no longer belong to me, but they are ravaging what belongs to you." 89. The reply of Crœsus attracted the attention of Cyrus; he therefore ordered all the rest to withdraw, and asked Crœsus what he thought should be done in the present conjuncture. He answered: "Since the gods have made me your servant, I think it my duty to acquaint you if I perceive any thing deserving of remark. The Persians, who are by nature overbearing, are poor. If, therefore, you permit them to plunder and possess great riches, you may expect the following results: whoso acquires the greatest possessions, be assured will be ready to rebel. Therefore, if you approve what I say, adopt the following plan: place some of your body-guard as sentinels at every gate, with orders to take the booty from all those who would go out, and to acquaint them that the tenth must of necessity be consecrated to Jupiter: thus you will not incur the odium of taking away their property; and they, acknowledging your intention to be just, will readily obey." 90. Cyrus, when he heard this, was exceedingly delighted, as he thought the suggestion a very good one. Having, therefore, commended it highly, and ordered his guards to do what Crœsus suggested, he addressed Crœsus as follows: "Crœsus, since you are resolved to display the deeds and words of a true king, ask whatever boon you desire on the instant." "Sir," he answered, "the most acceptable favor you can bestow upon me is to let me send my fetters to the god of the Grecians, whom I have honored more than any other deity, and to ask him if it be his custom to deceive those who deserve well of him." Cyrus asked him what cause he had to complain, that induced him to make this request: upon which Crœsus recounted to him all his projects, and the answers of the oracles, and particularly the offerings he had presented; and how he was incited by the oracle to make war against the Persians. When he had said this, he again besought him to grant him leave to reproach the god with these things. But Cyrus, smiling, said, "You shall not only receive this boon from me, but whatever else you may at any time desire." When Crœsus heard this, he sent certain Lydians to Delphi, with orders to lay his fetters at the entrance of the temple, and to ask the god if he were not ashamed to have encouraged Crœsus by his oracles to make war on the Persians, *assuring him* that he would put an end to the power of Cyrus, of which war such were the first-fruits (*commanding them at these words* to show the fetters), and at the same time to ask if it were the custom of the Grecian gods to be ungrateful. 91. When the Lydians arrived at Delphi, and had delivered their message, the Pythian is reported to have made this answer: "The god himself even can not avoid the decrees of fate; and Crœsus has atoned the crime of his ancestor in the fifth generation,[1] who, being one of the body-guard of the Heraclidæ, was induced by the artifice of a woman to murder his master, and to usurp his dignity, to which he had no right. But although Apollo was desirous that the fall of Sardis might happen in the time of the sons of Crœsus, and not during his reign, yet it was not in his power to avert the fates; but so far as he allowed they accomplished, and conferred the boon on him; for he delayed the capture of Sardis for the space of three years. Let Crœsus know, therefore, that he was taken prisoner three years later than the fates had ordained; and in the next place, he came to his relief when he was upon the point of being burned alive. Then, as to the prediction of the oracle, Crœsus has no right to complain; for Apollo foretold him that if he made war on the Persians, he would subvert a great empire; and had he desired to be truly informed, he ought to have sent again to inquire whether his own or that of Cyrus was meant. But since he neither understood the oracle, nor inquired again, let him lay the blame on himself. And when he last consulted the oracle, he did not understand the answer concerning the mule; for Cyrus was that mule; inasmuch as he was born of parents of different nations, the mother superior, but the father inferior. For she was a Mede, and daughter of Astyages, king of Media; but he was a Persian, subject to the Medes; and though in every respect inferior, he married his own mistress." The Pythian gave this answer to the Lydians, and they carried it back to Sardis, and reported it to Crœsus, and he, when he heard it, acknowledged

[1] Crœsus was the fifth descendant of Gyges, if we include the two extremes; for the house of the Mermnadæ was as follows: Gyges, Ardys, Sadyattes, Alyattes, Crœsus. See chap. 13.

the fault to be his, and not the god's. Such is the account of the kingdom of Crœsus, and the first subjection of Ionia.

92. Many other offerings were also consecrated by Crœsus in Greece, besides those already mentioned; for at Thebes of Bœotia there is a golden tripod, which he dedicated to Ismenian Apollo; and in Ephesus, the golden heifers, and several of the pillars; and in the Pronæa at Delphi a large golden shield. All these were in existence in my day; but others have been lost. The offerings he dedicated in Branchis, a city of the Milesians, were, as I am informed, equal in weight and similar to those at Delphi. Now the offerings which he made to Delphi and to Amphiaraus were his own property and the first-fruits of his patrimonial riches; but the rest were the produce of the property of an enemy, who, before he came to the throne, had set up an adverse faction, endeavoring to raise Pantaleon to the throne: now Pantaleon was the son of Alyattes, but of the same mother as Crœsus; for Alyattes had Crœsus by a Carian, and Pantaleon by an Ionian woman. When, therefore, Crœsus, by the will of his father, obtained the kingdom, he put his opponent to death by tearing his flesh with a fuller's thistle; and having already vowed all his treasure to the gods, he dedicated it in the manner above described to the places I have mentioned. And this may suffice respecting the offerings.

93. The Lydian territory does not present many wonders worthy of description, like some other countries, except the gold dust brought down from Mount Tmolus. It exhibits, however, one work the greatest of all, except those of the Egyptians and Babylonians. There is there a monument to Alyattes, father of Crœsus, the basis of which is composed of large stones, the rest is a mound of earth. This fabric was raised by merchants, artificers, and prostitutes. On the summit of this monument there remained, even in my day, five termini, upon which were inscriptions, showing how much of the work each class executed, and when measured the work of the females proved to be the greatest. For the daughters of the Lydian common people all prostitute themselves, for the purpose of providing themselves with dowries; and they continue to do so until they marry; and they dispose of themselves in marriage. This monument is six stades and two plethra in circumference, and in breadth thirteen plethra;

contiguous to it is a large lake, which the Lydians say is fed by perpetual springs, and it is called the Gygean lake. This may suffice for this subject.

94. The customs of the Lydians differ little from those of the Grecians, except that they prostitute their females. They are the first of all nations we know of that introduced the art of coining gold and silver; and they were the first retailers. The Lydians themselves say that the games which are now common to themselves and the Greeks were their invention; and they say they were invented about the time they sent a colony to Tyrrhenia, of all which they give the following account. During the reign of Atys, son of Manes, king of Lydia, a great scarcity of corn pervaded all Lydia: for some time the Lydians supported it with constancy; but when they saw the evil still continuing, they sought for remedies, and some devised one thing, some another; and at that time the games of dice, hucklebones, ball, and all other kinds of games except draughts, were invented, for the Lydians do not claim the invention of this last; and having made these inventions to alleviate the famine, they employed them as follows: they used to play one whole day that they might not be in want of food; and on the next, they ate and abstained from play; thus they passed eighteen years; but when the evil did not abate, on the contrary became still more virulent, their king divided the whole people into two parts, and cast lots which should remain and which quit the country, and over that part whose lot it should be to stay he appointed himself king, and over that part which was to emigrate he appointed his own son, whose name was Tyrrhenus. Those to whose lot it fell to leave their country went down to Smyrna, built ships, and, having put all their movables which were of use on board, set sail in search of food and land, till, having passed by many nations, they reached the Ombrici, where they built towns, and dwell to this day. From being called Lydians, they changed their name to one after the king's son, who led them out; from him they gave themselves the appellation of Tyrrhenians. The Lydians then were reduced under the power of the Persians.

95. My history hence proceeds to inquire who Cyrus was that overthrew the power of Crœsus, and how the Persians became masters of Asia; in which narration I shall fol-

low those Persians who do not wish to magnify the actions of Cyrus, but to relate the plain truth, though I am aware that there are three other ways of relating Cyrus's history. After the Assyrians had ruled over Upper Asia five hundred and twenty years, the Medes first began to revolt from them; and they, it seems, in their struggle with the Assyrians for liberty, proved themselves brave men; and having shaken off the yoke, became free: afterward the other nations also did the same as the Medes. When all throughout the continent were independent, they were again reduced under a despotic government in the following manner. 96. There was among the Medes a man famous for wisdom, named Deioces, son of Phraortes. This Deioces, aiming at absolute power, had recourse to the following plan. The Medes were at that time distributed into villages, and Deioces, who was already highly esteemed in his own district, applied himself with great zeal to the exercise of justice; and this he did, since great lawlessness prevailed throughout the whole of Media, and he knew that injustice and justice are ever at variance. The Medes of the same village, observing his conduct, chose him for their judge; and he, constantly keeping the sovereign power in view, showed himself upright and just. By this conduct he acquired no slight praise from his fellow-citizens, so much so that the inhabitants of other villages, hearing that Deioces was the only one who judged uprightly, having before met with unjust sentences, when they heard of him gladly came from all parts to Deioces, in order to submit their quarrels to his decision; and at last they would commit the decision to no one else. 97. In the end, when the number of those who had recourse to him continually increased as men heard of the justice of his decisions, Deioces, seeing the whole devolved upon himself, would no longer occupy the seat where he used to sit to determine differences, and refused to act as judge any more, for that it was no advantage to him to neglect his own affairs, and spend the day in deciding the quarrels of others. Upon this, rapine and lawlessness growing far more frequent throughout the villages than before, the Medes called an assembly and consulted together about the present state of things, but, as I suspect, the partisans of Deioces spoke to the following purpose: "Since it is impossible for us to inhabit the country if we continue in our present condition, let us constitute a king over us, and so the country will be governed by good laws, and we ourselves shall be able to attend to our business, nor be any longer driven from our homes by lawlessness." By some such words they persuaded them to submit to a kingly government. 98. Upon their immediately putting the question whom they should appoint king, Deioces was unanimously preferred and commended; so that at last they agreed that he should be their king. But he required them to build him a palace suitable to the dignity of a king, and guards for the security of his person. The Medes accordingly did so; and built him a spacious and strong palace in the part of the country that he selected, and permitted him to choose guards for his person out of all the Medes. Being thus possessed of the power, he compelled the Medes to build one city, and having carefully adorned that, to pay less attention to the others. And as the Medes obeyed him in this also, he built lofty and strong walls, which now go under the name of Ecbatana,[2] one placed in a circle within the other; and this fortification is so contrived that each circle was raised above the other by the height of the battlements only. The situation of the ground, rising by an easy ascent, was very favorable to the design. But that which was particularly attended to is, that there being seven circles altogether, the king's palace and the treasury are situated within the innermost of them. The largest of these walls is about equal in circumference to the city of Athens; the battlements of the first circle are white, of the second black, of the third purple, of the fourth blue, of the fifth bright red. Thus the battlements of all the circles are painted with different colors; but the two last have their battlements plaited, the one with silver, the other with gold.

99. Deioces then built these fortifications for himself, and round his own palace; and he commanded the rest of the people to fix their habitations round the fortification; and when all the buildings were completed, he, for the first time, established the following regulations: that no man should be admitted to the king's presence, but every one should consult him by means of messengers, and that none should be permitted to see him; and, moreover, that it should be accounted

[2] For the Scripture account of Ecbatana, see Judith i. 1—4.

indecency for any to laugh or spit before him. He established such ceremony about his own person, for this reason, that those who were his equals, and who were brought up with him, and of no meaner family, nor inferior to him in manly qualities, might not, when they saw him, grieve and conspire against him; but that he might appear to be of a different nature to them who did not see him. 100. When he had established these regulations, and settled himself in the tyranny, he was very severe in the distribution of justice. And the parties contending were obliged to send him their case in writing; and he, having come to a decision on the cases so laid before him, sent them back again. This, then, was his plan in reference to matters of litigation; and all other things were regulated by him; so that, if he received information that any man had injured another, he would presently send for him, and punish him in proportion to his offense; and for this purpose he had spies and eaves-droppers in every part of his dominions.

101. Now Deioces collected the Medes into one nation, and ruled over that. The following are the tribes of the Medes: the Busæ, Parataceni, Struchates, Arizanti, Budii, and the Magi. Such are the tribes of the Medes. 102. Deioces had a son, Phraortes, who, when his father died, after a reign of fifty-three years, succeeded him in the kingdom; but, having so succeeded, he was not content to rule over the Medes only, but, having made war on the Persians, he attacked them first, and reduced them under the dominion of the Medes. And afterward, being master of these two nations, both of them powerful, he subdued Asia, attacking one nation after another, till at last he invaded the Assyrians, who inhabited the city of Nineveh, and who had before been supreme, though at that time they were abandoned by their confederates (who had revolted), but who were otherwise in good condition: Phraortes then, having made war on them, perished with the greater part of his army, after he had reigned twenty-two years.

103. When Phraortes was dead, Cyaxares his son, grandson of Deioces, succeeded him. He is said to have been more warlike than his ancestors. He first divided the people of Asia into cohorts, and first divided them into spearmen, archers, and cavalry; whereas before they had been confusedly mixed together. It was he that fought with the Lydians,

when the day was turned into night,[3] as they were fighting; and who subjected the whole of Asia above the river Halys. He assembled the forces of all his subjects, and marched against Nineveh to avenge his father, and destroy that city. However, when he had obtained a victory over the Assyrians, and while he was besieging Nineveh, a great army of Scythians came upon him, under the conduct of their king Madyes, son of Protothyas. These Scythians had driven the Cimmerians out of Europe, and pursuing them into Asia, by that means entered the territories of the Medes. 104. The distance from the lake Mæotis to the river Phasis and to Colchis is a journey of thirty days to a well-girt man,[4] but the route from Colchis to Media is not long, for there is only one nation, the Saspires, between them; when one has passed over this, one finds one's self in Media. The Scythians, however, did not pass by this way, but turned to the higher road by a much longer route, having Mount Caucasus on the right,[5] and there the Medes, coming to an engagement with the Scythians, and being worsted in the battle, lost their dominion; but the Scythians became masters of all Asia. 105. From thence they proceeded to Egypt, and when they reached Palestine in Syria, Psammitichus, king of Egypt, having met them with presents and prayers, diverted them from advancing farther. In their return, however, they came to Ascalon, a city of Syria, and when most of them had marched through without doing any injury, some few, who were left behind, pillaged the temple of Celestial Venus. This temple, as I find by inquiry, is the most ancient of all the temples dedicated to this goddess; for that in Cyprus was built after this, as the Cyprians themselves confess; and that in Cythera was erected by Phœnicians who came from the same part of Syria. However, the goddess inflicted on the Scythians who robbed her temple at Ascalon, and on all their posterity, a female disease; so that the Scythians confess that they are afflicted with it on this account, and those who visit Scythia may see in what a state they are whom the Scythians call Enarees. 106. For twenty-eight years, then, the Scythians governed Asia, and every thing was overthrown by their licentiousness and neglect; for, besides the usual tribute, they exacted from

[3] See chap. 74. [4] See chap. 72, *n.*
[5] See B. IV. chap. 12, and B. VII. chap. 20.

each whatever they chose to impose; and, in addition to the tribute, they rode round the country and plundered them of all their possessions. Now Cyaxares and the Medes invited the greatest part of them to a feast, and having made them drunk, put them to death; and so the Medes recovered their former power, and all they had possessed before; and they took Nineveh (how they took it I will relate in another work),[6] and reduced the Assyrians into subjection, with the exception of the Babylonian district. Having accomplished these things, Cyaxares died, after he had reigned forty years, including the time of the Scythian dominion.

107. Astyages, the son of Cyaxares, succeeded him in the kingdom. He had a daughter, to whom he gave the name of Mandane. He dreamed that she made so great a quantity of water as not only filled his own city, but overflowed all Asia; and having communicated this dream to those of the Magi who interpret dreams, he was exceedingly alarmed when informed by them of every particular; and he afterward gave this Mandane, when arrived at a marriageable age, to no one of the Medes who was worthy of her, through dread of the vision; but to a Persian, named Cambyses, whom he found descended of a good family, and of a peaceful disposition, deeming him far inferior to a Mede of moderate rank. 108. In the first year after Mandane was married to Cambyses, Astyages saw another vision; it appeared to him that a vine grew up from his daughter's womb, and that the vine covered all Asia. Having seen this and communicated it to the interpreters of dreams, he sent to Persia for his daughter, who was then near her time of delivery; and upon her arrival he put her under a guard, resolving to destroy whatever should be born of her; for the Magian interpreters had signified to him from his vision that the issue of his daughter would reign in his stead. Astyages therefore, guarding against this, as soon as Cyrus was born, sent for Harpagus, a kinsman of his, and the most faithful of all the Medes, and the manager of all his affairs, and said to him, "Harpagus, on no account fail to perform the business I now charge you

[6] Several passages of our author seem to prove that Herodotus wrote other histories than those which have come down to us. In the 184th chapter of this book he speaks of his Assyrian history; in the 161st, of the 2d of the Libyan.

with; nor expose me to danger by deceiving me; nor, by preferring another, draw ruin upon thy own head. Take the child that Mandane has given birth to, carry him to your own house and kill him, and afterward bury him in whatever way you think fit." Harpagus answered, "O king, you have never yet observed any ingratitude in me, and I shall take care never to offend you for the future. If, therefore, it is your pleasure that this thing should be done, it is fitting that I readily obey you." 109. Harpagus, having given this answer, when the child had been put into his hands, adorned as if for death, returned home weeping; and upon his arrival he told his wife all that Astyages had said. She asked him, "What, then, do you purpose to do?" He answered, "Not as Astyages has commanded; though he should be yet more outrageous and mad than he is, I will not comply with his wishes, nor will I submit to him by performing such a murder; and for many reasons I will not murder the child; both because he is my own relation, and because Astyages is old, and has no male offspring; besides, if, after his death, the sovereignty should devolve on this daughter, whose son he would now murder by my means, what else remains for me but the greatest danger? It is necessary, however, for my safety, that the child should die, but as necessary that one of Astyages's people should be the executioner, and not one of mine." 110. Thus he spoke, and immediately sent a messenger for one of Astyages's herdsmen, who he knew grazed his cattle on pastures most convenient for the purpose, and on mountains abounding with wild beasts. His name was Mitradates, and he had married his fellow-servant. The name of the woman to whom he was married, in the language of Greece, was *Cyno*, and in that of the Medes, *Spaco*, for the Medes call a bitch Spaca. The foot of the mountains at which this herdsman grazed his cattle lies to the north of Ecbatana, toward the Euxine Sea; for the Medic territory on this side toward the Saspires is very mountainous, lofty, and covered with forests, whereas all the rest of Media is level. When, therefore, the herdsman, being summoned in great haste, arrived, Harpagus addressed him as follows: "Astyages bids thee take this infant, and expose him on the bleakest part of the mountains, that he may speedily perish; and has charged me to add, that if thou by any means shouldst save the child, thou shalt die by the most cruel death; and I am appointed to see the child exposed." 111. The herdsman, having heard these words, took the infant, returned back by the same way, and reached his cottage. It so happened that his own wife, whose confinement had been daily expected, was brought to bed while he was absent in the city, and each had been in a state of anxiety for the other; he being alarmed about his wife's delivery, and the woman, because Harpagus, who had not been accustomed to do so, had sent for her husband. When he returned and came up to her, she seeing him thus unexpectedly, first asked him why Harpagus had sent for him in such haste. "Wife," said he, "when I reached the city, I saw and heard what I wish I had never seen, nor had ever befallen our masters. The whole house of Harpagus was filled with lamentations; I, greatly alarmed, went in, and as soon as I entered, I saw an infant lying before me, panting and crying, dressed in gold and a robe of various colors. When Harpagus saw me, he ordered me to take up the child directly, and carry him away, and expose him in the part of the mountain most frequented by wild beasts; telling me at the same time that it was Astyages who imposed this task on me, and threatening the severest punishment if I should fail to do it. I took up the infant and carried him away, supposing him to belong to one of the servants; for I had then no suspicion whence he came, though I was astonished at seeing him dressed in gold and fine apparel, and also at the sorrow which evidently prevailed in the house of Harpagus. But soon after, on my way home, I learned the whole truth from a servant who accompanied me out of the city, and delivered the child into my hands; that he was born of Mandane, Astyages's daughter, and of Cambyses, son of Cyrus, and that Astyages had commanded him to be put to death."

112. As the herdsman uttered these last words, he uncovered the child, and showed it to his wife; she, seeing that the child was large, and of a beautiful form, embraced the knees of her husband, and with tears besought him by no means to expose it. He said that it was impossible to do otherwise; for that spies would come from Harpagus to see the thing done, and he must himself die the most cruel death if he should fail to do it. The woman, finding she could not persuade her husband, again addressed him as follows: "Since,

then, I can not persuade you not to expose the child, do this, at least, if it is absolutely necessary that he should be seen exposed: now I too have been delivered, and delivered of a still-born child; then take this and expose it, and let us bring up the son of Astyages's daughter as our own. Thus you will neither be convicted of having wronged our masters, nor shall we have consulted ill for our own interests; for the child that is dead will have a royal burial, and the one that survives will not be deprived of life." 113. The herdsman thought his wife spoke very much to the purpose, under existing circumstances, and immediately proceeded to act accordingly. The child that he had brought for the purpose of putting to death he delivered to his wife; his own, which was dead, he put into the basket in which he had brought the other, and having dressed it in all the finery of the other child, he exposed it in the most desolate part of the mountains. On the third day after the infant had been exposed, the herdsman, having left one of his assistants as a guard, went to the city, and, arriving at the house of Harpagus, told him he was ready to show the dead body of the infant. Harpagus accordingly sent some of the most trusty of his guards, and by that means saw the body, and buried the herdsman's child. Thus this child was buried. The other, who afterward had the name of Cyrus, was brought up by the herdsman's wife, who gave him some other name, and not that of Cyrus.

114. When the child attained the age of ten years, a circumstance of the following nature discovered him. He was playing in the village in which the ox-stalls were, with boys of his own age, in the road. The boys who were playing chose this reputed son of the herdsman for their king. But he appointed some of them to build houses, and others to be his body-guards; one of them to be the king's eye, and to another he gave the office of bringing messages to him, assigning to each his proper duty. Now one of these boys who was playing with him, being son of Artembares, a man of rank among the Medes, refused to obey the orders of Cyrus; he therefore commanded the others to seize him, and when they obeyed, Cyrus scourged the boy very severely. But the boy, as soon as he was let loose, considering that he had been treated with great indignity, took it very much to heart, and hastening to the city, complained to his father of the treat-

ment he had met with from Cyrus; not, indeed, saying from Cyrus (for he was not yet known by that name), but from the son of Astyages's herdsman. Artembares, in a transport of anger, went immediately to Astyages, and taking his son with him, said that he suffered treatment that was not to be borne, adding, "Thus, O king, are we insulted by your slave, the son of a herdsman," showing the boy's shoulders. 115. Astyages having heard and seen what was done, resolving, on account of the rank of Artembares, to avenge the indignity offered to the youth, sent for the herdsman and his son. When both came into his presence, Astyages, looking upon Cyrus, said, "Have you, who are the son of such a man as this, dared to treat the son of one of the principal persons in my kingdom with such indignity?" But Cyrus answered, "Sir, I treated him as I did with justice; for the boys of our village, of whom he was one, in their play made me their king, because I appeared to them the most fitted to that office. Now all the other boys performed what they were ordered, but he alone refused to obey, and paid no attention to my commands; wherefore he was punished. If, then, on this account I am deserving of punishment, here I am, ready to submit to it." 116. As the boy was speaking thus, Astyages recognized who he was; both the character of his face appeared like his own, and his answer more free than accorded with his condition; the time, also, of the exposure seemed to agree with the age of the boy. Alarmed at this discovery, he was for some time speechless; and at last, having with difficulty recovered himself (being desirous of sending Artembares away, in order that he might examine the herdsman in private), he said, "Artembares, I will take care that neither you nor your son shall have any cause of complaint." Thus he dismissed Artembares; but the servants, at the command of Astyages, conducted Cyrus into an inner room; and when the herdsman remained alone, he asked him, in the absence of witnesses, whence he had the boy, and from whose hands he received him? He affirmed that the boy was his own son, and that the mother who bore him was still living with him. Astyages told him that he did not consult his own safety in wishing to be put to the torture; and as he said this, he made a signal to his guards to seize him. The man, when brought to the torture, discovered the whole matter, and beginning from the outset he went through it, speaking the truth throughout, and concluded with prayers and entreaties for pardon. 117. Astyages, when the herdsman had confessed the truth, did not concern himself much about him afterward; but attaching great blame to Harpagus, he ordered his guards to summon him; and when Astyages asked, "Harpagus, by what kind of death did you dispose of the child which I delivered to you, born of my daughter?" Harpagus, seeing the herdsman present, had not recourse to falsehood, lest he should be detected and convicted, but said, "O king, when I had received the infant, I carefully considered how I could act according to your wish and command, and, without offending you, I might be free from the crime of murder both in your daughter's sight and in yours. I therefore acted as follows: having sent for this herdsman, I gave him the child, saying that you had commanded him to put it to death; and in saying this I did not speak falsely, for such indeed were your orders. In this manner I delivered the infant to him, charging him to place it in some desert mountain, and to stay and watch till the child was dead, threatening the severest punishment if he should not fully carry out these injunctions. When he had executed these orders, and the child was dead, I sent some of the most trusty of my eunuchs, and by means of them beheld the body and buried it. This is the whole truth, O king, and such was the fate of the child."

118. Thus Harpagus told the real truth; but Astyages, dissembling the anger which he felt on account of what had been done, again related to Harpagus the whole matter as he had heard it from the herdsman; and afterward, when he had repeated it throughout, he ended by saying that the child was alive and all was well. "For," he added, "I suffered much on account of what had been done regarding this child, and could not easily bear the reproaches of my daughter; therefore, since fortune has taken a more favorable turn, do you, in the first place, send your own son to accompany the boy I have recovered; and, in the next place (for I purpose to offer a sacrifice for the preservation of the child to the gods, to whom that honor is due), do you be with me at supper." 119. Harpagus, on hearing these words, when he had paid his homage, and had congratulated himself that his fault had turned to so good account, and that he was invited to

the feast under such auspicious circumstances, went to his own home, and as soon as he entered he sent his only son, who was about thirteen years of age, and bade him go to Astyages, and do whatever he should command; and then, being full of joy, he told his wife what had happened. But when the son of Harpagus arrived, having slain him and cut him into joints, Astyages roasted some parts of his flesh and boiled others, and having had them well dressed, kept them in readiness. At the appointed hour, when the other guests and Harpagus were come, tables full of mutton were placed before the rest and Astyages himself, but before Harpagus all the body of his son, except the head, the hands, and the feet; these were laid apart in a basket covered over. When Harpagus seemed to have eaten enough, Astyages asked him if he was pleased with the entertainment; and when Harpagus replied that he was highly delighted, the officers appointed for the purpose brought him the head of his son, covered up with the hands and feet, and standing before Harpagus, they bade him uncover the basket and take what he chose. Harpagus doing as they desired, and uncovering the basket, saw the remains of his son's body, but he expressed no alarm at the sight, and retained his presence of mind; whereupon Astyages asked him if he knew of what animal he had been eating. He said he knew very well, and that whatever a king did was agreeable to him. After he had given this answer he gathered the remains of the flesh and went home, purposing, as I conjecture, to collect all he could and bury it.

120. Astyages thus punished Harpagus; and then considering what he should do with Cyrus, summoned the Magi, who had formerly interpreted his dream. When they were come, Astyages asked them in what way they had interpreted his vision. They gave the same answer as before; and said that if the boy was still alive, and had not already died, he must of necessity be king. He answered them as follows: "The boy is and still survives, and while living in the country, the boys of the village made him king, and he has already performed all such things as kings really do, for he has appointed guards, door-keepers, messengers, and all other things in like manner; and now I desire to know to what do these things appear to you to tend." The Magi answered, "If the boy be living, and has already been a king by no settled plan, you may take

courage on his account and make your mind easy, for he will not reign a second time; for some of our predictions terminate in trifling results; and dreams, and things like them, are fulfilled by slight events." To this Astyages replied, "I too, O Magi, am very much of the same opinion, that since the child has been named king, the dream is accomplished, and that the boy is no longer an object of alarm to me; yet consider well, and carefully weigh what will be the safest course for my family and yourselves." The Magi answered, "O king, it is of great importance to us that your empire should be firmly established, for otherwise it is alienated, passing over to this boy, who is a Persian, and we, who are Medes, shall be enslaved by Persians, and held in no account as being foreigners; whereas while you, who are of our own country, are king, we have a share in the government, and enjoy great honors at your hands. Thus, then, we must on every account provide for your safety and that of your government; and now, if we saw any thing to occasion alarm, we should tell you of it beforehand; but now, since the dream has issued in a trifling event, we ourselves take courage, and advise you to do the like, and to send the boy out of your sight to his parents in Persia." 121. When, therefore, Astyages heard this, he was both delighted, and, having called for Cyrus, said to him, "Child, I have been unjust to you, by reason of a vain dream; but you survive by your own destiny. Now go in happiness to Persia, and I will send an escort to attend you: when you arrive there, you will find a father and mother very different from the herdsman Mitradates and his wife."

122. Astyages, having spoken thus, sent Cyrus away, and, upon his arrival at the house of Cambyses, his parents received him; and having received him, when they heard who he was they embraced him with the greatest tenderness, having been assured that he had died immediately after his birth; and they inquired of him by what means his life had been preserved. He told them, saying, that before he knew not, but had been very much mistaken; however, that on his road he had heard the whole case; for that till that time he believed he was the son of Astyages's herdsman. He related that he had been brought up by the herdsman's wife; and he went on constantly praising her; and Cyno was the

chief subject of his talk. His parents, having taken up this name (in order that the Persians might suppose that the child was somewhat miraculously preserved for them), spread about a report that a bitch had nourished him when exposed; hence this report was propagated. 123. When Cyrus had reached man's estate, and proved the most manly and beloved of his equals in age, Harpagus paid great court to him, sending him presents, from his desire to be avenged on Astyages; for he did not see that he himself, who was but a private man, could be able to take vengeance on Astyages; perceiving, therefore, that Cyrus was growing up to be his avenger, he contracted a friendship with him, comparing the sufferings of Cyrus with his own. And before this he had made the following preparations. Seeing Astyages severe in his treatment of the Medes, Harpagus, holding intercourse with the chief persons of the nation, one after another, persuaded them that they ought to place him at their head, and depose Astyages. When he had effected his purpose in this respect, and all was ready, Harpagus, wishing to discover his designs to Cyrus, who resided in Persia, and having no other way left, because the roads were all guarded, contrived the following artifice. Having cunningly contrived a hare, by opening its belly, and tearing off none of the hair, he put a letter, containing what he thought necessary to write, into the body; and having sewed up the belly of the hare, he gave it with some nets to the most trusty of his servants, dressed as a hunter, and sent him to Persia; having by word of mouth commanded him to bid Cyrus, as he gave him the hare, to open it with his own hand, and not to suffer any one to be present when he did so. 124. This was accordingly done; and Cyrus, having received the hare, opened it; and finding the letter which was in it, he read it; and it was to the following purport: "Son of Cambyses, seeing the gods watch over you (for otherwise you could never have arrived at your present fortune), do you now avenge yourself on your murderer Astyages; for as far as regards his purpose you are long since dead, but by the care of the gods and of me you survive. I suppose you have been long since informed both what was done regarding yourself, and what I suffered at the hands of Astyages because I did not put you to death, but gave you to the herdsman. If, then, you will follow my counsel, you shall rule over the whole territory that Astyages now governs. Persuade the Persians to revolt, and invade Media; and whether I or any other illustrious Mede be appointed to command the army opposed to you, every thing will turn out as you wish; for they, on the first onset, having revolted from him, and siding with you, will endeavor to depose him. Since, then, every thing is ready here, do as I advise, and do it quickly."

125. Cyrus, having received this intelligence, began to consider by what measures he could best persuade the Persians to revolt; and after mature consideration, he fixed upon the following as the most proper; and accordingly he put it in practice. Having written such a letter as he thought fit, he called an assembly of the Persians, and then, having opened the letter and read it, he said that Astyages had appointed him general of the Persians: "Now," he continued, "I require you to attend me, every man with a sickle." Cyrus then issued such an order. Now the Persians are divided into many tribes; and some of them Cyrus assembled together, and persuaded to revolt from the Medes; these are they upon whom the rest of the Persians are dependent: the Pasargadæ, the Maraphians, and the Maspians: of these the Pasargadæ are the most noble; among them is the family of the Achæmenidæ, from which the kings of Persia are descended. The rest are as follows: the Panthialæans, the Derusiæans, and the Germanians; these are all husbandmen: the rest are pastoral; Daians, Mardians, Dropicians, and Sagartians. 126. When all were come with their sickles, as had been ordered, Cyrus *selected* a tract of land in Persia, which was overgrown with briers, and about eighteen or twenty stadia square, and directed them to clear it during the day: when the Persians had finished the appointed task, he next told them to come again on the next day, having first washed themselves. In the mean time, Cyrus, having collected together all his father's flocks and herds, had them killed and dressed, as purposing to entertain the Persian forces, and he provided wine and bread in abundance. The next day, when the Persians were assembled, he made them lie down on the turf, and feasted them; and after the repast was over, Cyrus asked them whether the treatment they had received

the day before, or the present, were preferable. They answered that the difference was great; for on the preceding day they had every hardship, but on the present every thing that was good. Cyrus, therefore, having received this answer, discovered his intentions, and said, "Men of Persia, the case stands thus: if you will hearken to me, you may enjoy these, and numberless other advantages, without any kind of servile labor; but if you will not hearken to me, innumerable hardships like those of yesterday await you. Now, therefore, obey me, and be free; for I am persuaded I am born by divine providence to undertake this work; and I deem you to be men in no way inferior to the Medes, either in other respects or in war: since, then, these things are so, revolt with all speed from Astyages."

127. The Persians then having obtained a leader, gladly asserted their freedom, having for a long time felt indignant at being governed by the Medes. Astyages, being informed of what Cyrus was doing, sent a messenger and summoned him; but Cyrus bade the messenger take back word "that he would come to him sooner than Astyages desired." When Astyages heard this, he armed all the Medes; and, as if the gods had deprived him of understanding, made Harpagus their general, utterly forgetting the outrage he had done him. And when the Medes came to an engagement with the Persians, such of them as knew nothing of the plot, fought; but others went over to the Persians; and the far greater part purposely behaved as cowards and fled. 128. The army of the Medes being thus shamefully dispersed, as soon as the news was brought to Astyages, he exclaimed, threatening Cyrus, "Not even so shall Cyrus have occasion to rejoice." Having so said, he first impaled the Magi, who had interpreted his dream and advised him to let Cyrus go; then he armed all the Medes that were left in the city, both young and old; and leading them out, he engaged the Persians, and was defeated. Astyages himself was made prisoner, and he lost all the Medes whom he had led out. 129. Harpagus, standing by Astyages after he was taken, exulted over him and jeered him; and among other galling words, he asked him also about the supper at which he had feasted him with his son's flesh, and inquired "how he liked slavery in exchange for a kingdom." Astyages, looking steadfastly on Harpagus, asked in return whether he

thought himself the author of Cyrus's success. Harpagus said he did, for, as he had written, the achievement was justly due to himself. Astyages thereupon proved him to be "the weakest and most unjust of all men; the weakest, in giving the kingdom to another, which he might have assumed to himself, if indeed he had effected this change; and the most unjust, because he had enslaved the Medes on account of the supper; for if it were absolutely necessary to transfer the kingdom to some one else and not to take it himself, he might, with more justice, have conferred this benefit on some one of the Medes than on a Persian; whereas now the Medes, who were not at all in fault, had become slaves instead of masters, and the Persians, who before were slaves to the Medes, had now become their masters."

130. So Astyages, after he had reigned thirty-five years, was thus deposed; and by reason of his cruelty, the Medes bent under the Persian yoke after they had ruled over all Asia beyond the river Halys for the space of one hundred and twenty-eight years,[7] excepting the interval of the Scythian dominion. At a later period, however, they repented of what they had done, and revolted from Darius; but, being conquered in battle, were again subdued; but now, in the time of Astyages, the Persians, under the conduct of Cyrus, having risen against the Medes, have from that time been masters of Asia. As for Astyages, Cyrus kept him with him till he died, without doing him any farther injury. Cyrus therefore, having been thus born and educated, came to the throne; and after these events he conquered Crœsus, who gave the first provocation, as I have already related, and having subdued him, he became master of all Asia.

131. The Persians, according to my own knowledge, observe the following customs. It is not their practice to erect statues, or temples, or altars, but they charge those with folly

[7] According to Herodotus, Deioces reigned 53 years,

Deioces	53 years
Phraortes	22
Cyaxares.....	40
Astyages.....	35
	150

If from this number we subtract 28, the time that the Scythians reigned, there remain but 122; so that in all probability a mistake has been made in the text by some copyist.—*Larcher.*

who do so; because, as I conjecture, they do not think the gods have human forms, as the Greeks do. They are accustomed to ascend the highest parts of the mountains, and offer sacrifice to Jupiter, and they call the whole circle of the heavens by the name of Jupiter. They sacrifice to the sun and moon, to the earth, fire, water, and the winds. To these alone they have sacrificed from the earliest times; but they have since learned from the Arabians and Assyrians to sacrifice to Venus Urania, whom the Assyrians call Venus Mylitta, the Arabians, Alitta, and the Persians, Mitra. 132. The following is the established mode of sacrifice to the abovementioned deities: they do not erect altars nor kindle fires when about to sacrifice; they do not use libations, or flutes, or fillets, or cakes; but when any one wishes to offer sacrifice to any one of these deities, he leads the victim to a clean spot, and invokes the god, usually having his tiara decked with myrtle. He that sacrifices is not permitted to pray for blessings for himself alone; but he is obliged to offer prayers for the prosperity of all the Persians, and the king, for he is himself included in the Persians. When he has cut the victim into small pieces, and boiled the flesh, he strews under it a bed of tender grass, generally trefoil, and then lays all the flesh upon it: when he has put every thing in order, one of the Magi standing by sings an ode concerning the original of the gods, which they say is the incantation; and without one of the Magi it is not lawful for them to sacrifice. After having waited a short time, he that has sacrificed carries away the flesh and disposes of it as he thinks fit. 133. It is their custom to honor their birth-day above all other days; and on this day they furnish their table in a more plentiful manner than at other times. The rich then produce an ox, a horse, a camel, and an ass, roasted whole in an oven, but the poor produce smaller cattle. They are moderate at their meals, but eat of many after dishes, and those not served up together. On this account the Persians say "that the Greeks rise hungry from table, because nothing worth mentioning is brought in after dinner, and that if any thing were brought in, they would not leave off eating." The Persians are much addicted to wine; they are not allowed to vomit or make water in presence of another. These customs are observed to this day. They are used to debate the most important affairs when intoxicated; but whatever they have determined on in such deliberations is, on the following day, when they are sober, proposed to them by the master of the house where they have met to consult; and if they approve of it when sober also, then they adopt it; if not, they reject it; and whatever they have first resolved on when sober, they reconsider when intoxicated. 134. When they meet one another in the streets, one may discover by the following custom whether those who meet are equals; for, instead of accosting one another, they kiss on the mouth; if one be a little inferior to the other, they kiss the cheek; but if he be of a much lower rank, he prostrates himself before the other. They honor, above all, those who live nearest to themselves; in the second degree, those that are second in nearness; and after that, as they go farther off, they honor in proportion; and least of all they honor those who live at the greatest distance; esteeming themselves to be by far the most excellent of men in every respect, and that others make approaches to excellence according to the foregoing gradations, but that they are the worst who live farthest from them. During the empire of the Medes, each nation ruled over its next neighbor, the Medes over all, and especially over those who were nearest to them; these, again, over the bordering people, and the last, in like manner, over their next neighbors; and in the same gradations the Persians honor; for that nation went on extending its government and guardianship. 135. The Persians are of all nations most ready to adopt foreign customs; for they wear the Medic costume, thinking it handsomer than their own; and in war they use the Egyptian cuirass; and they practice all kinds of indulgences with which they become acquainted; among others, they have learned from the Greeks a passion for boys: they marry, each of them, many wives, and keep a still greater number of concubines. 136. Next to bravery in battle, this is considered the greatest proof of manliness, to be able to exhibit many children; and to such as can exhibit the greatest number, the king sends presents every year; for numbers are considered strength. Beginning from the age of five years to twenty, they instruct their sons in three things only—to ride, to use the bow, and to speak truth. Before he is five years of age, a son is not admitted to the presence of his father, but lives entirely with the women: the reason of this custom is, that if he should die in childhood, he may occasion no grief to his father.

137. Now I much approve of the above custom, as also of the following, that not even the king is allowed to put any one to death for a single crime, nor any private Persian exercise extreme severity against any of his domestics for one fault, but if, on examination, he should find that his misdeeds are more numerous and greater than his services, he may, in that case, give vent to his anger. They say that no one ever yet killed his own father or mother, but whenever such things have happened they affirm that, if the matter were thoroughly searched into, they would be found to have been committed by supposititious children, or those born in adultery, for they hold it utterly impossible that a true father should be murdered by his own son. 138. They are not allowed even to mention the things which it is not lawful for them to do. To tell a lie is considered by them the greatest disgrace; next to that, to be in debt, and this for many other reasons, but especially because they think that one who is in debt must of necessity tell lies. Whosoever of the citizens has the leprosy or scrofula, is not permitted to stay within a town, nor to have communication with other Persians; and they say that from having committed some offense against the sun a man is afflicted with these diseases. Every stranger that is seized with these distempers many of them even drive out of the country; and they do the same to white pigeons, making the same charge against them. They neither make water, nor spit, nor wash their hands in a river, nor defile the stream with urine, nor do they allow any one else to do so, but they pay extreme veneration to all rivers. 139. Another circumstance is also peculiar to them, which has escaped the notice of the Persians themselves, but not of us. Their names, which correspond with their personal forms and their rank, all terminate in the same letter which the Dorians call *San*, and the Ionians *Sigma*; and if you inquire into this, you will find that all Persian names, without exception, end in the same letter. 140. These things I can with certainty affirm to be true, since I myself know them. But what follows, relating to the dead, is only secretly mentioned, and not openly; viz., that the dead body of a Persian is

never buried until it has been torn by some bird or dog; but I know for a certainty that the Magi do this, for they do it openly. The Persians then, having covered the body with wax, conceal it in the ground. The Magi differ very much from all other men, and particularly from the Egyptian priests; for the latter hold it matter of religion not to kill any thing that has life, except such things as they offer in sacrifice; whereas the Magi kill every thing with their own hands, except a dog or a man; and they think they do a meritorious thing when they kill ants, serpents, and other reptiles, and birds. And with regard to this custom, let it remain as it existed from the first. I will now return to my former subject.

141. The Ionians and Æolians, as soon as the Lydians were subdued by the Persians, sent embassadors to Cyrus at Sardis, wishing to become subject to him on the same terms as they had been to Crœsus. But he, when he heard their proposal, told them this story: "A piper, seeing some fishes in the sea, began to pipe, expecting that they would come to shore; but finding his hopes disappointed, he took a casting-net, and inclosed a great number of fishes, and drew them out. When he saw them leaping about, he said to the fishes, 'Cease your dancing, since when I piped you would not come out and dance.'" Cyrus told this story to the Ionians and Æolians, because the Ionians, when Cyrus pressed them, by his embassador, to revolt from Crœsus, refused to consent; and now, when the business was done, were ready to listen to him. He, therefore, under the influence of anger, gave them this answer. But the Ionians, when they heard this message brought back to their cities, severally fortified themselves with walls, and met together at the Panionium, with the exception of the Milesians; for Cyrus made an alliance with them only, on the same terms as the Lydians had done. The rest of the Ionians resolved unanimously to send embassadors to Sparta, to implore them to succor the Ionians. 142. The Ionians, to whom the Panionium belongs, have built their cities under the finest sky and climate of the world that we know of; for neither the regions that are above it, nor those that are below, nor the parts to the east or west, are at all equal to Ionia; for some of them are oppressed by cold and rain, others by heat and drought. These Ionians do not all use the same language, but have four varieties of dialect. Miletus, the first of

them, lies toward the south; next are Myus and Priene: these are situate in Caria, and use the same dialect. The following are in Lydia: Ephesus, Colophon, Lebedus, Teos, Clazomenæ, Phocæa. These cities do not at all agree with those before mentioned in their language, but they speak a dialect common to themselves. There are three remaining of the Ionian cities, of which two inhabit islands, Samos and Chios; and one, Erythræ, is situated on the continent. Now the Chians and Erythræans use the same dialect, but the Samians have one peculiar to themselves. And these are the four different forms of language.

143. Of these Ionians, the Milesians were sheltered from danger, as they had made an alliance. The islanders also had nothing to fear; for the Phœnicians were not yet subject to the Persians, nor were the Persians themselves at all acquainted with maritime affairs. Now the Milesians had seceded from the rest of the Ionians only for this reason, that, weak as the Grecian race then was, the Ionian was weakest of all, and of least account; for, except Athens, there was no other city of note. The other Ionians, therefore, and the Athenians, shunned the name, and would not be called Ionians; and even now many of them appear to me to be ashamed of the name. But these twelve cities gloried in the name, and built a temple for their own use, to which they gave the name of Panionium; and they resolved not to communicate privileges to any other of the Ionians; nor, indeed, have any others, except the Smyrnæans, desired to participate in them. 144. In the same manner, the Dorians of the present Pentapolis, which was before called Hexapolis, take care not to admit any of the neighboring Dorians into the temple at Triopium, but excluded from participation such of their own community as have violated the sacred laws; for in the games in honor of Triopian Apollo, they formerly gave brazen tripods to the victors; and it was usual for those who gained them, not to carry them out of the temple, but to dedicate them there to the god: however, a man of Halicarnassus, whose name was Agasicles, having won the prize, disregarded their custom, and, carrying away the tripod, hung it up in his own house. For this offense, the five cities, Lindus, Ialyssus, Cameirus, Cos, and Cnidus, excluded the sixth city, Halicarnassus, from participation; on them, therefore, they imposed

this punishment. 145. The Ionians appear to me to have formed themselves into twelve cities, and to have refused to admit more, for the following reason: because, when they dwelt in Peloponnesus, there were twelve divisions of them, as now there are twelve divisions of Achæans, who drove out the Ionians. Pellene is the first toward Sicyon; next, Ægyra and Æge, in which is the overflowing river Crathis, from which the river in Italy derived its name; then Bura and Helice, to which the Ionians fled when they were defeated by the Achæans; Ægium, Rhypes, Patrees, Pharees, and Olenus, in which is the great river Pirus; lastly, Dyma and Tritæes, the only inland places among them. 146. These now are the twelve divisions of the Achæans, which formerly belonged to the Ionians; and, on that account, the Ionians erected twelve cities; for to say that these are more properly Ionians, or of more noble origin than other Ionians, would be great folly, since the Abantes, from Eubœa, who had no connection, even in name, with Ionia, are no inconsiderable part of this colony; and Minyan-Orchomenians are intermixed with them, and Cadmæans, Dryopians, Phocians (who separated themselves from the rest of their countrymen), and Molossians, Pelasgians of Arcadia, Dorian Epidaurians, and many other people, are intermixed with them; and those of them who set out from the Prytaneum of Athens, and who deem themselves the most noble of the Ionians, brought no wives with them when they came to settle in this country, but seized a number of Carian women after they had killed their men; and on account of this massacre, these women established a law, and imposed on themselves an oath, and transmitted it to their daughters, that they would never eat with their husbands, nor ever call them by the name of husband, because they had killed their fathers, their husbands, and their children, and then, after so doing, had forced them to become their wives. This was done in Miletus. 147. The Ionians appointed kings to govern them; some choosing Lycians, of the posterity of Glaucus, son of Hippolochus; others Cauconian Pylians, descended from Codrus, son of Melanthus; others, again, from both those families. However, they are more attached to the name of Ionians than any others; let it be allowed, then, that they are genuine Ionians. Still, all are Ionians who derive their original from Athens, and celebrate the Apaturian festival; but all do so except the Ephesians and Colophonians; for these alone do not celebrate the Apaturian festival, on some pretext of a murder. 148. The Panionium is a sacred place in Mycale, looking to the north, and by the Ionians consecrated in common to Heliconian Neptune; and Mycale is a headland on the continent, stretching westward toward Samos. At this place the Ionians, assembling from the various cities, were accustomed to celebrate the festival to which they gave the name of Panionia; and not only do the festivals of the Ionians, but the festivals of all the Greeks terminate, like the Persian names,[8] in the same letter. These, then, are the Ionian cities.

149. The following are the Æolian: Cyme, called also Phriconis, Larissæ, Neon-teichos, Temnos, Cilla, Notium, Ægiroessa, Pitane, Ægææ, Myrina, and Grynia. These are eleven of the ancient cities of the Æolians; for one of them, Smyrna, was taken away from them by the Ionians; for they too had twelve cities on the continent. These Æolians have settled in a more fertile country than the Ionians, but not equal in climate. 150. The Æolians lost Smyrna in the following manner. They received into their city certain Colophonians, who were unsuccessful in a sedition and driven from their country. But, some time after, the Colophonian exiles, having watched the opportunity while the Smyrnæans were celebrating a festival to Bacchus outside the walls, shut to the gates, and seized the city. But when all the Æolians came to the assistance of the Smyrnæans, an agreement was made that the Ionians should restore the movable property, and that the Æolians should abandon Smyrna. When the Smyrnæans did this, the other eleven cities distributed them among themselves, and gave them the privilege of citizens. 151. These, then, are the Æolian cities on the continent, besides those settled on Mount Ida; for these are altogether distinct. But of those that occupy islands, five cities are situated in Lesbos; for the sixth in Lesbos, Arisba, the Methymnæans reduced to slavery, although they were of kindred blood; one city is situated in Tenedos, and another in what are called the Hundred Islands. Accordingly, the Lesbians and Tenedians, as well as the Ionians of the islands, had nothing to fear; but

[8] See ch. 130.

all the other cities resolved with one accord to follow the Ionians, wherever they should lead the way.

152. When the embassadors of the Ionians and Æolians arrived at Sparta (for this was done with all possible speed), they made choice of a Phocæan, whose name was Pythermus, to speak in behalf of all; he then, having put on a purple robe, in order that as many as possible of the Spartans might hear of it and assemble, and having stood forward, addressed them at length, imploring their assistance. But the Lacedæmonians would not listen to him, and determined not to assist the Ionians: they therefore returned home. Nevertheless, the Lacedæmonians, though they had rejected the Ionian embassadors, dispatched men in a penteconter, as I conjecture, to keep an eye upon the affairs of Cyrus and Ionia. These men, arriving in Phocæa, sent the most eminent person among them, whose name was Lacrines, to Sardis, to warn Cyrus, in the name of the Lacedæmonians, "not to injure any city on the Grecian territory, for in that case they would not pass it by unnoticed." 153. When the herald gave this message, it is related that Cyrus inquired of the Grecians who were present who the Lacedæmonians were, and how many in number, that they sent him such a warning. And when informed, he said to the Spartan herald, "I was never yet afraid of those who in the midst of their city have a place set apart in which they collect and cheat one another by false oaths; and if I continue in health, not the calamities of the Ionians shall be talked about, but their own." This taunt of Cyrus was leveled at the Grecians in general, who have markets for the purposes of buying and selling; for the Persians themselves are not accustomed to use markets, nor have they such a thing as a market. After this, Cyrus, having intrusted Tabalus, a Persian, with the government of Sardis, and appointed Pactyas, a Lydian, to bring away the gold, both that belonging to Crœsus and to the other Lydians, took Crœsus with him, and departed for Ecbatana, for from the first he took no account of the Ionians. But Babylon was an obstacle to him, as were also the Bactrians, the Sacæ, and the Egyptians; against whom he resolved to lead an army in person, and to send some other general against the Ionians. 154. But as soon as Cyrus had marched from Sardis, Pactyas prevailed on the Lydians to revolt from Tabalus and Cyrus; and going down to the sea-coast with all

having the gold taken from Sardis in his possession, he hired mercenaries, and persuaded the inhabitants of the coast to join him; and then, having marched against Sardis, he besieged Tabalus, who was shut up in the citadel.

155. When Cyrus heard this news on his march, he said to Crœsus, "Crœsus, what will be the end of these things? The Lydians, it seems, will never cease to give trouble to me and to themselves. I am in doubt whether it will not be better to reduce them to slavery; for I appear to have acted like one who, having killed the father, has spared the children; so I am carrying away you, who have been something more than a father to the Lydians, and have intrusted their city to the Lydians themselves; and then I wonder at their rebellion!" Now he said what he had in contemplation to do; but Crœsus, fearing lest he should utterly destroy Sardis, answered, "Sir, you have but too much reason for what you say; yet do not give full vent to your anger, nor utterly destroy an ancient city, which is innocent as well of the former as of the present offence; for of the former I myself was guilty, and now bear the punishment on my own head; but in the present instance Pactyas, to whom you intrusted Sardis, is the culprit; let him, therefore, pay the penalty; but pardon the Lydians, and enjoin them to observe the following regulations, to the end that they may never more revolt, nor be troublesome to you: send to them and order them to keep no weapons of war in their possession; and enjoin them to wear tunics under their cloaks, and buskins on their feet; and require them to teach their sons to play on the cithara, to strike the guitar, and to sell by retail; and then you will soon see them becoming women instead of men, so that they will never give you any apprehensions about their revolting." 156. Crœsus suggested this plan, thinking it would be more desirable for the Lydians than that they should be sold for slaves; and being persuaded that unless he could suggest some feasible proposal, he should not prevail with him to alter his resolution; and he dreaded also lest the Lydians, if they should escape the present danger, might hereafter revolt from the Persians, and bring utter ruin on themselves. Cyrus, pleased with the expedient, laid aside his anger, and said that he would follow his advice; then, having sent for Mazares, a Mede, he commanded him to order the Lydians to conform themselves to the regulations proposed by

Crœsus, and moreover to enslave all the rest who had joined the Lydians in the attack on Sardis; but by all means to bring Pactyas to him alive. 157. Cyrus then, having given these orders on his way, proceeded to the settlements of the Persians; but Pactyas, hearing that the army which was coming against him was close at hand, fled in great consternation to Cyme; and Mazares the Mede having marched against Sardis with an inconsiderable division of Cyrus's army, when he found that Pactyas and his party were no longer there, in the first place compelled the Lydians to conform to the injunctions of Cyrus; and by his order the Lydians completely changed their mode of life: after this Mazares dispatched messengers to Cyme, requiring them to deliver up Pactyas. But the Cymæans, in order to come to a decision, resolved to refer the matter to the deity at Branchidæ, for there was there an oracular shrine, erected in former times, which all the Ionians and Æolians were in the practice of consulting: this place is situated in Milesia, above the port of Panormus.[9] 158. The Cymæans therefore, having sent persons to consult the oracle at Branchidæ, asked "what course they should pursue respecting Pactyas that would be most pleasing to the gods:" the answer to their question was, that they should deliver up Pactyas to the Persians. When the Cymæans heard this answer reported, they determined to give him up; but, though most of them came to this determination, Aristodicus, the son of Heraclides, a man of high repute among the citizens, distrusting the oracle, and suspecting the sincerity of the consulters, prevented them from doing so; till at last other messengers, among whom was Aristodicus, went to inquire a second time concerning Pactyas. 159. When they arrived at Branchidæ, Aristodicus consulted the oracle in the name of all, inquiring in these words: "O king, Pactyas, a Lydian, has come to us as a suppliant, to avoid a violent death at the hands of the Persians. They now demand him, and require the Cymæans to give him up. We, however, though we dread the Persian power, have not yet dared to surrender the suppliant, till it be plainly declared by thee what we ought to do." Such was the inquiry of Aristodicus; but the oracle gave the same answer

[9] It will be proper to remark that there were two places of that name, and that this must not be confounded with the port of Panormus, in the vicinity of Ephesus.—*Beloe.*

as before, and bade them surrender Pactyas to the Persians. Upon this Aristodicus deliberately acted as follows; walking round the temple, he took away the sparrows and all other kinds of birds that had built nests in the temple; and while he was doing this, it is reported that a voice issued from the sanctuary, and addressing Aristodicus, spoke as follows: "O most impious of men, how darest thou do this? Dost thou tear my suppliants from my temple?" Aristodicus without hesitation answered, "O king, art thou then so careful to succor thy suppliants, but biddest the Cymæans to deliver up theirs?" The oracle again rejoined: "Yes, I bid you do so; that, having acted impiously, ye may the sooner perish, and never more come and consult the oracle about the delivering up of suppliants." 160. When the Cymæans heard this last answer, they, not wishing to bring destruction on themselves by surrendering Pactyas, or to subject themselves to a siege by protecting him, sent him away to Mitylene. But the Mitylenæans, when Mazares sent a message to them requiring them to deliver up Pactyas, were preparing to do so for some remuneration; what, I am unable to say precisely, for the proposal was never completed; for the Cymæans, being informed of what was being done by the Mitylenæans, dispatched a vessel to Lesbos, and transported Pactyas to Chios, whence he was torn by violence from the temple of Minerva Poliuchus by the Chians and delivered up. The Chians delivered him up in exchange for Atarneus: this Atarneus was a place situate in Mysia, opposite Lesbos. In this manner Pactyas fell into the hands of the Persians; therefore, having got possession of Pactyas, they kept him under guard in order that they might deliver him up to Cyrus. And for a long time after this, none of the Chians would offer barley-meal from Atarneus to any of the gods, or make any cakes of the fruit that came from thence; but all the productions of that country were excluded from the temples. Thus the Chians gave up Pactyas. 161. Mazares, after this, marched against those who had assisted in besieging Tabalus; and, in the first place, he reduced the Prienians to slavery, and in the next overran the whole plain of the Mæander, and gave it to his army to pillage; and he treated Magnesia in the same manner; and shortly afterward he fell sick and died.

162. On his death Harpagus came down as his successor in the command; he also was by birth a Mede, the same whom

Astyages, king of the Medes, entertained at an impious feast, and who assisted Cyrus in ascending the throne. This man, being appointed general by Cyrus on his arrival in Ionia, took several cities by means of earthworks; for he forced the people to retire within their fortifications, and then, having heaped up mounds against the walls, he carried the cities by storm. Phocæa was the first place in Ionia that he attacked.

163. These Phocæans were the first of all the Grecians who undertook long voyages, and they are the people who discovered the Adriatic and Tyrrhenian seas, and Iberia, and Tartessus.[1] They made their voyages in fifty-oared galleys, and not in merchant-ships.[2] When they arrived at Tartessus they were kindly received by the king of the Tartessians, whose name was Arganthonius; he reigned eighty years over Tartessus, and lived to the age of one hundred and twenty. The Phocæans became such great favorites with him, that he at first solicited them to abandon Ionia, and to settle in any part of his territory they should choose; but afterward, finding he could not prevail with the Phocæans to accept his offer, and hearing from them the increasing power of the Mede, he gave them money for the purpose of building a wall round their city; and he gave it unsparingly, for the wall is not a few stades in circumference, and is entirely built of large and well-compacted stone. 164. Now the wall of the Phocæans had been built in the above manner; but when Harpagus marched his army against them, he besieged them, having first offered terms; "that he would be content if the Phocæans would throw down only one of their battlements, and consecrate one house *to the king's use*." The Phocæans, detesting slavery, said "that they wished for one day to deliberate, and would then give their answer;" but while they were deliberating, they required him to draw off his forces from the wall. Harpagus said that, "though he well knew their design, yet he would permit them to consult together." In the interval, then, during which Harpagus withdrew his army from the wall, the Phocæans launched their fifty-oared galleys, and having put their wives, children, and goods on board, together with the images from the temples, and other offerings, except works of

[1] Tartessus was situated between the two branches of the Bœtis (now Guadalquiver), through which it discharges itself into the sea.

[2] See Note [5], B. I. c. 2.

brass, or stone, or pictures—*with these exceptions*, having put every thing on board, and embarked themselves, they set sail for Chios; and the Persians took possession of Phocæa, abandoned by all its inhabitants. 165. The Phocæans, when the Chians refused to sell them the Œnyssæ islands, for fear they should become the seat of trade, and their own island be thereby excluded, thereupon directed their course to Cyrnus; where, by the admonition of an oracle, they had twenty years before built a city, named Alalia. But Arganthonius was at that time dead. On their passage to Cyrnus, having first sailed down to Phocæa, they put to death the Persian garrison which had been left by Harpagus to guard the city. Afterward, when this was accomplished, they pronounced terrible imprecations on any who should desert the fleet; besides this, they sunk a mass of red-hot iron, and swore "that they would never return to Phocæa till this burning mass should appear again." Nevertheless, as they were on their way toward Cyrnus, more than one half of the citizens were seized with regret and yearning for their city and dwellings in the country, and violating their oaths, sailed back to Phocæa; but such of them as kept to their oath weighed anchor and sailed from the Œnyssæ islands. 166. On their arrival at Cyrnus they lived for five years in common with the former settlers; but as they ravaged the territories of all their neighbors, the Tyrrhenians and Carthaginians combined together to make war against them, each with sixty ships; and the Phocæans, on their part, having manned their ships, consisting of sixty in number, met them in the Sardinian Sea; and having engaged, the Phocæans obtained a kind of Cadmean victory;[3] for forty of their own ships were destroyed, and the twenty that survived were disabled, for their prows were blunted. They therefore sailed back to Alalia, and took on board their wives and children, with what property their ships were able to carry, and leaving Cyrnus, sailed to Rhegium. 167. As to the men belonging to the ships destroyed, most of them fell into the hands[4] of the

[3] A proverbial expression, importing "that the victors suffered more than the vanquished."

[4] I have ventured to depart from the usual rendering of this passage, even though it has the sanction of Baehr. It is commonly inferred from the use of the word ἔλαχόν that the Carthaginians and Tyrrhenians "divided their prisoners by lot." That word appears to me, however,

Carthaginians and Tyrrhenians, who took them on shore, and stoned them to death. But afterward, all animals belonging to the Agyllæans that passed by the spot where the Phocæans who had been stoned lay, became distorted, maimed, and crippled, as well sheep as beasts of burden and men. The Agyllæans, therefore, being anxious to expiate the guilt, sent to Delphi; and the Pythia enjoined them to use those rites which the Agyllæans still observe; for they commemorate their death with great magnificence, and have established gymnastic and equestrian contests. This was the fate of these Phocæans; but the others who fled to Rhegium left that place, and got possession of that town in the territory of Œnotria, which is now called Hyela, and they colonized this town by the advice of a certain Posidonian, who told them the Pythia had directed them to establish sacred rites to Cyrnus, as being a hero, but not to colonize the island of that name.

168. The Teians also acted nearly in the same manner as the Phocæans; for when Harpagus, by means of his earthworks, had made himself master of their walls, they all went on board their ships, and sailed away to Thrace, and there settled in the city of Abdera, which Timesius of Clazomenæ having formerly founded, did not enjoy, but was driven out by the Thracians, and is now honored as a hero by the Teians of Abdera.

169. These were the only Ionians who abandoned their country rather than submit to servitude. The rest, except the Milesians, gave battle to Harpagus, and as well as those who abandoned their country, proved themselves brave men, each fighting for his own; but, being defeated and subdued, they severally remained in their own countries, and submitted to the commands imposed on them. But the Milesians, as I have before mentioned,[5] having made a league with Cyrus, remained quiet. Thus, then, was Ionia a second time enslaved;[6] and when Harpagus had subdued the Ionians on the continent, those that occupied the islands, dreading the same fate, made their submission to Cyrus. 170. When the Ionians were

only to mean that "they *happened* to take them"—"it was their *lot* to take them." Indeed, I believe that wherever Herodotus speaks of an actual casting of lots, he always adds some word that expresses the action or method of allotting, as κλήρῳ λαχόντα, iii. 83; παλλομένων δὲ λαγχάνει, iii. 128; τὸν πάλῳ λαχόντα, iv. 94 and 153.

[5] Ch. 143. [6] See ch. 6 and 28.

brought to this wretched condition, and nevertheless still held assemblies at Panionium, I am informed that Bias, of Priene, gave them most salutary advice, which if they had hearkened to him, would have made them the most flourishing of all the Grecians. He advised "that the Ionians, having weighed anchor, should sail in one common fleet to Sardinia, and then build one city for all the Ionians: thus, being freed from servitude, they would flourish, inhabiting the most considerable of the islands, and governing the rest; whereas, if they remained in Ionia, he saw no hope of recovering their liberty." This was the advice of Bias, the Prienean, after the Ionians were ruined. But, before Ionia was ruined, the advice of Thales, the Milesian, who was of Phœnician extraction, was also good. He advised the Ionians to constitute one general council in Teos, which stands in the centre of Ionia, and that the rest of the inhabited cities should nevertheless be governed as independent states. Such was the advice they severally gave.

171. Harpagus, having subdued Ionia, marched against the Carians, Caunians, Lycians, Ionians, and Æolians. Of these the Carians had come from the islands to the continent; for, being subjects of Minos, and anciently called Leleges, they occupied the islands without paying any tribute, as far as I am able to discover, by inquiring into the remotest times; but, whenever he required them, they manned his ships; and as Minos subdued a large territory, and was successful in war, the Carians were by far the most famous of all nations in those times. They also introduced three inventions which the Greeks have adopted. For the Carians set the example of fastening crests upon helmets, and of putting devices on shields: they are also the first who put handles to shields; but, until their time, all who used shields carried them without handles, guiding them with leathern thongs, having them slung round their necks and left shoulders. After a long time had elapsed, the Dorians and Ionians drove the Carians out of the islands, and so they came to the continent. This, then, is the account that the Cretans give of the Carians. The Carians themselves, however, do not admit its correctness, but consider themselves to be aboriginal inhabitants of the continent, and always to have gone under the same name as they now do; and, in testimony of this, they show an ancient temple of Jupiter Carius at Mylasa, which the Mysians and Lydians share, as

kinsmen to the Carians, for they say that Lydus and Mysus were brothers to Car. Now they do share the temple, but none who are of a different nation, though of the same language with the Carians, are allowed to share it. 172. The Caunians, in my opinion, are aboriginals, though they say they are from Crete. However, they have assimilated their language to that of the Carians, or the Carians to theirs; for this I can not determine with certainty. Their customs are totally distinct from those of other nations, even from the Carians; for they account it very becoming for men, women, and boys to meet together to drink according to their age and intimacy. They had formerly erected temples to foreign deities, but afterward, when they changed their minds (for they resolved to have none but their own national deities), all the Caunians armed themselves, both young and old, and, beating the air with their spears, marched in a body to the Calindian confines, and said they were expelling strange gods. They then have such customs. 173. The Lycians were originally sprung from Crete, for in ancient time Crete was entirely in the possession of barbarians. But a dispute having arisen between Sarpedon and Minos, sons of Europa, respecting the sovereign power, when Minos got the upper hand in the struggle, he drove out Sarpedon with his partisans; and they, being expelled, came to the land of Milyas in Asia; for the country which the Lycians now occupy was anciently called Milyas; but the Milyans were then called Solymi. So long as Sarpedon reigned over them, they went by the name of Termilæ, which they brought with them, and the Lycians are still called by that name by their neighbors. But when Lycus, son of Pandion, who was likewise driven out by his brother Ægeus, came from Athens, the Termilæ, under Sarpedon, in course of time, got to be called Lycians after him. Their customs are partly Cretan and partly Carian; but they have one peculiar to themselves, in which they differ from all other nations; for they take their name from their mothers and not from their fathers; so that if any one ask another who he is, he will describe himself by his mother's side, and reckon up his maternal ancestry in the female line. And if a free-born woman marry a slave, the children are accounted of pure birth; but if a man who is a citizen, even though of high rank, marry a foreigner or cohabit with a concubine, the children are infamous.

174. Now the Carians were subdued by Harpagus without having done any memorable action in their own defense; and not only the Carians, but all the Grecians that inhabit those parts, behaved themselves with as little courage; and among others settled there are the Cnidians, colonists from the Lacedæmonians, whose territory juts on the sea, and is called the Triopean; but the region of Bybassus commenced from the peninsula, for all Cnidia, except a small space, is surrounded by water (for the Ceramic gulf bounds it on the north, and on the south the sea by Syme and Rhodes): now this small space, which is about five stades in breadth, the Cnidians, wishing to make their territory insular, designed to dig through while Harpagus was subduing Ionia; for the whole of their dominions were within the isthmus; and where the Cnidian territory terminates toward the continent, there is the isthmus that they designed to dig through. But as they were carrying on the work with great diligence, the workmen appeared to be wounded to a greater extent and in a more strange manner than usual, both in other parts of the body, and particularly in the eyes, by the chipping of the rock; they therefore sent deputies to Delphi to inquire what was the cause of the obstruction; and, as the Cnidians say, the Pythian answered as follows in trimeter verse: "Build not a tower on the isthmus, nor dig it through, for Jove would have made it an island had he so willed." When the Pythia had given this answer, the Cnidians desisted from their work, and surrendered without resistance to Harpagus as soon as he approached with his army. 175. The Pedasians were situate inland above Halicarnassus; when any mischief is about to befall them or their neighbors, the priestess of Minerva has a long beard: this has three times occurred. Now these were the only people about Caria who opposed Harpagus for any time, and gave him much trouble by fortifying a mountain called Lyda. 176. After some time, however, the Pedasians were subdued. The Lycians, when Harpagus marched his army toward the Xanthian plain, went out to meet him, and, engaging with very inferior numbers, displayed great feats of valor; but, being defeated and shut up within their city,

they collected their wives, children, property, and servants within the citadel, and then set fire to it and burned it to the ground. When they had done this, and engaged themselves by the strongest oaths, all the Xanthians went out and died fighting. Of the modern Lycians, who are said to be Xanthians, all, except eighty families, are strangers; but these eighty families happened at the time to be away from home, and so survived. Thus Harpagus got possession of Xanthus and Caunia almost in the same manner; for the Caunians generally followed the example of the Lycians.

177. Harpagus therefore reduced the lower parts of Asia, but Cyrus conquered the upper parts, subduing every nation without exception. The greatest part of these I shall pass by without notice; but I will make mention of those which gave him most trouble, and are most worthy of being recorded.

178. When Cyrus had reduced all the other parts of the continent, he attacked the Assyrians. Now Assyria contains many large cities, but the most renowned and the strongest, and where the seat of government was established after the destruction of Nineveh, was Babylon, which is of the following description. The city stands in a spacious plain, and is quadrangular, and shows a front on every side of one hundred and twenty stades; these stades make up the sum of four hundred and eighty in the whole circumference. Such is the size of the city of Babylon. It was adorned in a manner surpassing any city we are acquainted with. In the first place, a moat deep, wide, and full of water, runs entirely around it; next, there is a wall fifty royal cubits in breadth, and in height two hundred; but the royal cubit is larger than the common one by three fingers' breadth. 179. And here I think I ought to explain how the earth taken out of the moat was consumed, and in what manner the wall was built. As they dug the moat they made bricks of the earth that was taken out, and when they had moulded a sufficient number they baked them in kilns. Then, making use of hot asphalt for cement, and laying wattled reeds between the thirty bottom courses of bricks, they first built up the sides of the moat, and afterward the wall itself in the same manner; and on the top of the wall, at the edges, they built dwellings of one story, fronting each other, and they left a space between these dwellings

sufficient for turning a chariot with four horses. In the circumference of the wall there were a hundred gates, all of brass, as also are the posts and lintels. Eight days' journey from Babylon stands another city, called Is, on a small river of the same name, which discharges its stream into the Euphrates. Now this river brings down with its water many lumps of bitumen, from whence the bitumen used in the wall of Babylon was brought. 180. In this manner Babylon was encompassed with a wall; and the city consists of two divisions, for a river, called the Euphrates, separates it in the middle: this river, which is broad, deep, and rapid, flows from Armenia, and falls into the Red Sea. The wall, therefore, on either bank, has an elbow carried down to the river; from thence, along the curvatures of each bank of the river, runs a wall of baked bricks. The city itself, which is full of houses three and four stories high, is cut up into straight streets, as well all the other as the transverse ones that lead to the river. At the end of each street a little gate is formed in the wall along the river-side, in number equal to the streets; and they are all made of brass, and lead down to the edge of the river. 181. This outer wall, then, is the chief defense, but another wall runs round within, not much inferior to the other in strength, though narrower. In the middle of each division of the city fortified buildings were erected; in one, the royal palace, with a spacious and strong inclosure, brazen-gated; and in the other, the precinct of Jupiter Belus, which in my time was still in existence, a square building of two stades on every side. In the midst of this precinct is built a solid tower of one stade both in length and breadth, and on this tower rose another, and another upon that, to the number of eight; and an ascent to these is outside, running spirally round all the towers. About the middle of the ascent there is a landing-place and seats to rest on, on which those who go up sit down and rest themselves; and in the uppermost tower stands a spacious temple, and in this temple is placed, handsomely furnished, a large couch, and by its side a table of gold. No statue has been erected within it, nor does any mortal pass the night there, except only a native woman, chosen by the god out of the whole nation, as the Chaldeans, who are priests of this deity, say. 182. These same priests assert, though I can not credit what they say, that the god himself comes to the temple and reclines on the bed, in the same manner as the Egyptians say happens at Thebes in Egypt, for there also a woman lies in the temple of Theban Jupiter, and both are said to have no intercourse with men; in the same manner also the priestess who utters the oracles at Pataræ in Lycia, when the god is there, for there is not an oracle there at all times, but when there she is shut up during the night in the temple with the god. 183. There is also another temple below, within the precinct at Babylon; in it is a large golden statue of Jupiter seated, and near it is placed a large table of gold, the throne also and the step are of gold, which together weigh eight hundred talents, as the Chaldæans affirm. Outside the temple is a golden altar, and another large altar, where full-grown sheep are sacrificed; for on the golden altar only sucklings may be offered. On the great altar the Chaldæans consume yearly a thousand talents of frankincense when they celebrate the festival of this god. There was also at that time within the precincts of this temple a statue of solid gold, twelve cubits high: I, indeed, did not see it; I only relate what is said by the Chaldæans. Darius, son of Hystaspes, formed a design to take away this statue, but dared not do so; but Xerxes, son of Darius, took it, and killed the priest who forbade him to remove it. Thus, then, this temple was adorned; and, besides, there are many private offerings.

184. There were many others who reigned over Babylon, whom I shall mention in my Assyrian history, who beautified the walls and temples, and among them were two women. The first of these, named Semiramis, lived five generations before the other. She raised mounds along the plain which are worthy of admiration; for, before, the river used to overflow the whole plain like a sea. 185. But the other, who was queen next after her, and whose name was Nitocris (she was much more sagacious than the queen before her), in the first place, left monuments of herself which I shall presently describe; and, in the next place, when she saw the power of the Medes growing formidable and restless, and that, among other cities, Nineveh was captured by them, she took every possible precaution for her own defense. First of all, with respect to the river Euphrates, which before ran in a straight line, and which flows through the middle of the city, this, by

having channels dug above, she made so winding that in its course it touches three times at one and the same village in Assyria: the name of this village at which the Euphrates touches is Arderica; and to this day, those who go from our sea to Babylon, if they travel by the Euphrates, come three times to this village on three successive days. She also raised on either bank of the river a mound, astonishing for its magnitude and height. At a considerable distance above Babylon, she had a reservoir for a lake dug, carrying it out some distance from the river, and in depth digging down to water, and in width making its circumference of four hundred and twenty stades: she consumed the soil from this excavation by heaping it up on the banks of the river, and when it was completely dug, she had stones brought, and built a casing to it all round. She had both these works done, the river made winding, and the whole excavation a lake, in order that the current, being broken by frequent turnings, might be more slow, and the navigation to Babylon tedious, and that after the voyage a long march round the lake might follow. All this was done in that part of the country where the approach to Babylon is the nearest, and where is the shortest way for the Medes, in order that the Medes might not, by holding intercourse with her people, become acquainted with her affairs. 186. She inclosed herself, therefore, with these defenses by digging, and immediately afterward made the following addition. As the city consisted of two divisions, which were separated by the river, during the reign of former kings, when any one had occasion to cross from one division to the other, he was obliged to cross in a boat; and this, in my opinion, was very troublesome. She therefore provided for this; for, after she had dug the reservoir for the lake, she left this other monument, built by similar toil. She had large blocks of stone cut, and when they were ready, and the place was completely dug out, she turned the whole stream of the river into the place she had dug: while this was filled, and the ancient channel had become dry, in the first place, she lined with burned bricks the banks of the river throughout the city, and the descents that lead from the gates to the river, in the same manner as the walls. In the next place, about the middle of the city she built a bridge with the stones she had prepared, and bound them together with plates of lead and iron. Upon these stones she laid, during the day, square planks of timber, on which the Babylonians might pass over; but at night these planks were removed, to prevent people from crossing by night and robbing one another. When the hollow that was dug had become a lake filled by the river, and the bridge was finished, she brought back the river to its ancient channel from the lake. And thus, the excavation having been turned into a marsh, appeared to answer the purpose for which it was made, and a bridge was built for the use of the inhabitants.

187. This same queen also contrived the following deception. Over the most frequented gate of the city she prepared a sepulchre for herself, high up above the gate itself; and on the sepulchre she had engraved, SHOULD ANY ONE OF MY SUCCESSORS, KINGS OF BABYLON, FIND HIMSELF IN WANT OF MONEY, LET HIM OPEN THIS SEPULCHRE, AND TAKE AS MUCH AS HE CHOOSES; BUT IF HE BE NOT IN WANT, LET HIM NOT OPEN IT, FOR THAT WERE NOT WELL. This monument remained undisturbed until the kingdom fell to Darius; but it seemed hard to Darius that this gate should be of no use, and that when money was lying there, and this money inviting him to take it, he should not do so; but no use was made of this gate for this reason, that a dead body was over the head of any one who passed through it. He therefore opened the sepulchre, and instead of money, found only the body, and these words written: HADST THOU NOT BEEN INSATIABLY COVETOUS, AND GREEDY OF THE MOST SORDID GAIN, THOU WOULDST NOT HAVE OPENED THE CHAMBERS OF THE DEAD. Such, then, is the account given of this queen.

188. Cyrus made war against the son of this queen, who bore the name of his father Labynetus, and had the empire of Assyria. Now when the great king leads his army in person, he carries with him from home provisions well prepared and cattle; and he takes with him water from the river Choaspes, which flows past Susa, of which alone, and no other, the king drinks. A great number of four-wheeled carriages, drawn by mules, carry the water of this river, after it has been boiled in silver vessels, and follow him from place to place wherever he marches. 189. When Cyrus, in his march against Babylon, arrived at the river Gyndes, whose fountains are in the Matianian mountains, and which flows through the

land of the Dardanians, and falls into another river, the Tigris; which latter, flowing by the city of Opis, discharges itself into the Red Sea: now, when Cyrus was endeavoring to cross this river Gyndes, which can be passed only in boats, one of the sacred white horses, through wantonness, plunged into the stream, and attempted to swim over, but the stream having carried him away and drowned him, Cyrus was much enraged with the river for this affront, and threatened to make his stream so weak that henceforth women should easily cross it without wetting their knees. After this menace, deferring his expedition against Babylon, he divided his army into two parts; and having so divided it, he marked out by lines one hundred and eighty channels, on each side of the river, diverging every way; then having distributed his army, he commanded them to dig. His design was indeed executed by the great numbers he employed, but they spent the whole summer in the work. 190. When Cyrus had avenged himself on the river Gyndes by distributing it into three hundred and sixty channels, and the second spring began to shine, he then advanced against Babylon. But the Babylonians, having taken the field, awaited his coming; and when he had advanced near the city, the Babylonians gave battle, and, being defeated, were shut up in the city. But as they had been long aware of the restless spirit of Cyrus, and saw that he attacked all nations alike, they had laid up provisions for many years, and therefore were under no apprehensions about a siege. On the other hand, Cyrus found himself in difficulty, since much time had elapsed, and his affairs were not at all advanced. 191. Whether, therefore, some one else made the suggestion to him in his perplexity, or whether he himself devised the plan, he had recourse to the following stratagem. Having stationed the bulk of his army near the passage of the river where it enters Babylon, and again having stationed another division beyond the city, where the river makes its exit, he gave orders to his forces to enter the city as soon as they should see the stream fordable. Having thus stationed his forces and given these directions, he himself marched away with the ineffective part of his army; and having come to the lake, Cyrus did the same with respect to the river and the lake as the queen of the Babylonians had done; for having diverted the river, by means of a canal, into the lake, which was before a swamp, he made the ancient channel fordable by the sinking of the river. When this took place, the Persians who were appointed to that purpose close to the stream of the river, which had now subsided to about the middle of a man's thigh, entered Babylon by this passage. If, however, the Babylonians had been aware of it beforehand, or had known what Cyrus was about, they would not have suffered the Persians to enter the city, but would have utterly destroyed them; for, having shut all the little gates that lead down to the river, and mounting the walls that extend along the banks of the river, they would have caught them as in a net; whereas the Persians came upon them by surprise. It is related by the people who inhabited this city, that, by reason of its great extent, when they who were at the extremities were taken, those of the Babylonians who inhabited the centre knew nothing of the capture (for it happened to be a festival); but they were dancing at the time, and enjoying themselves, till they received certain information of the truth. And thus Babylon was taken for the first time.[7]

192. How great was the power of the Babylonians I can prove by many other circumstances, and especially by the following. The whole territory over which the great king reigns is divided into districts, for the purpose of furnishing subsistence for him and his army, in addition to the usual tribute; now, whereas there are twelve months in the year, the Babylonian territory provides him with subsistence for four months, and all the rest of Asia for the remaining eight. Thus the territory of Assyria amounts to a third part of the power of all Asia, and the government of this region, which the Persians call a satrapy, is considerable, since it yielded a full artabe of silver every day to Tritæchmes, son of Artabazus, who held this district from the king. The artabe is a Persian measure, containing three Attic chœnices more than the Attic medimnus. And he had a private stud of horses, in addition to those used in war, of eight hundred stallions, and sixteen thousand mares; for each stallion served twenty mares. He kept, too, such a number of Indian dogs, that four considerable towns in the plain were exempted from all other taxes, and appointed to find food for the dogs. Such were the advantages accruing

[7] It was again taken by Darius. See Book III. chap. 159.

to the governor of Babylon. 193. The land of Assyria is but little watered by rain, and that little nourishes the root of the corn; however, the stalk grows up, and the grain comes to maturity by being irrigated from the river, not, as in Egypt, by the river overflowing the fields, but it is irrigated by the hand and by engines. For the Babylonian territory, like Egypt, is intersected by canals, and the largest of these is navigable, stretching in the direction of the winter sunrise;[8] and it extends from the Euphrates to another river, the river Tigris, on which the city of Nineveh stood. This is, of all lands with which we are acquainted, by far the best for the growth of corn; but it does not carry any show of producing trees of any kind, neither the fig, nor the vine, nor the olive; yet it is so fruitful in the produce of corn, that it yields continually two hundred-fold, and when it produces its best, it yields even three hundred-fold. The blades of wheat and barley grow there to full four fingers in breadth; and though I well know to what a height millet and sesama grow, I shall not mention it; for I am well assured that, to those who have never been in the Babylonian country, what has been said concerning its productions will appear to many incredible. They use no other oil than such as is drawn from sesama. They have palm-trees growing all over the plain; most of these bear fruit, from which they make bread, wine, and honey. These they cultivate as fig-trees, both in other respects, and they also tie the fruit of that which the Grecians call the male palm about those trees that bear dates, in order that the fly, entering the date, may ripen it, lest otherwise the fruit fall before maturity; for the males have flies in the fruit, just like wild fig-trees.

194. The most wonderful thing of all here, next to the city itself, is what I now proceed to describe: their vessels that sail down the river to Babylon are circular, and made of leather; for when they have cut the ribs out of willows that grow in Armenia above Babylon, they cover them with hides extended on the outside, by way of a bottom; neither making any distinction in the stern, nor contracting the prow, but making them circular like a buckler; then having lined this vessel throughout with reeds, they suffer it to be carried down by the river, freighted with merchandise; but they chiefly

[8] That is, southeast.

take down casks of palm wine. The vessel is steered by two spars, and two men standing upright, one of whom draws his spar in and the other thrusts his out. Some of these vessels are made very large, and others of a smaller size; but the largest of them carry a cargo of five thousand talents. Every vessel has a live ass on board, and the larger ones more; for after they arrive at Babylon, and have disposed of their freight, they sell the ribs of the boat and all the reeds by public auction; then, having piled the skins on the asses, they return by land to Armenia, for it is not possible by any means to sail up the river by reason of the rapidity of the current: and for this reason they make their vessels of skins and not of wood, and at their return to Armenia with their asses they construct other vessels in the same manner. Such, then, is the description of their boats. 195. For their dress, they wear a linen tunic that reaches down to the feet; over this they put another garment of wool, and over all a short white cloak; they have sandals peculiar to the country, very like the Bœotian clogs. They wear long hair, binding their heads with turbans, and anoint the whole body with perfumes. Every man has a seal, and a staff curiously wrought; and on every staff is carved either an apple, a rose, a lily, an eagle, or something of the kind; for it is not allowable to wear a stick without a device. Such, then, is their manner of adorning the body.

196. The following customs prevail among them. This, in my opinion, is the wisest, which I hear the Venetians, of Illyria, also practice. Once in every year the following course is pursued in every village. Whatever maidens were of a marriageable age, they used to collect together and bring in a body to one place; around them stood a crowd of men. Then a crier, having made them stand up one by one, offered them for sale, beginning with the most beautiful; and when she had been sold for a large sum, he put up another who was next in beauty. They were sold on condition that they should be married. Such men among the Babylonians as were rich and desirous of marrying, used to bid against one another, and purchase the handsomest; but such of the lower classes as were desirous of marrying did not require a beautiful form, but were willing to take the plainer damsels with a sum of money; for when the crier had finished selling the handsomest of the maidens, he made the ugliest stand up, or one that was

a cripple, and put her up to auction, for the person who would marry her with the least sum, until she was adjudged to the man who offered to take the smallest sum. This money was obtained from *the sale of* the handsome maidens; and thus the beautiful ones portioned out the ugly and the crippled. A father was not allowed to give his daughter in marriage to whom he pleased, neither might a purchaser carry off a maiden without security, but he was first obliged to give security that he would certainly marry her, and then he might take her away. If they did not agree, a law was enacted that the money should be repaid. It was also lawful for any one who pleased to come from another village and purchase. Such was their best institution; it has not, however, continued to exist. They have lately adopted another regulation to prevent them from ill-treating the women, or carrying them away to another city; for now that, since the taking of the city, they have been harshly treated and ruined in fortune, all the meaner sort, from want of a livelihood, prostitute their daughters. 197. They have also this other custom, second to the former in wisdom. They bring out their sick to the market-place, for they have no physicians; then those who pass by the sick person confer with him about the disease, *to discover* whether they have themselves been afflicted with the same disease as the sick person, or have seen others so afflicted: thus the passers-by confer with him, and advise him to have recourse to the same treatment as that by which they escaped a similar disease, or as they have known cure others. And they are not allowed to pass by a sick person in silence, without inquiring into the nature of his distemper. 198. They embalm the dead in honey, and their funeral lamentations are like those of the Egyptians. As often as a Babylonian has had intercourse with his wife, he sits over burning incense, and his wife does the same in some other place; at break of day both wash, for they will not touch any vessel till they have washed. The same practice is observed by the Arabians.

199. The most disgraceful of the Babylonian customs is the following: every native woman is obliged, once in her life, to sit in the temple of Venus, and have intercourse with some stranger; and many, disdaining to mix with the rest, being proud on account of their wealth, come in covered carriages, and take up their station at the temple with a numerous train

of servants attending them. But the far greater part do thus: many sit down in the temple of Venus, wearing a crown of corn round their heads; some are continually coming in, and others are going out. Passages marked out in a straight line lead in every direction through the women, along which strangers pass and make their choice. When a woman has once seated herself, she must not return home till some stranger has thrown a piece of silver into her lap, and lain with her outside the temple. He who throws the silver must say thus: "I beseech the goddess Mylitta to favor thee;" for the Assyrians call Venus Mylitta. The silver may be ever so small, for she will not reject it, inasmuch as it is not lawful for her to do so, for such silver is accounted sacred. The woman follows the first man that throws, and refuses no one. But when she has had intercourse and has absolved herself from her obligation to the goddess, she returns home; and after that time, however great a sum you may give her, you will not gain possession of her. Those that are endowed with beauty and symmetry of shape are soon set free; but the deformed are detained a long time, from inability to satisfy the law, for some wait for a space of three or four years. In some parts of Cyprus there is a custom very similar. 200. These customs, then, prevail among the Babylonians. There are three tribes among them that eat nothing but fish; these, when they have taken and dried them in the sun, they treat in the following manner; they put them into a mortar, and having pounded them with a pestle, sift them through a fine cloth; then, whoever pleases, kneads them into a cake, or bakes them like bread.

201. When Cyrus had conquered this nation, he was anxious to reduce the Massagetæ to subjection. Now this nation is said to be both powerful and valiant, dwelling toward the east and the rising sun beyond the river Araxes, over against the Issedonians: there are some who say that this nation is Scythian. 202. The Araxes is reported by some persons to be greater, by others less, than the Ister; they say that there are many islands in it, some nearly equal in size to Lesbos; and that in them are men who, during the summer, feed upon all manner of roots, which they dig out of the ground; and that they store up for food ripe fruits which they find on the trees, and feed upon these during the winter. *They add*

that they have discovered other trees that produce fruit of a peculiar kind, which the inhabitants, when they meet together in companies, and have lit a fire, throw on a fire, as they sit round in a circle; and that by inhaling the fumes of the burning fruit that has been thrown on, they become intoxicated by the odor, just as the Greeks do by wine; and that the more fruit is thrown on, the more intoxicated they become, until they rise up to dance and betake themselves to singing. In this manner these islanders are reported to live. The river Araxes flows from the Matienian mountains, whence also springs the river Gyndes, which Cyrus distributed into the three hundred and sixty trenches; and it gushes out from forty springs, all of which, except one, discharge themselves into fens and swamps, in which it is said men live who feed on raw fish, and clothe themselves in the skins of sea-calves; but the one stream of the Araxes flows through an unobstructed channel into the Caspian Sea. The Caspian is a sea by itself, having no communication with any other sea; for the whole of that which the Grecians navigate, and that beyond the Pillars, called the Atlantic, and the Red Sea, are all one. 203. But the Caspian is a separate sea of itself; being in length a fifteen days' voyage for a rowing boat, and in breadth, where it is widest, an eight days' voyage. On the western shore of this sea stretches the Caucasus, which is in extent the largest, and in height the loftiest of all mountains: it contains within itself many and various nations of men, who for the most part live upon the produce of wild fruit-trees. In this country, it is said, there are trees which produce leaves of such a nature, that by rubbing them and mixing them with water the people paint figures on their garments; these figures, they say, do not wash out, but grow old with the wool, as if they had been woven in from the first. It is said that sexual intercourse among these people takes place openly, as with cattle. 204. The Caucasus, then, bounds the western side of this sea, which is called the Caspian; and on the east, toward the rising sun, succeeds a plain in extent unbounded in the prospect. A great portion of this extensive plain is inhabited by the Massagetæ, against whom Cyrus resolved to make war; for the motives that urged and incited him to this enterprise were many and powerful; first of all his birth, which he thought was something more than human; and, secondly, the good fortune which had attended him in his wars; for wherever Cyrus directed his arms, it was impossible for that nation to escape.

205. A woman whose husband was dead was queen of the Massagetæ; her name was Tomyris; and Cyrus sent embassadors under pretense of wooing her, and made her an offer of marriage. But Tomyris, being aware that he was not wooing her, but the kingdom of the Massagetæ, forbade their approach. Upon this Cyrus, perceiving his artifice ineffectual, marched to the Araxes, and openly prepared to make war on the Massagetæ, by throwing bridges over the river, and building turrets on the boats which carried over his army. 206. While he was employed in this work, Tomyris sent a herald to him with this message; "King of the Medes, desist from your great exertions; for you can not know if they will terminate to your advantage; and having desisted, reign over your own dominions, and bear to see me governing what is mine. But if you will not attend to my advice, and prefer every thing before peace—*in a word*, if you are very anxious to make trial of the Massagetæ, toil no longer in throwing a bridge over the river, but do you cross over to our side, while we retire three days' march from the river; or if you had rather receive us on your side, do you the like." When Cyrus heard this proposal, he called a council of the principal Persians; and having assembled them, he laid the matter before them, and demanded their opinion as to what he should do; they unanimously advised him to let Tomyris pass with her army into his territory. 207. But Crœsus the Lydian, who was present and disapproved this advice, delivered a contrary opinion to that which was put forward, and said: "O king, I assured you long ago that, since Jupiter delivered me into your hands, I would to the utmost of my power avert whatever misfortune I should see impending over your house; and my own calamities,[9] sad as they are, have been lessons to me. If you think yourself immortal, and that you command an army that is so too, it were needless for me to make known to you my opinion; but if you know that you too are a man, and that you command such as are men, learn this first of all, that there is a wheel in human affairs, which, continually revolv-

[9] This appears to have been a proverb παθήματα μαθήματα.

ing, does not suffer the same persons to be always successful. Now, therefore, I hold an opinion touching the matter before us wholly at variance with that already given; for if we shall receive the enemy into this country, there is this danger in so doing, if you are defeated, you will lose, besides, your whole empire; for it is plain that if the Massagetæ are victorious, they will not flee home again, but will march upon your territories; and if you are victorious, your victory is not so complete as if, having crossed over into their territory, you should conquer the Massagetæ, and pursue them in their flight; for I will carry the comparison throughout, *it is plain* that if you are victorious over your adversaries you will march directly into the dominions of Tomyris. In addition to what has been now stated, it were a disgrace and intolerable that Cyrus, the son of Cambyses, should give way and retreat before a woman. My opinion therefore is, that you should pass over and advance as far as they retire; and then, by the following stratagem, endeavor to get the better of them. As I hear, the Massagetæ are unacquainted with the Persian luxuries, and are unused to the comforts of life. *My opinion then is*, that, having cut up and dressed abundance of cattle, you should lay out a feast in our camp for these men; and besides, bowls of unmixed wine without stint, and all other provisions; and that, having done this, and having left the weakest part of your army behind, the rest should return again toward the river; for the Massagetæ, if I mistake not, when they see so much excellent fare, will turn to immediately, and after that there remains for us the display of mighty achievements."

208. Now these two contrary opinions were given. Cyrus, rejecting the former, and approving that of Crœsus, bade Tomyris retire, for that he would cross over to her. She accordingly retired, as she had promised at first. But Cyrus, having placed Crœsus in the hands of his son Cambyses, to whom he also intrusted the kingdom, and having strictly charged him to honor Crœsus, and treat him well, in case his inroad on the Massagetæ should fail—having given these injunctions, and sent them back to Persia, he himself crossed the river with his army. 209. When he had passed the Araxes, and night came on, he saw the following vision, as he was sleeping in the country of the Massagetæ. Cyrus fancied in his sleep that he saw the eldest son of Hystaspes

with wings on his shoulders; and that with one of these he overshadowed Asia, and with the other Europe. Now Darius, who was then about twenty years of age, was the eldest son of Hystaspes, son of Arsames, one of the Achæmenides; and he had been left in Persia, for he had not yet attained the age of military service. When, therefore, Cyrus awoke, he considered his dream with attention; and as it seemed to him of great moment, he summoned Hystaspes, and taking him aside, said, "Hystaspes, your son has been detected plotting against me and my empire; and I will show you how I know it for a certainty. The gods watch over me, and forewarn me of every thing that is about to befall me. Now, in the past night, as I was sleeping, I saw the eldest of your sons with wings on his shoulders, and with one of these he overshadowed Asia, and Europe with the other; from this vision, it can not be otherwise than that your son is forming designs against me; do you, therefore, go back to Persia with all speed, and take care that, when I have conquered these people and return home, you bring your son before me to be examined." 210. Cyrus spoke thus under a persuasion that Darius was plotting against him; but the deity forewarned him that he himself would die in that very expedition, and that his kingdom would devolve on Darius. Hystaspes, however, answered in these words: "God forbid, O king, that a Persian should be born who would plot against you! But if any such there be, may sudden destruction overtake him; for you have made the Persians free instead of being slaves, and instead of being ruled over by others, to rule over all; but if any vision informs you that my son is forming any plot against you, I freely surrender him to you to deal with as you please." Hystaspes, having given this answer, repassed the Araxes and went to Persia, for the purpose of keeping his son Darius in custody for Cyrus.

211. Cyrus, having advanced one day's march from the Araxes, proceeded to act according to the suggestion of Crœsus. After this, when Cyrus and the effective part of the Persian army had marched back to the Araxes, leaving the ineffective part behind, a third division of the army of the Massagetæ attacked those of Cyrus's forces that had been left behind, and, after some resistance, put them to death. Then, seeing the feast laid out, as soon as they had overcome their enemies

they lay down and feasted, and being filled with food and wine, fell asleep. But the Persians having attacked them, put many of them to death, and took a still greater number prisoners, and among them the son of Queen Tomyris, who commanded the Massagetæ, and whose name was Spargapises. 212. She, when she heard what had befallen her army and her son, sent a herald to Cyrus with the following message: "Cyrus, insatiate with blood, be not elated with what has now happened, that by the fruit of the vine, with which ye yourselves, when filled with it, so rave, that when it descends into your bodies evil words float on your lips—*be not elated* that by such a poison you have deceived and conquered my son, instead of by prowess in battle. Now, however, take the good advice that I offer you. Restore my son; depart out of this country unpunished for having insolently disgraced a third division of the army of the Massagetæ. But if you will not do this, I swear by the sun, the Lord of the Massagetæ, that, insatiable as you are, I will glut you with blood." 213. Cyrus, however, paid no attention to this message; but Spargapises, the son of Queen Tomyris, as soon as he recovered from the effects of the wine, and perceived in what a plight he was, begged of Cyrus that he might be freed from his fetters; but as soon as he was set free, and found his hands at liberty, he put himself to death. Such was the end he met with. 214. But Tomyris, finding Cyrus did not listen to her, assembled all her forces, and engaged with him. I think that this battle was the most obstinate that was ever fought between barbarians; and I am informed that it took place in the following manner: it is related that, first of all, they stood at a distance and used their bows, and that afterward, when they had emptied their quivers, they engaged in close fight with their swords and spears, and that thus they continued fighting for a long time, and neither were willing to give way; but at length the Massagetæ got the better, and the greater part of the Persian army was cut in pieces on the spot, and Cyrus himself killed, after he had reigned twenty-nine years. But Tomyris, having filled a skin with human blood, sought for the body of Cyrus among the slain of the Persians, and having found it, thrust the head into the skin, and insulting the dead body, said: "Thou hast indeed ruined me, though alive and victorious in battle, since thou hast taken my son by stratagem; but I will now glut thee with blood, as I threatened." Of the many accounts given of the end of Cyrus, this appears to me most worthy of credit.

215. The Massagetæ resemble the Scythians in their dress and mode of living. They have both horse and foot; for they have some of each; and bow-men, and javelin-men, who are accustomed to carry battle-axes. They use gold and brass for every thing; for, in whatever concerns spears, and arrow-points, and battle-axes, they use brass; but for the head, and belts, and shoulder-pieces, they are ornamented with gold. In like manner, with regard to the chests of horses, they put on breast-plates of brass; but the bridle-bit and cheek-pieces are ornamented with gold. They make no use of silver or iron, for neither of those metals are found in their country, but they have brass and gold in abundance. 216. Their manners are as follows: each man marries a wife, but they use the women promiscuously; for what the Grecians say the Scythians do, is a mistake, for they do it not, but the Massagetæ; for when a Massagetan desires to have the company of a woman, he hangs up his quiver in front of her chariot, and has intercourse with her without shame. No particular term of life is prescribed to them; but when a man has attained a great age, all his kinsmen meet, and sacrifice him, together with cattle of several kinds; and when they have boiled the flesh, they feast on it. This death they account the most happy; for they do not eat the bodies of those who die of disease, but bury them in the earth, and think it a great misfortune that they did not reach the age to be sacrificed. They sow nothing, but live on cattle and fish, which the river Araxes yields in abundance, and they are drinkers of milk. They worship the sun only of all the gods, and sacrifice horses to him; and this is the reason of this custom—they think it right to offer the swiftest of all animals to the swiftest of all the gods.

BOOK II.

EUTERPE.

After the death of Cyrus, Cambyses succeeded to the kingdom. He was son of Cyrus and Cassandane, the daughter of Pharnaspes, who having died some time before, Cyrus both deeply mourned for her himself and commanded all his subjects to mourn. Cambyses then, being son of this lady and Cyrus, considered the Ionians and Æolians as his hereditary slaves; *when, therefore,* he made an expedition against Egypt, he took with him others of his subjects, and also some of the Greeks over whom he bore rule.

2. The Egyptians, before the reign of Psammitichus, considered themselves to be the most ancient of mankind. But after Psammitichus, having come to the throne, endeavored to ascertain who were the most ancient, from that time they consider the Phrygians to have been before them, and themselves before all others. Now, when Psammitichus was unable, by inquiry, to discover any solution of this question, who were the most ancient of men, he devised the following expedient. He gave two new-born children of poor parents to a shepherd, to be brought up among his flocks in the following manner: he gave strict orders that no one should utter a word in their presence, that they should lie in a solitary room by themselves, and that he should bring goats to them at certain times, and that, when he had satisfied them with milk, he should attend to his other employments. Psammitichus contrived and ordered this for the purpose of hearing what word the children would first articulate after they had given over their insignificant mewlings; and such accordingly was the result; for, when the shepherd had pursued this plan for the space of two years, one day, as he opened the door and went in, both the children, falling upon him, and holding

out their hands, cried "Becos." The shepherd, when he first heard it, said nothing; but when this same word was constantly repeated to him whenever he went and tended the children, he at length acquainted his master, and by his command brought the children into his presence. When Psammitichus heard the same, he inquired what people call any thing by the name of "Becos;" and on inquiry, he discovered that the Phrygians call bread by that name. Thus the Egyptians, convinced by the above experiment, allowed that the Phrygians were more ancient than themselves. 3. This relation I had from the priests of Vulcan at Memphis. But the Greeks tell many other foolish things, and, moreover, that Psammitichus, having had the tongues of some women cut out, then had the children brought up by these women. Such is the account they gave of the nurture of the children. I heard other things also at Memphis in conversation with the priests of Vulcan; and on this very account I went also to Thebes, and to Heliopolis, in order to ascertain whether they would agree with the accounts given at Memphis; for the Heliopolitans are esteemed the most learned in history of all the Egyptians. The parts of the narration that I heard concerning divine things I am not willing to relate, except only their names, and with these I suppose all men are equally well acquainted; but what more I shall relate of these matters I shall relate from a necessity to keep up the thread of my story.

4. But as concerns human affairs, they agree with one another in the following account: that the Egyptians were the first to discover the year, which they divided into twelve parts; and they say that they made this discovery from the stars; and so far, I think, they act more wisely than the Grecians, in that the Grecians insert an intercalary month every third year, on account of the seasons; whereas the Egyptians, reckoning twelve months of thirty days each, add five days each year above that number, and so with them the circle of the seasons comes round to the same point. They say, also, that the Egyptians were the first who introduced the names of the twelve gods, and that the Greeks borrowed those names from them; that they were the first to assign altars, images, and temples to the gods, and to carve the figures of animals on stone; and most of these things they proved were so in fact. They added that Menes was the first mortal who reigned over

Egypt, and that in his time all Egypt, except the district of Thebes, was a morass, and that no part of the land that now exists below Lake Myris was then above water: to this place from the sea is a seven days' passage up the river. 5. And they seemed to me to give a good account of this region. For it is evident to a man of common understanding, who has not heard it before, but sees it, that the part of Egypt which the Greeks frequent with their shipping is land acquired by the Egyptians and a gift from the river; and the parts above this lake, during a three days' passage, of which, however, they said nothing, are of the same description. For the nature of the soil of Egypt is of this kind; when you are fast sailing to it, and are at the distance of a day's sail from land, if you cast the lead you will bring up mud, and will find yourself in eleven fathoms water: this so far shows that there is an alluvial deposit.

6. The length of Egypt along the sea-coast is sixty schœni, according as we reckon it to extend from the Plinthinetic bay to Lake Serbonis, near which Mount Casius stretches: from this point, then, the length is sixty schœni. Now all men who are short of land measure their territory by fathoms; but those who are less short of land, by stades; and those who have much, by parasangs; and such as have a very great extent, by schœni. Now a parasang is equal to thirty stades, and each schœnus, which is an Egyptian measure, is equal to sixty stades. So the whole coast of Egypt is three thousand six hundred stades in length. 7. From thence, as far as Heliopolis, inland, Egypt is wide, being all flat, without water, and a swamp. The distance to Heliopolis, as one goes up from the sea, is about equal in length to the road from Athens, *that is to say*, from the altar of the twelve gods, to Pisa and the temple of Olympian Jupiter; for whoever will compare these roads will find, by computation, that the difference between them is but little, not exceeding fifteen stades, for the road from Athens to Pisa is only fifteen stades short of one thousand five hundred stades; but the road from the sea to Heliopolis amounts to just that number. 8. From Heliopolis upward Egypt is narrow, for on one side the mountain of Arabia extends from north to south and southwest, stretching up continuously to that which is called the Red Sea. In this mountain are the stone quarries which were cut for the pyramids at Memphis; here, then, the mountain, deviating, turns to the parts above

mentioned. But where its length is the greatest, I have heard that it is a two months' journey from east to west; and that eastward its confines produce frankincense. On that side of Egypt which borders upon Libya extends another rocky mountain, and covered with sand, on which the pyramids stand; and this stretches in the same direction as that part of the Arabian mountain that runs southward; so that from Heliopolis, the territory which belongs to Egypt is not very extensive; but for four days' sail up the river it is very narrow. Between the mountains before mentioned the land is level, and in the narrowest part appeared to me to be not more than two hundred stades in breadth from the Arabian mountain to that called the Libyan; but above this Egypt again becomes wide. Such, then, is the character of this country. 9. From Heliopolis to Thebes is a voyage up of nine days: the length of this journey is, in stades, four thousand eight hundred and sixty, which amount to eighty-one schœni. Now, if we compute these stades together, the coast of Egypt, as I before explained, contains, in length, three thousand and six hundred stades. How far it is from the sea inland, as far as Thebes, I will next show, namely, six thousand one hundred and twenty stades; and from Thebes to the city called Elephantine, one thousand eight hundred stades.

10. The greater part of all this country, as the priests informed me, and as appeared to me also to be the case, has been acquired by the Egyptians; for the space between the above-mentioned mountains, that are situate beyond the city of Memphis, seem to me to have been formerly a bay of the sea; as is the case, also, with the parts about Ilium, Teuthrania, Ephesus, and the plain of the Mæander, if I may be permitted to compare small things with great; for of the rivers that have thrown up the soil that forms these countries, not one can justly be brought into comparison, as to size, with any one of the five mouths of the Nile. But there are other rivers, not equal in size to the Nile, which have wrought great works: of these I could mention the names, and among them, one of the most remarkable is the Achelous, which, flowing through Acarnania, and falling into the sea, has already converted one half of the Echinades islands into continent. 11. There is also in the Arabian territory, not far from Egypt, branching from the Red Sea, a bay of the sea, of the length and width

I shall here describe. The length of the voyage, beginning from the innermost part of this bay, to the broad sea, occupies forty days for a vessel with oars; and the width, where the bay is widest, half a day's passage; and in it an ebb and flow takes place daily; and I am of opinion that Egypt was formerly a similar bay—this stretching from the Northern Sea toward Ethiopia; and the Arabian Bay, which I am describing, from the south toward Syria—and that they almost perforated their recesses so as to meet each other, overlapping* to some small extent. Now if the Nile were to turn its stream into this Arabian gulf, what could hinder it from being filled with soil by the river within twenty thousand years? for my part, I think it would be filled within ten thousand. How, then, in the time that has elapsed before I was born, might not even a much greater bay than this have been filled up by such a great and powerful river? 12. I therefore both give credit to those who relate these things concerning Egypt, and am myself persuaded of their truth, when I see that Egypt projects beyond the adjoining land; that shells are found on the mountains; that a saline humor forms on the surface so as even to corrode the pyramids; and that this mountain, which is above Memphis, is the only one in Egypt that abounds in sand; add to which, that Egypt, in its soil, is neither like Arabia on its confines, nor Libya, nor Syria (Syrians occupy the sea-coast of Arabia), but is black and crumbling, as if it were mud and alluvial deposit, brought down by the river from Ethiopia; whereas we know that the earth of Libya is reddish. and somewhat more sandy, and that of Arabia and Syria is more clayey and flinty.

13. The priests told me this, also, as a great proof of what they related concerning this country, that in the reign of Mœris, when the river rose at least eight cubits, it irrigated all Egypt below Memphis; and yet Mœris had not been nine hundred years dead when I received this information. But now, unless the river rises sixteen cubits, or fifteen, at least, it does not overflow the country. It appears to me, therefore, that if the soil continues to grow in height in the same proportion, and to contribute in like manner toward its increase,

* I have adopted the meaning given to παραλλάσσοντας by Liddell and Scott, instead of the usual interpretation, that "the two bays were but little distant from each other."

those Egyptians below Lake Mœris, who inhabit other districts and that which is called Delta, must, by reason of the Nile not overflowing their land, forever suffer the same calamity which they used to say the Greeks would suffer from; for, having heard that all the lands of Greece were watered by rain, and not by rivers, as their own was, they said "that the Grecians at some time or other would be disappointed in their great expectations, and suffer miserably from famine;" meaning, "that if the deity should not vouchsafe rain to them, but visit them with a long drought, the Greeks must perish by famine, since they had no other resource for water except from Jupiter only." 14. And the Egyptians are right in saying this to the Greeks; but now let me state how the matter stands with the Egyptians themselves: if, as I said before, the land below Memphis (for this it is that increases) should continue to increase in height in the same proportion as it has in time past, what else will happen but that the Egyptians who inhabit this part will starve, if their land shall neither be watered by rain, nor the river be able to inundate the fields? Now, indeed, they gather in the fruits of the earth with less labor than any other people, and than the rest of the Egyptians, for they have not the toil of breaking up the furrows with the plow, nor of hoeing, nor of any other work which all other men must labor at to obtain a crop of corn; but when the river has come of its own accord and irrigated their fields, and having irrigated them, has subsided, then each man sows his own land and turns swine into it; and when the seed has been trodden in by the swine, he afterward waits for harvest-time: then having trod out the corn with his swine, he gathers it in.

15. But if we should adopt the opinion of the Ionians respecting Egypt, who say that the Delta alone is properly Egypt, stating that its sea-coast extends from what is called the tower of Perseus to the Tarichæa of Pelusium, forty schœni in length; and who say that from the sea inland it stretches to the city of Cercasorus, where the Nile divides, and flows toward Pelusium and Canopus, and who attribute the rest of Fgypt partly to Libya and partly to Arabia—if we adopted this account, we should show that the Egyptians had not formerly any country of their own; for the Delta, as the Egyptians themselves acknowledge, and as I think, is alluvial, and (if I may so express myself) has lately come to

light. If, then, they formerly had no country, how foolish they were to think themselves the most ancient of all people! nor was there any use in their having recourse to the experiment of the children to ascertain what language they would first speak. For my own part, I am not of opinion that the Egyptians commenced their existence with the country which the Ionians call Delta, but that they always were since men have been; and that as the soil gradually increased, many of them remained in their former habitations, and many came lower down; for, anciently, Thebes was called Egypt, and is six thousand one hundred and twenty stades in circumference. 16. If, therefore, I judge correctly of these things, the Ionians are mistaken with respect to Egypt; but if their opinion is correct, then I will show that neither the Greeks nor the Ionians themselves know how to reckon, when they say that the whole earth consists of three divisions, Europe, Asia, and Libya; for they ought to add a fourth, the Delta of Egypt, if it be not a part either of Asia or of Libya; for, by this account, the Nile does not separate Asia from Libya, but is divided at the point of Delta, so that it must be between Asia and Libya. But I will dismiss the opinion of the Ionians, and proceed to give my own account of the matter. 17. *I consider* that the whole country inhabited by Egyptians is Egypt, as that inhabited by Cilicians is Cilicia, and that by Assyrians, Assyria; and, strictly speaking, I know of no other boundary to Asia and Libya except the frontier of Egypt. But if we follow the opinion received by the Greeks, we shall suppose that all Egypt, beginning from the cataracts and the city of Elephantine, is divided into two parts, and partakes of both names; and that one part belongs to Libya, and the other to Asia; for the Nile, beginning from the cataracts, flows to the sea, dividing Egypt in the middle. Now, as far as the city of Cercasorus, the Nile flows in one stream, but from that point it is divided into three channels; and that which runs eastward is called the Pelusiac mouth; another of the channels bends westward, and is called the Canopic mouth; but the direct channel of the Nile is the following: descending from above, it comes to the point of the Delta, and after this it divides the Delta in the middle, and discharges itself into the sea, supplying by this channel not by any means the least quantity of water, nor that the least renowned; this is called the Sebennytic mouth. There are also two other mouths, that diverge from the Sebennytic and flow into the sea. To these the following names are given: to one the Saitic, to the other the Mendesian mouth. The Bolbitine and Bucolic mouths are not natural, but artificial. 18. My opinion that Egypt is of the extent I have above declared it to be is confirmed by an oracle delivered at Ammon, which I heard after I had formed my own opinion respecting Egypt. For the people who inhabit the cities of Marea and Apis, in the part of Egypt bordering on Libya, deeming themselves Libyans and not Egyptians, and being discontented with the institutions regarding victims, were desirous not to be restricted from the use of cow's flesh, and therefore sent to Ammon, saying "that they had no relation to the Egyptians, because they lived out of Delta, and did not speak the same language with them; and desired to be allowed to eat all manner of food." The god, however, did not permit them to do so, saying "that all the country which the Nile irrigated was Egypt, and that all those were Egyptians who dwell below the city Elephantine, and drink of that river. Such was the answer given them. 19. But the Nile, when full, inundates not only Delta, but also part of the country said to belong to Libya and Arabia, to the extent of about two days' journey on either side, more or less.

Respecting the nature of this river I was unable to gain any information, either from the priests or any one else. I was very desirous, however, of learning from them why the Nile, beginning at the summer solstice, fills and overflows for a hundred days; and when it has nearly completed this number of days, falls short in its stream, and retires; so that it continues low all the winter, until the return of the summer solstice. Of these particulars I could get no information from the Egyptians, though I inquired whether this river have any peculiar quality that makes it differ in nature from other rivers. Being anxious, then, of knowing what was said about this matter, I made inquiries, and also how it comes to pass that this is the only one of all rivers that does not send forth breezes from its surface. 20. Nevertheless, some of the Greeks, wishing to be distinguished for their wisdom, have attempted to account for these indications in three different ways: two of these ways are scarcely worth mentioning, except that I wish to show what they are. One of them says that the Etesian winds are the cause of the swelling of the river, by preventing the Nile from discharging itself into the sea. But frequently the Etesian winds have not blown, yet the Nile produces the same effects; besides, if the Etesian winds were the cause, all other rivers that flow opposite to the same winds must of necessity be equally affected, and in the same manner as the Nile; and even so much the more, as they are less and have weaker currents: yet there are many rivers in Syria and many in Libya which are not all affected as the Nile is. 21. The second opinion shows still more ignorance than the former, but, if I may so say, is more marvellous. It says that the Nile, flowing from the ocean, produces this effect; and that the ocean flows all round the earth. 22. The third way of resolving this difficulty is by far the most specious, but most untrue; for by saying that the Nile flows from melted snow, it says nothing, for this river flows from Libya through the middle of Ethiopia, and discharges itself into Egypt; how, therefore, since it runs from a very hot to a colder region, can it flow from snow? Many reasons will readily occur to men of good understanding to show the improbability of its flowing from snow. The first and chief proof is derived from the winds, which blow hot from those regions; the second is, that the country, destitute of rain, is always free from ice, but after snow has fallen it must of necessity rain within five days; so that, if snow fell, it would also rain in these regions. In the third place, the inhabitants become black from the excessive heat; kites and swallows continue there all the year; and the cranes, to avoid the cold of Scythia, migrate to these parts as winter quarters. If, then, ever so little snow fell in this country through which the Nile flows, and from which it derives its source, none of these things would happen, as necessity proves. 23. But the person who speaks about the ocean, since he has referred his account to some obscure fable, produces no conviction at all; for I do not know any river called the Ocean; but suppose that Homer, or some other ancient poet, having invented the name, introduced it into poetry.

24. Yet if, after I have found fault with the opinions advanced *by others*, it becomes me to declare my own concerning so obscure a question, I will describe what, in my opinion,

causes the Nile to overflow in summer. During the winter season, the sun, being driven by storms from his former course, retires to the upper parts of Libya; this, in few words, comprehends the whole matter; for it is natural that that country which this god is nearest to, and over which he is, should be most in want of water, and that the native river streams should be dried up. 25. But, to explain my meaning more at length, the case is this: the sun, passing over the upper parts of Libya, produces the following effect: as the air in these regions is always serene, and the soil always hot, since there are no cold winds passing over, he produces just the same effect as he usually does in the summer, when passing through the middle of the firmament; for he attracts the water to himself, and, having so attracted it, throws it back upon the higher regions; there the winds, taking it up and dispersing it, melt it; and therefore, with good reason, the winds that blow from this country, from the south and southwest, are by far the most rainy of all. I do not think, however, that the sun on each occasion discharges the annual supply of water from the Nile, but that some remains about him. When, however, the winter grows mild, the sun returns again to the middle of the heavens, and from that time attracts water equally from all rivers. Up to this time, those other rivers, having much rain-water mixed with them, flow with full streams; but as the country has been watered by showers and torn up by torrents, when the showers fail them, and they are attracted in summer by the sun, they become weak; but the Nile, being destitute of rain, and attracted by the sun, is the only river that, with good reason, flows much weaker than usual at this time than in summer; for in summer it is attracted equally with all other waters, but in winter it alone is hard pressed. Thus I consider that the sun is the cause of these things. 26. The same cause, in my opinion, occasions also the dryness of the air in those parts, the sun scorching every thing in his passage: in consequence of this, heat always prevails in the upper parts of Libya. But if the order of the seasons were changed, and that part of the heaven where the north and winter are now placed could be made the position of the south and mid-day, and the north were transferred to the south—if such a change were made, the sun, driven from the middle of the firmament by the winter and the north wind, would go to the upper parts of Europe, as he now does through those of Libya; and I suppose he would produce in his passage the same effects on the Ister which he now does on the Nile. 27. Then, with regard to the reason why no breezes blow from the Nile, my opinion is that it is very improbable they should blow from hot countries, for they generally blow from some cold one.

28. But I leave these things as they are, and as they were at the beginning. With regard to the sources of the Nile, no man of all the Egyptians, Libyans, or Grecians with whom I have conversed ever pretended to know any thing, except the registrar of Minerva's treasury at Sais in Egypt. He, indeed, seemed to be trifling with me when he said he knew perfectly well; yet his account was as follows: "That there are two mountains rising into a sharp peak, situated between the city of Syene in Thebais and Elephantine; the names of these mountains are, the one Crophi, the other Mophi; that the sources of the Nile, which are bottomless, flow from between these mountains, and that half of the water flows over Egypt, and to the north, the other half over Ethiopia and the south. That the fountains of the Nile are bottomless, he said, Psammitichus, king of Egypt, proved by experiment; for having caused a line to be twisted many thousand fathoms in length, he let it down, but could not find a bottom." Such, then, was the opinion the registrar gave, if indeed he spoke the real truth, *proving*, in my opinion, that there are strong whirlpools and an eddy here; so that, the water beating against the rocks, a sounding-line, when let down, can not reach the bottom. 29. I was unable to learn any thing more from any one else; but thus much I learned by carrying my researches as far as possible, having gone and made my own observations as far as Elephantine, and beyond that obtaining information from hearsay. As one ascends the river, above the city of Elephantine the country is steep; here, therefore, it is necessary to attach a rope on both sides of a boat, as one does with an ox in a plow, and so proceed; but if the rope should happen to break, the boat is carried away by the force of the stream. This kind of country lasts for a four days' passage, and the Nile here winds as much as the Mæander. There are twelve schœni which it is necessary to sail through in this manner, and after that you will come to a level plain, where the Nile flows round an island; its name is Tachompso. Ethiopians inhabit the country immediately above Elephantine, and one half of the island; the other half

is inhabited by Egyptians. Near to this island lies a vast lake, on the borders of which Ethiopian nomades dwell; after sailing through this lake, you will come to the channel of the Nile, which flows into it; then you will have to land and travel forty days by the side of the river, for sharp rocks rise in the Nile, and there are many sunken ones, through which it is not possible to navigate a boat: having passed this country in the forty days, you must go on board another boat, and sail for twelve days, and then you will arrive at a large city called Meroe: this city is said to be the capital of all Ethiopia. The inhabitants worship no other gods than Jupiter and Bacchus, but these they honor with great magnificence; they have also an oracle of Jupiter; and they make war whenever that god bids them by an oracular warning, and against whatever country he bids them. 30. Sailing from this city, you will arrive at the country of the Automoli in a space of time equal to that which you took in coming from Elephantine to the capital of the Ethiopians. These Automoli are called by the name of Asmak, which in the language of Greece signifies "those that stand at the left hand of the king." These, to the number of two hundred and forty thousand of the Egyptian war-tribe, revolted to the Ethiopians on the following occasion. In the reign of king Psammitichus garrisons were stationed at Elephantine against the Ethiopians, and another at the Pelusian Daphnæ against the Arabians and Syrians, and another at Marea against Libya; and even in my time garrisons of the Persians are stationed in the same places as they were in the time of Psammitichus, for they maintain guards at Elephantine and Daphnæ. Now these Egyptians, after they had been on duty three years, were not relieved; therefore, having consulted together, and come to a unanimous resolution, they all revolted from Psammitichus, and went to Ethiopia. Psammitichus, hearing of this, pursued them; and when he overtook them, he entreated them by many arguments, and adjured them not to forsake the gods of their fathers, and their children and wives. But one of them is reported to have uncovered his private parts, and to have said, "that wheresoever these were, there they should find both children and wives." These men, when they arrived in Ethiopia, offered their services to the king of the Ethiopians, who made them the following recompense. There were certain Ethiopians disaffected toward him; these he bade them expel, and take possession of their land: by the settlement of these men among the Ethiopians, the Ethiopians became more civilized, and learned the manners of the Egyptians.

31. Now for a voyage and land journey of four months, the Nile is known, in addition to the part of the stream that is in Egypt; for upon computation, so many months are known to be spent by a person who travels from Elephantine to the Automoli. This river flows from the west and the setting of the sun; but beyond this no one is able to speak with certainty, for the rest of the country is desert by reason of the excessive heat. 32. But I have heard the following account from certain Cyrenæans, who say that they went to the oracle of Ammon, and had a conversation with Etearchus, king of the Ammonians, and that, among other subjects, they happened to discourse about the Nile—that nobody knew its sources; whereupon Etearchus said that certain Nasamonians once came to him: this nation is Libyan, and inhabits the Syrtis, and the country for no great distance eastward of the Syrtis; and that when these Nasamonians arrived, and were asked if they could give any farther information touching the deserts of Libya, they answered that there were some daring youths among them, sons of powerful men, and that they, having reached man's estate, formed many other extravagant plans, and, moreover, chose five of their number by lot to explore the deserts of Libya, to see if they could make any farther discovery than those who had penetrated the farthest. (For as respects the parts of Libya along the Northern Sea, beginning from Egypt to the promontory of Solois, where is the extremity of Libya, Libyans and various nations of Libyans reach all along it, except those parts which are occupied by Grecians and Phœnicians; but as respects the parts above the sea, and those nations which reach down to the sea, in the upper parts Libya is infested by wild beasts; and all beyond that is sand, dreadfully short of water, and utterly desolate.) *They farther related*, "that when the young men deputed by their companions set out, well furnished with water and provisions, they passed first through the inhabited country; and having traversed this, they came to the region infested by wild beasts; and after this they crossed the desert, making their way toward the west; and when they had traversed much sandy

ground, during a journey of many days, they at length saw some trees growing in a plain, and that they approached and began to gather the fruit that grew on the trees; and while they were gathering, some diminutive men, less than men of middle stature, came up, and having seized them, carried them away; and that the Nasamonians did not at all understand their language, nor those who carried them off the language of the Nasamonians. However, they conducted them through vast morasses, and when they had passed these, they came to a city, in which all the inhabitants were of the same size as their conductors, and black in color; and by the city flowed a great river, running from the west to the east, and that crocodiles were seen in it." 33. Thus far I have set forth the account of Etearchus the Ammonian; to which may be added, as the Cyrenæans assured me, "that he said the Nasamonians all returned safe to their own country, and that the men whom they came to were all necromancers." Etearchus also conjectured that this river, which flows by their city, is the Nile; and reason so evinces; for the Nile flows from Libya, and intersects it in the middle; and (as I conjecture, inferring things unknown from things known) it sets out from a point corresponding with the Ister; for the Ister, beginning from the Celts and the city of Pyrene, divides Europe in its course; but the Celts are beyond the pillars of Hercules, and border on the territories of the Cynesians, who lie in the extremity of Europe to the westward; and the Ister terminates by flowing through all Europe into the Euxine Sea, where a Milesian colony is settled in Istria. 34. Now the Ister, as it flows through a well-peopled country, is generally known; but no one is able to speak about the sources of the Nile, because Libya, through which it flows, is uninhabited and desolate. Respecting this stream, therefore, as far as I was able to reach by inquiry, I have already spoken. It, however, discharges itself into Egypt; and Egypt lies, as near as may be, opposite to the mountains of Cilicia; from whence to Sinope, on the Euxine Sea, is a five day's journey in a straight line to an active man; and Sinope is opposite to the Ister, where it discharges itself into the sea. So I think that the Nile, traversing the whole of Libya, may be properly compared with the Ister. Such, then, is the account that I am able to give respecting the Nile.

35. I now proceed to give a more particular account of Egypt. It possesses more wonders than any other country, and exhibits works greater than can be described, in comparison with all other regions; therefore more must be said about it. The Egyptians, besides having a climate peculiar to themselves, and a river differing in its nature from all other rivers, have adopted customs and usages in almost every respect different from the rest of mankind. Among them the women attend markets and traffic, but the men stay at home and weave. Other nations, in weaving, throw the wool upward; the Egyptians, downward. The men carry burdens on their heads; the women, on their shoulders. The women stand up when they make water, but the men sit down. They ease themselves in their houses, but eat out of doors; alleging that whatever is indecent, though necessary, ought to be done in private; but what is not indecent, openly. No woman can serve the office for any god or goddess; but men are employed for both offices. Sons are not compelled to support their parents unless they choose, but daughters are compelled to do so, whether they choose or not. 36. In other countries the priests of the gods wear long hair; in Egypt they have it shaved. With other men it is customary in mourning for the nearest relations to have their heads shorn; the Egyptians, on occasions of death, let the hair grow both on the head and face, though till then used to shave. Other men live apart from beasts; but the Egyptians live with them. Others feed on wheat and barley, but it is a very great disgrace for an Egyptian to make food of them; but they make bread from spelt, which some call zea. They knead the dough with their feet, but mix clay and take up dung with their hands. Other men leave their private parts as they are formed by nature, except those who have learned otherwise from them; but the Egyptians are circumcised. Every man wears two garments; the women, but one. Other men fasten the rings and sheets of their sails outside; but the Egyptians, inside. The Grecians write and cipher moving the hand from left to right; but the Egyptians, from right to left; and doing so, they say they do it right-ways, and the Greeks left-ways. They have two sorts of letters, one of which is called sacred, the other common.

37. They are of all men the most excessively attentive to

the worship of the gods, and observe the following ceremonies. They drink from cups of brass, which they scour every day; nor is this custom practiced by some and neglected by others, but all do it. They wear linen garments, constantly fresh washed, and they pay particular attention to this. They are circumcised for the sake of cleanliness, thinking it better to be clean than handsome. The priests shave their whole body every third day, that neither lice nor any other impurity may be found upon them when engaged in the service of the gods. The priests wear linen only, and shoes of byblus, and are not permitted to wear any other garments, or other shoes. They wash themselves in cold water twice every day, and twice every night; and, in a word, they use a number of ceremonies. On the other hand, they enjoy no slight advantages, for they do not consume or expend any of their private property; but sacred food is cooked for them, and a great quantity of beef and geese is allowed each of them every day, and wine from the grape is given them; but they may not taste of fish. Beans the Egyptians do not sow at all in their country, neither do they eat those that happen to grow there, nor taste them when dressed. The priests, indeed, abhor the sight of that pulse, accounting it impure. The service of each god is performed, not by one, but by many priests, of whom one is chief priest, and when any one of them dies, his son is put in his place. 38. The male kine they deem sacred to Epaphus, and to that end prove them in the following manner. If the examiner finds one black hair upon him, he adjudges him to be unclean; and one of the priests appointed for this purpose makes this examination, both when the animal is standing up and lying down; and he draws out the tongue, to see if it is pure as to the prescribed marks, which I shall mention in another part of my history. He also looks at the hairs of his tail, whether they grow naturally. If the beast is found pure in all these respects, he marks it by rolling a piece of byblus round the horns, and then having put on it some sealing earth, he impresses it with his signet; and so they drive him away. Any one who sacrifices one that is unmarked is punished with death. In this manner the animal is proved. 39. The established mode of sacrifice is this: having led the victim, properly marked, to the altar where they intend to sacrifice, they kindle a fire. Then, having poured wine upon the altar, near the victim, and having invoked the god, they kill it, and after they have killed it they cut off the head; but they flay the body of the animal; then, having pronounced many imprecations on the head, they who have a market and Grecian merchants dwelling among them carry it there, and having so done, they usually sell it; but they who have no Grecians among them throw it into the river; and they pronounce the following imprecations on the head: "If any evil is about to befall either those that now sacrifice, or Egypt in general, may it be averted on this head." With respect, then, to the heads of beasts that are sacrificed, and to the making libations of wine, all the Egyptians observe the same customs in all sacrifices alike; and, from this custom, no Egyptian will taste of the head of any animal. 40. But a different mode of disemboweling and burning the victims prevails in different sacrifices. I proceed, therefore, to speak of the practice with regard to the goddess whom they consider the greatest, and in whose honor they celebrate the most magnificent festival. When they have flayed the bullocks, having first offered up prayers, they take out all the intestines, and leave the vitals with the fat in the carcass; and they then cut off the legs and the extremity of the hip, with the shoulders and neck, and having done this, they fill the body of the bullock with fine bread, honey, raisins, figs, frankincense, myrrh, and other perfumes; and after they have filled it with these, they burn it, pouring on it a great quantity of oil. They sacrifice after they have fasted, and while the sacred things are being burned they all beat themselves, and when they have done beating themselves they spread a banquet of what remains of the victims.

41. All the Egyptians, therefore, sacrifice the pure male kine and calves, but they are not allowed to sacrifice the females, for they are sacred to Isis; for the image of Isis is made in the form of a woman with the horns of a cow, as the Grecians represent Io; and all Egyptians alike pay a far greater reverence to cows than to any other cattle; so that no Egyptian man or woman will kiss a Grecian on the mouth, or use the knife, spit, or caldron of a Greek, or taste of the flesh of a pure ox that has been divided by a Grecian knife. They bury the kine that die in the following manner: the females they throw into the river, and the males they sever-

ally inter in the suburbs, with one horn, or both, appearing above the ground for a mark. When it is putrefied and the appointed time arrives, a raft comes to each city from the island called Prosopitis: this island is in the Delta, and is nine schœni in circumference. Now in this island Prosopitis there are several cities; but that from which the rafts come to take away the bones of the oxen is called Atarbechis; in it a temple of Venus has been erected. From this city, then, many persons go about to other towns; and having dug up the bones, all carry them away, and bury them in one place; and they bury all other cattle that die in the same way that they do the oxen; for they do not kill any of them. 42. All those who have a temple erected to Theban Jupiter, or belong to the Theban district, abstain from sheep, and sacrifice goats only; for the Egyptians do not all worship the same gods in the same manner, except Isis and Osiris, who, they say, is Bacchus; but these deities they all worship in the same manner. On the other hand, those who frequent the temple of Mendes, and belong to the Mendesian district, abstain from goats, and sacrifice sheep. Now the Thebans, and such as abstain from sheep after their example, say that this custom was established among them in the following way: that Hercules was very desirous of seeing Jupiter, but Jupiter was unwilling to be seen by him; at last, however, as Hercules persisted, Jupiter had recourse to the following contrivance: having flayed a ram, he cut off the head, and held it before himself, and then having put on the fleece, he in that form showed himself to Hercules. From this circumstance the Egyptians make the image of Jupiter with a ram's face; and from the Egyptians the Ammonians, who are a colony of Egyptians and Ethiopians, and who speak a language between both, *have adopted the same practice;* and, as I conjecture, the Ammonians from hence derived their name, for the Egyptians call Jupiter, Ammon. The Thebans, then, do not sacrifice rams, but they are for the above reason accounted sacred by them; on one day in the year, however, at the festival of Jupiter, they kill and flay one ram, and put it on the image of Jupiter, and then they bring another image of Hercules to it; when they have done this, all who are in the temple beat themselves in mourning for the ram, and then bury him in a sacred vault.

43. Of this Hercules I have heard this account, that he is one of the twelve gods; but of the other Hercules, who is known to the Grecians, I could never hear in any part of Egypt. And that the Egyptians did not derive the name of Hercules from the Grecians, but rather the Grecians (and especially those who gave the name of Hercules to the son of Amphitryon) from the Egyptians, I have both many other proofs to show, and moreover the following, that the parents of this Hercules, Amphitryon and Alcmene, were both of Egyptian descent, and because the Egyptians say they do not know the names of Neptune and the Dioscuri, and that they have never been admitted into the number of their gods; yet if they had derived the name of any deity from the Grecians, they would certainly have mentioned these above all others, since even at that time they made voyages, and some of the Grecians were sailors, so that I believe, and am persuaded, that the Egyptians must have learned the names of these gods, rather than that of Hercules. But Hercules is one of the ancient gods of the Egyptians; and as they say themselves, it was seventeen thousand years before the reign of Amasis, when the number of their gods was increased from eight to twelve, of whom Hercules was accounted one. 44. And being desirous of obtaining certain information from whatever source I could, I sailed to Tyre in Phœnicia, having heard that there was there a temple dedicated to Hercules; and I saw it richly adorned with a great variety of offerings, and in it were two pillars, one of fine gold, the other of emerald stone, both shining exceedingly* at night. Conversing with the priests of this god, I inquired how long this temple had been built, and I found that neither did they agree with the Greeks; for they said that the temple was built at the time when Tyre was founded, and that two thousand three hundred years had elapsed since the foundation of Tyre. In this city I also saw another temple dedicated to Hercules by the name of Thasian; I went therefore to Thasos, and found there a temple of Hercules built by the Phœnicians, who, having set sail in search of Europa, founded Thasos; and this occurred five generations before Hercules, the son of Amphitryon, appeared in Greece. The researches, then, that I have made evidently prove that

* Μέγαθος must be here construed as an adverb; but Baehr thinks that the text is corrupt.

Hercules is a god of great antiquity, and therefore those Grecians appear to me to have acted most correctly, who have built two kinds of temples sacred to Hercules, and who sacrificed to one as an immortal, under the name of Olympian, and paid honor to the other as a hero. 45. But the Grecians say many other things *on this subject* inconsiderately; for instance, this is a silly story of theirs which they tell of Hercules: that, "when he arrived in Egypt, the Egyptians, having crowned him with a garland, led him in procession, as designing to sacrifice him to Jupiter, and that for some time he remained quiet, but when they began the preparatory ceremonies upon him at the altar, he set about defending himself, and slew every one of them." Now the Greeks who tell this story appear to me to be utterly ignorant of the character and customs of the Egyptians; for how can they who are forbidden to sacrifice any kind of animal, except swine, and such bulls and calves as are without blemish, and geese, sacrifice human beings? Moreover, since Hercules was but one, and, besides, a mere man, as they confess, how is it probable that he should slay many thousands? And in thus speaking of them may I meet with indulgence both from gods and heroes.

46. The reason why the Egyptians above mentioned do not sacrifice the goat, either male or female, is as follows: the Mendesians consider Pan one of the eight gods, and they say that these eight existed prior to the twelve gods. And, indeed, their painters and sculptors represent Pan with the face and legs of a goat, as the Grecians do; not that they imagine this to be his real form, for they think him like other gods; but why they represent him in this way I had rather not mention. However, the Mendesians pay reverence to all goats, and more to the males than to the females (and the goatherds who tend them receive greater honor), and particularly one he-goat, on whose death public mourning is observed throughout the whole Mendesian district. In the language of Egypt, both a goat and Pan are called Mendes; and in my time the following prodigy occurred in this district: a goat had connection with a woman in open day. This came to the knowledge of all men. 47. The Egyptians consider the pig to be an impure beast, and therefore, if a man, in passing by a pig, should touch him only with his garments, he forthwith goes to the river and plunges in; and, in the next place, swineherds, although

native Egyptians, are the only men who are not allowed to enter any of their temples; neither will any man give his daughter in marriage to one of them, nor take a wife from among them; but the swineherds intermarry among themselves. The Egyptians, therefore, do not think it right to sacrifice swine to any other deities; but to the moon and Bacchus they do sacrifice them, at the same time, that is, at the same full moon, and then they eat of the flesh. A tradition is related by the Egyptians in relation to this matter, giving an account why they abhor swine on all other festivals, and sacrifice them in that; but it is more becoming for me, though I know it, not to mention it. This sacrifice of pigs to the moon is performed in the following manner: when the sacrificer has slain the victim, he puts together the tip of the tail, with the spleen and the caul, and then covers them with the fat found about the belly of the animal; and next he consumes them with fire. The rest of the flesh they eat during the full moon in which they offer the sacrifices, but in no other day would any one even taste it. The poor among them, through want of means, form pigs of dough, and, having baked them, offer them in sacrifice. 48. On the eve of the festival of Bacchus, every one slays a pig before his door, and then restores it to the swineherd that sold it, that he may carry it away. The rest of this festival to Bacchus, except as regards the pigs, the Egyptians celebrate much in the same manner as the Greeks do, but only, instead of phalli, they have invented certain images, as much as a cubit in height, moved by strings, which women carry about the villages, and which have the member nodding, in size not much less than the rest of the body; a pipe leads the way, and the women follow, singing the praises of Bacchus. But why it has the member so large, and moves no other part of the body, is accounted for by a sacred story. 49. Now Melampus, son of Amytheon, appears to me not to have been ignorant of this sacrifice, but perfectly well acquainted with it; for Melampus is the person who first introduced among the Greeks the names and sacrifices of Bacchus, and the procession of the phallus; he did not, however, fully explain every particular, but other learned persons who lived after him revealed them more accurately. Melampus, then, is the person who introduced the procession of the phallus in honor of Bacchus, and from him the Greeks having learned it, do as they do. For my part, I think that Melampus, being a wise man, both acquired the art of divination, and having learned many other things in Egypt, introduced them among the Greeks, and particularly the worship of Bacchus, changing only some few particulars; for I can not admit that the ceremonies adopted in Egypt in honor of this god, and those among the Greeks, coincide by chance; in that case they would be conformable to Grecian customs, and not have been lately introduced; neither can I admit that the Egyptians borrowed either this or any other usage from the Greeks. But I am of opinion that Melampus obtained his information respecting the ceremonies of Bacchus chiefly from Cadmus the Tyrian, and those who accompanied him from Phœnicia to the country now called Bœotia.

50. And indeed the names of almost all the gods came from Egypt into Greece; for that they came from barbarians I find on inquiry to be the case; and I think they chiefly proceeded from Egypt; for, with the exception of Neptune and the Dioscuri, as I before mentioned, and Juno, Vesta, Themis, the Graces, and the Nereids, the names of all the others have always existed among the Egyptians: in this I repeat what the Egyptians themselves affirm; but the gods whose names they say they are not acquainted with, I think, derived their names from the Pelasgians, with the exception of Neptune; this god they learned from the Libyans, for no people except the Libyans originally possessed the name of Neptune, and they have always worshiped him. Moreover, the Egyptians pay no religious honor to heroes. 51. These, and other customs besides, which I shall hereafter mention, the Grecians received from the Egyptians. The practice of making the images of Mercury with the member erect, they did not learn from the Egyptians, but from the Pelasgians: the Athenians were the first of all the Greeks who adopted this practice, and others from them; for the Pelasgians dwelt in the same country as the Athenians, who were already ranked among Greeks, whence they also began to be reckoned as Grecians. Whoever is initiated in the mysteries of the Cabiri, which the Samothracians have adopted from the Pelasgians, knows what I mean; for these Pelasgians dwelt in the same country as the Athenians formerly inhabited, Samothrace, and from them the Samothracians learned the mysteries:

the Athenians, therefore, were the first of the Grecians who, having learned the practice from the Pelasgians, made the images of Mercury with the member erect; but the Pelasgians assign a certain sacred reason for this, which is explained in the mysteries of Samothrace. 52. Formerly the Pelasgians sacrificed all sorts of victims to the gods with prayer, as I was informed at Dodona, but they gave no surname or name to any of them, for they had not yet heard of them; but they called them gods, because they had set in order and ruled over all things. Then, in course of time, they learned the names of the other gods that were brought from Egypt, and after some time, that of Bacchus. Concerning the names, they consulted the oracle of Dodona, for this oracle is accounted the most ancient of those that are in Greece, and was then the only one. When, therefore, the Pelasgians inquired at Dodona "whether they should receive the names that came from barbarians," the oracle answered "that they should." From that time, therefore, they adopted the names of the gods in their sacrifices, and the Grecians afterward received them from the Pelasgians. 53. Whence each of the gods sprung, whether they existed always, and of what form they were, was, so to speak, unknown till yesterday. For I am of opinion that Hesiod and Homer lived four hundred years before my time, and not more, and these were they who framed a theogony for the Greeks, and gave names to the gods, and assigned to them honors and arts, and declared their several forms. But the poets, said to have been before them, in my opinion, were after them. The first part of the above statement is derived from the Dodonæan priestesses; but the latter, that relates to Hesiod and Homer, I say on my own authority.

54. Concerning the two oracles, one in Greece, the other in Libya, the Egyptians give the following account. The priests of the Theban Jupiter say "that two women, employed in the temple, were carried away from Thebes by certain Phœnicians, and that one of them was discovered to have been sold into Libya, the other to the Greeks, and that these two women were the first who established oracles in the nations above mentioned." When I inquired how they knew this for a certainty, they answered "that they made diligent search for these women, and were never able to find them, but had afterward heard the account they gave of them." 55. This

then is the account I heard from the priests at Thebes; but the prophetesses at Dodona say "that two black pigeons flew away from Thebes in Egypt; that one of them went to Libya, and the other to them; that this last, sitting perched on an oak-tree, proclaimed in a human voice that it was fitting an oracle should be erected there to Jupiter; and that the people believed this to be a divine message to them, and did accordingly. They add, that the other pigeon, which flew into Libya, commanded the Libyans to found the oracle of Ammon:" this also belongs to Jupiter. The priestesses of Dodona, of whom the eldest is named Promenia, the second Timarete, and the youngest Nicandra, gave this account; and the rest of the Dodonæans engaged in the service of the temple agreed with them. 56. My opinion of these things is this: if the Phœnicians did really carry off the women employed in the temple, and sold the one of them into Libya and the other into Greece, this last woman, as I think, was sold to some Thesprotians, in that part which is now called Hellas, but was formerly called Pelasgia; then, being reduced to slavery, she erected a temple to Jupiter, under an oak that grew there; nothing being more natural than that she, who had been an attendant in the temple of Jupiter at Thebes, should retain the memory of it wherever she came. And after this, when she had learned the Greek language, she instituted an oracle; and she said that her sister in Libya had been sold by the same Phœnicians by whom she herself was sold. 57. The women, I conjecture, were called doves by the Dodonæans because they were barbarians, and they seemed to them to chatter like birds; but after a time, when the woman spoke intelligibly to them, they presently reported that the dove had spoken with a human voice; for as long as she used a barbarous language, she appeared to them to chatter like a bird; for how could a dove speak with a human voice? But in saying that the dove was black, they show that the woman was an Egyptian. The manner in which oracles are delivered at Thebes in Egypt, and at Dodona, is very similar; and the art of divination from victims came likewise from Egypt.

58. The Egyptians were also the first who introduced public festivals, processions, and solemn supplications; and the Greeks learned them from them; for these rites appear to have been established for a very long time, but those in Greece have

been lately introduced. 59. The Egyptians hold public festivals not only once in a year, but several times: that which is best and most rigidly observed is in the city of Bubastis, in honor of Diana; the second, in the city of Busiris, is in honor of Isis; for in this city is the largest temple of Isis, and it is situated in the middle of the Egyptian Delta. Isis is in the Grecian language called Demeter. The third festival is held at Sais, in honor of Minerva; the fourth, at Heliopolis, in honor of the sun; the fifth, at the city of Buto, in honor of Latona; the sixth, at the city of Papremis, in honor of Mars. 60. Now, when they are being conveyed to the city Bubastis, they act as follows: for men and women embark together, and great numbers of both sexes in every barge: some of the women have castanets on which they play, and the men play on the flute during the whole voyage; the rest of the women and men sing and clap their hands together at the same time. When, in the course of their passage, they come to any town, they lay their barge near to land, and do as follows: some of the women do as I have described; others shout and scoff at the women of the place; some dance, and others stand up and pull up their clothes: this they do at every town by the river side. When they arrive at Bubastis, they celebrate the feast, offering up great sacrifices; and more wine is consumed at this festival than in all the rest of the year. What with men and women, besides children, they congregate, as the inhabitants say, to the number of seven hundred thousand. 61. I have already related how they celebrate the festival of Isis in the city of Busiris; and besides, all the men and women, to the number of many myriads, beat themselves after the sacrifice; but for whom they beat themselves it were impious for me to divulge. All the Carians that are settled in Egypt do still more than this, in that they cut their foreheads with knives, and thus show themselves to be foreigners and not Egyptians. 62. When they are assembled at the sacrifice in the city of Sais, they all, on a certain night, kindle a great number of lamps in the open air around their houses; the lamps are flat vessels filled with salt and oil, and the wick floats on the surface, and this burns all night; and the festival is thence named "the lighting of lamps." The Egyptians who do not come to this public assembly observe the rite of sacrifice, and all kindle lamps, and this not only in Sais, but throughout all Egypt. A religious reason is given why this night is illuminated and so honored. 63. Those who assemble at Heliopolis and Buto perform sacrifices only; but in Papremis they offer sacrifices and perform ceremonies, as in other places; but, when the sun is on the decline, a few priests are occupied about the image, but the greater number stand, with wooden clubs, at the entrance of the temple, while others, accomplishing their vows, amounting to more than a thousand men, each armed in like manner, stand in a body on the opposite side. But the image, placed in a small wooden temple, gilded all over, they carry out to another sacred dwelling: then the few who were left about the image draw a four-wheeled carriage, containing the temple and the image that is in it. But the priests, who stand at the entrance, refuse to give them admittance; and the votaries, bringing succor to the god, oppose, and then strike; whereupon an obstinate combat with clubs ensues, and they break one another's heads, and, as I conjecture, many die of their wounds, though the Egyptians deny that any one dies. 64. The inhabitants say they instituted this festival on the following occasion: they say that the mother of Mars dwelt in this temple, and that Mars, who had been educated abroad, when he reached to man's estate, came, and wished to converse with his mother; and that his mother's attendants, as they had never seen him before, did not allow him to pass them, but repelled him; whereupon he, having collected men from another city, handled the servants roughly, and got access to his mother. In consequence of this, they say that they have instituted this combat on this festival in honor of Mars.

The Egyptians were likewise the first who made it a point of religion that men should abstain from women in the sacred precincts, and not enter unwashed after the use of a woman; for almost all other nations except the Egyptians and Grecians have intercourse in sacred places, and enter them unwashed, thinking mankind to be like other animals; therefore, since they see other animals and birds coupling in the shrines[1] and temples of the gods, they conclude that if this were displeasing to the god, the brute creatures even would not do it. Now they who argue thus act in a manner that I can not approve. The Egyptians, then, are beyond measure scrupulous

[1] See Book I. ch. 199.

in all things concerning religion, and especially in the abovementioned particulars.

65. Egypt, though bordering on Libya, does not abound in wild beasts; but all that they have are accounted sacred, as well those that are domesticated as those that are not. But, if I should give the reasons why they are consecrated, I must descend in my history to religious matters, which I avoid relating as much as I can, and such as I have touched upon in the course of my narrative I have mentioned from necessity. They have a custom relating to animals of the following kind. Superintendents, consisting both of men and women, are appointed to feed every kind separately; and the son succeeds the father in this office. All the inhabitants of the cities perform their vows to the superintendents in the following manner: having made a vow to the god to whom the animal belongs, they shave either the whole heads of their children, or a half, or a third part of the head, and then weigh the hair in a scale against silver, and, whatever the weight may be, they give to the superintendent of the animals, and she, in return, cuts up some fish, and gives it as food to the animals. Such is the usual mode of feeding them. Should any one kill one of these beasts, if willfully, death is the punishment; if by accident, he pays such fine as the priests choose to impose. But whoever kills an ibis or a hawk, whether willfully or by accident, must necessarily be put to death. 66. Although the domesticated animals are many, they would be much more numerous were it not for the following accidents which befall the cats. When the females have littered, they no longer seek the company of the males, and they, being desirous of having intercourse with them, are not able to do so, wherefore they have recourse to the following artifice: having taken the young from the females, and carried them away secretly, they kill them, though, when they have killed them, they do not eat them. The females, being deprived of their young, and desirous of others, again seek the company of the males; for this animal is very fond of its young. When a conflagration takes place, a supernatural impulse seizes on the cats; for the Egyptians, standing at a distance, take care of the cats, and neglect to put out the fire; but the cats, making their escape, and leaping over the men, throw themselves into the fire; and when this happens, great lament-

ations are made among the Egyptians. In whatever house a cat dies of a natural death, all the family shave their eyebrows only; but if a dog die, they shave the whole body and the head. 67. All cats that die are carried to certain sacred houses, where, being first embalmed, they are buried in the city of Bubastis. All persons bury their dogs in sacred vaults within their own city; and ichneumons are buried in the same manner as the dogs; but field-mice and hawks they carry to the city of Buto; the ibis to Hermopolis; the bears, which are few in number, and the wolves, which are not much larger than foxes, they bury wherever they are found lying.

68. The following is the nature of the crocodile. During the four coldest months it eats nothing, and though it has four feet, it is amphibious. It lays its eggs on land, and there hatches them. It spends the greater part of the day on the dry ground, but the whole night in the river; for the water is then warmer than the air and dew. Of all living things with which we are acquainted, this, from the least beginning, grows to be the largest; for it lays eggs little larger than those of a goose, and the young is at first in proportion to the egg; but when grown up it reaches to the length of seventeen cubits, and even more. It has the eyes of a pig, large teeth, and projecting tusks, in proportion to the body: it is the only animal that has no tongue; it does not move the lower jaw, but is the only animal that brings down its upper jaw to the under one. It has strong claws, and a skin covered with scales, that can not be broken on the back. It is blind in the water, but very quick-sighted on land; and because it lives for the most part in the water, its mouth is filled with leeches. All other birds and beasts avoid him, but he is at peace with the trochilus, because he receives benefit from that bird; for when the crocodile gets out of the water on land, and then opens its jaws, which it does most commonly toward the west, the trochilus enters its mouth and swallows the leeches: the crocodile is so well pleased with this service that it never hurts the trochilus. 69. With some of the Egyptians crocodiles are sacred; with others not, but they treat them as enemies. Those who dwell about Thebes, and Lake Mœris, consider them to be very sacred; and they each of them train up a crocodile, which is taught to be quite

tame; and they put crystal and gold ear-rings into their ears, and bracelets on their fore paws; and they give them appointed and sacred food, and treat them as well as possible while alive, and when dead they embalm them, and bury them in sacred vaults. But the people who dwell about the city of Elephantine eat them, not considering them sacred. They are not called crocodiles by the Egyptians, but "champsæ;" the Ionians gave them the name of crocodiles, because they thought they resembled lizards, *which are also so called, and* which are found in the hedges in their country. 70. The modes of taking the crocodile are many and various, but I shall only describe that which seems to me most worthy of relation. When the fisherman has baited a hook with the chine of a pig, he lets it down into the middle of the river, and holding a young live pig on the brink of the river, beats it; the crocodile, hearing the noise, goes in its direction, and meeting with the chine, swallows it; but the men draw it to land: when it is drawn out on shore, the sportsman first of all plasters its eyes with mud; and having done this, afterward manages it very easily; but until he has done this, he has a great deal of trouble. 71. The hippopotamus is esteemed sacred in the district of Papremis, but not so by the rest of the Egyptians. This is the nature of its shape. It is a quadruped, cloven-footed, with the hoofs of an ox, snub nosed, has the mane of a horse, projecting tusks, and the tail and neigh of a horse. In size he is equal to a very large ox: his hide is so thick that spear-handles are made of it when dry. 72. Otters are also met with in the river, which are deemed sacred; and among fish, they consider that which is called the lepidotus, and the eel, sacred; these, they say, are sacred to the Nile; and among birds, the vulpanser.

73. There is also another sacred bird, called the phœnix, which I have never seen except in a picture; for it seldom makes its appearance among them, only once in five hundred years, as the Heliopolitans affirm: they say that it comes on the death of its sire. If he is like the picture, he is of the following size and description: the plumage of his wings is partly golden-colored and partly red; in outline and size he is very like an eagle. They say that he has the following contrivance, which, in my opinion, is not credible. They say that he comes from Arabia, and brings the body of his father to

the temple of the sun, having inclosed him in myrrh, and there buries him in the temple. He brings him in this manner: first he moulds an egg of myrrh as large as he is able to carry; then he tries to carry it, and when he has made the experiment, he hollows out the egg, and puts his parent into it, and stops up with some more myrrh the hole through which he had introduced the body, so when his father is put inside the weight is the same as before; then, having covered it over, he carries him to the temple of the sun in Egypt. This, they say, is done by this bird.

74. In the neighborhood of Thebes there are sacred serpents not at all hurtful to men: they are diminutive in size, and carry two horns that grow on the top of the head. When these serpents die they bury them in the temple of Jupiter; for they say they are sacred to that god. 75. There is a place in Arabia, situated very near the city of Buto, to which I went on hearing of some winged serpents; and when I arrived there, I saw bones and spines of serpents in such quantities as it would be impossible to describe: there were heaps of these spinal bones, some large, some smaller, and others still less; and there were great numbers of them. The place in which these spinal bones lie scattered is of the following description: it is a narrow pass between two mountains into a spacious plain; this plain is contiguous to the plain of Egypt; it is reported that, at the beginning of spring, winged serpents fly from Arabia toward Egypt; but that ibises, a sort of bird, meet them at the pass, and do not allow the serpents to go by, but kill them: for this service the Arabians say that the ibis is highly reverenced by the Egyptians, and the Egyptians acknowledge that they reverence these birds for this reason. 76. The ibis is of the following description: it is all over a deep black, it has the legs of a crane, its beak is much curved, and it is about the size of the crex. Such is the form of the black ones that fight with the serpents; but those that are commonly conversant among men (for there are two species) are bare on the head and the whole neck, have white plumage except on the head, the throat, and the tips of the wings and extremity of the tail; in all these parts that I have mentioned they are of a deep black; in their legs and beak they are like the other kind. The form of the serpent is like that of the

water-snake; but he has wings without feathers, and as like as possible to the wings of a bat. This must suffice for the description of sacred animals.

77. Of the Egyptians, those who inhabit that part of Egypt which is sown with corn, in that they cultivate the memory of past events more than any other men, are the best informed of all with whom I have had intercourse. Their manner of life is this. They purge themselves every month, three days successively, seeking to preserve health by emetics and clysters; for they suppose that all diseases to which men are subject proceed from the food they use. And, indeed, in other respects, the Egyptians, next to the Libyans, are the most healthy people in the world, as I think, on account of the seasons, because they are not liable to change; for men are most subject to disease at periods of change, and, above all others, at the change of the seasons. They feed on bread made into loaves of spelt, which they call cyllestis; and they use wine made of barley, for they have no vines in that country. Some fish they dry in the sun, and eat raw, others salted with brine; and of birds they eat quails, ducks, and smaller birds raw, having first salted them: all other things, whether birds or fishes, that they have, except such as are accounted sacred, they eat either roasted or boiled. 78. At their convivial banquets, among the wealthy classes, when they have finished supper, a man carries round in a coffin the image of a dead body carved in wood, made as like as possible in color and workmanship, and in size generally about one or two cubits in length; and showing this to each of the company, he says, "Look upon this, then drink and enjoy yourself; for when dead you will be like this." This practice they have at their drinking parties.

79. They observe their ancient customs, but acquire no new ones. Among other memorable customs, they have one song, Linus, which is sung in Phœnicia, Cyprus, and elsewhere; in different nations it bears a different name, but it agrees so exactly as to be the same which the Greeks sing, under the name of Linus. So that among the many wonderful things seen in Egypt, this is especially wonderful, whence they got this Linus; for they seem to have sung it from time immemorial. The Linus, in the Egyptian language, is called Maneros; and the Egyptians say that he was the only son of

the first king of Egypt, and that happening to die prematurely, he was honored by the Egyptians in this mourning dirge; and this is the first and only song they have. 80. In this other particular the Egyptians resemble the Lacedæmonians only among all the Grecians: the young men, when they meet their elders, give way and turn aside, and when they approach, rise up from their seats. In the following custom, however, they do not resemble any nation of the Greeks; instead of addressing one another in the streets, they salute by letting the hand fall down as far as the knee. 81. They wear linen tunics fringed round the legs, which they call calasiris, and over these they throw white woolen mantles; woolen clothes, however, are not carried into the temples, nor are they buried with them, for that is accounted profane. In this respect they agree with the worshipers of Orpheus and Bacchus, who are Egyptians and Pythagoreans; for it is considered profane for one who is initiated in these mysteries to be buried in woolen garments, and a religious reason is given for this custom.

82. These other things were also invented by the Egyptians. Each month and day is assigned to some particular god; and according to the day on which each person is born, *they determine* what will befall him, how he will die, and what kind of person he will be. And these things the Grecian poets have made use of. They have also discovered more prodigies than all the rest of the world; for when any prodigy occurs, they carefully observe and write down the result; and if a similar occurrence should happen afterward, they think the result will be the same. 83. The art of divination is in this condition: it is attributed to no human being, but only to some of the gods; for they have among them an oracle of Hercules, Apollo, Minerva, Diana, Mars, and Jupiter; and that which they honor above all others is the oracle of Latona, in the city of Buto. Their modes of delivering oracles, however, are not all alike, but differ from each other. 84. The art of medicine is thus divided among them: each physician applies himself to one disease only, and not more. All places abound in physicians; some physicians are for the eyes, others for the head, others for the teeth, others for the parts about the belly, and others for internal disorders.

85. Their manner of mourning and burying is as follows. When in a family a man of any consideration dies, all the

females of that family besmear their heads and faces with mud, and then leaving the body in the house, they wander about the city, and beat themselves, having their clothes girt up, and exposing their breasts, and all their relations accompany them. On the other hand, the men beat themselves, being girt up, in like manner. When they have done this, they carry out the body to be embalmed. 86. There are persons who are appointed for this very purpose; they, when the dead body is brought to them, show to the bearers wooden models of corpses, made exactly like by painting. And they show that which they say is the most expensive manner of embalming, the name of which I do not think it right to mention on such an occasion; they then show the second, which is inferior and less expensive; and then the third, which is the cheapest. Having explained them all, they learn from them in what way they wish the body to be prepared; then the relations, when they have agreed on the price, depart; but the embalmers remaining in the work-shops thus proceed to embalm in the most expensive manner. First they draw out the brains through the nostrils with an iron hook, taking part of it out in this manner, the rest by the infusion of drugs. Then with a sharp Ethiopian stone they make an incision in the side, and take out all the bowels; and having cleansed the abdomen and rinsed it with palm-wine, they next sprinkle it with pounded perfumes. Then, having filled the belly with pure myrrh pounded, and cassia, and other perfumes, frankincense excepted, they sew it up again; and when they have done this, they steep it in natrum, leaving it under for seventy days; for a longer time than this it is not lawful to steep it. At the expiration of the seventy days they wash the corpse, and wrap the whole body in bandages of flaxen cloth, smearing it with gum, which the Egyptians commonly use instead of glue. After this the relations, having taken the body back again, make a wooden case in the shape of a man, and having made it, they inclose the body; and thus, having fastened it up, they store it in a sepulchral chamber, setting it upright against the wall. In this manner they prepare the bodies that are embalmed in the most expensive way. 87. Those who, avoiding great expense, desire the middle way, they prepare in the following manner. When they have charged their syringes with oil made from cedar, they fill the abdomen of the corpse without making any incision or taking out the bowels, but inject it at the fundament; and having prevented the injection from escaping, they steep the body in natrum for the prescribed number of days, and on the last day they let out from the abdomen the oil of cedar which they had before injected, and it has such power that it brings away the intestines and vitals in a state of dissolution; the natrum dissolves the flesh, and nothing of the body remains but the skin and the bones. When they have done this they return the body without any farther operation. 88. The third method of embalming is this, which is used only for the poorer sort: having thoroughly rinsed the abdomen in syrmaea, they steep it with natrum for the seventy days, and then deliver it to be carried away. 89. But the wives of considerable persons, when they die, they do not immediately deliver to be embalmed, nor such women as are very beautiful and of celebrity, but when they have been dead three or four days they then deliver them to the embalmers; and they do this for the following reason, that the embalmers may not abuse the bodies of such women; for they say that one man was detected in abusing a body that was fresh, and that a fellow-workman informed against him. 90. Should any person, whether Egyptian or stranger, no matter which, be found to have been seized by a crocodile, or drowned in the river, to whatever city the body may be carried, the inhabitants are by law compelled to have the body embalmed, and having adorned it in the handsomest manner, to bury it in the sacred vaults. Nor is it lawful for any one else, whether relations or friends, to touch him; but the priests of the Nile bury the corpse with their own hands, as being something more than human.

91. They avoid using Grecian customs, and, in a word, the customs of all other people whatsoever. All the other Egyptians are particular in this. But there is a large city called Chemmis, situate in the Thebaic district, near Neapolis, in which is a quadrangular temple dedicated to Perseus, the son of Danae; palm-trees grow round it, and the portico is of stone, very spacious, and over it are placed two large stone statues. In this inclosure is a temple, and in it is placed a statue of Perseus. The Chemmitæ affirm that Perseus has frequently appeared to them on earth, and frequently within the temple, and that a sandal worn by him is sometimes

found, which is two cubits in length; and that after its appearance all Egypt flourishes. This they affirm. They adopt the following Grecian customs in honor of Perseus: they celebrate gymnastic games, embracing every kind of contest; and they give as prizes cattle, cloaks, and skins. When I inquired why Perseus appeared only to them, and why they differed from the rest of the Egyptians in holding gymnastic games, they answered "that Perseus derived his origin from their city; for that Danaus and Lynceus, who were both natives of Chemmis, sailed from them into Greece;" and, tracing the descent down from them, they came to Perseus; and "that he, coming to Egypt for the same reason, as the Greeks allege, in order to bring away the Gorgon's head from Libya, they affirmed that he came to them also, and acknowledged all his kindred; and that, when he came to Egypt, he was well acquainted with the name of Chemmis, having heard it from his mother. They add that, by his order, they instituted gymnastic games in honor of him."

92. The Egyptians who dwell above the morasses observe all these customs; but those who live in the morasses have the same customs as the rest of the Egyptians, and as in other things, so in this, that each man has but one wife, like the Greeks. But, to obtain food more easily, they have the following inventions: when the river is full, and has made the plains like a sea, great numbers of lilies, which the Egyptians call lotus, spring up in the water. These they gather and dry in the sun; then having pounded the middle of the lotus, which resembles a poppy, they make a bread of it and bake it. The root also of this lotus is fit for food, and is tolerably sweet, and is round, and of the size of an apple. There are also other lilies, like roses, that grow in the river, the fruit of which is contained in a separate pod, that springs up from the root in form very like a wasp's nest. In this there are many berries fit to be eaten, of the size of an olive-stone, and they are eaten both fresh and dried. The byblus, which is an annual plant, when they have pulled it up in the fens, they cut off the top of it and put to some other uses, but the lower part that is left, to the length of a cubit, they eat and sell. Those who are anxious to eat the byblus dressed in the most delicate manner, stew it in a hot pan and then eat it. Some of them live entirely on

fish, which they catch, and gut, and dry in the sun, and then eat them dried.

93. Fishes that are gregarious are seldom found in the rivers, but, being bred in the lakes, they proceed as follows: when the desire of engendering comes upon them, they swim out in shoals to the sea; the males lead the way, scattering the sperm, and the females following swallow it, and are thus impregnated. When they find themselves full in the sea, they swim back, each to their accustomed haunts; however, the males no longer take the lead, but this is done by females: they, leading the way in shoals, do as the males did before; for they scatter their spawn by degrees, and the males following devour them; but, from the spawn that escapes and is not devoured, the fish that grow up are engendered. Any of these fish that happen to be taken in their passage toward the sea are found bruised on the left side of the head; but those that are taken on their return are bruised on the right; and this proceeds from the following cause: they swim out to the sea keeping close to the land on the left side, and when they swim back again they keep to the same shore, hugging it and touching it as much as possible, for fear of losing their way by the stream. When the Nile begins to overflow, the hollow parts of the land and the marshes near the river first begin to be filled by the water oozing through from the river; and as soon as they are full, they are immediately filled with little fishes; the reason of which, as I conjecture, is this: in the preceding year, when the Nile retreated, the fish that had deposited their eggs in the marshy ground went away with the last of the waters; but when, as the time came round, the water has risen again, fishes are immediately produced from these eggs. Thus it happens with respect to the fishes.

94. The Egyptians who live about the fens use an oil drawn from the fruit of the sillicypria, which they call cici, and they make it in the following manner: they plant these sillicypria, which in Greece grow spontaneous and wild, on the banks of the rivers and lakes. These, when planted in Egypt, bear abundance of fruit, though of an offensive smell. When they have gathered it, some bruise it and press out the oil; others boil and stew it, and collect the liquid that flows from it; this is fat, and no less suited for lamps than olive oil, but it emits an offensive smell. 95. They have the following contrivance

to protect themselves from the musquitoes, which abound very much. The towers are of great service to those who inhabit the upper parts of the marshes; for the musquitoes are prevented by the winds from flying high; but those who live round the marshes have contrived another expedient instead of the towers. Every man has a net, with which in the day he takes fish, and at night uses it in the following manner: in whatever bed he sleeps, he throws the net around it, and then getting in, sleeps under. If he should wrap himself up in his clothes or in linen, the musquitoes would bite through them, but they never attempt to bite through the net.

96. Their ships in which they convey merchandise are made of the acacia, which in shape is very like the Cyrenæan lotus, and its exudation is gum. From this acacia they cut planks about two cubits in length, and join them together like bricks, building their ships in the following manner. They fasten the planks of two cubits length round stout and long ties: when they have thus built the hulls, they lay benches across them. They make no use of ribs, but caulk the seams inside with byblus. They make only one rudder, and that is driven through the keel. They use a mast of acacia and sails of byblus. These vessels are unable to sail up the stream unless a fair wind prevails, but are towed from the shore. They are thus carried down the stream: there is a hurdle made of tamarisk, wattled with a band of reeds, and a stone bored through the middle, of about two talents in weight; of these two, the hurdle is fastened to a cable, and let down at the prow of the vessel to be carried on by the stream; and the stone by another cable at the stern; and by this means the hurdle, by the stream bearing hard upon it, moves quickly and draws along "the baris" (for this is the name given to these vessels), but the stone being dragged at the stern, and sunk to the bottom, keeps the vessel in its course. They have very many of these vessels, and some of them carry many thousand talents. 97. When the Nile inundates the country, the cities alone are seen above its surface, very like the islands in the Ægean Sea; for all the rest of Egypt becomes a sea, and the cities alone are above the surface. When this happens, they navigate no longer by the channel of the river, but across the plain. To a person sailing from Naucratis to Memphis, the passage is by the pyramids; this, however, is not the usual

course, but by the point of the Delta and the city of Cercasorus; and in sailing from the sea and Canopus to Naucratis across the plain, you will pass by the city of Anthylla and that called Archandropolis. 98. Of these, Anthylla, which is a city of importance, is assigned to purchase shoes for the wife of the reigning king of Egypt; and this has been so as long as Egypt has been subject to the Persians. The other city appears to me to derive its name from the son-in-law of Danaus, Archander, son of Phthius, and grandson of Achæus, for it is called Archandropolis. There may, indeed, have been another Archander, but the name is certainly not Egyptian.

99. Hitherto I have related what I have seen, what I have thought, and what I have learned by inquiry; but from this point I proceed to give the Egyptian account, according to what I heard, and there is added to it something also of my own observation. The priests informed me that Menes, who first ruled over Egypt, in the first place protected Memphis by a mound; for the whole river formerly ran close to the sandy mountain on the side of Libya; but Menes, beginning about a hundred stades above Memphis, filled in the elbow toward the south, dried up the old channel, and conducted the river into a canal, so as to make it flow between the mountains:[2] this bend of the Nile, which flows excluded from *its ancient course*, is still carefully upheld by the Persians, being made secure every year; for if the river should break through and overflow in this part, there would be danger lest all Memphis should be flooded. When the part cut off had been made firm land by this Menes, who was first king, he, in the first place, built on it the city that is now called Memphis; for Memphis is situate in the narrow part of Egypt; and outside of it he excavated a lake from the river toward the north and the west; for the Nile itself bounds it toward the east. In the next place, *they relate* that he built in it the temple of Vulcan, which is vast and well worthy of mention. 100. After this, the priests enumerated from a book the names of three hundred and thirty other kings. In so many generations of men, there were eighteen Ethiopians and one native queen; the rest were Egyptians. The name of this woman who reigned was the same as that of the Babylonian queen, Nitocris: they said that she avenged her brother,

[2] That is, those of Arabia and Libya

whom the Egyptians had slain while reigning over them; and after they had slain him they then delivered the kingdom to her, and she, to avenge him, destroyed many of the Egyptians by stratagem; for having caused an extensive apartment to be made under ground, she pretended that she was going to consecrate it, but in reality had another design in view, and having invited those of the Egyptians whom she knew to have been principally concerned in the murder, she gave a great banquet, and when they were feasting, she let in the river upon them through a large concealed channel. This is all they related of her, except that when she had done this she threw herself into a room full of ashes, in order that she might escape punishment. 101. Of the other kings they did not mention any memorable deeds, nor that they were in any respect renowned, except one, the last of them, Mœris; but he accomplished some memorable works, as the portal of Vulcan's temple, facing the north wind, and dug a lake (the dimensions of which I shall describe hereafter), and built pyramids in it, the size of which I shall also mention when I come to speak of the lake itself. He, then, achieved these several works, but none of the others achieved any thing.

102. Having, therefore, passed them by, I shall proceed to make mention of the king that came after them, whose name was Sesostris. The priests said that he was the first who, setting out in ships of war[3] from the Arabian Gulf, subdued those nations that dwell by the Red Sea, until, sailing onward, he arrived at a sea which was not navigable on account of the shoals; and afterward, when he came back to Egypt, according to the report of the priests, he assembled a large army, and marched through the continent, subduing every nation that he fell in with; and whenever he met with any who were valiant, and who were very ardent in defense of their liberty, he erected columns in their territory, with inscriptions declaring his own name and country, and how he had conquered them by his power; but when he subdued any cities without fighting and easily, he made inscriptions on columns in the same way as among the nations that had proved themselves valiant, and he had besides engraved on them the secret parts of a woman, wishing to make it known that they were cowardly. 103. Thus doing, he traversed the

[3] See Book I. chap. 2, note [6]

continent, until, having crossed from Asia into Europe, he subdued the Scythians and Thracians: to these the Egyptian army appears to me to have reached, and no farther; for in their country the columns appear to have been erected, but nowhere beyond them. From thence, wheeling round, he went back again; and when he arrived at the river Phasis, I am unable after this to say with certainty whether king Sesostris himself, having detached a portion of his army, left them there to settle in that country, or whether some of the soldiers, being wearied with his wandering expedition, of their own accord remained by the river Phasis. 104. For the Colchians were evidently Egyptians, and I say this having myself observed it before I heard it from others; and as it was a matter of interest to me, I inquired of both people, and the Colchians had more recollection of the Egyptians than the Egyptians had of the Colchians; yet the Egyptians said that they thought the Colchians were descended from the army of Sesostris; and I formed my conjecture, not only because they are swarthy and curly-headed, for this amounts to nothing, because others are so likewise, but chiefly from the following circumstances, because the Colchians, Egyptians, and Ethiopians are the only nations of the world who, from the first, have practiced circumcision; for the Phœnicians, and the Syrians in Palestine, acknowledge that they learned the custom from the Egyptians; and the Syrians about Thermodon and the river Parthenius, with their neighbors the Macrones, confess that they very lately learned the same custom from the Colchians. And these are the only nations that are circumcised, and thus appear evidently to act in the same manner as the Egyptians. But of the Egyptians and Ethiopians, I am unable to say which learned it from the other, for it is evidently a very ancient custom. And this appears to me a strong proof that the Phœnicians learned this practice through their intercourse with the Egyptians, for all the Phœnicians who have any commerce with Greece no longer imitate the Egyptians in this usage, but abstain from circumcising their children. 105. I will now mention[4] another fact respecting the Colchians, how they resemble the Egyptians. They alone and the Egyptians manufacture[5] linen in the same manner; and the whole way of living, and the language, is similar in both

[4] "Come, now, I will also mention." [5] See chap. 35.

nations; but the Colchian linen is called by the Greeks Sardonic, though that which comes from Egypt is called Egyptian. 106. As to the pillars which Sesostris, king of Egypt, erected in the different countries, most of them are evidently no longer in existence, but in Syrian Palestine I myself saw some still remaining, and the inscriptions before mentioned still on them, and the private parts of a woman. There are also in Ionia two images of this king, carved on rocks, one on the way from Ephesia to Phocæa, the other from Sardis to Smyrna. In both places a man is carved, four cubits and a half high, holding a spear in his right hand, and in his left a bow, and the rest of his equipment in unison, for it is partly Egyptian and partly Ethiopian; from one shoulder to the other across the breast extend sacred Egyptian characters engraved, which have the following meaning: "I ACQUIRED THIS REGION BY MY OWN SHOULDERS." Who or whence he is he does not here show, but has elsewhere made known. Some, however, who have seen these monuments, have conjectured them to be images of Memnon, herein being very far from the truth.

107. The priests said, moreover, of this Egyptian Sesostris, that returning and bringing with him many men from the nations whose territories he had subdued, when he arrived at the Pelusian Daphnæ, his brother, to whom he had committed the government of Egypt, invited him to an entertainment, and his sons with him, and caused wood to be piled up round the house, and having caused it to be piled up, set it on fire; but that Sesostris, being informed of this, immediately consulted with his wife, for he took his wife with him; and she advised him to extend two of his six sons across the fire, and form a bridge over the burning mass, and that the rest should step on them and make their escape. Sesostris did so, and two of his sons were in this manner burned to death, but the rest, together with their father, were saved. 108. Sesostris having returned to Egypt, and taken revenge on his brother, employed the multitude of prisoners whom he brought from the countries he had subdued in the following works: these were the persons who drew the huge stones which, in the time of this king, were conveyed to the temple of Vulcan; they, too, were compelled to dig all the canals now seen in Egypt; by their involuntary labor they made Egypt, which before was throughout practicable for horses and carriages,

unfit for these purposes; for from that time Egypt, though it was one level plain, became impassable for horses or carriages; and this is caused by the canals, which are numerous and in every direction. But the king intersected the country for this reason: such of the Egyptians as occupied the cities not on the river, but inland, when the river receded, being in want of water, were forced to use a brackish beverage which they drew[6] from wells; and for this reason Egypt was intersected. 109. They said also that this king divided the country among all the Egyptians, giving an equal square allotment to each; and from thence he drew his revenues, having required them to pay a fixed tax every year; but if the river happened to take away a part of any one's allotment, he was to come to him and make known what had happened; whereupon the king sent persons to inspect and measure how much the land was diminished, that in future he might pay a proportionate part of the appointed tax. Hence land-measuring appears to me to have had its beginning, and to have passed over into Greece; for the pole[7] and the sun-dial, and the division of the day into twelve parts, the Greeks learned from the Babylonians. 110. This king, then, was the only Egyptian that ruled over Ethiopia, and he left as memorials before Vulcan's temple statues of stone, two of thirty cubits, himself and his wife; and his four sons, each of twenty cubits. A long time after, the priest of Vulcan would not suffer Darius the Persian to place his statue before them, saying "that deeds had not been achieved by him equal to those of Sesostris the Egyptian; for that Sesostris had subdued other nations, not fewer than Darius had done, and the Scythians besides; but that Darius was not able to conquer the Scythians; wherefore it was not right for one who had not surpassed him in achievements to place his statue before his offerings." They relate, however, that Darius pardoned these observations.

111. After the death of Sesostris, they said that his son Pheron succeeded to the kingdom; that he undertook no military expedition, and happened to become blind through the following occurrence: the river having risen to a very great

[6] Literally, "using it from wells."

[7] Πόλος here means "a concave dial," shaped like the vault of heaven. See *Baehr*.

height for that time, to eighteen cubits, when it overflowed the fields, a storm of wind arose, and the river was tossed about in waves; whereupon they say that the king with great arrogance laid hold of a javelin, and threw it into the midst of the eddies of the river, and that immediately afterward he was seized with a pain in his eyes, and became blind. He continued blind for ten years; but in the eleventh year an oracle reached him from the city of Buto, importing "that the time of his punishment was expired, and he should recover his sight by washing his eyes with the urine of a woman who had had intercourse with her own husband only, and had known no other man. He therefore made trial of his own wife first, and afterward, when he did not recover his sight, he made trial of others indifferently; and at length, having recovered his sight, he collected the women of whom he had made trial, except the one by washing with whose urine he had recovered his sight, into one city, which is now called Erythrebolus, and when he had assembled them together he had them all burned, together with the city; but the woman, by washing in whose urine he recovered his sight, he took to himself to wife. Having escaped from this calamity in his eyes, he dedicated other offerings throughout all the celebrated temples, and, what is most worthy of mention, he dedicated to the temple of the sun works worthy of admiration, two stone obelisks, each consisting of one stone, and each a hundred cubits in length and eight cubits in breadth.

112. They said that a native of Memphis succeeded him in the kingdom, whose name in the Grecian language is Proteus: there is to this day an inclosure sacred to him at Memphis, which is very beautiful and richly adorned, situated to the south side of the temple of Vulcan. Tyrian Phœnicians dwell round this inclosure, and the whole tract is called the Tyrian camp.[8] In this inclosure of Proteus is a temple which is called after the foreign Venus; and I conjecture that this is the temple of Helen, the daughter of Tyndarus, both because I have heard that Helen lived with Proteus, and also because it is named from the foreign Venus; for of all the other temples of Venus, none is any where called by the name

[8] In chap. 154 we meet with "the camp of the Ionians and Carians."

of foreign. 113. When I inquired about Helen, the priests told me that the case was thus: that when Paris had carried Helen off from Sparta, he sailed away to his own country, and when he was in the Ægean, violent winds drove him out of his course into the Egyptian sea, and from thence (for the gale did not abate) he came to Egypt, and in Egypt to that which is now called the Canopic mouth of the Nile, and to Taricheæ. On that shore stood a temple of Hercules, which remains to this day; in which, if the slave of any person whatsoever takes refuge, and has sacred marks impressed on him, so devoting himself to the god, it is not lawful to lay hands on him. This custom continues the same to my time as it was from the first. The attendants of Paris, therefore, when informed of the custom that prevailed respecting the temple, revolted from him, and, sitting as suppliants of the god, accused Paris with a view to injure him, relating the whole account, how things stood with regard to Helen, and his injustice toward Menelaus. These accusations were made to the priests, and the governor of that mouth, whose name was Thonis. 114. Thonis having heard this, immediately sends a message to Proteus at Memphis, to the following effect: "A stranger of Trojan race has arrived, after having committed a nefarious deed in Greece; for having beguiled the wife of his own host, he has brought her with him, and very great treasures, having been driven by winds to this land. Whether, then, shall we allow him to depart unmolested, or shall we seize what he has brought with him?" Proteus sends back a messenger with the following answer: "Seize this man, whoever he may be, that has acted so wickedly toward his host, and bring him to me, that I may know what he will say for himself." 115. Thonis, having received this message, seizes Paris, and detains his ships; and then sent him up to Memphis with Helen and his treasures, and, besides, the suppliants also. When all were carried up, Proteus asked Paris who he was, and whence he had sailed; and he gave him an account of his family, and told him the name of his country, and, moreover, described his voyage and from whence he had set sail. Then Proteus asked him whence he got Helen; and when Paris prevaricated in his account, and did not speak the truth, they who had become suppliants accused him, relating the whole account of his crime. At last Proteus pronounced this judgment, saying, "If I did not think it of great moment not to put any stranger to death who, being prevented by the winds from pursuing his course, has come to my territory, I would take vengeance on you on behalf of the Grecian, you basest of men, who, after you had met with hospitable treatment, have committed the most nefarious deed; you seduced the wife of your host, and this did not content you, but, having excited her passions,[9] you have taken her away by stealth. Nor even did this content you, but you have also robbed the house of your host and come hither with the spoils; now therefore, since I deem it of great moment not to put a stranger to death, I will not suffer you to carry away this woman or this treasure, but I will keep them for your Grecian host until he please to come himself and take them away; as for you and your shipmates, I bid you depart out of my territory to some other within three days; if not, you shall be treated as enemies."

116. The priests gave this account of the arrival of Helen at the court of Proteus. And Homer appears to me to have heard this relation; but it was not equally suited to epic poetry as the other which he has made use of, wherefore he has rejected it, though he has plainly shown that he was acquainted with this account also. And this is evident, since he has described in the Iliad (and has nowhere else retraced his steps) the wanderings of Paris, how, while he was carrying off Helen, he was driven out of his course, and wandered to other places, and how he arrived at Sidon of Phœnicia; and he has mentioned it in the exploits of Diomede; his verses are as follows: "Where were the variegated robes, works of Sidonian women, which god-like Paris himself brought from Sidon, sailing over the wide sea, along the course by which he conveyed high-born Helen."[1] He mentions it also in the Odyssey, in the following lines: "Such well-chosen drugs had the daughter of Jove, of excellent quality, which Polydamna gave her, the Egyptian wife of Thonis, where the fruitful earth produces many drugs, many excellent when mixed, and many noxious."[2] Menelaus also says the following to Telemachus: "The gods detained me in Egypt,

[9] Literally, "having raised the wings."
[1] Iliad, vi. 289.
[2] Odyssey, iv. 227.

though anxious to return hither, because I did not offer perfect hecatombs to them."[3] He shows in these verses that he was acquainted with the wandering of Paris in Egypt; for Syria borders on Egypt, and the Phœnicians, to whom Sidon belongs, inhabit Syria. 117. From these verses, and this first passage especially, it is clear that Homer was not the author of the Cyprian verses, but some other person; for in the Cyprian verses it is said that Paris reached Ilium from Sparta on the third day, when he carried off Helen, having met with a favorable wind and a smooth sea; whereas Homer, in the Iliad, says that he wandered far, while taking her with him. And now I take my leave of Homer and the Cyprian verses.

118. When I asked the priests whether the Greeks tell an idle story about the Trojan war or not, they gave me the following answer, saying that they knew it by inquiry from Menelaus himself: That, after the rape of Helen, a vast army of Grecians came to the land of Teucria to assist Menelaus; and that, when the army had landed and pitched their camp, they sent embassadors to Ilium, and that Menelaus himself went with them. When they reached the walls, they demanded the restitution of Helen, and the treasures that Paris had stolen from him, and satisfaction for the injuries done: that the Trojans told the same story then and ever after, both when put to the oath and when not swearing, that they had neither Helen nor the treasures about which they were accused, but that they were all in Egypt; and that they could not with justice be answerable for what Proteus, the Egyptian king, had in his possession. But the Greeks, thinking they were derided by them, therefore besieged them until they took their city. When, however, after they had taken the fortifications, Helen was nowhere found, but they heard the same story as before, then they gave credit to the first account, and sent Menelaus himself to Proteus. 119. When Menelaus reached Egypt, he sailed up to Memphis, and related the real truth. He both met with very hospitable entertainment, and received back Helen unharmed, and, besides, all his treasures. Menelaus, however, though he met with this treatment, behaved very iniquitously to the Egyptians; for, when he was desirous of sailing away, contrary winds detained him; and

[3] Odyssey, iv. 351.

when this continued the same for a long time, he had recourse to a nefarious expedient; for having taken two children of the people of the country, he sacrificed them;[4] but afterward, when it was discovered that he had done this deed, he was detested and persecuted by the Egyptians, and fled with his ships to Libya. Whither he bent his course from thence the Egyptians were unable to say; but of the above particulars they said they knew some by inquiry, and others, having taken place among themselves, they were able, from their own knowledge, to speak of with certainty. 120. These things the priests of the Egyptians related, and I myself agree with the account that is given respecting Helen, from the following considerations. If Helen had been in Ilium, she would have been restored to the Grecians, whether Paris were willing or not; for surely Priam could not have been so infatuated, nor the others his relatives, as to be willing to expose their own persons, their children, and the city to danger, in order that Paris might cohabit with Helen. But even if at first they had taken this resolution, yet, seeing that many of the other Trojans perished whenever they engaged with the Greeks, and that on every occasion when a battle took place, two or three, or even more, of Priam's own sons fell, if we may speak on the authority of the epic poets—when such things happened, I think that, if Priam himself were cohabiting with Helen, he would have restored her to the Greeks in order to be delivered from such present evils. Neither would the kingdom devolve upon Paris, so that when Priam was now old, the administration of affairs should fall upon him; but Hector, who was both older and more a man than he was, would succeed to the throne on the death of Priam; nor did it become him to give way to his brother when acting unjustly, and this, too, when through his means so many evils were falling on himself, and on all the rest of the Trojans. But, indeed, they had it not in their power to restore Helen, nor, when they spoke the truth, did the Greeks give credit to them; Providence ordaining, as I am of opinion, that they, by utterly perishing, should make it clear to all men, that for great crimes great punishments at the hands of the gods are

[4] Literally, "he made victims of them:" by ἔντομα are meant "victims slain to appease the infernal deities."

in store. Thus these things have been related as they appear to me.

121. The priests also informed me that Rhampsinitus succeeded Proteus in the kingdom: he left as a monument the portico of the temple of Vulcan, fronting to the west; and he erected two statues before the portico, twenty-five cubits high. Of these, the one standing to the north the Egyptians call Summer, and that to the south Winter; and the one that they call Summer they worship and do honor to, but the one called Winter they treat in a quite contrary way.

1. This king, they said, possessed a great quantity of money, such as no one of the succeeding kings was able to surpass, or even nearly come up to; and he, wishing to treasure up his wealth in safety, built a chamber of stone, of which one of the walls adjoined the outside of the palace. But the builder, forming a plan against it, devised the following contrivance; he fitted one of the stones so that it might be easily taken out by two men, or even one. When the chamber was finished, the king laid up his treasures in it; but in course of time, the builder, finding his end approaching, called his sons to him, for he had two, and described to them how (providing for them that they might have abundant sustenance) he had contrived when building the king's treasury; and having clearly explained to them every thing relating to the removal of the stone, he gave them its dimensions, and told them, if they would observe his instructions, they would be stewards of the king's riches. He accordingly died, and the sons were not long in applying themselves to the work; but having come by night to the palace, and having found the stone in the building, they easily removed it, and carried off a great quantity of treasure. 2. When the king happened to open the chamber, he was astonished at seeing the vessels deficient in treasure; but he was not able to accuse any one, as the seals were unbroken, and the chamber well secured. When, therefore, on his opening it two or three times, the treasures were always evidently diminished (for the thieves did not cease plundering), he adopted the following plan: he ordered traps to be made, and placed them round the vessels in which the treasures were. But when the thieves came as before, and one of them had entered, as soon as he went near a vessel he was straightway caught in the trap; perceiving, there-

fore, in what a predicament he was, he immediately called to his brother, and told him what had happened, and bade him enter as quick as possible and cut off his head, lest, if he was seen and recognized, he should ruin him also: the other thought that he spoke well, and did as he was advised; then, having fitted in the stone, he returned home, taking with him his brother's head. 3. When day came, the king, having entered the chamber, was astonished at seeing the body of the thief in the trap without the head, but the chamber secure, and without any means of entrance or exit. In this perplexity he contrived the following plan: he hung up the body of the thief from the wall, and having placed sentinels there, he ordered them to seize and bring before him whomsoever they should see weeping or expressing commiseration at the spectacle. The mother was greatly grieved at the body being suspended, and coming to words with her surviving son, commanded him, by any means he could, to contrive how he might take down and bring away the corpse of his brother; but, should he neglect to do so, she threatened to go to the king, and inform him that he had the treasures. 4. When the mother treated her surviving son harshly, and when, with many entreaties, he was unable to persuade her, he contrived the following plan: having got some asses, and having filled some skins with wine, he put them on the asses, and then drove them along; but when he came near the sentinels that guarded the suspended corpse, having drawn out two or three of the necks of the skins that hung down, he loosened them; and when the wine ran out, he beat his head, and cried out aloud, as if he knew not to which of the asses he should turn first: but the sentinels, when they saw wine flowing in abundance, ran into the road, with vessels in their hands, caught the wine that was being spilled, thinking it all their own gain; but the man, feigning anger, railed bitterly against them all; however, as the sentinels soothed him, he at length pretended to be pacified, and to forego his anger; at last he drove his asses out of the road, and set them to rights again. When more conversation passed, and one of the sentinels joked with him and moved him to laughter, he gave them another of the skins; and they, just as they were, lay down and set to to drink, and joined him to their party, and invited him to stay and drink with them: he was persuaded, forsooth, and remained with them; and as they treated him kindly during the drinking, he gave them another of the skins; and the sentinels, having taken very copious draughts, became exceedingly drunk, and, being overpowered by the wine, fell asleep on the spot where they had been drinking. But he, as the night was far advanced, took down the body of his brother, and, by way of insult, shaved the right cheeks of all the sentinels; then, having laid the corpse on the asses, he drove home, having performed his mother's injunctions. 5. The king, when he was informed that the body of the thief had been stolen, was exceedingly indignant, and, resolving by any means to find out the contriver of this artifice, had recourse, *as it is said,* to the following plan, a design which to me seems incredible: he placed his own daughter in a brothel, and ordered her to admit all alike to her embraces, but before they had intercourse with her to compel each one to tell her what he had done during his life most clever and most wicked, and whosoever should tell her the facts relating to the thief, she was to seize, and not suffer him to escape. When, therefore, the daughter did what her father commanded, the thief, having ascertained for what purpose this contrivance was had recourse to, and being desirous to outdo the king in craftiness, did as follows: having cut off the arm of a fresh corpse at the shoulder, he took it with him, under his cloak; and having gone in to the king's daughter, and being asked the same questions as all the rest were, he related that he had done the most wicked thing when he cut off his brother's head who was caught in a trap in the king's treasury; and the most clever thing when, having made the sentinels drunk, he took away the corpse of his brother that was hung up: she, when she heard this, endeavored to seize him, but the thief in the dark held out to her the dead man's arm, and she seized it and held it fast, imagining that she had got hold of the man's own arm; then the thief, having let it go, made his escape through the door. 6. When this also was reported to the king, he was astonished at the shrewdness and daring of the man; and at last, sending throughout all the cities, he caused a proclamation to be made, offering a free pardon, and promising great reward to the man if he would discover himself. The thief, relying on this promise, went to the king's palace; and Rhampsinitus greatly admired him, and gave him his daughter in marriage, accounting him the most knowing of all men; for that the Egyptians are superior to all others, but he was superior to the Egyptians.

122. After this, they said that this king descended alive into the place which the Greeks call Hades, and there played at dice with Ceres, and sometimes won, and other times lost; and that he came up again, and brought with him, as a present from her, a napkin of gold. On account of the descent of Rhampsinitus, since he came back again they said that the Egyptians celebrated a festival: this I know they observed even in my time; but whether they held this feast for some other reason or for that above mentioned, I am unable to say. However, on that same day, the priests, having woven a cloak, bind the eyes of one of their number with a scarf, and having conducted him with the cloak on him to the way that leads to the temple of Ceres, they then return: upon which they say this priest, with his eyes bound, is led by two wolves to the temple of Ceres, twenty stades distant from the city, and afterward the wolves lead him back to the same place. 123. Any person to whom such things appear credible may adopt the accounts given by the Egyptians; it is my object, however, throughout the whole history, to write what I hear from each people. The Egyptians say that Ceres and Bacchus hold the chief sway in the infernal regions; and the Egyptians also were the first who asserted the doctrine that the soul of man is immortal, and that when the body perishes it enters into some other animal, constantly springing into existence; and when it has passed through the different kinds of terrestrial, marine, and aerial beings, it again enters into the body of a man that is born, and that this revolution is made in three thousand years. Some of the Greeks have adopted this opinion, some earlier, others later, as if it were their own; but, although I know their names, I do not mention them.

124. Now they told me that to the reign of Rhampsinitus there was a perfect distribution of justice, and that all Egypt was in a high state of prosperity; but that after him Cheops, coming to reign over them, plunged into every kind of wickedness; for that, having shut up all the temples, he first of all forbade them to offer sacrifice, and afterward he ordered all the Egyptians to work for himself; some, accordingly, were

appointed to draw stones from the quarries in the Arabian mountain down to the Nile, others he ordered to receive the stones when transported in vessels across the river, and to drag them to the mountain called the Libyan; and they worked to the number of a hundred thousand men at a time, each party during three months. The time during which the people were thus harassed by toil lasted ten years on the road which they constructed, along which they drew the stones, a work, in my opinion, not much less than the pyramid; for its length is five stades, and its width ten orgyæ, and its height, where it is the highest, eight orgyæ; and it is of polished stone, with figures carved on it: on this road, then, ten years were expended, and in forming the subterraneous apartments on the hill, on which the pyramids stand, which he had made as a burial vault for himself, in an island, formed by draining a canal from the Nile. Twenty years were spent in erecting the pyramid itself: of this, which is square, each face is eight plethra, and the height is the same; it is composed of polished stones, and jointed with the greatest exactness: none of the stones are less than thirty feet. 125. This pyramid was built thus, in the form of steps, which some call crossæ, others bomides. When they had first built it in this manner, they raised the remaining stones by machines made of short pieces of wood: having lifted them from the ground to the first range of steps, when the stone arrived there, it was put on another machine that stood ready on the first range, and from this it was drawn to the second range on another machine, for the machines were equal in number to the ranges of steps; or they removed the machine, which was only one, and portable, to each range in succession, whenever they wished to raise the stone higher, for I should relate it in both ways, as it is related. The highest parts of it, therefore, were first finished, and afterward they completed the parts next following; but last of all they finished the parts on the ground, and that were lowest. On the pyramid is shown an inscription, in Egyptian characters, how much was expended in radishes, onions, and garlic for the workmen; which the interpreter, as I well remember, reading the inscription, told me amounted to one thousand six hundred talents of silver; and if this be really the case, how much more was probably expended in iron tools, in bread, and in clothes for the laborers, since they occupied in building the works the time which I mentioned, and no short time besides, as I think, in cutting and drawing the stones, and in forming the subterraneous excavation. 126. *It is related* that Cheops reached such a degree of infamy, that, being in want of money, he prostituted his own daughter in a brothel, and ordered her to extort, they did not say how much, but she exacted a certain sum of money, privately, as much as her father ordered her, and contrived to leave a monument of herself, and asked every one that came in to her to give her a stone toward the edifice she designed: of these stones they said the pyramid was built that stands in the middle of the three, before the great pyramid, each side of which is a plethron and a half in length. 127. The Egyptians say that this Cheops reigned fifty years; and when he died, his brother Chephren succeeded to the kingdom, and he followed the same practice as the other, both in other respects, and in building a pyramid, which does not come up to the dimensions of his brother's, for I myself measured them; nor has it subterraneous chambers; nor does a channel from the Nile flow to it, as to the other; but this flows through an artificial aqueduct round an island within, in which they say the body of Cheops is laid. Having laid the first course of variegated Ethiopian stones, less in height than the other by forty feet, he built it near the large pyramid. They both stand on the same hill, which is about a hundred feet high. Chephren, they said, reigned fifty-six years. 128. Thus one hundred and six years are reckoned, during which the Egyptians suffered all kinds of calamities, and for this length of time the temples were closed and never opened. From the hatred they bear them, the Egyptians are not very willing to mention their names, but call the pyramids after Philition, a shepherd, who at that time kept his cattle in those parts.

129. They said that after him, Mycerinus, son of Cheops, reigned over Egypt; that the conduct of his father was displeasing to him; and that he opened the temples, and permitted the people, who were worn down to the last extremity, to return to their employments and to sacrifices; and that he made the most just decisions of all their kings. On this account, of all the kings that ever reigned in Egypt, they praise him most, for he both judged well in other respects, and

moreover, when any man complained of his decision, he used to make him some present out of his own treasury and pacify his anger. To this Mycerinus, who was thus beneficent toward his subjects, and who followed these practices, the first beginning of misfortunes was the death of his daughter, who was his only child; whereupon he, being extremely afflicted with the calamity that had befallen him, and wishing to bury her in a more costly manner than usual, caused a hollow wooden image of a cow to be made, and then, having covered it with gold, he put the body of his deceased daughter into it. 130. This cow was not interred in the ground, but even in my time was exposed to view, being in the city of Sais, placed in the royal palace, in a richly-furnished chamber; and they burn near it all kinds of aromatics every day, and a lamp is kept burning by it throughout each night. In another chamber near to this cow are placed the images of Mycerinus's concubines, as the priests of Sais affirmed; and, indeed, wooden statues, about twenty in number, all formed naked, are placed there: however, as to who they are I am unable to say, except what was told me. 131. Some people, however, give the following account of this cow and these statues: that Mycerinus fell in love with his own daughter, and had intercourse with her against her will; but afterward, they say, that the girl strangled herself through grief, and he entombed her in this cow; but her mother cut off the hands of the servants who had betrayed her daughter to the father, and that now their images have suffered the same that they did when alive. But these things, as I conjecture, are trifling fables, both in other respects and in what relates to the hands of the statues, for I myself saw that they had lost their hands from age, which were seen lying at their feet even in my time. 132. The cow is in other parts covered with a purple cloth, but shows the head and the neck, covered over with very thick gold; and the orb of the sun imitated in gold is placed between the horns. The cow is not standing up, but kneeling: in size it is equal to a large living cow. It is carried every year out of the chamber. When the Egyptians beat[5] themselves for the god that is not to be named by me on this occasion, they then carry out the cow to the light; for they say that she, when she was dying, entreated her father Mycerinus to permit her

[5] See Chap. 61.

to see the sun once every year. 133. After the loss of his daughter, this second calamity befell this king: an oracle reached him from the city of Buto, importing "that he had no more than six years to live, and should die in the seventh;" but he, thinking this very hard, sent a reproachful message to the god, complaining "that his father and uncle, who had shut up the temples, and paid no regard to the gods, and, moreover, had oppressed men, had lived long; whereas he, who was religious, must die so soon." But a second message came to him from the oracle, stating "that for this very reason his life was shortened, because he had not done what he ought to have done; for it was needful that Egypt should be afflicted during one hundred and fifty years; and the two who were kings before him understood this, but he did not." When Mycerinus heard this, seeing that this sentence was now pronounced against him, he ordered a great number of lamps to be made, and having lighted them, whenever night came on, he drank and enjoyed himself, never ceasing night or day, roving about the marshes and groves, wherever he could hear of places most suited for pleasure; and he had recourse to this artifice for the purpose of convicting the oracle of falsehood, that by turning the nights into days he might have twelve years instead of six.

134. This king also left a pyramid much less than that of his father, being on each side twenty feet short of three plethra; it is quadrangular, and built half way up of Ethiopian stone. Some of the Grecians erroneously say that this pyramid is the work of the courtesan Rhodopis; but they evidently appear to me ignorant who Rhodopis was, for they would not else have attributed to her the building such a pyramid, on which, so to speak, numberless thousands of talents were expended; besides, Rhodopis flourished in the reign of Amasis, and not at this time; for she was very many years later than those kings who left these pyramids. By birth she was a Thracian, servant to Iadmon, son of Hephæstopolis, a Samian, and fellow-servant with Æsop, the writer of fables, for he too belonged to Iadmon, as is clearly proved by this circumstance. When the Delphians frequently made proclamation, in obedience to the oracle, for "any one who would require satisfaction for the death of Æsop," no one else appeared, but another Iadmon, the grandson of this Iadmon, required it; thus Æsop must have belonged to Iadmon.

135. Rhodopis came to Egypt under the conduct of Xanthus the Samian; and having come to gain money by her person, she was ransomed for a large sum by Charaxus of Mitylene, son to Scamandronymus, and brother of Sappho the poetess. Thus Rhodopis was made free, and continued in Egypt, and being very lovely, acquired great riches for a person of her condition, though no way sufficient to erect such a pyramid; for as any one who wishes may to this day see the tenth of her wealth, there is no need to attribute any great wealth to her; for Rhodopis was desirous of leaving a monument to herself in Greece, and, having had such a work made as no one ever yet devised and dedicated in a temple, to offer it at Delphi as a memorial of herself; having, therefore, made from the tenth of her wealth a great number of iron spits for roasting oxen, as far as the tenth allowed, she sent them to Delphi; which are still piled up behind the altar, which the Chians dedicated opposite the temple itself. The courtesans of Naucratis are generally very lovely; for, in the first place, this one, of whom this account is given, became so famous that all the Greeks became familiar with the name of Rhodopis; and, in the next place, after her, another, whose name was Archidice, became celebrated throughout Greece, though less talked about than the former. As for Charaxus, when, having ransomed Rhodopis, he returned to Mitylene, Sappho gibed him very much in an ode. Now I have done speaking of Rhodopis.

136. After Mycerinus, the priests said that Asychis became king of Egypt, and that he built the eastern portico to the temple of Vulcan, which is far the most beautiful and the largest; for all the porticoes have sculptured figures, and an infinite variety of architecture, but this most of all. They related that, during his reign, there being a great want of circulation of money, a law was made by the Egyptians that a man, by giving the dead body of his father in pledge, might borrow money; and it was also added to this law that the lender should have power over the whole sepulchre of the borrower; and that on any one who gave this pledge, the following punishment should be inflicted if he afterward refused to repay the debt, that neither he himself, when he died, should be buried in his family sepulchre, or in any other, nor have the liberty of burying any other of his own dead. This king, being de-

sirous of surpassing his predecessors who were kings of Egypt, left a pyramid as a memorial, made of bricks, on which is an inscription, carved on stone, in the following words: "Do not despise me in comparison with the pyramids of stone, for I excel them as much as Jupiter the other gods; for by plunging a pole into a lake, and collecting the mire that stuck to the pole, men made bricks, and in this manner built me." Such were the works that this king performed.

137. After him there reigned a blind man of the city of Anysis, whose name was Anysis. During his reign, the Ethiopians, and Sabacon, king of the Ethiopians, invaded Egypt with a large force; whereupon this blind king fled to the fens; and the Ethiopian reigned over Egypt for fifty years, during which time he performed the following actions. When any Egyptian committed any crime, he would not have any of them put to death, but passed sentence upon each according to the magnitude of his offense, enjoining them to heap up mounds against their own city to which each of the offenders belonged; and by this means the cities were made much higher; for first of all they had been raised by those who dug the canals in the time of king Sesostris,[6] and secondly, under the Ethiopian they were made very high. Although other cities in Egypt were carried to a great height, in my opinion, the greatest mounds were thrown up about the city of Bubastis, in which is a temple of Bubastis well worthy of mention; for, though other temples may be larger and more costly, yet none is more pleasing to look at than this. Bubastis, in the Grecian language, answers to Diana. 138. Her sacred precinct is thus situated: all except the entrance is an island; for two canals from the Nile extend to it, not mingling with each other, but each reaches as far as the entrance of the precinct, one flowing round it on one side, the other on the other. Each is a hundred feet broad, and shaded with trees. The portico is ten orgyæ in height, and is adorned with figures six cubits high, that are deserving of notice. This precinct, being in the middle of the city, is visible on every side to a person going round it; for as the city has been mounded up to a considerable height, but the temple has not been moved, it is conspicuous as it was originally built. A wall sculptured with figures runs round it; and within is a grove of lofty trees, planted round a large temple in which the

[6] See II. 108.

image is placed. The width and length of the precinct is each way a stade. Along the entrance is a road paved with stone, about three stades in length, leading through the square eastward; and in width it is about four plethra. On each side of the road grow trees of enormous height: it leads to the temple of Mercury. Such, then, is the situation of this precinct. 139. They related that the final departure of the Ethiopian occurred in the following manner: that he, having seen a vision of the following kind in his sleep, fled away: it appeared to him that a man, standing by him, advised him to assemble all the priests in Egypt, and to cut them in two down the middle; but he, having seen this vision, said that he thought the gods held this out as a pretext to him, in order that he, having been guilty of impiety in reference to sacred things, might draw down some evil on himself from gods or from men. He would not, therefore, do so; but as the time was expired during which it was foretold that he should reign over Egypt, he would depart from the country; for, while he was yet in Ethiopia, the oracles which the Ethiopians have recourse to answered that he was fated to reign over Egypt fifty years. Since, then, this period had elapsed, and the vision of the dream troubled him, Sabacon, of his own accord, withdrew from Egypt. 140. When, therefore, the Ethiopian departed from Egypt, the blind king resumed the government, having returned from the fens, where he had lived fifty years, having formed an island of ashes and earth; for when any of the Egyptians came to him bringing provisions, as they were severally ordered unknown to the Ethiopian, he bade them bring some ashes also as a present. No one, before Amyrtæus, was able to discover this island; but, for more than seven hundred years, the kings who preceded Amyrtæus were unable to find it out. The name of this island was Elbo; its size is about ten stades in each direction.

141. After him reigned the priest of Vulcan, whose name was Sethon. He held in no account and despised the military caste of the Egyptians, as not having need of their services; and accordingly, among other indignities, he took away their lands, to each of whom, under former kings, twelve chosen acres[7] had been assigned. After this, Sennacherib, king of the

[7] The arura, here rendered "acre," was an Egyptian measure, containing a square of 100 Egyptian cubits.

Arabians and Assyrians, marched a large army against Egypt; whereupon the Egyptian warriors refused to assist him; and the priest, being reduced to a strait, entered the temple, and bewailed before the image the calamities he was in danger of suffering. While he was lamenting, sleep fell upon him, and it appeared to him in a vision that the god stood by and encouraged him, assuring him that he should suffer nothing disagreeable in meeting the Arabian army, for he would himself send assistants to him. Confiding in this vision, he took with him such of the Egyptians as were willing to follow him, and encamped in Pelusium, for here the entrance *into Egypt* is; but none of the military caste followed him, but tradesmen, mechanics, and sutlers. When they arrived there, a number of field-mice, pouring in upon their enemies, devoured their quivers and their bows, and, moreover, the handles of their shields; so that, on the next day, when they fled bereft of their arms, many of them fell; and to this day a stone statue of this king stands in the temple of Vulcan, with a mouse in his hand, and an inscription to the following effect: "Whoever looks on me, let him revere the gods."

142. Thus much of the account the Egyptians and the priests related, showing that from the first king to this priest of Vulcan who last reigned were three hundred forty and one generations of men, and during these generations there were the same number of chief priests and kings. Now three hundred generations are equal to ten thousand years, for three generations of men are one hundred years; and the forty-one remaining generations that were over the three hundred make one thousand three hundred and forty years. Thus, they said, in eleven thousand three hundred and forty years, no god had assumed the form of a man; neither, they said, had any such thing happened before or afterward, in the time of the remaining kings of Egypt. During this time, they related that the sun had four times risen out of his usual quarter, and that he had twice risen where he now sets, and twice set where he now rises; yet that no change in the things in Egypt was occasioned by this, either with regard to the productions of the earth or the river, or with regard to diseases, or with respect to deaths. 143. In former time, the priests of Jupiter did to Hecatæus the historian, when he was tracing his own genealogy, and connecting his family

with a god in the sixteenth degree, the same as they did to me, though I did not trace my genealogy. Conducting me into the interior of an edifice that was spacious, and showing me wooden colossuses to the number I have mentioned, they reckoned them up; for every high priest places an image of himself there during his lifetime; the priests, therefore, reckoning them and showing them to me, pointed out that each was the son of his own father; going through them all, from the image of him that died last until they had pointed them all out. But when Hecatæus traced his own genealogy, and connected himself with a god in the sixteenth degree, they controverted his genealogy by computation, not admitting that a man could be born from a god; and they thus controverted his genealogy, saying that each of the colossuses was a Piromis sprung from a Piromis, until they pointed out the three hundred and forty-five colossuses, each a Piromis sprung from a Piromis, and they did not connect them with any god or hero. Piromis means, in the Grecian language, "a noble and good man." 144. They pointed out to me, therefore, that all those of whom there were images were of that character, but were very far from being gods; that, indeed, before the time of these men, gods had been the rulers of Egypt, and had dwelt among men, and that one of them always had the supreme power, and that Orus, the son of Osiris, whom the Greeks call Apollo, was the last who reigned over it; he, having deposed Typhon, was the last who reigned over Egypt. Now Osiris, in the Grecian language, means Bacchus.

145. Among the Greeks, the most recent of the gods are thought to be Hercules, Bacchus, and Pan; but by the Egyptians Pan is esteemed the most ancient, and one of the eight called original; but Hercules is among the second, among those called the twelve; and Bacchus is of the third, who were sprung from the twelve gods. I have already declared[8] how many years the Egyptians say there were from Hercules to the reign of Amasis; but from Pan a still greater number of years are said to have intervened, and from Bacchus fewest of all; and from him there are computed to have been fifteen thousand years to the reign of Amasis. The Egyptians say they know these things with accuracy, because they always compute and register the years. Now from Bacchus, who is

[8] See chap. 43.

said to have been born of Semele, the daughter of Cadmus, to my time, is about sixteen hundred years, and from Hercules, the son of Alcmena, about nine hundred years; but from Pan, born of Penelope (for Pan is said by the Greeks to have sprung from her and Mercury), is a less number of years than from the siege of Troy, about eight hundred, to my time. 146. Of these two accounts, each person may adopt that which he thinks most credible; I have therefore declared my own opinion respecting them; for, if these deities had been well known, and had grown old in Greece, as Hercules, who was sprung from Amphitryon, and especially Bacchus, the son of Semele, and Pan, who was borne by Penelope, some one might say that these later ones, though mere men, bore the names of the gods who were long before them. Now the Greeks say of Bacchus that Jupiter sewed him into his thigh as soon as he was born, and carried him to Nyssa, which is above Egypt in Ethiopia; and concerning Pan, they are unable to say whither he was taken at his birth. It is evident to me, therefore, that the Grecians learned their names later than those of the other gods, and from the time when they learned them they trace their origin; therefore they ascribe their generation to that time, and not higher. These things, then, the Egyptians themselves relate.

147. What things both other men and the Egyptians agree in saying occurred in this country, I shall now proceed to relate, and shall add to them some things of my own observation. The Egyptians having become free after the reign of the priest of Vulcan, for they were at no time able to live without a king, established twelve kings, having divided all Egypt into twelve parts. These, having contracted intermarriages, reigned, adopting the following regulations: that they would not attempt the subversion of one another, nor one seek to acquire more than another, and that they should maintain the strictest friendship. They made these regulations, and strictly upheld them, for the following reason: it had been foretold them by an oracle, when they first assumed the government, "that whoever among them should offer a libation in the temple of Vulcan from a brazen bowl, should be king of all Egypt;" for they used to assemble in all the temples. 148. Now they determined to leave in common a memorial of themselves, and having so determined, they built a labyrinth a little above the lake of Mœris, situated

near that called the city of Crocodiles; this I have myself seen, *and found it* greater than can be described; for if any one should reckon up the buildings and public works of the Grecians, they would be found to have cost less labor and expense than this labyrinth, though the temple in Ephesus is deserving of mention, and also that in Samos. The pyramids, likewise, were beyond description, and each of them comparable to many of the great Grecian structures. Yet the labyrinth surpasses even the pyramids; for it has twelve courts inclosed with walls, with doors opposite each other, six facing the north and six the south, contiguous to one another, and the same exterior wall incloses them. It contains two kinds of rooms, some under ground and some above ground over them, to the number of three thousand, fifteen hundred of each. The rooms above ground I myself went through and saw, and relate from personal inspection; but the under ground rooms I only know from report; for the Egyptians who have charge of the building would on no account show me them, saying that there were the sepulchres of the kings who originally built this labyrinth, and of the sacred crocodiles. I can therefore only relate what I have learned by hearsay concerning the lower rooms; but the upper ones, which surpass all human works, I myself saw; for the passages through the corridors, and the windings through the courts, from their great variety, presented a thousand occasions of wonder, as I passed from a court to the rooms, and from the rooms to halls, and to other corridors from the halls, and to other courts from the rooms. The roofs of all these are of stone, as also are the walls; but the walls are full of sculptured figures. Each court is surrounded with a colonnade of white stone, closely fitted; and adjoining the extremity of the labyrinth is a pyramid, forty orgyæ in height, on which large figures are carved, carved, and a way to it has been made under ground.

149. Although this labyrinth is such *as I have described*, yet the lake named from Mœris, near which this labyrinth is built, occasions greater wonder: its circumference measures three thousand six hundred stades, or sixty schœnes, equal to the sea-coast of Egypt. The lake stretches lengthways, north and south, being in depth in the deepest part fifty orgyæ. That it is made by hand and dry, this circumstance proves, for about the middle of the lake stand two pyramids,

each rising fifty orgyæ above the surface of the water, and the part built under water extends to an equal depth: on each of these is placed a stone statue, seated on a throne. Thus these pyramids are one hundred orgyæ in height; and a hundred orgyæ are equal to a stade of six plethra; the orgyæ measuring six feet, or four cubits; the foot being four palms, and the cubit six palms. The water in this lake does not spring from the soil, for these parts are excessively dry, but it is conveyed through a channel from the Nile, and for six months it flows into the lake, and six months out again into the Nile; and during the six months that it flows out it yields a talent of silver every day to the king's treasury from the fish; but when the water is flowing into it, twenty minæ. 150. The people of the country told me that this lake discharges itself under ground into the Syrtis of Libya, running westward toward the interior by the mountain above Memphis; but when I did not see any where a heap of soil from this excavation, for this was an object of curiosity to me, I inquired of the people who lived nearest the lake where the soil that had been dug out was to be found; they told me where it had been carried, and easily persuaded me, because I had heard that a similar thing had been done at Nineveh, in Assyria; for certain thieves formed a design to carry away the treasures of Sardanapalus, king of Nineveh, which were very large, and preserved in subterraneous treasuries; the thieves, therefore, beginning from their own dwellings, dug under ground by estimated measurement to the royal palace, and the soil that was taken out of the excavations, when night came on, they threw into the river Tigris, that flows by Nineveh; *and so they proceeded* until they had effected their purpose. The same method I heard was adopted in digging the lake in Egypt, except that it was not done by night, but during the day; for the Egyptians who dug out the soil carried it to the Nile, and the river receiving it, soon dispersed it. Now this lake is said to have been excavated in this way.

151. While the twelve kings continued to observe justice, in course of time, as they were sacrificing in the temple of Vulcan, and were about to offer a libation on the last day of the festival, the high priest, mistaking the number, brought out eleven of the twelve golden bowls with which he used to make the libation; whereupon he who stood last of them, Psam-

mitichus, since he had not a bowl, having taken off his helmet, which was of brass, held it out and made the libation. All the other kings were in the habit of wearing helmets, and at that time had them on. Psammitichus therefore, without any sinister intention, held out his helmet; but they, having taken into consideration what was done by Psammitichus, and the oracle that had foretold to them "that whoever among them should offer a libation from a brazen bowl should be sole king of Egypt;" calling to mind the oracle, they did not think it right to put him to death, since upon examination they found that he had done it by no premeditated design. But they determined to banish him to the marshes, having divested him of the greatest part of his power; and they forbade him to leave the marshes, or have any intercourse with the rest of Egypt.

152. This Psammitichus, who had before fled from Sabacon the Ethiopian, who had killed his father Neco—having at that time fled into Syria, the Egyptians, who belong to the Saitic district, brought back when the Ethiopian withdrew in consequence of the vision in a dream.[9] And afterward, having been made king, he was a second time constrained[1] by the eleven kings to go into exile among the marshes on account of the helmet. Knowing, then, that he had been exceedingly injured by them, he entertained the design of avenging himself on his persecutors; and when he sent to the city of Buto to consult the oracle of Latona, where is the truest oracle that the Egyptians have, an answer came "that vengeance would come from the sea, when men of brass should appear." He, however, was very incredulous[2] that men of brass would come te assist him. But when no long time had elapsed, stress of weather compelled some Ionians and Carians, who had sailed out for the purpose of piracy, to bear away to Egypt; and when they had disembarked and were clad in brazen armor, an Egyptian, who had never before seen men clad in brass, went to the marshes to Psammitichus, and told him that men of brass, having arrived from the sea, were ravaging the plains. He, perceiving that the oracle was accomplished, treated these Ionians and Carians in a friendly manner, and having promised them great things, persuaded them to join with him; and when he had succeeded in persuading them, he thus, with the

[9] See II. 139. [1] Literally, "it befell him."

[2] Literally, "great incredulity was poured secretly into him."

help of such Egyptians as were well affected to him, and with these allies, overcame the other kings.

153. Psammitichus, having made himself master of all Egypt, constructed the portico to Vulcan's temple at Memphis that faces the south wind; and he built a court for Apis, in which he is fed whenever he appears opposite the portico, surrounded by a colonnade, and full of sculptured figures; and instead of pillars, statues twelve cubits high are placed under the piazza. Apis, in the language of the Greeks, means Epaphus. 154. To the Ionians, and those who with them had assisted him, Psammitichus gave lands opposite each other, with the Nile flowing between; to these lands was given the name of Camps; and besides these lands he gave them all that he had promised; and he, moreover, put Egyptian children under their care, to be instructed in the Greek language; and from those who learned the language the present interpreters in Egypt are descended. The Ionians and the Carians continued for a long time to inhabit these lands, and they are situated near the sea, a little below the city of Bubastis, on that which is called the Pelusiac mouth of the Nile; these, in after time, king Amasis removed and settled at Memphis, making them his body-guard against the Egyptians. From the time of the settlement of these people in Egypt, we Greeks have had such constant communication with them, that we are accurately informed of all that has happened in Egypt, beginning from the reign of Psammitichus to the present time. These were the first people of a different language who settled in Egypt. The docks for their ships, and the ruins of their buildings, were to be seen in my time in the places from which they were removed. Thus, then, Psammitichus became master of Egypt.

155. Of the oracle that is in Egypt I have already made frequent mention;[3] and I shall now give an account of it, as well deserving notice. This oracle in Egypt is a temple sacred to Latona, situated in a large city, near that which is called the Sebennytic mouth of the Nile, as one sails upward from the sea. The name of this city, where the oracle is, is Buto, as I have already mentioned. There is also in this Buto a precinct sacred to Apollo and Diana; and the temple of Latona, in which the oracle is, is spacious, and has a portico ten

[3] See II. 83, 133, 152.

orgyæ in height. But of all the things I saw there, I will describe that which occasioned most astonishment. There is in this inclosure a temple of Latona made from one stone, both in height and length, and each wall is equal to them;[4] each of these measures forty cubits: for the roof, another stone is laid over it, having a cornice four cubits deep.[5] 156. This temple, then, is the most wonderful thing that I saw about this precinct. Next to it is the island called Chemmis, situated in a deep and broad lake near the precinct in Buto. This is said by the Egyptians to be a floating island, but I myself saw it neither floating nor moving, and I was astonished when I heard that there really was a floating island. In this, then, is a spacious temple of Apollo, and in it three altars are placed; and there grow in it great numbers of palms, and many other trees, both such as produce fruit and such as do not. The Egyptians, when they affirm that it floats, add the following story: *they say* that in this island, which before did not float, Latona, who was one of the eight primary deities, dwelling in Buto, where this oracle of hers now is, received Apollo as a deposit from the hands of Isis, and saved him by concealing him in this, which is now called the floating island, when Typhon arrived, searching every where, and hoping to find the son of Osiris; for they say that Apollo and Diana are the offspring of Bacchus and Isis, and that Latona was their nurse and preserver. In the language of Egypt, Apollo is called Orus; Ceres, Isis; and Diana, Bubastis. Now from this account, and no other, Æschylus, the son of Euphorion, alone among the earlier poets, derived the tradition that I will mention, for he made Diana to be the daughter of Ceres. On this account *they say* that the island was made to float. Such is the account they give.

157. Psammitichus reigned in Egypt fifty-four years, during twenty-nine of which he sat down before and besieged Azotus, a large city of Syria, until he took it. This Azotus, of all the cities we know of, held out against a siege the longest period. 158. Neco was son of Psammitichus, and became king of Egypt. He first set about the canal that leads

[4] That is to say, its external surface forms a perfect cube.

[5] This is usually translated "having a projecting roof to the extent of four cubits;" but see Letronne's remark in Baehr.—*Cary's Lexicon*, παρωροφὶς.

to the Red Sea, which Darius the Persian afterward completed. Its length is a voyage of four days, and in width it was dug so that two triremes might sail rowed abreast. The water is drawn into it from the Nile, and it enters it a little above the city Bubastis, *passes* near the Arabian city Patumos, and reaches to the Red Sea. The parts of the Egyptian plain that lie toward Arabia were dug first; above this plain is situated the mountain that stretches toward Memphis, in which are the quarries. Along the base of this mountain, therefore, the canal is carried lengthways from the west to the east, and then it stretches to the defiles, passing from the mountain toward the meridian and the south inward, as far as the Arabian Gulf. But in the part where is the shortest and most direct passage from the northern sea to the southern, which is the same as that called the Red Sea, *namely*, from Mount Cesius, that separates Egypt from Syria, from this point the distance is a thousand stades to the Arabian Gulf: this, then, is the most direct way; but the canal is very much longer, in that it is more winding, in the digging of which one hundred and twenty thousand Egyptians perished in the reign of Neco. Now Neco stopped digging it in the middle of the work, the following oracle having caused an impediment, "that he was working for a barbarian;" for the Egyptians call all men barbarians who do not speak the same language as themselves. 159. But Neco, having put a stop to his excavation, turned his attention to military affairs; and triremes were constructed, some on the northern sea, and others in the Arabian Gulf or the Red Sea, of which the docks are still to be seen. These he used as he had occasion; and Neco, having come to an engagement with the Syrians on land at Magdolus, conquered them, and after the battle took Cadytis, which is a large city in Syria. The garments he wore during these actions he consecrated to Apollo, having sent them to Branchidæ of the Milesians. Afterward, having reigned sixteen years in all, he died, and left the kingdom to his son Psammis.

160. While this Psammis was reigning over Egypt, embassadors arrived from the Eleans, boasting that they had established the Olympian games under the most just and excellent regulations in the world, and believing that not even the Egyptians, the wisest of mankind, could invent any thing

surpassing them. When the Eleans, having arrived in Egypt, mentioned for what purpose they had come, this king thereupon summoned those who were reputed to be the wisest among the Egyptians; and the Egyptians, having met together, heard the Eleans relate what was settled for them to do with regard to the games; and they, having mentioned every thing, said they had come to inquire "whether the Egyptians could invent any thing more equitable;" and they, having consulted together, asked the Eleans whether their own citizens were permitted to enter the lists; they said that they and all other Grecians who wished were allowed to contend; but the Egyptians replied, "that in making such enactments they had totally deviated from the rules of justice, for that they could not contrive so as not to favor a citizen of their own to the prejudice of a stranger; but if they really wished to make just enactments, and had come into Egypt for this purpose, they advised them to establish games for foreign candidates, and to allow no Elean to enter the lists." Such was the suggestion that the Egyptians made to the Eleans.

161. When Psammis had reigned only six years over Egypt, and made an expedition into Ethiopia, and shortly afterward died, Apries his son succeeded to the kingdom. He, next to his grandfather Psammitichus, enjoyed greater prosperity than any of the former kings, during a reign of five-and-twenty years, in which period he marched an army against Sidon, and engaged the Tyrian by sea. But when it was destined for him to meet with adversity, it happened on an occasion which I shall narrate more fully in my Libyan history,[6] and briefly in this place; for Apries, having sent an army against the Cyrenæans, met with a signal defeat; but the Egyptians, complaining of this, revolted from him, suspecting that Apries had designedly sent them to certain ruin, in order that they might be destroyed, and he might govern the rest of the Egyptians with greater security; both those that returned and the friends of those who perished, being very indignant at this, openly revolted against him. 162. Apries, having heard of this, sent Amasis to appease them by persuasion; but when he, having come to them, was endeavoring to restrain them, as he was urging them to desist from their enterprise, one of the Egyptians standing behind him placed a helmet on his head,

[6] See B. IV. chap. 159.

and as he put it on, said "that he put it on him to make him king." And this action was not at all disagreeable to Amasis, as he presently showed; for when the revolters had appointed him king of the Egyptians, he prepared to lead an army against Apries; but Apries, being informed of this, sent to Amasis a considerable person among the Egyptians that adhered to him, whose name was Patarbemis, with orders to bring Amasis alive into his presence. When Patarbemis arrived and summoned Amasis, Amasis, raising his leg (for he happened to be on horseback), broke wind, and bade him carry that to Apries. Nevertheless, Patarbemis begged of him, since the king had sent for him, to go to him; but he answered "that he had been some time preparing to do so, and that Apries should have no cause of complaint, for that he would not only appear himself, but would bring others with him." Patarbemis, perceiving his design from what was said, and seeing preparations being made, returned in haste, as he wished to inform the king as soon as possible of what was going on. When, however, he came to Apries without bringing Amasis, Apries, taking no time for deliberation, in a transport of passion commanded his ears and nose to be cut off. The rest of the Egyptians, who still adhered to him, seeing one of the most distinguished among them treated in so unworthy a manner, did not delay a moment, but went immediately over to the others and gave themselves to Amasis. 163. When Apries heard of this, he armed his auxiliaries and marched against the Egyptians; but he had with him Carian and Ionian auxiliaries to the number of thirty thousand; and he had a palace in the city of Sais that was spacious and magnificent. Now Apries's party advanced against the Egyptians, and the party of Amasis against the foreigners. They met near the city Momemphis, and prepared to engage with each other.

164. There are seven classes of Egyptians, and of these some are called priests, others warriors, others herdsmen, others swineherds, others tradesmen, others interpreters, and, lastly, pilots: such are the classes of Egyptians: they take their names from the employments they exercise. Their warriors are called Calasiries or Hermotybies, and they are of the following districts, for all Egypt is divided into districts. 165. The following are the districts of the Hermotybies,

Busiris, Sais, Chemmis, Papremis, the island called Prosopitis, and the half of Natho. From these districts are the Hermotybies, being in number, when they are most numerous, a hundred and sixty thousand. None of these learn any mechanical art, but apply themselves wholly to military affairs. 166. These next are the districts of the Calasiries: Thebes, Bubastis, Aphthis, Tanis, Mendes, Sebennys, Athribis, Pharbæthis, Thmuis, Onuphis, Anysis, Mycephoris: this district is situated in an island opposite the city of Bubastis. These are the districts of the Calasiries, being in number, when they are most numerous, two hundred and fifty thousand men. Neither are these allowed to practice any art, but they devote themselves to military pursuits alone, the son succeeding to his father. 167. Whether the Greeks learned this custom from the Egyptians, I am unable to determine with certainty, seeing that the Thracians, Scythians, Persians, Lydians, and almost all barbarous nations, hold in less honor than their other citizens those who learn any art and their descendants, but deem such to be noble as abstain from handicrafts, and particularly those who devote themselves to war. All the Greeks, moreover, have adopted the same notion, and especially the Lacedæmonians; but the Corinthians hold handicraftsmen in least disesteem. 168. To these alone, of all the Egyptians, besides the priests, the following special privileges are attached: to each, twelve chosen acres[7] free from tribute. The acre contains a square of one hundred Egyptian cubits, and the Egyptian cubit is equal to that of Samos. These privileges were attached to them all, but others enjoyed them by turns, and the same persons never *more than once.* A thousand of the Calasiries, and as many of the Hermotybies, each served for a year as the king's body-guard. To these, accordingly, was given the following allowance daily, in addition to the acres, to each five minæ in weight of baked bread, two minæ of beef, and four arysters of wine. This was the constant allowance of the body-guard.

169. When, therefore, Apries, leading his auxiliaries, and Amasis, all the Egyptians, met together at Momemphis, they came to an engagement, and the foreigners fought well, but being far inferior in numbers, were, on that account, defeated.

[7] See chap. 141, and note there.

Apries is said to have been of opinion that not even a god could deprive him of his kingdom, so securely did he think himself established. Now, however, when he came to an engagement, he was beaten, and, being taken prisoner, he was carried back to Sais, to that which was formerly his own palace, but which now belonged to Amasis. Here he was maintained for some time in the royal palace, and Amasis treated him well. But, at length, the Egyptians complaining that he did not act rightly in preserving a man who was the greatest enemy both to them and to him, he thereupon delivered Apries to the Egyptians; but they strangled him, and afterward buried him in his ancestral sepulchre: this is in the sacred precinct of Minerva, very near the temple, on the left hand as you enter. The Saitæ used to bring all the kings sprung from this district within the sacred precinct; however, the tomb of Amasis is farther from the temple than that of Apries and his progenitors, but even[8] this is in the court of the sacred precinct, consisting of a large stone chamber, adorned with columns, made in imitation of palm-trees, and with other ornaments; inside this chamber are placed folding doors, and within the doors is the sepulchre. 170. At Sais, also, in the sacred precinct of Minerva, behind the chapel and joining the whole of the wall, is the tomb of one whose name I consider it impious to divulge on such an occasion; and in the inclosure stand large stone obelisks, and there is a lake near, ornamented with a stone margin, formed in a circle, and in size, as appeared to me, much the same as that in Delos, which is called the Circular. 171. In this lake they perform by night the representation of that person's adventures, which they call mysteries. On these matters, however, though accurately acquainted with the particulars of them, I must observe a discreet silence; and respecting the sacred rites of Ceres, which the Greeks call Thesmyphoria, although I am acquainted with them, I must observe silence except so far as it is lawful for me to speak of them. The daughters of Danaus were they who introduced these ceremonies from Egypt, and taught them to the Pelasgian women; but afterward, when almost the whole Peloponnese was depopulated by the Dorians, these rites were lost; but the Arcadians, who

[8] All former translators of Herodotus have misconstrued this passage, by neglecting to give the force of the word μέντοι.

were the only Peloponnesians left, and not expelled, alone preserved them.

172. Apries being thus dethroned, Amasis, who was of the Saitic district, reigned in his stead; the name of the city from which he came was Siuph. At first the Egyptians despised, and held him in no great estimation, as having been formerly a private person, and of no illustrious family; but afterward he conciliated them by his address, without any arrogance. He had an infinite number of other treasures, and, besides, a golden foot-pan, in which Amasis himself, and all his guests, were accustomed to wash their feet. Having then broken this in pieces, he had made from it the statue of a god, and placed it in the most suitable part of the city; but the Egyptians, flocking to the image, paid it the greatest reverence. But Amasis, informed of their behavior, called the Egyptians together, and explained the matter to them, saying "that the statue was made out of the foot-pan in which the Egyptians formerly vomited, made water, and washed their feet, and which they then so greatly reverenced; now, then, he proceeded to say, the same had happened to him as to the foot-pan; for, though he was before but a private person, yet he was now their king;" he therefore required them to honor and respect him: by this means he won over the Egyptians, so that they thought fit to obey him. 173. He adopted the following method of managing his affairs: early in the morning, until the time of full market, he assiduously dispatched the business brought before him; after that he drank and jested with his companions, and he talked loosely and sportively. But his friends, offended at this, admonished him, saying, "You do not, O king, control yourself properly in making yourself too common; for it becomes you, who sit on a venerable throne, to pass the day in transacting public business; thus the Egyptians would know that they are governed by a great man, and you would be better spoken of; but now you act in a manner not at all becoming a king." But he answered them as follows: "They who have bows, when they want to use them, bend them; but when they have done using them, they unbend them; for if it were kept always bent, it would break, so that he could not use it when he had need. Such is the condition of man; if he should incessantly attend to serious business, and not give

himself up sometimes to sport, he would unawares become mad or stupefied. I, being well aware of this, give up a portion of my time to each." Thus he answered his friends.

174. Amasis is said to have been, even when a private person, fond of drinking and jesting, and by no means inclined to serious business; and when the means failed him for drinking and indulging himself, he used to go about pilfering. Such persons as accused him of having their property, on his denying it, used to take him to the oracle of the place, and he was oftentimes convicted by the oracles, and oftentimes acquitted. When, therefore, he came to the throne, he acted as follows: whatever gods had absolved him from the charge of theft, of their temples he neither took any heed, nor contributed any thing toward their repair; neither did he frequent them, and offer sacrifices, considering them of no consequence at all, and as having only lying responses to give. But as many as had convicted him of the charge of theft, to them he paid the highest respect, considering them as truly gods, and delivering authentic responses.

175. Moreover, he built an admirable portico to the temple of Minerva at Sais, far surpassing all others both in height and size, as well as in the dimensions and quality of the stones; he likewise dedicated large statues, and huge andro-sphinxes, and brought other stones of a prodigious size for repairs: of these he brought some from the quarries near Memphis; but those of the greatest magnitude from the city of Elephantine, distant from Sais a passage of twenty days. But of these, that which I not the least, rather the most admire, is this; he brought a building of one stone from the city of Elephantine, and two thousand men, who were appointed to convey it, were occupied three whole years in its transport, and these men were all pilots. The length of this chamber, outside, is twenty-one cubits, the breadth fourteen, and the height eight. This is the measure of the outside of the one-stoned chamber. But inside, the length is eighteen cubits and twenty digits, and the width twelve cubits, and the height five cubits. This chamber is placed near the entrance of the sacred precinct; for they say that he did not draw it within the precinct for the following reason: the architect, as the chamber was being drawn along, heaved a deep sigh, being wearied with the work, over which so long a time had been

spent; whereupon Amasis, making a religious scruple of this, would not suffer it to be drawn any farther. Some persons, however, say that one of the men employed at the levers was crushed to death by it, and that on that account it was not drawn into the precinct. 176. Amasis dedicated in all the most famous temples works admirable for their magnitude; and among them at Memphis, the reclining colossus before the temple of Vulcan, of which the length is seventy-five feet; and on the same base stand two statues of Ethiopian stone, each twenty feet in height, one on each side of the temple. There is also at Sais another similar statue, lying in the same manner as that at Memphis. It was Amasis also who built the temple to Isis at Memphis, which is spacious and well worthy of notice.

177. Under the reign of Amasis Egypt is said to have enjoyed the greatest prosperity, both in respect to the benefits derived from the river to the land, and from the land to the people; and it is said to have contained at that time twenty thousand inhabited cities. Amasis it was who established the law among the Egyptians that every Egyptian should annually declare to the governor of his district by what means he maintained himself; and if he failed to do this, or did not show that he lived by honest means, he should be punished with death. Solon the Athenian, having brought this law from Egypt, established it at Athens; and that people still continue to observe it, as being an unobjectionable regulation. 178. Amasis, being partial to the Greeks, both bestowed other favors on various of the Greeks, and, moreover, gave the city of Naucratis for such as arrived in Egypt to dwell in; and to such as did not wish to settle there, but only to trade by sea, he granted places where they might erect altars and temples to the gods. Now the most spacious of these sacred buildings, which is also the most renowned and frequented, called the Hellenium, was erected at the common charge of the following cities: of the Ionians, Chios, Teos, Phocæa, and Clazomenæ; of the Dorians, Rhodes, Cnidus, Halicarnassus, Phaselis; and of the Æolians, Mitylené alone; so that this temple belongs to them, and these cities appoint officers to preside over the mart; and whatever other cities claim a share in it, claim what does not belong to them. Besides this, the people of Ægina built a temple to Jupiter

for themselves; and the Samians another to Juno, and the Milesians one to Apollo. 179. Naucratis was anciently the only place of resort for merchants, and there was no other in Egypt; and if a man arrived at any other mouth of the Nile, he was obliged to swear "that he had come there against his will;" and, having taken such an oath, he must sail in the same ship to the Canopic mouth: but if he should be prevented by contrary winds from doing so, he was forced to unload his goods, and carry them in barges round the Delta until he reached Naucratis. So great were the privileges of Naucratis. 180. When the Amphictyons contracted to build the temple that now stands at Delphi for three hundred talents (for the temple that was formerly there had been burned by accident, and it fell upon the Delphians to supply a fourth part of the sum), the Delphians went about from city to city, and solicited contributions; and doing this, they brought home no small amount from Egypt; for Amasis gave them a thousand talents of alum, and the Grecians who were settled in Egypt twenty minæ.

181. Amasis also contracted a friendship and an alliance with the Cyrenæans, and resolved to take a wife from that country, either out of a desire of having a Grecian woman, or from some peculiar affection to the Cyrenæans. He therefore married, as some say, the daughter of Battus; others, of Arcesilaus; though others, of Critobulus, a person of distinction among the citizens: her name was Ladice. Whenever Amasis lay with her, he was unable to have connection with her, which was not the case with respect to other women; upon the continuance of this for a long time, Amasis said to this woman, who was called Ladice, "O woman, you have used charms against me, and no contrivance can prevent your perishing by the most cruel death of all women." But Ladice, finding that Amasis was not at all appeased by her denial of the fact, made a mental vow to Venus, that if Amasis should have intercourse with her that night (for this was the only remedy left), she would send a statue of the goddess to Cyrene. Immediately after the vow, Amasis had intercourse with her; and from that time forward, whenever he came to her, he was able to have connection; and after this he was exceedingly fond of her. But Ladice performed her vow to the goddess, for, having caused a statue to be made, she sent it to

Cyrene, and it was still safe in my time, facing out of the city of Cyrene. When Cambyses had conquered Egypt, and learned who this Ladice was, he sent her back unharmed to Cyrene.

182. Amasis also dedicated offerings in Greece. In the first place, a gilded statue of Minerva at Cyrene, and his own portrait painted; secondly, to Minerva in Lindus two stone statues and a linen corslet well worthy of notice; thirdly, to Juno at Samos two images of himself carved in wood, which stood in the large temple even in my time, behind the doors. Now he made this offering at Samos on account of the friendship that subsisted between himself and Polycrates, the son of Æaces; but those at Lindus, not on account of any friendship, but because it is reported that the daughters of Danaus founded the temple of Minerva at Lindus when they touched there in their flight from the sons of Egyptus: and these were the offerings that Amasis made. He was the first who conquered Cyprus, and subjected it to the payment of tribute.

BOOK III.

THALIA.

Against this Amasis, Cambyses, son of Cyrus, made war, leading with him both others, his own subjects, and of the Grecians, Ionians and Æolians. The cause of the war was this: Cambyses, having sent a herald into Egypt, demanded the daughter of Amasis; and he made this demand at the suggestion of an Egyptian physician, who out of spite served Amasis in this manner, because, *having selected* him out of all the physicians in Egypt, and torn him from his wife and children, he had sent him as a present to the Persians, when Cyrus, having sent to Amasis, required of him the best oculist in Egypt. The Egyptian, therefore, having this spite against him, urged on Cambyses by his suggestions, bidding him demand the daughter of Amasis, in order that if he should comply he might be grieved, or, if he refused, he might incur the hatred of Cambyses. But Amasis, dreading the power of the Persians, and being alarmed, knew not whether to give or to deny; for he was well aware that Cambyses purposed to take her, not as his wife, but his mistress. Having considered these things, he did as follows. There was a daughter of Apries, the former king, very tall and beautiful, the only survivor of the family; her name was Nitetis. This damsel, Amasis, having adorned with cloth of gold, sent to Persia as his own daughter. After a time, when Cambyses saluted her, addressing her by her father's name, the damsel said to him, "O king, you do not perceive that you have been imposed upon by Amasis, who, having dressed me in rich attire, sent me to you, presenting me as his own daughter; whereas, in truth, I am the daughter of Apries, whom he, though he was his own master, put to death after he had incited the Egyptians to revolt." These words and this accusation induced

Cambyses, the son of Cyrus, being greatly enraged, to invade Egypt. Such is the account the Persians give. 2. But the Egyptians claim Cambyses as their own, saying that he was born from this daughter of Apries; for that it was Cyrus, and not Cambyses, who sent to Amasis for his daughter; but in saying this they err. Nor, indeed, could it escape their notice (for if any people are well acquainted with the Persian customs, the Egyptians are so), that, first of all, it is not customary with them for a natural son to reign when there is a legitimate son living; and, secondly, that Cambyses was the son of Cassandane, daughter of Pharnaspes, one of the Achæmenidæ, and not of the Egyptian woman; but they pervert the truth, claiming to be related to the family of Cyrus; and this is the real state of the case. 3. This other story is also told, which seems to me incredible. A certain Persian lady visited Cyrus's women, and when she saw the children of Cassandane, beautiful and tall, standing by her, praised them highly, being exceedingly struck with them; but Cassandane, wife of Cyrus, said, "Though I am the mother of such children, Cyrus holds me in disdain, and honors her whom he has obtained from Egypt." This she said through envy of Nitetis; but the eldest of her sons, Cambyses, said, "Therefore, mother, when I am a man, I will turn all Egypt upside down." He said this when he was about ten years of age, and the women were much astonished; but he, bearing it in mind when he grew up and was possessed of the kingdom, accordingly invaded Egypt.

4. The following other incident also occurred to promote this invasion. There was among the auxiliaries of Amasis a man, by birth a Halicarnassian, whose name was Phanes, one able in counsel and valiant in war. This Phanes, owing some spite to Amasis, escaped in a ship from Egypt with a design to confer with Cambyses. But, as he was a man of no small consequence among the auxiliaries, and was very accurately acquainted with the affairs of Egypt, Amasis sent in pursuit of him, making every effort to take him; and he sent the most trusty of his eunuchs in pursuit of him, with a trireme, who caught him in Lycia, but, having taken him, did not bring him back to Egypt, for Phanes overreached him by artifice; for, having intoxicated his guards, he got away to the Persians, and coming over to Cambyses as he was preparing

to march against Egypt, and was in doubt about his route, how he should pass the arid desert, he informed him both of other affairs of Amasis, and explained to him the route, thus advising him: to send to the king of the Arabians, and ask him to grant him a safe passage through his territories. 5. By this way only is there an open passage into Egypt; for from Phœnicia to the confines of the city of Cadytis, which belongs to those who are called the Syrians of Palestine, and from Cadytis, which is a city, in my opinion, not much less than Sardis, the sea-ports as far as the city of Jenysus belong to the Arabian king; and again, from Jenysus as far as the lake Serbonis, near which Mount Casius stretches to the sea, belongs to the Syrians; and from the lake Serbonis, in which Typhon is reported to have been concealed, Egypt begins. Now the country between the city of Jenysus, Mount Casius, and the lake Serbonis, which is no small tract, but about a three days' journey, is utterly destitute of water. 6. A circumstance that few of those who have made voyages to Egypt have noticed I shall now proceed to mention. From every part of Greece, and also from Phœnicia, earthen vessels filled with wine are imported into Egypt twice every year, and yet, so to speak, not a single one of these wine jars is afterward to be seen. In what way, then, some one may ask, are they disposed of? This I will also relate. Every magistrate is obliged to collect all the vessels from his own city and send them to Memphis; but the people of that city, having filled them with water, convey them to those arid parts of Syria; so the earthen vessels continually imported and landed in Egypt are added to those already in Syria. 7. Thus the Persians, as soon as they became masters of Egypt, facilitated the passage into that country by supplying it with water in the manner above mentioned. But as at that time water was not provided, Cambyses, by the advice of the Halicarnassian stranger, sent embassadors to the Arabian, and requested a safe passage, which he obtained, giving to and receiving from him pledges of faith.

8. The Arabians observe pledges as religiously as any people, and they make them in the following manner: when any wish to pledge their faith, a third person, standing between the two parties, makes an incision with a sharp stone in the palm of the hand, near the longest fingers, of both the

contractors; then taking some of the nap from the garment of each, he smears seven stones, placed between them, with the blood; and as he does this, he invokes Bacchus and Urania. When this ceremony is completed, the person who pledges his faith binds his friends as sureties to the stranger, or the citizen, if the contract be made with a citizen, and the friends also hold themselves obliged to observe the engagement. They acknowledge no other gods than Bacchus and Urania, and they say that their hair is cut in the same way as Bacchus's is cut; but they cut it in a circular form, shearing it round the temples. They call Bacchus, Orotal; and Urania, Alilat. 9. When, therefore, the Arabian had exchanged pledges with the embassadors who came from Cambyses, he adopted the following contrivance: having filled camels' skins with water, he loaded them on all his living camels; and having done this, he drove them to the arid region, and there awaited the army of Cambyses. This is the most credible of the accounts that are given; yet it is right that one less credible should be mentioned, since it is likewise affirmed. There is a large river in Arabia called Corys, which discharges itself into that called the Red Sea. From this river, then, it is said that the king of the Arabians, having sewn together a pipe of ox hides and other skins, reaching in length to the arid region, conveyed the water through it; and that in the arid region he dug large reservoirs, to receive and preserve the water. It is a twelve days' journey from the river to the arid region; he therefore conveyed water through three several pipes into three different places.

10. Psammenitus, the son of Amasis, lay encamped at that called the Pelusiac mouth of the Nile, awaiting Cambyses; for Cambyses did not find Amasis alive when he marched against Egypt; but Amasis died after a reign of forty-four years, during which no great calamity had befallen him. But having died, and being embalmed, he was buried in the sepulchre that is in the sacred precinct, which he himself had built.[1] During the reign of Psammenitus, son of Amasis, a most remarkable prodigy befell the Egyptians; for rain fell at Egyptian Thebes, which had never happened before, nor since, to my time, as the Thebans themselves affirm; for no

[1] See Book II. chap. 169.

rain ever falls in the upper regions of Egypt; but at that time rain fell in drops at Thebes. 11. The Persians, having marched through the arid region, halted near the Egyptians, as if with a design of engaging; there the auxiliaries of the Egyptians, consisting of Greeks and Carians, condemning Phanes because he had led a foreign army against Egypt, adopted the following expedient against him: Phanes had left his sons in Egypt; these they brought to the camp, within sight of their father, and placed a bowl midway between the two armies; then, dragging the children one by one, they slew them over the bowl. When they slaughtered all the children, they poured wine and water into the bowl; and, after all the auxiliaries had drank of the blood, they immediately joined battle. A hard battle having been fought, and when great numbers had fallen on both sides, the Egyptians were put to flight. 12. Here I saw a very surprising fact, which the people of the country informed me of; for as the bones of those who were killed in that battle lie scattered about separately (for the bones of the Persians lay apart in one place, as they did at first, and those of the Egyptians in another), the skulls of the Persians were so weak, that if you should hit them only with a single pebble, you would break a hole in them; whereas those of the Egyptians are so hard, that you could scarcely fracture them by striking them with a stone. The cause of this, they told me, is as follows, and I readily assented; that the Egyptians begin from childhood and shave their heads, and the bone is thickened by exposure to the sun; from the same cause, also, they are less subject to baldness, for one sees fewer persons bald in Egypt than in any other country. This, then, is the cause of their having such strong skulls; and the reason why the Persians have weak skulls is this: they shade them from the first, wearing tiaras for hats. Now I myself saw that such was the case; and I also observed the same thing at Papremis, with respect to those who were slain with Achæmenes,[2] son of Darius, by Inarus the Libyan.

13. The Egyptians, when they were defeated, fled in complete disorder from the battle. When they had shut themselves up in Memphis, Cambyses sent a Mitylenæan bark up the river, with a Persian herald on board, to invite the Egyptians to terms. But they, when they saw the bark

[2] See book VII. chap. 7.

entering Memphis, rushed in a mass from the wall, destroyed the ship, and having torn the crew to pieces, limb by limb, they carried them into the citadel. After this the Egyptians were besieged, and at length surrendered. The neighboring Libyans, fearing what had befallen Egypt, gave themselves up without resistance, and submitted to pay a tribute, and sent presents. In like manner, the Cyrenæans and Barcæans, being equally alarmed with the Libyans, did as they had done. But Cambyses received very graciously the presents that came from the Libyans, but was displeased with those of the Cyrenæans, as I suppose, because they were inconsiderable; for the Cyrenæans sent only five hundred minæ of silver, which he grasped and dispersed with his own hand among the soldiers. 14. On the tenth day after Cambyses had taken the citadel of Memphis, having seated Psammenitus, the king of the Egyptians, who had reigned only six months, at the entrance of the city, by way of insult —having seated him with other Egyptians, he made trial of his courage by the following means. Having dressed his daughter in the habit of a slave, he sent her with a pitcher to fetch water; and he sent with her other virgins selected from the principal families, dressed in the same manner as the king's daughter. As the virgins, with loud lamentation and weeping, came into the presence of their fathers, all the other fathers answered them with wailing and weeping, when they beheld their children thus humiliated. But Psammenitus alone, when he saw and knew what was going on, only bent his eyes to the ground. When these water-carriers had passed by, he next sent his son, with two thousand Egyptians of the same age, with halters about their necks, and a bridle in their mouths; and they were led out to suffer retribution for those Mitylenæans who had perished at Memphis with the ship; for the royal judges had given sentence, that for each man, ten of the principal Egyptians should be put to death. Yet he, when he saw them passing by, and knew that his son was being led out to death, though all the rest of the Egyptians who sat round him wept and made loud lamentations, did the same as he had done in his daughter's case. When these had passed by, it happened that one of his boon companions, a man somewhat advanced in years, who had lost his all, and possessed nothing but such things as a beggar has, asking alms of the soldiery, passed by Psammenitus, the son of Amasis, and the

Egyptians seated in the suburbs; but Psammenitus, when he saw him, weeping bitterly, and calling his companion by name, smote his head. There were, however, spies there who communicated to Cambyses every thing that was done by him at each procession; but Cambyses, surprised at this behavior, sent a messenger and inquired of him as follows: "Psammenitus, your master Cambyses inquires why, when you saw your daughter humiliated and your son led to execution, you did not bewail or lament; and have been so highly concerned for a beggar, who is no way related to you, as he is informed." He then asked this question, but Psammenitus answered as follows: "Son of Cyrus, the calamities of my family are too great to be expressed by lamentation; but the griefs of my friend were worthy of tears, who, having fallen from abundance and prosperity, has come to beggary on the threshold of old age." When this answer was brought back by the messenger, it appeared to Cambyses to be well said; and, as the Egyptians relate, Crœsus wept, for he had attended Cambyses into Egypt, and the Persians that were present wept also; and Cambyses himself was touched with pity, and gave immediate orders to preserve his son out of those who were to perish, and to remove him, and bring him from the suburbs into his presence.

15. Those who were sent found the son no longer alive, having been the first that suffered; but having removed Psammenitus himself, they conducted him to Cambyses, with whom he afterward lived without experiencing any violence; and had it not been suspected[3] that he was planning innovations, he would probably have recovered Egypt, so as to have the government intrusted to him; for the Persians are accustomed to honor the sons of kings, and even if they have revolted from them, nevertheless bestow the government upon their children: that such is their custom may be proved from many other examples, and among them by that of Thannyras, the son of Inarus the Libyan, who recovered the government which his father had; and by that of Pausiris, son of Amyrtæus, for he also recovered his father's government; yet none ever did more mischief to the Persians than Inarus and Amyrtæus. But now Psammenitus, devising mischief, received his reward, for he was discovered inciting the Egyptians to revolt; and when he was detected by Cambyses, he

[3] See Cary's Lexicon, v. Ἀπιστέειν.

was compelled to drink the blood of a bull, and died immediately. Such, then, was his end.

16. Cambyses proceeded from Memphis to the city of Sais, purposing to do what he did effect; for when he entered the palace of Amasis, he presently commanded the dead body of Amasis to be brought out of the sepulchre; and when this was done, he gave orders to scourge it, to pull off the hair, to prick it, and to abuse it in every possible manner. But when they were wearied with this employment (for the dead body, since it was embalmed, resisted, and did not at all fall in pieces), Cambyses gave orders to burn it, commanding what is impious; for the Persians consider fire to be a god; therefore to burn the dead is on no account allowed by either nation; not by the Persians, for the reason above mentioned, for they say it is not right to offer to a god the dead body of a man; and by the Egyptians fire is held to be a living beast, and that it devours every thing it can lay hold of, and when it is glutted with food it expires with what it has consumed; therefore it is their law on no account to give a dead body to wild beasts, and for that reason they embalm them, that they may not lie and be eaten by worms. Cambyses, therefore, commanded a thing repugnant to the customs of both nations. However, as the Egyptians say, it was not Amasis that was thus treated, but some other Egyptian of the same stature as Amasis whom the Persians insulted, thinking they insulted Amasis; for they say that Amasis, having been informed by an oracle of what should happen to him after death, in order to remedy the impending evil, buried the body of this very man who was scourged near the door of his own sepulchre,[4] and charged his son to deposit his own in the remotest part of the vault. Now these commands of Amasis touching his own burial and this man appear to me never to have been given, but the Egyptians falsely boast of them.

17. After this, Cambyses planned three several expeditions; one against the Carthaginians, another against the Ammonians, and a third against the Macrobian Ethiopians, who inhabit that part of Libya which lies upon the South Sea. And in forming his plans, he determined to send a naval force against the Carthaginians, and against the Ammonians a detachment of his land forces; and against the Ethiopians, spies in the

[4] See Book II. chap. 169.

first instance, who were to see the table of the sun, which was said to exist among the Ethiopians, and, besides, to explore other things, and to cover their design they were to carry presents to the king. 18. The table of the sun is said to be of the following description: there is a meadow in the suburbs filled with the cooked flesh of all sorts of quadrupeds; in this the several magistrates of the city, for some purpose, place the flesh at night, and in the day-time whoever chooses comes and feasts on it. The inhabitants say that the earth itself, from time to time, produces these things. Such is the description given of what is called the table of the sun. 19. When Cambyses had determined to send the spies, he immediately sent to Elephantine for some of the Ichthyophagi, who understood the Ethiopian language; and while they were fetching these, he commanded the naval force to sail against Carthage. But the Phœnicians refused to obey, for that they were bound by solemn oaths, and that they should act impiously if they made war against their own descendants. As the Phœnicians would not go, the rest were not fit for such an enterprise. Thus, therefore, the Carthaginians escaped slavery at the hands of the Persians; for Cambyses did not think it right to employ force toward the Phœnicians, because they had voluntarily submitted to the Persians, and the whole naval force depended on them. The Cyprians, too, having given themselves up to the Persians, joined the expedition against Egypt. 20. When the Ichthyophagi came to Cambyses from Elephantine, he dispatched them to the Ethiopians, having instructed them what to say, carrying presents, consisting of a purple cloak, a golden necklace, bracelets, an alabaster box of ointment, and a cask of palm wine. These Ethiopians, to whom Cambyses sent, are said to be the tallest and handsomest of all men; and they say that they have customs different from those of other nations, and especially the following, with regard to the regal power; for they confer the sovereignty upon the man whom they consider to be of the largest stature, and to possess strength proportionable to his size.

21. When, therefore, the Ichthyophagi arrived among this people, they gave the presents to the king, and addressed him as follows: "Cambyses, king of the Persians, desirous of becoming your friend and ally, has sent us, bidding us

confer with you, and he presents you with these gifts, which are such as he himself most delights in." But the Ethiopian, knowing that they came as spies, spoke thus to them: "Neither has the king of Persia sent you with these presents to me, because he valued my alliance; nor do you speak the truth; for you are come as spies of my kingdom. Nor is he a just man; for if he were just, he would not desire any other territory than his own; nor would he reduce people into servitude who have done him no injury. However, give him this bow, and say these words to him: 'The king of the Ethiopians advises the king of the Persians, when the Persians can thus easily draw a bow of this size, then to make war on the Macrobian Ethiopians with more numerous forces; but until that time, let him thank the gods, who have not inspired the sons of the Ethiopians with a desire of adding another land to their own.'" 22. Having spoken thus and unstrung the bow, he delivered it to the comers. Then taking up the purple cloak, he asked what it was, and how made; and when the Ichthyophagi told him the truth respecting the purple, and the manner of dyeing, he said that the men are deceptive, and their garments are deceptive also. Next he inquired about the necklace and bracelets, and when the Ichthyophagi explained to him their use as ornaments, the king laughing, and supposing them to be fetters, said that they have stronger fetters than these. Thirdly, he inquired about the ointment; and when they told him about its composition and use, he made the same remark as he had on the cloak. But when he came to the wine, and inquired how it was made, being very much delighted with the draught, he farther asked what food the king made use of, and what was the longest age to which a Persian lived. They answered that he fed on bread, describing the nature of wheat; and that the longest period of the life of a Persian was eighty years. Upon this the Ethiopian said that he was not at all surprised if men who fed on dung lived so few years; and they would not be able to live so many years if they did not refresh themselves with this beverage, showing the wine to the Ichthyophagi; for in this *he admitted* they were surpassed by the Persians. 23. The Ichthyophagi inquiring in turn of the king concerning the life and diet of the Ethiopians, *he said* that most of them attained to a hundred and twenty years, and some even exceeded that term, and that their food was boiled flesh, and their drink milk. And when the spies expressed their astonishment at the number of years, he led them to a fountain, by washing in which they became more sleek, as if it had been of oil, and an odor proceeded from it as of violets. The water of this fountain, the spies said, is so weak, that nothing is able to float upon it, neither wood, nor such things as are lighter than wood; but every thing sinks to the bottom. If this water is truly such as it is said to be, it may be they are long-lived by reason of the abundant use of it. Leaving this fountain, he conducted them to the common prison, where all were fettered with golden chains; for among these Ethiopians brass is the most rare and precious of all metals. After having viewed the prison, they next visited that which is called the table of the sun. 24. After this, they visited last of all their sepulchres, which are said to be prepared from crystal in the following manner. When they have dried the body, either as the Egyptians do, or in some other way, they plaster it all over with gypsum, and paint it, making it as much as possible resemble real life; they then put round it a hollow column made of crystal, which they dig up in abundance, and is easily wrought. The body being in the middle of the column is plainly seen, nor does it emit an unpleasant smell, nor is it in any way offensive; and it is all visible[5] as the body itself. The nearest relations keep the column in their houses for a year, offering to it the first-fruits of all, and performing sacrifices; after that time they carry it out and place it some where near the city.

25. The spies, having seen every thing, returned home; and when they had reported all that had passed, Cambyses, being greatly enraged, immediately marched against the Ethiopians, without making any provision for the subsistence *of his army*, or once considering that he was going to carry his arms to the remotest part of the world; but as a madman, and not in possession of his senses, as soon as he heard the report of the Ichthyophagi, he set out on his march, ordering the Greeks who were present to stay behind, and taking with him all his land forces. When the army reached Thebes, he

[5] The Egyptian mummies could only be seen in front, the back being covered by a box or coffin; the Ethiopian bodies could be seen all round, as the column of glass was transparent.

detached about fifty thousand men, and ordered them to reduce the Ammonians to slavery, and to burn the oracular temple of Jupiter, while he, with the rest of his army, marched against the Ethiopians; but before the army had passed over a fifth part of the way, all the provisions[6] that they had were exhausted, and after the provisions, the beasts of burden were eaten, and likewise failed. Now if Cambyses, when he learned this, had altered his purpose, and had led back his army, even after his first error, he would have proved himself to be a wise man; but now, without any reflection, he still continued advancing. The soldiers, as long as they could gather any from the earth, supported life by eating herbs; but when they reached the sands, some of them had recourse to a horrid expedient, for, taking one man in ten by lot, they devoured him. When Cambyses heard this, shocked at their eating one another, he abandoned his expedition against the Ethiopians, marched back, and reached Thebes, after losing a great part from his army. From Thebes he went down to Memphis, and suffered the Greeks to sail away. Thus ended the expedition against the Ethiopians. 26. Those who had been sent on the expedition against the Ammonians, after having set out from Thebes, marched under the conduct of guides, and are known to have reached the city Oasis, which is inhabited by Samians, said to be of the Æschrionian tribe; and they are distant seven days' march from Thebes, across the sands. This country, in the Greek language, is called the Island of the Blessed. It is said, then, that the army reached this country; but afterward none, except the Ammonians and those who have heard their report, are able to give any account of them; for they neither reached the Ammonians nor returned back. But the Ammonians make the following report: when they had advanced from this Oasis toward them across the sands, and were about half way between them and Oasis, as they were taking dinner, a strong and vehement south wind blew, and carrying with it heaps of sand, covered them over, and in this manner they disappeared. The Ammonians say that such was the fate of this army.

27. When Cambyses arrived at Memphis, Apis, whom the

[6] The Greek is *σιτιων ἐχόμενα*. This expression is very common in Herodotus. So Book I. 120, *τὰ τῶν ὀνειράτων ἐχόμενα*, *dreams*. So also V. 44, and VIII. 142.

Greeks call Epaphus, appeared to the Egyptians; and when this manifestation took place, the Egyptians immediately put on their richest apparel, and kept festive holiday. Cambyses, seeing them thus occupied, and concluding that they made these rejoicings on account of his ill success, summoned the magistrates of Memphis; and when they came into his presence, he asked "why the Egyptians had done nothing of the kind when he was at Memphis before, but did so now, when he had returned with the loss of a great part of his army." They answered that their god appeared to them, who was accustomed to manifest himself at distant intervals, and that when he did appear, then all the Egyptians were used to rejoice, and keep a feast. Cambyses, having heard this, said they lied, and as liars he put them to death. 28. Having slain them, he next summoned the priests into his presence; and when the priests gave the same account, he said that he would find out whether a god so tractable had come among the Egyptians; and having said this, he commanded the priests to bring Apis to him; they therefore went away to fetch him. This Apis, or Epaphus, is the calf of a cow incapable of conceiving another offspring; and the Egyptians say that lightning descends upon the cow from heaven, and that from thence it brings forth Apis. This calf, which is called Apis, has the following marks: it is black, and has a square spot of white on the forehead; and on the back the figure of an eagle; and in the tail double hairs; and on the tongue a beetle. 29. When the priests brought Apis, Cambyses, like one almost out of his senses, drew his dagger, meaning to strike the belly of Apis, but hit the thigh; then falling into a fit of laughter, he said to the priests, "Ye blockheads, are there such gods as these, consisting of blood and flesh, and sensible of steel? This, truly, is a god worthy of the Egyptians. But you shall not mock me with impunity." Having spoken thus, he commanded those, whose business it was, to scourge the priests, and to kill all the Egyptians whom they should find feasting. Thus the festival of the Egyptians was put an end to, and the priests were punished; but Apis, being wounded in the thigh, lay and languished in the temple; and at length, when he had died of the wound, the priests buried him without the knowledge of Cambyses.

30. But Cambyses, as the Egyptians say, immediately became

mad in consequence of this atrocity, though indeed he was not of sound mind before. His first crime he committed against his brother Smerdis, who was born of the same father and mother; him he sent back from Egypt to Persia through envy, because he alone of all the Persians had drawn the bow which the Ichthyophagi brought from the Ethiopian within two fingers' breadth: of the other Persians no one was able to do this. After the departure of Smerdis for Persia, Cambyses saw the following vision in his sleep: he imagined that a messenger arrived from Persia, and informed him that Smerdis was seated on the royal throne, and touched the heavens with his head. Upon this, fearing for himself lest his brother should kill him, and reign, he sent Prexaspes, who was a man the most faithful to him of the Persians, to Persia, with orders to kill Smerdis; and he, having gone up to Susa, killed Smerdis; some say when he had taken him out to hunt, but others, that he led him to the Red Sea and drowned him. 31. This, they say, was the first of the crimes of Cambyses: the second he committed against his sister, who had accompanied him into Egypt, and whom he married, and who was his sister by both parents. He married her in the following way; for before, the Persians were on no account accustomed to intermarry with their sisters. Cambyses became enamored of one of his sisters, and then, being desirous of making her his wife, because he purposed doing what was not customary, he summoned the royal judges, and asked them if there was any law permitting one who wished to marry his sister. The royal judges are men chosen from among Persians, *who continue in office* until they die or are convicted of some injustice. They determine causes between the Persians, and are the interpreters of the ancient constitutions, and all questions are referred to them. When, therefore, Cambyses put the question, they gave an answer that was both just and safe, saying that they could find no law permitting a brother to marry his sister, but had discovered another law which permitted the king of Persia to do whatever he pleased. Thus they did not abrogate the law through fear of Cambyses; but, that they might not lose their lives by upholding the law, they found out another that favored his desire of marrying his sister; thereupon Cambyses married her of whom he was enamored, and shortly afterward he had another sister. The youngest of these, then, who followed him into Egypt, he put to death. 32. With respect to her death, as well as that of Smerdis, a twofold account is given. The Greeks say that Cambyses made the whelp of a lion fight with a young dog, and that this wife was also looking on; and that the dog being over-matched, another puppy of the same litter broke his chain and came to his assistance, and thus the two dogs united got the better of the whelp. Cambyses was delighted at the sight, but she, sitting by him, shed tears. Cambyses, observing this, asked her why she wept. She answered that she wept seeing the puppy come to the assistance of its brother, remembering Smerdis, and knowing that there was no one to avenge him. The Greeks say that for this speech she was put to death by Cambyses; but the Egyptians say that, as they were sitting at table, his wife took a lettuce, and stripped off its leaves, and then asked her husband "whether the lettuce stripped of its leaves, or thick with foliage, was the handsomer." He said, "When thick with foliage." Whereupon she remarked, "Then you have imitated this lettuce in dismembering the house of Cyrus." Whereupon he, being enraged, kicked her when she was with child, and she miscarried and died.

33. Thus madly did Cambyses behave toward his own family, whether on account of Apis, or from some other cause, from which, in many ways, misfortunes are wont to befall mankind; for Cambyses is said, even from infancy, to have been afflicted with a certain severe malady, which some called the sacred disease.[7] In that case, it was not at all surprising that, when his body was so diseased, his mind should not be sound. 34. And toward the other Persians he behaved madly in the following instances: for it is reported that he said to Prexaspes, whom he highly honored, and whose office it was to bring messages to him, and whose son was cup-bearer to Cambyses, and this is no trifling honor: he is reported to have spoken as follows: "Prexaspes, what sort of a man do the Persians think me, and what remarks do they make about me?" He answered, "Sir, you are highly extolled in every other respect, but they say you are too much addicted to wine." Prexaspes said this of the Persians; but the king, enraged, answered as follows: "Do the Persians

[7] Epilepsy.

indeed say that, by being addicted to wine, I am beside myself, and am not in my senses? then their former words were not true." For, on a former occasion, when the Persians and Crœsus were sitting with him, Cambyses asked what sort of a man he appeared to be in comparison with his father Cyrus; they answered that he was superior to his father, for that he held all that Cyrus possessed, and had acquired besides Egypt and the empire of the sea. Crœsus, being present, not being pleased with this decision, spoke thus to Cambyses: "To me now, O son of Cyrus, you do not appear comparable to your father, for you have not yet such a son as he left behind him." Cambyses was delighted at hearing this, and commended the judgment of Crœsus. 35. Therefore, remembering this, he said in anger to Prexaspes, "Observe now yourself whether the Persians have spoken the truth, or whether they who say such things are not out of their senses; for if I shoot that son of yours who stands under the portico, and hit him in the heart, the Persians will appear to have said nothing to the purpose; but if I miss, then say that the Persians have spoken truth, and that I am not of sound mind." Having said this and bent his bow, he hit the boy; and when the boy had fallen, he ordered them to open him and examine the wound; and when the arrow was found in the heart, he said to the boy's father, laughing, "Prexaspes, it has been clearly shown to you that I am not mad, but that the Persians are out of their senses. Now tell me, did you ever see a man take so true an aim?" But Prexaspes, perceiving him to be out of his mind, and being in fear for his own life, said, "Sir, I believe that a god himself could not have shot so well." At that time he committed such an atrocity; and at another time, having, without any just cause, seized twelve Persians of the first rank, he had them buried alive up to the head.

36. While he was acting in this manner, Crœsus the Lydian thought fit to admonish him in the following terms: "O king, do not yield entirely to your youthful impulses and anger, but possess and restrain yourself. It is a good thing to be provident, and wise to have forethought. You put men to death who are your own subjects, having seized them without any just cause; and you slay their children. If you persist in such a course, beware lest the Persians revolt from

you. Your father Cyrus strictly charged me to admonish you, and suggest whatever I might discover for your good." He then manifested his good-will in giving this advice; but Cambyses answered, "Do you presume to give me advice, you, who so wisely managed your own country; and so well advised my father, when you persuaded him to pass the river Araxes, and advance against the Massagetæ, when they were willing to cross over into our territory? You have first ruined yourself by badly governing your own country, and then ruined Cyrus, who was persuaded by your advice. But you shall have no reason to rejoice; for I have long wanted to find a pretext against you." So saying, he took up his bow for the purpose of shooting him; but Crœsus jumped up and ran out. Cambyses, when he was unable to shoot him, commanded his attendants to seize him, and put him to death. But the attendants, knowing his temper, concealed Crœsus for the following reason, that if Cambyses should repent, and inquire for Crœsus, they, by producing him, might receive rewards for preserving him alive; or if he should not repent, or regret him, then they would put him to death. Not long afterward Cambyses did regret Crœsus, and the attendants, knowing this, acquainted him that he was still living; on which Cambyses said, "I am rejoiced that Crœsus is still alive; they, however, who saved him, shall not escape with impunity, but I will have them put to death." And he made good his word.

37. He, then, committed many such mad actions, both against the Persians and his allies, while he staid at Memphis, both opening ancient sepulchres, and examining the dead bodies; he also entered the temple of Vulcan, and derided the image, for the image of Vulcan is very like the Phœnician Pataici, which the Phœnicians place at the prows of their triremes. For the benefit of any one who has not seen them, I will describe them; it is a representation of a pigmy. He likewise entered the temple of the Cabeiri (into which it is unlawful for any one except the priest to enter), and these images he burned, after he had ridiculed them in various ways: these also are like that of Vulcan; and they say that they are the sons of this latter. 38. It is then in every way clear to me that Cambyses was outrageously mad, otherwise he would not have attempted to deride things sacred and established

customs; for if any one should propose to all men to select the best institutions of all that exist, each, after considering them all, would choose their own; so certain is it that each thinks his own institutions by far the best. It is not, therefore, probable that any but a madman would make such things the subject of ridicule. That all men are of this mind respecting their own institutions may be inferred from many and various proofs, and among them by the following. Darius having summoned some Greeks under his sway, who were present, asked them "for what sum they would feed upon the dead bodies of their parents." They answered that they would not do it for any sum. Darius afterward having summoned some of the Indians called Callatians, who are accustomed to eat their parents, asked them, in the presence of the Greeks, and who were informed of what was said by an interpreter, "for what sum they would consent to burn their fathers when they die;" but they, making loud exclamations, begged he would speak words of good omen. Such, then, is the effect of custom; and Pindar appears to me to have said rightly, "That custom is the king of all men."

39. While Cambyses was invading Egypt, the Lacedæmonians made an expedition against Samos and Polycrates, the son of Æaces, who had made an insurrection and seized on Samos. At first, having divided the state into three parts, he shared it with his brothers Pantagnotus and Syloson; but afterward, having put one of them to death, and expelled Syloson, the younger, he held the whole of Samos; and holding it, made a treaty of friendship with Amasis, king of Egypt, sending presents, and receiving others from him in return. In a very short time the power of Polycrates increased, and was noised abroad throughout Ionia and the rest of Greece; for wherever he turned his arms, every thing turned out prosperously. He had a hundred fifty-oared galleys, and a thousand archers; and he plundered all without distinction; for he said that he gratified a friend more by restoring what he had seized than by taking nothing at all. He accordingly took many of the islands, and many cities on the continent; he moreover overcame in a sea-fight, and took prisoners, the Lesbians, who came to assist the Milesians with all their forces: these, being put in chains, dug the whole trench that surrounds the walls of Samos. 40. Some-

how the exceeding good fortune of Polycrates did not escape the notice of Amasis, but was the cause of uneasiness to him; and when his successes continued to increase, having written a letter in the following terms, he dispatched it to Samos: "Amasis to Polycrates says thus: It is pleasant to hear of the successes of a friend and ally. But your too great good fortune does not please me, knowing, as I do, that the divinity is jealous. As for me, I would rather choose that both I and those for whom I am solicitous should be partly successful in our undertakings, and partly suffer reverses; and so pass life, meeting with vicissitudes of fortune, than being prosperous in all things; for I can not remember that I ever heard of any man, who, having been constantly successful, did not at last utterly perish. Be advised, therefore, by me, and act thus with regard to your good fortune. Having considered what you can find that you value most, and the loss of which would most pain your soul, this so cast away that it may never more be seen of man; and if, after this, successes are not mingled interchangeably with reverses, again have recourse to the remedy I have suggested." 41. Polycrates, having read this letter, and conceived that Amasis had given him good advice, inquired of himself by the loss of which of his valuables he should most afflict his soul; and, on inquiry, he discovered the following: he had a seal which he wore, set in gold, made of an emerald, and it was the workmanship of Theodorus, the son of Telecles, a Samian; when, therefore, he had determined to cast this away, he did as follows. Having manned a fifty-oared galley, he went on board it, and then ordered to put out to sea; and when he was a considerable distance from the island, he took off the seal, and in the sight of all on board, threw it into the sea. This done, he sailed back again; and having reached his palace, he mourned it as a great misfortune. 42. But on the fifth or sixth day after this, the following circumstance occurred: a fisherman, having caught a large and beautiful fish, thought it a present worthy to be given to Polycrates; he accordingly carried it to the gates, and said that he wished to be admitted to the presence of Polycrates; and when this was granted, he presented the fish, and said, "O king, having caught this, I did not think it right to take it to market, although I get my living by hard labor; but it seemed to me worthy of you and your empire: I bring it therefore, and present it to you." He, pleased with these words, replied, "You have done well, and I give you double thanks for your speech and your present, and I invite you to supper." The fisherman, thinking a great deal of this, went away to his own home; but the servants, opening the fish, found the seal of Polycrates in its belly; and as soon as they had seen it and taken it out, they carried it with great joy to Polycrates, and as they gave him the seal, they acquainted him in what manner it had been found. But when it occurred to him that the event was superhuman, he wrote an account of what he had done and of what had happened, and having written, he dispatched the account to Egypt. 43. But Amasis, having read the letter that came from Polycrates, felt persuaded that it was impossible for man to rescue man from the fate that awaited him, and that Polycrates would not come to a good end, since he was fortunate in every thing, and even found what he had thrown away. Having, therefore, sent a herald to Samos, he said that he must renounce his friendship. He did this for the following reason, lest, if some dreadful and great calamity befell Polycrates, he might himself be grieved for him as for a friend.

44. Against this Polycrates, then, who was so universally prosperous, the Lacedæmonians made war, at the solicitation of those Samians who afterward founded Cydonia in Crete.[8] Polycrates, having sent to Cambyses, the son of Cyrus, as he was collecting an army for the invasion of Egypt, begged that he would send to him at Samos and demand some troops. When Cambyses heard this, he readily sent to Samos, requesting Polycrates to furnish a naval force to attend him in his invasion of Egypt; whereupon he, having selected those citizens whom he most suspected of seditious designs, sent them away in forty galleys, enjoining Cambyses not to send them home again. 45. Now some say that these Samians who were sent out by Polycrates never reached Egypt, but, when they were off Carpathius, they conferred together, and resolved to sail no farther. Others say that, having arrived in Egypt, and finding themselves watched, they made their escape from thence; and as they were sailing back to Samos, Polycrates met them with a fleet, and came to an

8 See chap. 59.

engagement; and they who were returning gained the victory and landed on the island, and there having fought on land, they were worsted, and so set sail for Lacedæmon. There are some who say that the party from Egypt conquered Polycrates; in my opinion, giving an erroneous account; for there would have been no need of their calling in the Lacedæmonians if they were themselves able to get the better of Polycrates. Besides, it is not at all probable that one who had a numerous body of foreign mercenaries and of native archers should be beaten by the Samians who returned, who were few in number. Moreover, Polycrates, having shut up together in the arsenal the children and wives of the citizens who were subject to him, had them ready to burn, together with the arsenals themselves, in case they should go over to those who were returning. 46. When the Samians expelled by Polycrates arrived at Sparta, having presented themselves before the magistrates, they made a long harangue, as people very much in earnest; but they, at this first audience, answered them that they had forgotten the first part of their speech, and did not understand the last. After this, having presented themselves a second time, they brought a sack, and said nothing else than "the sack wants meal;" but the Lacedæmonians replied that the word "*sack*" was superfluous: it was, however, decreed that they should assist them. 47. Then the Lacedæmonians, having made preparations, set out with an army against Samos; as the Samians say, requiting a former kindness, because they had formerly assisted them with some ships against the Messenians; but as the Lacedæmonians say, they undertook this expedition, not so much for the purpose of assisting the Samians who entreated them, as from a desire to revenge the seizure of the bowl[9] which they sent to Crœsus, and the corslet which Amasis, king of Egypt, had sent to them as a present; for the Samians had robbed them of the corslet the year before they took the bowl. *This corslet* was made of linen, with many figures of animals inwrought, and adorned with gold and cotton-wool; and on this account each thread of the corslet makes it worthy of admiration; for though it is fine, it contains three hundred and sixty threads, all distinct. Such another is that which Amasis dedicated to Minerva at Lindus.[1]

[9] See Book I. ch. 70.

[1] See Book II. ch. 182.

48. The Corinthians readily assisted in abetting the expedition against Samos, because an injury had been also done to them by the Samians in the age preceding this expedition, done about the same time as the seizure of the bowl; for Periander, son of Cypselus, had sent three hundred youths, of the noblest families of the Corcyræans, to Alyattes at Sardis, for the purpose of emasculation; but when the Corinthians who were conducting the youths touched at Samos, the Samians, having ascertained for what purpose they were being conducted to Sardis, first of all instructed the youths to touch the temple of Diana, and afterward would not suffer the Corinthians to remove the suppliants from the sanctuary; and when the Corinthians denied the youths any sustenance, the Samians instituted a festival, which they still observe in the same way; for when night came on, as long as the youths continued suppliants, they instituted choruses of virgins and young men, and made a law that they should carry cakes of sesame and honey, in order that the Corcyræan youths might seize them and have food. This was continued until the Corinthians, who had charge of the youths, went away and left them; then the Samians sent home the youths to Corcyra. 49. Now if, after the death of Periander, the Corinthians had been on friendly terms with the Corcyræans, they would not have assisted in the expedition against Samos for the above-mentioned cause; but, in fact, from the first colonization of the island, they have always been at variance with one another; for this reason, therefore, the Corinthians remembered their grudge against the Samians. But Periander had selected the sons of the Corcyræan nobles, and sent them to Sardis to be emasculated, in revenge of an insult offered him; for the Corcyræans had first committed an outrageous deed against him. 50. When Periander had killed his own wife Melissa, it happened that another calamity succeeded the former. He had two sons by Melissa, one seventeen, the other eighteen years of age. These their maternal grandfather, Procles, who was tyrant of Epidaurus, sent for, and treated affectionately, as was natural, they being the sons of his own daughter; but when he sent them home, as he escorted them on their way, he said, "Do you know, my sons, who killed your mother?" The elder of them took no notice of these words; but the younger, whose name was Lycophron, when he heard it, was so grieved at hearing

this, that on his return to Corinth, he neither addressed his father, regarding him as the murderer of his mother, nor entered into conversation with him, nor answered a word to his questions. At last Periander, being exceedingly angry, drove him from the palace. 51. Having driven him out, he inquired of the elder one what their grandfather had said to them. He related to him how kindly he had received them, but he did not mention the words Procles said as he was escorting them, for he had paid no attention to them; but Periander affirmed that it was impossible but that he had suggested something to them; and he persevered in his inquiries, till the young man recovered his memory, and mentioned this also. Periander, reflecting on this, and resolving not to show any indulgence, sent a messenger to the persons by whom the son who was driven out was entertained, and forbade them to receive him in their houses; but he, when being driven out from one house he came to another, was driven from this also, since Periander threatened all that received him, and required them to expel him. Being thus driven about, he went to some other of his friends; and they, though in dread, yet received him as the son of Periander. 52. At last Periander made a proclamation, that whoever should either receive him in his house, or converse with him, should pay a sacred fine to Apollo, mentioning the amount. In consequence of this proclamation, therefore, no one would either converse with him, or receive him into their houses; besides, he himself did not think it right to attempt what was forbidden, but persisting in his purpose, strayed among the porticoes. On the fourth day, Periander, seeing him reduced to a state of filth and starvation, felt compassion, and relaxing his anger, approached him, and said, "My son, which of these is preferable, your present mode of life, or, by accommodating yourself to your father's wishes, to succeed to the power and riches which I now possess? You, who are my son, and a prince of wealthy Corinth, have chosen a vagabond life, by opposing and showing anger toward him, whom, least of all, you ought so to treat; for if any calamity has occurred in our family on account of which you have conceived any suspicion of me, it has fallen upon me, and I bear the chief burden of it, inasmuch as I murdered her. Do you, therefore, having learned how much better it is to be envied than pitied, and at the same time what it is to be angry with parents and superiors, return to your home." With these words Periander endeavored to restrain him. He, however, gave his father no other answer, but said that he had made himself liable to pay the sacred fine to the god by having spoken to him. Periander therefore perceiving that the distemper of his son was impracticable and invincible, put him on board a ship, and sent him out of his sight to Corcyra, for he was also master of that island. Periander, having sent him away, made war on his father-in-law, Procles, as being the principal author of the present troubles; and he took Epidaurus, and took Procles himself and kept him prisoner. 53. But when, in lapse of time, Periander grew old, and became conscious that he was no longer able to superintend and manage public affairs, having sent to Corcyra, he recalled Lycophron to assume the government, for he did not perceive in his eldest son *any capacity for government*,[2] but he appeared to him dull of intellect. But Lycophron did not deign to give an answer to the bearer of the message. Nevertheless, Periander, having a strong affection for the youth, next sent to him his sister, who was his own daughter, thinking she would be most likely to persuade him. On her arrival she thus addressed him: "Brother, would you that the government should pass to others, and that your father's family should be utterly destroyed, rather than yourself return and possess it? Come home, then, and cease to punish yourself. Obstinacy is a sorry possession: think not to cure one evil by another. Many have preferred equity to strict justice; and many, ere this, in seeking their mother's rights, have lost their father's inheritance. A kingdom is an uncertain possession, and many are suitors for it. He is now old, and past the vigor of life. Do not give your own to others." Thus she, having been instructed by her father, said what was most likely to persuade him; but he, in answer, said that he would never return to Corinth so long as he should hear his father was living. When she brought back this answer, Periander sent a third time by a herald *to say* that he himself intended to go to Corcyra, and urged him to return to Corinth and become his successor in the kingdom. The son consenting to this proposal, Periander prepared to set out for Corcyra, and his son for Cor-

[2] After ἐνεώρα, τὸ εἶναι δυνατὸν τὰ πράγματα διέπειν must be supplied to complete the sentence.

inth; but the Corcyræans being informed of each particular, in order that Periander might not come to their country, killed the young man; and in return for this, Periander took vengeance on the Corcyræans.

54. The Lacedæmonians, arriving with a great armament, besieged Samos, and having attacked the fortifications, they had passed beyond the tower that faced the sea near the suburbs; but afterward, when Polycrates himself advanced with a large force, they were driven back. Immediately after, the auxiliaries and many of the Samians poured down from the upper tower, which stands on the ridge of the mountain; and having withstood the Lacedæmonians for a short time, they fled back again, and the enemy pursued them with great slaughter. 55. Now if all the Lacedæmonians who were present on that day had behaved themselves as well as Archias and Lycopas, Samos would have been taken; for Archias and Lycopas alone, rushing on with the Samians as they fled to the wall, and being shut out from retreat, died in the city of the Samians. Another Archias, the son of Samius, son of Archias, the third in descent from this Archias, I myself met with in Pitane, for he was of that tribe. He esteemed the Samians above all other strangers, and said that the surname of Samian was given to his father because he was son to that Archias who fell so gloriously at Samos; and he said that he honored the Samians because his grandfather had been buried by them at the public charge. 56. The Lacedæmonians, after forty days had been spent in besieging Samos, finding their affairs were not at all advanced, returned to Peloponnesus; though a groundless report has gone abroad, *for* it is said that Polycrates, having coined a large quantity of the country money in lead, had it gilt and gave it to them; and that they, having received it, thereupon took their departure. This was the first expedition that the Lacedæmonian Dorians undertook against Asia.

57. Those of the Samians who had fomented the war against Polycrates, when the Lacedæmonians were about to abandon them, set sail for Siphnus, for they were in want of money. The affairs of the Siphnians were at that time in a flourishing condition, and they were the richest of all the islanders, having in the island gold and silver mines, so that from the tenth of the money accruing from thence, a treasure

is laid up at Delphi equal to the richest; and they used every year to divide the riches that accrued *from the mines.* When, therefore, they established this treasure, they consulted the oracle, whether their present prosperity should continue with them for a long time; but the Pythian answered as follows: "When the Prytaneum in Siphnus shall be white, and the market white-fronted, then there is need of a prudent man to guard against a wooden ambush and a crimson herald." The market and Prytaneum of the Siphnians were then adorned with Parian marble. 58. This response they were unable to comprehend, either then on the moment or when the Samians arrived; for, as soon as the Samians reached Siphnus, they sent one of their ships, conveying embassadors, to the city. Formerly, all ships were painted red; and this it was that the Pythian forewarned the Siphnians, bidding them beware of a wooden ambush and a crimson herald. These embassadors, then, having arrived, requested the Siphnians to lend them ten talents; but when the Siphnians refused the loan, the Samians ravaged their territory; but the Siphnians having heard of it, came out to protect their property, and having engaged, were beaten, and many of them were cut off from the city by the Samians, and they afterward exacted from them a hundred talents. 59. From the Hermionians they received an island instead of money, Thyrea, near Peloponnesus, and gave it in charge to the Trœzenians; and they themselves founded Cydonia in Crete, though they did not sail thither for that purpose, but to expel the Zacynthians from the island. They continued in this settlement, and were prosperous for five years, so much so that these are the people who erected the sacred precincts that are now in Cydonia, and the temple of Dictynna; but in the sixth year the Æginetæ, having vanquished them in a sea-fight, reduced them to slavery, together with the Cretans; and they cut off the prows of their ships, which represented the figure of a boar, and dedicated them in the temple of Minerva, in Ægina. The Æginetæ did this on account of a grudge they bore the Samians; for former Samians, when Amphicrates reigned in Samos, having made war against Ægina, did the Æginetæ much mischief, and suffered in return. This, then, was the cause.

60. I have dwelt longer on the affairs of the Samians, because they have three works the greatest that have been ac-

complished by all the Greeks. The first is of a mountain, one hundred and fifty orgyæ in height; in this is dug a tunnel, beginning from the base, with an opening at each side. The length of the excavation is seven stades, and the height and breadth eight feet each; through the whole length of it is dug another excavation twenty cubits deep, and three feet broad, through which the water conveyed by pipes reaches the city, drawn from a copious fountain. The architect of this excavation was a Megarian, Eupalinus, son of Naustrophus. This, then, is one of the three. The second is a mound in the sea round the harbor, in depth about one hundred orgyæ, and the length of the mound is more than two stades. The third work of theirs is a temple, the largest of all we have ever seen; of this, the architect was Rhœcus, son of Phileus, a native. On account of these things I have dwelt longer on the affairs of the Samians.

61. While Cambyses, son of Cyrus, tarried in Egypt, and was acting madly, two magi, who were brothers, revolted. One of these Cambyses had left steward of his palace. He accordingly revolted, having been informed of the death of Smerdis, and that it was kept secret, and that there were few of the Persians who were acquainted with it, for the generality thought him still alive. Therefore, having formed the following design, he determined to make an attempt on the throne. He had a brother who, I have said, joined him in the revolt, in person very like Smerdis, son of Cyrus, whom Cambyses, although he was his own brother, had put to death. The magus Patizithes, having persuaded this man that he would manage every thing for him, set him on the throne; and having done this, he sent heralds in various directions, and particularly to Egypt, to proclaim to the army that they must in future obey Smerdis, son of Cyrus, and not Cambyses. 62. The other heralds, therefore, made this proclamation; and he, moreover, who was appointed to Egypt, finding Cambyses and his army at Ecbatana, in Syria, standing in the midst, proclaimed what had been ordered by the magus. Cambyses having heard this from the herald, and believing that he spoke the truth, and that he had himself been betrayed by Prexaspes (for that he, when sent to kill Smerdis, had not done so), looked toward Prexaspes, and said, "Prexaspes, hast thou thus performed the business I en-

joined thee?" But he answered, "Sir, it is not true that your brother Smerdis has revolted against you, nor that you can have any quarrel, great or small, with him, for I myself put your order in execution, and buried him with my own hands; if, however, the dead rise again, expect that Astyages the Mede will rise up against you; but if it is now as formerly, nothing new can spring up to you from him. It appears to me, however, that we should pursue the herald, and find out by inquiry from whom he comes to proclaim to us that we are to obey king Smerdis." 63. When Prexaspes had spoken thus, as the advice was approved by Cambyses, the herald was immediately pursued and brought back. When he arrived, Prexaspes questioned him as follows: "Friend, since you say that you come as the messenger of Smerdis, son of Cyrus, now speak the truth, and depart in peace. Whether did Smerdis himself appear in person before you, and give these orders, or some one of his ministers?" He answered, "I have not so much as seen Smerdis, son of Cyrus, since king Cambyses marched for Egypt; but the magus whom Cambyses appointed steward of his palace gave me these orders, saying that Smerdis, son of Cyrus, was the person who charged me to deliver this message to you." Thus the man spoke without adding any untruth. But Cambyses said, "Prexaspes, you, like a faithful man, having executed your instructions, have escaped all blame; but what Persian can this be who has revolted against me, usurping the name of Smerdis?" He replied, "I think I understand the whole matter, O king: the magi are the persons who have revolted against you—Patizithes, whom you left steward of the palace, and his brother Smerdis." 64. When Cambyses heard the name of Smerdis, the truth of this account and of the dream[3] struck him: *for* he fancied in his sleep that some one announced to him that Smerdis, seated on the royal throne, touched the heavens with his head. Perceiving, therefore, that he had destroyed his brother without a cause, he wept for Smerdis, and after he had lamented him, and bitterly deplored the whole calamity, he leaped upon his horse, resolving with all speed to march to Susa against the magus. But as he was leaping on his horse, the chape of his sword's scabbard fell off, and the blade, being laid bare, struck the thigh, being wounded in that part where he him-

[3] See chap. 30.

self had formerly smitten the Egyptian god Apis. Cambyses, when he thought that he was mortally wounded, asked what was the name of the city. They said it was Ecbatana. And it had been before prophesied to him from the city of Buto that he should end his life in Ecbatana. He therefore imagined he should die an old man in Ecbatana of Media, where all his treasures were; but the oracle, in truth, meant in Ecbatana of Syria. When he had thus been informed, on inquiry, of the name of the city, though smitten by his misfortune, as well that proceeding from the magus as from the wound, he returned to his right mind, and comprehending the oracle, said, "Here it is fated that Cambyses, son of Cyrus, should die."

65. So much he said at that time; but about twenty days after, having summoned the principal men of the Persians who were with him, he addressed them as follows: "I am constrained to disclose to you a matter which above all others I desired to conceal. When I was in Egypt I saw a vision in my sleep which I wish I had never seen. I thought that a messenger arrived from my palace and announced to me that Smerdis, seated on the royal throne, touched the heavens with his head. Fearing lest I should be deprived of my kingdom by my brother, I acted with more precipitation than wisdom; for, in truth, it belongs not to human nature to avert what is destined to happen. But I foolishly sent Prexaspes to Susa to put Smerdis to death. Since that crime was perpetrated I have lived in security, never considering whether, now that Smerdis was removed, some other mortal might not rise up against me. But, utterly mistaking what was about to happen, I became a fratricide to no purpose, and am nevertheless deprived of my kingdom; for Smerdis the magus was the person who the deity forewarned me in the vision would rise up against me. The deed, then, has been perpetrated by me; consider, therefore, that Smerdis, son of Cyrus, is no more; but the magi have possessed themselves of the throne—he whom I left steward of my palace and his brother Smerdis. Now he who of right should have revenged the indignity I suffer from the magi has perished impiously by the hand of his nearest relation. Since, therefore, he is no more, in the next place, of the other injunctions that I have to lay upon you, O Persians, the most necessary is, to

let you know what I would have you do after my death. I therefore, in the name of the gods who protect the throne, charge you, and all of you, especially those of the Achæmenidæ who are present, never to permit the government to return into the hands of the Medes; and if they have possessed themselves of it by craft, by craft be it recovered by you; or if they accomplish it by force, by force to the utmost win it back again. And if you do thus, may the earth bring forth her increase; may your wives and your flocks be fruitful, and you remain forever free; but if you do not win back, nor attempt to win back the sovereign power, I imprecate upon you the contrary of all these things; and, moreover, may such an end befall every Persian as has befallen me." When Cambyses had spoken thus, he deplored his whole fortunes. 66. The Persians, when they saw their king weep, all rent the garments they had on, and gave themselves to abundant lamentation; but afterward, when the bone became infected and the thigh mortified, it carried off Cambyses, son of Cyrus, after he had reigned in all seven years and five months, having never had any children, either male or female. Great incredulity stole over the Persians who were present *as to the story* that the magi had possession of the government, but they thought that Cambyses said what he did calumniously respecting the death of Smerdis, in order that the whole Persian nation might be made hostile to him. They therefore believed that Smerdis, son of Cyrus, had risen up and seized the kingdom: Prexaspes, moreover, vehemently denied that he had killed Smerdis; for it was not safe for him, now that Cambyses was dead, to own that he had killed the son of Cyrus with his own hand.

67. Accordingly, the magus, after the death of Cambyses, relying on his having the same name as Smerdis, the son of Cyrus, reigned securely during the seven months that remained to complete the eighth year of Cambyses; in which time he treated all his subjects with such beneficence, that at his death, all the people of Asia, except the Persians, regretted his loss; for the magus, having dispatched messengers to every nation he ruled over, proclaimed a general exemption from military service and tribute for the space of three years; and he made this proclamation immediately on assuming the sovereignty. 68. But in the eighth month he was discovered

in the following manner. Otanes, son of Pharnaspes, was by birth and fortune equal to the first of the Persians. This Otanes first suspected the magus not to be Smerdis, the son of Cyrus, but the person who he really was; forming his conjecture from this circumstance, that he never went out of the citadel, and that he never summoned any of the principal men of Persia to his presence. Having conceived suspicion of him, he contrived the following artifice. Cambyses had married his daughter, whose name was Phædyma; the magus, therefore, had her as his wife, and cohabited with her, as well as with all the rest of the wives of Cambyses. Otanes therefore, sending to this daughter, inquired with what man she lay, whether with Smerdis, son of Cyrus, or some other person. She sent back word to him, saying that she did not know, for that she had never seen Smerdis, son of Cyrus, nor knew who it was that cohabited with her. Otanes sent a second time, saying, "If you do not yourself know Smerdis, son of Cyrus, then inquire of Atossa who this man is with whom she as well as you cohabits, for she must of necessity know her own brother." To this his daughter replied, "I can neither have any conversation with Atossa, nor see any of the women who used to live with me; for as soon as this man, whoever he is, succeeded to the throne, he dispersed us all, assigning us separate apartments." 69. When Otanes heard this, the matter appeared much more plain; and he sent a third message to her in these words: "Daughter, it becomes you, being of noble birth, to undertake any peril that your father may require you to incur; for if this Smerdis is not the son of Cyrus, but the person whom I suspect, it is not fit that he, lying with you and possessing the empire of the Persians, should escape with impunity, but suffer the punishment due to his offenses. Now, therefore, follow my directions: when he sleeps with you, and you know him to be sound asleep, touch his ears; and if you find he has ears, be assured that you cohabit with Smerdis, son of Cyrus; but if he has none, with Smerdis the magus." To this message Phædyma answered, saying "that she should incur very great danger by doing so; for if he had no ears, and she should be discovered touching him, she well knew that he would put her to death; nevertheless, she would make the attempt." She accordingly promised to accomplish this for her father. Now Cyrus, son of Cambyses, during his reign, had cut off the ears of this Smerdis, the magus, for some grave offense. This Phædyma, daughter of Otanes, therefore, determining to execute all that she had promised her father, when her turn came to approach the magus (for in Persia the wives visit their husbands in regular succession), went and slept with him; and when the magus was sound asleep, she felt for his ears, and perceiving without any difficulty that the man had no ears, as soon as it was day, she sent and made known to her father what the case was.

70. Thereupon Otanes, having taken with him Aspathines and Gobryas, who were the noblest of the Persians, and persons on whom he could best rely, related to them the whole affair: they too had themselves suspected that the case was so; and when Otanes had adduced his reasons, they admitted *their force;* and they agreed that each should associate with himself a Persian in whom he could place most reliance. Otanes accordingly introduced Intaphernes; Gobryas, Megabyzus; and Aspathines, Hydarnes. These six being associated, Darius, son of Hystaspes, arrived at Susa from Persia, where his father was governor. When, therefore, he arrived, the six Persians determined to admit Darius to the confederacy. 71. These seven having met, exchanged pledges with each other and conferred together. When it came to the turn of Darius to declare his opinion, he addressed them as follows: "I thought that I was the only person who knew that it was the magus who reigns, and that Smerdis, son of Cyrus, is dead; and for this very reason I hastened hither in order to contrive the death of the magus; but since it proves that you also are acquainted with the fact, and not I only, it appears to me that we should act immediately, and not put it off, for that would be of no advantage." Otanes said to this, "Son of Hystaspes, you are born of a noble father, and show yourself not at all inferior to him; do not, however, so inconsiderately hasten this enterprise, but set about it with more caution; for we must increase our numbers, and then attempt it." Darius replied to this, "Be assured, ye men who are here present, if you adopt the plan proposed by Otanes, you will all miserably perish; for some one will discover it to the magus, consulting

his own private advantage; and, indeed, you ought to have carried out your project immediately, without communicating it to any one else;[4] but since you have thought fit to refer it to others, and ye have disclosed it to me, let us carry it out this very day, or be assured that, if this day passes over, no one shall be beforehand with me and become my accuser, but I myself will denounce you to the magus." 72. Otanes, seeing Darius so eager, replied, "Since you compel us to precipitate our enterprise, and will not permit us to defer it, come, do you tell us in what way we are to enter the palace and attack them; for you yourself know, if not having seen them, yet surely by report, that guards are stationed at intervals, and how shall we pass them?" Darius answered Otanes, "There are many things that can not be made clear by words, but may by action; and there are other things that seem practicable in description, but no signal effect proceeds from them. Be assured that the guards stationed there will not be at all difficult to pass by; for, in the first place, seeing our rank, there is no one who will not allow us to pass, partly from respect, and partly from fear; and, in the next place, I have a most specious pretext by which we shall gain admission, for I will say that I am just arrived from Persia, and wish to report a message to the king from my father; for when a lie must be told, let it be told, for we all aim at the same ends, both they who tell lies, and they who keep to the truth. Some tell lies when, by persuading with falsehoods, they are likely to gain some advantage; while others speak the truth, in order that, by the truth, they may acquire some advantage, and something farther may be intrusted to them: thus by different processes we aim at the same end. But if nothing were likely to be gained, as well he who speaks truth would lie, and he who lies would speak truth. Whoever of the doorkeepers, therefore, shall willingly let us pass, shall be rewarded in due time; but whoever offers to oppose us must instantly be treated as an enemy; and when we have forced our passage, we must accomplish our work. 73. After this Gobryas said, "Friends, shall we ever have a better opportunity to recover the sovereign power, or, if we shall be unable to do so, to die?

[4] More literally, "deliberating upon it by yourselves," or "having kept your own counsel."

seeing we who are Persians are governed by a Medic magus, and one without ears. Those among you who were present with Cambyses when he lay sick, well remember the imprecations he uttered at the point of death against the Persians if they should not attempt to repossess themselves of the sovereign power: we did not then believe his story, but thought that Cambyses spoke from ill-will. I therefore give my voice that we yield to Darius, and that on breaking up this conference we go nowhere else but direct to the magus." Thus spoke Gobryas, and all assented to his proposal.

74. While they were deliberating on these things, the following events happened to take place. The magi, on consultation, determined to make Prexaspes their friend, both because he had suffered grievous wrong from Cambyses, who shot his son dead with an arrow, and because he alone of all the Persians knew of the death of Smerdis, son of Cyrus, having dispatched him with his own hand; and, moreover, because Prexaspes was in high repute with the Persians. For these reasons, therefore, having sent for Prexaspes, they endeavored to win his friendship, binding him by pledges and oaths that he would keep to himself, and never divulge to any man, the cheat they had put upon the Persians, assuring him that they would give him every thing in abundance. When Prexaspes had promised that he would do as the magi persuaded him, they made a second proposal, saying that they would assemble all the Persians under the walls of the palace, and desired that he would ascend a tower, and harangue them, *assuring them* that they were governed by Smerdis, son of Cyrus, and by no one else. This they enjoined him, as being a man most trusted by the Persians, and as having frequently affirmed his belief that Smerdis, son of Cyrus, was still living, and having utterly denied his murder. 75. When Prexaspes said that he was ready to do that also, the magi having convoked the Persians, placed him on the top of a turret, and commanded him to harangue the people. But he purposely forgot what they desired him to say, and, beginning from Achæmenes, described the genealogy of Cyrus's family; and afterward, when he came down to him, he ended by telling them what great benefits Cyrus had done the Persians; and having gone through these, he declared the whole truth, saying that he had before concealed it, as it was not safe for

him to tell what had happened; but that in the present emergency, necessity constrained him to make it known. He accordingly told them that he, being compelled by Cambyses, had put Smerdis, son of Cyrus, to death, and that the magi then reigned. After he had uttered many imprecations against the Persians if they should not recover back the sovereign power and punish the magi, he threw himself headlong from the tower. Thus died Prexaspes, a man highly esteemed during the course of his whole life.

76. The seven Persians, having resolved to attack the magi without delay, set out after they had offered prayers to the gods; and while they were in the midst of their way, they were informed of all that had occurred with respect to Prexaspes; whereupon, standing aside out of the way, they again conferred together; and some, with Otanes, strongly advised to defer the enterprise, and not to attempt it while affairs were in such a ferment; but others, with Darius, *urged* to proceed at once, and to do what had been determined on, and on no account to defer it. While they were hotly disputing there appeared seven pairs of hawks pursuing two pairs of vultures, and plucking and tearing them. The seven, on seeing this, all approved the opinion of Darius, and forthwith proceeded to the palace, emboldened by the omen. 77. When they approached the gates, it happened as Darius had supposed; for the guards, out of respect for men of highest rank among the Persians, and not suspecting any such design on their part, let them pass by, moved *as they were* by divine impulse; nor did any one question them; but when they reached the hall, they fell in with the eunuchs appointed to carry in messages, who inquired of them for what purpose they had come; and at the same time that they questioned them, they threatened the door-keepers for permitting them to pass, and endeavored to prevent the seven from proceeding any farther; but they, having exhorted each other, and drawn their daggers, stabbed all that opposed their passage on the spot, and then rushed to the men's apartment. 78. The magi happened to be both within at the time, and were consulting about the conduct of Prexaspes. When, therefore, they saw the eunuchs in confusion, and heard their outcry, they both hurried out, and when they perceived what was going on, put themselves on the defensive. One of them accordingly snatched up a bow, and the other

had recourse to a javelin, and thereupon the parties engaged with each other. The one who had taken up the bow, seeing his enemies were near and pressing upon them, found it of no use; but the other made resistance with his spear, and first wounded Aspathines in the thigh, and next Intaphernes in the eye; and Intaphernes lost his eye from the wound, but did not die. Thus one of the magi wounded those two; but the other, when he found his bow of no service, fled to a chamber adjoining the men's apartment, purposing to shut to the door, and two of the seven, Darius and Gobryas, rushed in with him; and as Gobryas was grappling with the magus, Darius, standing by, was in perplexity, fearing lest he should strike Gobryas in the dark; but Gobryas, seeing that he stood by inactive, asked him why he did not use his hand; he answered, "Fearing for you, lest I should strike you." But Gobryas replied, "Drive your sword even through both of us." Darius, obeying, made a thrust with his dagger, and, by good fortune, hit the magus.

79. Having slain the magi and cut off their heads, they left the wounded of their own party there, as well on account of their exhaustion as to guard the acropolis; but the other five of them, carrying the heads of the magi, ran out with shouting and clamor, and then called upon the rest of the Persians, relating what they had done, and showing them the heads; and at the same time they slew every one of the magi that came in their way. The Persians, informed of what had been done by the seven, and of the fraud of the magi, determined themselves also to do the like; and, having drawn their daggers, they slew every magus they could find; and if night coming on had not prevented, they would not have left a single magus alive. This day the Persians observe in common more than any other, and in it they celebrate a great festival, which they call "the slaughter of the magi." On that day no magus is allowed to be seen in public, but they shut themselves up in their own houses during the whole of that day.

80. When the tumult had subsided, and five days had elapsed, those who had risen up against the magi deliberated on the state of affairs, and speeches were made that are disbelieved by some of the Greeks, however they were made. Otanes advised that they should commit the government to the Per-

sians at large, speaking as follows: "It appears that no one of us should henceforward be a monarch, for it is neither agreeable nor good; for you know to what a pitch the insolence of Cambyses reached, and you have experienced the insolence of the magus; and, indeed, how can a monarchy be a well-constituted government, where one man is allowed to do whatever he pleases without control? For if even the best of men were placed in such power, he would depart from his wonted thoughts; for insolence is engendered in him by the advantages that surround him, and envy is implanted in man from his birth, and having these two, he has every vice; for, puffed up by insolence, he commits many nefarious actions, and others through envy. One would think that a man who holds sovereign power should be free from envy, since he possesses every advantage; but the contrary to this takes place in his conduct toward the citizens, for he envies the best who continue to live, and delights in the worst men of the nation; he very readily listens to calumny, and is the most inconsistent of all men; for if you show him respect in moderation, he is offended because he is not sufficiently honored; and if any one honors him very much, he is offended as with a flatterer. But I proceed to relate what is most important. He changes the institutions of our ancestors, violates women, and puts men to death without trial. But a popular government bears the fairest name of all, equality of rights; and, secondly, is guilty of none of those excesses that a monarch is. *The magistrate* obtains his office by lot, and exercises it under responsibility, and refers all plans to the public. I therefore give my opinion that we should do away with monarchy, and exalt the people, for in the many all things are found." Otanes accordingly advanced this opinion. 81. Megabyzus advised them to intrust the government to an oligarchy, and spoke as follows: "I concur with what Otanes has said about abolishing tyranny; but in bidding us transfer the power to the people, he has erred from the best opinion; for nothing is more foolish and insolent than a useless crowd; therefore it is on no account to be endured, that men, who are endeavoring to avoid the insolence of a tyrant, should fall under the insolence of an unrestrained multitude. The former, when he does any thing, does it knowingly, but the latter have not the means of knowing; for how should they know who have neither been taught, nor are acquainted with any thing good or fitting; they who, rushing on without reflection, precipitate affairs like a winter torrent. Let those, then, who desire the ruin of the Persians adopt a democracy; but let us, having chosen an association of the best men, commit the sovereign power to them, for among them we ourselves shall be included, and it is reasonable to expect that the best counsels will proceed from the best men." Megabyzus accordingly advanced this opinion. 82. Darius expressed his opinion the third, saying, "In what Megabyzus has said concerning the people, he appears to me to have spoken rightly; but concerning an oligarchy, not so; for if three forms are proposed, and each of these which I allude to the best in its kind, the best democracy, and oligarchy, and monarchy, I affirm that the last is far superior; for nothing can be found better than one man, who is the best; since acting upon equally wise plans, he would govern the people without blame, and would keep his designs most secret from the ill-affected. But in an oligarchy, while many are exerting their energies for the public good, strong private enmities commonly spring up; for each wishing to be chief, and to carry his own opinions, they come to deep animosities one against another, from whence seditions arise; and from seditions, murder; and from murder it results in anarchy; and thus it is proved how much this form of government is the best. But when the people rule, it is impossible but that evil should spring up; when, therefore, evil springs up, mutual enmities do not arise among the bad, but powerful combinations, for they who injure the commonweath act in concert; and this lasts until some one of the people stands forward and puts them down; and on this account he is admired by the people, and being admired, he becomes a monarch; and in this he too shows that a monarchy is best. But to comprehend all in one word, whence came our freedom? and who gave it? Was it from the people, or an oligarchy, or a monarch? My opinion, therefore, is, that if we were made free by one man, we should maintain the same kind of government; and, moreover, that we should not subvert the institutions of our ancestors, seeing they are good; for that were not well."

83. These three opinions were proposed, and four of the

seven adhered to the last. When the opinion of Otanes, who was anxious to introduce equality among the Persians, was overruled, he thus spoke in the midst of them: "Associates, since it is evident that some one of us must be made king, either appointed by lot, or by the body of the Persians, intrusting the government to whom they may choose, or by some other way; now I will not enter into competition with you, for I wish neither to govern nor to be governed. But on this condition I give up all claim to the government, that neither I nor any of my posterity may be subject to any one of you." When he had said this, and the six had agreed to these terms, he did not join in the contest, but withdrew from the assembly; and this family alone, of all the Persians, retains its liberty to this day, and yields obedience so far as it pleases, but without transgressing the laws of the Persians. 84. The rest of the seven consulted how they might appoint a king on the most equitable terms; and they determined that to Otanes and his posterity forever, if the kingdom should devolve on any other of the seven, should be given a Median vest yearly, by way of distinction, together with all such presents as are accounted most honorable among the Persians. They decreed that these things should be given him for this reason, because he first advanced the enterprise, and associated them together. These honors were conferred on Otanes by way of distinction. And they made the following resolutions with regard to the whole body: that every one of the seven should have liberty to enter into the palace without being introduced, unless the king should happen to be in bed with one of his wives; and that the king should not be allowed to marry a wife out of any other family than of the conspirators. With regard to the kingdom, they came to the following determination, that he whose horse should first neigh in the suburbs at sunrise, while they were mounted, should have the kingdom.

85. Darius had a groom, a shrewd man, whose name was Œbares; to this person, when the assembly had broken up, Darius spoke as follows: "Œbares, we have determined with respect to the kingdom to do in this manner: he whose horse shall neigh first at sunrise, when we ourselves are mounted, is to have the kingdom. Now, therefore, if you have any

ingenuity, contrive that I may obtain this honor, and not another." Œbares answered, "If, sir, it indeed depends on this whether you shall be king or not, be confident on this point, and keep up your spirits; for no one else shall be king before you; I have a charm for the occasion." Darius said, "If you have any such contrivance, it is time to put it in practice, and not to delay, for to-morrow our trial is to be." Œbares, having heard this, did as follows: as soon as it was night, he led the mare which Darius's horse was most fond of to the suburbs, tied her up, and led Darius's horse to her; and he led him several times round near the mare, gradually bringing him nearer, and at last let the horse cover her. 86. At dawn of day, the six, as they had agreed, met together on horseback; and, as they were riding round the suburbs, when they came to the spot where the mare had been tied the preceding night, Darius's horse ran forward and neighed; and as the horse did this, lightning and thunder came from a clear sky. These things, happening to Darius, consummated the auspices, as if done by appointment. The others, dismounting from their horses, did obeisance to Darius as king. 87. Some say that Œbares had recourse to the foregoing artifice; others to the following (for the story is told both ways by the Persians): that, having rubbed his hand upon the genital part of the mare, he kept it concealed under his trowsers, and at sunrise, when the horses were about to start, Œbares drew out his hand and put it to the nostrils of Darius's horse, and that he, taking the scent, began to snort and neigh.

88. Accordingly, Darius, son of Hystaspes, was declared king, and all the people of Asia except the Arabians were subject to him, Cyrus having first subdued them, and afterward Cambyses. The Arabians never submitted to the Persian yoke, but were on friendly terms, and gave Cambyses a free passage into Egypt; for, without the consent of the Arabians, the Persians could not have penetrated into Egypt. Darius contracted his first marriages with Persians: *he married* two daughters of Cyrus, Atossa and Artystona. Atossa had been before married to her brother Cambyses, and afterward to the magus, but Artystona was a virgin. He married another also, daughter of Smerdis, son of Cyrus, whose name was Parmys; and he had, besides, the

daughter of Otanes, who detected the magus. His power was fully established on all sides. Having, then, first of all, made a stone statue, he had it erected; and a figure was upon it *representing* a man on horseback; and he had engraved on it the following inscription, DARIUS, SON OF HYSTASPES, BY THE SAGACITY OF HIS HORSE (here mentioning the name), AND BY THE ADDRESS OF ŒBARES, HIS GROOM, OBTAINED THE EMPIRE OF THE PERSIANS. 89. Having done this in Persia, he constituted twenty governments, which they call satrapies; and having constituted the governments and set governors over them, he appointed tributes to be paid to him from each nation, both connecting the adjoining people with the several nations, and omitting some neighboring people, he annexed to some others that were more remote. He distributed the governments and the annual payment of tribute in the following manner. Such of them as contributed silver were required to pay it according to the standard of the Babylonian talent; and such as contributed gold, according to the Euboic talent. The Babylonian talent is equal to seventy Euboic minæ. During the reign of Cyrus, and afterward of Cambyses, there was no fixed regulation with regard to tribute, but they brought in presents. In consequence of this imposition of tribute, and other things of a similar kind, the Persians say Darius was a trader, Cambyses a master, and Cyrus a father. The first, because he made profit of every thing; the second, because he was severe and arrogant; the latter, because he was mild, and always aimed at the good of his people. 90. From the Ionians, the Magnesians in Asia,[5] the Æolians, Carians, Lycians, Milyens, and Pamphylians, for one and the same tribute was imposed on them all, there came in a revenue of four hundred talents in silver; this, then, composed the first division. From the Mysians, Lydians, Lasonians, Cabalians, and Hygennians, five hundred talents; this was the second division. From the Hellespontians, who dwell on the right as one sails in, the Phrygians, the Thracians in Asia, Paphlagonians, Mariandynians, and Syrians, there was a tribute of three hundred and sixty talents; this was the third division. From the Cilicians, three hundred and sixty white horses, one for every day, and five hundred

[5] There were also Magnesians in Thessaly. See Book VII. ch. 183.

talents of silver; of these a hundred and forty were expended on the cavalry that guarded the Cilician territory, and the remaining three hundred and sixty went to Darius; this was the fourth division. 91. From the city of Poseideium, which Amphilochus, son of Amphiaraus, founded on the confines of the Cilicians and Syrians, beginning from this down to Egypt, except a district belonging to Arabians, which was exempt from taxation, was paid a tribute of three hundred and fifty talents; and in this division is *included* all Phœnicia, Syria which is called Palæstine, and Cyprus; this was the fifth division. From Egypt and the Libyans bordering on Egypt, and from Cyrene and Barce (for these were annexed to the Egyptian division), accrued seven hundred talents, besides the revenue arising from lake Mœris, which was derived from the fish; in addition, then, to this money, and the fixed supply of corn, there accrued seven hundred talents; for they furnish in addition 120,000 measures of corn for the Persians who occupy the white fortress at Memphis, and their allies; this was the sixth division. The Sattagydæ, Gandarians, Dadicæ, and Aparytæ, joined together, contributed one hundred and seventy talents; this was the seventh division. From Susa, and the rest of the country of the Cissians, three hundred talents; this was the eighth division. 92. From Babylon and the rest of Assyria there accrued to him a thousand talents of silver and five hundred young eunuchs; this was the ninth division. From Ecbatana and the rest of Media, and the Paricanians and Orthocorybantes, four hundred and fifty talents; this was the tenth division. The Caspians, Pausicæ, Pantimathians, and Daritæ, contributing together, paid two hundred talents; this was the eleventh division. From the Bactrians as far as the Æglæ was a tribute of three hundred and sixty talents; this was the twelfth division. 93. From Pactyica, and the Armenians, and the neighboring people as far as the Euxine Sea, four hundred talents; this was the thirteenth division. From the Sagartians, Sarangeans, Thamanæans, Utians, Mycians, and those who inhabit the islands on the Red Sea, in which the king settles transported convicts, from all these came a tribute of six hundred talents; this was the fourteenth division. The Sacæ and Caspians paid two hundred and fifty talents; this was the fifteenth division. The Parthians, Chorasmians, Sogdians, and Arians, three hundred talents; this was the sixteenth division. 94. The Paricanians and Asiatic Ethiopians paid four hundred talents; this was the seventeenth division. The Matienians, Saspires, and Alarodians were taxed at two hundred talents; this was the eighteenth division. From the Moschians, Tibarenians, Macronians, Mosynœcians, and Marsians, three hundred talents were demanded; this was the nineteenth division. Of the Indians the population is by far the greatest of all nations whom we know of, and they paid a tribute proportionally larger than all the rest—three hundred and sixty talents of gold dust; this was the twentieth division. 95. Now the Babylonian standard, compared with the Euboic talent, makes the total nine thousand five hundred and forty talents; and the gold, estimated at thirteen times the value of silver, the gold dust will be found to amount to four thousand six hundred and eighty Euboic talents. Therefore, if the total of all these are computed together, fourteen thousand five hundred and sixty Euboic talents were collected by Darius as an annual tribute; and passing over sums less than these, I do not mention them. 96. This tribute accrued to Darius from Asia and a small part of Libya; but, in the course of time, another tribute accrued from the islands and the inhabitants of Europe as far as Thessaly. This tribute the king treasures up in the following manner: having melted it, he pours it into earthen jars, and having filled it, he takes away the earthen mould, and when he wants money, he cuts off so much as he wants from time to time.

97. These, then, were the governments and the imposts on each. The Persian territory alone has not been mentioned as subject to tribute, for the Persians occupy their land free from taxes. They, indeed, were not ordered to pay any tribute, but brought gifts. The Ethiopians bordering on Egypt, whom Cambyses subdued when he marched against the Macrobian Ethiopians, and who dwell about the sacred city of Nysa, and celebrate festivals of Bacchus—these Ethiopians and their neighbors use the same grain as the Calantian Indians, and live in subterraneous dwellings—both these bring every third year, and they continued to do so to my time, two chœnices of unmolten gold, two hundred blocks of ebony, five Ethiopian boys, and twenty large elephants' tusks. The Colchians numbered themselves among those who gave presents,

as well as the neighboring nations, as far as Mount Caucasus; for to this mountain the dominions of Persia extend; but the people to the north side of the Caucasus pay no regard to the Persians. These, then, for the gifts they imposed on themselves, furnished, even to my time, every five years, one hundred boys and one hundred virgins. The Arabians also furnished every year a thousand talents of frankincense. These, then, brought to the king the above gifts, besides the tribute.

98. The Indians obtain the great quantity of gold, from which they supply the before-mentioned dust to the king, in the manner presently described. That part of India toward the rising sun is all sand; for of the people with whom we are acquainted, and of whom any thing certain is told, the Indians live the farthest toward the east and the sunrise of all the inhabitants of Asia; for the Indians' country toward the east is a desert, by reason of the sands. There are many nations of Indians, and they do not speak the same language as each other; some of them are nomades, and others not. Some inhabit the marshes of the river, and feed on raw fish, which they take going out in boats made of reeds: one joint of the reed makes a boat. These Indians wear a garment made of rushes, which, when they have cut the reed from the river and beaten it, they afterward plait like a mat, and wear it as a corslet. 99. Other Indians, living to the east of these, are nomades, and eat raw flesh; they are called Padæans. They are said to use the following customs. When any one of the community is sick, whether it be a woman or a man, if it be a man, the men who are his nearest connections put him to death, alleging that if he wasted by disease his flesh would be spoiled; but if he denies that he is sick, they, not agreeing with him, kill and feast upon him; and if a woman be sick, in like manner the women who are most intimate with her do the same as the men; and whoever reaches to old age, they sacrifice and feast upon; but few among them attain to this state; for before that, they put to death every one that falls into any distemper. 100. Other Indians have the following different custom: they neither kill any thing that has life, nor sow any thing, nor are they wont to have houses, but they live upon herbs, and they have a grain of the size of millet in a pod, which springs spontaneously from the earth; this they gather,

and boil it, and eat it with the pod. When any one of them falls into any disorder, he goes and lies down in the desert, and no one takes any thought about him, whether dead or sick. 101. The intercourse of all these Indians whom I have mentioned takes place openly, as with cattle; and all have a complexion closely resembling the Ethiopians. The seed they emit is not white, as that of other men, but black as their skin; the Ethiopians also emit similar seed. These Indians are situated very far from the Persians, toward the south, and were never subject to Darius.

102. There are other Indians bordering on the city of Caspatyrus and the country of Pactyica, settled northward of the other Indians, whose mode of life resembles that of the Bactrians. They are the most warlike of the Indians, and these are they who are sent to procure the gold; for near this part is a desert, by reason of the sand. In this desert, then, and in the sand, there are ants, in size somewhat less indeed than dogs, but larger than foxes. Some of them are in the possession of the king of the Persians, which were taken there. These ants, forming their habitations under ground, heap up the sand, as the ants in Greece do, and in the same manner; and they are very like them in shape. The sand that is heaped up is mixed with gold. The Indians, therefore, go to the desert to get this sand, each man having three camels, on either side a male one harnessed to draw by the side, and a female in the middle; this last the man mounts himself, having taken care to yoke one that has been separated from her young as recently born as possible; for camels are not inferior to horses in swiftness, and are much better able to carry burdens. 103. What kind of figure the camel has I shall not describe to the Greeks, as they are acquainted with it, but what is not known respecting it I will mention. A camel has four thighs and four knees in his hinder legs, and his private parts are turned between the hinder legs to the tail. 104. The Indians then, adopting such a plan and such a method of harnessing, set out for the gold, having before calculated the time, so as to be engaged in their plunder during the hottest part of the day; for during the heat the ants hide themselves under ground. Among these people the sun is hottest in the morning, and not, as among others, at mid-day, from the time that it has risen some way to the break-

ing up of the market; during this time it scorches much more than at midday in Greece; so that, it is said, they then refresh themselves in water. Midday scorches other men much the same as the Indians; but as the day declines, the sun becomes to them as it is in the morning to others; and after this, as it proceeds, it becomes still colder until sunset; then it is very cold. 105. When the Indians arrive at the spot, having sacks with them, they fill these with the sand, and return with all possible expedition; for the ants, as the Persians say, immediately discovering them by the smell, pursue them, and they are equaled in swiftness by no other animal, so that if the Indians did not get the start of them while the ants were assembling, not a man of them could be saved. Now the male camels (for they are inferior in speed to the females) slacken their pace, dragging on,[6] not both equally; but the females, mindful of the young they have left, do not slacken their pace. Thus the Indians, as the Persians say, obtain the greatest part of their gold; and they have some small quantity more that is dug in the country.

106. The extreme parts of the inhabited world somehow possess the most excellent products, as Greece enjoys by far the best-tempered climate; for, in the first place, India is the farthest part of the inhabited world toward the east, as I have just observed; in this part, then, all animals, both quadrupeds and birds, are much larger than they are in other countries, with the exception of horses; in this respect they are surpassed by the Medic breed called the Nysæan horses. In the next place, there is abundance of gold there, partly dug, partly brought down by the rivers, and partly seized in the manner I have described. And certain wild trees there bear wool instead of fruit, that in beauty and quality excels that of sheep; and the Indians make their clothing from these trees. 107. Again, Arabia is the farthest of the inhabited countries toward the south; and this is the only region in which grow frankincense, myrrh, cassia, cinnamon, and ledanum. All these, except myrrh, the Arabians gather with difficulty. The frankincense they gather by burning styrax, which the Phœnicians import into Greece; they take it by burning this; for winged serpents, small in size, and various

[6] For the various modes of translating this difficult passage, see *Baehr's Note* or *Cary's Lexicon*.

in form, guard the trees that bear frankincense, a great number round each tree. These are the same serpents that invade Egypt.[7] They are driven from the trees by nothing else but the smoke of the styrax. 108. The Arabians say this also, that the whole land would be filled by these serpents if some such thing did not take place with regard to them, as I know happens to vipers. And the providence of God, as was likely, proves itself wise: whatever creatures are timid, and fit for food, have been made very prolific, lest the species should be destroyed by constant consumption; but such as are savage and noxious, unprolific. For instance, the hare, which is hunted by all, beasts, birds, and men, is so prolific that it alone of all beasts conceives to superfetation, having in its womb some of its young covered with down, others bare, others just formed, and at the same time conceives again. Such, then, is the case. Whereas a lioness, which is the strongest and fiercest of beasts, bears only one once in her life; for in bringing forth she ejects her matrix with the whelp; and this is the cause: when the whelp begins to move in the womb, he, having claws much sharper than those of any other beast, lacerates the womb; and as he increases in strength, he continues tearing it much more; and when the birth approaches, not a single part of it remains sound. 109. So, also, if vipers and the winged serpents of Arabia multiplied as fast as their nature admits, men could not possibly live. But now, when they couple together, and the male is in the very act of impregnating, as he emits the seed, the female seizes him by the neck, and clinging to him, never lets him go until she has gnawed through him. In this manner the male dies, and the female pays the following retribution to the male: the offspring, while yet in the womb, avenging their father, eat through the matrix; and having gnawed through her bowels, thus make their entrance into the world. But other serpents, which are not hurtful to men, lay eggs, and hatch a vast number of young. Now vipers are found in all parts of the world; but flying serpents are abundant in Arabia, and nowhere else: there they appear to be very numerous.

110. The Arabians obtain the frankincense in the manner I have described; and the cassia as follows: when they have covered their whole body and face, except the eyes, with hides

[7] See Book II. chap. 75.

and other skins, they go to the cassia; it grows in a shallow lake; and around the lake and in it lodge winged animals, very like bats, and they screech fearfully, and are exceedingly fierce. These they keep off from their eyes, and so gather the cassia. 111. The cinnamon they collect in a still more wonderful manner. Where it grows, and what land produces it, they are unable to tell, except that some, giving a probable account, say that it grows in those countries in which Bacchus was nursed. And they say that large birds bring those rolls of bark, which we, from the Phœnicians, call cinnamon, the birds bring them for their nests, which are built with clay, against precipitous mountains, where there is no access for man. The Arabians, to surmount this difficulty, have invented the following artifice: having cut up into large pieces the limbs of dead oxen, and asses, and other beasts of burden, they carry them to these spots, and having laid them near the nests, they retire to a distance. But the birds flying down carry up the limbs of the beasts to their nests, which not being strong enough to support the weight, break and fall to the ground. Then the men, coming up, in this manner gather the cinnamon, and being gathered by them, it reaches other countries. 112. But the ledanum, which the Arabians call ladanum, is still more wonderful than this; for though it comes from a most stinking place, it is itself most fragrant; for it is found sticking like gum to the beards of he-goats, *which collect it* from the wood. It is useful for many ointments, and the Arabians burn it very generally as a perfume. 113. It may suffice to have said thus much of these perfumes; and there breathes from Arabia, as it were, a divine odor. They have two kinds of sheep worthy of admiration, which are seen nowhere else. One kind has large tails, not less than three cubits in length, which, if suffered to trail, would ulcerate, by the tails rubbing on the ground. But every shepherd knows enough of the carpenter's art *to prevent this*, for they make little carts and fasten them under the tails, binding the tail of each separate sheep to a separate cart. The other kind of sheep have broad tails, even to a cubit in breadth. 114. Where the meridian declines[8] toward the setting sun, the Ethiopian territory reaches, being the extreme part of the habitable world. It produces much gold, huge elephants, wild

[8] That is, "southwest."

trees of all kinds, ebony, and men of large stature, very handsome, and long-lived.

115. These, then, are the extremities of Asia and Libya. Concerning the western extremities of Europe I am unable to speak with certainty, for I do not admit that there is a river called by barbarians Eridanus, which discharges itself into the sea toward the north, from which amber is said to come; nor am I acquainted with the Cassiterides islands, from whence our tin comes; for, in the first place, the name Eridanus shows that it is Grecian and not barbarian, and feigned by some poet; in the next place, though I have diligently inquired, I have never been able to hear from any man who has himself seen it that there is a sea on that side of Europe. However, both tin and amber come to us from the remotest parts. 116. Toward the north of Europe there is evidently a very great quantity of gold, but how procured I am unable to say with certainty, though it is said that the Arimaspians, a one-eyed people, steal it from the griffins. Neither do I believe this, that men are born with one eye, and yet in other respects resemble the rest of mankind. However, the extremities of the world seem to surround and inclose the rest of the earth, and to possess those productions which we account most excellent and rare.

117. There is a plain in Asia shut in on every side by a range of mountains, and there are five defiles in the mountain. This plain formerly belonged to the Chorasmians, situated on the confines of these Chorasmians, of the Hyrcanians, Parthians, Sarangæans, and Thamanæans; but since the Persians have had the empire it belongs to the king. From this range of mountains, then, that shuts in this plain, there flows a great river, the name of which is Aces; it formerly, being divided into five several channels, used to irrigate the lands of the nations before mentioned, being conducted to each nation through each separate defile. But since they have become subject to the Persian, they have suffered the following calamity. The king, having caused the clefts of the mountains to be blocked up, placed gates at each cleft, and the passage of the water being stopped, the plain within the mountains has become a sea, as the river continued to pour in, and had nowhere any exit. The people, therefore, who before were in the habit of using the water, not being able to use it any longer, were reduced to

great extremities; for though in winter heaven supplies them with rain, as it does other men, yet, in summer, when they sow millet and sesame, they stood in need of water. When, therefore, no water was allowed them, they and their wives going to the Persians, and standing before the king's palace, raised a great outcry. But the king gave order that the gates should be open toward those lands that were most in need; and when their land was satiated by imbibing water, these gates were shut, and he ordered others to be opened to those who were next in greatest need; and, as I have been informed, he opens them after he has exacted large sums of money, in addition to the tribute. Now these things are so.

118. Of the seven men that conspired against the magus, it happened that one of them, Intaphernes, having committed the following act of insolence, lost his life shortly after the revolution. He wished to enter the palace in order to confer with Darius; for the law was so settled among those who had conspired against the magus, that they should have access to the king without a messenger, unless the king should happen to be in bed with one of his wives. Intaphernes, therefore, determined that no one should announce him; but, because he was one of the seven, chose to enter; the door-keeper, however, and the messenger, would not let him pass, saying that the king was then in bed with one of his wives. But Intaphernes, suspecting they told a falsehood, did as follows: having drawn his cimeter, he cut off their ears and noses, and having strung them to the bridle of his horse, he hung them round their necks, and so dismissed them. 119. They presented themselves to the king, and told him the cause for which they had been so treated. Darius, fearing lest the six had done this in concert, sent for them, one by one, and endeavored to discover their opinions, whether they approved of what had been done. But when he discovered that Intaphernes had not done this with their privity, he seized Intaphernes himself, and his children, and all his family, having reason to suspect that he, with his relations, would raise a rebellion against him; and having seized them, he bound them as for death. But the wife of Intaphernes, going to the gates of the palace, wept and lamented aloud; and having done this continually, she prevailed on Darius to have compassion on her. He therefore, having sent a messenger, spoke as follows:

"Madam, king Darius allows you to release one of your relations who are now in prison, whichever of them all you please." But she, having deliberated, answered as follows: "Since the king grants me the life of one, I choose my brother from them all." Darius, when he heard this, wondering at her choice, having sent again, asked, "Madam, the king inquires the reason why, leaving your husband and children, you have chosen that your brother should survive, who is not so near related to you as your children, and less endeared to you than your husband?" She answered as follows: "O king, I may have another husband, if God will, and other children if I lose these; but, as my father and mother are no longer alive, I can not by any means have another brother; for this reason I spoke as I did." The woman appeared to Darius to have spoken well, and he granted her the one whom she asked, and her eldest son, he was so well pleased with her. All the rest he put to death. Of the seven, therefore, one very soon perished in the manner now mentioned.

120. Near about the time of Cambyses's illness, the following events took place. Orœtes, a Persian, had been appointed governor of Sardis by Cyrus; this man conceived an impious project; for, without having sustained any injury, or heard a hasty word from Polycrates the Samian, and without having seen him before, he conceived the design of seizing him and putting him to death, as most people say, for some such cause as this. Orœtes and another Persian, whose name was Mitrobates, governor of the district of Dascylium, were sitting together at the palace gates, and fell into a dispute. As they were quarreling about valor, Mitrobates said to Orœtes tauntingly, "Are you to be reckoned a brave man, who have not yet acquired for the king the island of Samos, that lies near your government, and is so easy to be subdued? which one of its own inhabitants, having made an insurrection with fifteen armed men, obtained possession of, and now reigns over?" Some say that he, having heard this, and being stung with the reproach, conceived a desire, not so much to revenge himself on the man who said it as of utterly destroying Polycrates, on whose account he had been reproached.

121. A fewer number say that Orœtes sent a herald to Samos to make some demand which is not mentioned, and that Polycrates happened to be reclining in the men's apartment, and

that Anacreon of Teos was with him; and somehow (whether designedly disregarding the business of Orœtes, or by chance it so happened), when the herald of Orœtes came forward and delivered his message, Polycrates, as his face chanced to be turned toward the wall, neither turned about nor made any answer. 122. These twofold causes are assigned for the death of Polycrates: every man may give credit to whichever he pleases. However, Orœtes, who resided in Magnesia, situated on the river Mæander, being acquainted with the intentions of Polycrates, sent Myrsus, a Lydian, son of Gyges, with a message to Samos; for Polycrates is the first of the Grecians of whom we know who formed a design to make himself master of the sea, except Minos the Cnossian, or any other, who before his time obtained the empire of the sea; but, within what is called the historical[9] age, Polycrates is the first who had entertained great expectations of ruling Ionia and the islands. Orœtes, therefore, having ascertained that he had formed this design, sent a message to the following effect: "Orœtes to Polycrates says as follows: I understand that you are planning vast enterprises, and that you have not money answerable to your projects. Now if you will do as I advise, you will promote your own success, and preserve me; for king Cambyses meditates my death, and of this I have certain information. Now do you convey me and my wealth out of the country, and take part of it, and suffer me to enjoy the rest. By means of the wealth you will become master of all Greece. If you doubt what I say concerning my riches, send to me the most trusty of your servants, to whom I will show them." 123. Polycrates, having heard this, was delighted, and accepted the offer; and, as he was very eager for wealth, he first sent Mæandrius, son of Mæandrius, to view it, a citizen who was his secretary. He not long after dedicated to the temple of Juno all the ornamental furniture from the men's apartment of Polycrates, which was indeed magnificent. Orœtes, having learned that an inspector might be expected, did as follows: having filled eight chests with stones, except a very small space round the brim, he put gold on the surface of the stones, and having made the chests fast with cords, he kept them in readiness. But Mæandrius,

[9] In opposition to "the fabulous."

having come and inspected *the chests*, took back a report to Polycrates. 124. He, though earnestly dissuaded by the oracles and by his friends, resolved to go in person; and, moreover, though his daughter had seen in a dream this vision: she imagined she saw her father elevated in the air, washed by Jupiter, and anointed by the sun. Having seen this vision, she endeavored by all possible means to divert Polycrates from going from home to Orœtes; and, as he was going on board a fifty-oared galley, she persisted in uttering words of bad omen; but he threatened her, if he should return safe, that she should long continue unmarried; and she prayed that so it might be brought to pass; for she chose to continue a longer time unmarried than be deprived of her father. 125. Thus Polycrates, disregarding all advice, set sail to visit Orœtes, taking with him many others of his friends, and among them Democedes, son of Calliphon, a Crotonian, who was a physician, and the most skillful practitioner of his time. But Polycrates, on his arrival at Magnesia, was put to death in a horrid manner, unworthy of himself and his lofty thoughts; for, with the exception of those who have been tyrants of Syracuse, not one of all the Grecian tyrants deserves to be compared with Polycrates for magnificence. But Orœtes, having put him to death in a manner not to be described, caused him to be crucified. Of those who accompanied Polycrates, as many as were Samians he dismissed, bidding them to feel thankful to him for their liberty; but as many as were strangers and servants he detained and treated as slaves. Thus Polycrates, being crucified, fulfilled the vision of his daughter in every particular; for he was washed by Jupiter when it rained, and was anointed by the sun, himself emitting moisture from his body. Thus the constant good fortune of Polycrates ended as Amasis, king of Egypt, had foretold.[1]

126. Not long after, vengeance on account of Polycrates overtook Orœtes; for, after the death of Cambyses, and during the reign of the magi, Orœtes, continuing at Sardis, gave no assistance to the Persians, who had been deprived of the government by the Medes; but he, in this confusion, put to death Mitrobates, governor of Dascylium, who had upbraided him with his conduct to Polycrates, together with Mitrobates's son Cranaspes, men of high repute among the Persians; and he

[1] See chapters 40—43.

committed various other atrocities; and a certain courier of Darius who came to him, because he brought him an unwelcome message, he had assassinated on his return, having set men to way-lay him; and when he had caused him to be slain, he had him and his horse put out of sight. 127. Darius, therefore, when he got possession of the throne, was anxious to punish Orœtes for all his iniquities, and especially for the death of Mitrobates and his son; but he did not think it prudent to send an army against him openly, as his affairs were still in a ferment, and he had but just got possession of the throne, and he heard that Orœtes had great strength; for he had a body-guard of a thousand Persians, and held the government of Phrygia, Lydia, and Ionia. Under these circumstances, therefore, Darius had recourse to the following plan: having called the most eminent of the Persians together, he addressed them as follows: "Which of you, O Persians, will undertake to accomplish for me this by address, and not by force and numbers? for where skill is required, force is of no avail. Which of you, then, will either bring me Orœtes alive, or put him to death? He has never done the Persians any service, but he has brought great mischiefs upon them. In the first place, he destroyed two of us, Mitrobates and his son; and, in the next place, he slew the messenger sent by me to recall him, displaying intolerable insolence. He must therefore be stopped by death before he has perpetrated any greater evils against the Persians." 128. Darius asked the above questions; and thirty men offered to undertake it, each being willing to accomplish the plan alone. But Darius put an end to their competitions by desiring them to cast lots; and when they cast lots, it fell to Bagæus, son of Artontes. Bagæus, having obtained it, did as follows: having written several letters relating to a variety of affairs, he affixed to them Darius's seal, and then proceeded with them to Sardis. On his arrival, having come into the presence of Orœtes, he opened the letters one by one, and gave them to the royal secretary to read; for all the governors have royal secretaries. Bagæus gave the letters in order to make trial of the guards, whether they would listen to a revolt from Orœtes; and perceiving they paid great respect to the letters, and still more to the contents, he gave one in which were these words: "Persians, King Darius forbids you to be guards to Orœtes."

They, when they heard this, lowered their lances to him. When Bagæus saw them so obedient to the letter, he thereupon took confidence, and delivered the last letter to the secretary, in which was written, "King Darius commands the Persians at Sardis to put Orœtes to death." The guards, when they heard this, drew their cimeters and killed him immediately. Thus vengeance overtook Orœtes the Persian on account of Polycrates the Samian.

129. When the treasures of Orœtes had been removed, and had arrived at Susa, it happened not long after that Darius, in leaping from his horse while hunting, twisted his foot, and it was twisted with such violence that the ankle-bone was dislocated; and at first, thinking he had about him those of the Egyptians who had the first reputation for skill in the healing art, he made use of their assistance; but they, by twisting the foot, and using force, made the evil worse; and from the pain which he felt, Darius lay seven days and seven nights without sleep. On the eighth day, as he still continued in a bad state, some one who had before heard at Sardis of the skill of Democedes the Crotonian, made it known to Darius, and he ordered them to bring him to him as quickly as possible. They found him among the slaves of Orœtes, altogether neglected, and brought him forward, dragging fetters behind him, and clothed in rags. 130. As he stood before him, Darius asked him whether he understood the art. He denied that he did, fearing lest, if he discovered himself, he should be altogether precluded from returning to Greece. But he appeared to Darius to dissemble, although he was skilled in the art; he therefore commanded those who had brought him thither to bring out whips and goads; whereupon he discovered himself, saying that he did not know it perfectly, but having been intimate with a physician, he had some poor knowledge of the art. Upon which, when Darius put himself under his care, by using Grecian medicines, and applying lenitives after violent remedies, he caused him to sleep, and in a little time restored him to his health, though he had before despaired of ever recovering the use of his foot. After this cure, Darius presented him with two pair of golden fetters; but Democedes asked him if he purposely gave him a double evil because he had restored him to health. Darius, pleased with the speech, sent him to his own wives; and the eunuchs,

introducing him, said to the women that this was the man who had saved the king's life; whereupon each of them, dipping a goblet into a chest of gold, presented Democedes with such a munificent gift, that a servant whose name was Sciton, following behind, picked up the staters that fell from the goblets, and collected a large quantity of gold.

131. This Democedes visited Polycrates, after having left Crotona on the following account. He was harshly treated at Crotona by his father, who was of a severe temper, and being unable to endure this, he left him and went to Ægina; having settled there, in the first year, though he was unprovided with means, and had none of the instruments necessary for the exercise of his art, he surpassed the most skillful of their physicians; and in the second year, the Æginetæ engaged him for a talent out of the public treasury; and in the third year, the Athenians, for a hundred minæ; and in the fourth year, Polycrates, for two talents: thus he came to Samos. From this man the Crotonian physicians obtained a great reputation; for at this period the physicians of Crotona were said to be the first throughout Greece, and the Cyrenæans the second. At the same time, the Argives were accounted the most skillful of the Greeks in the art of music. 132. At that time, then, Democedes, having completely cured Darius at Susa, had a very large house, and had a seat at the king's table; and he had every thing he could wish for, except the liberty of returning to Greece. And, in the first place, he obtained from the king a pardon for the Egyptian physicians, who first attended the king, and were about to be impaled, because they had been outdone by a Greek physician; and, in the next place, he procured the liberty of a prophet of Elis, who had attended Polycrates, and lay neglected among the slaves. In short, Democedes had great influence with the king.

133. Not long after these things the following events took place: Atossa, daughter of Cyrus, and wife to Darius, had a tumor on her breast; after some time it burst, and spread considerably. As long as it was small she concealed it, and from delicacy informed no one of it; when it became dangerous, she sent for Democedes and showed it to him. He, saying that he could cure her, exacted from her a solemn promise, that she, in return, would perform for him whatever he should require of her, but *added* that he would ask nothing which

might bring disgrace upon her. 134. When, therefore, he had healed her, and restored her to health, Atossa, instructed by Democedes, addressed Darius, as he lay in bed, in the following words: "O king, you who possess so great power, sit idle, and do not add any nation or power to the Persians. It were right that a man who is both young and master of such vast treasures should render himself considerable by his actions, that the Persians may know that they are governed by a man. Two motives should influence you to such a course; first, that the Persians may know that it is a man who rules over them, and, secondly, that they may be worn in war, and not tempted by too much ease to plot against you. You should therefore perform some illustrious action while you are in the flower of your age; for the mind grows with the growth of the body, and as it grows old, grows old with it, and dull for every action." She spoke thus according to her instructions, and he answered, "Lady, you have mentioned the very things that I myself purpose to do; for I have determined to make a bridge and march from this continent to the other, against the Scythians; and this shall shortly be put in execution." Atossa replied, "Look you now, give up the thought of marching first against the Scythians, for they will be in your power whenever you choose; but take my advice, and lead an army into Greece; for, from the account I have heard, I am anxious to have Lacedæmonian, Argive, Athenian, and Corinthian attendants; and you have the fittest man in the world to show and inform you of every thing concerning Greece; I mean the person who cured your foot." Darius answered, "Lady, since you think I ought to make my first attempt against Greece, I think it better first to send some Persians thither as spies with the man you mention; they, when they are informed of and have seen every particular, will make a report to me; and then, being thoroughly informed, I will turn my arms against them." 135. Thus he spoke; and no sooner said than done; for, as soon as day dawned, having summoned fifteen eminent Persians, he commanded them to accompany Democedes, and pass along the maritime parts of Greece, and to take care that Democedes did not escape from them, but they must by all means bring him back again. Having given these commands to them, he next summoned Democedes himself, and requested him, when he had conducted the Persians through all Greece, and shown it to them, to return back again; he also commanded him to take with him all his movables as presents to his father and brothers, promising to give him many times as much instead. Moreover, he said that, for the purpose of transporting the presents, he would give a merchant ship, filled with all kinds of precious things, which should accompany him on his voyage. Now Darius, in my opinion, promised him these things without any deceitful intention; but Democedes, fearing lest Darius was making trial of him, received all that was given without eagerness, but said that he would leave his own goods where they were, that he might have them on his return; the merchant ship which Darius promised him to convey the presents to his brothers he said he would accept of. Darius, having given him these instructions, sent them down to the coast.

136. Accordingly, going down to Phœnicia and Sidon, a city of Phœnicia, they manned two triremes, and with them also a large trading vessel, *laden* with all kinds of precious things, and having prepared every thing, they set sail for Greece; and keeping to the shore, they surveyed the coasts, and made notes in writing. At length, having inspected the greatest part of it, and whatever was most remarkable, they proceeded to Tarentum, in Italy. There, out of kindness toward Democedes, Aristophilides, king of the Tarentines, first took off the rudders of the Median ships, and next shut up the Persians as spies. While they were in this condition Democedes went to Crotona, and when he had reached his own home, Aristophilides set the Persians at liberty, and restored what he had taken from their ships. 137. The Persians sailing from thence, and pursuing Democedes, arrived at Crotona, and having found him in the public market, they laid hands on him. Some of the Crotonians, dreading the Persian power, were ready to deliver him up; but others seized the Persians in turn, and beat them with staves, though they expostulated in these terms: "Men of Crotona, have a care what you do: you are rescuing a man who is a runaway from the king; how will king Darius endure to be thus insulted? How can what you do end well, if you force this man from us? What city shall we sooner attack than this? What sooner shall we endeavor to reduce to slavery?" Saying this, they

did not persuade the Crotonians; but, being forcibly deprived of Democedes, and having had the trading vessel which they brought with them taken from them, they sailed back to Asia; nor, as they were deprived of their guide, did they attempt to explore Greece any farther. At their departure Democedes enjoined them to tell Darius that he had Milo's daughter affianced to him as his wife, for the name of Milo, the wrestler, stood high with the king; and on this account it appears to me that Democedes spared no expense to hasten this marriage, that he might appear to Darius to be a man of consequence in his own country. 138. The Persians, having set sail from Crotona, were driven to Iapygia, and being made slaves there, Gillus, a Tarentine exile, ransomed them, and conducted them to king Darius; and he, in return for this, professed himself ready to give him whatever he should desire. But Gillus, having first related his misfortunes, asked to be restored to Tarentum; but that he might not disturb Greece, if on his account a great fleet should sail to Italy, he said that the Cnidians alone would suffice to effect his restoration; thinking that by them, as they were on terms of friendship with the Tarentines, his return would be most easily effected. Darius having promised this, performed it; for, having dispatched a messenger to Cnidus, he bade them restore Gillus to Tarentum; but the Cnidians, though they obeyed Darius, could not persuade the Tarentines, and were not strong enough to employ force. Thus these things ended; and these were the first Persians who came from Asia to Greece, and they, on that occasion, were spies.

139. After these things, king Darius took Samos, first of all the cities, either Grecian or barbarian, *and he took it* for the following reason. When Cambyses, son of Cyrus, invaded Egypt, many Grecians resorted thither; some, as one may conjecture, on account of trade; others, to serve as soldiers; others, to view the country. Of these, the last was Syloson, son of Æaces, brother to Polycrates, and an exile from Samos. The following piece of good luck befell this Syloson: having put on a scarlet cloak, he walked in the streets of Memphis; and Darius, who was one of Cambyses's guard, and as yet a man of no great account, seeing him, took a fancy to the cloak, and coming up, wished to purchase it. But Syloson, perceiving that Darius was very anxious to have the cloak,

impelled by a divine impulse, said, "I will not sell it for any sum, but I will give it you for nothing, if so it must needs be." Darius, having accepted his offer with thanks, took the cloak. 140. Syloson thought afterward that he had lost it through his good nature; but when, in course of time, Cambyses died, and the seven rose up against the magus, and of the seven, Darius possessed the throne, Syloson heard that the kingdom had devolved on the man to whom he had given his cloak in Egypt on his requesting it; so, having gone up to Susa, he seated himself at the threshold of the king's palace, and said he had been a benefactor to Darius. The porter, having heard this, reported it to the king; but he, wondering, said to the man, "What Grecian is my benefactor, to whom I owe a debt of gratitude, having so lately come to the throne? Scarcely one of them has as yet come up hither, nor can I mention any thing that I owe to a Greek. However, bring him in, that I may know the meaning of what he says." The porter introduced Syloson, and, as he stood in the midst, the interpreters asked him who he was, and what he had done that he said he had been a benefactor to the king. Then Syloson related all that had passed respecting the cloak, and that he was the person who gave it. To this the king answered, "Most generous of men! art thou, then, the man who, when as yet I had no power, made me a present, small as it was? yet the obligation is the same as if I were now to receive a thing of great value. In return, I will give thee abundance of gold and silver, so that thou shalt never repent having conferred a favor on Darius, son of Hystaspes." To this Syloson replied, "O king, give me neither gold nor silver, but recover and give me back my country, Samos, which now, since my brother Polycrates died by the hands of Orœtes, a slave of ours has possessed himself of. Give me this without bloodshed and bondage. 141. When Darius heard this, he sent an army under the conduct of Otanes, one of the seven, with orders to accomplish whatever Syloson should desire. Whereupon Otanes, going down to the sea, embarked his army.

142. Mæandrius, son of Mæandrius, held the government of Samos, having had the administration intrusted to him by Polycrates. Though he wished to prove himself the most just of men, he was unable to effect his purpose; for when the death of Polycrates was made known to him, he did as fol-

lows: First he erected an altar to Jupiter Liberator, and marked round it the sacred inclosure which is now in the suburbs. Afterward, when he had done this, he summoned an assembly of all the citizens, and spoke as follows: "To me, as you know, the sceptre and all the power of Polycrates has been intrusted, and I am now able to retain the government. But what I condemn in another, I will myself, to the utmost of my ability, abstain from doing; for neither did Polycrates please me in exercising despotic power over men equal to himself, nor would any other who should do the like. Now Polycrates has accomplished his fate, and I, surrendering the government into your hands, proclaim equality to all. I require, however, that the following remuneration should be granted to myself; that six talents should be given me out of the treasures of Polycrates; and, in addition, I claim for myself and my descendants forever, the priesthood of the temple of Jupiter Liberator, to whom I have erected an altar, and under whose auspices I restore to you your liberties." He then made these demands of the Samians, but one of them rising up said, "You, forsooth, are not worthy to rule over us, being as you are a base and pestilent fellow; rather think how you will render an account of the wealth that you have had the management of." 143. Thus spoke a man of eminence among the citizens, whose name was Telesarchus. But Mæandrius, perceiving that if he should lay down the power, some other would set himself up as tyrant in his place, no longer thought of laying it down. To which end, when he had withdrawn to the citadel, sending for each one severally, as if about to give an account of the treasures, he seized them and put them in chains. They were then kept in confinement; but, after this, disease attacked Mæandrius, and his brother, whose name was Lycaretus, supposing that he would die, in order that he might the more easily possess himself of the government of Samos, put all the prisoners to death; for, as it seems, they were not willing to be free.

144. When, therefore, the Persians arrived at Samos, bringing Syloson with them, no one raised a hand against them, and the partisans of Mæandrius, and Mæandrius himself, said they were ready to quit the island under a treaty; and when Otanes had assented to this, and had ratified the agreement, the principal men of the Persians, having had seats placed for

them, sat down opposite the citadel. 145. The tyrant Mæandrius had a brother somewhat out of his senses, whose name was Charilaus; he, for some fault he had committed, was confined in a dungeon; and having at that time overheard what was doing, and having peeped through his dungeon, when he saw the Persians sitting quietly down, he shouted and said that he wished to speak with Mæandrius; but Mæandrius, having heard this, commanded him to be released and brought into his presence; and as soon as he was brought there, upbraiding and reviling his brother, he urged him to attack the Persians, saying, "Me, O vilest of men, who am your own brother, and have done nothing worthy of bonds, you have bound and adjudged to a dungeon; but when you see the Persians driving you out and making you houseless, you dare not avenge yourself, though they are so easy to be subdued; but if you are in dread of them, lend me your auxiliaries, and I will punish them for coming here, and I am ready, also, to send you out of the island." 146. Thus spoke Charilaus; and Mæandrius accepted his offer, as I think, not that he had reached such a pitch of folly as to imagine that his own power could overcome that of the king, but rather out of envy to Syloson, if, without a struggle, he should possess himself of the city uninjured. Having, therefore, provoked the Persians, he wished to make the Samian power as weak as possible, and then to give it up; being well assured that the Persians, if they suffered any ill-treatment, would be exasperated against the Samians; and knowing, also, that he had for himself a safe retreat from the island, whenever he chose, for he had had a secret passage dug leading from the citadel to the sea. Accordingly, Mæandrius himself sailed away from Samos; but Charilaus, having armed all the auxiliaries, and having thrown open the gates, sallied out upon the Persians, who did not expect any thing of the kind, but thought every thing had been agreed upon; and the auxiliaries, falling on, slew those of the Persians who were seated in chairs,[2] and who were the principal men among them. But the rest of the Persian army came to their assistance, and the auxiliaries, being hard pressed, were shut up again within the

[2] Διφροφορευμένους, Baehr thinks, refers to those Persians who were before described as seated opposite the citadel; Coray, quoted by Larcher and others, thinks it means "those who were carried on litters."

citadel. 147. But Otanes, the general, when he saw that the Persians had suffered great loss, purposely[3] neglected to obey the orders which Darius had given him at his departure, that he should neither kill nor take prisoner any of the Samians, but deliver the island to Syloson without damage; on the contrary, he commanded his army to put to death every one they met with, both man and child alike; whereupon one part of the army besieged the citadel, and the rest killed every one that came in their way, all they met as well within the temples as without. 148. Mæandrius, having escaped from Samos, sailed to Lacedæmon; and having arrived there, and carried with him all the treasures that he had when he set out, he did as follows. When he had set out his silver and golden cups, his servants began to clean them; and he, at the same time, holding a conversation with Cleomenes, son of Anaxandrides, then king of Sparta, led him on to his house. When the king saw the cups, he was struck with wonder and astonishment; upon which Mæandrius bade him take away whatever he pleased; and when Mæandrius had repeated this offer two or three times, Cleomenes showed himself a man of the highest integrity, who refused to accept what was offered; and being informed that by giving to other citizens he would gain their support, he went to the Ephori, and said that it would be better for Sparta that this Samian stranger should quit the Peloponnesus, lest he should persuade him, or some other of the Spartans, to become base; but they, having assented, banished Mæandrius by public proclamation. 149. The Persians, having drawn Samos as with a net,[4] delivered it to Syloson, utterly destitute of inhabitants. Afterward, however, Otanes, the general, repeopled it, in consequence of a vision in a dream, and a distemper which seized him in his private parts.

150. While the naval armament was on its way to Samos, the Babylonians revolted, having very well prepared themselves; for while the magus reigned, and the seven rose up against him, during all that time, and in the confusion, they had made preparations for a siege, and somehow, in doing this, had escaped observation; but when they openly revolt-

[3] *μεμνημένος ἐπελάνθανετο*, literally, "remembering he forgot." Just as *τοῦ ἐπιστάμενος τὸ οὔνομα ἑκὼν ἐπιλήθομαι*, B. IV. chap. 43.

[4] For a description of this mode of taking an island, see B. VI. chap. 31.

ed they did as follows: having excepted their mothers, each man selected one woman besides, whomever he chose, from his own family, but all the rest they assembled together and strangled: the one woman each man selected to cook his food. They strangled them, that they might not consume their provisions. 151. Darius, being informed of this, and having collected all his forces, marched against them; and having advanced to Babylon, he besieged them, who were not at all solicitous about the event, for the Babylonians, mounting on the ramparts of the wall, danced, and derided Darius and his army, and one of them spoke as follows: "Why sit ye there, O Persians? will ye not be off? for ye will then take us when mules bring forth young." One of the Babylonians said this who never expected that a mule would breed. 152. When a year and seven months had now passed, Darius was vexed, and all his army, that they were not able to take the Babylonians; though Darius had recourse to every kind of stratagem and artifice against them. But even so he could not take them; and having tried other stratagems, he made trial of that also by which Cyrus had taken them. However, the Babylonians kept strict guard, and he was not able to surprise them.

153. Thereupon, in the twentieth month, to Zopyrus, son of that Megabyzus who was one of the seven who dethroned the magus—to this Zopyrus, son of Megabyzus, the following prodigy happened: one of his sumpter-mules brought forth young; but when the news was told him, Zopyrus himself, not believing it, went to see the foal, and having strictly charged his servants not to tell any one what had happened, he considered on it; and in consequence of the words of the Babylonian, who at the beginning said, "When even mules bring forth young, then would the city be taken"—in consequence of this omen, he thought that Babylon could now be taken; for that the man had spoken under divine influence, and that his own mule had brought forth young. 154. When he thought that it was fated for Babylon to be now taken, he went to Darius, and asked him whether he deemed the taking of Babylon as of very great importance; and having learned that he valued it at a high price, he next considered how he might be the person to take it, and the work might be his own; for among the Persians great achievements are honored in the

highest degree. Now he concluded that he should not be able to reduce it in any other way than if he should mutilate himself and desert to the enemy. Thereupon, considering that as a light matter, he inflicted on himself an irremediable mutilation; for having cut off his nose and ears, and having cut his hair in a disgraceful manner, and having scourged himself, he presented himself before Darius. 155. Darius was very much grieved when he beheld a man of high rank so mutilated, and having started from his throne, he shouted aloud and asked who had mutilated him, and for what cause. He answered, "O king, there is no man except yourself who could have power to treat me thus; no stranger has done this, O king, but I have done it to myself, deeming it a great indignity that the Assyrians should deride the Persians." He replied, "Most wretched of men, you have given the fairest name to the foulest deed in saying that you have injured yourself thus incurably on account of those who are besieged. How, foolish man, because you are mutilated, will the enemy sooner submit? Have you lost your senses, that you have thus ruined yourself?" He said in answer, "If I had communicated to you what I was about to do, you would not have permitted me; but now, having deliberated with myself, I have done it; now, therefore, if you are not wanting to your own interests, we shall take Babylon; for I, as I am, will desert to the city, and will tell them that I have been thus treated by you; and I think that when I have persuaded them that such is the case, I shall obtain the command of their army. Do you then, on the tenth day after I shall have entered the city, of that part of your army whose loss you would least regret, station a thousand men over against the gates called after Semiramis; again after that, on the seventh day after the tenth, station two thousand more against the gate called from Nineveh; and from the seventh day let an interval of twenty days elapse, and then place four thousand more against the gate called from the Chaldæans; but let neither the first nor these carry any defensive arms except swords, but let them have those. After the twentieth day, straightway command the rest of the army to invest the wall on all sides, but station the Persians for me at those called the Belidian and Cissian gates; for as I think, when I have performed great exploits, the Babylonians will intrust every thing to me, and, moreover, the keys of the gates, and then it will be mine and the Persians' care to do what remains to be done.

156. Having given these injunctions, he went to the gates, turning round as if he were really a deserter. But those who were stationed in that quarter, seeing him from the turrets, ran down, and having opened one door of the gate a little, asked him who he was, and for what purpose he came. He told them that he was Zopyrus, and had deserted to them; the door-keepers therefore, when they heard this, conducted him to the assembly of the Babylonians, and, standing before them, he deplored his condition, saying that he had suffered from Darius the injuries he had inflicted on himself, and that he was so treated because he had advised to raise the siege, since there appeared no means of taking the city. "Now, therefore," he said, "I come to you, O Babylonians, the greatest blessing; and to Darius, his army, and the Persians, the greatest mischief; for he shall not escape with impunity, having thus mutilated me; and I am acquainted with all his designs." 157. Thus he spoke; but the Babylonians, seeing a man of distinction among the Persians deprived of his ears and nose, and covered with stripes and blood, thoroughly believing that he spoke the truth, and that he had come as an ally to them, were ready to intrust him with whatever he should ask; and he asked the command of the forces. But he, having obtained this from them, acted as he had preconcerted with Darius; for on the tenth day, leading out the army of the Babylonians, and having surrounded the thousand, whom he had instructed Darius to station there first, he cut them all in pieces. The Babylonians therefore perceiving that he had performed deeds suitable to his promises, were exceedingly rejoiced, and were ready to obey him in every thing. He, therefore, having suffered the appointed number of days to elapse, and again having selected a body of Babylonians, led them out and slaughtered the two thousand of Darius's soldiers. But the Babylonians witnessing this action also, all had the praises of Zopyrus on their tongues. Then he again, having suffered the appointed number of days to elapse, led out his troops according to the settled plan, and having surrounded the four thousand, he cut them in pieces. And when he had accomplished this, Zopyrus was every thing to the Babylonians, and he was appointed commander-in-chief, and guardian of the walls. 158. But when

Darius, according to agreement, invested the wall all round, then Zopyrus discovered his whole treachery; for the Babylonians, mounting on the wall, repelled the army of Darius that was attacking them; but Zopyrus, having opened the Cissian and Belidian gates, led the Persians within the wall. Those of the Babylonians who saw what was done fled into the temple of Jupiter Belus, and those who did not see it remained each at their post, until they also discovered that they had been betrayed.

159. Thus Babylon was taken a second time. But when Darius had made himself master of the Babylonians, first of all he demolished the walls and bore away all the gates; for when Cyrus had taken Babylon before, he did neither of these things; and, secondly, Darius impaled about three thousand of the principal citizens, and allowed the rest of the Babylonians to inhabit the city. And that the Babylonians might have wives, in order that offspring might grow up from them, Darius made the following provision; for the Babylonians had strangled their wives, as already has been mentioned, to prevent the consumption of their provisions; and to that end he enjoined the neighboring provinces to send women to Babylon, taxing each at a certain number, so that a total of fifty thousand women came together; and from these the Babylonians of our time are descended. 160. No Persian, in the opinion of Darius, either of those who came after or lived before, surpassed Zopyrus in great achievements, Cyrus only excepted; for with him no Persian ever ventured to compare himself. It is also reported that Darius frequently expressed this opinion, that he would rather Zopyrus had not suffered ignominious treatment, than acquire twenty Babylons in addition to that he had. And he honored him exceedingly; for he every year presented him with those gifts which are most prized by the Persians, and he assigned him Babylon to hold free from taxes during his life, and gave him many other things in addition. From this Zopyrus sprung Megabyzus, who commanded the army in Egypt against the Athenians and their allies; and from this Megabyzus sprung Zopyrus, who deserted to the Athenians from the Persians.

BOOK IV.

MELPOMENE.

After the capture of Babylon, Darius's expedition against the Scythians took place; for as Asia was flourishing in men, and large revenues came in, Darius was desirous of revenging himself upon the Scythians, because they formerly, having invaded the Median territory, and defeated in battle those that opposed them, were the first beginners of violence. For the Scythians, as I have before mentioned,[1] ruled over Upper Asia for eight-and-twenty years; for while in pursuit of the Cimmerians, they entered Asia, and overthrew the empire of the Medes; for these last, before the arrival of the Scythians, ruled over Asia. Those Scythians, however, after they had been abroad eight-and-twenty years, and returned to their own country, after such an interval, a task no less than the invasion of Media awaited; for they found an army of no inconsiderable force ready to oppose them; for the wives of the Scythians, seeing their husbands were a long time absent, had sought the company of their slaves. 2. The Scythians deprive all their slaves of sight for the sake of the milk which they drink, doing as follows: when they have taken bone tubes very like flutes, they thrust them into the genital parts of the mares, and blow with their mouths; while some blow, others milk. They say they do this for the following reason: because the veins of the mare, being inflated, become filled, and the udder is depressed. When they have finished milking, they pour it into hollow wooden vessels, and having placed the blind men round about the vessels, they agitate the milk; and having skimmed off that which swims on the surface, they consider it the most valuable, but that which subsides is of less value than the oth-

[1] See Book I. ch. 103, 105.

er. On this account the Scythians put out the eyes of every prisoner they take; for they are not agriculturists, but feeders of cattle. 3. From these slaves, then, and the women, a race of youths had grown up, who, when they knew their own extraction, opposed those who were returning from Media. And first they cut off the country by digging a wide ditch, stretching from Mount Taurus to the lake Mæotis, which is of great extent, and afterward encamping opposite, they came to an engagement with the Scythians, who were endeavoring to enter. When several battles had been fought, and the Scythians were unable to obtain any advantage, one of them said, "Men of Scythia, what are we doing? by fighting with our slaves, both we ourselves by being slain become fewer in number, and by killing them we shall hereafter have fewer to rule over. Now, therefore, it seems to me that we should lay aside our spears and bows, and that every one, taking a horsewhip, should go directly to them; for so long as they saw us with arms, they considered themselves equal to us, and born of equal birth; but when they shall see us with our whips instead of arms, they will soon learn that they are our slaves, and being conscious of that, will no longer resist." 4. The Scythians, having heard this, adopted the advice; and the slaves, struck with astonishment at what was done, forgot to fight, and fled. Thus the Scythians both ruled over Asia, and being afterward expelled by the Medes, returned in this manner to their own country; and for the above-mentioned reasons, Darius, desiring to take revenge, assembled an army to invade them.

5. As the Scythians say, theirs is the most recent of all nations; and it arose in the following manner. The first man that appeared in this country, which was a wilderness, was named Targitaus; they say that the parents of this Targitaus —in my opinion relating what is incredible—they say, however, that they were Jupiter and a daughter of the river Borysthenes; that such was the origin of Targitaus; and that he had three sons, who went by the names of Lipoxais, Apoxais, and the youngest, Colaxais; that during their reign a plow, a yoke, an axe, and a bowl of golden workmanship, dropping down from heaven, fell on the Scythian territory; that the eldest, seeing them first, approached, intending to take them up, but as he came near, the gold began to burn; when he

had retired the second went up, and it did the same again; accordingly the burning gold repulsed these; but when the youngest went up the third, it became extinguished, and he carried the things home with him, and that the elder brothers, in consequence of this giving way, surrendered the whole authority to the youngest. 6. From Lipoxais, *they say*, are descended those Scythians who are called Auchatæ; from the second, Apoxais, those who are called Catiari and Traspies; and from the youngest of them, the royal race, who are called Paralatæ; but all have the name of Scoloti, from the surname of their king, but the Grecians call them Scythians. 7. The Scythians say that such was their origin, and they reckon the whole number of years from their first beginning, from king Targitaus to the time that Darius crossed over against them, to be not more than a thousand years, but just that number. This sacred gold the kings watch with the greatest care, and annually approach it with magnificent sacrifices to render it propitious. If he who has the sacred gold happens to fall asleep in the open air on the festival, the Scythians say he can not survive the year, and on this account they give him as much land as he can ride round on horseback in one day. The country being very extensive, Colaxais established three of the kingdoms for his sons, and made that one the largest in which the gold is kept. The parts beyond the north of the inhabited districts, the Scythians say, can neither be seen nor passed through, by reason of the feathers[2] shed there; for that the earth and air are full of feathers, and that it is these which intercept the view.

8. Such is the account the Scythians give of themselves and of the country above them, but the Greeks who inhabit Pontus give the following account: *they say* that Hercules, as he was driving away the herds of Geryon, arrived in this country, that was then a desert, and which the Scythians now inhabit; that Geryon, fixing his abode outside the Pontus, inhabited the island which the Greeks call Erythia, situate near Gades, beyond the columns of Hercules in the ocean. The ocean, they say, beginning from the sun-rise, flows round the whole earth, but they do not prove it in fact; that Hercules thence came to the country now called Scythia, and as a storm and frost overtook him, he drew his lion's skin over him, and

[2] See chap. 31.

went to sleep, and in the mean while his mares, which were feeding apart from his chariot, vanished by some divine chance. 9. *They add* that when Hercules awoke, he sought for them, and that having gone over the whole country, he at length came to the land called Hylæa; there he found a monster having two natures, half virgin, half viper, of which the upper parts, from the buttocks, resembled a woman, and the lower parts a serpent: when he saw he was astonished, but asked her if she had any where seen his strayed mares. She said that she herself had them, and would not restore them to him before she had laid with him: Hercules accordingly lay with her on these terms. She, however, delayed giving back the mares, out of a desire to enjoy the company of Hercules as long as she could; he, however, was desirous of recovering them and departing. At last, as she restored the mares, she said, "These mares that strayed hither I preserved for you, and you have paid me salvage, for I have three sons by you; tell me, therefore, what must I do with them when they are grown up? whether shall I establish them here, for I possess the rule over this country, or shall I send them to you?" She asked this question, but he replied, they say, "When you see the children arrived at the age of men, you can not err if you do this; whichever of them you see able thus to bend this bow, and thus girding himself with this girdle, make him an inhabitant of this country; and whichever fails in these tasks which I enjoin, send out of the country. If you do this, you will please yourself and perform my injunctions." 10. Then, having drawn out one of his bows, for Hercules carried two at that time, and having shown her the belt, he gave her both the bow and the belt, which had a golden cup at the extremity of the clasp, and having given them, he departed. But she, when the sons who were born to her attained to the age of men, in the first place gave them names: to the first, Agathyrsis; to the second, Gelonus; and to the youngest, Scythes; and, in the next place, remembering the orders, she did what had been enjoined; and two of her sons, Agathyrsis and Gelonus, being unable to come up to the proposed task, left the country, being expelled by their mother; but the youngest of them, Scythes, having accomplished it, remained there. From this Scythes, son of Hercules, are descended those who have been successively kings of the Scythi- and from the cup, the Scythians even to this day wear cups from their belts. This thing only the mother did for Scythes. Such is the account given by the Greeks who inhabit Pontus.

11. There is another account, to the following effect, to which I myself rather incline. *It is said* that the Scythian nomades who dwelt in Asia, being harassed in war by the Massagetæ, crossed the river Araxes, and entered the Cimmerian territory; for the country which the Scythians now inhabit is said to have formerly belonged to the Cimmerians. The Cimmerians, when the Scythians invaded them, deliberated, seeing a large army was coming against them; however, their opinions were divided, which both vehemently upheld, though that of the kings was the best; for the opinion of the people was, that it was necessary to retire, and that there was no need[3] to hazard a battle against superior numbers; but the opinion of the kings was, that they should fight to the last for their country against the invaders. When, therefore, neither the people would submit to the kings, nor the kings to the people; and one party resolved to depart without fighting, and abandon the country to the invaders, while the kings determined to die and be buried in their own country, and not fly with the people, considering what great advantages they had enjoyed, and how many misfortunes would probably befall them if they fled from their country: when they had come to this resolution, having divided, and being equal in numbers, they fought with one another; and the one party, *the royal race*, having all perished, the people of the Cimmerians buried them near the river Tyras; and their sepulchre is still to be seen. After they had buried them, they then abandoned the country; and the Scythians coming up, took possession of the deserted country. 12. And there are now in Scythia Cimmerian fortifications and Cimmerian Porthmia;[4] there is also a district named Cimmeria, and a bosphorus called Cimmerian. The Cimmerians evidently appear to have fled from the Scythians into Asia, and settled in the peninsula in which the Grecian city Sinope now stands; and it is evident that the Scythians, pursuing them, and entering the Median territory, missed their way, for the Cimmerians fled constantly by the sea-coast; whereas the Scythians pursued, keeping Caucasus on the right, until they entered the Median territory, toward

[3] See Cary's Lexicon. v. Δέειν, *num.* 3. [4] Passages *or* ferries.

the midland. This last account is given in common both by Greeks and barbarians.

13. But Aristeas, son of Caystrobius, a native of Proconnesus, says in his epic verses that, inspired by Apollo, he came to the Issedones; that beyond the Issedones dwell the Arimaspians, a people that have only one eye; and beyond them the gold-guarding griffins; and beyond these the Hyperboreans, who reach to the sea: that all these, except the Hyperboreans, beginning from the Arimaspians, continually encroached upon their neighbors; that the Issedones were expelled from their country by the Arimaspians, the Scythians by the Issedones, and that the Cimmerians, who inhabited on the south sea, being pressed by the Scythians, abandoned their country. Thus he does not agree with the Scythians respecting this country. 14. Of what country Aristeas, who made these verses, was, has already been mentioned, and I shall now relate the account I heard of him in Proconnesus and Cyzicus. They say that Aristeas, who was inferior to none of the citizens by birth, entering into a fuller's shop in Proconnesus, died suddenly; and that the fuller, having closed his work-shop, went to acquaint the relatives of the deceased. When the report had spread through the city that Aristeas was dead, a certain Cyzicenian, arriving from Artace, fell into a dispute with those who made the report, affirming that he had met and conversed with him on his way to Cyzicus, and he vehemently disputed the truth of the report; but the relations of the deceased went to the fuller's shop, taking with them what was necessary for the purpose of carrying the body away, but when the house was opened, Aristeas was not to be seen either dead or alive. *They say* that afterward, in the seventh year, he appeared in Proconnesus, composed those verses which by the Greeks are now called Arimaspian, and having composed them, disappeared a second time. Such is the story current in these cities. 15. But these things I know happened to the Metapontines in Italy, three hundred and forty years after the second disappearance of Aristeas, as I discovered by computation in Proconnesus and Metapontium. The Metapontines say that Aristeas himself, having appeared in their country, exhorted them to erect an altar to Apollo, and to place near it a statue bearing the name of Aristeas, the Proconnesian; for he said that Apollo had visited their [illegible]-

try only of all the Italians, and that he himself, who was now Aristeas, accompanied him; and that when he accompanied the god, he was a crow; and after saying this, he vanished; and the Metapontines say they sent to Delphi to inquire of the god what the apparition of the man meant; but the Pythian bade them obey the apparition, and if they obeyed it would conduce to their benefit. They accordingly, having received this answer, fulfilled the injunctions; and now a statue bearing the name of Aristeas is placed near the image of Apollo, and around it laurels are planted. The image is placed in the public square. Thus much concerning Aristeas.

16. No one knows with certainty what is beyond the country about which this account proceeds to speak; for I have not been able to hear of any one who says he has seen them with his own eyes; nor even did Aristeas, of whom I have just now made mention, say in his poems that he went farther than the Issedones, but of the parts beyond he spoke by hearsay, stating that the Issedones gave him his information; but, as far as we have been able to arrive at the truth with accuracy from hearsay, the whole shall be related. 17. From the port of the Borysthenitæ, for this is the most central part of the sea-coast of all Scythia, the first people are the Callipidæ, being Greek-Scythians; beyond these is another nation, called Alazones. These and the Callipidæ, in other respects, follow the usages of the Scythians, but they both sow and feed on wheat, onions, garlic, lentils, and millet; but beyond the Alazones dwell husbandmen who do not sow wheat for food, but for sale. Beyond these the Neuri[5] dwell, and to the north of the Neuri the country is utterly uninhabited, as far as I know. These nations are by the side of the river Hypanis, to the west of the Borysthenes. 18. But if one crosses the Borysthenes, the first country from the sea is Hylæa; and from this higher up live Scythian agriculturists, where the Greeks settled on the river Hypanis, called Borysthenitæ, but they call themselves Olbiopolitæ. These Scythian husbandmen, then, occupy the country eastward, for three days' journey, extending to the river whose name is Panticapes; and northward, a passage of eleven days up the Borysthenes. Beyond this region the country is desert for a great distance; and beyond the desert Androphagi[6] dwell, who are a distinct

[5] See chap. 51, 105.

[6] See chap. 106.

people, and not in any respect Scythian. Beyond this is really desert, and no nation of men is found there as far as we know. 19. The country eastward of these Scythian agriculturists, when one crosses the Panticapes, nomades occupy, who neither sow at all, nor plow; and all this country is destitute of trees except Hylæa. These nomades occupy a tract eastward for fourteen days' journey, stretching to the river Gerrhus. 20. Beyond the Gerrhus are the parts called the Royal, and the most valiant and numerous of the Scythians, who deem all other Scythians to be their slaves. These extend southward to Taurica, and eastward to the trench, which those sprung from the blind men dug, and to the port on the lake Mæotis, which is called Cremni, and some of them reach to the river Tanais. The parts above, to the north of the Royal Scythians, the Melanchlæni[7] inhabit, a distinct race, and not Scythian; but above the Melanchlæni are lakes, and an uninhabited desert, as far as we know.

21. After one crosses the river Tanais, it is no longer Scythian, but the first region belongs to the Sauromatæ,[8] who, beginning from the recess of the lake Mæotis, occupy the country northward, for a fifteen days' journey, all destitute both of wild and cultivated trees. Above these dwell the Budini,[9] occupying the second region, and possessing a country thickly covered with all sorts of trees. 22. Above the Budini, toward the north, there is first a desert of seven days' journey, and next to the desert, if one turns somewhat toward the east, dwell the Thyssagetæ, a numerous and distinct race, and they live by hunting. Contiguous to these, in the same regions, dwell those who are called Iyrcæ, who also live by hunting in the following manner: *the huntsman*, having climbed a tree, lies in ambush (and the whole country is thickly wooded), and each man has a horse ready, taught to lie on his belly, that he may not be much above the ground, and a dog besides. When he sees any game from the tree, having let fly an arrow and mounted his horse, he goes in pursuit, and the dog keeps close to him. Above these, as one bends toward the east, dwell other Scythians, who revolted from the Royal Scythians, and so came to this country. 23. As far as the territory of these Scythians, the whole country

[7] See chap. 107. [8] See chap. 116. [9] See chap. 108.

that has been described is level and deep-soiled, but after this it is stony and rugged. When one has passed through a considerable extent of the rugged country, a people are found living at the foot of lofty mountains who are said to be all bald from their birth, both men and women alike, and they are flat-nosed, and have large chins; they speak a peculiar language, wear the Scythian costume, and live on the fruit of a tree: the name of the tree on which they live is called ponticon, about the size of a fig-tree; it bears fruit like a bean, and has a stone. When this is ripe they strain it through a cloth, and a thick and black liquor flows from it; the name of what flows from it is aschy; this they suck, and drink mingled with milk; from the thick sediment of the pulp they make cakes, and feed on them; for they have not many cattle in these parts, as the pastures there are not good. Every man lives under a tree in the winter, when he has covered the tree with a thick white woolen covering; but in summer, without the woolen covering. No man does any injury to this people, for they are accounted sacred; nor do they possess any warlike weapon. And, in the first place, they determine the differences that arise among their neighbors; and, in the next place, whoever takes refuge among them is injured by no one. They are called Argippæi.

24. As far, then, as these bald beople, our knowledge respecting the country and the nations before them is very good, for some Scythians frequently go there, from whom it is not difficult to obtain information, as also from Greeks belonging to the port of the Borysthenes, and other ports in Pontus. The Scythians who go to them transact business by means of seven interpreters and seven languages. 25. So far, then, is known; but beyond the bald men no one can speak with certainty, for lofty and impassable mountains form their boundary, and no one has ever crossed them; but these bald men say, what to me is incredible, that men with goat's feet inhabit these mountains; and when one has passed beyond them, other men are found, who sleep six months at a time, but this I do not at all admit. However, the country eastward of the bald men is well known, being inhabited by Issedones, though the country above to the north, either of the bald men or the Issedones, is utterly unknown, except only

such things as these people relate. 26. The Issedones are said to observe these customs. When a man's father dies, all his relations bring cattle, and then, having sacrificed them and cut up the flesh, they cut up also the dead parent of their host, and, having mingled all the flesh together, they spread out a banquet; then, having made bare and cleansed his head, they gild it; and afterward they treat it as a sacred image,[1] performing grand annual sacrifices to it. A son does this to his father, as the Greeks celebrate the anniversary of their fathers' death. These people are likewise accounted just; and the women have equal authority with the men. These, then, are well known.

27. Above them, the Issedones affirm, are the men with only one eye, and the gold-guarding griffins. The Scythians repeat this account, having received it from them; and we have adopted it from the Scythians, and call them, in the Scythian language, Arimaspi; for *Arima*, in the Scythian language, signifies one, and *Spou*, the eye. 28. All this country which I have been speaking of is subject to such a severe winter, that for eight months the frost is so intolerable, that if you pour water on the ground you will not make mud, but if you light a fire you will make mud. Even the sea freezes, and the whole Cimmerian bosphorus; and the Scythians who live within the trench lead their armies and drive their chariots over the ice to the Sindians, on the other side. Thus winter continues eight months, and during the other four it is cold there. And this winter is different in character from the winters in all other countries; for in this no rain worth mentioning falls in the usual season, but during the summer it never leaves off raining. At the time when there is thunder elsewhere there is none there, but in summer it is violent; if there should be thunder in winter, it is accounted a prodigy to be wondered at; so, should there be an earthquake, whether in summer or winter, in Scythia, it is accounted a prodigy. Their horses endure this cold, but their asses and mules can not endure it at all; but in other places, horses that stand exposed to frost become frost-bitten in

[1] I have adopted Baehr's interpretation of ἀγάλματι in preference to that of Schweighæuser, who considers it to mean "a sacred ornament," or to that of Larcher, who takes it to mean "a precious vessel."

the cold, waste away, but asses and mules endure it. 29. On this account, also, the race of beeves appears to me to be defective there, and not to have horns; and the following verse of Homer, in his Odyssey,[2] confirms my opinion: "And Libya, where the lambs soon put forth their horns;" rightly observing, that in warm climates horns shoot out quickly; but in very severe cold, the cattle either do not produce them at all, or if they do produce them, they do so with difficulty. Here, then, such are the effects of the cold. 30. I am surprised (for my narrative has from its commencement sought for digressions), that in the whole territory of Elis no mules are able to breed, though neither is the climate cold, nor is there any other visible cause. The Eleans themselves say that mules do not breed with them in consequence of a curse; therefore, when the time for the mares breeding approaches, they lead them to the neighboring districts, and there put the he-asses with them until they are in foal; then they drive them home again. 31. With respect to the feathers with which the Scythians say the air is filled, and that on account of them it is not possible either to see farther upon the continent or to pass through it, I entertain the following opinion: in the upper parts of this country it continually snows, less in summer than in winter, as is reasonable: now whoever has seen snow falling thick near him will know what I mean, for snow is like feathers; and on account of the winter being so severe, the northern parts of this continent are uninhabited. I think, then, that the Scythians and their neighbors call the snow feathers, comparing[3] them together. These regions, therefore, which are said to be the most remote, have been sufficiently described.

32. Concerning the Hyperboreans, neither the Scythians say any thing, nor any people of those parts, except the Issedones; and, as I think, neither do they say any thing, for then the Scythians would mention it, as they do the one-eyed people. Hesiod, however, has made mention of the Hyperboreans, and Homer, in the Epigoni, if indeed Homer was in reality the author of that poem. 33. But the Delians say very much more than any others about them, affirming that sacred things, wrapped in wheat-straw, were brought from the Hyperboreans and came to the Scythians; and from the

[2] B. IV. l. 85.

[3] That is, "speaking figuratively."

Scythians each contiguous nation receiving them in succession, carried them to the extreme west as far as the Adriatic; that, being forwarded thence toward the south, the Dodonæans, the first of the Greeks, received them; that from them they descended to the Maliac Gulf, and passed over into Eubœa, and that one city sent them on to another as far as Carystus; that after this Andros was passed by, for the Carystians conveyed them to Tenos, and the Tenians to Delos: in this manner they say these sacred things reached Delos. *They add* that the Hyperboreans first sent two virgins, whom they call by the names of Hyperoche and Laodice, to carry these sacred things; and with them, for the sake of safety, the Hyperboreans sent five of their citizens as attendants, the same who are now called Perpherees, and are held in high honor at Delos. But when those who were sent out by the Hyperboreans did not return, they, thinking it a grievous thing if it should always happen to them not to receive back those whom they sent out, therefore carried their offerings wrapped in wheat-straw to their borders, and enjoined their neighbors to forward them to the next nation; and these being so forwarded, they say, reached Delos. I myself know that the following practice is observed, resembling that of these sacred things: the Thracian and Pæonian women, when they sacrifice to Royal Diana, do not offer their sacrifices without wheat-straw; and I know that they do this. 34. In honor of these Hyperborean virgins who died in Delos, both the virgins and youths of the Delians shear their hair: the former, having cut off a lock before marriage, and having wound it about a distaff, lay it upon the sepulchre; the sepulchre is within the temple of Diana, on the left as one enters, and on it grows an olive-tree: the youths of the Delians having wound some of their hair round a plant, place it also on the sepulchre. These virgins receive such honor from the inhabitants of Delos. 35. These same persons also affirm that Arge and Opis, who were Hyperborean virgins, passing through the same nations, came to Delos even before Hyperoche and Laodice: that these last came to bring the tribute they had agreed to pay to Ilithya for a speedy delivery; but they say that Arge and Opis arrived with the gods themselves, and that different honors are paid them by themselves, for that the women collect contributions for them, calling on their names in a hymn, which Olen, a Lycian, composed for them; and that the islanders and Ionians afterward, having learned it from them, celebrate Opis and Arge in song, mentioning their names, and collecting contributions (now this Olen, coming from Lycia, composed also the other ancient hymns which are sung in Delos); and that the ashes of the thighs burned on the altar are thrown and expended on the sepulchre of Opis and Arge; but their sepulchre is behind the temple of Diana, facing the east, very near the banqueting-room of the Ceians. 36. And thus much may be said concerning the Hyperboreans, for I do not relate the story concerning Abaris, who was said to be an Hyperborean, to the effect that he carried an arrow round the whole earth without eating any thing. If, however, there are Hyperboreans, there must also be Hypernotians. But I smile when I see many persons describing the circumference of the earth, who have no sound reason to guide them; they describe the ocean flowing round the earth, which is made circular as if by a lathe, and make[4] Asia equal to Europe. I will therefore briefly show the dimensions of each of them, and what is the figure of each.

37. The Persian settlements extend to the southern sea, called the Erythræan; above them, to the north, are the Medes; above the Medes, the Saspires; and above the Saspires, the Colchians, who reach to the northern sea, into which the river Phasis discharges itself. These four nations occupy the space from sea to sea. 38. Thence westward two tracts stretch out to the sea, which I shall describe. On one side, the one tract, beginning at the north from the Phasis, extends along the Euxine and the Hellespont, as far as the Trojan Sigæum; and on the south, this same tract, beginning from the Myriandrian Gulf, which is adjacent to Phœnicia, stretches toward the sea as far as the Triopian promontory. In this tract dwell thirty different nations. This, then, is one of the tracts. 39. The other, beginning at Persia, reaches to the Red Sea; *it comprises* Persia, and after that Assyria, and after Assyria, Arabia; it terminates (terminating only by custom) at the Arabian Gulf, into which Darius carried a canal[5] from

[4] Baehr observes that ποιεύντων is the genitive participle, depending on γελῶ preceding; "I smile when they make Asia equal to Europe." It would be difficult to express the connection in an English version.

[5] See B. II. chap. 158.

the Nile. Now as far as Phœnicia from Persia the country is wide and open, but from Phœnicia the same tract stretches along this sea by Syrian Palestine and Egypt, where it terminates; in it are only three nations. These, then, are the parts of Asia that lie westward of Persia. 40. Beyond the Persians, Medes, Saspires, and Colchians, toward the east and rising sun, extends the Red Sea, and on the north the Caspian Sea, and the river Araxes, which flows toward the rising sun. Asia is inhabited as far as India; but beyond this, it is all desert toward the east, nor is any one able to describe what it is. Such and so great is Asia.

41. Libya is in the other tract; for Libya commences from Egypt. Now in Egypt this tract is narrow; for from this sea to the Red Sea are a hundred thousand orgyæ, which make one thousand stades. But from this narrow neck the tract which is called Libya becomes very wide. 42. I wonder, therefore, at those who have described the limits of and divided Libya, Asia, and Europe, for the difference between them is not trifling; for in length Europe extends along both of them, but with respect to width it is evidently not to be compared.[6] Libya shows itself to be surrounded by water, except so much of it as borders upon Asia. Neco, king of Egypt, was the first whom we know of that proved this; he, when he had ceased digging the canal leading from the Nile to the Arabian Gulf, sent certain Phœnicians in ships, with orders to sail back through the pillars of Hercules into the northern sea,[7] and so to return to Egypt. The Phœnicians accordingly, setting out from the Red Sea, navigated the southern sea; when autumn came, they went ashore, and sowed the land, by whatever part of Libya they happened to be sailing, and waited for harvest; then having reaped the corn, they put to sea again. When two years had thus passed, in the third, having doubled the pillars of Hercules, they arrived in Egypt, and related what to me does not seem credible, but may to others, that as they sailed round Libya, they had the sun on their right hand. Thus was Libya first known. 43. Subsequently the Carthaginians say *that Libya is surrounded by water;* for Sataspes, son of Teaspes, one of the Achæmenidæ, did not sail round Libya,

[6] He means, "it is much wider than either of them."

[7] Meaning "the Mediterranean," which was north of Libya.

though sent for that very purpose; but dreading the length of the voyage and the desolation, returned home and did not accomplish the task which his mother imposed upon him; for he had violated a virgin, daughter of Zopyrus, son of Megabyzus; whereupon, when he was about to be impaled for this offense by king Xerxes, the mother of Sataspes, who was sister to Darius, begged him off, promising that she would inflict a greater punishment upon him than he would, for she would constrain him to sail round Libya, until, sailing round, he should reach the Arabian Gulf. Xerxes having agreed on these terms, Sataspes went into Egypt, and having taken a ship and men from thence, sailed through the pillars of Hercules; and having sailed through, and doubled the cape of Libya, whose name is Solois, he steered to the southward; but after traversing a vast extent of sea in many months, when he found that he had still more to pass, he turned back and sailed away for Egypt. From thence going to king Xerxes, he told him that in the most distant part he sailed past a nation of little men, who wore garments made of palm leaves, who, whenever they drew to shore, left their cities and flew to the mountains; that his men, when they entered their country, did them no injury, but only took some cattle from them. Of his not sailing completely round Libya, this he said was the cause: that his ship could not proceed any farther, but was stopped. Xerxes, however, being persuaded that he did not speak the truth, as he had not accomplished the task imposed upon him, impaled him, inflicting the original sentence. A eunuch of this Sataspes, as soon as he heard of his master's death, ran away to Samos with great wealth, which a Samian detained: though I know his name, I purposely conceal it.

44. A great part of Asia was explored under the direction of Darius. He, being desirous to know in what part the Indus, which is the second river that produces crocodiles, discharges itself into the sea, sent in ships both others on whom he could rely to make a true report, and also Scylax of Caryanda. They accordingly, setting out from the city of Caspatyrus and the country of Pactyice, sailed down the river toward the east and sunrise to the sea; then sailing on the sea westward, they arrived in the thirtieth month at that place where the king of Egypt dispatched the Phœnicians, whom I before mentioned, to sail round Libya. After these persons had sailed round, Darius

subdued the Indians and frequented this sea. Thus the other parts of Asia, except toward the rising sun, are found to exhibit things similar to Libya.

45. Whether Europe is surrounded by water either toward the east or toward the north, has not been fully discovered by any man; but in length it is known to extend beyond both *the other continents.* Nor can I conjecture for what reason three different names have been given to the earth, which is but one, and those derived from the names of women; nor why the Egyptian river Nile and the Colchian Phasis have been assigned as boundaries to it (some say, the Mæotian river Tanais and the Cimmerian Porthmeia); nor can I learn the names of those who made this division, nor from whence they derived the appellations. Libya is said by most of the Greeks to take its name from a native woman of the name of Libya, and Asia from the wife of Prometheus; but the Lydians claim this name, saying that Asia was so called after Asius, son of Cotys, son of Manes, and not after Asia, the wife of Prometheus, from whom also a tribe in Sardis is called the Asian tribe. Whether Europe, then, is surrounded by water, is known by no man; nor is it clear whence it received this name, nor who gave it, unless we will say that the region received the name from the Tyrian Europa, but was before without a name, like the others; yet she evidently belonged to Asia, and never came into that country which is now called Europe by the Grecians, but only passed from Phœnicia to Crete, and from Crete to Lycia. Thus much may suffice for this subject, for we shall adopt the names in common use.

46. The Euxine Sea, to which Darius led an army of all countries, except the Scythians, exhibits the most ignorant nations; for we are unable to mention any one nation of those on this side the Pontus that has any pretensions to intelligence; nor have we ever heard of any learned man among them except the Scythian nation and Anacharsis. By the Scythian nation one the most important of human devices has been contrived more wisely than by any others whom we know; their other customs, however, I do not admire. This most important device has been so contrived that no one who attacks them can escape, and that, if they do not choose to be found, no one is able to overtake them; for they who have neither cities nor fortifications, but carry their houses with them, who are

all equestrian archers, living not from the cultivation of the earth, but from cattle, and whose dwellings are wagons—how must not such a people be invincible, and difficult to engage with? 47. This device has been contrived by them, as the country is fit for it, and the rivers aid them; for the country, being level, abounds in herbage and is well watered, and rivers flow through it almost as numerous as the canals in Egypt. Such of them as are celebrated and navigable from the sea I will mention: the Ister, that has five mouths; then the Tyres, the Hypanis, the Borysthenes, the Panticapes, the Hypacyris, the Gerrhus, and the Tanais. These flow as follows:

48. The Ister, which is the greatest of all the rivers we know, flows always with an equal stream both in summer and winter. Flowing the first of those in Scythia from the west, it is on this account the greatest, because other rivers discharge themselves into it. The following are those that make it great: there are five that flow through Scythia; one which the Scythians call Porata, but the Grecians Pyretos; another the Tiarantus, then the Aratus, the Naparis, and the Ordessus. The first-mentioned of these rivers is large, and, flowing toward the east, communicates its water with the Ister; that mentioned second, the Tiarantus, is more to the west and less; the Aratus, the Naparis, and Ordessus, passing between these, fall likewise into the Ister. These indigenous Scythian rivers assist in filling it. 49. The river Maris, flowing from the Agathyrsi, mingles with the Ister. From the summits of Mount Hæmus three other large rivers, flowing toward the north, empty themselves into it, the Atlas, the Auras, and the Tibisis. The Athres, the Noes, and the Atarnes, flowing through Thrace and the Thracian Crobyzi, discharge themselves into the Ister; and from the Pæonians and Mount Rhodope, the river Scios, dividing the Hæmus in the middle, discharges itself into it; and the river Angrus, flowing from the Illyrians toward the north, empties itself into the Triballic plain and into the river Brongus, and the Brongus into the Ister; thus the Ister receives both these, which are considerable. From the country above Umbrici, the river Carpis and another river, Alpis, flowing toward the north, also discharge themselves into it; for the Ister flows through all Europe, beginning from the Celts, who, next to the Cynetæ,[8] inhabit the

[8] See B. II. chap. 33.

remotest parts of Europe toward the west, and flowing through all Europe, enters the borders of Scythia. 50. By these, then, that have been mentioned, and many other rivers that contribute their waters, the Ister becomes the greatest of all rivers; for, if we compare one stream with another, the Nile surpasses in quantity; for into this no river or fountain discharging itself contributes to its increase. But the Ister always flows equal in summer and in winter, for the following reason, as I think: during the winter it is about as large as it usually is, and perhaps a little larger; for this country is very little moistened by rain during the winter, but is entirely covered with snow. In the summer, the snow that fell in the winter in vast quantities, dissolving on all sides, flows into the Ister; and this snow flowing into it assists in filling it, and frequent and violent rains besides; for it rains much in summer. By how much, therefore, the sun draws up to himself more water in summer than in winter, by so much the waters mingled with the Ister are greater in summer than in winter; and these things, therefore, being opposed, an equilibrium results, so that it is always found to be equal.

51. One of the rivers, then, of the Scythians is the Ister; after this is the Tyres, which proceeds from the north, and begins flowing from a vast lake, which separates Scythia and Neuris. At its mouth are settled Grecians, who are called Tyritæ. 52. The third river, the Hypanis, proceeds from Scythia, and flows from a vast lake, around which wild white horses graze. This lake is rightly called the mother of the Hypanis. The river Hypanis, then, rising from this, is small and still sweet for a five days' voyage, but from thence, for a four days' voyage to the sea, it is exceedingly bitter; for a bitter fountain discharges itself into it, which is so very bitter, though small in size, that it taints the Hypanis, which is a considerable river among small ones. This fountain is on the borders of the territory of the Scythian husbandmen and the Alazones; the name of the fountain, and of the district whence it flows, is, in the Scythian language, Exampæus, but in the language of the Greeks, "The Sacred Ways." The Tyres and Hypanis contract their boundaries in the country of the Alazones; but after that, each turning away, flows on widening the intermediate space.

53. The fourth is the river Borysthenes, which is the

largest of these after the Ister, and, in my opinion, the most productive, not only of the Scythian rivers, but of all others, except the Egyptian Nile, for to this it is impossible to compare any other river, but of the rest the Borysthenes is the most productive. It affords the most excellent and valuable pasture for cattle, and fish of the highest excellence and in great quantities; it is most sweet to drink; it flows pure in the midst of turbid rivers; the sown land near it is of the best quality, and the herbage where the land is not sown is very tall; at its mouth abundance of salt is crystallized spontaneously; and it produces large whales, without any spinal bones, which they call Antacæi, fit for salting, and many other things that deserve admiration. As far as the country of Gerrhus, a voyage of forty days, *this river* is known to flow from the north, but above that, through what people it flows no one is able to tell; but it evidently flows through a desert to the country of the agricultural Scythians; for these Scythians dwell near it for the space of a ten days' voyage. Of this river only and of the Nile I am unable to describe the sources, and I think that no Greek can do so. The Borysthenes continues flowing near the sea, and the Hypanis mingles with it, discharging itself into the same morass. The space between these rivers, which is a projecting piece of land, is called the promontory of Hippoleon, and in it a temple of Ceres is built; beyond the temple, on the Hypanis, the Borysthenitæ are settled. Thus much concerning these rivers.

54. After these is the fifth river, the name of which is the Panticapes; this also flows from the north and out of a lake, and between this and the Borysthenes dwell the agricultural Scythians; it discharges itself into Hylæa, and having passed through that region, mingles with the Borysthenes. 55. The Hypacyris is the sixth river, which proceeds from a lake, and flowing through the middle of the Scythian nomades, discharges itself near the city Carcinitis, skirting Hylæa on the right, and that which is called the Course of Achilles. 56. The seventh river, the Gerrhus, is separated from the Borysthenes near the place at which the Borysthenes is first known. It is separated, then, from this very spot, and has the same name as the country, Gerrhus; and flowing toward the sea, it divides the territory of the Nomadic and the Royal Scy-

thians, and discharges itself into the Hypacyris. 57. The eighth river is the Tanais, which flows originally from a vast lake, and discharges itself into a still larger lake, called Mæotis, which divides the Royal Scythians and the Sauromatæ. Into this river Tanais runs another river, the name of which is Hyrgis. 58. Thus the Scythians are provided with these celebrated rivers. The grass that grows in Scythia is the most productive of bile for cattle of any with which we are acquainted, and when the cattle are opened one may infer that such is the case.

59. Thus the greatest commodities are furnished them in abundance. Their other customs are established as follows. They propitiate the following gods only: Vesta, most of all; then Jupiter, deeming the Earth to be the wife of Jupiter; after these, Apollo, and Venus Urania, and Hercules, and Mars. All the Scythians acknowledge these, but those who are called Royal Scythians, sacrifice also to Neptune. Vesta, in the Scythian language, is named Tabiti; Jupiter is, in my opinion, very rightly called Papæus; the Earth, Apia; Apollo, Œtosyrus; Venus Urania, Artimpasa; and Neptune, Thamimasadas. They are not accustomed to erect images, altars, and temples, except to Mars; to him they are accustomed. 60. The same mode of sacrificing is adopted by all, with respect to all kinds of victims alike, being as follows: the victim itself stands with its fore feet tied together; he who sacrifices, standing behind the beast, having drawn the extremity of the cord, throws it down, and as the victim falls he invokes the god to whom he is sacrificing; then he throws a halter round its neck, and having put in a stick, he twists it round and strangles it, without kindling any fire, or performing any preparatory ceremonies, or making any libation, but having strangled and flayed it, he applies himself to cook it. 61. As the Scythian country is wholly destitute of wood, they have invented the following method of cooking flesh. When they have flayed the victims, they strip the flesh from the bones, then they put it into caldrons made in the country, if they happen to have any, which very much resemble Lesbian bowls, except that they are much larger; having put it into these, they cook it by burning underneath the bones of the victims. If they have no caldron at hand, they put all the flesh into the paunches of the victims, and having poured in

water, burn the bones underneath; they burn very well, and the paunches easily contain the flesh stripped from the bones; thus the ox cooks himself, and all other victims each cooks itself. When the flesh is cooked, he that sacrifices, offering the first-fruits of the flesh and entrails, throws it before him. They sacrifice both other cattle, and chiefly horses.

62. In this manner, then, and these victims, they sacrifice to the other gods; but to Mars as follows. In each district, in the place where the magistrates assemble, is erected a structure sacred to Mars, of the following kind. Bundles of fagots are heaped up to the length and breadth of three stades, but less in height; on the top of this a square platform is formed; and three of the sides are perpendicular, but on the fourth it is accessible. Every year they heap on it one hundred and fifty wagon-loads of fagots, for it is continually sinking by reason of the weather. On this heap an old iron cimeter is placed by each tribe, and this is the image of Mars; and to this cimeter they bring yearly sacrifices of cattle and horses; and to these *cimeters* they offer more sacrifices than to the rest of the gods. Whatever enemies they take alive, of these they sacrifice one in a hundred, not in the same manner as they do the cattle, but in a different manner; for after they have poured a libation of wine on their heads, they cut the throats of the men over a bowl; then, having carried *the bowl* on the heap of fagots, they pour the blood over the cimeter. This, then, they carry up; but below, at the sacred precinct, they do as follows: having cut off all the right shoulders of the men that have been killed, with the arms, they throw them into the air; and then, having finished the rest of the sacrificial rites, they depart; but the arm lies wherever it has fallen, and the body apart. 63. Such, then, are the sacrifices instituted among them. Swine they never use, nor suffer them to be reared in their country at all.

64. Their military affairs are ordered as follows. When a Scythian overthrows his first enemy, he drinks his blood; and presents the king with the heads of the enemies he has killed in battle; for if he brings a head, he shares the booty that they take, but not if he does not bring one. He skins it in the following manner. Having made a circular incision round the ears and taking hold of the skin, he shakes it from

the skull; then, having scraped off the flesh with the rib of an ox, he softens the skin with his hands, and having made it supple, he uses it as a napkin: each man hangs it on the bridle of the horse which he rides, and prides himself on it, for whoever has the greatest number of these skin napkins is accounted the most valiant man. Many of them make cloaks of these skins to throw over themselves, sewing them together like shepherd's coats; and many, having flayed the right hands of their enemies that are dead, together with the nails, make coverings for their quivers: the skin of a man, which is both thick and shining, surpasses almost all other skins in the brightness of its white. Many, having flayed men whole, and stretched the skin on wood, carry it about on horseback. Such usages are received among them. 65. The heads themselves, not indeed of all, but of their greatest enemies, they treat as follows: each, having sawn off all below the eye-brows, cleanses it, and if the man is poor, he covers only the outside with leather, and so uses it; but if he is rich, he covers it indeed with leather, and, having gilded the inside, he so uses it for a drinking-cup. And they do this to their relatives if they are at variance, and one prevails over another in the presence of the king. When strangers of consideration come to him, he produces these heads, and relates how, though they were his relatives, they made war against him, and he overcame them, considering this a proof of bravery. 66. Once in every year, the governor of a district, each in his own district, mingles a bowl of wine, from which those Scythians drink by whom enemies have been captured; but they who have not achieved this do not taste of this wine, but sit at a distance in dishonor; this is accounted the greatest disgrace: such of them as have killed very many men, having two cups at once, drink them together.

67. Soothsayers among the Scythians are numerous, who divine by the help of a number of willow rods, in the following manner. When they have brought with them large bundles of twigs, they lay them on the ground and untie them; and, having placed each rod apart, they utter their predictions; and while they are pronouncing them, they gather up the rods again, and put them together again one by one. This is their national mode of divination. But the Enarees,[9] or An-

[9] See Book I. chap. 105.

drogyni, say that Venus gave them the power of divining. They divine by means of the bark of a linden-tree: when a man has split the linden-tree in three pieces, twisting it round his own fingers, and then untwisting it, he utters a response. 68. When the king of the Scythians is sick, he sends for three of the most famous of these prophets, who prophesy in the manner above mentioned; and they generally say as follows, that such or such a citizen has sworn falsely by the royal hearth, mentioning the name of the citizen of whom they speak; for it is a custom with the Scythians in general to swear by the royal hearth when they would use the most solemn oath. The person who they say has sworn falsely is immediately seized and brought forward, and when he is come, the prophets charge him with being clearly proved by their prophetic art to have sworn falsely by the royal hearth, and for this reason the king is ill. He denies it, affirming that he has not sworn falsely, and complains bitterly. On his denial, the king sends for twice as many more prophets; and if they also, examining into the prophetic art, condemn him with having sworn falsely, they straightway cut off his head, and the first prophets divide his property between them; but if the prophets who came last acquit him, other prophets are called in, and others after them. If, then, the greater number acquit the man, it is decreed that the first prophets shall be put to death. 69. They accordingly put them to death in the following manner: when they have filled a wagon with fagots, and have yoked oxen to it, having tied the feet of the prophets and bound their hands behind them, and having gagged them, they inclose them in the midst of the fagots; then having set fire to them, they terrify the oxen and let them go. Many oxen, therefore, are burned with the prophets, and many escape very much scorched, when the pole has been burned asunder. In this manner, and for other reasons, they burn the prophets, calling them false prophets. The king does not spare the children of those whom he puts to death, but kills all the males, and does not hurt the females. 70. The Scythians make solemn contracts in the following manner, with whomsoever they make them. Having poured wine into a large earthen vessel, they mingle with it blood taken from those who are entering into covenant, having struck with an awl or cut with a knife a small part of the body; then, having dipped a cimeter, some arrows, a hatchet, and a javelin in the vessel, when they have done this, they make many solemn prayers, and then both those who make the contract, and the most considerable of their attendants, drink up *the mixture.*

71. The sepulchres of the kings are in the country of the Gerrhi, as far as which the Borysthenes is navigable. There, when their king dies, they dig a large square hole in the ground; and having prepared this, they take up the corpse, having the body covered with wax, the belly opened and cleaned, filled with bruised cypress, incense, and parsley and anise-seed, and then sewn up again, and carry it in a chariot to another nation: those who receive the corpse brought to them do the same as the Royal Scythians; they cut off part off their ear, shave off their hair, wound themselves on the arms, lacerate their forehead and nose, and drive arrows through their left hand. Thence they carry the corpse of the king to another nation whom they govern, and those to whom they first came accompany them. When they have carried the corpse round all the provinces, they arrive among the Gerrhi, who are the most remote of the nations they rule over, and at the sepulchres. Then, when they have placed the corpse in the grave on a bed of leaves, having fixed spears on each side of the dead body, they lay pieces of wood over it, and cover it over with mats. In the remaining space of the grave they bury one of the king's concubines, having strangled her, and his cup-bearer, a cook, a groom, a page, a courier, and horses, and firstlings of every thing else, and golden goblets: they make no use of silver or brass. Having done this, they all heap up a large mound, striving and vieing with each other to make it as large as possible. 72. When a year has elapsed, they then do as follows: having taken the most fitting of his remaining servants—they are all native Scythians, for they serve him whomsoever the king may order, and they have no servants bought with money—when, therefore, they have strangled fifty of these servants, and fifty of the finest horses, having taken out their bowels and cleansed them, they fill them with chaff, and sew them up again. Then, having placed the half of a wheel, with its concave side uppermost, on two pieces of wood, and the other half on two other pieces of wood, and having fixed many of these in the same manner, then having thrust thick pieces of

wood through the horses lengthwise up to the neck, they mount them on the half wheels; and of these the foremost part of the half wheels supports the shoulders of the horses, and the hinder part supports the belly near the thighs, but the legs on both sides are suspended in the air; then, having put bridles and bits on the horses, they stretch them in front, and fasten them to a stake; they then mount upon a horse each, one of the fifty young men that have been strangled, mounting them in the following manner: when they have driven a straight piece of wood along the spine as far as the neck, but a part of this wood projects from the bottom, they fix it into a hole bored in the other piece of wood that passes through the horse. Having placed such horsemen round the monument, they depart.

73. Thus they bury their kings. But the other Scythians, when they die, their nearest relations carry about among their friends, laid in chariots; and of these each one receives and entertains the attendants, and sets the same things before the dead body as before the rest. In this manner private persons are carried about for forty days, and then buried. The Scythians, having buried them, purify themselves in the following manner: having wiped and thoroughly washed their heads, they do thus with regard to the body: when they have set up three pieces of wood leaning against each other, they extend around them woolen cloths; and having joined them together as closely as possible, they throw red-hot stones into a vessel placed in the middle of the pieces of wood and the cloths. 74. They have a sort of hemp growing in this country, very like flax, except in thickness and height; in this respect the hemp is far superior: it grows both spontaneously and from cultivation, and from it the Thracians make garments very like linen; nor would any one who is not well skilled in such matters distinguish whether they are made of flax or hemp; but a person who has never seen this hemp would think the garment was made of flax. 75. When, therefore, the Scythians have taken some seed of this hemp, they creep under the cloths, and then put the seed on the red-hot stones; but this being put on smokes, and produces such a steam that no Grecian vapor-bath would surpass it. The Scythians, transported with the vapor, shout aloud;[1] and this serves them instead of

[1] See Book I. chap. 202.

washing, for they never bathe the body in water. Their women, pouring on water, pound on a rough stone *pieces of* cypress, cedar, and incense-tree; and then this pounded matter, when it is thick, they smear over the whole body and face; and this at the same time gives them an agreeable odor, and when they take off the cataplasm on the following day they become clean and shining.

76. They studiously avoid the use of foreign customs; not only, therefore, *will they* not *adopt* those of each other, but, least of all, Grecian usages,[2] as the example of Anacharsis, and afterward of Scylas, sufficiently demonstrated; for, in the first place, Anacharsis, having visited many countries, and having displayed great wisdom during his progress, was returning to the abodes of the Scythians, and sailing through the Hellespont toward Cyzicus, and as he found the Cyzicenians celebrating a festival to the mother of the gods with great magnificence, Anacharsis made a vow to the goddess, that if he should return safe and sound to his own country, he would sacrifice in the same manner as he saw the inhabitants of Cyzicus doing, and would also institute a vigil. Accordingly, when he arrived in Scythia, he returned into the country called Hylæa; it is near the Course of Achilles, and is full of trees of all kinds; to this Anacharsis having retired, performed all the rites to the goddess, holding a timbrel in his hand, and fastening images about his person; but one of the Scythians, having observed him doing this, gave information to the king, Saulius; but he, having come in person, when he saw Anacharsis thus employed, shot at him with an arrow, and killed him; and now, if any one speaks about Anacharsis, the Scythians say they do not know him, because he traveled into Greece and adopted foreign customs. However, I heard from Timnes, the guardian of Ariapithes, that Anacharsis was paternal uncle to Idanthyrsus, king of the Scythians, and that he was son of Gnurus, son of Lycus, son of Spargapithes; if, then, Anacharsis was of this family, let him know he was killed by his own brother; for Idanthyrsus was son of Saulius,

[2] The simplest method of rendering this obscure passage appears to me to be that suggested by Letronne, as quoted by Baehr, according to which the usual signification of the word *ἥκιστα* is retained without any violence to the construction. It is as follows: *μή τι γε ὦν ἀλλήλων (νομαίοισι χρέωνται), Ἑλληνικοῖσι δὲ καὶ ἥκιστα.*

and it was Saulius who killed Anacharsis. 77. However, I have heard another story told by the Peloponnesians, that Anacharsis, being sent abroad by the king of the Scythians, became a disciple of the Grecians; and on his return home he said to the king who sent him abroad that all the Greeks were employed in acquiring all kinds of knowledge except the Lacedæmonians, but that they only were able to give and receive a reason with prudence. But this story is told in sport by the Greeks themselves. The man, then, was killed in the manner before mentioned. Thus, therefore, he fared because of foreign customs and intercourse with the Grecians.

78. Many years afterward, Scylas, son of Ariapithes, met with a similar fate; for Ariapithes, king of the Scythians, had, among other children, Scylas; he was born of an Istrian woman, who did not in any way belong to the country. His mother taught him the Grecian language and letters; afterward, in course of time, Ariapithes met his death by treachery at the hands of Spargapithes, king of the Agathyrsi, and Scylas succeeded to the kingdom, and his father's wife, whose name was Opœa; this Opœa was a native, by whom Ariapithes had a son, Oricus. Scylas, though reigning over the Scythians, was by no means pleased with the Scythian mode of life, but was much more inclined to the Grecian manners, on account of the education he had received; he therefore acted thus. Whenever he led the Scythian army to the city of the Borysthenitæ (now these Borysthenitæ say they are Milesians), as soon as Scylas reached them, he used to leave his army in the suburbs, and, when he himself had gone within the walls, and had closed the gates, having laid aside his Scythian dress, he used to assume the Grecian habit, and in this dress he walked in public, unattended by guards or any one else; and they kept watch at the gates, that no Scythian might see him wearing this dress; and in other respects he adopted the Grecian mode of living, and performed sacrifices to the gods according to the rites of the Grecians. When he had staid a month or more, he used to depart, resuming the Scythian habit. This he used frequently to do; he also built a palace in the Borysthenes, and married a native woman to inhabit it. 79. Since, however, it was fated that misfortune should befall him, it happened on this occasion. He was very desirous to be initiated in the mysteries of Bacchus;

and as he was just about to commence the sacred rites, a very great prodigy occurred. He had in the city of the Borysthenitæ a large and magnificent mansion,[3] of which I have just now made mention; round it were placed sphinxes and griffins of white marble; on this the god hurled a bolt, and it was entirely burned down; Scylas, nevertheless, accomplished his initiation. Now the Scythians reproach the Grecians on account of their Bacchic ceremonies, for they say it is not reasonable to discover such a god as this, who drives men to madness. When Scylas had been initiated in the Bacchic mysteries, one of the Borysthenitæ carried the information to the Scythians, saying, "You Scythians laugh at us because we celebrate Bacchic rites, and the god takes possession of us. Now this same deity has taken possession of your king, and he celebrates the rites of Bacchus, and is maddened by the god; but if you disbelieve me, follow, and I will show you." The chief men of the Scythians followed him; and the Borysthenite, conducting them in, placed them secretly on a tower; but when Scylas went past with a thyasus, and the Scythians saw him acting the bacchanal, they regarded it as a very great calamity; and, having returned, they acquainted all the army with what they had seen. 80. After this, when Scylas returned to his own home, the Scythians, having set up his brother Octamasades, born of the daughter of Tereus, revolted from Scylas; but he, being informed of what was being done against him, and the reason for which it was done, fled to Thrace. Octamasades, being informed of this, marched against Thrace, but when he arrived on the Ister, the Thracians advanced to meet him. As they were about to engage, Sitalces sent to Octamasades saying as follows: "Why need we try each other's strength? You are the son of my sister, and have with you my brother. Do you restore him to me, and I will deliver up Scylas to you, and so neither you nor I shall expose our army to peril." Sitalces sent this message to him by a herald; for there was with Octamasades a brother of Sitalces, who had fled from the latter. Octamasades acceded to this proposal, and having surrendered his maternal uncle to Sitalces, received his brother Scylas in exchange. Now Sitalces, having got his brother in his power, drew off

[3] Literally, "a circumference of a large and magnificent mansion."

his forces; but Octamasades beheaded Scylas on the same spot. Thus the Scythians maintain their own customs, and impose such punishments on those who introduce foreign usages.

81. I have never been able to learn with accuracy the amount of the population of the Scythians, but I heard different accounts concerning the number; for some pretend that they are exceedingly numerous, and others that there are very few real Scythians: thus much, however, they exposed to my sight. There is a spot between the river Borysthenes and the Hypanis, called Exampæus,[4] which I mentioned a little before, saying that there was in it a fountain of bitter water, from which the water flowing made the Hypanis unfit to be drunk. In this spot lies a brass caldron, in size six times as large as the bowl at the mouth of the Pontus, which Pausanias, son of Cleombrotus, dedicated. For the benefit of any one who has never seen this, I will here describe it: the brass caldron among the Scythians easily contains six hundred amphoræ; and this Scythian vessel is six fingers in thickness. Now the inhabitants say it was made from the points of arrows, for that their king, whose name was Ariantus, wishing to know the population of the Scythians, commanded all the Scythians to bring him each severally one point of an arrow, and he threatened death on whosoever should fail to bring it. Accordingly, a vast number of arrow points were brought, and he resolved to leave a monument made from them; he therefore made this brass bowl, and dedicated it at Exampæus. This I heard concerning the population of the Scythians. 82. Their country has nothing wonderful, except the rivers, which are very large and very many in number; but what it affords also worthy of admiration, besides the rivers and the extent of the plains, shall be mentioned: they show the print of the foot of Hercules upon a rock: it resembles the footstep of a man, is two cubits in length, near the river Tyras. Such, then, is this; but I will now return to the subject I at first set out to relate.

83. While Darius was making preparations against the Scythians, and sending messengers to command some to contribute land forces, and others a fleet, and others to bridge over the Thracian Bosphorus, Artabanus, the son of Hystaspes, and brother of Darius, entreated him on no account to make

[4] See chap. 52.

an expedition against the Scythians, representing the poverty of Scythia; but when he found that although he gave him good counsel he could not persuade him, he desisted: Darius therefore, when every thing was prepared, marched his army from Susa. 84. At that time Œobazus, a Persian, who had three sons all serving in the army, besought Darius that one might be left at home for him. The king answered him, as a friend, and one who made a moderate request, that he would leave him all his sons; he therefore was exceedingly delighted, hoping that his sons would be discharged from the army. But Darius commanded the proper officers to put all the sons of Œobazus to death; and they, being slain, were left on the spot.

85. When Darius, marching from Susa, reached Chalcedon on the Bosphorus, where a bridge was already laid across, from thence going on board a ship he sailed to those called the Cyanean islands, which the Grecians say formerly floated. There, sitting in the temple, he took a view of the Euxine Sea, which is worthy of admiration; for of all seas it is by nature the most wonderful: its length is eleven thousand one hundred stades, and its width, in the widest part, three thousand three hundred stades. The mouth of this sea is four stades in width, and the length of the mouth, *that is*, the neck, which is called the Bosphorus, where the bridge was laid across, amounts to about a hundred and twenty stades; and the Bosphorus extends to the Propontis. The Propontis, which is five hundred stades in breadth, and one thousand four hundred in length, discharges itself into the Hellespont, which in the narrowest part is seven stades, and in length four hundred; the Hellespont falls into an expanse of the sea, which is called the Ægean. 86. These seas have been measured as follows: a ship commonly makes in a long day about seventy thousand orgyæ, and in a night about sixty thousand. Now from the mouth to the Phasis (for this is the greatest length of the Pontus) is a voyage of nine days and eight nights; these make one million one hundred and ten thousand orgyæ, and these orgyæ are equal to eleven thousand one hundred stades. From Sindica to Themiscyra, on the river Thermodon (for here is the broadest part of the Pontus) is a voyage of three days and two nights; these make three hundred and thirty thousand orgyæ, or three thousand three hundred stades. The Pontus, therefore, and the Bosphorus, and the Hellespont, have been thus measured

by me, and are such as I have described. Moreover, this Pontus possesses a lake that discharges itself into it, not much less than itself. It is called Mæotis, and the mother of the Pontus.

87. Darius, when he had viewed the Pontus, sailed back to the bridge, of which Mandrocles, a Samian, was the architect; and having also viewed the Bosphorus, he erected two columns of white marble on the shore, engraving on one in Assyrian characters, and on the other in Grecian, *the names of* all the nations he had in his army, and he had some from all whom he ruled over; of these, besides the navy, seven hundred thousand were reckoned, including cavalry; and six hundred ships were assembled. Now these columns the Byzantians some time afterward removed into their city, and used in building the altar of the Orthosian Diana, except one stone; this was left near the temple of Bacchus in Byzantium, covered with Assyrian letters. The spot of the Bosphorus which king Darius caused the bridge to be laid over was, as I conjecture, midway between Byzantium and the temple at the mouth.

88. Darius, after this, being pleased with the bridge, presented its architect, Mandrocles the Samian, with ten of every thing. From these, then, Mandrocles, having painted a picture of the whole junction of the Bosphorus, with king Darius seated on a throne, and his army crossing over; having painted this, he dedicated it as first-fruits in the temple of Juno, with this inscription: "Mandrocles, having thrown a bridge across the fishy Bosphorus, dedicated to Juno a memorial of the raft; laying up for himself a crown, and for the Samians glory, having completed it to the satisfaction of king Darius." This, then, was the memorial of the man who constructed the bridge.

89. Darius, having rewarded Mandrocles, crossed over into Europe, having commanded the Ionians to sail by the Pontus as far as the river Ister; and when they should have reached the Ister, to throw a bridge over the river, and there wait his arrival; for the Ionians, Æolians, and Hellespontines conducted the naval armament. The fleet accordingly, having sailed through the Cyanian islands, stood direct for the Ister; and having sailed up the river a two days' voyage from the sea, they joined the neck of the river with a bridge, at the point where the several mouths of the river are separated.

But Darius, when he had passed over the Bosphorus by the bridge of boats, marched through Thrace, and having arrived at the sources of the river Tearus, encamped there three days. 90. The Tearus is said by the inhabitants of the country to be the best of all rivers, both for its other healing qualities, and especially for curing the itch in men and horses. Its springs are thirty eight, *flowing* from the same rock, and some of them are cold, others hot. The distance to them is the same from Heræopolis, near Perinthus, and from Apollonia on the Euxine Sea, each a two days' journey. This Tearus empties itself into the river Contadesdus, the Contadesdus into the Agrianes, the Agrianes into the Hebrus, and this last into the sea near the city of Ænus. 91. Darius, then, having reached this river, when he had encamped, was so delighted with the river, that he erected a pillar here also, with the following inscription: THE SPRINGS OF THE TEARUS YIELD THE BEST AND FINEST WATER OF ALL RIVERS; AND A MAN, THE BEST AND FINEST OF ALL MEN, CAME TO THEM, LEADING AN ARMY AGAINST THE SCYTHIANS, DARIUS, SON OF HYSTASPES, KING OF THE PERSIANS, AND OF THE WHOLE CONTINENT. 92. Darius, having set out from thence, came to another river, the name of which is Artiscus, which flows through the Odrysæ. When he arrived at this river, he did as follows: having marked out a certain spot of ground to the army, he commanded every man as he passed by to place a stone on this spot that was marked out; and when the army had executed his order, having left vast heaps of stones there, he continued his march.

93. But before he reached the Ister, he subdued the Getæ first, who think themselves immortal; for the Thracians who occupy Salmydessus, and those who dwell above the cities of Apollonia and Mesambria, who are called Scyrmiadæ and Nypsæi, surrendered themselves to Darius without resistance; but the Getæ, having recourse to obstinate resistance, were soon reduced to slavery, though they are the most valiant and the most just of the Thracians. 94. They think themselves immortal in this manner. They imagine that they themselves do not die, but that the deceased goes to the deity Zalmoxis, and some of them think that he is the same with Gebeleizis. Every fifth year they dispatch one of themselves, taken by lot, to Zalmoxis, with orders to let him know on each occasion what they want. Their mode of sending

him is this. Some of them who are appointed hold three javelins; while others, having taken up the man who is to be sent to Zalmoxis by the hands and feet, swing him round, and throw him into the air, upon the points. If he should die, being transfixed, they think the god is propitious to them; if he should not die, they blame the messenger himself, saying that he is a bad man; and having blamed him, they dispatch another, and they give him his instructions while he is yet alive. These same Thracians, in time of thunder and lightning, let fly their arrows toward heaven, and threaten the god, thinking that there is no other god but their own. 95. But, as I am informed by the Greeks who dwell about the Hellespont and the Pontus, this Zalmoxis was a man, and lived in slavery at Samos; he was slave to Pythagoras, son of Mnesarchus; and after that, having procured his liberty, he acquired great riches, and having acquired them, he returned to his own country; but finding the Thracians lived wretchedly and in a very uncivilized manner, this Zalmoxis, being acquainted with the Ionian way of living, and with manners more polite than those of Thrace, in that he had been familiar with Greeks, and with Pythagoras, who was not the meanest sage in Greece, had a hall built, in which, receiving and entertaining the principal persons of the country, he taught them that neither he nor any of his guests, nor their posterity forever, would die, but would go into a place where they should live eternally, and have every kind of blessing. While he did and said as above described, he, in the mean time, had a subterraneous habitation made, and when the building was completed, he disappeared from among the Thracians; and having gone down to the subterraneous habitation, he abode there three years. But they both regretted him, and lamented him as dead; but in the fourth year he appeared to the Thracians, and thus what Zalmoxis said became credible to them. Thus they say that he acted. 96. For my own part, I neither disbelieve nor entirely believe the account of this person and the subterraneous habitation; but I am of opinion that this Zalmoxis lived many years before Pythagoras. Yet, whether Zalmoxis were a man or a native deity among the Getæ, I take my leave of him. These people, then, who observe such a custom, when they were subdued by the Persians, followed the rest of the army.

97. When Darius and his land forces with him reached the Ister, all crossed over the river, and Darius commanded the Ionians to loose the bridge, and follow him on the continent with the forces from the ships; but, as they were about to loose *the bridge* and execute his orders, Coes, son of Erxandrus, general of the Mitylenians, spoke as follows to Darius, having first inquired whether it would be agreeable to him to hear an opinion from one who wished to give it: "O king, since you are about to invade a country in which no cultivated land will be seen, nor any inhabited city, do you let this bridge remain where it is, leaving these men who constructed it as its guard; and if, having met with the Scythians, we succeed according to our wishes, we have a way to return; but if we should not be able to meet with them, we shall at least have a secure retreat; for I am not at all afraid that we shall be conquered in battle by the Scythians, but rather that, being unable to find them, we may suffer somewhat in our wanderings. Perhaps some one may think I say this for my own sake, that I may remain here; but, O king, I advance the opinion which I think is best for you; nevertheless, I will follow you myself, and would by no means be left behind." Darius was much pleased with the advice, and answered him as follows: "Lesbian friend, when I am safe back in my own palace, fail not to present yourself to me, that I may requite you for good advice with good deeds." 98. Having spoken thus and tied sixty knots in a thong, and having summoned the Ionian commanders to his presence, he addressed them as follows: "Men of Ionia, I have changed my former resolution concerning the bridge; therefore, take this thong and do thus: as soon as you see me march against the Scythians, beginning from that time, untie one of these knots every day; and if I return not within that time, but the days *numbered* by the knots have passed, do you sail away to your own country. Till that time, since I have changed my determination, do you guard the bridge, and apply the utmost care to preserve and secure it; and if you do this, you will oblige me exceedingly." Darius, having spoken thus, hastened forward.

99. Thrace, in the part next the sea, projects before the Scythian territory; and where a bay is formed in this country Scythia begins, and the Ister discharges itself, having its mouth turned toward the east. But, beginning from the Ister,

I now proceed to describe by measurement the part of the Scythian country that is on the sea-coast. Now from the Ister, that is ancient Scythia that lies toward the meridian and the south wind, as far as the city called Carcinitis—next to that, the Tauric nation inhabits the land extending along the same sea, which is a mountainous country, and projects into the Pontus as far as the Chersonesus called Trachea; and it reaches to the sea toward the east; for the two parts of the boundaries of Scythia extend to the sea, one toward the south, and the other toward the east, as is the case with the region of Attica; and the Tauri inhabit parts of Scythia similar to this, just as if any other people instead of the Athenians possessed the promontory of Sunium, which extends more into a point into the sea from the borough of Thoricus to that of Anaphlystus. I mention this, if I may compare small things with great. Such, then, is Taurica. But for any one who has never sailed by that part of Attica, I will explain the matter in another way: it is as if a nation distinct from Japygia, and not the Japygians, beginning from the port of Brundusium, should cut off the country as far as Tarentum, and occupy the promontory. Mentioning these two, I might mention many others, to which Taurica is like. 100. From Taurica, Scythians inhabit the country above the Tauri, and the parts along the eastern sea, and the parts westward of the Cimmerian Bosphorus and the lake Mæotis, as far as the river Tanais, which flows into the farthest recess of that lake. Now from the Ister at the parts above, stretching to the interior, Scythia is shut off first by the Agathyrsi, next by the Neuri, then by the Androphagi, and last by the Melanchlæni. 101. Of Scythia, therefore, which is quadrangular, with two parts reaching to the sea, that which stretches to the interior and that along the coast is in every way equal; for from the Ister to the Borysthenes is a journey of ten days, and from the Borysthenes to the lake Mæotis ten more; from the sea to the interior, as far as the Melanchlæni, who inhabit above the Scythians, is a journey of twenty days. The day's journey has been computed by me at two hundred stades. Thus the extent of Scythia crossways would be four thousand stades, and the direct route leading to the interior would be the same number of stades. Such is the extent of this country.

102. The Scythians, considering with themselves that they were not able alone to repel the army of Darius in a pitched battle, sent messengers to the adjoining nations; and the kings of those nations, having met together, consulted, since so great an army was advancing against them. The kings who met together were those of the Tauri, the Agathyrsi, the Neuri, the Androphagi, the Melanchlæni, the Geloni, the Budini, and the Sauromatæ. 103. Of these, the Tauri observe the following customs: they sacrifice to the virgin all who suffer shipwreck, and any Greeks they meet with driven on their coasts, in the following manner: having performed the preparatory ceremonies, they strike the head with a club; some say they throw the body down from a precipice (for their temple is built on a precipice), and impale the head; but others agree with respect to the head, but say that the body is not thrown from the precipice, but buried in the earth. The Tauri themselves say, that this deity to whom they sacrifice is Iphigenia, daughter of Agamemnon. Enemies whom they subdue they treat as follows: each having cut off a head, carries it home with him, then having fixed it on a long pole, he raises it far above the roof of his house, at all events above the chimney; they say that these are suspended as guards over the whole household. This people live by rapine and war. 104. The Agathyrsi are a most luxurious people, and wear a profusion of gold. They have promiscuous intercourse with women, to the end that they may be brethren one of another, and being all of one family, may not entertain hatred toward each other. In other respects they approach the usages of the Thracians. 105. The Neuri observe Scythian customs. One generation before the expedition of Darius, it happened to them to be driven out of their whole country by serpents; for their country produced many serpents, and a much greater number came down upon them from the deserts above; until, being hard pressed, they abandoned their territory, and settled among the Budini. These men seem to be magicians, for it is said of them by the Scythians and the Greeks settled in Scythia, that once every year each Neurian becomes a wolf for a few days, and then is restored again to the same state. Though they affirm this, however, they do not persuade me; they affirm it nevertheless, and support their assertion with an oath. 106. The Androphagi have the most savage cus-

toms of all men; they pay no regard to justice, nor make use of any established law. They are nomades, and wear a dress like the Scythian; *they speak* a peculiar language; and of those nations, are the only people that eat human flesh. 107. The Melanchlæni all wear black garments, from which circumstance they take their name. These follow Scythian usages. 108. The Budini, who are a great and populous nation, *paint* their whole bodies with a deep blue and red. There is in their country a city built of wood; its name is Gelonus; each side of the wall is thirty stades in length; it is lofty, and made entirely of wood. Their houses, also, and their temples are of wood; for there are there temples of the Grecian gods, adorned after the Grecian manner, with images, altars, and shrines of wood. They celebrate the triennial festivals of Bacchus, and perform the bacchanalian ceremonies; for the Geloni were originally Grecians, but being expelled from the trading ports, settled among the Budini: and they use a language partly Scythian and partly Grecian. 109. The Budini, however, do not use the same language as the Geloni, nor the same mode of living; for the Budini, being indigenous, are nomades, and are the only people of those parts who eat vermin; whereas the Geloni are tillers of the soil, feed upon corn, cultivate gardens, and are not at all like the Budini in form or complexion. By the Greeks, however, the Budini are called Geloni, though erroneously so called. Their country is thickly covered with trees of all kinds, and in the thickest wood is a spacious and large lake, and a morass, and reeds around it: in this, otters are taken, and beavers, and other square-faced animals: their skins are sewn as borders to cloaks, and their testicles are useful for the cure of diseases of the womb.

110. Concerning the Sauromatæ, the following account is given. When the Grecians had fought with the Amazons (the Scythians call the Amazons *Aiorpata*, and this name in the Grecian language means manslayers, for they call *Aior* a man, and *Pata* to kill), the story goes that the Greeks, having been victorious in the battle at the Thermodon, sailed away, taking with them in three ships as many Amazons as they had been able to take alive; but the Amazons, attacking them out at sea, cut the men to pieces. However, as they had no knowledge of navigation, nor any skill in the use of the rud-

der, sails, or oars, when they had cut the men to pieces, they were carried by the waves and wind, and arrived at Cremni, on the lake Mæotis; but Cremni belongs to the territory of the free Scythians. Here the Amazons, landing from the vessels, marched to the inhabited parts and seized the first herd of horses they happened to fall in with, and mounting on them, plundered the lands of the Scythians. 111. The Scythians knew not what to make of the matter; for they were not acquainted either with their language, dress, or nation, but wondered from whence they came. They conjectured that they were men of the same stature, and therefore gave them battle; but after the battle the Scythians got possession of the dead, and so discovered that they were women. On deliberation, therefore, they resolved on no account to kill them any more, but to send out to them the youngest of their own party, guessing a number equal to theirs; these were to encamp near them, and do the same as they did; should the Amazons pursue them, they were not to fight, but fly; and when they halted, were to come and encamp near them. The Scythians resolved on this out of a desire to have children by these women. 112. The young men, being dispatched, did as they were ordered. When the Amazons found that they had not come to hurt them, they let them alone, and they drew one camp nearer to the other every day. The youths, as well as the Amazons, had nothing except their arms and horses, but obtained their subsistence in the same way that the Amazons did, by hunting and pillage. 113. The Amazons, about midday, were wont to do as follows: they separated themselves into parties of one and two, at a distance from each other, being dispersed for the purpose of easing themselves. The Scythians, observing this, did the same; and one of them drew near one of the Amazons who was alone; and she did not repel him, but suffered him to enjoy her person. She could not speak to him, because they did not understand each other, but she made signs to him by her hand to come the next day to the same place, and to bring another with him, signifying that they should be two, and she would bring another with her. When the youth departed, he related this to the rest, and on the next day he himself went to the place, and took another with him, and found the Amazon with a companion waiting for him. The rest of the youths, when they heard this, conciliated the rest of the Amazons. 114. Afterward, having joined their camps, they lived together, each having for his wife the person he first attached himself to. The men were not able to learn the language of the women, but the women soon attained that of the men. When, therefore, they understood one another, the men spoke to the Amazons as follows: "We have parents and possessions; let us, then, no longer lead this kind of life, but let us return to the bulk of our people and live with them; we will have you as our wives, and no others." To this they answered: "We never could live with the women of your country, because we have not the same customs with them. We shoot with the bow, throw the javelin, and ride on horseback, and have never learned the employments of women. But your women do none of the things we have mentioned, but are engaged in women's employments, remaining in their wagons, and do not go out to hunt, or any where else; we could not, therefore, consort with them. If, then, you desire to have us for your wives, and to prove yourselves honest men, go to your parents, claim your share of their property, then return, and let us live by ourselves." 115. The youths yielded, and acted accordingly; but when they came back to the Amazons, having received what fell to their share of the possessions, the women spoke to them as follows: "Alarm and fear come upon us *when we consider* that we must live in this country; in the first place, because we have deprived you of your parents; and in the next, have committed great depredations in your territory. Since, therefore, you think us worthy to be your wives, do thus with us: come, let us leave this country, and, having crossed the river Tanais, let us settle there." 116. The youths consented to this also; accordingly, having crossed the Tanais, they advanced a journey of three days eastward from the Tanais, and three from the lake Mæotis northward, and, having reached the country in which they are now settled, they took up their abode there. From that time the wives of the Sauromatæ retain their ancient mode of living, both going out on horseback to hunt with their husbands and without their husbands, and joining in war, and wearing the same dress as the men. 117. The Sauromatæ use the Scythian language, speaking it corruptly from the first, since the Amazons never learned it correctly. Their rules respecting marriage are thus settled; no virgin is permitted to marry until she has killed an enemy; some of them, therefore, die of old age without being married, not being able to satisfy the law.

118. The messengers of the Scythians, therefore, coming to the assembled kings of the nations above mentioned, informed them that the Persian, when he had subdued all the nations on the other continent, had constructed a bridge over the neck of the Bosphorus, and crossed over to this continent; and, having crossed over and subdued the Thracians, he was building a bridge over the river Ister, designing to make all these regions also subject to him: "Do you, therefore, on no account, sit aloof, and suffer us to be destroyed, but with one accord let us oppose the invader. If you will not do this, we, being pressed, shall either abandon the country, or, if we stay, shall submit to terms; for what would be our condition if you refuse to assist us? Nor will it fall more lightly on you on that account; for the Persian is advancing not more against us than against you; nor will he be content to subdue us and abstain from you; and we will give you a strong proof of what we say; for if the Persian had undertaken this expedition against us only, wishing to revenge his former subjection, he would have abstained from all others, and have marched directly against our territories, and would have made it clear to all that he was marching against the Scythians, and not against others. But now, as soon as he crossed over to this continent, he subdued all that laid in his way; and holds in subjection the rest of the Thracians, and more particularly our neighbors, the Getæ." 119. When the Scythians had made this representation, the kings who had come from the several nations consulted together, and their opinions were divided. The Gelonian, Budinian, and Sauromatian, agreeing together, promised to assist the Scythians; but the Agathyrsian, Neurian, Androphagian, and the Melanchlænian and Taurian princes gave this answer to the Scythians: "If you, who make the request that you now do, had not been the first to injure the Persians and begin war, you would have appeared to us to speak rightly, and we, yielding to your wishes, would have acted in concert with you; but, in fact, you have invaded their territory without us, had the mastery of the Persians as long as the god allowed you; and they, when the same god instigates them, repay you like for like. We, how-

ever, neither on that occasion injured these men at all, nor will we now be the first to attempt to injure them. Nevertheless, should he invade our territory also, and become the aggressor, we will not submit to it. But until we see that, we will remain quiet at home, for we think that the Persians are not coming against us, but against those who were the authors of wrong."

120. When the Scythians heard this answer brought back, they determined to fight no battle in the open field, because these allies did not come to their assistance; but to retreat and draw off covertly, and fill up the wells they passed by, and the springs, and destroy the herbage on the ground, having divided their forces into two bodies, and *they resolved* that to one of the divisions, which Scopasis commanded, the Sauromatæ should attach themselves, and that they should retire if the Persian should take that course, retreating direct to the river Tanais, along the lake Mæötis; and when the Persian marched back, they were to follow him and harass his rear. This was one division of the kingdom appointed to pursue its march in the way that .has been described. The two other divisions of the kingdom, the greater one, which Indathyrsus commanded, and the third, which Taxacis ruled over, *were directed* to act in conjunction, and, with the addition of the Geloni and Budini, to keep a day's march before the Persians, and gradually retreat, retiring slowly, and doing as had been determined; and, first of all, they were to withdraw direct toward the territories of those who had renounced their alliance, in order that they might bring the war upon them; so that, though they would not willingly take part in the war against the Persians, they might be compelled to engage in it against their will; afterward they were to return to their own country, and attack the enemy, if, on consultation, it should seem advisable. 121. The Scythians, having come to this determination, went out to meet Darius's army, having sent forward the best of their cavalry as an advanced guard; but the wagons, in which all their children and wives lived, and all the cattle, except so many as were necessary for their subsistence, which they left behind—the rest they sent forward with the wagons, ordering them to march continually toward the north. These, therefore, were carried to a distance.

122. When the advanced guard of the Scythians fell in with the Persians, about three days' march from the Ister, they, having fallen in with them, kept a day's march in advance, and encamped, and destroyed all the produce of the ground; but the Persians, when they saw the Scythian cavalry before them, followed their track, while they continually retired; and then, for they directed their march after one of the divisions, the Persians pursued toward the east and the Tanais; and when they had crossed the river Tanais, the Persians also crossed over and pursued them, until, having passed through the country of the Sauromatæ, they reached that of the Budini. 123. As long as the Persians were marching through the Scythian and Sauromatian regions, they had nothing to ravage, as the country was all barren; but when they entered the territory of the Budini, there meeting with the wooden town, the Budini having abandoned it, and the town being emptied of every thing, they set it on fire. Having done this, they continued to follow in the track of *the enemy*, until, having traversed this region, they reached the desert: this desert is destitute of inhabitants, and is situate above the territory of the Budini, and is a seven days' march in extent. Beyond the desert the Thyssagetæ dwell; and four large rivers, flowing from them through the Mæotians, discharge themselves into the lake called Mæotis; their names are these, Lycus, Oarus, Tanais, and Syrgis. 124. When Darius came to the desert, having ceased his pursuit, he encamped his army on the river Oarus; and having done this, he built eight large forts, equally distant from each other, about sixty stades apart, the ruins of which remain to this day. While he was employed about these, the Scythians who were pursued, having made a circuit of the upper parts, returned into Scythia: these having entirely vanished, when they could no longer be seen, Darius left the forts half finished, and himself wheeling round, marched westward, supposing them to be all the Scythians, and that they had fled to the west.

125. Advancing with his army as quick as possible, when he reached Scythia, he fell in with the two Scythian divisions, and having fallen in with them, he pursued them, but they kept a day's march before him. The Scythians, for Darius did not relax his pursuit, fled, as had been determined,

toward those nations that had refused to assist them, and first they entered the territories of the Melanchlæni; and when the Scythians and the Persians, entering into their country, had put all things into confusion, the Scythians led the way into the country of the Androphagi; and when they had been thrown into confusion, they retreated to Neuris; and when they were thrown into confusion, the Scythians advanced in their flight toward the Agathyrsi; but the Agathyrsi, seeing their neighbors flying before the Scythians, and thrown into confusion before the Scythians entered, dispatched a herald, and forbade the Scythians to cross their borders, warning them that if they should attempt to force their way they must fight with them. The Agathyrsi, having sent this message beforehand, advanced to protect their frontiers, determined to repel the invaders; whereas the Melanchlæni, Androphagi, and Neuri, when the Persians and Scythians together invaded them, offered no resistance, but, forgetting their former menaces, fled continually in great confusion northward toward the desert. The Scythians no longer advanced toward the Agathyrsi when they warned them not to do so, but, departing from the Neurian territory, they led the Persians into their own.

126. When this had continued for a considerable time, and did not cease, Darius sent a horseman to Indathyrsus, king of the Scythians, with the following message: "Most miserable of men, why dost thou continually fly, when it is in thy power to do one of these two other things? For, if thou thinkest thou art able to resist my power, stand, and having ceased thy wanderings, fight; but if thou art conscious of thy inferiority, in that case also cease thy hurried march, and, bringing earth and water as presents to thy master, come to a conference." 127. To this Indathyrsus, the king of the Scythians, made answer as follows: "This is the case with me, O Persian: I never yet fled from any man out of fear, neither before, nor do I now so flee from thee; nor have I done any thing different now from what I am wont to do even in time of peace; but why I do not forthwith fight thee, I will now explain. We have no cities nor cultivated lands for which we are under any apprehension lest they should be taken or ravaged, and therefore should hastily offer you battle. Yet if it is by all means necessary to come to this at once, we have the

sepulchres of our ancestors; come, find these, and attempt to disturb them, then you will know whether we will fight for our sepulchres or not; but before that, unless we choose, we will not engage with thee. Thus much about fighting. The only masters I acknowledge are Jupiter, my progenitor, and Vesta, queen of the Scythians; but to thee, instead of presents of earth and water, I will send such presents as are proper to come to thee; and in answer to thy boast that thou art my master, I bid thee weep." (This is a Scythian saying.) The herald therefore departed, carrying this answer to Darius.

128. The kings of the Scythians, when they heard the name of servitude, were filled with indignation; whereupon they sent the division united with the Sauromatæ, which Scopasis commanded, with orders to confer with the Ionians, who guarded the bridge over the Ister. Those who were left resolved no longer to lead the Persians about, but to attack them whenever they were taking their meals. Accordingly, observing the soldiers of Darius taking their meals, they put their design in execution. The Scythian cavalry always routed the Persian cavalry, but the Persian horsemen, in their flight, fell back on the infantry, and the infantry supported them. The Scythians, having beaten back the cavalry, wheeled round through fear of the infantry. The Scythians also made similar attacks at night. 129. A very remarkable circumstance, that was advantageous to the Persians and adverse to the Scythians when they attacked the camp of Darius, I will now proceed to mention: *this was* the braying of the asses and the appearance of the mules; for Scythia produces neither ass nor mule, as I have before observed;[5] nor is there in the whole Scythian territory a single ass or mule, by reason of cold. The asses, then, growing wanton, put the Scythian horse into confusion; and frequently, as they were advancing upon the Persians, when the horses heard, midway, the braying of the asses, they wheeled round in confusion and were greatly amazed, pricking up their ears, as having never before heard such a sound nor seen such a shape. Now this circumstance in some slight degree affected the fortune of the war.

130. The Scythians, when they saw the Persians in great

[5] See chap. 28.

commotion, in order that they might remain longer in Scythia, and by remaining might be harassed through want of all things necessary, adopted the following expedient: when they had left some of their own cattle in the care of the herdsmen, they themselves withdrew to another spot, and the Persians coming up, took the cattle, and having taken them, exulted in what they had done. 131. When this had happened several times, at last Darius was in a great strait, and the kings of the Scythians, having ascertained this, sent a herald, bearing as gifts to Darius a bird, a mouse, a frog, and five arrows. The Persians asked the bearer of the gifts the meaning of this present; but he answered that he had no other orders than to deliver them and return immediately; and he advised the Persians, if they were wise, to discover what the gifts meant. The Persians, having heard this, consulted together. 132. Darius's opinion was that the Scythians meant to give themselves up to him, as well as earth and water, forming his conjecture thus: since a mouse is bred in the earth, and subsists on the same food as a man; a frog lives in the water; a bird is very like a horse; and the arrows they deliver up as their whole strength. This was the opinion given by Darius. But the opinion of Gobryas, one of the seven who had deposed the magus, did not coincide with this; he conjectured that the presents intimated, "Unless, O ye Persians, ye become birds and fly into the air, or become mice and hide yourselves beneath the earth, or become frogs and leap into the lakes, ye shall never return home again, but be stricken by these arrows." And thus the other Persians interpreted the gifts.

133. In the mean time, that division of the Scythians that had been before appointed to keep guard about the lake Mæotis, and then to confer with the Ionians at the Ister, when they arrived at the bridge, spoke as follows: "Men of Ionia, we are come bringing freedom to you, if only you will listen to us. We have heard that Darius commanded you to guard the bridge sixty days only, and if he did not come up within that time, then to return into your own country. Now, therefore, if you do this, you will be free from all blame as regards him and as regards us; when you have waited the appointed number of days, after that depart." On the Ionians

promising to do so, the Scythians hastened back with all expedition.

134. The rest of the Scythians, after they had sent the presents to Darius, drew themselves opposite the Persians, with their foot and horse, as if they intended to come to an engagement; and as the Scythians were standing in their ranks, a hare started in the midst of them, and each of them, as they saw the hare, went in pursuit of it. The Scythians being in great confusion, and shouting loudly, Darius asked the meaning of the uproar in the enemy's ranks; but when he heard that they were pursuing a hare, he said to those he was accustomed to address on such occasions, "These men treat us with great contempt, and I am convinced that Gobryas spoke rightly concerning the Scythian presents. Since, then, I am of opinion that the case is so, we have need of the best advice how our return home may be effected in safety." To this Gobryas answered, "O king, I was in some measure acquainted by report with the indigence of these men, but I have learned much more since I came hither, and seen how they make sport of us. My opinion therefore is, that as soon as night draws on, we should light fires, as we are accustomed to do, and having deceived those soldiers who are least able to bear hardships, and having tethered all the asses, should depart before the Scythians direct their march to the Ister for the purpose of destroying the bridge, or the Ionians take any resolution which may occasion our ruin." Such was the advice of Gobryas. 135. Afterward night came on, and Darius acted on this opinion: the infirm among the soldiers, and those whose loss would be of the least consequence, and all the asses tethered, he left on the spot in the camp. And he left the asses and the sick of his army for the following reason: that the asses might make a noise; and the men were left on this pretext, namely, that he, with the strength of his army, was about to attack the Scythians, and they, during that time, would defend the camp. Darius, having laid these injunctions on those he was preparing to abandon, and having caused the fires to be lighted, marched away with all speed toward the Ister. The asses, being deserted by the multitude, began to bray much louder than usual, so that the Scythians, hearing the asses, firmly believed that the

Persians were still at their station. 136. When day appeared, the men that were abandoned, discovering that they had been betrayed by Darius, extended their hands to the Scythians, and told them what had occurred. When they heard this, the two divisions of the Scythians, and the single one, the Sauromatæ, Budini, and Geloni, having joined their forces together as quickly as possible, pursued the Persians straight toward the Ister. But as a great part of the Persian army consisted of infantry, and they did not know the way, there being no roads cut, and as the Scythian army consisted of cavalry, and knew the shortest route, they missed each other, and the Scythians arrived at the bridge much before the Persians. And having learned that the Persians were not yet arrived, they spoke to the Ionians who were on board the ships in these terms: "Men of Ionia, the number of days appointed for your stay is already passed, and you do not as you ought in continuing here; but if you remained before through fear, now break up the passage and depart as quickly as possible, rejoicing that you are free, and give thanks to the gods and the Scythians. As for the man who before was your master, we will so deal with him that he shall never hereafter make war on any people."

137. Upon this the Ionians held a consultation. The opinion of Miltiades the Athenian, who commanded and reigned over the Chersonesites on the Hellespont, was, that they should comply with the request of the Scythians, and restore liberty to Ionia. But Histiæus the Milesian was of a contrary opinion, and said "that every one reigned over his own city through Darius; and if Darius's power should be destroyed, neither would he himself continue master of Miletus, nor any of the rest of other places, because every one of the cities would choose to be governed rather by a democracy than a tyranny. Histiæus had no sooner delivered this opinion than all went over to his side who had before assented to that of Miltiades. 138. These were they who gave their votes and were in high estimation with Darius; the tyrants of the Hellespontines, Daphnis of Abydos, Hippocles of Lampsacus, Herophantus of Parium, Metrodorus of Proconnesus, Aristagoras of Cyzicum, and Ariston of Byzantium; these were from the Hellespont. From Ionia, Strattis of Chios, Æaces of Samos, Laodamas of Phocæa, and Histiæus of Miletus, whose opinion was opposed

to that of Miltiades. Of the Æolians, the only person of consideration present was Aristagoras of Cyme.

139. When these men had approved the opinion of Histiæus, they determined to add to it the following acts and words: to break up the bridge on the Scythian side, as far as a bowshot might reach, that they might seem to do something, when in effect they did nothing; and that the Scythians might not attempt to use violence and purpose to cross the Ister by the bridge; and to say, while they were breaking up the bridge on the Scythian side, they would do every thing that might be agreeable to the Scythians. This, then, they added to the opinion of Histiæus. And, afterward, Histiæus delivered the answer in the name of all, saying as follows: "Men of Scythia, you have brought us good advice, and urge it seasonably; you, on your part, have pointed out the right way to us, and we, on ours, readily submit to you; for, as you see, we are breaking up the passage, and will use all diligence, desiring to be free. But while we are breaking it up, it is fitting you should seek for them, and having found them, avenge us and yourselves on them, as they deserve." 140. The Scythians, believing a second time that the Ionians were sincere, turned back to seek the Persians, but entirely missed the way they had taken. The Scythians themselves were the cause of this, having destroyed the pastures for the horses in this direction, and having filled in the wells; for if they had not done this, they might easily have found the Persians if they wished; but now they erred in the very thing which they thought they had contrived for the best; for the Scythians sought the enemy by traversing those parts of the country where there was forage and water for the horses, thinking that they too would make their retreat by that way. But the Persians, carefully observing their former track, returned by it, and thus with difficulty found the passage. As they arrived in the night, and perceived the bridge broken off, they fell into the utmost consternation lest the Ionians had abandoned them. 141. There was with Darius an Egyptian, who had an exceedingly loud voice. This man Darius commanded to stand on the bank of the Ister, and call Histiæus the Milesian. He did so, and Histiæus, having heard the first shout, brought up all the ships to carry the army across, and joined the bridge. Thus the Persians escaped. 142. The Scythians,

in their search, missed them a second time; and, on the one hand, considering the Ionians free and cowardly, they deem them to be the most base of men; but, on the other, accounting the Ionians as slaves, they say that they are most attached to their masters, and least inclined to run away. These reproaches the Scythians fling out against the Ionians.

143. Darius, marching through Thrace, reached Sestos in the Chersonesus; and thence he himself crossed over on shipboard into Asia, and left Megabazus, a Persian, to be his general in Europe. Darius once paid this man great honor, having expressed himself in this manner in the presence of the Persians: Darius being about to eat some pomegranates, as soon as he opened the first, his brother Artabanus asked him, Of what thing he would wish to possess a number equal to the grains in the pomegranate. Darius said that he would rather have as many Megabazuses, than Greece subject to him. By saying this, he honored him in the presence of the Persians, and now he left him as general with eighty thousand men of his own army. 144. This Megabazus, by making the following remark, left an everlasting memorial of himself among the Hellespontines; for when he was at Byzantium, he was informed that the Chalcedonians had settled in that country seventeen years before the Byzantians; but when he heard it, he said that the Chalcedonians must have been blind at that time, for if they had not been blind, they would never have chosen so bad a situation, when they might have had so beautiful a spot to settle in. This Megabazus, then, being left as general in the country of the Hellespontines, subdued those nations who were not in the interest of the Medes. He accordingly did this.

145. About the same time another great expedition was undertaken against Libya, on what pretext I will relate, when I have first given the following account by way of preface. The descendants of the Argonauts, being expelled from Lemnos by the Pelasgians, who carried off the Athenian women from Brauron,[6] set sail for Lacedæmon, and seating themselves on Mount Taygetus, lighted fires. The Lacedæmonians, having seen this, dispatched a messenger to demand who and whence they were. They said to the messenger who question-

[6] See Book VI. chap. 138.

ed them that "they were Minyæ, descendants of those heroes who sailed in the Argo, and that they, having touched at Lemnos, begot them." The Lacedæmonians, having heard this account of the extraction of the Minyæ, sent a second time to inquire with what design they had come to their territory and lighted fires; they said that, being ejected by the Pelasgians, they had come to their fathers; for that it was most proper for them so to do; and they requested leave to dwell with them, participating in their honors, and being allotted a portion of land. The Lacedæmonians determined to receive the Minyæ on the terms they themselves proposed; and the sailing of the Tyndaridæ in the Argo especially induced them to do this: having, therefore, received the Minyæ, they assigned them a portion of land, and distributed them among their tribes, and they immediately contracted marriages, and gave to others the wives they brought from Lemnos. 146. But when no long time had elapsed, the Minyæ became insolent, and demanded a share in the sovereignty, and committed other crimes. The Lacedæmonians therefore determined to put them to death, and having seized them, they threw them into prison. Now those whom they kill, the Lacedæmonians kill by night, but no one by day. When, therefore, they were about to put them to death, the wives of the Minyæ, who were citizens, and daughters to the principal Spartans, begged permission to enter the prison, and confer each with her husband. The Lacedæmonians gave them permission, not suspecting any fraud on their part; but they, when they entered, did as follows: having given all the clothes they had on to their husbands, themselves took their husbands' clothes. Upon which, the Minyæ, having put on the women's dress, passed out as women, and having thus escaped, again seated themselves on Mount Taygetus.

147. At the same time, Theras, son of Austesion, son to Tisamenus, son of Thersander, son of Polynices, set out from Lacedæmon on a colonizing expedition. This Theras was by birth a Cadmæan, brother to the mother of Aristodemus's sons, Eurysthenes and Procles; and while these youths were yet infants, Theras had the kingdom of Sparta under his guardianship. But when the youths were grown up and assumed the government, Theras, not brooking to be ruled by others after he had tasted the pleasures of power, declared

that he would not remain at Lacedæmon, but would sail away to his own kindred. In the island now called Thera, the same that was formerly Callista, lived the descendants of Membliares, the son of Pæciles a Phœnician. For Cadmus, son of Agenor, when in quest of Europa, touched at the island now called Thera; and whether when he touched at it the country pleased him, or whether for some other reason he chose to do so, he left in this island both others of the Phœnicians, and, moreover, his own kinsman, Membliares: these men occupied the island, then called Callista, during eight generations, before Theras came from Lacedæmon. 148. To these people, then, Theras went, having, with a multitude drawn out of the tribes, set out, purposing to dwell with them, and on no account to drive them out, but by all means to conciliate them. But when the Minyæ who had escaped from the prison seated themselves on Mount Taygetus, as the Lacedæmonians determined to destroy them, Theras begged that they might not be put to death, and promised that he would himself take them out of the country. The Lacedæmonians acceding to his request, he set sail with three thirty-oared galleys, to the descendants of Membliares, taking with him not only the Minyæ, but some few of them; for the greater number of them went over to Paroreates and Caucones; and having driven them out from their country, distributed themselves into six divisions, and then founded the following cities there: Leprium, Macistus, Phrixas, Pyrgus, Epium, and Nudium: most of these the Eleans have destroyed in my time. The name of Thera was given to the island after the founder. 149. His son refused to accompany him in his voyage, therefore he said that he would leave him as a sheep among wolves; in consequence of this speech, the name of Oiolycus was given to this youth, and this name chanced to prevail. To this Oiolycus was born Ægeus, from whom the Ægidæ, a principal tribe in Sparta, are named. As the children of the men of this tribe did not survive, they erected a temple, in obedience to an oracle, to the furies of Laius and Œpidus; and after that, the same thing happened in Thera to those who were descended from these men.

150. To this part of the story the Lacedæmonians agree with the Theræans; but after this, the Theræans only say

that what follows took place. Grinus, son of Æsanius, who was a descendant of this Theras, and reigned over the island Thera, came to Delphi, bringing a hecatomb from the city; and divers of the citizens attended him, and among them Battus, son to Polymnestus, who was of the family of Euphemus, one of the Minyæ. And as Grinus, king of the Theræans, was consulting the oracle concerning other affairs, the Pythian admonished him to "build a city in Libya." But he answered, "I, O prince, am now too old and heavy to move myself; therefore command one of these young men to do this;" and as he said these words, he pointed to Battus. At that time so much passed. But after their departure, they paid no attention to the oracle, neither knowing in what part of the world Libya was, nor daring to send out a colony on an uncertainty. 151. For seven years after this, no rain fell in Thera; during which period, every tree in the island, except one, was withered up; and when the Theræans consulted the oracle, the Pythian objected to them the colonization of Libya. When they found no remedy for the evil, they dispatched messengers to Crete, to inquire if any of the Cretans, or strangers settled among them, had ever gone to Libya. These messengers, wandering about the island, arrived in the city of Itanus; and here they became acquainted with a purple-dyer, whose name was Corobius; he said that, being driven by the winds, he had gone to Libya, and to Platea, an island of Libya: having persuaded this man by a promise of reward, they took him to Thera. At first, men sailed from Thera to explore, not many in number; and when Corobius had conducted them to this island Platea, they left Corobius there with provisions for a few months, and themselves sailed back with all speed to give the Theræans tidings of the island. 152. But these men staying away longer than the time agreed upon, Corobius was reduced to the last necessity; when a Samian vessel, whose master was Colæus, sailing for Egypt, was driven to this Platea. The Samians, having heard the whole account from Corobius, left him provisions for a year; and they, having got under weigh from the island, and being anxious to reach Egypt, set sail, and were carried away by an east wind; and as the wind did not abate, having passed through the columns of Hercules, they arrived at Tartessus, under divine guidance. That port was at that time unfrequented; so that these men returning home, gained from their cargo the largest profits of any of the Grecians we know of with certainty, next to Sostratus, son of Laodamas of Ægina, for with him it is impossible for any one to compete. The Samians, therefore, having set apart the tenth of their gains, amounting to six talents, made a vessel of brass, after the fashion of an Argolic bowl, and around it the heads of griffins project over, and they dedicated it in the temple of Juno, having placed under it three colossal figures of brass, seven cubits in height, leaning on their knees. And on this occasion the Cyrenæans and Theræans first contracted a great friendship with the Samians. 153. The Theræans, when they left Corobius in the island and returned to Thera, took back word that they had taken possession of an island off the coast of Libya. The Theræans, therefore, resolved to send one of every family,[7] chosen by lot; and *to send* men from all their districts, which were seven in number, and appointed Battus to be their leader and king. Thus, then, they fitted out two fifty-oared galleys for Platea.

154. The Theræans give this account; in the rest of the story the Theræans are supported by the Cyrenæans; for the Cyrenæans in no respect agree with the Theræans in what relates to Battus, for they tell the story thus. There is a city of Crete called Axus, in which Etearchus was king; he, having a motherless daughter, whose name was Phronima, married another wife; she, coming into the family, thought proper to be a stepmother indeed to Phronima, treating her shamefully, and contriving every mischief she could against her; and at last, having charged her with unchastity, persuaded her husband that such was the case. He, prevailed on by his wife, formed a wicked design against his daughter. There was then at Axus one Themison, a Theræan merchant; this man Etearchus received hospitably, and made him swear that he would serve him in any thing he should desire. When he had bound him by oath, he delivered his daughter to him, and commanded him to take her away, and throw her into the sea. But Themison, grieved at the deceitfulness of the oath, broke off the compact of friendship, and did as follows: having taken the damsel with him, he set sail; and

[7] Literally, "brother from brother."

when he was in the open sea, for the purpose of absolving himself from the oath imposed by Etearchus, he bound her round with ropes, and let her down into the sea; then, having drawn her up again, he departed for Thera. 155. After that, Polymnestus, a man of distinction among the Theræans, took Phronima as his concubine, and after some time he had a son by her who had an impediment in his speech, and lisped, to whom the name of Battus was given, as both the Theræans and Cyrenæans say; but, as I am of opinion, some other name, and it was afterward changed to Battus when he arrived in Libya, deriving that name both from the oracle pronounced to him at Delphi and from the rank to which he attained; for the Libyans call a king Battus, and for this reason I think that the Pythian, when delivering the oracle, addressed him in the Libyan tongue, knowing that he would be a king in Libya; for when he had reached man's estate, he came to Delphi about his voice. and to his inquiries the Pythian gave the following answer: "Battus, you have come about your voice; king Phœbus Apollo sends you to found a colony in Libya, abounding in sheep." As if she had said in the Grecian language, "O king, you are come about your voice." He answered as follows: "O king, I came indeed to consult you about my voice, but you give me an answer as to other impossible things, bidding me colonize Libya: with what power? with what force?" By saying this he did not persuade the Pythian to give him any other answer; and as she was repeating the same response as before, he in the mean while left her, and returned to Thera. 156. After this, Battus himself and the other Theræans fell anew into troubles, but the Theræans, not knowing whence their misfortunes came, sent to Delphi to inquire concerning their present sufferings. The Pythian answered that it would fare better with them when, with Battus, they had founded Cyrene in Libya. Upon this, the Theræans dispatched Battus with two fifty-oared galleys; but these having sailed to Libya, for they had nothing else that they could do, returned back to Theræa. The Theræans, however, beat them off as they drew to shore, and would not suffer them to approach the land, but commanded them to sail back again. Thus compelled, they sailed back again, and settled in an island that lies off Libya, whose name, as I before mentioned, is Platea. This island is said to be equal in extent to the present city of the Cyrenæans.

157. Having inhabited this island for two years, as nothing turned out prosperously for them, they left one of their company behind, and the rest set sail for Delphi; and having come to the oracle, they consulted it, saying, that they had settled in Libya, and fared no better since they had settled there. But the Pythian gave them the following answer: "If you, who have never been there, know Libya abounding in sheep, better than I who have been there, I very much admire your wisdom." When Battus and his companions heard this, they sailed back again; for the god did not release them from founding the colony until they had come to Libya itself. Having, therefore, arrived at the island, they took on board the man they had left there, and settled in a place on Libya itself, opposite the island: its name was Aziris, and most beautiful hills inclose it on two sides, and a river flows by it on the third. 158. They inhabited this spot for six years, but in the seventh, the Libyans, having promised to conduct them to a better place, persuaded them to leave it. But the Libyans, having removed them, conducted them from thence toward the west; and in order that the Greeks might not see the most beautiful part of their country as they passed through, they computed the time of the day, so as to lead them through it by night: the name of this country is Irasa. Having conducted them to a fountain, accounted sacred to Apollo, they said, "Grecians, here it is fitting for you to dwell, for here the heavens are open." 159. Now, during the life of Battus the founder, who reigned forty years, and of his son Arcesilaus, who reigned sixteen years, the Cyrenæans continued the same in number as when they were first sent to settle the colony; but under the third king, Battus, surnamed the Fortunate, the Pythian by an oracle encouraged all Grecians to sail to Libya, and join the Cyrenæans in colonizing it; for the Cyrenæans invited them to a division of the country. The words of the oracle were these: "He who shall come too late to lovely Libya, when the land is divided, shall hereafter one day repent." A great multitude having assembled at Cyrene, the neighboring Libyans and their king, whose name was Adicran, being curtailed of much of

their land, finding that they were deprived of their territory, and injuriously treated by the Cyrenæans, sent an embassy to Egypt, and gave themselves up to Apries, king of Egypt; but he, having assembled a large army of Egyptians, sent it against Cyrene; and the Cyrenæans, having drawn out their forces to the district of Irasa, and near the fountain Thestes, came to an engagement with the Egyptians, and conquered them; for the Egyptians, not having before made trial of the Greeks, and despising them, were so thoroughly defeated, that only a few of them returned to Egypt. In consequence of this, the Egyptians, laying the blame on Apries, revolted from him.

160. This Battus had a son, Arcesilaus, who, having come to the throne, first of all quarreled with his own brothers, so that they left him, and went to another part of Libya; and consulting among themselves, they founded the city which was then and is still called Barce; and as they were building it, they persuaded the Libyans to revolt from the Cyrenæans; but afterward Arcesilaus led an army against those Libyans who had received them, and against the revolters themselves; but the Libyans, through dread of him, fled to the eastern Libyans. Arcesilaus pursued them in their flight, until he overtook them at Leucon in Libya, and the Libyans resolved to attack him; and having come to an engagement, they conquered the Cyrenæans so completely, that seven thousand heavy-armed of the Cyrenæans fell upon the spot. After this blow, his brother Learchus strangled Arcesilaus, who was sick, and under the influence of some drug. The wife of Arcesilaus, whose name was Eryxo, put Learchus to death by stratagem.

161. Battus, the son of Arcesilaus, a lame man, and not perfect in his feet, succeeded to the kingdom. The Cyrenæans, on account of the disaster that had befallen them, sent to Delphi to inquire of the Delphian oracle under what form of government they might live most happily; the Pythian commanded them to procure an arbitrator from Mantinea, a city of the Arcadians. The Cyrenæans accordingly asked, and the Mantineans gave them a man, highly esteemed among the citizens, whose name was Demonax. This person, therefore, having arrived in Cyrene, and become acquainted with the state of affairs, first of all formed them into three tribes, dividing them as follows: of the Theræans and their immediate neighbors he formed one division; another of Peloponnesians and Cretans; and a

third of all the Islanders; and, in the next place, having reserved certain portions of land and the office of the priesthood for king Battus, he restored to the people every thing else that the kings had before.

162. During the reign of this Battus matters continued in this state, but in the time of his son Arcesilaus great disorders arose about the public offices; for Arcesilaus, son of the lame Battus and Pheretime, declared he would not submit to the constitutions of Demonax, but demanded back the prerogatives of his ancestors; and thereupon having raised a sedition, he was defeated, and fled to Samos; and his mother fled to Salamis, in Cyprus. At that time Euelthon bore rule over Salamis, the same who dedicated the curious censer at Delphi, which is deposited in the treasury of the Corinthians. Pheretime, having come to him, asked for an army which should reinstate them in Cyrene; but Euelthon would give her any thing rather than an army; but she, accepting what was given, said, "This indeed is handsome, but it would be still more handsome to give the army she asked for:" this she said at every present that was made. At last Euelthon sent her a golden spindle and distaff, and some wool was on it; and when Pheretime again made the same speech, Euelthon said "that women should be presented with such things, and not with armies." 163. In the mean time, Arcesilaus, continuing at Samos, collected men of all classes by a promise of a division of lands; and when a large army was collected, Arcesilaus set out to Delphi, to consult the oracle concerning his return; and the Pythian gave him the following answer: "Apollo grants you to reign over Cyrene during the time of four Battuses and four Arcesilauses, eight generations of men; he advises you, however, not to attempt any more than this. Do you therefore be quiet and return home; and if you find a furnace full of amphoræ, do not bake the amphoræ, but send them away with a favorable wind. But if you heat the furnace, enter not into a place surrounded with water, otherwise you will perish yourself, and the most beautiful bull." 164. The Pythian gave this answer to Arcesilaus; but he, having taken with him the men from Samos, returned to Cyrene; and having recovered the mastery, he forgot the oracle, and exacted vengeance of the adverse party for his own exile, so that some of them

abandoned their country altogether, and others Arcesilaus seized and sent to Cyprus to be put to death: now these last, being carried to their country, the Cnidians rescued, and sent away to Thera. Some others of the Cyrenians, who had taken refuge in a large private tower belonging to Aglomachus, Arcesilaus surrounded with wood and burned. After this was done, understanding that this was the meaning of the oracle, that the Pythian forbade him, when he found amphoræ in a furnace, to bake them, he of his own accord withdrew from the city of the Cyrenæans, dreading the predicted death, and supposing that Cyrene was the place surrounded with water. He had a wife who was his own kinswoman, and daughter to the king of the Barcæans, whose name was Alazir; to him he retired; and the Barcæans, and some of the exiles from Cyrene, having discovered him in the public place, killed him, and, moreover, his father-in-law Alazir. Thus Arcesilaus, whether willfully or otherwise, disobeying the oracle, accomplished his own destiny.

165. While Arcesilaus was living at Barce, working out his own destruction, his mother Pheretime held the honors of her son at Cyrene, both exercising his other functions and taking her seat in the council; but when she heard that her son had been put to death at Barce, she fled to Egypt; for Arcesilaus had performed some services for Cambyses, son of Cyrus, for it was this Arcesilaus who gave Cyrene to Cambyses, and imposed a tribute on himself. Pheretime having arrived in Egypt, seated herself as a suppliant of Aryandes, entreating him to avenge her, alleging as a pretext that her son had died in consequence of his attachment to the Medes. 166. Aryandes had been appointed governor of Egypt by Cambyses; he in succeeding time was put to death for attempting to make himself equal with Darius; for having been informed that Darius desired to leave such a memorial of himseif as had been accomplished by no other king, he imitated him until he received the reward *of his presumption;* for Darius, having refined gold to the utmost perfection, coined money; and Aryandes, governor of Egypt, made the same in silver; now this Aryandian silver is the purest; but Darius, when informed that he had done this, brought another charge against him, that he designed to rebel, and put him to death. 167. At that time, however, this Aryandes, taking

compassion on Pheretime, gave her all the forces of Egypt, both army and navy; and he appointed Amasis, a Maraphian, commander of the army; and of the fleet, Brades, a Parsagadian by birth. But, before he dispatched the forces, he sent a herald to Barce to inquire who it was that had slain Arcesilaus. All the Barcæans took it upon themselves, for that they had suffered many injuries at his hands; and when Aryandes received their answer, he dispatched the army with Pheretime. Now this cause was only a pretext for his proceeding; but, in my opinion, the expedition was undertaken with the intention of subduing the Libyans; for there are many and various nations of Libyans, and some few of them were subject to the king, but the greater part paid no regard to Darius.

168. The Libyans dwell as follows. Beginning from Egypt, the Adrymachidæ are the first of the Libyans we meet with; they, for the most part, observe the usages of Egypt, but they wear the same dress as the other Libyans. The women wear a chain of brass on each leg; they let their hair grow long, and when they catch vermin, each bites those from her own person, and then throws them away; these alone of the Libyans do this, and they alone exhibit to the king their virgins who are about to marry, and should any one be agreeable to the king, she is deflowered by him. These Adrymachidæ reach from Egypt to the harbor named Plunus. 169. Next to these are the Giligammæ, who occupy the country westward, as far as the island Aphrodisias. Midway on this coast the island of Platea is situate, which the Cyrenæans colonized, and on the continent is the port of Menelaus, with Azaris, which the Cyrenæans inhabited. At this place *the plant* Silphium is first found, and extends from the island of Platea to the mouth of the Syrtis. These people use nearly the same customs as the others. 170. The Asbystæ adjoin the Giligammæ westward; they inhabit the country above Cyrene, but the Asbystæ do not reach to the sea, for the Cyrenæans occupy the sea-coast. They drive four-horsed chariots more than any of the Libyans, and endeavor to imitate most of the customs of the Cyrenæans. 171. The Auschisæ adjoin the Asbystæ westward; these are situate above Barce, extending to the sea near the Euesperides. In the midst of the territory of the Auschisæ, the

Cabales, a small nation, dwell, extending to Tauchira, a city of Barcæa. They observe the same customs as those who dwell above Cyrene. 172. The Nasamones, a very numerous people, adjoin these Auschisæ westward. In summer they leave their cattle on the coast, and go up to the region of Augila, in order to gather the fruit of the palm-trees, which grow in great numbers and of a large size, and are all productive. When they have caught locusts, they dry them in the sun, reduce them to powder, and, sprinkling them in milk, drink them. Every man, by the custom of the country, has several wives, and they have intercourse with them in common; and much the same as the Massagetæ, they have intercourse when they have set up a staff before them. When a Nasamonian first marries, it is the custom for the bride on the first night to lie with all the guests in turn, and each, when he has intercourse with her, gives her some present which he has brought from home. In their oaths and divinations they observe the following custom: they swear, laying their hands on the sepulchres of those who are generally esteemed to have been the most just and excellent persons among them; and they divine, going to the tombs of their ancestors, and after having prayed, they lie down to sleep, and whatever dream they have, this they avail themselves of. In pledging their faith they observe the following method: each party gives the other to drink out of his hand, and drinks in turn from the other's hand, and if they have no liquid, they take up some dust from the ground and lick it.

173. The Psylli border on the Nasamonians; these perished in the following manner: the south wind blowing upon them dried up all their water tanks, and the whole country within the Syrtis was dry; they, therefore, having consulted together, with one consent determined to make war against that wind (I only repeat what the Libyans say); and when they arrived at the sands, the south wind, blowing, covered them over, and when they had perished the Nasamonians took possession of their territory. 174. Above these, to the north, in a country abounding with wild beasts, live the Garamantes, who avoid all men and the society of any others; they do not possess any warlike weapon, nor do they know how to defend themselves. 175. These, then, live above the Nasamonians, and the Macæ adjoin them on the sea-coast, westward; these shave their heads so as to

leave a tuft, and allowing the middle hair to grow, they shave both sides close to the skin; in war they wear the skins of ostriches for defensive armor. The river Cinyps, flowing through their country from a hill called the Graces, discharges itself into the sea. The hill of the Graces is thickly covered with trees, though all the rest of Libya above mentioned is bare. From the sea to this hill is a distance of two hundred stades. 176. The Gindanes adjoin these Macæ; their women wear bands of leather round their ankles, each several on the following account, as is said: she binds round a band for every man that has intercourse with her; and she who has the most is most esteemed, as being loved by the greatest number of men. 177. The Lotophagi occupy the coast that projects to the sea in front of these Gindanes; they subsist only on the fruit of the lotus; and the fruit of the lotus is equal in size to the mastic berry, and in sweetness it resembles the fruit of the palm-tree. The Lotophagi make wine also from this fruit.

178. The Machlyes, who also use the lotus, but in a less degree than those before mentioned, adjoin the Lotophagi on the sea-coast. They extend as far as a large river called Triton; and this river discharges itself into the great lake Tritonis; and in it is an island named Phla. They say that the Lacedæmonians were commanded by an oracle to colonize this island. 179. The following story is also told: that Jason, when the Argo was finished building at the foot of Mount Pelion, having put a hecatomb on board, and, moreover, a brazen tripod, sailed round the Peloponnesus, purposing to go to Delphi; and, as he was sailing off Malea, a north wind caught him and drove him to Libya; and before he could discern the land, he found himself in the shallows of the lake Tritonis; and as he was in doubt how to extricate *his ship*, the story goes that a Triton appeared to him, and bid Jason give him the tripod, promising that he would both show them the passage and conduct them away in safety. When Jason consented, the Triton thereupon showed them the passage out of the shallows, and placed the tripod in his own temple; then pronouncing an oracle from the tripod, he declared to Jason and his companions all that should happen, that "when one of the descendants of those who sailed with him in the Argo should carry away the tripod, then it was fated

that a hundred Grecian cities should be built about the lake Tritonis:" the neighboring nations of the Libyans, when they heard this, concealed the tripod. 180. The Auses adjoin these Machlyes; they, as well as the Machlyes, dwell round the lake Tritonis, and the Triton forms the boundary between them. The Machlyes let the hair grow on the back of the head, and the Auses on the front. At the annual festival of Minerva, their virgins, dividing themselves into two companies, fight together with stones and staves, affirming that they perform the ancient rites to their native goddess, whom we call Minerva; and those of the virgins who die from their wounds they call false virgins. But before they leave off fighting, they do as follows: with one consent they on each occasion deck the virgin that excels in beauty with a Corinthian helmet and a suit of Grecian armor, and, having placed her in a chariot, conduct her round the lake. In what way they formerly decorated the virgins before the Grecians settled in their neighborhood I am unable to say; but I conjecture that they were decked in Egyptian armor, for I am of opinion that the shield and helmet were brought from Egypt into Greece. They say that Minerva is the daughter of Neptune and the lake Tritonis; and that she, being for some reason offended with her father, gave herself to Jupiter, and that Jupiter adopted her as his own daughter: this they say. They have promiscuous intercourse with the women, and do not cohabit, and associate like beasts. The men meet together every third month, and when a woman has a son grown up, he is considered to be the son of that man whom he most resembles.

181. Those, then, of the Libyan nomades who live on the sea-coast have been mentioned. Above these, inland, Libya abounds in wild beasts; and beyond the wild beast tract is a ridge of sand, stretching from the Egyptian Thebes to the columns of Hercules. At intervals of a ten days' journey in this ridge there are pieces of salt in large lumps on hills; and at the top of each hill, from the midst of the salt, cold and sweet water gushes up; and around it dwell people the farthest toward the desert, and beyond the wild-beast tract. The first, after a ten days' journey from Thebes, are the Ammonians, who have a temple resembling that of Theban Jupiter; for, as I said before, the image of Jupiter at Thebes has the head of a ram. They have also another kind of spring water,

which in the morning is tepid, becomes colder about the time of full forum, and at midday is very cold; then they water their gardens. As the day declines it gradually loses its coldness till the sun sets, then the water becomes tepid again, and continuing to increase in heat till midnight, it then boils and bubbles up; when midnight is passed, it gets cooler until morning. This fountain is called after the sun. 182. Next to the Ammonians, along the ridge of sand, at the end af another ten days' journey, there is a hill of salt, like that of the Ammonians, and water, and men live round it: the name of this region is Augila; to this place the Nasamonians go to gather the dates. 183. From the Augilæ at the end of another ten days' journey is another hill of salt and water, and many fruit-bearing palm-trees, as also in the other places; and men inhabit it who are called Garamantes, a very powerful nation; they lay earth upon the salt, and then sow their ground. From these to the Lotophagi the shortest route is a journey of thirty days: among them the kine that feed backward are met with; they feed backward for this reason: they have horns that are bent forward, therefore they draw back as they feed; for they are unable to go forward, because their horns would stick in the ground. They differ from other kine in no other respect than this, except that their hide is thicker and harder. These Garamantes hunt the Ethiopian Troglodytes in four-horse chariots; for the Ethiopian Troglodytes are the swiftest of foot of all men of whom we have heard any account given. The Troglodytes feed upon serpents and lizards, and such kind of reptiles: they speak a language like no other, but screech like bats.

184. At the distance of another ten days' journey from the Garamantes is another hill of salt, and water, and men live round it who are called Atarantes; they are the only people we know of who have not personal names. For the name Atarantes belongs to them collectively, but to each one of them no name is given. They curse the sun as he passes over their heads, and, moreover, utter against him the foulest invectives, because he consumes them by his scorching heat, both the men themselves and their country. Afterward, at the end of another ten days' journey, there is another hill of salt, and water, and men live round it; and near this salt is a mountain which is called Atlas; it is narrow and circular on

all sides, and is said to be so lofty that its top can never be seen; for it is never free from clouds, either in summer or winter. The inhabitants say that it is the Pillar of Heaven. From this mountain these men derive their appellation, for they are called Atlantes. They are said neither to eat the flesh of any animal, nor to see visions. 185. As far, then, as these Atlantes, I am able to mention the names of the nations that inhabit this ridge, but not beyond them. This ridge, however, extends as far as the pillars of Hercules, and even beyond them; and there is a mine of salt in it at intervals of ten days' journey, and men dwelling there. The houses of them all are built of blocks of salt, for in these parts of Libya no rain falls; for walls being of salt could not stand long if rain did fall. The salt dug out there is white and purple in appearance. Above this ridge, to the south and interior of Libya, the country is desert, without water, without animals, without rain, and without wood; and there is no kind of moisture in it.

186. Thus, then, as far as the lake Tritonis from Egypt, the Libyans are nomades, eat flesh, and drink milk, but they do not taste the flesh of cows, for the same reason as the Egyptians, nor do they breed swine. Indeed, not only do the women of the Cyrenæans think it right to abstain from the flesh of cows, out of respect to Isis in Egypt, but they also observe the fasts and festivals in honor of her: and the women of the Barcæans do not taste the flesh of swine in addition to that of cows. These things, then, are so. 187. Westward of the lake Tritonis, the Libyans are no longer nomades, nor do they follow the same customs, nor do they do with respect to their children what the nomades are accustomed to do; for the nomadic Libyans, whether all I am unable to say with certainty, but many of them do as follows: when their children are four years old, they burn the veins on the crown of their heads with uncleaned sheep's wool, and some of them *do it* on the veins in the temples, to the end that humors flowing down from the head may not injure them as long as they live; and, for this reason, they say they are so very healthy, for the Libyans are in truth the most healthy of all men with whom we are acquainted; whether from this cause, I am unable to say with certainty; however, they are the most healthy. But if convulsions seize the children when

they are burning them, they have a remedy discovered; by sprinkling them with the urine of a he-goat, they restore them. I repeat what the Libyans themselves say. 188. These Libyan nomades have the following sacrificial rites. When they have first cut off the ear of the victim, they throw it over the house; and having done this, they twist its neck. They sacrifice only to the sun and moon: to them, indeed, all the Libyans offer sacrifice; but those who live about the lake Tritonis sacrifice principally to Minerva, and next to Triton and Neptune. 189. From the Libyan women the Grecians derived the attire and ægis of Minerva's statues; for, except that the dress of the Libyan women is leather, and the fringes that hang from the ægis are not serpents, but made of thongs, in all other respects they are equipped in the same way; and, moreover, the very name proves that the garb of the Palladia comes from Libya; for the Libyan women throw over their dress goats' skins without the hair, fringed and dyed with red. From these goats' skins the Grecians have borrowed the name of Ægis; and the howlings in the temples were, I think, first derived from thence; for the Libyan women practice the same custom, and do it well. The Grecians also learned from the Libyans to yoke four horses abreast. 190. All the nomades, except the Nasamonians, inter their dead in the same manner as the Grecians: these bury them in a sitting posture, watching when one is about to expire, that they may set him up, and he may not die supine. Their dwellings are compacted of the asphodel shrub interwoven with rushes, and are portable. Such are the customs of these people.

191. To the west of the river Triton, Libyans who are husbandmen next adjoin the Auses; they are accustomed to live in houses, and are called Maxyes. They let the hair grow on the right side of the head, and shave the left, and bedaub the body with vermilion: they say that they are descended from men *who came* from Troy. This region, and all the rest of Libya westward, is much more infested by wild beasts, and more thickly wooded than the country of the nomades; for the eastern country of Libya, which the nomades inhabit, is low and sandy, as far as the river Triton; but the country westward of this, which *is occupied* by agriculturists, is very mountainous, woody, and abounds with wild beasts. For among them there are enormous serpents, and lions, elephants,

bears, asps, and asses with horns, and monsters with dogs' heads and without heads, who have eyes in their breasts, at least, as the Libyans say, and wild men and wild women, and many other wild beasts *which are* not fabulous. 192. None of these things are found among the nomades, but others of the following kind: pygargi, antelopes, buffaloes, and asses; not such as have horns, but others that do not drink; for they never drink; and oryes, from the horns of which are made the elbows of the Phœnician citherns: in size this beast is equal to an ox; and foxes, hyænas, porcupines, wild rams, dictyes, thoes, panthers, boryes, and land crocodiles about three cubits long, very much like lizards; ostriches, and small serpents, each with one horn. These, then, are the wild animals in that country, besides such as are met with elsewhere, except the stag and the wild boar; but the stag and the wild boar are never seen in Libya. They have three sorts of mice there; some called dipodes, *or two-footed;* others, zegeries: this name is Libyan, and means the same as the word signifying hillocks in Greek; and hedgehogs. There are also weasels produced in the silphium very like those at Tartessus. The land of the Libyan nomades produces wild animals of the above description, as far as I, by the most diligent inquiry, have been able to ascertain.

193. The Zaveces adjoin the Maxyan Libyans; their women drive their chariots in war. 194. The Gyzantes adjoin them; among them bees make a great quantity of honey, and it is said that confectioners make much more. All these paint themselves with vermilion, and eat monkeys, which abound in their mountains. 195. Near them, the Carthaginians say, lies an island called Cyraunis, two hundred stades in length, inconsiderable in breadth, easy of access from the continent, and abounding in olive-trees and vines. *They add* that in it is a lake, from the mud of which the virgins of the country draw up gold dust by means of feathers daubed with pitch. Whether this is true I know not, but I write what is related; it may be so, however, for I have myself seen pitch drawn up out of a lake and from water in Zacynthus; and there are several lakes there; the largest of them is seventy feet every way, and two orgyæ in depth; into this they let down a pole with a myrtle branch fastened to the end, and then draw up pitch adhering to the myrtle; it has the

smell of asphalt, but is in other respects better than the pitch of Pieria. They pour it into a cistern dug near the lake, and when they have collected a sufficient quantity, they pour it off from the cistern into jars. All that falls into the lake passes under ground, and appears again upon the surface of the sea, which is about four stades distant from the lake. Thus, then, the account given of the island that lies off Libya may probably be true. 196. The Carthaginians farther say that beyond the pillars of Hercules there is a region of Libya and men who inhabit it: when they arrive among these people and have unloaded their merchandise, they set it in order on the shore, go on board their ships, and make a great smoke: that the inhabitants, seeing the smoke, come down to the sea, and then deposit gold in exchange for the merchandise, and withdraw to some distance from the merchandise; that the Carthaginians then, going ashore, examine *the gold*, and if the quantity seems sufficient for the merchandise, they take it up and sail away; but if it is not sufficient, they go on board their ships again and wait; the natives then approach and deposit more gold, until they have satisfied them: neither party ever wrongs the other; for they do not touch the gold before it is made adequate to the value of the merchandise, nor do the natives touch the merchandise before the other party has taken the gold.

197. Such are the Libyans, whose names I have been able to mention; and most of these neither now nor at that time paid any regard to the king of the Medes. But I have still this much to say about this country, that four distinct races inhabit it, and no more, as far as we know: two of these races are indigenous, and two not. The Libyans and Ethiopians are indigenous, the one inhabiting the northern, the other the southern parts of Libya; but the Phœnicians and Greeks are foreigners. 198. No part of Libya appears to me so good in fertility as to be compared with Asia or Europe, except only the district of Cinyps; for the land bears the same name as the river, and is equal to the best land in the production of corn; nor is it at all like the rest of Libya; for the soil is black, and well watered with springs; and it is neither affected at all by drought, nor is it injured by imbibing too much rain; for rain falls in this part of Libya. The proportion of the produce of this land equals that of

Babylon. The land also which the Euesperides occupy is good, for when it yields its best, it produces a hundred-fold, but that in Cinyps three hundred-fold. 199. The district of Cyrene, which is the highest of that part of Libya which the nomades occupy, has three seasons, *a circumstance* worthy of admiration; for the first fruits near the sea swell so as to be ready for the harvest and vintage; and when these are gathered in, the fruits of the middle region, away from the sea, swell so as to be gathered in, these they call uplands; and when this middle harvest has been gathered in, that in the highest part becomes ripe and swells. So that when the first crop has been drunk and eaten, the last comes in. Thus harvest occupies the Cyrenæans during eight months. This may be sufficient to say concerning these things.

200. The Persians sent to avenge Pheretime, when, having been dispatched from Egypt by Aryandes, they arrived at Barce, laid siege to the city, demanding the surrender of the persons concerned in the death of Arcesilaus; but as the whole people were implicated, they did not listen to the proposal. Thereupon they besieged Barce for nine months, digging passages under ground that reached to the walls, and making vigorous assaults. Now the excavations a worker of brass discovered by means of a brazen shield, having recourse to the following expedient: carrying it round within the wall, he applied it to the ground within the city; in other places to which he applied it, it made no noise, but at the parts that were excavated, the brass of the shield sounded. The Barcæans, therefore, countermining them in that part, slew the Persians who were employed in the excavation; thus, then, this was discovered; but the assaults the Barcæans repulsed. 201. When much time had been spent, and many had fallen on both sides, and not the fewest on the side of the Persians, Amasis, general of the land forces, had recourse to the following stratagem: finding that the Barcæans could not be taken by force, but might be by artifice, he did thus: having dug a wide pit by night, he laid weak planks of wood over it, and on the surface over the planks he spread a heap of earth, making it level with the rest of the ground. At daybreak he invited the Barcæans to a conference, but they gladly assented, so that at last they were pleased to come to terms; and they made an agreement of the following nature, concluding the

treaty over the concealed pit: "That as long as this earth shall remain as it is, the treaty should continue in force; and that the Barcæans should pay a reasonable tribute to the king, and that the Persians should form no new designs against the Barcæans." After the treaty, the Barcæans, confiding in the Persians, both themselves went out of the city, and allowed any one of the Persians who chose to pass within the wall, having thrown open all the gates. But the Persians having broken down the concealed bridge, rushed within the wall; and they broke down the bridge that they had made for the following reason, that they might keep their oath, having made a compact with the Barcæans that the treaty should continue so long as the earth should remain as it then was; but when they had broken down the bridge, the treaty no longer remained in force.

202. Those of the Barcæans who were most to blame Pheretime impaled round the walls when they had been delivered up to her by the Persians, and having cut off the breasts of their wives, she also studded the wall with them. The rest of the Barcæans she gave up as booty to the Persians, except such as were Battiadæ, and had not participated in the murder; to these Pheretime intrusted the city. 203. The Persians, therefore, having reduced the rest of the Barcæans to slavery, took their departure; and when they halted at the city of the Cyrenæans, the Cyrenæans, to absolve themselves from obedience to some oracle, permitted them to pass through the city; but as the army was going through, Bares, the commander of the naval forces, urged them to take the city, but Amasis, the commander of the land forces, would not allow it, "for that he was sent against no other Grecian city than that of Barce." However, when they had passed through, and encamped on the hill of the Lycæan Jupiter, they began to repent that they had not possessed themselves of Cyrene, and attempted to enter it a second time. But the Cyrenæans would not suffer them, and a panic struck the Persians, although no one attacked them; and having run away for a distance of sixty stades, they pitched their camp. When the army was encamped here, a messenger came from Aryandes to recall them. The Persians, having requested the Cyrenæans to give them provisions for their march, obtained their request, and having received them, marched away toward Egypt; and from thence the Libyans, laying wait for them, put to death those that

strayed and loitered behind, for the sake of their dress and baggage, until they reached Egypt. 204. The farthest point of Africa to which this Persian army penetrated was the country of the Euesperides. The Barcæans, whom they had enslaved, they transported from Egypt to the king, and king Darius gave them a village in the district of Bactria to dwell in. They gave, then, the name of Barce to this village, which was still inhabited in my time, in the Bactrian territory. 205. Pheretime, however, did not close her life happily; for immediately after she returned from Libya to Egypt, having avenged herself on the Barcæans, she died miserably, for even while alive she swarmed with maggots. So odious to the gods are the excesses of human vengeance. Such and so great was the vengeance of Pheretime, wife of Battus, on the Barcæans.

BOOK V.

TERPSICHORE.

The Persians, left in Europe by Darius under the command of Megabazus,[1] subdued the Perinthians first of the Hellespontines, who were unwilling to submit to Darius, and had been before roughly handled by the Pæonians. For the Pæonians from the Strymon, an oracle having admonished them to invade the Perinthians, and if the Perinthians, when encamped over against them, should challenge them, shouting to them by name, then to attack, but if they should not shout out to them, not to attack; the Pæonians did accordingly. The Perinthians having encamped opposite to them in the suburbs, a threefold single combat there took place according to a challenge; for they matched a man with a man, a horse with a horse, and a dog with a dog. But the Perinthians being victorious in two of these combats, when through excess of joy they sang the Pæon, the Pæonians conjectured that this was the meaning of the oracle, and said among themselves, "Now surely the oracle must be accomplished; now it is our part to act." Thus the Pæonians attacked the Perinthians as they were singing the Pæon, and gained a complete victory, and left but few of them alive. 2. Such, then, had formerly been the achievements of the Pæonians; but at that time, though the Perinthians proved themselves valiant in defense of their liberty, the Persians and Megabazus overcame them by numbers. When Perinthus was subdued, Megabazus marched his army through Thrace, subjecting to the king every city and every nation of those dwelling in that country; for this command had been given him by Darius, to subdue Thrace.

3. The nation of the Thracians is the greatest of any among

[1] See B. IV. chap. 144.

men, except at least the Indians; and if they were governed by one man, or acted in concert, they would, in my opinion, be invincible, and by far the most powerful of all nations. But as this is impracticable, and it is impossible that they should ever be united, they are therefore weak. They have various names, according to their respective regions, but all observe similar customs in every respect, except the Getæ, the Trausi, and those who dwell above the Crestonæans. 4. Of these, what are the customs of the Getæ, who pretend to be immortal, I have already described.[2] The Trausi, in all other respects, observe the same usages as the rest of the Thracians; but with regard to one born among them, or that dies, they do as follows. The relations, seating themselves around one that is newly born, bewail him, *deploring* the many evils he must needs fulfill, since he has been born; enumerating the various sufferings incident to mankind; but one that dies they bury in the earth, making merry and rejoicing, recounting the many evils from which being released, he is now in perfect bliss. 5. Those above the Crestonæans do as follows: each man has several wives; when, therefore, any of them dies, a great contest arises among the wives, and violent disputes among their friends, on this point, which of them was most loved by the husband. She who is adjudged to have been so, and is so honored, having been extolled both by men and women, is slain on the tomb by her own nearest relative, and when slain is buried with her husband; the others deem this a great misfortune, for this is the utmost disgrace to them. 6. There is, moreover, this custom among the rest of the Thracians: they sell their children for exportation. They keep no watch over their unmarried daughters, but suffer them to have intercourse with what men they choose; but they keep a strict watch over their wives, and purchase them from their parents at high prices. To be marked with punctures is accounted a sign of noble birth; to be without punctures, ignoble. To be idle is most honorable; but to be a tiller of the soil, most dishonorable; to live by war and rapine is most glorious. These are the most remarkable of their customs. 7. They worship the following gods only, Mars, Bacchus, and Diana. But their kings, to the exception of the other citizens, reverence Mercury most

[2] B. IV. chap. 93, 94.

of all the gods; they swear by him only, and say that they are themselves sprung from Mercury. 8. The funerals of the wealthy among them are celebrated in this manner. They expose the corpse during three days; and having slain all kinds of victims, they feast, having first made lamentation. Then they bury them, having first burned them, or, at all events, placing them under ground; then, having thrown up a mound, they celebrate all kinds of games, in which the greatest rewards are adjudged to single combat, according to the estimation in which they are held. Such are the funeral rites of the Thracians.

9. To the north of this region no one is able to say with certainty who are the people that inhabit it; but beyond the Ister appears to be a desert and interminable tract. The only men that I am able to hear of as dwelling beyond the Ister are those called Sigynnæ, who wear the Medic dress; their horses are shaggy all over the body, to five fingers in depth of hair; they are small, flat-nosed, and unable to carry men; but when yoked to chariots they are very fleet, therefore the natives drive chariots. Their confines extend as far as the Eneti on the Adriatic; and they say that they are a colony of Medes. How they can have been a colony of the Medes I can not comprehend; but any thing may happen in course of time. Now the Ligyes, who live above Massilia, call traders *Sigynnæ*, and the Cyprians *give that name to* spears. 10. The Thracians say bees occupy the parts beyond the Ister, and by reason of them it is impossible to penetrate farther; to me, however, in saying this, they appear to say what is improbable, for these creatures are known to be impatient of cold; but the regions beneath the Bear seem to be uninhabited by reason of the cold. Such is the account given of this country. Megabazus, then, subjected its maritime parts to the Persians.

11. Darius, as soon as he had crossed the Hellespont and reached Sardis, remembered the good offices of Histiæus the Milesian, and the advice of Coes the Mitylenian. Having therefore sent for them to Sardis, he gave them their choice of a recompense. Histiæus, as being already tyrant of Miletus, desired no other government in addition, but asked for Myrcinus of Edonia, wishing to build a city there; but Coes, as not being a tyrant, but a private citizen, asked for the government of Mitylene. When their requests were granted to both of them, they

betook themselves to the places they had chosen. 12. It happened that Darius, having witnessed a circumstance of the following kind, was desirous of commanding Megabazus to seize the Pæonians and transplant them out of Europe into Asia. Pigres and Mantyes were Pæonians, who, when Darius had crossed over into Asia, being desirous to rule over the Pæonians, came to Sardis, bringing with them their sister, who was tall and beautiful; and having watched the opportunity when Darius was seated in public in the suburb of the Lydians, they did as follows. Having dressed their sister in the best manner they could, they sent her for water, carrying a pitcher on her head, leading a horse on her arm, and spinning flax. As the woman passed by, it attracted the attention of Darius, for what she was doing was neither according to the Persian or Lydian customs, nor of any other people in Asia; when, therefore, it attracted his attention, he sent some of his body-guard, bidding them observe what the woman would do with the horse. The guards accordingly followed her, and she, when she came to the river, watered the horse; and having watered it, and filled her pitcher, returned by the same way, carrying the water on her head, leading the horse on her arm, and turning her spindle. 13. Darius, surprised at what he heard from the spies, and at what he himself had seen, commanded them to bring her into his presence; and when she was brought, her brothers also made their appearance, who were keeping a lookout some where not far off; and when Darius asked of what country she was, the young men said that they were Pæonians, and that she was their sister. He then inquired, "Who are the Pæonians, in what part of the world do they live, and for what purpose have they come to Sardis?" They told him that "they had come to deliver themselves up to him, and that Pæonia was situated on the river Strymon, and the Strymon was not far from the Hellespont; and that they were a colony of Teucrians, from Troy." They then mentioned these several particulars; and he asked "if all the women of that country were so industrious:" they readily answered that such was the case, for they had formed their plan for this very purpose.

14. Thereupon Darius writes letters to Megabazus, whom he had left general in Thrace, commanding him to remove the Pæonians from their abodes, and to bring to him themselves,

their children, and their wives. A horseman immediately hastened to the Hellespont with the message; and having crossed over, delivered the letter to Megabazus; but he, having read it, and taken guides from Thrace, marched against Pæonia. 15. The Pæonians, having heard that the Persians were coming against them, assembled, and drew out their forces toward the sea, thinking that the Persians would attempt to enter and attack them in that direction: the Pæonians, accordingly, were prepared to repel the army of Megabazus at its first onset. But the Persians, understanding that the Pæonians had assembled, and were guarding the approaches on the coast, having guides, went the upper road; and having escaped the notice of the Pæonians, came suddenly on their towns, which were destitute of inhabitants, and as they fell upon them when empty, they easily got possession of them. But the Pæonians, as soon as they heard that their cities were taken, immediately dispersed themselves, and repaired each to his own home, and gave themselves up to the Persians. Thus the Siropæonians and Pæoplæ, and those tribes of Pæonians as far as the lake Prasias, were removed from their abodes, and transported into Asia. 16. But those around Mount Pangæus and near the Doberes, the Agrianæ, Odomanti, and those who inhabit Lake Prasias itself, were not at all subdued by Megabazus. Yet he attempted to conquer those who live upon the lake in dwellings contrived after this manner: planks fitted on lofty piles are placed in the middle of the lake, with a narrow entrance from the main land by a single bridge. These piles that support the planks all the citizens anciently placed there at the common charge; but afterward they established a law to the following effect: whenever a man marries, for each wife he sinks three piles, bringing wood from a mountain called Orbelus: but every man has several wives. They live in the following manner: every man has a hut on the planks, in which he dwells, with a trap-door closely fitted in the planks, and leading down to the lake. They tie the young children with a cord round the foot, fearing lest they should fall into the lake beneath. To their horses and beasts of burden they give fish for fodder; of which there is such an abundance, that when a man has opened his trap-door, he lets down an empty basket by a cord into the lake, and, after waiting a short time, draws it up full of fish. They have two kinds of fish, which they call papraces and tilones. Those of the Pæonians, then, who were subdued, were taken to Asia.

17. When Megabazus had subdued the Pæonians, he sent into Macedonia seven Persians as embassadors, who, next to himself, were the most illustrious in the army. They were sent to Amyntas to demand earth and water for king Darius. From the lake Prasias the distance to Macedonia is very short; for near adjoining the lake is a mine, from which, in later times, a talent of silver came in daily to Alexander. Beyond the mine, when one has passed the mountain called Dysorum, one is in Macedonia. 18. When, therefore, the Persians who were sent arrived at the court of Amyntas, on going into the presence of Amyntas, they demanded earth and water for king Darius. He both promised to give these, and invited them to partake of his hospitality; and having prepared a magnificent feast, he entertained the Persians with great courtesy. But after supper, the Persians, who were drinking freely, spoke as follows: "Macedonian host, it is a custom with us Persians, when we have given a great feast, to introduce our concubines and lawful wives to sit by our side. Since, therefore, you have received us kindly, and have entertained us magnificently, and promise to give earth and water to king Darius, do you follow our custom." To this Amyntas answered, "O Persians, we have no such custom, but that the men should be separated from the women; yet since you, who are our masters, require this also, this shall also be granted to you." Amyntas, having spoken thus, sent for the women, and they, when they had come, being summoned, sat down in order opposite to the Persians. Thereupon the Persians, seeing the women were beautiful, spoke to Amyntas, saying "that what had been done was not at all wise, for that it were better that the women should not have come at all, than that, when they had come, they should not be placed beside them, but sit opposite to them as a torment to their eyes." Upon this, Amyntas, compelled by necessity, ordered them to sit down by the men; and when the women obeyed, the Persians, as being very full of wine, began to feel their breasts, and some one even attempted to kiss them. 19. Amyntas, when he beheld this, though very indignant, remained quiet, through excessive fear of the Persians; but Alexander, son of Amyntas, who was present, and witnessed this behavior, being a young man

and inexperienced in misfortune, was no longer able to restrain himself; so that, bearing it with difficulty, he addressed Amyntas as follows: "Father, yield to your years, and retire to rest, nor persist in drinking. I will stay here and furnish the guests with all things necessary." Amyntas, perceiving that Alexander was about to put some new design into execution, said, "Son, I pretty well discern by your words that you are burning with rage, and that you wish to dismiss me that you may attempt some new design. I charge you, therefore, to plan nothing new against these men, lest you cause our ruin, but endure to behold what is being done; with respect to my retiring, I will comply with your wishes." 20. When Amyntas, having made this request, had retired, Alexander said to the Persians, "Friends, these women are entirely at your service; and whether you desire to have intercourse with them all, or with any of them, on this point make known your own wishes; but now, as the time for retiring is fast approaching, and I perceive that you have had abundance to drink, let these women, if that is agreeable to you, go and bathe, and when they have bathed, expect their return." Having spoken thus, as the Persians approved his proposal, he sent away the women, as they came out, to their own apartment; and Alexander himself, having dressed a like number of smoothfaced young men in the dress of the women, and having furnished them with daggers, led them in; and as he led them in, he addressed the Persians as follows: "Persians, you appear to have been entertained with a sumptuous feast; for we have given you not only all we had, but whatever we could procure; and, which is more than all the rest, we now freely give up to you our mothers and sisters, that you may perceive that you are thoroughly honored by us with whatever you deserve; and also that you may report to the king who sent you, that a Greek, the prince of the Macedonians, gave you a good reception both at table and bed." Having thus spoken, Alexander placed by the side of each Persian a Macedonian man, as if a woman; but they, when the Persians attempted to touch them, put them to death. 21. By this death these perished, both they and their attendants, for they were followed by carriages, and attendants, and all kinds of baggage; but all these, with the whole of the men, disappeared. But after no long time, a great search was made by the Persians for these men; but Alexander by his prudence checked their inquiry, by giving a considerable sum of money, and his own sister, whose name was Gygæa, to Bubares a Persian, the chief of those sent to search for those who were lost: thus the inquiry into the death of these Persians, being suppressed, was hushed up. 22. That these princes, who are sprung from Perdiccas, are Greeks, as they themselves affirm, I myself happen to know; and in a future part of my history[3] I will prove that they are Greeks. Moreover, the judges presiding at the games of the Grecians in Olympia have determined that they are so; for when Alexander wished to enter the lists, and went down there for that very purpose, his Grecian competitors wished to exclude him, alleging that the games were not instituted for barbarian combatants, but Grecians. But Alexander, after he had proved himself to be an Argive, was pronounced to be a Greek, and when he was to contend in the stadium, his lot fell out with that of the first combatant. In this manner were these things transacted.

23. Megabazus, leading with him the Pæonians, arrived at the Hellespont; and having crossed over from thence, came to Sardis. In the mean time, Histiæus the Milesian was building a wall round the place, which, at his own request, he had received from Darius as a reward for his services in preserving the bridge: this place was near the river Strymon, and its name was Myrcinus. But Megabazus, having heard what was being done by Histiæus, as soon as he reached Sardis, bringing the Pæonians with him, addressed Darius as follows: "O king, what have you done, in allowing a crafty and subtle Greek to possess a city in Thrace, where there is abundance of timber fit for building ships, and plenty of wood for oars, and silver mines? A great multitude of Greeks and barbarians dwell around, who, when they have obtained him as a leader, will do whatever he may command both by day and by night. Put a stop, therefore, to the proceedings of this man, that you may not be harassed by a domestic war; but, having sent for him in a gentle manner, stop him; and when you have got him in your power, take care that he never returns to the Greeks." 24. Megabazus, speaking thus, easily persuaded Darius, since he wisely fore-

[3] See B. VIII. chap. 137.

saw what was likely to happen. Thereupon Darius, having sent a messenger to Myrcinus, spoke as follows: "Histiæus, king Darius says thus: I find, on consideration, that there is no man better affected to me and my affairs than thyself; and this I have learned, not by words, but actions; now, therefore, since I have great designs to put in execution, come to me, by all means, that I may communicate them to thee." Histiæus, giving credit to these words, and at the same time considering it a great honor to become a counselor of the king, went to Sardis. When he arrived, Darius addressed him as follows: "Histiæus, I have sent for you on this occasion. As soon as I returned from Scythia, and you were out of my sight, I have wished for nothing so much as to see you and converse with you again, being persuaded that a friend who is both intelligent and well affected is the most valuable of all possessions, both of which I am able to testify from my own knowledge concur in you as regards my affairs. Now, then, for you have done well in coming, I make you this offer. Think no more of Miletus, nor of the new-founded city in Thrace, but follow me to Susa, have the same that I have, and be the partner of my table and counsels." 25. Darius having spoken thus, and having appointed Artaphernes, his brother by the same father, to be governor of Sardis, departed for Susa, taking Histiæus with him; and having nominated Otanes to be general of the forces on the coast, whose father Sisamnes, one of the royal judges, king Cambyses had put to death and flayed[1] because he had given an unjust judgment for a sum of money; and having had his skin torn off, he had it cut into thongs, and extended it on the bench on which he used to sit when he pronounced judgment; and Cambyses, having so extended it, appointed as judge in the room of Sisamnes, whom he had slain and flayed, the son of Sisamnes, admonishing him to remember on what seat he sat to administer justice. 26. This Otanes, then, who had been placed on this seat, being now appointed successor to Megabazus in the command of the army, subdued the Byzantians and Chalcedonians, and took Antandros, which belongs to the territory of Troas and Lamponium, and having obtained ships from the Lesbians, he took Lemnos and Imbrus, both of which were then inhabited by Pelasgians. 27. (Now the Lemnians fought valiantly, and having defended themselves for

[1] Literally, "he cut off all his human *skin*."

some time, were at length overcome, and over those who survived the Persians set up Lycaretus as governor, the brother of Mæandrius, who had reigned in Samos. This Lycaretus died while governor of Lemnos.) Otanes enslaved and subdued them all; his reasons for so doing were as follows: some he charged of desertion to the Scythians, others of having harassed Darius's army in their return home from the Scythians. Such was his conduct while general of the forces.

28. Afterward, *for* the intermission from misfortune was not of long duration, evils arose a second time to the Ionians from Naxos and Miletus; for, on the one hand, Naxos surpassed all the islands in opulence, and, on the other hand, Miletus at the same time had attained the summit of its prosperity, and was accounted the ornament of Ionia; though before this period it had for two generations suffered excessively from seditions, until the Parians reconciled them, for the Milesians had chosen them out of all the Greeks to settle their differences. 29. The Parians reconciled them in the following manner. When their most eminent men arrived at Miletus, as they saw their private affairs in a dreadful state, they said that they wished to go through their whole country; and in doing this, and going through all Milesia, wheresoever they saw in the devastated country any land well cultivated, they wrote down the name of the proprietor. And having traversed the whole country and found but few such, as soon as they came down to the city they called an assembly, and appointed to govern the city those persons whose lands they had found well cultivated; for they said they thought they would administer the public affairs as well as they had done their own. The rest of the Milesians, who before had been split into factions, they ordered to obey them. Thus the Parians reconciled the Milesians. 30. From these two cities at that time misfortunes began to befall Ionia in the following manner. Some of the opulent men were exiled from Naxos by the people, and being exiled, went to Miletus. The governor of Miletus happened to be Aristagoras, son of Molpagoras, son-in-law and cousin of Histiæus, son of Lysagoras, whom Darius detained at Susa; for Histiæus was tyrant of Miletus, and happened to be at that time at Susa when the Naxians came, who were before on terms of friendship with Histiæus. The Naxians, then, having arrived at Miletus, entreated Aristagoras if he could

by any means give them some assistance, that so they might return to their own country. But he, having considered that if by his means they should return to their city, he would get the dominion of Naxos, used the friendship of Histiæus as a pretense, and addressed the following discourse to them: "I am not able of myself to furnish you with a force sufficient to reinstate you against the wishes of the Naxians who are in possession of the city, for I hear that the Naxians have eight thousand heavy-armed men, and a considerable number of ships of war; yet I will contrive some way, and use my best endeavors; and I design it in this way: Artaphernes happens to be my friend; he is son of Hystaspes and brother of king Darius, and commands all the maritime parts of Asia, and has a large army and many ships. This man, I am persuaded, will do whatever we desire." The Naxians, having heard this, urged Aristagoras to bring it about in the best way he could, and bade him promise presents, and their expenses to the army, for that they would repay it, having great expectation that when they should appear at Naxos the Naxians would do whatever they should order, as also would the other islanders; for of these Cyclades islands not one was as yet subject to Darius.

31. Accordingly, Aristagoras, having gone to Sardis, told Artaphernes that Naxos was an island of no great extent, but otherwise beautiful and fertile, and near Ionia, and in it was much wealth and many slaves. "Do you therefore send an army against this country to reinstate those who have been banished from thence; and if you do this, I have, in the first place, a large sum of money ready, in addition to the expenses of the expedition, for it is just that we who lead you on should supply that; and, in the next, you will acquire for the king Naxos itself, and the islands dependent upon it, Paros, Andros, and the rest that are called Cyclades. Setting out from thence, you will easily attack Eubœa, a large and wealthy island, not less than Cyprus, and very easy to be taken. A hundred ships are sufficient to subdue them all." He answered him as follows: "You propose things advantageous to the king's house, and advise every thing well, except the number of ships; instead of one hundred, two hundred shall be ready at the commencement of the spring; but it is necessary that the king himself should approve of the design." 32. Now

Aristagoras, when he heard this, being exceedingly rejoiced, went back to Miletus. But Artaphernes, when, on his sending to Susa and communicating what was said by Aristagoras, Darius himself also approved the plan, made ready two hundred triremes, and a very numerous body of Persians and other allies; and he appointed Megabates general, a Persian of the family of the Achemenidæ, his own and Darius's nephew, whose daughter, if the report be true, was afterward betrothed to Pausanias, son of Cleombrotus the Lacedæmonian, who aspired to become tyrant of Greece. Artaphernes, having appointed Megabates general, sent forward the army to Aristagoras.

33. Megabates, having taken with him from Miletus Aristagoras, and the Ionian forces and the Naxians, sailed professedly for the Hellespont; but when he arrived at Chios, anchored at Caucasa, that he might cross over from thence to Naxos by a north wind. However, since it was fated that the Naxians were not to perish by his armament, the following event occurred. As Megabates was going round the watches on board the ships, he found no one on guard on board a Myndian ship; thereupon, being indignant at this, he ordered his body-guards to find the captain of this ship, whose name was Scylax, and to bind him, having passed him half way through the lower rowlock of the vessel, so that his head should be on the outside of the vessel, and his body within. When Scylax was bound, some one told Aristagoras that Megabates had bound and disgraced his Myndian friend. He went, therefore, and interceded for him with the Persian; but when he found he could obtain nothing, he went and released him. Megabates, hearing of this, was very indignant, and enraged with Aristagoras; but he said, "What have you to do with these matters? Did not Artaphernes send you to obey me, and to sail wheresoever I should command? Why do you busy yourself?" Aristagoras spoke thus. But Megabates, exasperated at this, as soon as night arrived, dispatched men in a ship to Naxos to inform the Naxians of the impending danger. 34. Now the Naxians did not at all expect that this armament was coming against them; when, therefore, they heard of it, they immediately carried every thing from the fields into the town, and prepared to undergo a siege, and brought food and drink within the walls. Thus they made

preparations, as if war was close at hand; but the Persians, when they crossed over from Chios to Naxos, had to attack men well fortified, and besieged them during four months; so that having consumed all the supplies they had brought with them, together with large sums furnished by Aristagoras, and wanting still more to carry on the siege, they therefore built a fortress for the Naxian exiles, and retired to the continent, having been unsuccessful.

35. Aristagoras was unable to fulfill his promise to Artaphernes; and, at the same time, the expense of the expedition, which was demanded, pressed heavy on him. He was alarmed, too, on account of the ill success of the army, and at having incurred the ill will of Megabates, and thought that he should be deprived of the government of Miletus. Dreading, therefore, each of these things, he meditated a revolt; for it happened, at the same time, that a messenger with his head punctured came from Susa, from Histiæus, urging Aristagoras to revolt from the king; for Histiæus, being desirous to signify to Aristagoras his wish for him to revolt, had no other means of signifying it with safety, because the roads were guarded; therefore, having shaved the head of the most trustworthy of his slaves, he marked it, and waited till the hair was grown again. As soon as it was grown again, he sent him to Miletus without any other instructions than that when he arrived at Miletus he should desire Aristagoras to shave off his hair and look upon his head: the punctures, as I said before, signified a wish for him to revolt. Histiæus did this because he looked upon his detention at Susa as a great misfortune; if, then, a revolt should take place, he had great hopes that he should be sent down to the coast; but if Miletus made no new attempt, he thought that he should never go there again. 36. Histiæus accordingly, under these considerations, sent off the messenger. All these things concurred together at the same time to Aristagoras; he therefore consulted with his partisans, communicating to them his own opinion and the message that had come from Histiæus: now all the rest concurred in the same opinion, urging him to revolt; but Hecatæus, the historian, at first endeavored to dissuade him from undertaking a war against the king of the Persians, enumerating all the nations whom Darius governed, and his power; but when he could not prevail, he, in the next place, advised that they should so

contrive as to make themselves masters of the sea. "Now," he continued, "he saw no other way of effecting this, for he was well aware that the power of the Milesians was weak; but if the treasures should be seized from the temple of the Branchidæ, which Crœsus the Lydian had dedicated, he had great hopes that they might acquire the dominion of the sea; and thus they would have money for their own use, and the enemy could not plunder that treasure." But this treasure was very considerable, as I have already related in the first part of my history.[5] This opinion, however, did not prevail. Nevertheless, it was resolved to revolt, and that one of them, having sailed to Myus to the force that had returned from Naxos, and which was then there, should endeavor to seize the captains on board the ships. 37. Iatragoras, having been dispatched for this very purpose, and having, by stratagem, seized Oliatus, son of Ibanolis of Mylassa, Histiæus, son of Tymnes of Termera, Coes, son of Erxandrus, to whom Darius had given Mitylene, Aristagoras, son of Heraclides, of Cyme, and many others; Aristagoras thus openly revolted, devising every thing he could against Darius; and first, in pretense, having laid aside the sovereignty, he established an equality in Miletus, in order that the Milesians might more readily join with them in the revolt; and afterward he effected the same throughout the rest of Ionia, expelling some of the tyrants; and he delivered up those whom he had taken from on board the ships that had sailed with him against Naxos to the cities, in order to gratify the people, giving them up generally to the respective cities from whence each came. 38. The Mityleneans, as soon as they received Coes, led him out and stoned him to death; but the Cymeans let their tyrant go, and in like manner most of the others let theirs go. Accordingly, there was a suppression of tyrants throughout the cities; but Aristagoras the Milesian, when he had suppressed the tyrants, and enjoined them all to appoint magistrates in each of the cities, in the next place went himself in a trireme as embassador to Sparta, for it was necessary for him to procure some powerful alliance.

39. Anaxandrides, son of Leon, no longer survived and reigned over Sparta, but was already dead; Cleomenes, son of Anaxandrides, held the sovereignty, not having acquired it

[5] See B. I. chap. 50, 51, 92.

by his virtues, but by his birth. Anaxandrides, who had married his own sister's daughter, though she was very much beloved by him, had no children: this being the case, the Ephori, having sent for him, said, "If you do not provide for your own interests, yet we must not overlook this, that the race of Eurysthenes should become extinct. Do you therefore put away the wife whom you have, since she bears no children, and marry another; and by so doing you will gratify the Spartans." He answered, saying "that he would do neither of these things; and that they did not advise him well in urging him to dismiss the wife he had, when she had committed no error, and to take another in her place, and therefore he would not obey them." 40. Upon this the Ephori and senators, having consulted, made the following proposal to Anaxandrides: "As we see you strongly attached to the wife whom you have, act as follows, and do not oppose it, lest the Spartans should come to some unusual resolution respecting you. We do not require of you the dismissal of your present wife; pay her the same attention as you have always done, and marry another besides her, who may bear you children." When they spoke to this effect, Anaxandrides consented; and afterward, having two wives, he inhabited two houses, doing what was not at all in accordance with Spartan usages. 41. When no long time had elapsed, the wife last married bore this Cleomenes, and presented to the Spartans an heir apparent to the throne; and the former wife, who had before been barren, by some strange fortune then proved to be with child; and though she was really so, yet the relations of the second wife, having heard of it, raised a disturbance, saying that she boasted vainly, purposing to bring forward a supposititious child. As they made a great noise, when the time approached, the Ephori, from distrust, sat around, and watched the woman in her labor. She, however, when she had borne Dorieus, shortly afterward had Leonidas, and after him, in due course, Cleombrotus; though some say that Cleombrotus and Leonidas were twins. But she who bore Cleomenes, and who was the second wife, and daughter to Prinetades, son of Demarmenus, never bore a second time.

42. Cleomenes, as it is said, was not of sound mind, but almost mad; whereas Dorieus was the first of the young men of his age, and was fully convinced that by his virtues he

should obtain the sovereignty; so that, being of this persuasion, when Anaxandrides died, and the Lacedæmonians, following the usual custom, appointed the eldest, Cleomenes, to be king, Dorieus, being very indignant, and disdaining to be reigned over by Cleomenes, demanded a draught of men from the Spartans, and led them out to found a colony, without having consulted the oracle at Delphi to what land he should go and settle, nor doing any of those things that are usual on such occasions; but as he was very much grieved, he directed his ships to Libya, and some Theræans piloted him. Having arrived at Cinyps, he settled near the river, in the most beautiful spot of the Libyans. But in the third year, being driven out from thence by the Macæ, Libyans, and Carthaginians, he returned to Peloponnesus. 43. There Antichares, a citizen of Eleon, from the oracles delivered to Laius, advised him to found Heraclea in Sicily, affirming that all the country of Eryx belonged to the Heraclidæ, Hercules himself having possessed himself of it. He, hearing this, went to Delphi to inquire of the oracle whether he should take the country to which he was preparing to go. The Pythian answered that he should take it. Dorieus therefore, taking with him the force which he had led to Libya, sailed along the coast of Italy. 44. At that time, as the Sybarites say, they and their king Telys were preparing to make war against Crotona; and the Crotonians, being much alarmed, implored of Dorieus to assist them, and obtained their request; whereupon Dorieus marched with them against Sybaris, and took Sybaris in concert with them. Now the Sybarites say that Dorieus, and those who were with him, did this. But the Crotonians affirm that no foreigner took part with them in the war against the Sybarites, except only Callias of Elis, a seer of the Iamidæ, and he did so under the following circumstances: he had fled from Telys, king of the Sybarites, and come over to them, when the victims did not prove favorable as he was sacrificing against Crotona. Such is the account they give. 45. Each party produces the following proofs of what they assert. The Sybarites allege a sacred inclosure and temple near the dry Crastis,[6] which they say Dorieus, when he had assisted in taking the city, erected to Minerva, surnamed Crastian; and, in the next place, they mention the death of Dorieus as the

[6] Called "dry" because its stream was dried up in summer.

greatest proof, for that he was killed for having acted contrary to the warnings of the oracle; for if he had not at all transgressed, but had done that for which he was sent, he would have taken and possessed the Erycinian country, and having taken it, would have retained it; nor would he and his army have been destroyed. On the other hand, the Crotonians show selected portions of land given to Callias the Elean, in the territories of Crotona, which the descendants of Callias continued to occupy even in my time; but to Dorieus, and the posterity of Dorieus, nothing *was given;* whereas, if Dorieus had assisted them in the Sybaritic war, much more would have been given to him than to Callias. These, then, are the proofs that each produces, and every man has the liberty of adhering to that which he judges most probable. 46. There sailed with Dorieus also other Spartans, joint-founders of a colony, as Thessalus, Paræbates, Celeas, and Euryleon; who, on their arrival with the whole armament in Sicily, were killed, being defeated in battle by the Phœnicians and Egestæans. Euryleon alone of the associates in founding the colony survived this disaster: he, having collected the survivors of the army, possessed himself of Minoa, a colony of the Selinuntians, and assisted in liberating the Selinuntians from their monarch Pythagoras. But afterward, when he had removed him, he himself seized the tyranny of Selinus, and continued monarch for a short time; for the Selinuntians, having risen up against him, put him to death, though he had taken sanctuary at the altar of the Forensian Jupiter. 47. Philippus, son of Butacides, a citizen of Crotona, accompanied Dorieus, and perished with him. He, having entered into a contract of marriage with the daughter of Telys the Sybarite, fled from Crotona, but, disappointed of his marriage, sailed to Cyrene; and setting out from thence, he accompanied Dorieus in a trireme of his own, with a crew maintained at his own expense; for he had been victorious in the Olympian games, and was the handsomest of the Greeks of his day; and on account of his beauty, he obtained from the Egestæans what no other person ever did; for, having erected a shrine on his sepulchre, they propitiate him with sacrifices. 48. Dorieus, then, met with his death in the manner above described; but if he had submitted to be governed by Cleomenes, and had continued in Sparta, he would have become king of Lacedæmon; for Cleomenes did not reign for any length of time, but died without a son, leaving a daughter only, whose name was Gorgo.

49. Aristagoras then, tyrant of Miletus, arrived at Sparta, when Cleomenes held the government; and he went to confer with him, as the Lacedæmonians say, having a brazen tablet, on which was engraved the circumference of the whole earth, and the whole sea, and all rivers. And Aristagoras, having come to a conference, addressed him as follows: "Wonder not, Cleomenes, at my eagerness in coming here, for the circumstances that urge are such *as I will describe*. That the children of Ionians should be slaves instead of free, is a great disgrace and sorrow to us, and above all others to you, inasmuch as you are at the head of Greece. Now, therefore, I adjure you, by the Grecian gods, rescue the Ionians, who are of your own blood, from servitude. It is easy for you to effect this, for the barbarians are not valiant; whereas you, in matters relating to war, have attained to the utmost height of glory: their mode of fighting is this, *with* bows and a short spear; and they engage in battle, wearing loose trowsers, and turbans on their heads, so they are easy to be overcome. Besides, there are treasures belonging to those who inhabit that continent such as are not possessed by all other nations together; beginning from gold, there is silver, brass, variegated garments, beasts of burden, and slaves; all these you may have if you will. They live adjoining one another, as I will show you. Next these Ionians are the Lydians, who inhabit a fertile country, and abound in silver." As he said this he showed the circumference of the earth, which he brought with him, engraved on a tablet. "Next the Lydians," proceeded Aristagoras, "are these Phrygians to the eastward, who are the richest in cattle and corn of all with whom I am acquainted. Next to the Phrygians are the Cappadocians, whom we call Syrians; and bordering on them, the Cilicians, extending to this sea in which the island of Cyprus is situate: they pay an annual tribute of five hundred talents to the king. Next to the Cilicians are these Armenians, who also abound in cattle; and next the Armenians are the Matienians, who occupy this country; and next them this territory of Cissia, in which Susa is situated on this river Choaspes: here the great king resides, and there are his treasures of wealth. If you take this city, you may boldly contend with Jupiter in

wealth. But now you must carry on war for a country of small extent, and not very fertile, and of narrow limits, with the Messenians, who are your equals in valor, and with the Arcadians and Argives, who have nothing akin to gold or silver, the desire of which induces men to hazard their lives in battle. But when an opportunity is offered to conquer all Asia with ease, will you prefer any thing else?" Aristagoras spoke thus, and Cleomenes answered him as follows: "Milesian friend, I defer to give you an answer until the third day." 50. On that day they got so far. When the day appointed for the answer was come, and they had met at the appointed place, Cleomenes asked Aristagoras how many days' journey it was from the sea of the Ionians to the king. But Aristagoras, though he was cunning in other things, and had deceived him with much address, made a slip in this; for he should not have told the real fact if he wished to draw the Spartans into Asia; whereas he told him plainly that it was a three months' journey up there. But he, cutting short the rest of the description which Aristagoras was proceeding to give of the journey, said, "Milesian friend, depart from Sparta before sunset, for you speak no agreeable language to the Lacedæmonians in wishing to lead them a three months' journey from the sea." Cleomenes, having spoken thus, went home. 51. But Aristagoras, taking an olive-branch in his hand, went to the house of Cleomenes, and having entered in, as a suppliant, besought Cleomenes to listen to him, having first sent away his little child; for his daughter, whose name was Gorgo, stood by him: she happened to be his only child, and was about eight or nine years of age. But Cleomenes bid him say what he would, and not refrain for the sake of the child. Thereupon Aristagoras began promising ten talents if he would do as he desired; and when Cleomenes refused, Aristagoras went on increasing in his offers until he promised fifty talents; then the girl cried out, "Father, this stranger will corrupt you unless you quickly depart." Cleomenes, pleased with the advice of the child, retired to another apartment; and Aristagoras left Sparta altogether, nor could he get an opportunity to give farther particulars of the route to the king's residence.

52. With respect to this road, the case is as follows. There are royal stations all along, and excellent inns, and the whole

road is through an inhabited and safe country. There are twenty stations extending through Lydia and Phrygia, and the distance is ninety-four parasangs and a half. After Phrygia, the river Halys is met with, at which there are gates, which it is absolutely necessary to pass through, and thus to cross the river; there is also a considerable fort on it. When you cross over into Cappadocia, and traverse that country to the borders of Cilicia, there are eight-and-twenty stations, and one hundred and four parasangs; and on the borders of these people you go through two gates, and pass by two forts. When you have gone through these and made the journey through Cilicia, there are three stations, and fifteen parasangs and a half. The boundary of Cilicia and Armenia is a river that is crossed in boats: it is called the Euphrates. In Armenia there are fifteen stations for resting-places, and fifty-six parasangs and a half; there is also a fort in the stations. Four rivers that are crossed in boats flow through this country, which it is absolutely necessary to ferry over. First, the Tigris; then the second and third have the same name, though they are not the same river, nor flow from the same source; for the first mentioned of these flows from the Armenians, and the latter from the Matienians. The fourth river is called the Gyndes, which Cyrus once distributed into three hundred and sixty channels. As you enter from Armenia into the country of Matiene, there are four stations; and from thence, as you proceed to the Cissian territory, there are eleven stations, and forty-two parasangs and a half, to the river Choaspes, which also must be crossed in boats: on this Susa is built. All these stations amount to one hundred and eleven;[7] accordingly, the resting-places at the stations are so many as you go up from Sardis to Susa. 53. Now if the royal road has been correctly measured in parasangs, and if the parasang is equal to thirty stades, as indeed it is, from Sardis to the royal palace, called Memnonia, is a distance of thirteen thousand five hundred stades, the parasangs being four hundred and fifty; and by those who travel one hundred and fifty stades every day, just ninety days are spent on the journey. 54. Thus Aristagoras the Milesian spoke correctly,

[7] The detail of stations above-mentioned gives only eighty-one instead of one hundred and eleven. The discrepancy can only be accounted for by a supposed defect in the manuscripts.

when he told Cleomenes the Lacedæmonian that it was a three months' journey up to the king's residence; but if any one should require a more accurate account than this, I will also point this out to him, for it is necessary to reckon with the above the journey from Ephesus to Sardis. I therefore say that the whole number of stades from the Grecian sea to Susa (for such is the name of the Memnonian city) amounts to fourteen thousand and forty; for from Ephesus to Sardis is a distance of five hundred and forty stades. And thus the three months' journey is lengthened by three days.

55. Aristagoras, being driven from Sparta, went to Athens, which had been delivered from tyrants in the following manner. When Aristogiton and Harmodius, who were originally Gephyræans by extraction, had slain Hipparchus, son of Pisistratus, and brother to the tyrant Hippias, and who had seen a vision in a dream manifestly showing his own fate, after this the Athenians, during the space of four years, were no less, but even more, oppressed by tyranny than before. 56. Now the vision in Hipparchus's dream was as follows. On the night preceding the Panathenaic festival, Hipparchus fancied that a tall and handsome man stood by him, and uttered these enigmatical words: "Lion, endure with enduring mind to bear unendurable ills; no one, among unjust men, shall escape retribution." As soon as it was day he laid these things before the interpreters of dreams, and afterward, having attempted to avert the vision, he conducted the procession in which he perished.

57. The Gephyræans, of whom were the murderers of Hipparchus, were, as they themselves say, originally sprung from Eretria; but, as I find by diligent inquiry, they were Phœnicians, of the number of those Phœnicians who came with Cadmus to the country now called Bœotia, and they inhabited the district of Tanagra, in this country, which fell to their share. The Cadmeans having been first expelled from thence by the Argives, these Gephyræans being afterward expelled by the Bœotians, betook themselves to Athens; and the Athenians admitted them into the number of their citizens, on certain conditions, enacting that they should be excluded from several privileges not worth mentioning. 58. These Phœnicians who came with Cadmus, and of whom the Gephyræans were, when they settled in this country, introduced among the

Greeks many other kinds of useful knowledge, and more particularly letters; which, in my opinion, were not before known to the Grecians. At first they used the characters which all the Phœnicians make use of; but afterward, in process of time, together with the sound, they also changed the shape of the letters. At that time Ionian Greeks inhabited the greatest part of the country round about them; they having learned these letters from the Phœnicians, changed them in a slight degree and made use of them; and in making use of them, they designated them Phœnician, as justice required they should be called, since the Phœnicians had introduced them into Greece. Moreover, the Ionians, from ancient time, call books made from papyrus, parchments, because formerly, from the scarcity of papyrus, they used the skins of goats and sheep; and even at the present day many of the barbarians write on such skins. 59. And I myself have seen in the temple of Ismenian Apollo at Thebes, in Bœotia, Cadmean letters engraved on certain tripods, for the most part resembling the Ionian. One of the tripods has this inscription: "Amphitryon dedicated me on his return from the Teleboans." These must be about the age of Laius, son of Labdacus, son of Polydorus, son of Cadmus. 60. Another tripod has these words in hexameter verse: "Scæus, a boxer, having been victorious, dedicated me, a very beautiful offering to thee, far-darting Apollo." Scæus must have been son of Hippocoon, if indeed it was he who made the offering, and not another person bearing the same name as the son of Hippocoon; and must have been about the time of Œdipus, son of Laius. 61. A third tripod has these words, also in hexameters: "Laodamas, being a monarch, dedicated this tripod, a very beautiful offering, to thee, far-seeing[8] Apollo." During the reign of this Laodamas, son of Eteocles, the Cadmeans were expelled by the Argives, and betook themselves to the Encheleæ. But the Gephyræans, who were then left, were afterward compelled by the Bœotians to retire to Attica; and they built temples in Athens, in which the rest of the Athenians do not participate, but they are distinct from the other temples, more particularly the temple and mysteries of the Achæan Ceres.

62. Thus I have related the vision of Hipparchus's dream,

[8] Or "well-aiming."

and whence were sprung the Gephyræans, of whom were the murderers of Hipparchus; and it is now proper to resume the account I originally set out to relate, *and show* how the Athenians were delivered from tyrants. While Hippias was tyrant, and embittered against the Athenians on account of the death of Hipparchus, the Alcmæonidæ, who were Athenians by extraction, and were then banished by the Pisistratidæ, when they with other Athenian exiles did not succeed in their attempt to effect their return by force, but were signally defeated in their endeavors to reinstate themselves and liberate Athens, having fortified Lipsydrium, which is above Pæonia; thereupon the Alcmæonidæ, practicing every scheme against the Pisistratidæ, contracted with the Amphictyons to build the temple which is now at Delphi, but then did not exist; and as they were wealthy, and originally men of distinction, they constructed the temple in a more beautiful manner than the plan required, both in other respects, and also, though it was agreed they should make it of porine stone, they built its front of Parian marble. 63. Accordingly, as the Athenians state, these men, while staying at Delphi, prevailed on the Pythian by money, when any Spartans should come thither to consult the oracle, either on their own account or that of the public, to propose to them to liberate Athens from servitude. The Lacedæmonians, when the same warning was always given them, sent Anchimolius, son of Aster, a citizen of distinction, with an army to expel the Pisistratidæ from Athens, though they were particularly united to them by the ties of friendship, for they considered their duty to the god more obligatory than their duty to men. These forces they sent by sea in ships, and he, having touched at Phalerum, disembarked his army; but the Pisistratidæ, having had notice of this beforehand, called in assistance from Thessaly, for they had entered into an alliance with them. In accordance with their request, the Thessalians with one consent dispatched a thousand horse to their assistance, and their king Cineas, a native of Conium. When the Pisistratidæ had these auxiliaries, they had recourse to the following plan: having cleared the plains of the Phalereans, and made the country practicable for cavalry, they sent the cavalry against the enemy's camp; and it having fallen on, killed many of the Lacedæmonians, and among them Anchimolius, and the survivors they drove to their ships. The first expedition from Lacedæmon thus got off; and the tomb of Anchimolius is at Alopecæ of Attica, near the temple of Hercules in Cynosarges. 64. Afterward, the Lacedæmonians, having fitted out a larger armament, sent it from Athens, having appointed king Cleomenes, son of Anaxandrides, commander-in-chief; they did not, however, send it again by sea, but by land. On their entrance into the Athenian territory, the Thessalian cavalry first engaged with them, and was soon defeated, and more than forty of their number fell: the survivors immediately departed straight for Thessaly. Cleomenes having reached the city, accompanied by those Athenians who wished to be free, besieged the tyrants who were shut up in the Pelasgian fort. 65. However, the Lacedæmonians would not by any means have been able to expel the Pisistratidæ; for they had no intention of forming a blockade, and the Pisistratidæ were well provided with meat and drink; and after they had besieged them for a few days, they would have returned to Sparta; but now an accident happened, unfortunate for one party, and at the same time advantageous to the other; for the children of the Pisistratidæ were taken as they were being secretly removed from the country; when this occurred, all their plans were thrown into confusion; and, to redeem their children, they submitted to such terms as the Athenians prescribed, so as to quit Attica within five days. They afterward retired to Sigeum, on the Scamander, having governed the Athenians for thirty-six years. They were by extraction Pylians, and Neleïdæ, being sprung from the same ancestors as Codrus and Melanthus, who, though formerly foreigners, became kings of Athens. For this reason Hippocrates gave the same name to his son, in token of remembrance, calling him Pisistratus, after Nestor's son Pisistratus. Thus the Athenians were delivered from tyrants; and what things worthy of recital they either did or suffered before Ionia revolted from Darius, and Aristagoras the Milesian came to Athens to desire their assistance, I shall now relate.

66. Athens, although it was before powerful, being now delivered from tyrants, became still more so. Two men in it had great influence, Clisthenes, one of the Alcmæonidæ, who is reported to have prevailed with the Pythian, and Isagoras, son of Tisander, who was of an illustrious family, though I

am not able to mention his extraction; his kinsmen, however, sacrifice to Carian Jupiter. These men disputed for power; and Clisthenes, being worsted, gained over the people to his side, and afterward he divided the Athenians, who consisted of four tribes, into ten; changing the names, derived from the sons of Ion, Geleon, Ægicores, Argades, and Hoples, and inventing names from other heroes who were all natives, except Ajax; him, though a stranger, he added as a near neighbor and ally. 67. Herein, I think, this Clisthenes imitated his maternal grandfather, Clisthenes, tyrant of Sicyon; for Clisthenes, when he made war on the Argives, in the first place put a stop to the rhapsodists in Sicyon, contending for prizes in reciting the verses of Homer, because the Argives and Argos are celebrated in almost every part; and in the next place, as there was, and still is, a shrine dedicated to Adrastus, son of Talaus, in the very forum of the Sicyonians, he was desirous of expelling him from the country, because he was an Argive. Going, therefore, to Delphi, he consulted the oracle, whether he should expel Adrastus; and the Pythian answered him, saying "that Adrastus indeed was king of the Sicyonians, but Clisthenes deserved to be stoned." Finding the god would not permit this, Clisthenes returned home and considered of a contrivance by which Adrastus might depart of himself. When he thought he had found out a way, he sent to Thebes of Bœotia, and said that he wished to introduce Melanippus, son of Astacus; and the Thebans assented. Clisthenes, therefore, having introduced Melanippus, appointed him a precinct in the very prytaneum, and placed it there in the strongest position. But Clisthenes introduced Melanippus, for it is necessary to mention this motive, because he was the greatest enemy of Adrastus, having killed his brother Mecistes, and his son-in-law Tydeus. When he had appointed him this precinct, he took away the sacrifices and festivals of Adrastus, and gave them to Melanippus. But the Sicyonians had been accustomed to honor Adrastus very highly; for the country itself belonged to Polybus, and Polybus dying without a son, gave the sovereignty to Adrastus, the son of his daughter. The Sicyonians paid other honors to Adrastus, and, moreover, celebrated his misfortune by tragic choruses: not honoring Bacchus, but Adrastus, to that time. But Clisthenes transferred these dances to the worship of

Bacchus, and the rest of the ceremonies to Melanippus. This he did with reference to Adrastus. 68. He also changed the names of the Dorian tribes, in order that the Sicyonians and Argives might not have the same; and in this he very much ridiculed the Sicyonians; for, changing their names into names derived from a swine and an ass, he added only the terminations, except in the case of his own tribe; to this he gave a name significant of his own sovereignty, for they were called Archelai; but others Hyatæ, some Oneatæ, and others Chœreatæ.[9] The Sicyonians adopted these names for their tribes, both during the reign of Clisthenes, and after his death, during sixty years; after that, however, by common consent they changed them into Hylleans, Pamphylians, and Dymanatæ; and they added a fourth, after Ægialeus, son of Adrastus, giving them the name of Ægialeans.

69. Now the Sicyonian Clisthenes had done these things; and the Athenian Clisthenes, who was son to the daughter of this Sicyonian, and had his name from him, from contempt for the Ionians, as appears to me, that *the Athenians* might not have the same tribes as the Ionians, imitated his namesake Clisthenes; for when he had brought over to his own side the whole of the Athenian people, who had been before alienated from him, he changed the names of the tribes, and augmented their number; and established ten phylarchs instead of four, and distributed the people into ten tribes; and having gained over the people, he became much more powerful than his opponents. 70. Isagoras, being overcome in his turn, had recourse to the following counterplot: he called in Cleomenes the Lacedæmonian, who had been on terms of friendship with him from the time of the siege of the Pisistratidæ, and besides, Cleomenes was suspected of having had intercourse with the wife of Isagoras. First of all, therefore, Cleomenes, sending a herald to Athens, required the expulsion of Clisthenes, and with him of many other Athenians, as being "under a curse." He sent this message under the instruction of Isagoras; for the Alcmæonidæ, and those of their party, were accused of the following murder; but neither he himself had any share in it, nor had his friends. 71. Those of the Athenians who were "accursed" obtained the name on the

[9] Hyatæ, from ὗς, *a sow;* Oneatæ, from ὄνος, *an ass;* Chœreatæ, from χοῖρος, *a pig.*

following occasion. Cylon, an Athenian, had been victorious in the Olympic games; he, through pride, aspired to the tyranny; and having associated with himself a band of young men about his own age, attempted to seize the Acropolis, and, not being able to make himself master of it, he seated himself as a suppliant at the statue *of the goddess*. The prytanes of the Naucrari, who then had the administration of affairs in Athens, removed them, under promise that they should not be punished with death. But the Alcmæonidæ are accused of having put them to death. These things were done before the time of Pisistratus.

72. When Cleomenes sent a herald to require the expulsion of Clisthenes and the accursed, Clisthenes himself withdrew. But, nevertheless, Cleomenes came afterward to Athens with a small force, and, on his arrival, banished seven hundred Athenian families, whom Isagoras pointed out to him. Having done this, he next attempted to dissolve the senate, and placed the magistracy in the hands of three hundred partisans of Isagoras. But when the senate resisted and refused to obey, Cleomenes and Isagoras, with his partisans, seized the Acropolis; and the rest of the Athenians, who sided with the senate, besieged them two days: on the third day, as many of them as were Lacedæmonians left the country under a truce. And thus an omen, addressed to Cleomenes, was accomplished; for when he went up to the Acropolis, purposing to take possession of it, he approached the sanctuary of the goddess to consult her; but the priestess, rising from her seat before he had passed the door, said, "Lacedæmonian stranger! retire, nor enter within this precinct; for it is not lawful for Dorians to enter here." He answered, "Woman, I am not a Dorian, but an Achæan." He, however, paying no attention to the omen, made the attempt, and was again compelled to withdraw with the Lacedæmonians. The Athenians put the rest in bonds for execution; and among them Timesitheus of Delphi, of whose deeds both of prowess and courage I could say much. These, then, died in bonds. 73. After this the Athenians, having recalled Clisthenes, and the seven hundred families that had been banished by Cleomenes, sent embassadors to Sardis, wishing to form an alliance with the Persians; for they were assured that the Lacedæmonians and Cleomenes would make war upon them. When the em-

bassadors arrived at Sardis, and had spoken according to their instructions, Artaphernes, son of Hystaspes, governor of Sardis, asked who they were, and what part of the world they inhabited, that they should desire to become allies of the Persians. And having been informed on these points by the embassadors, he answered in few words, that if the Athenians would give earth and water to king Darius, he would enter into an alliance with them; but if they would not give them, he commanded them to depart. The embassadors, having conferred together, said that they would give them, being anxious to conclude the alliance: they, however, on their return home, were greatly blamed.

74. Cleomenes, conceiving that he had been highly insulted in words and deeds by the Athenians, assembled an army from all parts of the Peloponnesus, without mentioning for what purpose he assembled it; but he both purposed to revenge himself upon the Athenians, and desired to establish Isagoras as tyrant, for he had gone with him out of the Acropolis. Cleomenes accordingly invaded the territory of Eleusis with a large force, and the Bœotians, by agreement, took Œnoe and Hysiæ, the extreme divisions of Attica, and the Chalcidians attacked and ravaged the lands of Attica on the other side. The Athenians, though in a state of doubt, resolved to remember the Bœotians and Chalcidians on a future occasion, and took up their position against the Peloponnesians, who were at Eleusis. 75. When the two armies were about to engage, the Corinthians first, considering that they were not acting justly, changed their purpose and withdrew; and afterward, Demaratus, son of Ariston, who was also king of the Spartans, and joined in leading out the army from Lacedæmon, and who had never before had any difference with Cleomenes, *did the same.* In consequence of this division, a law was made in Sparta that the two kings should not accompany the army when it went out *on foreign service;* for until that time both used to accompany it; and that when one of them was released from military service, one of the Tyndaridæ[1] likewise should be left at home; for before that time both these also used to accompany the army as auxiliaries. At that time the rest of the allies, perceiving that the kings of the La-

[1] Castor and Pollux, the guardian deities of Sparta.

cedæmonians did not agree, and that the Corinthians had quitted their post, likewise took their departure. 76. This, then, was the fourth time that the Dorians had come to Attica; having twice entered to make war, and twice for the good of the Athenian people. First, when they settled a colony in Megara, when Codrus was king of Athens, that may properly be called an expedition; a second and third, when they were sent from Sparta for the expulsion of the Pisistratidæ; and a fourth time, when Cleomenes, at the head of the Peloponnesians, invaded Eleusis. Thus the Dorians then invaded Athens for the fourth time.

77. When this army was ingloriously dispersed, the Athenians, desirous to avenge themselves, marched first against the Chalcidians. The Bœotians came out to assist the Chalcidians at the Euripus; and the Athenians, seeing the auxiliaries, resolved to attack the Bœotians before the Chalcidians. Accordingly, the Athenians came to an engagement with the Bœotians, and gained a complete victory; and having killed a great number, took seven hundred of them prisoners. On the same day, the Athenians, having crossed over to Eubœa, came to an engagement also with the Chalcidians; and having conquered them also, left four thousand men, settlers, in possession of the lands of the Hippobotæ;[2] for the most opulent of the Chalcidians were called Hippobotæ. As many of them as they took prisoners, they kept in prison with the Bœotians that were taken, having bound them in fetters; but in time they set them at liberty, having fixed their ransom at two minæ. The fetters in which they had been bound they hung up in the Acropolis, where they remained to my time, hanging on a wall that had been much scorched by fire by the Mede, opposite the temple that faces the west. And they dedicated a tithe of the ransoms, having made a brazen chariot with four horses, and this stands on the left hand as you enter the portico in the Acropolis; and it bears the following inscription: "The sons of the Athenians, having overcome the nations of the Bœotians and Chalcidians in feats of war, quelled their insolence in a dark iron dungeon: they have dedicated these mares, a tithe of the spoil, to Pallas." 78. The Athenians accordingly increased in power; and equality of rights shows, not in one instance only, but in every way, what an excel-

[2] "Feeders of horses."

lent thing it is; for the Athenians, when governed by tyrants, were superior in war to none of their neighbors, but when freed from tyrants, became by far the first. This, then, shows that as long as they were oppressed they purposely acted as cowards, as laboring for a master; but when they were free, every man was zealous to labor for himself. They accordingly did this.

79. After this the Thebans sent to the god, wishing to revenge themselves on the Athenians; but the Pythian said "that they would not obtain vengeance by their own power, but bade them refer the matter to the many-voiced people, and ask the assistance of their nearest friends." Those who were sent to consult the oracle having returned, called a general assembly, and referred the oracle to them. But when they heard them say that they were to ask the assistance of their nearest friends, the Thebans, on hearing this, said, "Do not the Tanagræans, Coronæans, and Thespians live nearest to us, and do not they always fight on our side, and heartily share with us in the toils of war? What need have we, then, to ask their assistance? But probably this is not the meaning of the oracle." 80. While they were discussing the matter, one, having at length comprehended it, said, "I think I understand what the oracle means. Thebe and Ægina are said to be daughters of Asopus. Now, because these were sisters, I think the god has admonished us to entreat the Æginetæ to become our avengers." As no better opinion than this was brought forward, they immediately sent and entreated the Æginetæ, calling upon them to assist them, according to the admonition of the oracle, as being their nearest friends; but they, on their petition, promised to send the Æacidæ[3] to their assistance. 81. The Thebans, relying on the assistance of the Æacidæ, having tried the fortunes of war, and being roughly handled by the Athenians, sent again, and restored the Æacidæ, and requested a supply of men; whereupon the Æginetæ, elated with their present prosperity, and calling to mind the ancient enmity they had toward the Athenians, at the request of the Thebans, levied war upon the Athenians without proclamation; for while they were pursuing the Bœotians, having sailed in long ships to Attica, they ravaged Phalerum, and many villages on the rest of the coast; and

[3] Meaning "the statues of the Æacidæ."

in doing this, they did considerable damage to the Athenians.

82. The enmity that was due of old from the Æginetæ to the Athenians proceeded from this origin. The land of the Epidaurians yielded no fruit; the Epidaurians, therefore, sent to consult the oracle at Delphi concerning this calamity. The Pythian bade them erect statues of Damia and Auxesia, and when they had erected them it would fare better with them. The Epidaurians then asked whether the statues should be of brass or stone; but the Pythian did not allow it to be of either, but of the wood of a cultivated olive. The Epidaurians thereupon requested the Athenians to permit them to cut down an olive-tree, thinking that they were the most sacred; and it is said that there were olive-trees in no other part of the world at that time. The Athenians said that they would permit them, on condition that they should annually bring victims to Minerva Polias and Erectheus. The Epidaurians, having agreed to these terms, obtained what they asked for, and having made statues from these olive-trees, erected them, and their land became fruitful, and they fulfilled their engagements to the Athenians. 83. At that time, and before, the Æginetæ obeyed the Epidaurians, both in other respects, and crossing over to Epidaurus, the Æginetæ gave and received[4] justice from one another. But afterward, having built ships, and having recourse to foolish confidence, they revolted from the Epidaurians, and being at variance, they did them much damage, as they were masters of the sea; and, moreover, they took away from them those statues of Damia and Auxesia, and carried them off, and erected them in the interior of their own territory, the name of which is Œa, and about twenty stades distant from the city. Having erected them in this spot, they propitiated them with sacrifices and derisive dances of women, ten men being assigned to each deity as leaders of the chorus, and the choruses reviled, not any men, but the women of the country. The Epidaurians also had such religious ceremonies, but their religious ceremonies are kept secret. 84. When these statues had been stolen, the Epidaurians ceased to fulfill their engagements to the Athenians. The Athenians sent to expostulate with the Epidaurians, but they demonstrated that they were not in

[4] That is, "brought and defended actions there."

reality guilty of injustice; for as long as they had the statues in their country they fulfilled their engagements, but when they had been deprived of them it was not just that they should still pay the tribute, but they bid them demand it of the Æginetæ who possessed them. Upon this the Athenians, having sent to Ægina, demanded back the statues; but the Æginetæ made answer that they had nothing to do with the Athenians. 85. The Athenians say that after this demand some of their citizens were sent in a single trireme, who, being sent by the commonwealth, and arriving at Ægina, attempted to drag these statues from the pedestals, as made from their wood, in order that they might carry them away; but not being able to get possession of them in that way, they threw cords about the statues, and hauled them along, and as they were hauling them, thunder, and with the thunder an earthquake, came on, and the crew of the trireme, who were hauling them, were in consequence deprived of their senses, and in this condition slew one another as enemies, till only one of the whole number was left and escaped to Phalerum. 86. Thus the Athenians say that it happened; but the Æginitæ say that the Athenians did not come with a single ship, for that they could easily have repulsed one, or a few more than one, even though they had no ships of their own. But *they say* that they sailed against their territory with many ships, and that they yielded and did not hazard a sea fight. They are, however, unable to explain this clearly, whether they yielded because they were conscious that they would be inferior in a sea fight, or with the purpose of doing what they did. They say, however, that the Athenians, when no one prepared to give them battle, disembarked from the ships and proceeded toward the statues; and that, not being able to wrench them from their pedestals, they then threw cords round them, and hauled them until the statues being hauled did the same thing; herein relating what is not credible to me, but may be so to some one else; for *they say* that they fell on their knees, and have ever since continued in that posture. The Æginitæ say that the Athenians did this; but concerning themselves, that, being informed that the Athenians were about to make war upon them, they prepared the Argives to assist them; and, accordingly, that the Athenians landed on the territory of Ægina, and that the Argives came to their assistance; and that they crossed over to the island from Epidaurus unperceived, and fell upon the Athenians unexpectedly, cutting off their retreat to the ships; and at this moment the thunder and earthquake happened. 87. Such is the account given by the Argives and Æginetæ; and it is admitted by the Athenians that only one of their number was saved, and escaped to Attica; but the Argives affirm that this one man survived when they destroyed the Attic army; the Athenians, on the contrary, say, when the deity destroyed it; and that this one did not survive, but perished in the following manner: on his return to Athens, he gave an account of the disaster, and the wives of the men who had gone on the expedition against Ægina, when they heard it, being enraged that he alone of the whole number should be saved, crowded round this man, and piercing him with the clasps of their garments, each asked him where her own husband was: thus he died. This action of the women seemed to the Athenians more dreadful than the disaster itself; however, they had no other way of punishing the women, they therefore compelled them to change their dress for the Ionian; for before that time the wives of the Athenians wore the Dorian dress, which closely resembles the Corinthian; they changed it, therefore, for a linen tunic, that they might not use clasps. Yet if we follow the truth, this garment is not originally Ionian, but Carian; for the whole ancient Grecian dress of the women was the same as that which we now call Dorian. 88. In consequence of this event, it became a custom with both the Argives and the Æginetæ to do this; to make their clasps one half larger than the measure before established, and that the women should chiefly dedicate clasps in the temple of these deities; and to bring no other Attic article within the temple, not even a pitcher; but a law was made that they should drink there in future from vessels of their own country. Accordingly, from that time the wives of the Argives and Æginetæ, on account of their quarrel with the Athenians, continued even to my time to wear clasps larger than formerly.

89. The origin of the enmity entertained by the Athenians against the Æginetæ was such as has been described. At that time, therefore, when the Thebans called upon them, the Æginetæ, recalling to mind what had taken place respecting

the statues, readily assisted the Bœotians. The Æginetæ therefore laid waste the maritime places of Attica, and when the Athenians were preparing to march against the Æginetæ, an oracle came from Delphi *enjoining them* "to wait for thirty years from the period of the injury committed by the Æginetæ, and in the thirty-first year, after building a temple to Æacus, to begin the war against the Æginetæ, and then they would succeed according to their wishes; but if they should march against them immediately, they should in the mean while endure much and also inflict much, but in the end would subdue them." When the Athenians heard this answer reported, they erected that temple to Æacus which now stands in the forum, yet they could not bear to wait thirty years, when they heard that they ought to wait, though they had suffered such indignities from the Æginetæ. 90. But as they were preparing to take their revenge, an affair, set on foot by the Lacedæmonians, became an impediment; for the Lacedæmonians, being informed of the practices of the Alcmæonidæ toward the Pythia, and those of the Pythia against themselves and the Pisistratidæ, considered it a double misfortune, because they had expelled men who were their own friends out of their country, and because, when they had done this, no gratitude was shown them by the Athenians. In addition to this, the oracles urged them on, telling them that they would suffer many and grievous indignities from the Athenians, of which oracles they knew nothing before, but then became acquainted with them on the return of Cleomenes to Sparta. Cleomenes got the oracles from the Acropolis of the Athenians; the Pisistratidæ had had them before, and left them in the temple when they were expelled; and as they were left behind, Cleomenes took them away. 91. When the Lacedæmonians obtained the oracles, and saw the Athenians increasing in power, and not at all disposed to submit to them, taking into consideration that if the people of Attica should continue free they would become of equal weight with themselves, but if depressed by a tyranny would be weak and ready to obey; having considered each of these things, they sent for Hippias, son of Pisistratus, from Sigeum, on the Hellespont, to which place the Pisistratidæ had retired. And when Hippias came, in compliance with their invitation, the Spartans, having summoned also the embassadors of tho rest of their confederates, addressed them as follows: "Confederates, we are conscious that we have not acted rightly; for, being induced by lying oracles, the men who were our best friends, and who had promised to keep Athens subject to us, them we expelled from their country, and then, having done this, we delivered the city to an ungrateful people, who, after they had been set at liberty, and had lifted up their heads through our means, have insultingly ejected us and our king; and having obtained renown, are growing in power, as their neighbors the Bœotians and Chalcidians have already learned full well, and as others will soon learn to their cost.[5] Since, then, in doing these things, we have committed an error, we will now endeavor, with your assistance, to remedy the mischief and punish them; for on this very account we sent for, Hippias, who is here present, and *summoned* you from your cities, that by common consent, and combined forces, we may take him back to Athens, and restore to him what we took away."

92. Thus these spoke; but the majority of the confederates did not approve of their proposition. The rest kept silence, but Sosicles the Corinthian spoke as follows: "Surely the heavens will sink beneath the earth, and the earth ascend aloft above the heavens; men will live in the sea, and the fishes where men did before, now that you, O Lacedæmonians, abolish equality, dissolve a commonwealth, and prepare to restore tyrannies in the cities, than which there is nothing more unjust, nor more cruel among men. If, in truth, this appears to you a good thing, that cities should be ruled by tyrants, do you first set up a tyrant over yourselves, and then attempt to set them up over others. But now, while ye yourselves are altogether unacquainted with tyrannical power, and watch with jealousy that such a thing should not happen in Sparta, ye behave contemptuously toward your allies. But if ye had been taught by experience, as we have, ye would have a better proposal to make to us than you now do. (2.) The

[5] τάχα δέ τις καὶ ἄλλος ἐκμαθήσεται ἁμαρτών. I have ventured on a new mode of translating this passage, which appears to me more in accordance with the Greek idiom. Baehr, whose version is most simple and literal, renders it "and perhaps some one else will learn that he has committed an error;" meaning the Lacedæmonians themselves, to whom the speaker doubtless alludes.

constitution of the Corinthians was formerly of this kind: it was an oligarchy, and those who were called Bacchiadæ governed the city; they intermarried only within their own family. Amphion, one of these men, had a lame daughter; her name was Labda. As no one of the Bacchiadæ would marry her, Eetion, son of Echecrates, who was of the district of Petra, though originally one of the Lapithæ, and a descendant of Cæneus, had her. He had no children by this wife, nor by any other. He therefore went to Delphi to inquire about having offspring; and immediately as he entered, the Pythia saluted him in the following lines: "Eetion, no one honors thee, though worthy of much honor. Labda is pregnant, and will bring forth a round stone; it will fall on monarchs, and will vindicate Corinth." This oracle, pronounced to Eetion, was by chance reported to the Bacchiadæ, to whom a former oracle concerning Corinth was unintelligible, and which tended to the same end as that of Eetion, and was in these terms: "An eagle broods on rocks;[6] and shall bring forth a lion, strong and carnivorous; and it shall loosen the knees of many. Now ponder this well, ye Corinthians, who dwell around beauteous Pirene and frowning Corinth." (3.) Now this, which had been given before, was unintelligible to the Bacchiadæ; but now, when they heard that which was delivered to Eetion, they presently understood the former one, since it agreed with that given to Eetion. And though they comprehended, they kept it secret, purposing to destroy the offspring that should be born to Eetion. As soon as the woman brought forth, they sent ten of their own number to the district where Eetion lived, to put the child to death; and when they arrived at Petra, and entered the court of Eetion, they asked for the child; but Labda, knowing nothing of the purpose for which they had come, and supposing that they asked for it out of affection for the father, brought the child, and put it in the hands of one of them. Now it had been determined by them in the way, that whichever of them should first receive the child, should dash it on the ground. When, however, Labda brought and gave it to one of them, the child, by a divine providence, smiled on the man who received it;

[6] The words αἰετὸς, "an eagle," and πέτρῃσι, "rocks," bear an enigmatical meaning; the former intimating "Eetion," and the latter his birth-place, "Petra."

and when he perceived this, a feeling of pity restrained him from killing it; and, moved by compassion, he gave it to the second, and he to the third: thus the infant, being handed from one to another, passed through the hands of all the ten, and not one of them was willing to destroy it. Having therefore delivered the child again to his mother, and gone out, they stood at the door, and attacked each other with mutual recriminations; and especially the first who took the child, because he had not done as had been determined. At last, when some time had elapsed, they determined to go in again, and that every one should share in the murder. (4.) But it was fated that misfortunes should spring up to Corinth from the progeny of Eetion; for Labda, standing at the very door, heard all that had passed; and fearing that they might change their resolution, and having obtained the child a second time, might kill it, she took and hid it, in a place which appeared least likely to be thought of, in a chest; being very certain that if they should return and come back to search, they would pry every where, which in fact did happen; but when, having come and made a strict search, they could not find the child, they resolved to depart, and tell those who sent them that they had done all that they had commanded. (5.) After this, Eetion's son grew up, and having escaped this danger, the name of Cypselus was given him, from the chest. When Cypselus reached man's estate, and consulted the oracle, an ambiguous answer was given him at Delphi; relying on which, he attacked and got possession of Corinth. The oracle was this: 'Happy this man, who is come down to my dwelling; Cypselus, son of Eetion, king of renowned Corinth; he and his children, but not his children's children.' Such was the oracle. And Cypselus, having obtained the tyranny, behaved himself thus: he banished many of the Corinthians, deprived many of their property, and many more of their life. (6.) When he had reigned thirty years, and ended his life happily, his son Periander became his successor in the tyranny. Now Periander at first was more mild than his father; but when he had communicated by embassadors with Thrasybulus, tyrant of Miletus, he became far more cruel than Cypselus; for, having sent a nuncio to Thrasybulus, he asked in what way, having ordered affairs most securely, he might best govern the city. Thrasybulus conducted the persons who came from

Periander out of the city, and going into a field of corn, and as he went through the standing corn, questioning him about, and making him repeat over again, the account of his coming from Corinth, he cut off any ear that he saw taller than the rest, and having cut it off, he threw it away, till in this manner he had destroyed the best and deepest of the corn. Having gone through the piece of ground, and given no message at all, he dismissed the nuncio. When the nuncio returned to Corinth, Periander was anxious to know the answer of Thrasybulus; but he said that Thrasybulus had given him no answer, and wondered he should have sent him to such a man, for that he was crazy, and destroyed his own property, relating what he had seen done by Thrasybulus. (7.) But Periander, comprehending the meaning of the action, and understanding that Thrasybulus advised him to put to death the most eminent of the citizens, thereupon exercised all manner of cruelties toward his subjects; for whatever Cypselus had left undone, by killing and banishing, Periander completed. One day he stripped all the Corinthian women on account of his own wife Melissa;[7] for when he sent messengers to the Thesprotians, on the river Acheron, to consult the oracle of the dead respecting a deposit made by a stranger, Melissa having appeared, said that she would neither make it known, nor tell in what place the deposit lay, because she was cold and naked; for that there was no use in the garments in which he had buried her, since they had not been burned; and as a proof that she spoke truth, *she added* that Periander had put his bread into a cold oven. When this answer was brought back to Periander, for the token was convincing to him, since he had lain with Melissa after her death, he immediately, on receiving the message, made proclamation that all the women of Corinth should repair to the temple of Juno. They accordingly went, as to a festival, dressed in their best attire; but he, having privately introduced his guards, stripped them all alike, both the free women and attendants; and having collected them together in a pit, he invoked Melissa, and burned them. When he had done this, and sent a second time, the phantom of Melissa told in what place she had laid the stranger's deposit. Such, O Lacedæmonians, is a tyranny, and such are its deeds. Great astonishment, therefore, immediately seized us Corinthians,

[7] See B. III. chap. 50.

when we understood you had sent for Hippias; but now we are still more astonished at hearing you say what you do; and we entreat you, adjuring you by the Grecian gods, not to establish tyrannies in the cities. Nevertheless, if you will not desist, but against all right will endeavor to restore Hippias, know that the Corinthians, at least, do not approve of your design."

93. Sosicles, who was embassador from Corinth, spoke thus. But Hippias answered him, having invoked the same gods as he had, that the Corinthians would most of all regret the Pisistratidæ when the fated days should come for them to be harassed by the Athenians. Hippias answered thus, as being more accurately acquainted with the oracles than any other man. The rest of the confederates, until then, had kept silence; but when they heard Sosicles speak freely, every one of them, with acclamation, embraced the opinion of the Corinthian; and they adjured the Lacedæmonians not to introduce any innovation into a Grecian city; and thus that design was defeated. 94. When Hippias departed thence, Amyntas the Macedonian offered him Anthemus, and the Thessalians offered him Iolcus; he, however, accepted neither of them, but returned back to Sigeum, which Pisistratus had taken by force from the Mityleneans, and having got possession of it, he appointed his natural son, Hegesistratus, born of an Argive woman, to be tyrant; he, however, did not retain without a struggle what he had received from Pisistratus; for the Mityleneans and the Athenians, setting out from the city of Achilleïum and Sygeum, *respectively* carried on war for a long time; the former demanding restitution of the place, and the Athenians not only not conceding it, but showing by argument that the Æolians had no more right to the territories of Ilium than they, or any other of the Greeks, who had assisted Menelaus in avenging the rape of Helen. 95. While they were at war, various other events occurred in the different battles; and among them, Alcæus the poet, when an engagement took place, and the Athenians were victorious, saved himself by flight; but the Athenians got possession of his arms, and hung them up in the temple of Minerva at Sigeum. Alcæus having described this in an ode, sent it to Mitylene to inform his friend Melanippus of his misfortune. Periander, son of Cypselus, reconciled the Mityleneans and Athenians, for they referred to

him as arbitrator; and he reconciled them on these terms, that each should retain what they had. Thus, then, Sigeum became subject to the Athenians. 96. When Hippias returned from Lacedæmon to Asia, he set every thing in motion, accusing the Athenians falsely to Artaphernes, and contriving every means by which Athens might be subjected to himself and Darius. Hippias accordingly busied himself about this, and the Athenians, having heard of it, sent embassadors to Sardis, warning the Persians not to give ear to the Athenian exiles. But Artaphernes bade them, if they wished to continue safe, receive Hippias back again. The Athenians, however, would not consent to the proposed condition; and when they did not consent, it was determined openly to declare themselves enemies to the Persians.

97. When they were taking this resolution, and were being falsely accused to the Persians, at that very time Aristagoras the Milesian, having been expelled from Sparta by Cleomenes the Lacedæmonian, arrived at Athens; for this city was much more powerful than the rest. Aristagoras, presenting himself before the people, said the same he had done at Sparta respecting the wealth of Asia and the Persian mode of warfare, how they used neither shield nor spear, and would be easily conquered. He said this, and, in addition, that the Milesians were a colony of the Athenians, and it was but reasonable that they, having such great power, should rescue them; and there was nothing he did not promise, as being very much in earnest, until at length he persuaded them; for it appears to be more easy to impose upon a multitude than one man, since he was not able to impose upon Cleomenes the Lacedæmonian singly, but did so to thirty thousand Athenians. The Athenians accordingly, being persuaded, decreed to send twenty ships to succor the Ionians, having appointed Melanthius commander over them, a citizen who was universally esteemed. These ships were the source of calamities both to Greeks and barbarians. 98. Aristagoras having sailed first, and arrived at Miletus, had recourse to a project from which no advantage could result to the Ionians; nor did he employ it for that purpose, but that he might vex king Darius. He sent a man into Phrygia, to the Pæonians, who had been carried away captive by Megabazus from the river Strymon, and occupied a tract in Phrygia, and a village by themselves. When

he reached the Pæonians, he spoke as follows: "Men of Pæonia, Aristagoras, tyrant of Miletus, has sent me to suggest to you a mode of deliverance, if you will take his advice; for all Ionia has revolted from the king, and offers you an opportunity of returning safe to your own country; as far as the coast take care of yourselves, and we will provide for the rest." The Pæonians, when they heard these words, considered it a very joyful event, and having taken with them their children and wives, fled to the coast; but some of them, through fear, remained where they were. When the Pæonians reached the coast, they thence crossed over to Chios; and just as they had reached Chios, a large body of Persian cavalry came on their heels, pursuing the Pæonians; and when they did not overtake them, sent orders to Chios to the Pæonians commanding them to return; but the Pæonians did not listen to the proposal, but the Chians conveyed them to Lesbos, and the Lesbians forwarded them to Doriscus; thence proceeding on foot, they reached Pæonia.

99. But Aristagoras, when the Athenians arrived with twenty ships, bringing with them five triremes of the Eretrians, who engaged in this expedition, not out of good will to the Athenians, but of the Milesians themselves, in order to repay a former obligation; for the Milesians had formerly joined the Eretrians in the war against the Chalcidians, at the time when the Samians assisted the Chalcidians against the Eretrians and Milesians. When these, then, had arrived, and the rest of the allies had come up, Aristagoras resolved to make an expedition to Sardis. He himself did not march with the army, but remained at Miletus, and appointed others as generals of the Milesians, his own brother Charopinus, and of the other citizens Hermophantus. 100. The Ionians, having arrived at Ephesus with this force, left their ships at Coressus, in the Ephesian territory, and they advanced with a numerous army, taking Ephesians for their guides; and marching by the side of the river Cayster, from thence they crossed Mount Tmolus, and reached and took Sardis without opposition; and they took all except the citadel, but Artaphernes, with a strong garrison, defended the citadel. 101. The following accident prevented them, after they had taken the city, from plundering it. Most of the houses in Sardis were built with reeds; and such of them as were built with brick

had roofs of reeds. A soldier happened to set fire to one of these, and immediately the flame spread from house to house, and consumed the whole city. While the city was being burned, the Lydians, and as many of the Persians as were in the city, being inclosed on every side, since the fire had got possession of the extreme parts, and had no means of escaping from the city, rushed together to the market-place, and to the river Pactolus, which, bringing down grains of gold from Mount Tmolus, flows through the middle of the market-place, and then discharges itself into the river Hermus, and that into the sea. The Lydians and Persians, therefore, being assembled on this Pactolus and at the market-place, were constrained to defend themselves; and the Ionians, seeing some of the enemy standing on their defense, and others coming up in great numbers, retired through fear to the mountain called Tmolus, and thence under favor of the night retreated to their ships. 102. Thus Sardis was burned, and in it the temple of the native goddess Cybele; the Persians, making a pretext of this, afterward burned in retaliation the temples of Greece. As soon as the Persians who had settlements on this side the river Halys were informed of these things, they drew together, and marched to assist the Lydians; and they happened to find that the Ionians were no longer at Sardis; but following on their track, they overtook them at Ephesus; and the Ionians drew out in battle-array against them, and coming to an engagement, were sorely beaten; and the Persians slew many of them, and among other persons of distinction, Eualcis, general of the Eretrians, who had gained the prize in the contests for the crown, and had been much celebrated by Simonides the Cean. Those who escaped from the battle were dispersed throughout the cities.

103. At that time such was the result of the encounter. Afterward, the Athenians, totally abandoning the Ionians, though Aristagoras urgently solicited them by embassadors, refused to send them any assistance. The Ionians, being deprived of the alliance of the Athenians (for they had conducted themselves in such a manner toward Darius from the first), nevertheless prepared for war with the king; and having sailed to the Hellespont, they reduced Byzantium and all the other cities in that quarter to their obedience. Then having sailed out of the Hellespont, they gained over to their

alliance the greater part of Caria; for the city of Caunus, which before would not join their alliance, when they had burned Sardis, came over to their side. 104. And all the Cyprians, except the Amathusians, came over to them of their own accord; for they too had revolted from the Mede on the following occasion. Onesilus was younger brother of Gorgus, king of the Salaminians, and son of Chersis, son of Siromus, son of Euelthon: this man had frequently before exhorted his brother to revolt from the king; but when he heard that the Ionians had revolted, he pressed him very urgently; but, finding he could not persuade Gorgus, Onesilus with his partisans, thereupon having watched an opportunity when he had gone out of the city of the Salaminians, shut the gates against him. Gorgus, being thus deprived of his city, fled to the Medes; and Onesilus ruled over Salamis, and endeavored to persuade all the Cyprians to join in the revolt. The rest he persuaded; but the Amathusians, who would not listen to him, he sat down and besieged.

105. Onesilus accordingly besieged Amathus. But when it was told king Darius that Sardis had been taken and burned by the Athenians and Ionians, and that Aristagoras the Milesian was the chief of the confederacy, and the contriver of that enterprise, it is related that he, when he heard this, took no account of the Ionians, well knowing that they would not escape unpunished for their rebellion, but inquired where the Athenians were: then having been informed, he called for a bow, and having received one, and put an arrow into it, he let it fly toward heaven, and as he shot it into the air, he said, "O Jupiter, grant that I may revenge myself on the Athenians!" Having thus spoken, he commanded one of his attendants, every time dinner was set before him, to say thrice, "Sire, remember the Athenians." 106. Having given this order, and summoned to his presence Histiæus the Milesian, whom he had already detained a long time, Darius said, "I am informed, Histiæus, that your lieutenant, to whom you intrusted Miletus, has attempted innovations against me; for, having brought men from the other continent, and with them Ionians, who shall give me satisfaction for what they have done; having persuaded these to accompany them, he has deprived me of Sardis. Now can it appear to you that this is right? Could such a thing have been done without your advice? Be-

ware lest hereafter you expose yourself to blame." To this Histiæus answered, "O king, what have you said? that I should advise a thing from which any grief, great or little, should ensue to you! With what object should I do so? What am I in want of? I, who have all things the same as you, and am deemed worthy to share all your counsels? But if my lieutenant has done any such thing as you mention, be assured he has done it of his own contrivance. But, in the outset, I do not believe the account that the Milesians and my lieutenant have attempted any innovations against your authority; yet, if they have done any thing of the kind, and you have heard the truth, consider, O king, what mischief you have done in withdrawing me from the coast; for the Ionians seem, when I was out of their sight, to have done what they long ago desired to do; and had I been in Ionia, not one city would have stirred. Suffer me, therefore, to go with all speed to Ionia, that I may restore all things there to their former condition, and deliver into your hands this lieutenant of Miletus, who has plotted the whole. When I have done this according to your mind, I swear by the royal gods not to put off the garments which I shall wear when I go down to Ionia before I have made the great island Sardinia tributary to you." 107. Histiæus, speaking thus, deceived the king. But Darius was persuaded, and let him go, having charged him to return to him at Susa so soon as he should have accomplished what he had promised.

108. While the news concerning Sardis was going up to the king, and Darius, having done what has been described relating to the bow, held a conference with Histiæus, and while Histiæus, having been dismissed by Darius, was on his journey to the sea—during all this time the following events took place. Tidings were brought to Onesilus the Salaminian, as he was besieging the Amathusians, that Artybius, a Persian, leading a large Persian force on shipboard, was to be expected in Cyprus. Onesilus, having been informed of this, sent heralds to the different parts of Ionia, inviting them to assist him; and the Ionians, without any protracted deliberation, came with a large armament. The Ionians accordingly arrived at Cyprus, and the Persians, having crossed over in ships from Cilicia, marched by land against Salamis; but the Phœnicians in their ships doubled the promontory, which is

called the key of Cyprus. 109. This having taken place, the tyrants of Cyprus, having called together the general of the Ionians, said, "Men of Ionia, we Cyprians give you the choice, to engage with whichever you wish, the Persians or Phœnicians. If you choose to try your strength with the Persians drawn up on land, it is time for you to disembark from your ships, and to draw up on land, and for us to go on board your ships, in order to oppose the Phœnicians; but if you would rather try your strength with the Phœnicians, whichever of these you choose, it behooves you so to behave yourselves, that, as far as depends on you, both Ionia and Cyprus may be free." To this the Ionians answered: "The general council of the Ionians has sent us to guard the sea, and not that, having delivered our ships to the Cyprians, we ourselves should engage with the Persians by land. We therefore shall endeavor to do our duty in that post to which we have been appointed; and it behooves you, bearing in mind what you have suffered under the yoke of the Medes, to prove yourselves to be brave men." The Ionians made answer in these words. 110. Afterward, when the Persians had reached the plain of the Salaminians, the kings of the Cyprians drew up their forces in line, stationing the other Cyprians against the other soldiery *of the enemy*, but having selected the best of the Salaminians and Solians, they stationed them against the Persians. Onesilus voluntarily took up his position directly against Artybius, the general of the Persians. 111. Artybius used to ride on a horse that had been taught to rear up against an armed enemy. Onesilus, therefore, having heard of this, and having as a shield-bearer a Carian well skilled in matters of war, and otherwise full of courage, said to this man, "I am informed that the horse of Artybius rears up, and with his feet and mouth attacks whomsoever he is made to engage with; do you, therefore, determine at once, and tell me which you will watch and strike, whether the horse or Artybius himself." His attendant answered, "I am ready to do both, or either of them, and, indeed, whatever you may command; but I will declare how it appears to me to be most conducive to your interest. A king and a general ought, I think, to engage with a king and a general; for if you vanquish one who is a general, your glory is great; and, in the next place, if he should vanquish you, which may the gods avert, to fall by a noble hand is but half the calamity; but we servants should engage with other servants, and also against a horse, whose tricks do not you fear at all; for I promise you he shall never hereafter rear up against any man." 112. Thus he spoke, and forthwith the forces joined battle by land and sea. Now the Ionians, fighting valiantly on that day, defeated the Phœnicians at sea; and of these the Samians most distinguished themselves; but on land, when the armies met, they engaged in close combat; and the following happened with respect to the two generals: when Artybius, seated on his horse, bore down upon Onesilus, Onesilus, as he had concerted with his shield-bearer, struck Artybius himself as he was bearing down upon him; and as the horse was throwing his feet against the shield of Onesilus, the Carian thereupon struck him with a scythe, and cut off the horse's feet; so that Artybius, the general of the Persians, fell together with his horse on the spot. 113. While the rest were fighting, Stesenor, who was of Curium, deserted with no inconsiderable body of men; these Curians are said to be a colony of Argives; and when the Curians had deserted, the chariots of war belonging to the Salaminians did the same as the Curians: in consequence of this, the Persians became superior to the Cyprians; and the army being put to flight, many others fell, and among them Onesilus, son of Chersis, who had contrived the revolt of the Cyprians, and the king of the Solians, Aristocyprus, son of Philocyprus; of that Philocyprus whom Solon the Athenian, when he visited Cyprus, celebrated in his verses above all tyrants. 114. Now the Amathusians, having cut off the head of Onesilus because he had besieged them, took it to Amathus, and suspended it over the gates; and when the head was suspended, and had become hollow, a swarm of bees entered it, and filled it with honey-comb. When this happened, the Amathusians consulted the oracle respecting it, and an answer was given them "that they should take down the head and bury it, and sacrifice annually to Onesilus as to a hero; and if they did so, it would turn out better for them." 115. The Amathusians did accordingly, and *continued to do so* until my time. The Ionians, who had fought by sea at Cyprus, when they heard that the affairs of Onesilus were ruined, and that the rest of the Cyprian cities were besieged except Salamis, but this the Salaminians had restored to their former king

Gorgus; the Ionians, as soon as they learned this, sailed away to Ionia. Of the cities in Cyprus, Soli held out against the siege for the longest time; but the Persians, having undermined the wall all round, took it in the fifth month.

116. Thus the Cyprians, having been free for one year, were again reduced to servitude; but Daurises, who had married a daughter of Darius, and Hymees, and Otanes, and other Persian generals who also had married daughters of Darius, having pursued those of the Ionians who had attacked Sardis, and having driven them to their ships when they had conquered them in battle, next divided the cities among themselves and proceeded to plunder them. 117. Daurises, directing his march toward the cities on the Hellespont, took Dardanus; he also took Abydos, Percote, Lampsacus, and Pæsus: these he took each in one day; but as he was advancing from Pæsus against Parium, news was brought him that the Carians, having conspired with the Ionians, had revolted from the Persians; therefore, turning back from the Hellespont, he led his army against Caria. 118. Somehow news of this was brought to the Carians before Daurises arrived. The Carians, having heard of it, assembled at what are called the White Columns, on the river Marsyas, which, flowing from the territory of Idrias, flows into the Mæander. When the Carians were assembled on this spot, several other propositions were made, of which the best appeared to be that of Pixodarus, son of Mausolus, a Cyndian, who had married the daughter of Syennesis, king of the Cilicians. His opinion was, that the Carians, having crossed the Mæander, and having the river in their rear, should so engage, in order that the Carians, not being able to retreat, and being compelled to remain on their ground, might be made even braver than they naturally were. This opinion, however, did not prevail, but that the Mæander should rather be in the rear of the Persians than of themselves, to the end that if the Persians should be put to flight, and worsted in the engagement, they might have no retreat, and fall into the river. 119. Afterward, the Persians having come up and crossed the Mæander, the Carians thereupon came to an engagement with the Persians on the banks of the river Marsyas, and they fought an obstinate battle, and for a long time, but at last were overpowered by numbers. Of the Persians there fell about two thousand, and

of the Carians ten thousand. Such of them as escaped from thence were shut up in Labranda, a large precinct and sacred grove of plane-trees, dedicated to Jupiter Stratius. The Carians are the only people we know who offer sacrifices to Jupiter Stratius. They, then, being shut up in this place, consulted on the means of safety, whether they would fare better by surrendering themselves to the Persians, or by abandoning Asia altogether. 120. While they were deliberating about this, the Milesians and their allies came to their assistance; upon this the Carians gave up what they were before deliberating about, and prepared to renew the war; and they engaged with the Persians when they came up, and having fought, were more signally beaten than before; though in the whole many fell, the Milesians suffered most. 121. The Carians, however, afterward recovered this wound, and renewed the contest; for, hearing that the Persians designed to invade their cities, they placed an ambuscade on the way to Pedasus, into which the Persians falling by night, were cut in pieces, both they and their generals Daurises, Amorges, and Sisamaces; and with them perished Myrses, son of Gyges. The leader of this ambuscade was Heraclides, son of Ibanolis, a Mylassian. Thus the Persians were destroyed.

122. Hymees, who was also one of those who pursued the Ionians that had attacked Sardis, bending his march toward the Propontis, took Cius of Mysia; but having taken it, when he heard that Daurises had quitted the Hellespont, and was marching against Caria, he abandoned the Propontis, and led his army on the Hellespont; and he subdued all the Æolians who inhabited the territory of Ilium, and subdued the Gergithæ, the remaining descendants of the ancient Teucrians; but Hymees himself, having subdued these nations, died of disease in the Troad. 123. Thus, then, he died; but Artaphernes, governor of Sardis, and Otanes, one of the three generals,[8] were appointed to invade Ionia and the neighboring territory of Æolia. Of Ionia, accordingly, they took Clazomenæ; and of the Æolians, Cyme.

124. When these cities were taken, Aristagoras the[9] Milesian, for he was not, as it proved, a man of strong courage, who

[8] The two others were Daurises and Hymees; see ch. 116.

[9] The reader will observe that the sentence is broken and imperfect; it is so in the original.

having thrown Ionia into confusion, and raised great disturbances, thought of flight when he saw these results; and, besides, it seemed to him impossible to overcome king Darius; therefore, having called his partisans together, he conferred with them, saying "that it would be better for them to have some sure place of refuge in case they should be expelled from Miletus." *He asked*, therefore, whether he should lead them to Sardinia, to found a colony, or to Myrcinus of the Edonians, which Histiæus had begun to fortify, having received it as a gift from Darius. 125. However, the opinion of Hecatæus the historian, son of Hegesander, was, that they should set out for neither of these places, but that, having built a fortress in the island of Leros, they should remain quiet if they were compelled to quit Miletus; and that at some future time, proceeding from thence, they might return to Miletus. This was the advice of Hecatæus. 126. But Aristagoras himself was decidedly in favor of proceeding to Myrcinus; he therefore intrusted Miletus to Pythagoras, a citizen of distinction, and he himself, taking with him all who were willing, sailed to Thrace, and took possession of the region to which he was bound. But, setting out from thence, both Aristagoras himself and all his army perished by the hands of the Thracians as he was laying siege to a city, and the Thracians were willing to depart on terms of capitulation.

BOOK VI.

ERATO.

Aristagoras, having induced the Ionians to revolt, thus died; and Histiæus, tyrant of Miletus, having been dismissed by Darius, repaired to Sardis. When he arrived from Susa, Artaphernes, governor of Sardis, asked him for what reason he supposed the Ionians had revolted. Histiæus said he did not know, and seemed surprised at what had happened, as if he in truth knew nothing of the present state of affairs. But Artaphernes, perceiving that he was dissembling, and being aware of the exact truth as to the revolt, said, "Histiæus, the state of the case is this: you made the shoe, and Aristagoras has put it on." 2. Artaphernes spoke thus concerning the revolt; but Histiæus, fearing Artaphernes, as being privy to the truth, as soon as night came on, fled to the coast, having deceived king Darius; for, having promised to reduce the great island of Sardinia, he insinuated himself into the command of the Ionians in the war against Darius. Having crossed over to Chios, he was put in chains by the Chians, being suspected by them of planning some new design against them in favor of Darius. However, the Chians, having learned the whole truth, and that he was an enemy to the king, released him. 3. At that time, Histiæus being questioned by the Ionians why he had so earnestly pressed Aristagoras to revolt from the king, and had wrought so much mischief to the Ionians, he by no means made known to them the true reason, but told them that "king Darius had resolved to remove the Phœnicians, and settle them in Ionia, and the Ionians in Phœnicia; and for this reason he had pressed him." Although the king had formed no resolution of the kind, he terrified the Ionians. 4. After this, Histiæus, corresponding by means of a messenger, Hermippus, an Atarnian, sent letters to certain Persians in Sardis, as if they had before conferred with him on the subject of a revolt; but Hermippus did not deliver the letters to the persons to whom he had been sent, but put them into the hands of Artaphernes; he, having discovered all that was going on, commanded Hermippus to deliver the letters of Histiæus to the persons for whom he brought them, and to deliver to him the answers that should be sent back to Histiæus from the Persians. Thus they being discovered, Artaphernes thereupon put many of the Persians to death; and in consequence, there was a great commotion in Sardis. 5. Histiæus being disappointed of these hopes, the Chians conveyed him to Miletus at his own request; but the Milesians, delighted at being rid of Aristagoras, were by no means desirous to receive another tyrant in their country, as they had tasted of freedom. Thereupon Histiæus, going down to Miletus by night, endeavored to enter it by force, but was wounded in the thigh by one of the Milesians. When he was repulsed from his own country, he went back to Chios, and from thence, since he could not persuade the Chians to furnish him with ships, he crossed over to Mitylene, and prevailed with the Lesbians to furnish him with ships; and they, having manned eight triremes, sailed with Histiæus to Byzantium. There taking up their station, they took all the ships that sailed out of the Pontus, except such of them as said they were ready to submit to Histiæus.

6. Histiæus, then, and the Mitylenians, acted as above described; but a large naval and land force was expected against Miletus itself; for the Persian generals, having united their forces and formed one camp, marched against Miletus, deeming the other cities of less consequence. Of the maritime forces, the Phœnicians were the most zealous, and the Cyprians, who had been lately subdued, served with them, and the Cilicians and Egyptians. 7. They then advanced against Miletus and the rest of Ionia; but the Ionians, having heard of this, sent their respective deputies to the Panionium,[1] and when they arrived at that place and consulted together, it was determined not to assemble any land forces to oppose the Persians, but that the Milesians themselves should defend the walls, and that they should man their navy, without leaving a single ship behind; and after they had manned them, to assemble as soon as possible at Lade, to

[1] See B. I. chap. 143, 148.

fight in defense of Miletus. Lade is a small island lying off the city of the Milesians. 8. After this, the Ionians came up with their ships manned, and with them the Æolians who inhabit Lesbos; and they formed their line in the following order. The Milesians themselves, who furnished eighty ships, occupied the east wing; and next to these the Prienians with twelve ships, and the Myusians with three; the Teians were next to the Myusians, with seventeen ships; the Chians were next the Teians, with a hundred ships; next to these, the Erythræans and the Phocæans were drawn up, the Erythræans furnishing eight ships, and the Phocæans three; next the Phocæans were the Lesbians with seventy ships; last of all the Samians were drawn up, occupying the western wing with sixty ships. Of all these, the whole number amounted to three hundred and fifty-three triremes. Such was the fleet of the Ionians. 9. On the side of the barbarians the number of ships amounted to six hundred; but when they arrived on the Milesian coast, and all their land forces were come up, the Persian generals, hearing the number of the Ionian fleet, began to fear they should not be strong enough to overcome it, and so should be also unable to take Miletus, since they were not masters at sea, and then might be in danger of receiving punishment at the hands of Darius. Taking these things into consideration, they summoned the tyrants of the Ionians, who, having been deprived of their governments by Aristagoras, had fled to the Medes, and happened at that time to be serving in the army against Miletus; having called together such of these men as were at hand, they addressed them as follows: "Men of Ionia, let each of you now show his zeal for the king's house; for let each of you endeavor to detach his own countrymen from the rest of the confederacy, and hold out to them and proclaim this, that they shall suffer no hurt on account of their rebellion, nor shall their buildings, whether sacred or profane, be burned, nor shall they be treated with more severity than they were before. But if they will not do this, and will at all events come to the hazard of a battle, threaten them with this which will surely befall them; that when conquered in battle, they shall be enslaved; that we will make eunuchs of their sons, and transport their virgins to Bactra, and then give their country to others." 10. Thus they spoke; but the tyrants of the Ionians sent each by night to his own countrymen, to make known the warning. But the Ionians to whom these messages came continued firm to their purpose, and would not listen to treachery, for each thought that the Persians had sent this message to themselves only. This, then, took place immediately after the arrival of the Persians before Miletus.

11. Afterward, when the Ionians had assembled at Lade, councils were held, and on occasion others addressed them, and, among the rest, the Phocæan general Dionysius, who spoke as follows: "Our affairs are in a critical[2] state, O Ionians, whether we shall be freemen or slaves, and that, too, as runaway slaves: now, then, if you are willing to undergo hardships, for the present you will have toil, but will be enabled, by overcoming your enemies, to be free; on the other hand, if you abandon yourselves to ease and disorder, I have no hope of you that you will escape punishment at the hands of the king for your revolt; but be persuaded by me, and intrust yourselves to my guidance, and I promise you, if the gods are impartial, either that our enemies will not fight us at all, or, if they do fight with us, they shall be completely beaten." 12. The Ionians, having heard this, intrusted themselves to the guidance of Dionysius; and he, daily leading out the ships into a line, when he had exercised the rowers by practicing the manœuvre of cutting through one another's line, and had put the marines under arms, kept the ships at anchor for the rest of the day: thus he subjected the Ionians to toil throughout the day. Accordingly, for seven days they continued to obey, and did what was ordered, but on the following day the Ionians, unaccustomed to such toil, and worn down by hardships and the heat of the sun, spoke one to another as follows: "What deity having offended, do we fill up this measure of affliction? we who, being beside ourselves, and having lost our senses, have intrusted ourselves to the guidance of a presumptuous Phocæan, who has contributed three ships; but he, having got us under his control, afflicts us with intolerable hardships. Many of us have already fallen into distempers, and many must expect to meet with the same fate. Instead of these evils, it were better for us to suffer any thing else, and to endure the impending servitude, be it what

[2] Literally, "on a razor's edge."

it may, than be oppressed by the present. Come, then, let us no longer obey him." Thus they spoke, and from that moment no one would obey, but having pitched tents on the island, they continued under the shade, and would not go on board the ships or perform their exercise. 13. The generals of the Samians, observing what was passing among the Ionians, and at the same time seeing great disorder among them, thereupon accepted the proposal of Æaces, son of Syloson, which he had before sent them at the desire of the Persians, exhorting them to abandon the confederacy of the Ionians; and, moreover, it was clearly impossible for them to overcome the power of the king, because they were convinced that if they should overcome Darius with his present fleet, another, five times as large, would come against them. Therefore, laying hold of this pretext, as soon as they saw the Ionians refusing to behave well, they deemed it for their own advantage to preserve their own buildings, sacred and profane. This Æaces, from whom the Samians received the proposal, was son of Syloson, son of Æaces, and, being tyrant of Samos, had been deprived of his government by Aristagoras the Milesian, as the other tyrants of Ionia.

14. When, therefore, the Phœnicians sailed against them, the Ionians also drew out their ships in line to oppose them; but when they came near and engaged each other, after that I am unable to affirm with certainty who of the Ionians proved themselves cowards or brave men in this sea-fight, for they mutually accuse each other. The Samians, however, are said at that moment to have hoisted sail, in pursuance of their agreement with Æaces, and steered out of the line to Samos, with the exception of eleven ships: the captains of these staid and fought, refusing to obey their commanders, and for this action the commonwealth of the Samians conferred upon them the honor of having their names and ancestry engraved on a column, as having proved themselves valiant men, and this column now stands in the forum. The Lesbians also, seeing those stationed next them flee, did the same as the Samians, and in like manner most of the Ionians followed their example. 15. Of those that persisted in the battle, the Chians were most roughly handled, as they displayed signal proofs of valor, and would not act as cowards. They contributed, as has been before mentioned, one hundred ships,

and on board each of them, forty chosen citizens serving as marines; and though they saw most of the confederates abandoning the common cause, they disdained to follow the example of their treachery; but choosing rather to remain with the few allies, they continued the fight, cutting through the enemies' lines, until, after they had taken many of the enemies' ships, they lost most of their own. The Chians then fled to their own country with the remainder of their fleet. 16. Those Chians whose ships were disabled in the fight, when they were pursued, took refuge in Mycale; and having run their ships aground, left them there, and marched overland through the continent; but when the Chians, on their return, entered the territory of Ephesus, and arrived near the city by night, at a time when the women there were celebrating the Thesmophoria, the Ephesians thereupon, not having before heard how it had fared with the Chians, and seeing an army enter their territory, thinking they were certainly robbers, and were come to seize their women, rushed out in a body, and slew the Chians. Such was the fate they met with. 17. Dionysius the Phocæan, when he perceived that the affairs of the Ionians were utterly ruined, having taken three of the enemies' ships, sailed away, not indeed to Phocæa, well knowing that it would be enslaved with the rest of Ionia, but sailed directly, as he was, to Phœnicia; and there having disabled some merchantmen, and obtained great wealth, he sailed to Sicily; and sallying out from thence, he established himself as a pirate, *attacking* none of the Grecians, but only the Carthaginians and Tyrrhenians.

18. The Persians, when they had conquered the Ionians in the sea-fight, besieging Miletus both by land and sea, and undermining the walls, and bringing up all kinds of military engines against it, took it completely, in the sixth year after the revolt of Aristagoras; and they reduced the city to slavery, so that the event coincided with the oracle delivered concerning Miletus. 19. For when the Argives consulted the oracle at Delphi respecting the preservation of their city, a double answer was given; part concerning themselves, and the addition *the Pythian* uttered concerning the Milesians. The part relating to the Argives I will mention when I come to that part of the history;[3] the words she uttered relative to the Milesians, who were not present, were as follows: "Then Miletus,

[3] See chap. 77.

contriver of wicked deeds, thou shalt become a feast and a rich gift to many: thy wives shall wash the feet of many long-haired masters, and our temple at Didymi shall be tended by others." These things befell the Milesians at that time; for most of the men were killed by the Persians, who wear long hair; and their women and children were treated as slaves; and the sacred inclosure at Didymi, both the temple and the shrine, were pillaged and burned. Of the riches in this temple I have frequently made mention in other parts of my history.[4] 20. Such of the Milesians as were taken alive were afterward conveyed to Susa; and king Darius, without having done them any other harm, settled them on that which is called the Red Sea, in the city of Ampe, near which the Tigris, flowing by, falls into the sea. Of the Milesian territory, the Persians themselves retained the parts round the city and the plain; the mountainous parts they gave to the Carians of Pedasus to occupy. 21. When the Milesians suffered thus at the hands of the Persians, the Sybarites, who inhabited Laos and Scydrus, having been deprived of their country, did not show equal sympathy; for when Sybaris[5] was taken by the Crotonians, all the Milesians of every age shaved their heads and displayed marks of deep mourning; for these two cities had been more strictly united in friendship than any others we are acquainted with. The Athenians behaved in a very different manner; for the Athenians made it evident that they were excessively grieved at the capture of Miletus, both in many other ways, and more particularly when Phrynichus had composed a drama of the capture of Miletus, and represented it, the whole theatre burst into tears, and fined him a thousand drachms for renewing the memory of their domestic misfortunes; and they gave order that thenceforth no one should act this drama.

22. Miletus, therefore, was stripped of its Milesian population. But the Samians who had property were by no means pleased with what had been done by their generals in favor of the Medes, and determined, on a consultation immediately after the sea-fight, to sail away to a colony, before the tyrant Æaces should arrive in their country, and not, by remaining, become slaves to the Medes and Æaces; for the Zanclæans of Sicily, at this very time sending messengers to Ionia, invited the Ionians to Cale Acte, wishing them to found a city of

[4] See B. I. 92, II. 159, and V. 36. [5] See Book V. chap. 44.

Ionians there. This Cale Acte, as it is called, belongs to the Sicilians, and is in that part of Sicily that faces the Tyrrhenians. Accordingly, when they invited them, the Samians alone of all the Ionians set out, and with them such Milesians as had escaped by flight. 23. During this time, the following incident occurred. The Samians, on their way to Sicily, touched on the country of the Epizephyrian Locrians, and the Zanclæans, both they and their king, whose name was Scythes, were employed in the besieging of a Sicilian city, desiring to take it; and Anaxilaus, tyrant of Rhegium, who was then at variance with the Zanclæans, understanding this, held correspondence with the Samians, and persuaded them that it would be well not to trouble themselves about Cale Acte, to which they were sailing, but to seize the city of Zancle, which was destitute of inhabitants. The Samians were persuaded, and possessed themselves of Zancle, whereupon the Zanclæans, hearing that their city was occupied, went to recover it, and called to their assistance Hippocrates, tyrant of Gela, for he was their ally. But when Hippocrates came with his army, as if to assist them, he having thrown into chains Scythes, king of the Zanclæans, who had already lost his city, and his brother Pythogenes, sent them away to the city of Inycum. After having conferred with the Samians, and given and received oaths, he betrayed the rest of the Zanclæans; and this was the reward agreed upon by the Samians, that he should have one half of the movables and slaves in the city, and that Hippocrates should have for his share all that was in the country. Accordingly, having put in chains the greater part of the Zanclæans, he treated them as slaves; and three hundred of the principal citizens he delivered to the Samians to be put to death. The Samians, however, would not do this. 24. Scythes, king of the Zanclæans, made his escape from Inycum to Himera, and from thence passed over into Asia, and went up to king Darius. Darius considered him the most just of all the men who had come up to him from Greece; for, having asked permission of the king, he went to Sicily, and returned back from Sicily to the king, and at last, being very rich, died among the Persians of old age. Thus the Samians, being freed from the Medes, gained without toil the very beautiful city of Zancle. 25. After the sea-fight which took place off Miletus, the Phœnicians, by order of the Persians, conveyed Æaces, son of Syloson, to Samos, as one who had deserved much at their hands, and had performed great services. The Samians were the only people of those that revolted from Darius whose city and sacred buildings were not burned on account of the defection of their ships in the sea-fight. Miletus being taken, the Persians immediately got possession of Caria; some of the cities having submitted of their own accord, and others they reduced by force. Now these things happened thus.

26. While Histiæus the Milesian was near Byzantium, intercepting the trading ships of the Ionians that sailed out of the Pontus, news was brought him of what had taken place at Miletus. He therefore intrusted his affairs on the Hellespont to Bisaltes, son of Apollophanes of Abydos, and he himself, having taken the Lesbians with him, sailed to Chios, and engaged with a garrison of Chians, that would not admit him, at a place called Cœli in the Chian territory; and he killed great numbers of them; and the rest of the Chians, as they had been much shattered by the sea-fight, Histiæus, with the Lesbians, got the mastery of, setting out from Polichne of the Chians. 27. The deity is wont to give some previous warning when any great calamities are about to befall any city or nation, and before these misfortunes great warnings happened to the Chians; for, in the first place, when they sent to Delphi a band of one hundred youths, two of them only returned home, but the remaining ninety-eight a pestilence seized and carried off; in the next place, about the same time, a little before the sea-fight, a house in the city fell in upon some boys as they were learning to read, so that of one hundred and twenty boys one only escaped. These warnings the deity showed them beforehand. After this, the sea-fight following, threw the city prostrate; and after the sea-fight, Histiæus with the Lesbians came upon them; and as the Chians had been much shattered, he easily reduced them to subjection. 28. From thence Histiæus proceeded to attack Thasus with a large body of Ionians and Æolians; and while he was besieging Thasus, news came that the Phœnicians were sailing from Miletus against the rest of Ionia. When he heard this, he left Thasus untaken, and himself hastened to Lesbos with all his forces; and from Lesbos, because his army was suffering from want, he crossed to the opposite shore for the purpose of reaping the corn of

Atarneus, and the plain of Caicus, which belonged to the Mysians. But Harpagus, a Persian, general of a considerable army, happened to be in those parts; he engaged with him after his landing, took Histiæus himself prisoner, and destroyed the greater part of his army.

29. Histiæus was thus taken prisoner. When the Greeks were fighting with the Persians at Malene, in the district of Atarneus, they maintained their ground for a long time, but the cavalry at length coming up, fell upon the Greeks; then it was the work of the cavalry; and when the Greeks had betaken themselves to flight, Histiæus, hoping that he should not be put to death by the king for his present offense, conceived such a desire of preserving his life, that when in his flight he was overtaken by a Persian, and being overtaken was on the point of being stabbed by him, he, speaking in the Persian language, discovered himself to be Histiæus the Milesian. 30. Now if, when he was taken prisoner, he had been conducted to king Darius, in my opinion he would have suffered no punishment, and the king would have forgiven him his fault; but now, for this very reason, and lest, by escaping, he should again regain his influence with the king, Artaphernes, governor of Sardis, and Harpagus, who received him as soon as he was conducted to Sardis, impaled his body on the spot, and having embalmed the head, sent it to Darius at Susa. Darius having heard of this, and having blamed those that had done it because they had not brought him alive into his presence, gave orders that, having washed and adorned the head of Histiæus, they should inter it honorably, as the remains of a man who had been a great benefactor to himself and the Persians. Such was the fate of Histiæus.

31. The naval force of the Persians having wintered near Miletus, when it set sail in the second year, easily subdued the islands lying near the continent, Chios, Lesbos, and Tenedos; and when they took any one of these islands, the barbarians, as they possessed themselves of each, netted the inhabitants. They netted them in this manner. Taking one another by the hand, they extend from the northern to the southern sea, and so march over the island, hunting out the inhabitants. They also took the Ionian cities on the continent with the same ease; but they did not net the inhabitants, for that was impossible. 32. Then the Persian generals did not belie the threats which

they had uttered against the Ionians when arrayed against them; for when they had made themselves masters of the cities, they selected the handsomest youths, and castrated them, and made them eunuchs instead of men, and the most beautiful virgins they carried away to the king; this they did, and burned the cities with the very temples. Thus the Ionians were for the third time reduced to slavery; first by the Lydians, then twice successively by the Persians. 33. The naval force, departing from Ionia, reduced all the places on the left of the Hellespont as one sails in; for the places on the right, being on the continent, had already been subdued by the Persians. The following places on the Hellespont are in Europe: the Chersonese, in which are many cities, Perinthus, and the fortified towns toward Thrace, and Selybrie, and Byzantium. The Byzantians, however, and the Chalcedonians on the opposite side, did not wait the coming of the Phœnician fleet, but, having abandoned their country, went inward to the Euxine, and there founded the city of Mesambria; but the Phœnicians, having burned down the cities above mentioned, bent their course to Proconnesus, and Artace, and having devoted these also to flames, sailed back again to the Chersonese for the purpose of destroying the rest of the cities, which, when they passed near them before, they had not laid waste. Against Cyzicus they did not sail at all, for the Cyzicenians had of their own accord submitted to the king before the arrival of the Phœnicians, having capitulated with Œbares, son of Megabazus, governor of Dascylium. All the other cities of the Chersonese, except Cardia, the Phœnicians subdued.

34. Till that time Miltiades, son of Cimon, son of Stesagoras, was tyrant of these cities, Miltiades, son of Cypselus, having formerly acquired this government in the following manner. The Thracian Dolonci possessed this Chersonese; these Dolonci, then, being pressed in war by the Apsynthians, sent their kings to Delphi to consult the oracle concerning the war; the Pythian answered them "that they should take that man with them to their country to found a colony who, after their departure from the temple, should first offer them hospitality." Accordingly, the Dolonci, going by the sacred way, went through *the territories of* the Phocians and Bœotians, and when no one invited them, turned out of the road toward Athens. 35. At that time Pisistratus had the supreme power at Athens; but

Miltiades, son of Cypselus, had considerable influence. He was of a family that maintained horses for the chariot-races, and was originally descended from Æacus and Ægina, but in later times was an Athenian, Philæus, son of Ajax, having been the first Athenian of that family. This Miltiades, being seated in his own portico, and seeing the Dolonci passing by, wearing a dress not belonging to the country, and *carrying* javelins, called out to them; and upon their coming to him, he offered them shelter and hospitality. They having accepted his invitation, and having been entertained by him, made known to him the whole oracle, and entreated him to obey the deity. Their words persuaded Miltiades as soon as he heard them, for he was troubled with the government of Pisistratus, and desired to get out of his way. He therefore immediately set out to Delphi to consult the oracle, whether he should do that which the Dolonci requested of him. 36. The Pythian having bid him do so, thereupon Miltiades, son of Cypselus, who had formerly won the Olympic prize in the chariot-race, taking with him all such Athenians as were willing to join in the expedition, set sail with the Dolonci, and took possession of the country; and they who introduced him appointed him tyrant. He, first of all, built a wall on the isthmus of the Chersonese, from the city of Cardia to Pactya, in order that the Apsynthians might not be able to injure them by making incursions into their country. The width of this isthmus is thirty-six stades; and from this isthmus, the whole Chersonese inward is four hundred and twenty stades in length. 37. Miltiades, then, having built a wall across the neck of the Chersonese, and by that means repelled the Apsynthians, next made war upon the Lampsacenians; and the Lampsacenians, having laid an ambush, took him prisoner. But Miltiades was well known to Crœsus; Crœsus therefore, having heard of this event, sent and commanded the Lampsacenians to release Miltiades; if not, he threatened that he would destroy them like a pine-tree. The Lampsacenians, being in uncertainty in their interpretations as to what was the meaning of the saying with which Crœsus threatened them, that he would destroy them like a pine-tree, at length, with some difficulty, one of the elders, having discovered it, told the real truth, that the pine alone of all trees, when cut down, does not send forth any more shoots, but perishes entirely; whereupon the Lampsacenians, dreading the power of Crœsus, set Miltiades at liberty. 38. He accordingly escaped by means of Crœsus, and afterward died childless, having bequeathed the government and his property to Stesagoras, son of Cimon, his brother by the same mother; and when he was dead, the Chersonesians sacrificed to him, as is usual to a founder, and instituted equestrian and gymnastic exercises, in which no Lampsacenian is permitted to contend. The war with the Lampsacenians still continuing, it also befell Stesagoras to die childless, being stricken on the head with an axe in the prytaneum by a man who in pretense was a deserter, but was in fact an enemy, and that a very vehement one.

39. Stesagoras having died in that manner, the Pisistratidæ thereupon sent Miltiades, son of Cimon, and brother of Stesagoras who had died, with one ship to the Chersonese, to assume the government; they had also treated him with kindness at Athens, as if they had not been parties to the death of his father Cimon, the particulars of which I will relate in another place.[6] Miltiades, having arrived in the Chersonese, kept himself at home under color of honoring the memory of his brother Stesagoras; but the Chersonesians having heard of this, the principal persons of all the cities assembled together from every quarter, and having come in a body with the intention of condoling with him, were all thrown into chains by him. Thus Miltiades got possession of the Chersonese, maintaining five hundred auxiliaries, and married Hegesipyle, daughter of Olorus, king of the Thracians. 40. This Miltiades, son of Cimon, had lately arrived in the Chersonese; and, after his arrival, other difficulties, greater than the present,[7] befell him; for in the third year before these things, he fled from the Scythians; for the Scythian nomades, having been provoked by king Darius, had assembled their forces, and marched as far as this Chersonese: Miltiades, not daring to wait their approach, fled from the Chersonese, until the Scythians departed, and the Dolonci brought him back again. These things happened in the third year before the present affairs. 41. Miltiades, having heard that the Phœnicians were at Tenedos, loaded five triremes with the

[6] See chap. 103.

[7] By the present difficulties are meant those which Herodotus had begun to relate in chapter 33 of this Book.

property he had at hand, and sailed away for Athens; and when he had set out from the city of Cardia, he sailed through the Gulf of Melas, and as he was passing by the Chersonese, the Phœnicians fell in with his ships. Now Miltiades himself escaped with four of the ships to Imbrus, but the fifth the Phœnicians pursued and took: of this ship, Metiochus, the eldest of the sons of Miltiades, not by the daughter of Olorus the Thracian, but by another woman, happened to be commander, and him the Phœnicians took, together with the ship. When they heard that he was son of Miltiades, they took him up to the king, thinking that they should obtain great favor for themselves, because Miltiades had given an opinion to the Ionians advising them to comply with the Scythians when the Scythians requested them to loose the bridge and return to their own country; but Darius, when the Phœnicians had taken Metiochus, son of Miltiades, up to him, did him no injury, but many favors; for he gave him a house and estate, and a Persian wife, by whom he had children, who were reckoned among the Persians. But Miltiades arrived at Athens from Imbros.

42. During this year nothing more was done by the Persians relative to the war with the Ionians; on the contrary, the following things were done in this year which were advantageous to the Ionians. Artaphernes, governor of Sardis, having sent for deputies from the cities, compelled the Ionians to enter into engagements among themselves that they would submit to legal decisions, and not commit depredations one upon another. This he compelled them to do; and having measured their lands by parasangs, which name the Persians give to thirty stades—having measured them into these, he imposed tributes on each, which have continued the same from that time to the present, as they were imposed by Artaphernes; and they were imposed nearly at the same amount as they had been before. These things, then, tended to peace.

43. In the beginning of the spring, the other generals having been dismissed by the king, Mardonius, son of Gobryas, went down to the coast, taking with him a very large land army, and a numerous naval force: he was young in years, and had lately married king Darius's daughter Artazostra. Mardonius, leading this army, when he arrived in Cilicia, having gone in person on board ship, proceeded with the rest of the

fleet, but the other generals led the land army to the Hellespont. When Mardonius, sailing by Asia, reached Ionia, there *he did a thing*, which, when I mention it, will be a matter of very great astonishment to those Grecians who can not believe that Otanes, one of the seven Persians, gave an opinion that it was right for the Persians to be governed by a democracy; for Mardonius, having deposed the tyrants of the Ionians, established democracies in the cities. Having done this, he hastened to the Hellespont. And when a vast body of ships and a numerous land army was assembled, having crossed the Hellespont in ships, they marched through Europe, and directed their march against Eretria and Athens. 44. These cities, indeed, were the pretext of the expedition; but purposing to subdue as many Grecian cities as they could, in the first place they reduced the Thasians with their fleet, who did not even raise a hand to resist them; and in the next place, with their land forces they enslaved the Macedonians, in addition to those that were before subject to them; for all the nations on this side the Macedonians were already under their power. Then, crossing over from Thasus, they coasted along the continent as far as Acanthus; and proceeding from Acanthus, they endeavored to double Mount Athos, but a violent and irresistible north wind falling upon them as they were sailing round, very roughly dealt with a great number of the ships by driving them against Athos; for it is said that as many as three hundred ships were destroyed, and upward of twenty thousand men; for, as this sea around Athos abounds in monsters, some of them were seized and destroyed by these monsters; and others were dashed against the rocks, others knew not how to swim and so perished, and others from cold. Such, then, was the fate of the naval force. 45. Mardonius and the land forces, while encamped in Macedonia, the Thracian Brygi attacked in the night; and the Brygi slew many of them, and wounded Mardonius himself. Nevertheless, even they did not escape slavery at the hands of the Persians; for Mardonius did not quit those parts before he had reduced them to subjection. However, having subdued them, he led his army back again, having suffered a disaster with his land forces from the Brygi, and with his navy a greater one near Athos. Accordingly, this armament, having met with such disgraceful reverses, retreated into Asia.

46. In the second year after these events, the Thasians having been accused by their neighbors of designing a revolt, Darius sent a messenger and commanded them to demolish their walls, and to transport their ships to Abdera; for the Thasians, having been besieged by Histiæus the Milesian, and having large revenues, applied their wealth in building ships of war, and fortifying their city with a stronger wall. Their revenues arose both from the continent and from their mines. From the gold mines of Scapte-Hyle proceeded in all eighty talents yearly, and from those in Thasus less indeed than that amount, yet so much that, as they were exempt from taxes on the produce of the soil, there came in to the Thasians in all, from the continent and the mines, a revenue of two hundred talents yearly; and when the greatest quantity came in, three hundred talents. 47. I myself have seen these mines; and by far the most wonderful of them are those which the Phœnicians discovered, who with Thasus colonized this island, which on that occasion took its name from this Thasus the Phœnician. These Phœnician mines are in that part of Thasus between a place called Ænyra and Cœnyra, opposite Samothrace: a large mountain has been thrown upside down in the search. This, then, is of such a description. The Thasians, in obedience to the king, both demolished their walls, and transported all their ships to Abdera.

48. After this, Darius made trial of what were the intentions of the Greeks, whether to make war with him, or to deliver themselves up. He therefore dispatched heralds, appointing different persons to go to different parts throughout Greece, with orders to demand earth and water for the king. These, accordingly, he sent to Greece, and dispatched other heralds to the tributary cities on the coast, with orders to build ships of war and transports for horses. 49. They then set about preparing these things; and to the heralds who came to Greece many of the inhabitants of the continent gave what the Persian demanded, as did all the islanders to whom they came and made the demand. Indeed, the other islanders gave earth and water to Darius, and, moreover, the Æginetæ; but when they had done so, the Athenians forthwith threatened them, thinking that the Æginetæ had given *earth and water* out of ill will toward themselves, in order that they might make war on them in conjunction with the Persian; they therefore gladly laid

hold of the pretext, and going to Sparta, accused the Æginetæ of what they had done, as betraying Greece. 50. On this accusation, Cleomenes, son of Anaxandrides, who was then king of the Spartans, crossed over to Ægina, intending to seize the most culpable of the Æginetæ; but when he attempted to seize them, others of the Æginetæ opposed him, and among them especially Crius, son of Polycritus, who said "that he should not carry off any one of the Æginetæ with impunity; for that he was acting as he did without the consent of the commonwealth of the Spartans, being persuaded by bribes from the Athenians; and that if it had not been so, he would have come with the other king to seize them." He said this in consequence of a message from Demaratus. But Cleomenes, being driven from Ægina, asked Crius what his name was; and he told him the truth; whereupon Cleomenes said to him, "Now then tip your horns with brass, O Crius,[8] as you will have to contend with great misfortunes." 51. Meanwhile Demaratus, son of Ariston, who was likewise king of the Spartans, but of an inferior family, remaining in Sparta, aspersed the conduct of Cleomenes: he was in no other respect inferior, for they were sprung from the same origin, but somehow the family of Eurysthenes was more honored on account of seniority.

52. For the Lacedæmonians, agreeing with none of the poets, affirm that Aristodemus himself, son of Aristomachus, son of Cleodæus, son of Hyllus, being king, brought them to the country which they now inhabit, and not the sons of Aristodemus; and that after no long time Aristodemus's wife, whose name was Argia, brought forth: they say that she was daughter of Autesion, son of Tisamenes, son of Thersander, son of Polynices; and that she brought twins; and that Aristodemus, having looked on the children, died of disease: that the Lacedæmonians of that day resolved, according to custom, to make the eldest of the children king; but they knew not which to choose, since they were alike, and of equal size. Being unable to determine, they then, or perhaps before, asked the mother; she replied "that she herself was unable to distinguish:" she said this, although she knew very well, but was desirous, if it were possible, that both should be made kings. That the Lacedæmonians were consequently in

[8] Crius signifies "a ram."

doubt, and being in doubt, sent to Delphi, to inquire of the oracle what they should do in the matter. *They add* that the Pythian bade them consider both the children as kings, but to honor the eldest most. This answer the Pythian gave them; but the Lacedæmonians, being still in doubt how they should discover the eldest of them, a Messenian, whose name was Panites, made a suggestion to them. This Panites made the following suggestion to the Lacedæmonians, to observe which of the two children the mother would wash and feed first; and if she should be found constantly doing the same, they would then have all they were seeking for and desired to know; but if she should vary, attending to them interchangeably, it would be evident to them that she knew no more than they did; and then they must have recourse to some other expedient. Thereupon the Spartans, in pursuance of the suggestion of the Messenian, having watched the mother of Aristodemus's children, discovered that she constantly gave one the preference both in feeding and washing, she not knowing why she was watched. Therefore, considering that the child which was honored by its mother was the eldest, they educated it in the palace; and to him the name of Eurysthenes was given, and to the younger, Procles. They say that both these, though brothers, when they had reached manhood, were at variance with each other throughout the whole course of their lives, and that their descendants continued to be so. 53. The Lacedæmonians alone of the Grecians give this account; but I now describe these things in the way they are told by the rest of the Grecians; for they say that these kings of the Dorians up to Perseus, son of Danae, the deity being omitted, are rightly enumerated by the Greeks, and are proved to have been Greeks; for even at that time they were ranked among the Greeks. I have said up to Perseus for this reason, and have not carried it any higher, because no surname of any mortal father is attributed to Perseus, as Amphitryon to Hercules. I have, therefore, with good reason, and correctly, said up to Perseus; but if we reckon their progenitors upward from Danae, daughter of Acrisius, the leaders of the Dorians will prove to have been originally Egyptians. Such is the genealogy according to the account of the Greeks. 54. But as the account of the Persians is given, Perseus himself, being an Assyrian, became a Greek, though the ancestors of Perseus had not been so; but that the progenitors of Acrisius, being in no way related to Perseus, were Egyptians, as the Greeks also say. 55. Let this, then, suffice for this subject. But why, being Egyptians, and by what exploits, they obtained the sovereignty of the Dorians, I will omit to mention, as others have spoken of these matters. But such particulars as others have not taken in hand, of these I will make mention.

56. The Spartans have given the following privileges to their kings: two priesthoods, that of the Lacedæmonian Jupiter, and that of the Celestial Jupiter; and to levy war against whatever country they please; and no one of the Spartans may impede this, otherwise he falls under a curse. When they march out to war, the kings go first, and retire last; and a hundred chosen men guard them in the field. During the expeditions, they sacrifice as many cattle as they please, and take as their own share the skins and chines of all the victims. These are their privileges in time of war. 57. The others, those during peace, have been given them as follows. If any one make a public sacrifice, the kings sit first at the feast, and are first served, each receiving double of whatever is given to the other guests. They have the right of beginning the libations, and are entitled to the skins of the cattle that are sacrificed. At every new moon, and on the seventh day of the current month, a perfect victim is presented to each of them, at the public charge, for the temple of Apollo; and a medimnus of meal, and a Laconian quart of wine. At all public games they have seats appointed by way of distinction; and it is their prerogative to appoint such citizens as they please to be Proxeni;[9] and also to choose each two Pythii. The Pythii are persons who are sent to consult the oracle at Delphi, and are maintained with the kings at the public charge. When the kings do not come to the banquet, two chœnices of flour and a cotyle of wine are sent home to each of them; but when they are present, a double portion of every thing is given them; and when invited to a banquet by private persons, they are honored in the same manner. They have the keeping of the oracles that are pronounced, but the Pythii are also privy to them. The kings alone have to determine the following matters only: with respect to a virgin heiress, who is to marry her, if her

[9] Officers appointed to receive and entertain foreign embassadors.

father has not betrothed her; and with respect to the public highways; and if any one desires to adopt a son, it must be done in presence of the kings. They assist at the deliberations of the senators, who are twenty-eight in number; and if they do not attend, those of the senators who are most nearly connected with them enjoy the privileges of the kings, giving two votes, and a third, their own. 58. These privileges are given to the kings by the commonwealth of the Spartans during life; and when they die, the following. Horsemen announce through all Laconia what has happened; and women, going through the city, beat a caldron; when this accordingly is done, it is necessary for two free people of each house, a man and a woman, to make themselves squalid in token of grief; and if they neglect to do so, heavy fines are imposed on them. The Lacedæmonians have the same custom with regard to the deaths of their kings as the barbarians in Asia; for most of the barbarians observe the same custom with respect to the deaths of their kings; for when a king of the Lacedæmonians dies, it is required that from the whole territory of Lacedæmon, besides the Spartans, a certain number of the neighboring inhabitants should of necessity attend the funeral: when accordingly many thousands of these, and of the Helots and of the Spartans themselves, have assembled together in one place, they promiscuously with the women strike their foreheads vehemently, and give themselves up to unbounded lamentation, affirming that the king who died last was the best they ever had. Should one of their kings die in war, having prepared his effigy, they expose it to public view on a couch richly ornamented; and when they have buried him, no assembly takes place for ten days, nor is a meeting held for the election of magistrates, but they mourn during those days. 59. They also resemble the Persians in this other respect: when, on the death of a king, another king is appointed, he, on his accession, releases whatever debts may be due from any Spartan to the king or the public; and so among the Persians, a newly-appointed king remits to all the cities the arrears of tribute then due. 60. In this respect also the Lacedæmonians resemble the Egyptians: their heralds, musicians, and cooks succeed to their fathers' professions; so that a musician is son of a musician, a cook of a cook, and a herald of a herald; nor do others, on account of the clearness of their voice, apply themselves *to this profession* and exclude others; but they continue to practice it after their fathers. These things, then, are so.

61. At that time, therefore, while Cleomenes was at Ægina, and co-operating for the common good of Greece, Demaratus accused him; not so much caring for the Æginetæ, as moved by envy and hatred. But Cleomenes, having returned from Ægina, formed a plan to deprive Demaratus of the sovereignty, getting a handle against him by means of the following circumstance. When Ariston reigned in Sparta, and had married two wives, he had no children; and as he did not acknowledge himself to be the cause of this, he married a third wife; and he married her in this manner. He had a friend who was a Spartan, to whom he was more attached than to any other of the citizens. The wife of this man happened to be by far the most beautiful of all the women in Sparta, and this, moreover, having become the most beautiful from being the most ugly; for her nurse, perceiving that she was misshapen, and knowing her to be the daughter of opulent persons, and deformed, and seeing, moreover, that her parents considered her form a great misfortune, considering these several circumstances, devised the following plan. She carried her every day to the temple of Helen, which is in the place called Therapne, above the temple of Phœbus. When the nurse brought the child there, she stood before the image, and entreated the goddess to free the child from its deformity. And it is related that one day, as the nurse was going out of the temple, a woman appeared to her, and having appeared, asked what she was carrying in her arms; and she answered that she was carrying an infant; whereupon she bid her show it to her, but the nurse refused, for she had been forbidden by the parents to show the child to any one. The woman, however, urged her by all means to show it to her, and the nurse, seeing that the woman was so very anxious to see the child, at length showed it; upon which she, stroking the head of the child with her hands, said that she would surpass all the women in Sparta in beauty; and from that day her appearance began to change. When she reached the age for marriage, Agetus, son of Alcides, married her; this, then, was the friend of Ariston.

62. Now love for this woman excited Ariston; he, therefore, had recourse to the following stratagem. He promised he

would give his friend, whose wife this woman was, a present of any one thing he should choose out of all his possessions, and required his friend in return to do the like to him. He, having no apprehension on account of his wife, seeing that Ariston already had a wife, assented to the proposal; and they imposed oaths on each other on these terms. Accordingly, Ariston himself gave the thing, whatever it was, which Agetus chose out of all his treasures; and himself claiming to obtain the same compliance from him, thereupon attempted to carry off his wife with him. Agetus said that he had assented to any thing but this only; nevertheless, being compelled by his oath, and circumvented by deceit, he suffered him to take her away with him. 63. Thus, then, Ariston took to himself a third wife, having put away the second. But in too short a time, and before she had completed her ten months, this woman bore Demaratus; and as he was sitting on the bench with the Ephori, one of his servants announced to him that a son was born to him; but he, knowing the time at which he married the woman, and reckoning the months on his fingers, said with an oath, "It can not be mine." This the Ephori heard. However, at the time, they took no notice. The child grew up, and Ariston repented of what he had said, for he was fully persuaded that Demaratus was his son. He gave him the name of Demaratus for this reason: before this the Spartans had made public supplications that Ariston, whom they esteemed the most illustrious of all the kings that had ever reigned in Sparta, might have a son. For this reason the name of Demaratus[1] was given to him. 64. In process of time Ariston died, and Demaratus obtained the sovereignty. But it was fated, as it appears, that these things, when made known, should occasion the deposition of Demaratus from the sovereignty, for Demaratus had incurred the hatred of Cleomenes, because he had before led away the army from Eleusis,[2] and now more particularly when Cleomenes had crossed over against those Æginetæ who were inclined to Medism. 65. Cleomenes, then, being eager to avenge himself, made a compact with Leutychides, son of Menares, son of Agis, who was of the same family with Demaratus, on condition, that if he should make him king instead of Demaratus,

[1] Demaratus means "granted to the prayers of the people."

[2] See B. V. chap. 75.

he should accompany him against the Æginetæ. Leutychides had become an enemy to Demaratus chiefly for this reason. When Leutychides was affianced to Percalus, daughter of Chilon, son of Demarmenes, Demaratus, having plotted against him, disappointed Leutychides of his marriage, having himself anticipated him by seizing Percalus and retaining her as his wife. In this manner the enmity of Leutychides to Demaratus originated, and now, at the instigation of Cleomenes, Leutychides made oath against Demaratus, affirming "that he did not legitimately reign over the Spartans, not being the son of Ariston;" and after making oath against him, he prosecuted him, recalling the words which Ariston spoke, when the servant announced that a son was born to him; whereupon he, reckoning the months, denied with an oath, saying "that it was not his." Leutychides, insisting on this declaration, maintained that Demaratus was neither the son of Ariston, nor rightful king of Sparta; and he adduced as witnesses those Ephori who were then sitting by the king, and heard these words of Ariston. 66. At length, the matter coming to a trial,[3] the Spartans determined to inquire of the oracle at Delphi "whether Demaratus was the son of Ariston." But the matter being referred to the Pythian at the instance of Cleomenes, Cleomenes thereupon gained over one Cobon, son of Aristophantus, a man of very great influence at Delphi; and Cobon prevailed with Perialla, the prophetess, to say what Cleomenes wished to be said. The Pythian accordingly, when the persons sent to consult the oracle made the inquiry, decided that Demaratus was not the son of Ariston. In after time this came to be known, and Cobon fled from Delphi, and Perialla, the prophetess, was deposed from her office.

67. Thus, then, it happened with respect to the deposition of Demaratus from the sovereignty. But Demaratus fled from Sparta to the Medes on account of the following insult. After his deposition from the sovereignty, he was chosen to and held the office of magistrate. The Gymnopædiæ[4] were being celebrated; and, when Demaratus was looking on, Leutychides, who had been appointed king in his room, sent a servant and

[3] Baehr has pointed out the proper meaning of the word νεῖκος in this passage.

[4] An annual festival at Sparta, at which boys danced naked, and performed various athletic exercises.

asked him, by way of ridicule and mockery, "what kind of thing it was to be a magistrate after having been a king?" But he, being vexed with the question, answered, "that he indeed had tried both, but Leutychides had not; however, that this question would be the commencement either of infinite calamity or infinite prosperity to the Lacedæmonians." Having spoken thus and covered his face, he went out of the theatre to his own house, and having immediately made preparation, he sacrificed an ox to Jupiter, and having sacrificed, called for his mother. 68. When his mother came, he placed part of the entrails in her hands, and supplicated her, speaking as follows: "Mother, I beseech you, calling to witness both the rest of the gods and this Hectæan Jupiter, to tell me the truth, who is in reality my father; for Leutychides affirmed on the trial that you, being pregnant by your former husband, so came to Ariston: others tell even a more idle story, and say you kept company with one of the servants, a feeder of asses, and that I am his son. I adjure you, therefore, by the gods to speak the truth; for even if you have done any thing of what is said, you have not done it alone, but with many others; moreover, the report is common in Sparta that Ariston was incapable of begetting children, for that otherwise his former wives would have had offspring." Thus he spoke. 69. She answered as follows: "Son, since you implore me with supplications to speak the truth, the whole truth shall be told you. When Ariston had taken me to his own house, on the third night from the first, a spectre resembling Ariston came to me, and having lain with me, put on me a crown that it had: it departed, and afterward Ariston came, but when he saw me with the crown, he asked who it was that gave it me. I said he did, but he would not admit it, whereupon I took an oath, and said that he did not well to deny it, for that, having come shortly before and lain with me, he had given me the crown. Ariston, seeing that I affirmed with an oath, discovered that the event was superhuman; and, in the first place, the crown proved to have come from the shrine situate near the palace gates, which they call Astrabacus's; and, in the next place, the seers pronounced that it was the hero himself. Thus, then, my son, you have all that you wish to know; for you are sprung either from that hero, and the hero Astrabacus is your father, or Ariston, for I conceived you in that night.

As to that with which your enemies most violently attack you, affirming that Ariston himself, when your birth was announced to him, in the presence of many persons, denied you were his, for that the time, ten months, had not yet elapsed, he threw out those words through ignorance of such matters, for women bring forth at nine months and seven, and all do not complete ten months. But I bore you, my son, at seven months, and Ariston himself knew not long after that he had uttered those words thoughtlessly. Do not listen to any other stories respecting your birth, for you have heard the whole truth; and from feeders of asses may their wives bring forth children to Leutychides and such as spread such reports." Thus she spoke. 70. But he, having learned what he wished, and having taken provisions for his journey, proceeded to Elis, pretending that he was going to Delphi to consult the oracle; but the Lacedæmonians, suspecting that he was attempting to make his escape, pursued him, and by some means Demaratus got the start of them, crossing over from Elis to Zacynthus; but the Lacedæmonians, having crossed over after him, laid hands on him and took away his attendants. But afterward, for the Zacynthians would not give him up, he crossed over from thence to Asia to king Darius, and he received him honorably, and gave him land and cities. Thus Demaratus arrived in Asia, having met with such fortune, being renowned in many other respects among the Lacedæmonians, both by his deeds and counsels, and, moreover, having obtained an Olympic victory with a four-horse chariot, he procured this honor *for his native city*, being the only one of all the kings of Sparta who had done this.

71. Leutychides, son of Menares, when Demaratus was deposed, succeeded to the kingdom. A son was born to him named Zeuxidemus, whom some of the Spartans called Cyniscus. This Zeuxidemus was never king of Sparta, for he died before Leutychides, leaving a son, Archidamus. Leutychides, being bereaved of Zeuxidemus, married a second wife, Eurydame, who was sister of Menius, and daughter of Diactorides; by her he had no male offspring, but a daughter, Lampito; her Archidamus, son of Zeuxidemus, married, Leutychides having bestowed her upon him. 72. However, Leutychides did not grow old in Sparta, but made the following reparation, as it were, to Demaratus. He commanded the

Lacedæmonian army in Thessaly, and when it was in his power to have reduced the whole country to subjection, he accepted a large sum of money as a bribe; and being caught in the very act, sitting there in the camp on a sleeve full of silver, he was banished from Sparta, having been brought before a court of justice. His house was razed, and he fled to Tegea, where he died. These events happened some time after.

73. When Cleomenes had succeeded in his design against Demaratus, he immediately took Leutychides with him, and went against the Æginetæ, bearing a deep grudge against them on account of the insult he had received. The Æginetæ accordingly thought proper to make no farther resistance, as both kings were coming against them; they, therefore, having selected ten of the Æginetæ, the most eminent both in wealth and birth, and among them Crius, son of Polycritus, and Casambus, son of Aristocrates, who had the chief authority, and having carried them away to Attica, they delivered them as a pledge to the Athenians, the greatest enemies of the Æginetæ. 74. After this, fear of the Spartans seized upon Cleomenes, when discovered to have employed wicked artifices against Demaratus, and he withdrew secretly to Thessaly; and from thence passing into Arcadia, he began to form new designs, rousing the Arcadians against Sparta, and engaging them both by other oaths to follow him wherever he should lead them; and, moreover, he was desirous of leading the chief men of the Arcadians to the city of Nonacris, to make them swear by the water of the Styx, for in that city the water of the Styx is by the Arcadians said to be. And it is of the following description: a small quantity of water is seen and drops from a rock into a hollow, and a fence of masonry surrounds the hollow. Nonacris, in which this fountain happens to be, is a city of Arcadia near Pheneum. 75. The Lacedæmonians, being informed that Cleomenes was acting thus, through fear restored him to Sparta on the same terms as those on which he had reigned before; but as soon as he had returned, madness seized him, though he was before somewhat crazed; for whenever he met any one of the Spartans, he used to thrust the sceptre into his face. When he was found to do this, and to be clearly out of his mind, his relations confined him in wooden fetters; but he

being so confined, and seeing a single guard left alone by the rest, asked for a knife; and when the guard at first refused to give it, he threatened what he would do to him hereafter, till at last the guard, fearing his threats, for he was one of his Helots, gave him a knife. Then Cleomenes, having got hold of the blade, began to mutilate himself from the legs, for having cut the flesh lengthwise, he proceeded from the legs to the thighs, and from the thighs to the hips and loins; at last he came to the belly, and having gashed this, in that manner he died; as most of the Grecians say, because he persuaded the Pythian to say what she did concerning Demaratus; but as the Athenians alone say, because, when he invaded Eleusis, he cut down the grove of the goddesses;[5] but as the Argives say, because he, having called out those Argives who had fled from battle, from their sacred precinct of Argus, massacred them, and, holding the grove itself in contempt, set it on fire.

76. For when Cleomenes consulted the oracle at Delphi, an answer was given him that he should take Argos. When, therefore, leading the Spartans, he arrived at the river Erasinus, which is said to flow from the Stymphalian lake, for that this lake, discharging itself into an unseen chasm, reappears in Argos, and from that place this water is, by the Argives, called Erasinus—Cleomenes, therefore, having arrived at this river, offered to sacrifice to it; but as the victims by no means gave a favorable omen for his passing over, he said that he admired the Erasinus for not betraying its people, yet the Argives should not even thus escape with impunity. After this, having retired, he marched his forces to Thyrea; and having sacrificed a bull to the sea, he conveyed them in ships to the Tirynthian territory and Nauplia. 77. The Argives, being informed of this, went out to meet them on the coast; and when they were near Tiryns, at that place to which the name of Sepia is given, they encamped opposite the Lacedæmonians, leaving no great space between the two armies. There, then, they were not afraid of coming to a pitched battle, but lest they should be taken by stratagem; for it was to this event the oracle had reference which the Pythian pronounced in common to them and the Milesians,[6] running thus: "When the female, having conquered the male, shall drive him out, and obtain

[5] Ceres and Proserpine.

[6] For the part of the oracle relating to the Milesians, see chap. 19.

glory among the Argives, then shall she make many of the Argive women rend their garments; so that one of future generations shall say, a terrible triple-coiled serpent has perished, overcome by the spear." All these things concurring, spread alarm among the Argives, therefore they resolved to avail themselves of the herald of the enemy; and having so resolved, they did as follows: when the Spartan herald gave any signal to the Lacedæmonians, the Argives did the same. 78. Cleomenes, having observed that the Argives did whatever his herald gave the signal for, ordered his troops, when the herald should give the signal for going to dinner, then to seize their arms, and advance against the Argives. This, accordingly, was accomplished by the Lacedæmonians, for they fell upon the Argives as they were taking their dinner, according to the herald's signal; and they killed many of them, and a far greater number, who had taken refuge in the grove of Argus, they surrounded and kept watch over. 79. Cleomenes then adopted the following course: having some deserters with him, and having received information from them, he sent a herald and called them out, summoning by name those Argives who were shut up in the sacred precinct; and he called them out, saying that he had received their ransom; but the ransom among the Peloponnesians is a fixed sum of two minæ to be paid for each prisoner. Cleomenes therefore, having called them out severally, put to death about fifty of the Argives; and somehow this went on unknown to the rest who were within the precinct; for as the grove was thick, those within did not see those without, or what they were doing, until at last one of them, getting up into a tree, saw what was being done. They, therefore, no more went out when called for. 80. Thereupon Cleomenes ordered all the Helots to heap up wood around the grove, and when they had executed his orders, he set fire to the grove. When all was in a flame, he asked one of the deserters to which of the gods the grove belonged; he said that it belonged to Argus. Cleomenes, when he heard this, uttering a deep groan, said, "O prophetic Apollo! thou hast indeed greatly deceived me in saying that I should take Argos. I conjecture thy prophecy is accomplished." 81. After this, Cleomenes sent away the greater part of his army to Sparta; and he himself, taking a thousand chosen men with him, went to offer sacrifice at the temple of Juno; but when he wished himself to offer sacrifice on the altar, the priest forbade him, saying that it was not lawful for a stranger to offer sacrifice there; upon which Cleomenes commanded the Helots to drag the priest from the altar and scourge him, while he himself sacrificed; and having done this, he went away to Sparta. 82. On his return, his enemies accused him before the Ephori, alleging that he had been bribed not to take Argos, when he might easily have taken it. He said to them, whether speaking falsely or truly I am unable to say for certain; he affirmed, however, "that when he had taken the sacred precinct of Argus, he thought that the oracle of the god was accomplished, and therefore he did not think it right to attempt the city, before he had had recourse to victims, and ascertained whether the god would favor or obstruct him; and that while he was sacrificing favorably in the temple of Juno, a flame of fire shone forth from the breast of the image; and thus he learned for certain that he should not take Argos; for if it had shone forth from the head of the image, he should have taken the city completely; but as it shone forth from the breast, he thought that every thing had been done by him which the deity wished to happen." In saying this, he appeared to the Spartans to say what was credible and reasonable, and was acquitted by a large majority. 83. Argos, however, was left so destitute of men, that their slaves had the management of affairs, ruling and administering them, until the sons of those who had been killed grew up. Then they, having recovered Argos, expelled the slaves; and the slaves, being driven out, took Tiryns by assault. For a time concord subsisted between them, but then there came to the slaves one Cleander, a prophet, who was by birth a Phigalean of Arcadia; he persuaded the slaves to attack their masters. From this circumstance there was war between them for a long time, till at last the Argives with difficulty got the upper hand.

84. Now the Argives say that on this account Cleomenes became mad and perished miserably; but the Spartans themselves say that Cleomenes became mad from no divine influence, but that by associating with the Scythians he became a drinker of unmixed wine, and from that cause became mad; for that the Scythian nomades, since Darius had invaded their country, were afterward desirous to take venge-

ance on him, and having sent to Sparta to make an alliance, and agree that the Scythians themselves should endeavor to make an irruption into Media near the river Phasis, and to urge the Spartans to set out from Ephesus, and march upward, and then for both armies to meet at the same place. They say that Cleomenes, when the Scythians came for this purpose, associated with them too intimately; and being more intimate with them than was proper, contracted from them a habit of drinking unmixed wine; and the Spartans think that he became mad from this cause. And from that time, as they themselves say, when they wish to drink stronger drink, they say, "Pour out like a Scythian." Thus, then, the Spartans speak concerning Cleomenes. But Cleomenes appears to me to have suffered this retribution on account of Demaratus.

85. When the Æginetæ were informed of the death of Cleomenes, they sent embassadors to Sparta to complain loudly against Leutychides, on account of the hostages detained at Athens; and the Lacedæmonians, having assembled a court of judicature, determined that the Æginetæ had been very much injured by Leutychides, and condemned him to be delivered up and taken to Ægina, in the place of the men who were detained at Athens. But when the Æginetæ were about to take Leutychides away, Theasides, son of Leoprepes, an eminent man in Sparta, said to them, "Men of Ægina, what are you going to do, to take away the king of the Spartans, who has been delivered into your hands by the citizens? If the Spartans, yielding to anger, have so decided, take care lest, if you do these things, they hereafter pour into your country a calamity which will utterly destroy you." The Æginetæ, having heard this, refrained from taking him away, and came to this agreement, that Leutychides should accompany them to Athens, and restore the men to the Æginetæ. 86. When Leutychides, on his arrival at Athens, demanded back the pledges, the Athenians had recourse to evasions, not wishing to give them up; and said that two kings had deposited them, and it would not be right to deliver them up to one without the other. When the Athenians refused to give them up, Leutychides addressed them as follows: "O Athenians, do whichever you yourselves wish; for if you deliver them up, you will do what is just,

and if you do not deliver them up, the contrary. I will, however, tell you what once happened in Sparta respecting a deposit. We Spartans say, that about three generations before my time, there lived in Lacedæmon one Glaucus, son of Epicydes: we relate that this man both attained to the first rank in all other respects, and also bore the highest character for justice of all who at that time dwelt at Lacedæmon. We say that in due time the following events befell him. A certain Milesian, having come to Sparta, wished to have a conference with him, and made the following statement: 'I am a Milesian, and am come, Glaucus, with the desire of profiting by your justice; for since throughout all the rest of Greece, and particularly in Ionia, there was great talk of your justice, I considered with myself that Ionia is continually exposed to great dangers, and that, on the contrary, Peloponnesus is securely situated, and consequently that *with us* one can never see the same persons retaining property. Having, therefore, reflected and deliberated on these things, I have determined to change half of my whole substance into silver and deposit it with you, being well assured that, being placed with you, it will be safe. Do you, then, take this money, and preserve these tokens; and whosoever possessing these shall demand it back again, restore it to him.' (2.) The stranger who came from Miletus spoke thus. But Glaucus received the deposit on the condition mentioned. After a long time had elapsed, the sons of this man who had deposited the money came to Sparta, and having addressed themselves to Glaucus, and shown the tokens, demanded back the money. Glaucus repulsed them, answering as follows: I neither remember the matter, nor does it occur to me that I know any of the circumstances you mention; but if I can recall it to my mind, I am willing to do every thing that is just; and if, indeed, I have received it, *I wish* to restore it correctly; but if I have not received it at all, I shall have recourse to the laws of the Greeks against you. I therefore defer settling this matter with you for four months from the present time. (3.) The Milesians, accordingly, considering it a great calamity, departed, as being deprived of their money. But Glaucus went to Delphi to consult the oracle; and when he asked the oracle whether he should make a booty of the money by an oath, the Pythian assailed him in the following words: 'Glaucus, son of Epicydes, thus to prevail by an oath, and to make a booty of the money, will be a present gain: swear, then; for death even awaits the man who keeps his oath. But there is a nameless son of Perjury, who has neither hands nor feet; he pursues swiftly, until, having seized, he destroys the whole race, and all the house. But the race of a man who keeps his oath is afterward more blessed.' Glaucus, having heard this, entreated the god to pardon the words he had spoken; but the Pythian said that to tempt the gods and to commit the crime were the same thing. Glaucus, therefore, having sent for the Milesian strangers, restored them the money. With what design this story has been told you, O Athenians, shall now be mentioned. There is at present not a single descendant of Glaucus, nor any house which is supposed to have belonged to Glaucus; but he is utterly extirpated from Sparta. Thus it is right to have no other thought concerning a deposit than to restore it when it is demanded." Leutychides having said this, but finding the Athenians did not even then listen to him, departed.

87. But the Æginetæ, before they received punishment for the injuries they had done to the Athenians, to gratify the Thebans,[7] acted as follows. Being offended with the Athenians, and thinking themselves injured, they prepared to revenge themselves on the Athenians; and as the Athenians happened to have a five-benched galley at Sunium, they formed an ambuscade and took the ship Theoris,[8] filled with the principal Athenians; and having taken the men, they put them in chains. 88. The Athenians, having been treated thus by the Æginetæ, no longer delayed to devise all sorts of plans against them. Now there was in Ægina an eminent man named Nicodromus, son of Cnœthus; he, being incensed against the Æginetæ on account of his former banishment from the island, and now hearing that the Athenians were preparing to do a mischief to the Æginetæ, entered into an agreement with the Athenians for the betrayal of Ægina, mentioning on what day he would make the attempt, and on what it would be necessary for them to come to his assistance.

[7] See B. V. chap. 80, 81.

[8] The Theoris was a vessel which was sent every year to Delos to offer sacrifice to Apollo.

After this, Nicodromus, according to his agreement with the Athenians, seized that which is called the old town. 89. The Athenians, however, did not arrive at the proper time, for they happened not to have a sufficient number of ships to engage with the Æginetæ; and while they were entreating the Corinthians to furnish them with ships, their plan was ruined. The Corinthians, for they were then on very friendly terms with them, at their request supplied the Athenians with twenty ships; and they furnished them, letting them to hire for five drachmæ for each, because by their laws they were forbidden to give them for nothing. The Athenians, therefore, having taken these and their own, manned seventy ships in all, and sailed to Ægina, and arrived one day after that agreed upon. 90. Nicodromus, when the Athenians did not arrive at the proper time, embarked on shipboard and made his escape from Ægina; and others of the Æginetæ accompanied him, to whom the Athenians gave Sunium for a habitation; and they, sallying from thence, plundered the Æginetæ in the island. This, however, happened subsequently. 91. In the mean time, the most wealthy of the Æginetæ overpowered the common people, who, together with Nicodromus, had revolted against them, and afterward having subdued them, they led them out to execution; and on this occasion they incurred a guilt which they were unable to expiate by any contrivance; but they were ejected out of the island before the goddess became propitious to them; for, having taken seven hundred of the common people prisoners, they led them out to execution; and one of them, having escaped from his bonds, fled to the porch of Ceres the lawgiver, and seizing the door-handle, held it fast; but they, when they were unable, by dragging, to tear him away, cut off his hands, and so took him away; and the hands were left sticking on the door-handles. 92. Thus, then, the Æginetæ treated their own people. But when the Athenians arrived with their seventy ships, they came to an engagement, and being conquered in the sea-fight, they called on the same persons as before for assistance, *that is*, on the Argives. They, however, would not any longer succor them, but complained that the ships of the Æginetæ, having been forcibly seized by Cleomenes, had touched on the territory of Argos, and the crews had disembarked with the Lacedæmonians. Some men had also disembarked from Sicyonian ships in the same invasion; and a penalty was imposed upon them by the Argives, to pay a thousand talents, five hundred each. The Sicyonians, accordingly, acknowledging that they had acted unjustly, made an agreement to pay one hundred talents, and be free from the rest; but the Æginetæ would not own themselves in the wrong, and were very obstinate. On this account, therefore, none of the Argives were sent by the commonwealth to assist them; but, on their request, volunteers *went* to the number of a thousand: a general, whose name was Eurybates, and who had practiced for the pentathlon, led them: the greater number of these never returned home, but were slain by the Athenians in Ægina. The general, Eurybates, engaging in single combat, killed three several antagonists in that manner, but was slain by the fourth, Sophanes of Decelea. 93. The Æginetæ, however, having attacked the fleet of the Athenians when they were in disorder, obtained a victory, and took four of their ships, with the men on board.

94. War was accordingly kindled between the Athenians and Æginetæ. But the Persian pursued his own design, for the servant continually reminded him to remember the Athenians, and the Pisistratidæ constantly importuned him and accused the Athenians; and, at the same time, Darius, laying hold of this pretext, was desirous of subduing those people of Greece who had refused to give him earth and water. He therefore dismissed Mardonius from his command, because he had succeeded ill in his expedition; and having appointed other generals, he sent them against Eretria and Athens, *namely*, Datis, who was a Mede by birth, and Artaphernes, son of Artaphernes, his own nephew; and he dispatched them with strict orders, having enslaved Athens and Eretria, to bring the bondsmen into his presence. 95. When these generals who were appointed left the king, and reached the Aleian plain of Cilicia, bringing with them a numerous and well-equipped army, while they were there encamped the whole naval force required from each people came up: the horse-transports were also present, which Darius in the preceding year had commanded his tributaries to prepare. Having put the horses on board of these, and having embarked the land-forces in the ships, they sailed for Ionia with six hundred

triremes. From thence they did not steer their ships along the continent direct toward the Hellespont and Thrace, but, parting from Samos, they directed their course across the Icarian sea, and through the islands; as appears to me, chiefly dreading the circumnavigation of Athos, because in the preceding year, in attempting a passage that way, they had sustained great loss; and besides, Naxos compelled them, not having been before captured. 96. When, being carried out of the Icarian sea, they arrived off Naxos (for the Persians, bearing in mind what had formerly happened,[9] purposed to attack this place first), the Naxians fled to the mountains, and did not await their approach: the Persians, therefore, having seized as many of them as they could lay hold of, as slaves, set fire to both the sacred buildings and the city; and having done this, they proceeded against the rest of the islands.

97. While they were doing this, the Delians also, abandoning Delos, fled to Tenos; but as the fleet was sailing down toward it, Datis, having sailed forward, would not permit the ships to anchor near the island, but farther on, off Rhenea; and he, having ascertained where the Delians were, sent a herald and addressed them as follows: "Sacred men, why have you fled, forming an unfavorable opinion of me? for both I myself have so much wisdom, and am so ordered by the king, that in the region where the two deities[1] were born, no harm should be done either to the country itself or its inhabitants. Return, therefore, to your houses, and resume possession of the island." This message he sent to the Delians by means of a herald; and afterward having heaped up three hundred talents of frankincense upon the altar, he burned it. 98. Datis, accordingly, having done this, sailed with the army first against Eretria, taking with him both Ionians and Æolians. But after he had put out to sea from thence, Delos was shaken by an earthquake, as the Delians say, the first and last time that it was so affected to my time; and the deity assuredly by this portent intimated to men the evils that were about to befall them; for during the reigns of Darius, son of Hystaspes, of Xerxes, son of Darius, and of Artaxerxes, son of Xerxes—during these three successive

[9] See B. V. ch. 34.

[1] Apollo and Diana.

generations, more disasters befell Greece than during the twenty generations that preceded the time of Darius; partly brought upon it by the Persians, and partly by the chief men among them contending for power; so that it is nothing improbable that Delos should be moved at that time, having been until then unmoved; and in an oracle respecting it, it had been thus written: "I will move even Delos, although hitherto unmoved." And in the Grecian language these names mean, Darius, "one who restrains;" Xerxes, "a warrior;" and Artaxerxes, "a mighty warrior." Thus, then, the Greeks may rightly designate these kings in their language.

99. The barbarians, after they had parted from Delos, touched at the islands, and from thence they took with them men to serve in the army, and carried away the sons of the islanders for hostages; and when, having sailed round the islands, they touched at Carystus, as the Carystians would not give hostages, and refused to bear arms against their neighboring cities, meaning Eretria and Athens, they thereupon besieged them and ravaged their country, until at last the Carystians also submitted to the will of the Persians. 100. The Eretrians, being informed that the Persian armament was sailing against them, entreated the Athenians to assist them; and the Athenians did not refuse their aid, but gave them as auxiliaries those four thousand men to whom had been allotted the territory of the horse-feeding Chalcidians.[2] But the councils of the Eretrians were not at all sound: they sent for the Athenians indeed, but held divided opinions; for some of them proposed to abandon the city, *and to retire* to the fastnesses of Eubœa; but others of them, hoping that they should derive gain to themselves from the Persians, were planning to betray their country. But Æschines, son of Nothon, a man of rank among the Eretrians, being informed of the views of both parties, communicated to the Athenians who had come the whole state of their affairs, and entreated them to return to their own country, lest they too should perish. The Athenians followed this advice of Æschines, and, having crossed over to Oropus, saved themselves. 101. In the mean time, the Persians, sailing on, directed their ships' course to Tamynæ, Chœrea, and Ægilia, of the Eretrian territory; and having

See B. V. ch. 77.

taken possession of these places, they immediately disembarked the horses, and made preparations to attack the enemy. But the Eretrians had no thoughts of going out against them and fighting, but since that opinion had prevailed, that they should not abandon the city, their only care now was if by any means they could defend the walls. A violent attack on the walls ensuing, for six days many fell on both sides, but on the seventh, Euphorbus, son of Alcimachus, and Philargus, son of Cyneus, men of rank among the citizens, betrayed the city to the Persians. But they, having gained entrance into the city, in the first place pillaged and set fire to the temples, in revenge for those that had been burned at Sardis, and, in the next, they enslaved the inhabitants, in obedience to the commands of Darius.

102. Having subdued Eretria and rested a few days, they sailed to Attica, pressing them very close, and expecting to treat the Athenians in the same way as they had the Eretrians. Now, as Marathon was the spot in Attica best adapted for cavalry, and nearest to Eretria, Hippias, son of Pisistratus, conducted them there. 103. But the Athenians, when they heard of this, also sent their forces to Marathon; and ten generals led them, of whom the tenth was Miltiades, whose father, Cimon,[3] son of Stesagoras, had been banished from Athens by Pisistratus, son of Hippocrates. During his exile, it was his good fortune to obtain the Olympic prize in the four-horse chariot race, and having gained this victory, he transferred the honor to Miltiades, his brother by the same mother; and afterward, in the next Olympiad, being victorious with the same mares, he permitted Pisistratus to be proclaimed victor, and having conceded the victory to him, he returned home under terms; and after he had gained another Olympic prize with these same mares, it happened that he died by the hands of the sons of Pisistratus, when Pisistratus himself was no longer alive: they slew him near the Prytaneum, having placed men to waylay him by night. Cimon was buried in front of the city, beyond that which is called the road through Cœla, and opposite him these same mares were buried which won the three Olympic prizes. Other mares also had already done the same thing, belonging to Evagoras the Lacedæmonian, but besides these none others. Stesagoras,

[3] See ch. 39—41.

the elder of the sons of Cimon, was at that time being educated by his paternal uncle Miltiades in the Chersonese, but the younger by Cimon himself at Athens, and he had the name of Miltiades from Miltiades, the founder of the Chersonese. 104. At that time, then, this Miltiades, coming from the Chersonese, and having escaped a twofold death, became general of the Athenians; for, in the first place, the Phœnicians, having pursued him as far as Imbros, were exceedingly desirous of seizing him, and carrying him up to the king; and, in the next, when he had escaped them, and had returned to his own country, and thought himself in safety, his enemies thereupon, having attacked him, and brought him before a court of justice, prosecuted him for tyranny in the Chersonese; but having escaped these also, he was at length appointed general of the Athenians, being chosen by the people.

105. And, first, while the generals were yet in the city, they dispatched a herald to Sparta, one Phidippides, an Athenian, who was a courier by profession, one who attended to this very business. This man, then, as Phidippides himself said and reported to the Athenians, Pan met near Mount Parthenion, above Tegea; and Pan, calling out the name of Phidippides, bade him ask the Athenians why they paid no attention to him, who was well inclined to the Athenians, and had often been useful to them, and would be so hereafter. The Athenians, therefore, as their affairs were then in a prosperous condition, believed that this was true, and erected a temple to Pan beneath the Acropolis, and in consequence of that message they propitiate Pan with yearly sacrifices and the torch race. 106. This Phidippides, being sent by the generals at that time when he said Pan appeared to him, arrived in Sparta on the following day after his departure from the city of the Athenians, and on coming in presence of the magistrates, he said, "Lacedæmonians, the Athenians entreat you to assist them, and not to suffer the most ancient city among the Greeks to fall into bondage to barbarians; for Eretria is already reduced to slavery, and Greece has become weaker by the loss of a renowned city." He accordingly delivered the message according to his instructions, and they resolved indeed to assist the Athenians; but it was out of their power to do so immediately, as they were unwilling to violate the law; for it was the ninth day of the current month,

and they said they could not march out on the ninth day, the moon's circle not being full. They therefore waited for the full moon.

107. Meanwhile Hippias, son of Pisistratus, had led the barbarians to Marathon, having the preceding night seen the following vision in his sleep. Hippias fancied that he lay with his own mother; he inferred, therefore, from the dream, that, having returned to Athens and recovered the sovereignty, he should die an old man in his own country. He drew this inference from the vision. At that time, as he was leading the way, he first of all landed the slaves from Eretria on the island of the Styreans, called Ægilia; and next he moored the ships as they came from Marathon, and drew up the barbarians as they disembarked on land; and as he was busied in doing this, it happened that he sneezed and coughed more violently than he was accustomed; and as he was far advanced in years, several of his teeth were loose, so that through the violence of his cough he threw out one of these teeth; and as it fell on the sand, he used every endeavor to find it, but when the tooth could nowhere be found, he drew a deep sigh, and said to the by-standers, "This country is not ours, nor shall we be able to subdue it; whatever share belongeth to me, my tooth possesses." Hippias accordingly inferred that his vision had been thus fulfilled.

108. When the Athenians were drawn up in a place sacred to Hercules, the Platæans came to their assistance with all their forces; for the Platæans had given themselves up to the Athenians, and the Athenians had already undergone many toils on their account; and they gave themselves up on the following occasion. The Platæans, being hard pressed by the Thebans, first offered themselves to Cleomenes, son of Anaxandrides, and to the Lacedæmonians who happened to be present. They would not receive them, but addressed them as follows: "We live at too great a distance, and such assistance would be of little value to you; for you would often be enslaved before any of us could be informed of it. We advise you, therefore, to give yourselves up to the Athenians, who are your neighbors, and are not backward in assisting." The Lacedæmonians gave this advice, not so much from any good will to the Platæans, as from a desire that the Athenians might be subject to toil by being set at variance with the

Bœotians. The Lacedæmonians accordingly gave this advice to the Platæans, and they did not disregard it; but when the Athenians were performing the sacred rites to the twelve gods, they sat down at the altar as suppliants, and delivered themselves up. But the Thebans, having heard of this, marched against the Platæans, and the Athenians went to assist; and as they were about to engage in battle, the Corinthians interfered; for, happening to be present, and mediating between them, at the request of both parties, they prescribed the limits to the country in the following manner: that the Thebans should leave alone those of the Bœotians who did not wish to be ranked among the Bœotians. The Corinthians, having made this decision, returned home; but the Bœotians attacked the Athenians as they were departing, but, having attacked them, were worsted in the battle. The Athenians, therefore, passing beyond the limits which the Corinthians had fixed for the Platæans—passing beyond these, they made the Asopus and Hysiæ to be the boundary between the Thebans and Platæans. The Platæans, therefore, gave themselves up to the Athenians in the manner above described, and at that time came to assist them at Marathon.

109. The opinions of the Athenian generals were divided; one party not consenting to engage, "because they were too few to engage with the army of the Medes;" and the others, among whom was Miltiades, urging them *to give battle.* When, therefore, they were divided, and the worst opinion was likely to prevail, thereupon, for there was an eleventh voter who was appointed minister of war among the Athenians, for the Athenians in ancient times gave the minister of war an equal vote with the generals, and at that time Callimachus of Aphidnæ was minister of war—to him, therefore, Miltiades came, and spoke as follows: "It now depends on you, Callimachus, either to enslave Athens, or, by preserving its liberty, to leave a memorial of yourself to every age, such as not even Harmodius and Aristogiton have left; for the Athenians were never in so great danger from the time they were first a people; and if they succumb to the Medes, it has been determined what they are to suffer when delivered up to Hippias; but if the city survives, it will become the first of the Grecian cities. How, then, this can be brought to pass, and how the power of deciding this matter depends

on you, I will now proceed to explain. The opinions of us generals, who are ten, are divided, the one party urging that we should engage, the other that we should not engage. Now if we do not engage, I expect that some great dissension arising among us will shake the minds of the Athenians, so as to induce them to a compliance with the Medes; but if we engage before any dastardly thought arises in the minds of some of the Athenians, if the gods are impartial, we shall be able to get the better in the engagement. All these things, therefore, are now in your power, and entirely depend on you; for if you will support my opinion, your country will be free, and the city the first in Greece; but if you join with those who would dissuade us from an engagement, the contrary of the advantages I have enumerated will fall to your lot." 110. Miltiades, by these words, gained over Callimachus, and the opinion of the minister of war being added, it was determined to engage. Afterward the generals whose opinions had been given to engage, as the command for the day devolved upon each of them, gave it up to Miltiades; but he, having accepted it, would not come to an engagement before his own turn to command came.

111. When it came round to his turn, then the Athenians were drawn out in the following order for the purpose of engaging. The war-minister, Callimachus, commanded the right wing, for the law at that time was so settled among the Athenians that the war-minister should have the right wing. He having this command, the tribes succeeded as they were usually reckoned, adjoining one another; but the Platæans were drawn out last of all, occupying the left wing. Now, ever since that battle, when the Athenians offer sacrifices and celebrate the public festivals which take place every five years, the Athenian herald prays, saying, "May blessings attend both the Athenians and the Platæans." At that time, when the Athenians were drawn out at Marathon, the following was the case: their line was equal in extent to the Medic line, but the middle of it was but few deep, and there the line was weakest; but each wing was strong in numbers. 112. When they were thus drawn out, and the victims were favorable, thereupon the Athenians, as soon as they were ordered to charge, advanced against the barbarians in double-quick time; and the space between them was not less than eight stades. But the Persians,

seeing them charging at full speed, prepared to receive them; and they imputed madness to them, and that utterly destructive, when they saw that they were few in number, and that they rushed on at full speed, though they had no cavalry nor archers. So the barbarians surmised. The Athenians, however, when they engaged in close ranks with the barbarians, fought in a manner worthy of record; for they, the first of all the Greeks whom we know of, charged the enemy at full speed, and they first endured the sight of the Medic garb, and the men that wore it; but until that time the very name of the Medes was a terror to the Greeks. 113. The battle at Marathon lasted a long time; and in the middle of the line, where the Persians themselves and the Sacæ were arrayed, the barbarians were victorious; in this part, then, the barbarians conquered, and having broken the line, pursued to the interior; but in both wings the Athenians and the Platæans were victorious; and having gained the victory, they allowed the defeated portion of the barbarians to flee; and having united both wings, they fought with those who had broken their centre, and the Athenians were victorious. They followed the Persians in their flight, cutting them to pieces, till, reaching the shore, they called for fire and attacked the ships.

114. And, in the first place, in this battle the war-minister, Callimachus, was killed, having proved himself a brave man; and among the generals, Stesilaus, son of Thrasylas, perished; and, in the next place, Cynægeirus, son of Euphorion, having laid hold of a ship's poop, had his hand severed by an axe and fell; and, besides, many other distinguished Athenians *were slain*. 115. In this manner the Athenians made themselves masters of seven ships; but with the rest the barbarians, rowing rapidly back, and after taking off the Eretrian slaves from the island in which they had left them, sailed round Sunium, wishing to anticipate the Athenians in reaching the city. The charge prevailed among the Athenians that they formed this design by the contrivance of the Alcmæonidæ; for that they, having agreed with the Persians, held up a shield to them when they were on board their ships. 116. They then sailed round Sunium. But the Athenians marched with all speed to the assistance of the city, and were beforehand in reaching it before the barbarians arrived; and having come from the precinct of Hercules at Marathon, they took up their

station in another precinct of Hercules at Cynosarges; but the barbarians, having laid to with their fleet off Phalerum, for this was at that time the port of the Athenians, having anchored their ships there for a time, they sailed away for Asia. 117. In this battle at Marathon there died of the barbarians about six thousand four hundred men; and of the Athenians, one hundred and ninety-two: so many fell on both sides. The following prodigy occurred there: an Athenian, Epizelus, son of Cuphagoras, while fighting in the medley, and behaving valiantly, was deprived of sight, though wounded in no part of his body, nor struck from a distance; and he continued to be blind from that time for the remainder of his life. I have heard that he used to give the following account of his loss. He thought that a large heavy-armed man stood before him, whose beard shaded the whole of his shield; that this spectre passed by him, and killed the man that stood by his side. Such is the account, I have been informed, Epizelus used to give.

118. Datis, on his way back with the armament to Asia, when he came to Myconus, saw a vision in his sleep: what the vision was is not related; but he, as soon as day appeared, caused a search to be made through the ships; and having found in a Phœnician ship a gilded image of Apollo, he inquired whence it had been robbed; and having learned from what temple it was, he sailed in his own ship to Delos, and, as at that time the Delians had come back to the island, he deposited the image in the temple, and charged the Delians to convey the image to Delium of the Thebans; that place is on the coast, opposite Chalcis: Datis, accordingly, having given this charge, sailed away. The Delians, however, did not convey back this statue, but the Thebans themselves, twenty years afterward, carried it to Delium, in obedience to an oracle. 119. Those of the Eretrians who had been enslaved, Datis and Artaphernes, as soon as they reached Asia, took up to Susa; but king Darius, before the Eretrians were made captive, harbored deep resentment against them, as the Eretrians had been the first to begin acts of injustice; but when he saw them brought into his presence, and subject to his power, he did them no other harm, but settled them in the Cissian territory at a station of his own, the name of which is Ardericca: it is two hundred and ten stades distant from Susa, and forty from the well which produces three

different substances; for asphalt, salt, and oil are drawn up from it in the following manner. It is pumped up by means of a swipe, and, instead of a bucket, half of a wine-skin is attached to it; having dipped down with this, a man draws it up and then pours the contents into a receiver; and, being poured from this into another, it assumes three different forms: the asphalt and the salt immediately become solid, but the oil they collect, and the Persians call it rhadinace: it is black, and emits a strong odor. Here king Darius settled the Eretrians, who, even to my time, occupied this territory, retaining their ancient language. Such things took place with regard to the Eretrians. 120. Two thousand of the Lacedæmonians came to Athens after the full moon, making such haste to be in time that they arrived in Attica on the third day after leaving Sparta; but having come too late for the battle, they nevertheless desired to see the Medes; and having proceeded to Marathon, they saw *the slain;* and afterward, having commended the Athenians and their achievement, they returned home.

121. It is a marvel to me, and I can not credit the report, that the Alcmæonidæ ever held up a shield to the Persians by agreement, wishing that the Athenians should be subject to the barbarians and to Hippias; for they were evidently haters of tyrants more than, or equally with Callias, son of Phœnippus, and father of Hipponicus; for Callias was the only one of all the Athenians who, when Pisistratus was driven from Athens, dared to purchase his goods when put up to sale by the public crier; and he devised every thing else that was most hostile to him. 122. This Callias deserves to have frequent mention made of him by every one: first of all, on account of what has been already mentioned, as being a man ardent in asserting the freedom of his country; and, in the next place, on account of what he did at Olympia, having been victorious in the horse-race, and second in the chariot-race, and having before won the prize in the Pythian games, he was distinguished among all the Greeks for the greatest munificence. Moreover, with regard to his daughters, who were three in number, he behaved in the following manner: when they were of fit age for marriage, he gave them a most magnificent present, and gratified their wishes; for he gave each to that man of all the Athenians whom she wished to select for her own

husband. 123. And the Alcmæonidæ were haters of tyrants, equally with, or not at all less than him. It is therefore a marvel to me, and I can not admit the charge that they held up a shield, who at all times shunned the tyrants, and by whose contrivance the Pisistratidæ abandoned the tyranny.[4] Thus, in my judgment, these were the persons who liberated Athens much more than Harmodius and Aristogiton, for they, by slaying Hipparchus, exasperated the survivors of the Pisistratidæ, but did not any the more put an end to the tyranny of the rest; whereas the Alcmæonidæ manifestly liberated their country, if indeed they were the persons who persuaded the Pythian to enjoin the Lacedæmonians to liberate Athens, as I have already shown.[5] 124. But, perhaps, having some grudge against the Athenian people, they betrayed their country? There were not, however, any other men who were more highly esteemed among the Athenians than them, or who were more honored; so that it is not consistent with reason that a shield was held up by them from such a motive. Still, a shield was held up; and this can not be denied, for so it was; but who it was that held it up I am not able to say farther than this.

125. The Alcmæonidæ were even from a very early period distinguished at Athens; for through Alcmæon, and again through Megacles, they became very distinguished. For, in the first place, Alcmæon, son of Megacles, was coadjutor to the Lydians from Sardis, who came on the part of Crœsus to consult the oracle at Delphi,[6] and he assisted them zealously; and Crœsus being informed by the Lydians, who had gone to consult the oracle, that he had done him good service, sent for him to Sardis, and when he arrived, presented him with so much gold as he could carry away at once on his own person. Alcmæon, for the purpose of such a present, had recourse to the following expedient: having put on a large cloak, and having left a deep fold in the cloak, and having drawn on the widest boots he could find, he went into the treasury to which they conducted him; and meeting with a heap of gold-dust, he first stuffed around his legs as much gold as the boots would contain; and then, having filled the whole fold with gold, and having sprinkled the gold-dust over the hair of his head, and put more into his mouth, he went out of the treasury, dragging

[4] B. V. chap. 62—65. [5] B. V. chap. 63. [6] B. I. chap. 47, 53, 55.

his boots with difficulty, and resembling any thing rather than a man; for his mouth was stuffed, and he was all over swollen. Crœsus, when he saw him, burst into laughter; and he gave him all that, and, besides, presented him with other things not of less value than it. Thus this family became extremely rich; and this Alcmæon, having by these means bred horses, won the prize in the Olympic games. 126. In the second generation after, Clisthenes, tyrant of Sicyon, raised the family, so that it became far more celebrated among the Greeks than it had been before; for Clisthenes, son of Aristonymus, son of Myron, son of Andreas, had a daughter whose name was Agarista: her he resolved to give in marriage to the man whom he should find the most accomplished of all the Greeks. When, therefore, the Olympian games were being celebrated, Clisthenes, being victorious in them in the chariot race, made a proclamation, "that whoever of the Greeks deemed himself worthy to become the son-in-law of Clisthenes, should come to Sicyon on the sixtieth day, or even before; since Clisthenes had determined on the marriage in a year, reckoning from the sixtieth day." Thereupon such of the Greeks as were puffed up with themselves and their country came as suitors; and Clisthenes, having made a race-course and palæstra for them, kept it for this very purpose. 127. From Italy, accordingly, came Smindyrides, son of Hippocrates, a Sybarite, who more than any other man reached the highest pitch of luxury (and Sybaris was at that time in a most flourishing condition); and Damasus of Siris, son of Amyris called the Wise: these came from Italy. From the Ionian gulf, Amphimnestus, son of Epistrophus, an Epidamnian: he came from the Ionian gulf. An Ætolian came, Males, brother of that Titormus who surpassed the Greeks in strength, and fled from the society of men to the extremity of the Ætolian territory. And from Peloponnesus, Leocedes, son of Pheidon, tyrant of the Argives, *a descendant* of that Pheidon who introduced measures among the Peloponnesians, and was the most insolent of all the Greeks, who, having removed the Elean umpires, himself regulated the games at Olympia; his son accordingly came. And Amiantus, son of Lycurgus, an Arcadian from Trapezus; and an Azenian from the city of Pæos, Laphanes, son of Euphorion, who, as the story is told in Arcadia, received the Dioscuri in his house, and after that entertained all men; and an Elean, Onomastus, son of Agæus: these accordingly came from the Peloponnesus itself. From Athens there came Megacles, son of Alcmæon, the same who had visited Crœsus, and another, Hippoclides, son of Tisander, who surpassed the Athenians in wealth and beauty. From Eretria, which was flourishing at that time, came Lysanias: he was the only one from Eubœa. And from Thessaly there came, of the Scopades, Diactorides a Cranonian; and from the Molossi, Alcon. 128. So many were the suitors. When they had arrived on the appointed day, Clisthenes made inquiries of their country, and the family of each; then detaining them for a year, he made trial of their manly qualities, their dispositions, learning, and morals; holding familiar intercourse with each separately, and with all together, and leading out to the gymnasia such of them as were younger; but most of all he made trial of them at the banquet; for as long as he detained them, he did this throughout, and at the same time entertained them magnificently. And somehow, of all the suitors, those that had come from Athens pleased him most, and of these Hippoclides, son of Tisander, was preferred both on account of his manly qualities, and because he was distantly related to the Cypselidæ in Corinth. 129. When the day appointed for the consummation of the marriage arrived, and for the declaration of Clisthenes himself, whom he would choose of them all, Clisthenes, having sacrificed a hundred oxen, entertained both the suitors themselves and all the Sicyonians; and when they had concluded the feast, the suitors had a contest about music, and any subject proposed for conversation. As the drinking went on, Hippoclides, who much attracted the attention of the rest, ordered the flute-player to play a dance; and when the flute-player obeyed, he began to dance; and he danced, probably, so as to please himself; but Clisthenes, seeing it, beheld the whole matter with suspicion. Afterward, Hippoclides, having rested a while, ordered some one to bring in a table; and when the table came in, he first danced Laconian figures on it, and then Attic ones; and in the third place, having leaned his head on the table, he gesticulated with his legs. But Clisthenes, when he danced the first and second time, revolted from the thought of having Hippoclides for his son-in-law, on account of his dancing and want of decorum, yet restrained himself, not wishing to burst out against him; but when he saw him gesticulating with his legs, he was no longer able to restrain himself, and said, "Son of Tisander, you have danced away your marriage." But Hippoclides answered, "No matter to Hippoclides." Hence this answer became a proverb. 130. Clisthenes, having commanded silence, thus addressed the assembled company: "Gentlemen, suitors of my daughter, I commend you all, and, if it were possible, would gratify you all, not selecting one of you above the others, nor reject the rest; but as it is not possible, since I have to determine about a single damsel, to indulge the wishes of all, to such of you as are rejected from the marriage, I present a talent of silver to each, on account of your condescending to take a wife from my family, and of your absence from home; but to Megacles, son of Alcmæon, I betroth my daughter Agarista, according to the laws of the Athenians." When Megacles said that he accepted the betrothal, the marriage was celebrated by Clisthenes. 131. This happened respecting the decision between the suitors, and thus the Alcmæonidæ became celebrated throughout Greece. From this marriage sprung Clisthenes, who established the tribes and a democracy among the Athenians, taking his name from his maternal grandfather the Sicyonian; he was born to Megacles, as was also Hippocrates; and from Hippocrates, another Megacles, and another Agarista, who took her name from Agarista, daughter of Clisthenes; she having married Xanthippus, son of Ariphron, and being with child, saw a vision in her sleep, and fancied that she brought forth a lion; and after a few days she bore Pericles to Xanthippus.

132. After the defeat *of the Persians* at Marathon, Miltiades, who was before highly esteemed among the Athenians, then still more increased his reputation. Having, therefore, asked of the Athenians seventy ships, and troops and money, without telling them what country he purposed to invade, but saying that he would make them rich if they would follow him, for that he would take them to such a country, from whence they would easily bring abundance of gold; speaking thus, he asked for the ships; and the Athenians, elated by these hopes, granted them. 133. Miltiades, accordingly, having taken with him the troops, sailed against Paros, alleging as a pretext that the Parians had first begun hostilities

by sending a trireme with the Persian to Marathon. This was his pretended reason; but, in fact, he had a grudge against the Parians on account of Lysagoras, son of Tisias, who was a Parian by birth, and had calumniated him to Hydarnes the Persian. Miltiades, having arrived with his forces at the place to which he was sailing, besieged the Parians, who were driven within their walls; and, sending a herald to them, he demanded a hundred talents, saying that if they did not give him that sum, he would not draw off his army until he had destroyed them. The Parians never entertained the thought whether they should give Miltiades any money, but devised means by which they might defend the city; and, in addition to other plans, they also, in the several parts where the wall was most exposed to attack, there raised it, during the night, to double its former height. 134. Up to this point of the story all the Greeks agree; but after this, the Parians themselves say that it happened as follows: that when Miltiades was in a state of perplexity, a captive woman, who was by birth a Parian, and her name was Timo, conferred with him; she was an inferior priestess of the infernal goddesses. When she came into the presence of Miltiades, she advised him, if he deemed it of great consequence to take Paros, to act as she should suggest. She then made some suggestion; and he, coming to the mound that is before the city, leaped over the fence of Ceres Thesmophora, as he was unable to open the door; and having leaped over, he went to the temple, for the purpose of doing something within, either to move some of the things that may not be moved, or to do something or other; and he was just at the door, when suddenly a thrill of horror came over him, and he went back by the same way; and, in leaping over the fence, his thigh was dislocated; others say that he hurt his knee. 135. Miltiades, accordingly, being in a bad plight, sailed back home, neither bringing money to the Athenians, nor having reduced Paros, but having besieged it for six and twenty days, and ravaged the island. The Parians, being informed that Timo, the priestess of the goddesses, had directed Miltiades, and desiring to punish her for so doing, sent deputies to the oracle at Delphi as soon as they were relieved from the siege: they sent to inquire whether they should put to death the priestess of the goddesses for having made known to the enemy the means of capturing her country.

and for having discovered to Miltiades sacred things, which ought not to be revealed to the male sex. But the Pythian did not allow them, saying "that Timo was not to blame for this, but that it was fated Miltiades should come to a miserable end, and she had appeared to him as a guide to misfortunes." The Pythian gave this answer to the Parians. 136. When Miltiades returned from Paros, the Athenians were loud in their complaints against him, both all others, and especially Xanthippus, son of Ariphron, who, bringing a capital charge against Miltiades before the people, prosecuted him on a charge of deceiving the Athenians. Miltiades, though present in person, made no defense; for he was unable, and his thigh had begun to mortify. But while he lay on a couch, his friends made a defense for him, dwelling much on the battle that had been fought at Marathon, and on the capture of Lemnos; since, having taken Lemnos, and inflicted vengeance on the Pelasgians, he had given it up to the Athenians. The people so far favoring him as to acquit him of the capital offense, and having fined him fifty talents for the injury he had done, Miltiades soon after ended his life by the putrefaction and mortification of his thigh. His son Cimon paid the fifty talents.

137. Miltiades, son of Cimon, had possessed himself of Lemnos in the following manner. The Pelasgians, when they had been driven out of Attica by the Athenians, whether justly or unjustly—(for this I am unable to determine, except so far as is related), Hecatæus, however, son of Hegesander, says in his history that it was "unjustly, for that, when the Athenians saw the lands under Hymettus, which they had given to the Pelasgians in payment for the wall they had formerly built upon the Acropolis—when the Athenians saw this well cultivated, which was before barren and of no value, jealousy and a desire of the land took possession of them, and so the Athenians drove them out, without alleging any other pretense whatever." But as the Athenians say, "they justly expelled them; for that the Pelasgians, while settled under Mount Hymettus, made incursions from thence, and committed the following injuries: for that their daughters and sons used constantly to go for water to the Nine Springs, because at that time neither they nor the other Greeks had domestic servants; and whenever the young wom-

en went there, the Pelasgians used, out of insolence and contempt, to offer violence to them; nor were they satisfied with doing this, but at last they were discovered in the very act of plotting to attack *the city*. *They add* that they themselves showed themselves so much better men than them, in that, when it was in their power to put the Pelasgians to death, since they had found them plotting against them, they would not do so, but warned them to depart the country; and that they, accordingly, withdrawing, possessed themselves of other places, and among them of Lemnos." Hecatæus has given the former account, and the Athenians give the latter. 138. But these Pelasgians, who then inhabited Lemnos, and desired to be revenged on the Athenians, being well acquainted with the festivals of the Athenians, stationed fity-oared galleys and laid an ambuscade for the Athenian women, as they celebrated the festival of Diana in Brauron, and having carried many of them away from thence, they sailed off, and taking them to Lemnos, kept them as concubines. But when these women were fully supplied with children, they instructed their sons in the Attic language and the manners of the Athenians; they, therefore, would not hold any intercourse with the sons of the Pelasgian women, but if any one of their number was beaten by one of them, they all immediately assisted, and revenged one another; moreover, these boys thought they had a right to govern the other boys, and proved far superior to them. But the Pelasgians, observing this, consulted together, and, on consideration, considerable alarm came over them as to what these boys would do when they were grown up, if they already determined to assist each other against the sons of their lawful wives, and even now endeavored to rule over them. Thereupon they resolved to murder the children they had by the Attic women; and, accordingly, they did so, and, moreover, put their mothers to death. From this crime, and that which the women perpetrated before this, who, with the assistance of Thaos, killed their own husbands, all enormous actions are wont to be called Lemnian throughout Greece. 139. But when the Pelasgians had murdered their own children and women, neither did their land yield fruit, nor were their wives and flocks equally prolific as before; being, therefore, afflicted by famine and childlessness, they sent to Delphi to seek for some deliverance from their present distresses. But the Pythian bade them give such satisfaction to the Athenians as the Athenians themselves should impose. The Pelasgians, therefore, went to Athens, and professed themselves ready to give satisfaction for the whole injury. But the Athenians, having spread a couch in the Prytaneum in the handsomest way they were able, and having placed by it a table full of all sorts of good things, commanded the Pelasgians to surrender their country to them in such a condition. But the Pelasgians said, in answer, "When a ship shall perform the voyage in one day by the north wind from your country to ours, we will then deliver it up." This they said, supposing that it was impossible the thing should happen, because Attica lies far to the south of Lemnos. 140. This took place at that time. But very many years after this, when the Chersonese in the Hellespont became subject to the Athenians, Miltiades, son of Cimon, at a time when the Etesian winds prevailed, having performed the voyage in a ship from Elæus, on the Hellespont, to Lemnos, required the Pelasgians to quit the island, reminding them of the oracle, which the Pelasgians expected could never be accomplished. The Hephæstians accordingly obeyed; but the Myrinæans, not acknowledging the Chersonese to be Attica, were besieged until they also surrendered. Thus the Athenians and Miltiades got possession of Lemnos.

BOOK VII.

POLYMNIA.

When the news of the battle fought at Marathon reached Darius, son of Hystaspes, who was before much exasperated with the Athenians on account of the attack upon Sardis, he then became much more incensed, and was still more eager to prosecute the war against Greece. Having, therefore, immediately sent messengers to the several cities, he enjoined them to prepare an army, imposing on each a much greater number than they had furnished before, and ships, horses, corn, and transports. When these orders were proclaimed round about, Asia was thrown into agitation during the space of three years, the bravest men being enrolled and prepared for the purpose of invading Greece; but in the fourth year the Egyptians, who had been subdued by Cambyses, revolted from the Persians, whereupon Darius only became more eager to march against both. 2. When Darius was preparing for his expeditions against Egypt and Athens, a violent dissension arose between his sons concerning the sovereignty; for, by the customs of the Persians, he was obliged to nominate his successor before he marched out on any expedition. Now Darius, even before he became king, had three sons born to him by his former wife, the daughter of Gobryas; and after his accession to the throne, four others by Atossa, daughter of Cyrus. Of the former, Artabazanes was the eldest; of those after born, Xerxes: and these two, not being of the same mother, were at variance. Artabazanes *urged* that he was the eldest of all the sons, and that it was the established usage among all men that the eldest son should succeed to the sovereignty. On the other hand, Xerxes *alleged* that he was son of Atossa, daughter of Cyrus, and that it was Cyrus who had acquired freedom for the Persians. 3. When Darius had not yet declared his opinion, at this very conjuncture, Demaratus, son of Ariston, happened to come up to Susa, having been deprived of the kingly office at Sparta,[1] and having imposed on himself a voluntary exile from Lacedæmon. This man, having heard of the difference between the sons of Darius, went to Xerxes, as report says, and advised him to say, in addition to what he had already said, that "he was born to Darius after he had become a king, and was possessed of the empire of the Persians; whereas Artabazanes was born to Darius while he was yet a private person; wherefore it was not reasonable or just that any other should possess that dignity in preference to himself, since in Sparta, also," Demaratus continued to suggest, "this custom prevailed, that if some children were born before their father became king, and one was born subsequently when he had now come to the throne, this last-born son should succeed to the kingdom." Xerxes having availed himself of the suggestion of Demaratus, Da-

[1] See B. VI. chap. 70.

rius, acknowledging that he said what was just, declared him king. But it appears to me that even without this suggestion Xerxes would have been made king, for Atossa had unbounded influence. 4. Darius, having appointed Xerxes to be king over the Persians, prepared to march. However, after these things, and in the year after the revolt of Egypt, it happened that Darius himself, while he was making preparations, died, having reigned thirty-six years in all; nor was he able to avenge himself either on the Egyptians, who had revolted, or on the Athenians. When Darius was dead, the kingdom devolved on his son Xerxes.

5. Xerxes, however, was at first by no means inclined to make war against Greece, but he levied forces for the reduction of Egypt; but Mardonius, son of Gobryas, who was cousin to Xerxes, and son of Darius's sister, being present, and having the greatest influence with him of all the Persians, constantly held the following language, saying, "Sir, it is not right that the Athenians, having already done much mischief to the Persians, should go unpunished for what they have done. However, for the present, finish the enterprise you have in hand, and when you have quelled the insolence of Egypt, lead your army against Athens, that you may acquire a good reputation among men, and any one for the future may be cautious of marching against your territory." This language was used by him for the purposes of revenge, but he frequently made the following addition to it, that "Europe was a very beautiful country, and produced all kinds of cultivated trees, and was very fertile, and worthy to be possessed by the king alone of all mortals." 6. He spake thus, because he was desirous of new enterprises, and wished to be himself governor of Greece: in time he effected his purpose, and persuaded Xerxes to do as he advised, for other things happening favorably assisted him in persuading Xerxes. In the first place, messengers coming from Thessaly on the part of the Aleuadæ, invited the king, with earnest importunity, to invade Greece: these Aleuadæ were kings of Thessaly; and, in the next place, those of the Pisistratidæ who had gone up to Susa, holding the same language as the Aleuadæ, still more eagerly pressed him, having with them Onomacritus, an Athenian, a soothsayer, and dispenser of the oracles of Musæus; for they went up *to Susa*, having first reconciled their former

enmity *with him;* for Onomacritus had been banished from Athens by Hipparchus, son of Pisistratus, having been detected by Lasus the Hermionian in the very act of interpolating among the oracles of Musæus one importing that the islands lying off Lemnos would disappear beneath the sea: wherefore Hipparchus banished him, although he had before been very familiar with him. But at that time, having gone up with them, whenever he came into the presence of the king, as the Pisistratidæ spoke of him in very high terms, he recited some of the oracles; if, however, there was among them any that portended misfortune to the barbarians, of these he made no mention; but, selecting such as were most favorable, he said it was fated that the Hellespont should be bridged over by a Persian, describing the march. Thus he continually assailed[2] *the king*, rehearsing oracles, as did the Pisistratidæ and Aleuadæ, by declaring their opinions. 7. When Xerxes was persuaded to make war against Greece, he then, in the second year after the death of Darius, first made an expedition against those who had revolted; and, having subdued them and reduced all Egypt to a worse state of servitude than it was under Darius, he committed the government to Achæmenes, his own brother, and son of Darius. Some time after, Inarus,[3] son of Psammitichus, a Libyan, slew Achæmenes, to whom the government of Egypt was committed.

8. Xerxes, after the reduction of Egypt, when he was about to take in hand the expedition against Athens, convoked an assembly of the principal Persians, that he might both hear their opinions, and himself make known his intentions before them all. When they were assembled Xerxes addressed them as follows: (1.) "Men of Persia, I shall not be the first to introduce this custom among you, but shall adopt it, having received it from my forefathers; for, as I learn from older men, we have never remained inactive since we wrested the sovereign power from the Medes, and Cyrus overthrew Astyages: but the deity thus leads the way, and to us who follow his guidance many things result to our advantage. What deeds Cyrus, and Cambyses, and my father Darius have achieved, and what nations they have added to our empire, no one need mention to you who know them well; but I, since I have succeeded to the throne,

[2] Or "conducted himself." [3] See B. III. chap 12.

have carefully considered this, in what way I may not fall short of my predecessors in this honor, nor acquire less additional power to the Persians. And, on mature consideration, I find that we may at once acquire an increase of glory, and a country not inferior nor poorer, but even more productive than that we now possess; and, at the same time, that satisfaction and vengeance will accrue to us. Wherefore I have now called you together, that I may communicate to you what I purpose to do. (2.) I intend to throw a bridge over the Hellespont, and to march an army through Europe against Greece, that I may punish the Athenians for the injuries they have done to the Persians and to my father. You have already seen Darius preparing to make war against those people; but he died, and had it not in his power to avenge himself. But I, in his cause and that of the other Persians, will not rest till I have taken and burned Athens, for they first began by doing acts of injustice against my father and me. First of all, having come to Sardis with Aristagoras the Milesian, our servant, on their arrival they burned down both the groves and the temples; and, secondly, how they treated us on our making a descent on their territory, when Datis and Artaphernes led our forces, you all know well enough. (3.) For these reasons, therefore, I have resolved to make war upon them; and, on reflection, I find the following advantages in this course: if we shall subdue them, and their neighbors, who inhabit the country of Pelops the Phrygian, we shall make the Persian territory coextensive with the air of heaven; nor will the sun look down upon any land that borders on ours; but I, with your assistance, will make them all one territory, marching through the whole of Europe; for I am informed that such is the case; and that no city or nation of the world will remain, which will be able to come to a battle with us, when those whom I have mentioned have been brought into subjection. Thus both those who are guilty and those who are not guilty must equally submit to the yoke of servitude. (4.) But you, by doing what I require, will gratify me exceedingly; when I shall have informed you of the time, it will be the duty of each of you to come promptly; and whosoever shall appear with the best-appointed troops, to him I will give such presents as are accounted most honorable in our country. But that I may not appear to follow my own counsel only, I lay the matter before you, bidding any one of you who wishes to declare his opinion." Having said this, he ceased.

9. After him Mardonius spoke: "Sir, not only are you the most excellent of all the Persians that have yet been, but even of all that ever shall be; you also, in other respects, have in speaking touched upon the most important topics and the most exact truth, and especially will not suffer the Ionians, who dwell in Europe, to mock us, worthless as they are; for it would indeed be a great indignity if, having subdued the Sacæ, Indians, Ethiopians, and Assyrians, and other nations, many and powerful, which never did the Persians any wrong, but, in order only to enlarge our dominions, we hold them in servitude, and yet shall not avenge ourselves on the Greeks, who were the first to commit injustice. Having what to fear? what confluence of numbers? what power of wealth? (1.) We are acquainted with their manner of fighting; and we are acquainted with their power, that it is weak. We hold their children in subjection, those who dwell within their territories, and are called Ionians, Æolians, and Dorians. I myself have made trial of these men already, marching against them at the command of your father; and when I advanced as far as Macedonia, and was within a short distance of reaching Athens itself, no one opposed me in battle. (2.) And yet the Greeks are accustomed, as I am informed, to undertake wars without deliberation, from obstinacy and folly; for when they have declared war against one another, having found out the fairest and most level spot, they go down to it and fight; so that the conquerors depart with great loss, and of the conquered I say nothing at all, for they are utterly destroyed; whereas, being of the same language, they ought, by the intervention of heralds and embassadors, to adjust their differences, and in any way rather than by fighting; but if they must needs go to war with each other, they ought to find out where they are each least likely to be conquered, and there try *the issue of a battle*. The Greeks accordingly, adopting a disadvantageous method, when I marched as far as Macedonia, never ventured so far as to come to a battle. (3.) Will any one, then, O king, have recourse to war, and oppose you, when you lead the multitudes of Asia, and all her ships? In my opinion, indeed, the Grecians will never proceed to such a degree of audacity. But if I should happen to be deceived

in my opinion, and they, elated by folly, should come to battle with us, they will learn that of all men we are the most skilled in war. Let nothing, then, be untried; for nothing is accomplished of its own self, but all things are usually achieved by men through endeavors." Mardonius, having thus smoothed over the opinion of Xerxes, ceased to speak.

10. The rest of the Persians continuing silent, and not daring to declare an opinion to the one proposed, Artabanus, son of Hystaspes, being uncle to Xerxes, and relying on this, spoke as follows: (1.) "O king, unless opinions opposite to each other are spoken, it is impossible to choose the better, but it becomes necessary to adopt that which has been advanced; whereas, when various opinions have been given, it is possible: just as with unalloyed gold, we can not distinguish it by itself, but when we have rubbed it by the side of other gold, we do distinguish the better. I warned your father and my brother not to make war upon the Scythians,[4] a people who have no city in any part of their territory; but he, hoping to subdue the Scythian nomades, heeded not my advice, and, having led an army against them, returned with the loss of many brave men of his army. But you, O king, are about to make war upon men far superior to the Scythians, who are said to be most valiant both by sea and land; it is therefore right that I should inform you of the danger we have to fear. (2.) You say that, having thrown a bridge over the Hellespont, you will march an army through Europe into Greece; now it may happen that we shall be worsted either by land or by sea, or even by both, for the people are said to be valiant; and this we may infer, since the Athenians alone destroyed so great an army that invaded the Attic territory under Datis and Artaphernes. They were not, however, successful in both; but if they should attack us with their fleet, and, having obtained a naval victory, should sail to the Hellespont and destroy the bridge, this surely, O king, were a great danger. (3.) Nor do I found this conjecture on any wisdom of my own, but from the calamity that once all but befell us, when your father, having joined the shores of the Thracian Bosphorus, and thrown a bridge over the Ister, crossed over to attack the Scythians; then the Scythians used every means to induce the Ionians, to whom the guard of the

[4] See B. IV. ch. 83.

passage over the Ister had been intrusted, to break up the bridge; and if, at that time, Histiæus, tyrant of Miletus, had assented to the opinion of the other tyrants, and had not opposed it, the power of the Persians would have been utterly ruined. It is dreadful even to hear it said that the whole power of the king depended on a single man. (4.) Do not, therefore, willingly expose yourself to any such danger, when there is no necessity, but be persuaded by me; dismiss this assembly; and hereafter, whenever it shall seem fit to you, having considered with yourself, proclaim what appears to you to be most advantageous; for to deliberate well I find is the greatest gain; for if the result prove unfortunate, the matter has nevertheless been well deliberated on, but our deliberation is defeated by fortune; but he who has deliberated badly, if fortune attend him, has met with a success he had no right to expect, but has nevertheless formed bad plans. (5.) Do you see how the deity strikes with his thunder the tallest animals, and suffers them not to be ostentatious, but the smaller ones do not at all offend him? Do you see how he ever hurls his bolts against the loftiest buildings, and trees of the like kind? for the deity is wont to cut off every thing that is too highly exalted. Thus even a large army is often defeated by a small one in such a manner as this: when the deity, through jealousy, strikes them with terror or lightning, whereby they perish in a manner unworthy of themselves; for the deity will not suffer any one but himself to have high thoughts. (6.) Again, to hasten any matter produces failures, from whence great losses are wont to follow; but in delay there are advantages, which, though not immediately apparent, yet one may discover after a time. This, then, O king, is the advice I give you. (7.) But do you, Mardonius, son of Gobryas, cease to speak vain words of the Grecians, who do not deserve to be spoken lightly of; for by calumniating the Greeks you urge the king himself to lead an army against them; and to this end you appear to me to exert all your efforts. But it may not so be; for calumny is the worst of evils; in it there are two who commit injustice, and one who is injured; for he who calumniates another acts unjustly, by accusing one that is not present; and he acts unjustly who is persuaded before he has learned the exact truth; and he that is absent when the charge is made is thus doubly injured, being calumniated by the one, and by the other deemed to be base. (8.) But if, at all events, it must needs be that war must be made on these people, come, let the king himself remain in the abodes of the Persians; let both of us risk our children, and do you lead the expedition, having selected what men you choose, and taken with you as large a force as you think fit; and if matters succeed to the king in the manner you say, let my children be put to death, and me also with them; but if the event prove such as I foretell, then let your children suffer the same, and you also with them, if ever you return. If, however, you are unwilling to submit to these terms, and will at all events lead an army against Greece, I affirm that some of those who are left in this country will hear that Mardonius, having brought some great disaster upon the Persians, and being torn in pieces by dogs and birds, either in the territory of the Athenians or in that of the Lacedæmonians, if not sooner on his march, has discovered[5] against what sort of men you now persuade the king to make war."

11. Artabanus thus spoke, but Xerxes, inflamed with anger, answered as follows: "Artabanus, you are my father's brother; this will protect you from receiving the just recompense of your foolish words. However, I inflict this disgrace upon you, base and cowardly as you are, not to accompany me in my expedition against Greece, but to remain here with the women, and I, without your assistance, will accomplish all that I have said; for I should not be sprung from Darius, son of Hystaspes, son of Arsames, son of Ariaramnes, son of Teispes, son of Cyrus, son of Cambyses, son of Achæmenes, if I did not avenge myself on the Athenians, knowing full well that if we continue quiet, yet they will not, but will even invade our territories, if we may conjecture from what has been already done by them, who have both burned Sardis and advanced into Asia; wherefore it is not possible for either party to retreat, but the alternative lies before us, to do or suffer; so that all these dominions must fall under the power of the Grecians, or all theirs under that of the Persians, for there is no medium in this enmity. It is, therefore, honorable for us, who have first

[5] Larcher, with whom Baehr appears to agree, refers *γνόντα* to *τινα*: in that case, the meaning of the passage being that "those who remain at home will, when they hear of the disasters that have befallen Mardonius and the army, learn what an enemy they have had to contend with."

suffered, to take revenge, that I may also be informed of the danger to which I shall expose myself by marching against those men whom Pelops the Phrygian, who was a slave of my ancestors, so completely subdued that, even to this day, the people themselves and their country are called after the name of the conqueror."

12. These things were said so far, but afterward night came on, and the opinion of Artabanus occasioned uneasiness to Xerxes, and deliberating with himself during the night, he clearly discovered that it would not be to his interest to make war on Greece: having thus altered his resolution, he fell asleep, and some time in the night he saw the following vision, as is related by the Persians. Xerxes imagined that a tall and handsome man stood by him and said, "Do you, then, change your mind, O Persian, *and resolve* not to lead an army against Greece, after having ordered the Persians to assemble their forces? You do not well to change your resolution, nor is there any man who will agree with you; therefore pursue that course which you resolved upon in the day." Xerxes thought that the man, having pronounced these words, flew away. 13. When day dawned, he paid no attention to this dream, but having assembled those Persians whom he had before convened, he addressed them as follows: "Pardon me, O Persians, that I suddenly change my plans, for I have not yet attained to the highest perfection of judgment, and they who persuade me to this enterprise are never absent from me. When, therefore, I heard the opinion of Artabanus, my youth immediately boiled with rage against him, so that I threw out words more unbecoming than I ought to a person of his years; but now, conscious of my error, I will follow his advice: since, therefore, I have changed my resolution, *and determined* not to make war against Greece, do you remain quiet." The Persians, when they heard this, being transported with joy, did him homage. 14. When night came, the same dream, again standing by Xerxes as he slept, said, "Son of Darius, you have, then, openly renounced, in the presence of the Persians, the intended expedition, and make no account of my words, as if you had not heard them from any one. Be well assured, however, of this, that unless you immediately undertake this expedition, this will be the consequence to you: as you have become great and powerful in a short time, so you shall become low

again in an equally short space." 15. Xerxes, being alarmed by this vision, rushed from his bed, and sent a messenger to call Artabanus; and when he came, Xerxes spoke to him as follows: "Artabanus, I on the moment was not in my senses when I used hasty words to you in return for your good advice; however, after no long time I repented, and acknowledged that those measures which you suggested ought to be adopted by me. I am not, however, able to perform them, though desirous of doing so; for, after I had altered my resolution and acknowledged my error, a dream frequently presents itself to me by no means approving of my so doing; and it has just now vanished, after threatening me. If, then, it is a deity who sends this dream, and it is his pleasure that an expedition against Greece should at all events take place, this same dream will also flit before you, and give the same injunction as to me. This I think will happen, if you should take all my apparel, and, having put it on, should afterward sit on my throne, and then go to sleep in my bed." 16. Xerxes thus addressed him; but Artabanus not obeying the first order, as he did not think himself worthy to sit on the royal throne, when he was at last compelled, did as he was desired, after he had spoken as follows. (1.) "I deem it an equal merit, O king, to form good plans, and to be willing to yield to one who gives good advice; and though both of these qualities attach to you, the converse of wicked men leads you astray; just as blasts of wind falling on the sea, which of all things is the most useful to mankind, do not suffer it to follow its proper nature. As for me, grief did not so much vex me at hearing your reproaches, as that when two opinions were proposed by the Persians, one tending to increase their arrogance, the other to check it, and to show how hurtful it is to teach the mind to be constantly seeking for more than we already possess; that, when these two opinions were proposed, you should choose that which is more dangerous both to yourself and the Persians. (2.) Now, however, after you have changed to the better resolution, you say, that since you have given up the expedition against the Greeks, a dream has come to you, sent by some god, which forbids you to abandon the enterprise. But these things, my son, are not divine, for dreams which wander among men are such as I will explain to you, being many years older than you are. Those visions of dreams most commonly hover around men *respecting things* which one has thought of during the day; and we, during the preceding days, have been very much busied about this expedition. (3.) If, however, this is not such as I judge, but has something divine in it, you have correctly summed up the whole in few words; then let it appear, and give the same injunction to me as to you; and it ought not to appear to me any the more for my having your apparel than my own; nor the more because I go to sleep on your bed than on my own, if, indeed, it will appear at all; for that which has appeared to you in your sleep, whatever it be, can never arrive at such a degree of simplicity as to suppose that when it sees me, it is you, conjecturing from your apparel; but if it shall hold me in contempt, and not deign to appear to me, whether I be clothed in your robes or in my own, and if it shall visit you again, this indeed would deserve consideration; for if it should repeatedly visit you, I should myself confess it to be divine. If, however, you have resolved that so it should be, and it is not possible to avert this, but I must needs sleep in your bed, well, when this has been done, let it appear also to me. But till that time I shall persist in my present opinion." 17. Artabanus, having spoken thus, and hoping to show that Xerxes had said nothing of any moment, did what was ordered; and having put on the apparel of Xerxes, and sat in the royal throne, when he afterward went to bed, the same dream which had appeared to Xerxes came to him when he was asleep, and standing over Artabanus, spoke as follows: "Art thou, then, the man who dissuadeth Xerxes from invading Greece, as if thou wert very anxious for him? But neither hereafter nor at present shalt thou escape unpunished for endeavoring to avert what is fated to be. What Xerxes must suffer if he continues disobedient, has been declared to him himself." 18. Artabanus imagined that the dream uttered these threats, and was about to burn out his eyes with hot irons. He therefore, having uttered a loud shriek, leaped up, and seating himself by Xerxes, when he had related all the particulars of the vision in the dream, spoke to him in this manner: "I, O king, being a man who have seen already many and great powers overthrown by inferior ones, would not suffer you to yield entirely to youth; knowing how mischievous it is to desire much, calling to mind the expedition of Cyrus against the Massagetæ, how it fared, and calling to mind also that of Cambyses against the Ethiopians, and having accompanied Darius in the invasion of Scythia, knowing all these things, I was of opinion, that if you remained quiet, you must be pronounced happy by all men; but since some divine impulse has sprung up, and, as it seems, some heaven-sent destruction impends over the Greeks, I myself am converted, and change my opinion. Do you, then, make known to the Persians the intimation sent by the deity, and command them to follow the orders first given by you for the preparations; and act so, that, since the deity permits, nothing on your part may be wanting." When he had thus spoken, both being carried away by the vision, as soon as it was day Xerxes acquainted the Persians with what had happened; and Artabanus, who before was the only man who greatly opposed the expedition, now as openly promoted it.

19. After this, when Xerxes was resolved to undertake the expedition, another vision appeared to him in his sleep, which the magi, when they heard it, interpreted to relate to the whole world, and *to signify* that all mankind should serve him. The vision was as follows: Xerxes imagined that he was crowned with the sprig of an olive-tree, and that branches from this olive covered the whole earth; and that afterward the crown that was placed on his head disappeared. The magi having given this interpretation, every one of the Persians, who were then assembled, departed immediately to his own government, and used all diligence to execute what had been ordered; every man hoping to obtain the proposed reward. Xerxes thus levied his army, searching out every region of the continent. 20. For from the reduction of Egypt, he was employed four whole years in assembling his forces, and providing things necessary for the expedition. In the course of the fifth year he began his march with a vast multitude of men; for of the expeditions with which we are acquainted, this was by far the greatest, so that that of Darius against the Scythians appears nothing in comparison with this, nor the Scythian, when the Scythians, pursuing the Cimmerians, and invading the Medic territory, subdued almost the whole of the upper part of Asia, on account of which Darius afterward attempted to inflict vengeance on them; nor, according to what is related, that of the Atridæ against Ilium; nor that of the Mysians and Teucrians, which took place before the

Trojan war, who, having passed over into Europe by the Bosphorus, subdued all the Thracians, and went down to the Ionian Sea, and marched southward as far as the river Peneus. 21. All these expeditions, and any others, if there have been any besides them, are not to be compared with this one. For what nation did not Xerxes lead out of Asia against Greece? what stream, being drunk, did not fail him, except that of great rivers? Some supplied ships; others were ordered to furnish men for the infantry, from others cavalry were required, from others transports for horses, together with men to serve in the army; others had to furnish long ships for the bridges, and others provisions and vessels.

22. And first of all, as those who had first attempted to double Mount Athos had met with disasters, preparations were being made for nearly three years about Athos; for triremes were stationed at Eleus in the Chersonese, and proceeding from thence, men of every nation from the army dug under the lash; and they went in succession; and the people who dwelt round Athos dug also. Bubares, son of Megabazus, and Artachæus, son of Artæus, both Persians, presided over the work. Athos is a vast and celebrated mountain, stretching into the sea, and inhabited by men. Where the mountain terminates toward the continent, it is in the form of a peninsula, and is an isthmus of about twelve stades: this is a plain with hills of no great height from the sea of the Acanthians to the sea which is opposite Torone. On this isthmus, in which Mount Athos terminates, stands Sana, a Grecian city; but those within Sana, and situate on Athos itself, which the Persian then was proceeding to make insular instead of continental, are the following, Dion, Olophyxus, Acrothoon, Thyssus, and Cleonæ. These are the cities which occupy Mount Athos. 23. They made the excavation as follows: the barbarians divided the ground among the several nations, having drawn a straight line near the city of Sana; and when the trench was deep, some standing at the bottom continued to dig, and others handed the soil that was dug out to men who stood above on ladders; they again in turn handed it to others, until they reached those that were at the top; these last carried it off and threw it away. To all the rest, except the Phœnicians, the brink of the excavation falling in gave double labor, for as they made the upper opening and the lower of

equal dimensions, this must necessarily happen. But the Phœnicians show their skill in other works, and especially *did so* in this; for having received the portion that fell to their share, they dug it, making the upper opening of the trench twice as large as it was necessary for the trench itself to be; and as the work proceeded, they contracted it gradually, so that when they came to the bottom, the work was equal in width to the rest: near adjoining is a meadow, where they had a market and bazar, and great abundance of meal was brought to them from Asia. 24. According to my deliberate opinion,[6] Xerxes ordered this excavation to be made from motives of ostentation, wishing to display his power, and to leave a memorial of himself; for though it was possible, without any great labor, to have drawn the ships over the isthmus, he commanded them to dig a channel for the sea of such a width that two triremes might pass through rowed abreast. And the same persons, to whom the excavation was committed, were ordered also to throw a bridge over the river Strymon. 25. These things, then, he thus contrived: he also caused cables of papyrus and of white flax to be prepared for the bridges, having ordered the Phœnicians and Egyptians also to lay up provisions for the army, that neither the men nor the beasts of burden might suffer from famine on their march toward Greece; and having informed himself of the situations of the places, he ordered them to lay up the provisions where it was most convenient, conveying them to various quarters in merchant-ships and transports from all parts of Asia. Of these provisions the largest quantity they conveyed to a place called Leuce-Acte, in Thrace; some were ordered to Tyrodiza of the Perinthians, others to Doriscus, others to Eion on the Strymon, and others to Macedonia.

26. While these men were employed in their appointed task, the whole land forces, having been assembled, marched with Xerxes to Sardis, having set out from Critalla in Cappadocia, for it was ordered that all the troops throughout the continent, that were to march with Xerxes himself, should be assembled at that place. Now which of the generals, bringing the best-appointed troops, received the gifts promised by the king, I am unable to mention; for I am not at all aware

[6] Literally, "as I conjecturing discover."

that they came to any decision on this point. They then, when having crossed the river Halys they entered Phrygia, marching through that country, arrived at Celænæ, where rise the springs of the Mæander, and of another river not less than the Mæander, which is called the Catarractes, which, springing up in the very forum of the Celænians, discharges itself into the Mæander; in this city, also, the skin of Silenus Marsyas is suspended, which, as the Phrygians report, was stripped off and suspended by Apollo. 27. In this city Pythius, son of Atys, a Lydian, being in waiting, entertained the whole army of the king and Xerxes himself with most sumptuous feasts; and he offered money, wishing to contribute toward the expense of the war. When Pythius offered money, Xerxes asked the Persians near him who this Pythius was, and what riches he possessed, that he made such an offer. They answered, "O king, this is the person who presented your father Darius with the golden plane-tree and the vine; and he is now the richest man we know of in the world, next to yourself." 28. Xerxes, surprised with these last words, next asked Pythius what might be the amount of his wealth. He said, "O king, I will not conceal it from you, nor will I pretend to be ignorant of my own substance, but as I know it perfectly I will tell you the exact truth. As soon as I heard you were coming down to the Grecian sea, wishing to present you with money for the war, I made inquiry, and found by computation that I had two thousand talents of silver, and of gold four millions of Daric staters, all but seven thousand. These I freely give you; for myself, I have sufficient subsistence from my slaves and lands." 29. Thus he spoke; but Xerxes, delighted with his offer, replied: "My Lydian friend, since I left the Persian country I have met with no man to the present moment who was willing to entertain my army, or who, having come into my presence, has voluntarily offered to contribute money toward the war. But you have entertained my army magnificently, and have offered me vast sums; therefore, in return for this, I confer on you the following rewards: I make you my friend, and will make up the sum of four millions of staters from my own treasures, by adding the seven thousand; so that the four millions may not be short of seven thousand, but the full sum may be completed by me. Do you retain what you have acquired, and be careful always to continue such as you are; for if you do this, you shall never repent, either now or hereafter."

30. Having said this, and performed his promises, he continued his march; and passing by a city of the Phrygians called Anaua, and a lake from which salt is obtained, he arrived at Colossæ, a considerable city of Phrygia, in which the river Lycus, falling into a chasm of the earth, disappears; then reappearing after a distance of about five stades, it also discharges itself into the Mæander. From Colossæ the army, advancing toward the boundaries of the Phrygians and Lydians, arrived at the city of Cydrara, where a pillar, planted in the ground, and erected by Crœsus, indicates the boundaries by an inscription. 31. When from Phrygia he entered Lydia, the way dividing into two, that on the left leading to Caria, the other on the right to Sardis, by which latter a traveler is compelled to cross the river Mæander, and to pass by the city of Callatebus, in which confectioners make honey with tamarisk and wheat; Xerxes, going by this way, met with a plane-tree, which, on account of its beauty, he presented with golden ornaments, and, having committed it to the care of one of the immortals,[7] on the next day he arrived at Sardis, the capital of the Lydians. 32. On his arrival at Sardis, he first of all sent heralds to Greece to demand earth and water, and to require them to provide entertainment for the king; except that he did not send either to Athens or Lacedæmon,[8] but he did to every other place. And he sent the second time for earth and water for the following reason: such as had not given them before when Darius sent, he thought would then certainly do so through fear; wishing, therefore, to know this for certain, he sent. And after this he prepared to march to Abydos.

33. In the mean while, those who were appointed had joined the Hellespont from Asia to Europe. There is in the Chersonese on the Hellespont, between the city of Sestos and Madytus, a craggy shore extending into the sea, directly opposite Abydos: there, not long after these events, under Xanthippus, son of Ariphron, a general of the Athenians, having taken Artayctes, a Persian, governor of Sestos, they impaled him alive against a plank; for he, having brought women into the tem-

[7] One of the ten thousand chosen men called immortals, of whom we shall hear more hereafter. See chap. 83.

[8] See chap. 133.

ple of Protesilaus at Elæus, committed atrocious crimes.[9] 34. To this shore, then, beginning at Abydos, they, on whom this task was imposed, constructed bridges, the Phœnicians one with white flax, and the Egyptians the other with papyrus. The distance from Abydos to the opposite shore is seven stades. When the strait was thus united, a violent storm arising, broke in pieces and scattered the whole work. 35. When Xerxes heard of this, being exceedingly indignant, he commanded that the Hellespont should be stricken with three hundred lashes with a scourge, and that a pair of fetters should be let down into the sea. I have moreover heard that with them he likewise sent branding instruments to brand the Hellespont. He certainly charged those who flogged the waters to utter these barbarous and impious words: "Thou bitter water! thy master inflicts this punishment upon thee, because thou hast injured him, although thou hadst not suffered any harm from him; and king Xerxes will cross over thee, whether thou wilt or not; it is with justice that no man sacrifices to thee, because thou art both a deceitful and briny river!" He accordingly commanded them to chastise the sea in this manner, and to cut off the heads of those who had to superintend the joining of the Hellespont. 36. They on whom this thankless office was imposed, carried it into execution; and other engineers constructed bridges; and they constructed them in the following manner. They connected together penteconters and triremes, under that toward the Euxine sea, three hundred and sixty; and under the other, three hundred and fourteen, obliquely in respect of the Pontus, but in the direction of the current in respect of the Hellespont, that it might keep up the tension of the cables. Having connected them together, they let down very long anchors, some on the one bridge toward the Pontus, on account of the winds that blew from it within; others on the other bridge toward the west and the Ægean, on account of the south and south-east winds. They left an opening as a passage through between the penteconters, and that in three places, that any one who wished might be able to sail into the Pontus in light vessels, and from the Pontus outward. Having done this, they stretched the cables from the shore, twisting them with wooden capstans, not as before using the two kinds separately, but as-

[9] See B. IX. chap. 116.

signing to each two of white flax and four of papyrus. The thickness and quality was the same, but those of flax were stronger in proportion, every cubit weighing a full talent. When the passage was bridged over, having sawn up trunks of trees, and having made them equal to the width of the bridge, they laid them regularly upon the extended cables; and having laid them in regular order, they then fastened them together. And having done this, they put brush-wood on the top; and having laid the brush-wood in regular order, they put earth over the whole; and having pressed down the earth, they drew a fence on each side, that the beasts of burden and horses might not be frightened by looking down upon the sea.

37. When the works at the bridges were completed, and those at Mount Athos, as well as the mounds at the mouths of the canal, which had been made on account of the tide, in order that the mouths of the trench might not be choked up, and news was brought that the canal was entirely completed; thereupon the army, having wintered at Sardis, and being fully prepared, set out at the beginning of the spring from thence toward Abydos. But as it was on the point of setting out, the sun, quitting his seat in the heavens, disappeared, though there were no clouds, and the air was perfectly serene, and night ensued in the place of day. When Xerxes saw and perceived this, it occasioned him much uneasiness; he therefore inquired of the magi what the prodigy might portend. They answered that "the deity foreshows to the Greeks the extinction of their cities;" adding, "that the sun is the portender of the future to the Greeks, and the moon to the Persians." Xerxes, having heard this, was much delighted, and set out upon his march. 38. As he was leading his army away, Pythius the Lydian, terrified by the prodigy in the heavens, and emboldened by the gifts, went to Xerxes the king, and spoke thus: "Sire, would you indulge me by granting a boon I should wish to obtain, which is easy for you to grant, and of great importance to me." Xerxes, expecting that he would wish for any thing rather than what he did ask, said that he would grant his request, and bade him declare what he wanted; whereupon he, when he heard this, spoke confidently as follows: "Sire, I have five sons; and it happens that they are all attending you in the expedition against

Greece. But do you, O king, pity me, who am thus advanced in years, and release one of my sons from the service, that he may take care of me and my property. Take the other four with you, and, having accomplished your designs, may you return home." 39. Xerxes was highly incensed, and answered as follows: "Base man! hast thou dared, when I am marching in person against Greece, and taking with me my children, and brothers, and kinsmen, and friends, to make mention of thy son? thou, who art my slave, and who wert bound in duty to follow me with all thy family, even with thy wife. Now learn this well, that the spirit of man dwells in his ears; which, when it hears pleasing things, fills the whole body with delight, but when it hears the contrary, swells with indignation. When, therefore, you did well, and gave promise of the like, you can not boast of having surpassed the king in generosity; but now that you have adopted a more shameless conduct, you shall not receive your deserts, but less than your deserts; for your hospitality preserves four of your children, but you shall be punished with the loss of the one whom you cherish most." When he had given this answer, he immediately commanded those whose office it was to execute such orders, to find out the eldest of the sons of Pythius, and to cut his body in two; and having so done, to deposit the halves, one on the right of the road, the other on the left; and that the army should pass between them.

40. When they had done this, the army afterward passed between. The baggage-bearers and beasts of burden first led the way; after them *came* a host of all nations promiscuously, not distinguished: after more than one half of the army had passed, an interval was left, that they might not mix with the king's troops. Before him a thousand horsemen led the van, chosen from among all the Persians; and next to them a thousand spearmen, these also chosen from among all, carrying their lances turned downward to the earth. After these *came* ten sacred horses called Nisæan, gorgeously caparisoned. These horses are called Nisæan on the following account: there is a large plain in the Medic territory which is called the Nisæan; now this plain produces these large horses. Behind these ten horses was placed the sacred chariot of Jupiter, drawn by eight white horses; behind the horses followed a charioteer on foot, holding the reins; because no mortal ever

ascends this seat. Behind this *came* Xerxes himself, on a chariot drawn by Nisæan horses; and a charioteer walked at his side, whose name was Patiramphes, son of Otanes, a Persian. 41. In this manner, then, Xerxes marched out of Sardis, and whenever he thought right, he used to pass from the chariot to a covered carriage. Behind him *marched* a thousand spearmen, the bravest and most noble of the Persians, carrying their spears in the usual manner; and after them another body of a thousand horse, chosen from among the Persians: after the cavalry *came* ten thousand men chosen from the rest of the Persians; these were infantry; and of these, one thousand had golden pomegranates on their spears instead of ferules, and they inclosed the others all round; but the nine thousand, being within them, had silver pomegranates. Those also that carried their spears turned to the earth had golden pomegranates, and those that followed nearest to Xerxes had golden apples. Behind the ten thousand foot were placed ten thousand Persian cavalry; and after the cavalry was left an interval of two stades; and then the rest of the throng followed promiscuously. 42. The army directed its march from Lydia to the river Caicus and the Mysian territory; and proceeding from the Caicus, leaving Mount Canæ on the left, *passed* through Atarneus to the city Carina. From thence it marched through the plain of Thebes, and passing by the city of Adramyttium and the Pelasgian Antrandus, and keeping Mount Ida on the left, it entered the territory of Ilium. But before this, as the army halted during the night under Mount Ida, thunder and lightning fell upon them, and destroyed a considerable number of the troops on the spot. 43. When the army arrived at the Scamander, which was the first river since they had set out on their march from Sardis, whose stream failed and did not afford sufficient drink for the army and beasts of burden; when, accordingly, Xerxes arrived at this river, he went up to the Pergamus[1] of Priam, being desirous of seeing it; and having seen it, and inquired into every particular, he sacrificed a thousand oxen to the Ilian Minerva, and the magi poured out libations to the honor of the heroes. After they had done this, a panic fell on the camp during the night, and at the dawn of day they marched from thence, on the left skirting

[1] That is, "the citadel."

the city of Rhœtium, and Ophrynium, and Dardanus, which borders on Abydos, and on the right the Gergithæ Teucrians.

44. When they were at Abydos, Xerxes wished to behold the whole army; and there had been previously erected on a hill at this place, for his express use, a lofty throne of white marble; the people of Abydos had made it, in obedience to a previous order of the king. When he was seated there, looking down toward the shore, he beheld both the land army and the fleet; and when he beheld them, he desired to see a contest take place between the ships; and when it had taken place, and the Sidonian Phœnicians were victorious, he showed himself exceedingly gratified both with the contest and the army. 45. And when he saw the whole Hellespont covered by the ships, and all the shores and the plains of Abydos full of men, Xerxes thereupon pronounced himself happy, but afterward shed tears. 46. Artabanus, his paternal uncle, having observed him, the same who had before freely declared his opinion, and advised Xerxes not to invade Greece; this man, having perceived Xerxes shedding tears, addressed him thus: "O king, how very different from each other are what you are now doing and what you did a little while ago! for, having pronounced yourself happy, now you weep." He answered, "Commiseration seized me when I considered how brief all human life is, since of these, numerous as they are, not one shall survive to the hundredth year." But Artabanus replied, saying, "We suffer during life other things more pitiable than this; for in this so brief life, there is not one, either of these or of others, born so happy, that it will not occur to him, not only once but oftentimes, to wish rather to die than to live; for calamities befalling him, and diseases disturbing him, make life, though really short, appear to be long; so that death, life being burdensome, becomes the most desirable refuge for man; and the deity, having given us to taste of sweet existence, is found to be jealous of his gift." 47. Xerxes answered, saying, "Artabanus, of human life, which is such as you have described it, let us say no more, nor let us call evils to mind, now that we have good things before us. But tell me this: if the vision of the dream had not appeared so clearly, would you have retained your former opinion, and dissuaded me from making war against Greece, or would you have changed your opinion?

Come, tell me this explicitly." He answered, saying, "O king, may the vision of the dream that appeared terminate as we both desire; but I am still full of alarm, and not master of myself, when I consider many other circumstances, and, moreover, perceive two things of the greatest importance most hostile to you." 48. To this Xerxes answered as follows: "Strange man! what are these two things which you say are most hostile to me? whether do you find fault with the land army on account of numbers, and do you think that the Grecian army will be much more numerous than ours, or that our navy will fall short of theirs? or both these together? for, if you think our forces deficient in this respect, we can quickly assemble another army." 49. He answered, saying, "O king, no man of common understanding can find fault either with this army or the number of the ships. (1.) But even if you should muster more, the two things which I mean would become still more hostile. These two things are land and sea; for, as I conjecture, there is nowhere any harbor of the sea so large as to be capable, in case a storm should arise, of receiving this your navy, and sheltering the ships. And yet there is need, not only that there be one such harbor, but *others* along the whole continent, by which you are about to coast. Since there are not harbors sufficiently capacious, remember that accidents rule men, not men accidents. (2.) One of the two things having thus been mentioned, I now proceed to mention the other. The land will be hostile to you in this way: if nothing else should stand in your way, it will become more hostile to you the farther you advance, as you are continually drawn on unawares; for men are never satiated with success; and even if I should grant that no one will oppose you, I say that the country, becoming more extensive in process of time, will produce a famine. A man would therefore thus prove himself most wise if in deliberation he should be apprehensive, and consider himself likely to suffer every misfortune, but in action should be bold." 50. Xerxes answered in these words: "Artabanus, you have discussed each of these particulars plausibly; but do not fear every thing, nor weigh every circumstance with equal strictness. (1.) For if, in every matter that is proposed, you should weigh every thing with equal care, you would never do any thing at all; it is better, being confident on all occasions, to suffer half the evils, than, fearing every thing beforehand, never suffer any thing at all; but if you oppose every thing that is proposed, and do not advance something certain, you must fail in your plans equally with the person who has given a contrary opinion. This, therefore, comes to the same. (2.) Can any one who is a man know for a certainty what ought to be done?[2] I think certainly not. To those, however, who are ready to act, gain for the most part is wont to accrue; but to those that weigh every thing and are timid, it seldom does. You see to what a degree of power the empire of the Persians has advanced; if, then, they who were kings before me had entertained such opinions as you do, or, not entertaining such opinions, had such counselors, you would never have seen their power advanced to this pitch. But now, by hazarding dangers, they carried it to this height; for great undertakings are wont to be accomplished at great hazards. We, therefore, emulating them, set out at the most favorable season of the year, and having subdued all Europe, will return home, without having met with famine any where, or suffered any other reverse; for, in the first place, we march, carrying with us abundant provisions, and, in the next place, whatever land and nation we invade, we shall have their corn; and we are making war on men who are husbandmen, and not feeders of cattle." 51. After this Artabanus said, "O king, since you will not allow us to fear any thing, yet hearken to my advice; for it is necessary, when speaking on many topics, to extend one's discourse. Cyrus, son of Cambyses, subdued all Ionia except the Athenians, so as to be tributary to the Persians. I advise you, therefore, on no account to lead these men against their fathers; for even without them we are able to get the better of our enemies; for if they accompany you, they must either be most unjust in assisting to enslave their mother-city, or most just in endeavoring to maintain its freedom. Now if they should be most unjust, they will not add any great gain to us; but if just, they are able to damage your army to a great degree. Consider, therefore, on this ancient saying, since it has been well said, that the termination is not always evident at the beginning." 52. To this Xerxes an-

[2] I have followed the reading and punctuation of Matthiæ and Baehr. The latter, though he approves the mark of interrogation, omits it in his version of this passage.

swered, "Artabanus, of all the opinions you have given, you are deceived most in this, in fearing lest the Ionians should desert us; of whom we have the strongest proofs, and of whom you are a witness, as well as all the rest who accompanied Darius in his expedition against the Scythians, that the whole Persian army was in their power to destroy or to save, yet they evinced justice and fidelity, and *committed* nothing ungrateful. Besides this, since they have left their children, and wives, and possessions in our territories, we must not expect that they will form any new design. Do not, therefore, fear this, but be of good courage, and preserve my house and my government; for to you alone, of all men, I intrust my sceptre."

53. Having spoken thus, and dispatched Artabanus to Susa, Xerxes again summoned the most distinguished of the Persians, and when they were assembled he addressed them as follows: "O Persians, I have called you together to desire this of you, that you would acquit yourselves like brave men, and not disgrace the former exploits of the Persians, which are great and memorable; but let each and all of us together show our zeal, for this which we are endeavoring to accomplish is a good common to all. On this account, then, I call on you to apply yourselves earnestly to the war; for, as I am informed, we are marching against brave men; and if we conquer them, no other army in the world will dare to oppose us. Now, then, let us cross over, having first offered up prayers to the gods who protect the Persian territory." 54. That day they made preparations for the passage over; and on the following they waited for the sun, as they wished to see it rising, in the mean time burning all sorts of perfumes on the bridges, and strewing the road with myrtle branches. When the sun rose, Xerxes, pouring a libation into the sea out of a golden cup, offered up a prayer to the sun that no such accident might befall him as would prevent him from subduing Europe until he had reached its utmost limits. After having prayed, he threw the cup into the Hellespont, and a golden bowl, and a Persian sword, which they call acinace; but I can not determine with certainty whether he dropped these things into the sea as an offering to the sun, or whether he repented of having scourged the Hellespont, and presented these gifts to the sea as a compensation. 55. When these ceremonies were finished, the infantry and all

the cavalry crossed over by that bridge which was toward the Pontus, and the beasts of burden and attendants by that toward the Ægean. First of all, the ten thousand Persians led the van, all wearing crowns, and after them the promiscuous host of all nations. These crossed on that day. On the following, first the horsemen, and those who carried their lances downward: these also wore crowns; next came the sacred horses and the sacred chariot; afterward Xerxes himself, and the spearmen, and the thousand horsemen; after them the rest of the army closed the march, and at the same time the ships got under weigh to the opposite shore. I have also heard that Xerxes crossed over last of all. 56. Xerxes, when he had crossed over into Europe, saw the army crossing over under the lash: his army crossed over in seven days and seven nights without halting at all. On this occasion, it is related that when Xerxes had crossed over the Hellespont, a certain Hellespontine said, "O Jupiter, why, assuming the form of a Persian, and taking the name of Xerxes, do you wish to subvert Greece, bringing all mankind with you, since without them it was in your power to do this?"

57. When all had crossed over and were proceeding on their march, a great prodigy appeared to them, which Xerxes took no account of, although it was easy to be interpreted. A mare foaled a hare: this, then, might easily have been interpreted thus: that Xerxes was about to lead an army into Greece with exceeding pomp and magnificence, but would return to the same place running for his life. Another prodigy had also happened while he was at Sardis: a mule brought forth a colt with double parts, both those of a male and those of a female; those of the male were uppermost. 58. But, taking no account of either of these, he proceeded forward, and with him the land forces; but the fleet, sailing out of the Hellespont, stood along by the land, taking a contrary course to that of the army; for it sailed toward the west, steering for cape Sarpedon, where, on its arrival, it was ordered to wait; but the army on the continent marched toward the east and the rising sun, through the Chersonese, having on the right hand the sepulchre of Helle, daughter of Athamas, and on the left the city of Cardia, and going through the middle of a city, the name of which happened to be Agora; and from thence, bending round a bay called Melas, and hav-

ing come to the river Melas, whose stream did not suffice for the army, but failed—having crossed this river, from which the bay derives its name, they marched westward, passing by Ænos, an Æolian city, and the lake Stentoris, until they reached Doriscus. 59. Doriscus is a shore and extensive plain of Thrace. Through it flows a large river, the Hebrus. On it a royal fort had been built, the same that is now called Doriscus, and a Persian garrison had been established in it by Darius from the time that he marched against the Scythians. This place, therefore, appeared to Xerxes to be convenient for reviewing and numbering his army; this accordingly he did. All the ships, therefore, having arrived at Doriscus, the captains, at the command of Xerxes, brought them to the shore adjoining Doriscus. On this coast stood Sala, a Samothracian city, and Zona, and at its extremity Serrhium, a celebrated promontory: this region formerly belonged to the Ciconians. Having steered to this shore, they hauled up the ships and repaired them, and in the mean time Xerxes numbered his army at Doriscus. 60. How great a number of men each contributed I am unable to say with certainty, for it is not mentioned by any one, but the amount of the whole land forces was found to be seventeen hundred thousand. They were computed in this manner: having drawn together ten thousand men in one place, and having crowded them as close together as it was possible, they traced a circle on the outside, and having traced it, and removed the ten thousand, they threw up a stone fence on the circle, reaching to the height of a man's navel. Having done this, they made others enter within the inclosed space, until they had in this manner computed all, and having numbered them, they drew out according to nations.

61. Those who served in this expedition were the following. The Persians, equipped as follows: on their heads they wore loose coverings, called tiaras; on the body, various-colored sleeved breastplates, with iron scales like those of fish; and on their legs, loose trowsers; and, instead of shields, bucklers made of osiers; and under them their quivers were hung. They had short spears, long bows, and arrows made of cane; and, besides, daggers suspended from the girdle on the right thigh. They had for their general Otanes, father of Amestris, wife of Xerxes. They were formerly called Cephenes by the Grecians, but by themselves and neighbors Artæans; but

when Perseus, son of Danae and Jupiter, came to Cepheus, son of Belus, and married his daughter Andromeda, he had a son to whom he gave the name of Perses; and him he left in the country, for Cepheus had no male offspring; from him, therefore, they derived their appellation. 62. The Medes marched equipped in the same manner as the Persians, for the above is a Medic and not a Persian costume. The Medes had for their general Tigranes, of the family of the Achæmenidæ: they were formerly called Arians by all nations, but when Medea of Colchis came from Athens to these Arians, they also changed their names: the Medes themselves give this account of their nation. The Cissians, who served in the army, were in other respects accoutred like the Persians, except that, instead of turbans, they wore mitres. Anaphes, son of Otanes, commanded the Cissians. The Hyrcanians were also armed like the Persians, and had for their general Megapanus, who was afterward governor of Babylon. 63. The Assyrians who served in the army had helmets of brass, twisted in a barbarous manner not easy to be described, and they had shields, and spears, and daggers similar to those of the Egyptians, and, besides, wooden clubs knotted with iron, and linen cuirasses. By the Greeks they were called Syrians, but by the barbarians Assyrians. Among them were the Chaldeans, and Otaspes, son of Artachæus commanded them. 64. The Bactrians joined the army, having turbans on their heads very much like those of the Medes, and bows made of cane peculiar to their country, and short spears. The Sacæ, who are Scythians, had on their heads caps which came to a point and stood erect; they also wore loose trowsers, and carried bows peculiar to their country, and daggers, and also battle-axes *called* sagares. These, though they are Amyrgian Scythians, they called Sacæ, for the Persians call all the Scythians Sacæ. Hystaspes, son of Darius and Atossa, daughter of Cyrus, commanded the Bactrians and Sacæ. 65. The Indians, clad with garments made of cotton, had bows of cane, and arrows of cane tipped with iron. Thus the Indians were equipped, and they were marshaled under the command of Phanazathres, son of Artabates. 66. The Arians were furnished with Medic bows, and in other respects *were accoutred* like the Bactrians. Sisamnes, son of Hydarnes, commanded the Arians. The Parthians, Chorasmians, Sogdians, Gandarians, and Dadicæ joined the army, having the same accoutrements as the Bactrians. The following leaders commanded them. Artabazus, son of Pharnaces, *commanded* the Parthians and Chorasmians; Azanes, son of Artæus, the Sogdians; and Artyphius, son of Artabanus, the Gandarians and Dadicæ. 67. The Caspians, clothed in goat-skin mantles, and carrying bows made of cane peculiar to their country, and cimeters, joined the expedition. These were thus equipped, having for their general Ariomardus, brother of Artyphius. The Sarangæ were conspicuous by having dyed garments; they also wore buskins reaching up to the knee, and had bows and Medic javelins. Pherendates, son of Megabazus, commanded the Sarangæ. The Pactyes also wore goat-skin mantles, and had bows peculiar to the country and daggers. The Pactyes had for their general Artyntes, son of Ithamatres. 68. The Utians, Mycians, and Paricanians were equipped like the Pactyes. The following leaders commanded them. Arsamenes, son of Darius, led the Utians and Mycians; and Siromitres, son of Œobazus, the Paricanians. 69. The Arabians wore cloaks fastened by a girdle, and carried on their right sides long bows which bent backward. The Ethiopians were clothed in panthers' and lions' skins, and carried long bows, not less than four cubits in length, made from branches of the palm-tree; and on them *they placed* short arrows made of cane, instead of iron, tipped with a stone, which was made sharp, and of that sort on which they engrave seals. Besides, they had javelins, and at the tip was an antelope's horn, made sharp like a lance; they had also knotted clubs. When they were going to battle, they smeared one half of their body with chalk, and the other half with red ochre. The Arabians and Ethiopians who dwell above Egypt were commanded by Arsames, son of Darius and Artystone, daughter of Cyrus, whom Darius loved more than all his wives, and whose image he had made of beaten gold. 70. The Ethiopians from the sun-rise (for two kinds served in the expedition) were marshaled with the Indians, and did not at all differ from the others in appearance, but only in their language and their hair; for the eastern Ethiopians are straight-haired, but those of Libya have hair more curly than that of any other people. These Ethiopians from Asia were accoutred almost the same as the Indians; but they wore on their heads skins of horses' heads as masks, stripped off with the ears and mane; and the mane served instead of a crest, and the horses' ears were fixed erect; and as defensive armor they used the skins of cranes instead of shields. 71. The Libyans marched clad in leathern garments, and made use of javelins hardened by fire. They had for their general Massages, son of Oarizus. 72. The Paphlagonians joined the expedition, wearing on their heads plaited helmets, and carried small shields, and not large spears, and, besides, javelins and daggers; and on their feet they wore boots, peculiar to their country, reaching up to the middle of the leg. The Ligyes and the Matienians, the Mariandynians and Syrians, marched in the same dress as the Paphlagonians. These Syrians are called by the Persians Cappadocians. Now Dotus, son of Megasidrus, commanded the Paphlagonians and Matienians; and Gobryas, son of Darius and Artystone, the Mariandynians, Ligyes, and Syrians. 73. The Phrygians had very nearly the same dress as that of Paphlagonia, varying it a little. The Phrygians, as the Macedonians say, were called Briges, as long as they were Europeans, and dwelt with the Macedonians; but having passed over into Asia, they changed their name, with their country, into that of Phrygians. The Armenians, being colonists of the Phrygians, were equipped like the Phrygians. Artochmes, who had married a daughter of Darius, commanded both these. 74. The Lydians had arms very like the Grecian. The Lydians were formerly called Meïonians, but took their appellation from Lydus, the son of Atys, having changed their name. The Mysians wore on their heads a helmet peculiar to their country, and small shields; and they used javelins hardened by fire. They are colonists of the Lydians, and from the mountain Olympus are called Olympieni. Artaphernes, son of Artaphernes who invaded Marathon with Datis, commanded the Lydians and Mysians. 75. The Thracians joined the expedition, having fox-skins on their heads, and tunics around their body, and over them they were clothed with various-colored cloaks, and on their feet and legs they had buskins of fawn-skin, and, besides, they had javelins, light bucklers, and small daggers. These people, having crossed over into Asia, were called Bithynians; but formerly, as they themselves say, were called Strymonians, as they dwelt on the river Strymon: they say that they were removed from their original settlements by the

Teucrians and Mysians. Bassaces, son of Artabanus, commanded the Thracians of Asia. 76. The * * * * * * [3] had small shields made of raw hides, and each had two javelins used for hunting wolves, and on their heads brazen helmets; and in addition to the helmets, they wore the ears and horns of an ox in brass. And over these were crests; and as to their legs, they were enwrapped in pieces of purple cloth. Among these people there is an oracle of Mars. 77. The Cabalian Meionians, who are also called Lasonians, had the same dress as the Cilicians, which I shall describe when I come to speak of the army of the Cilicians. The Milyæ had short lances, and their garments were fastened by clasps. Some of them had Lycian bows, and on their heads helmets made of tanned skins. Badres, son of Hystanes, commanded all these. 78. The Moschians had on their heads wooden helmets, and small bucklers, and spears; but there were large points *on the spears.* The Tibarenians, Macrones, and Mosynœci joined the expedition equipped as the Moschians. The following generals marshaled these: the Moschians and Tibarenians, Ariomardus, son of Darius and Parmys, daughter of Smerdis, son of Cyrus; the Macrones and Mosynœci, Artayctes, son of Cherasmis, who was intrusted with the government of Sestos on the Hellespont. 79. The Mares wore helmets on their heads, painted after the manner of their country; and small shields made of skin, and javelins. The Colchians had about their heads wooden helmets, and small shields of raw hides, and short lances; and, besides, they had swords. Pherendates, son of Teaspes, commanded the Mares and Colchians. The Alarodi and the Saspires marched armed like the Colchians; Masistius, son of Siromitres, commanded them. 80. The insular nations that came from the Erythræan Sea, and from the islands in which the king makes those dwell who are called "the banished," had clothing and arms very similar to the Medic. Mardontes, son of Bagæus, who, when commanding the army at Mycale, two years after this, died in battle, commanded these islanders.

81. These were the nations that marched on the continent and composed the infantry. They, then, who have been mentioned commanded this army, and these were they who set in

[3] There is a hiatus in the manuscripts, which the ingenuity of annotators and editors has been unable to supply.

order, and numbered them, and appointed commanders of thousands and of ten thousands; but the commanders of ten thousands *appointed* the captains of hundreds and captains of tens. There were other subaltern officers over the troops and nations, but those who have been mentioned were the commanders. 82. Over these and the whole infantry were appointed as generals, Mardonius, son of Gobryas; Tritantæchmes, son of Artabanus, who gave his opinion against the invasion of Greece; Smerdomenes, son of Otanes (both these were sons to brothers of Darius, and cousins to Xerxes); Masistes, son of Darius and Atossa; Gergis, son of Arizus; and Megabyzus, son of Zopyrus. 83. These were generals of the whole land-forces, except the ten thousand; of these ten thousand chosen Persians, Hydarnes, son of Hydarnes, was general. These Persians were called Immortal for the following reason: if any one of them made a deficiency in the number, compelled either by death or disease, another was ready chosen to supply his place, so that they were never either more or less than ten thousand. The Persians displayed the greatest splendor of all, and were also the bravest; their equipment was such as has been described; but, besides this, they were conspicuous from having a great profusion of gold. They also brought with them covered chariots, and concubines in them, and a numerous and well-equipped train of attendants. Camels and other beasts of burden conveyed their provisions apart from that of the rest of the soldiers.

84. All these nations have cavalry; they did not, however, all furnish horse, but only the following. First, the Persians, equipped in the same manner as their infantry, except that on their heads some of them wore brazen and wrought-steel ornaments. 85. There is a certain nomadic race, called Sagartians, of Persian extraction and language; they wear a dress fashioned between the Persian and the Pactyan fashion; they furnished eight thousand horse, but they are not accustomed to carry arms either of brass or iron, except daggers: they use ropes made of twisted thongs; trusting to these, they go to war. The mode of fighting of these men is as follows: when they engage with the enemy, they throw out the ropes, which have nooses at the end, and whatever any one catches, whether horse or man, he drags toward himself, and they that are entangled in the coils are put to death. This is their

mode of fighting; and they were marshaled with the Persians. 86. The Medes had the same equipment as that used in the infantry, and the Cissians in like manner. The Indians were also equipped like their infantry, but they used saddle-horses and chariots, and in their chariots they yoked horses and wild asses. The Bactrians were equipped in the same manner as their infantry, and the Caspians likewise. The Libyans too *were accoutred* like their infantry, but they all drove chariots. In like manner, the Caspiri and Paricanii were equipped in the same way as their infantry; and the Arabians had the same dress as their infantry, but all rode camels not inferior to horses in speed. 87. These nations only furnished cavalry. The number of the horse amounted to eighty thousand, besides the camels and chariots. All the rest of the cavalry were marshaled in troops, but the Arabians were stationed in the rear; for as horses can not endure camels, they were stationed behind, that the horses might not be frightened. 88. Armamithres and Tithæus, sons of Datis, were generals of the cavalry. Their third colleague in command, Pharnuches, had been left at Sardis sick; for as they were setting out from Sardis he met with a sad accident; for when he was mounted, a dog ran under the legs of his horse, and the horse, not being aware of it, was frightened, and, rearing up, threw Pharnuches; upon which, he, having fallen, vomited blood, and the disease turned to a consumption. With respect to the horse, his servants immediately did as he ordered; for, leading him to the place where he had thrown his master, they cut off his legs at the knees. Thus Pharnuches was deprived of the command.

89. The number of the triremes amounted to twelve hundred and seven; the following nations furnished them. The Phœnicians, with the Syrians of Palestine, *furnished* three hundred, being thus equipped: on their heads they had helmets, made very nearly after the Grecian fashion, and, clothed in linen breastplates, they carried shields without rims, and javelins. These Phœnicians, as they themselves say, anciently dwelt on the Red Sea; and having crossed over from thence, they settled on the sea-coast of Syria: this part of Syria, and the whole as far as Egypt, is called Palestine. The Egyptians contributed two hundred ships. These had on their heads plaited helmets, and *carried* hollow shields, with large rims,

and pikes fit for a sea-fight, and large hatchets. The greater part of them had breastplates, and carried large swords. 90. The Cyprians contributed a hundred and fifty ships, and were equipped as follows: their kings had their heads wrapped in turbans; the rest wore tunics, and were in other respects attired like the Greeks. Of these there are the following nations: some from Salamis and Athens, others from Arcadia, others from Cythnus, others from Phœnicia, and others from Ethiopia, as the Cyprians themselves say. 91. The Cilicians contributed a hundred ships. These, again, wore on their heads helmets peculiar to their country, and had bucklers instead of shields, made of raw hides, and were clothed in woolen tunics; every one had two javelins, and a sword made very much like the Egyptian cimeters. They were anciently called Hypachæans, and took their present name from Cilix, son of Agenor, a Phœnician. The Pamphylians contributed thirty ships, and were equipped in Grecian armor. These Pamphylians are descended from those who, in their return from Troy, were dispersed with Amphilochus and Calchas. 92. The Lycians contributed fifty ships, and wore breastplates and greaves. They had bows made of cornel-wood, and cane arrows without feathers, and javelins; and, besides, goat-skins were suspended over their shoulders, and round their heads caps encircled with feathers; they had also daggers and falchions. The Lycians were called Termilæ, being sprung from Crete, but took their present name from Lycus, son of Pandion, an Athenian. 93. The Dorians of Asia contributed thirty ships, wearing Grecian armor, and sprung from the Peloponnesus. The Carians contributed seventy ships, and were in other respects accoutred like the Greeks, but had falchions and daggers. What these were formerly called I have mentioned in the first part[4] of my history. 94. The Ionians contributed a hundred ships, and were equipped as Greeks. The Ionians, as long as they inhabited that part of the Peloponnesus which is now called Achaia, and before Danaus and Xuthus arrived in the Peloponnesus, as the Greeks say, were called Pelasgian Ægialees; but Ionians from Ion, son of Xuthus. 95. The Islanders contributed seventeen ships, and were armed like the Greeks. This race is also Pelasgic, but was afterward called Ionian for the same reason as the Ionians of the twelve cities, who came

[4] See B. I. chap. 171.

from Athens. The Æolians contributed sixty ships, and were equipped like the Greeks; they were anciently called Pelasgians, as the Grecians say. The Hellespontines, except those of Abydos, for the people of Abydos were ordered by the king to stay at home and guard the bridges—the rest, however, who joined the expedition from the Pontus, contributed a hundred ships; they were equipped like the Greeks: these are colonists of the Ionians and Dorians.

96. Persians, Medes, and Sacæ served as marines on board all the ships. Of these the Phœnicians furnished the best sailing ships, and of the Phœnicians the Sidonians. Over all these, as well as over those that formed the land-army, native officers were appointed to each; but I do not mention their names, for I am not necessarily constrained to do so for the purpose of the history; nor were the officers of each nation worthy of mention; and in each nation, as many as the cities were, so many were the leaders. They did not, however, follow in the quality of generals, but like the other subjects who joined the expedition. Moreover, the generals, who had all the power, and were the commanders of the several nations, such of them as were Persians have been already mentioned by me. 97. The following were admirals of the navy: Ariabignes, son of Darius; Prexaspes, son of Aspathines; Megabazus, son of Megabates; and Achæmenes, son of Darius: of the Ionian and Carian force, Ariabignes, son of Darius and the daughter of Gobryas; Achæmenes, who was brother to Xerxes on both sides, commanded the Egyptians; and the other two commanded the rest of the fleet. Triëconters, penteconters, light boats, and long horse transports were found to assemble to the number of three thousand. 98. Of those who served in the fleet, the following, next to the admirals, were the most illustrious: Tetramnestus, son of Anysus, a Sidonian; Mapen, son of Siromus, a Tyrian; Merbalus, son of Agbalus, an Aridian; Syennesis, son of Oromedon, a Cilician; Cybernisus, son of Sicas, a Lycian; Gorgus, son of Chersis, and Timonax, son of Timagoras, Cyprians; and of the Carians, Histiæus, son of Tymnes; Pygres, son of Seldomus, and Damasithymus, son of Candaules. 99. Of the other captains I make no mention, as I deem it unnecessary, except of Artemisia, whom I most admire, as having, though a woman, joined this expedition against Greece; who, her husband being dead, herself hold-

T 2

ing the sovereignty while her son was under age, joined the expedition from a feeling of courage and manly spirit, though there was no necessity for her doing so. Her name was Artemisia, and she was the daughter of Lygdamis, and by birth she was of Halicarnassus on her father's side, and on her mother's a Cretan. She commanded the Halicarnassians, the Coans, the Nisyrians, and the Calydnians, having contributed five ships; and of the whole fleet, next to the Sidonians, she furnished the most renowned ships, and of all the allies, gave the best advice to the king. The cities which I have mentioned as being under her command, I pronounce to be all of Doric origin; the Halicarnassians being Trœzenians, and the rest Epidaurians. Thus far the naval armament has been spoken of.

100. Xerxes, when he had numbered his forces, and the army was drawn up, desired to pass through and inspect them in person. Accordingly he did so, and driving through on a chariot, by each separate nation, he made inquiries, and his secretaries wrote down the answers, until he had gone from one extremity to the other, both of the horse and foot. When he had finished this, and the ships had been launched into the sea, Xerxes thereupon removing from his chariot to a Sidonian ship, sat under a gilded canopy, and then sailed by the prows of the ships, asking questions of each, as he had done with the land-forces, and having the answers written down. The captains of the ships having drawn their vessels about four plethra from the beach, lay to, all having turned their ships frontwise to land, and having armed the marines as if for a battle; but Xerxes, sailing between the prows and the beach, inspected them.

101. When he had sailed through them, and had landed from the ship, he sent for Demaratus, son of Ariston, who accompanied him in the expedition against Greece; and having called him, he addressed him thus: "Demaratus, it is now my pleasure to ask of you certain questions that I wish. You are a Greek, and, as I am informed by you, and other Greeks who have conversed with me, of a city neither the least nor the weakest. Now, therefore, tell me this, whether the Grecians will venture to lift their hands against me; for, as I think, if all the Grecians, and all the rest of the nations that dwell toward the west, were collected together, they would

not be able to withstand my attack unless they were united together. However, I am desirous to know what you say on this subject." Such was the question he asked; but Demaratus answering, said, "O king, whether shall I speak truth to you, or what is pleasing?" He bade him speak truth, assuring him that he would not be at all less agreeable than he was before. 102. When Demaratus heard this, he spoke thus: "O king, since you positively require me to speak truth, I will say such things as whoever should utter them would not hereafter be convicted of falsehood. Poverty has ever been familiar to Greece, but virtue has been acquired, having been accomplished by wisdom and firm laws; by the aid of which, Greece has warded off poverty and tyranny. I commend, indeed, all those Greeks who dwell round those Doric lands; but I shall now proceed to speak, not of all, but of the Lacedæmonians only. In the first place, *I say* it is not possible that they should ever listen to your proposals, which bring slavery on Greece; secondly, that they will meet you in battle, even if all the rest of the Greeks should side with you. With respect to their number, you need not ask how many they are, that they are able to do this; for whether a thousand men, or more, or even less, should have marched out, they will certainly give you battle." 103. Xerxes, having heard this, replied, "Demaratus, what have you said? that a thousand men will fight with such an army as this? Come, tell me, you say that you were yourself king of these men; are you, then, willing on the spot to fight with ten men? And yet, if all your citizens are such as you represent, you, who are their king, ought, by your own institutions, to be matched against twice that number; for if each of them is a match for ten men in my army, I expect that you should be a match for twenty, so the opinion you have given utterance to would prove correct; but if, being such as yourself, and of the same stature as you and other Greeks who have conversed with me, ye boast so much, beware that the opinion you have uttered be not an idle vaunt; for come, let us consider every probability: how could a thousand men, or even ten thousand, or even fifty thousand, being all equally free, and not subject to the command of a single person, resist such an army as this? for if they are five thousand, we are more than a thousand against one. Were they, indeed, according to our custom, subject to the command of a single person, they might, through fear of him, prove superior to their natural courage; and, compelled by the lash, might, though fewer, attack a greater number; but now, being left to their own free will, they will do nothing of the kind. And I am of opinion that, even if they were equal in numbers, the Grecians would hardly contend with the Persians alone. For the valor that you speak of exists among us; it is not, however, common, but rare; for there are Persians among my body-guards who would readily encounter three Greeks at once; and you, having no experience of these men, talk very idly." 104. To this Demaratus replied, "O king, I knew from the first that by adhering to the truth I should not say what would be agreeable to you; but since you constrained me to speak the exact truth, I told you the real character of the Spartans. However, you yourself well know how tenderly I must love them, who, after they had deprived me of my paternal honors and dignity, have made me citiless and an exile; but your father, having received me, gave me maintenance and a home; it is not probable, therefore, that a prudent man should repel manifest benevolence, but should by all means cherish it. For my part, I do not pretend to be able to fight with ten men, nor with two; nor would I willingly fight with one; but if there was any necessity, or any great stake to rouse me, I would most willingly fight with one of those men who pretend to be singly a match for three Grecians. In like manner, the Lacedæmonians in single combat are inferior to none, but together are the bravest of all men; for, though free, they are not absolutely free, for they have a master over them, the law, which they fear much more than your subjects do you. They do, accordingly, whatever it enjoins; and it ever enjoins the same thing, forbidding them to fly from battle before any number of men, but to remain in their ranks, and conquer or die. If I appear to you, in saying this, to talk idly, I will for the future observe silence on this subject, and now I have spoken through compulsion; however, may events, O king, turn out according to your wish."

105. Such was the reply he made; but Xerxes turned it into ridicule, and evinced no anger, but dismissed him kindly. Xerxes, having held this conversation, and appointed Mas-

cames, son of Megadostes, to be governor of this Doriscus, and having deposed the person placed there by Darius, marched his army through Thrace toward Greece. 106. Mascames, whom he left, proved so excellent a man, that Xerxes used to send presents every year to him alone, as being the best of all the governors whom either he or Darius had appointed; and he used to send them every year, as did also Artaxerxes, son of Xerxes, to the descendants of Mascames; for even before this expedition governors had been appointed in Thrace, and throughout the Hellespont. Now all these, both in Thrace and on the Hellespont, except the one in Doriscus, were driven out by the Greeks after this invasion; but none were able to drive out Mascames, who was in Doriscus, though many made the attempt. On this account presents are sent to his family by the reigning king of Persia. 107. But of all those who were driven out by the Greeks, king Xerxes thought no one had behaved himself with courage except Boges, who was governor of Eion. Him he never ceased praising, and conferred the highest honors on his sons who survived in Persia. And, indeed, Boges deserves great praise; for when he was besieged by the Athenians under Cimon, son of Miltiades, and might have marched out by capitulation and returned to Asia, he would not do so, lest the king should think he saved his life through cowardice; but he held out to the last; and when there was no longer any food in the fort, having raised a great pile, he slew his children and wife, and concubines and servants, and then threw their bodies into the fire; after this he cast all the gold and silver that was in the tower from the fort into the Strymon, and, having done this, he threw himself into the fire, so that he is with justice commended by the Persians even to this day.

108. Xerxes set out from Doriscus toward Greece, and compelled such nations as he met with to join his army; for, as I before observed,[5] the whole country as far as Thessaly had been brought to subjection, and made tributary to the king, Megabazus, and afterward Mardonius, having subdued it. In his march from Doriscus, he first passed the Samothracian fortresses, the last of which is situate toward the west, and is a city called Mesambria; near this is Stryme, a city of the Thasians. Between these two places the river Lissus flows;

[5] See B. V. ch. 12, 15; and B. VI. ch. 43—45.

which did not supply sufficient water for the army of Xerxes, but failed. This country was anciently called Gallaica, but now Briantica; in strict right, however, it belongs to the Ciconians.

109. Xerxes, having crossed the dried-up channel of the river Lissus, passed by the following Grecian cities, Maronea, Dicæa, and Abdera; he accordingly went by these, and near them, the following celebrated lakes: the Ismaris, situate between Maronea and Stryme; and Bistonis, near Dicæa, into which two rivers empty their water, the Travus and Compsatus. Near Abdera Xerxes passed by no celebrated lake, but the river Nestus, which flows into the sea. After these places he passed in his march by several continental cities, in one of which is a lake about thirty stades in circumference: it abounds in fish, and is very brackish. The beasts of burden alone, being watered there, dried this up. The name of this city is Pistyrus. These cities, then, maritime and Grecian, he passed by, leaving them on the left hand. 110. The nations of Thrace, through whose country he marched, are these: the Pæti, Ciconians, Bistonians, Sapæi, Dersæi, Edoni, and Satræ. Of these, such as dwelt near the sea attended him with their ships; and such as dwelt inland, who have been enumerated by me, all, except the Satræ, were compelled to follow by land. 111. The Satræ. as far as we are informed, were never subject to any man, but alone, of all the Thracians, have continued free to this day; for they inhabit lofty mountains, covered with all kinds of wood and snow, and are courageous in war. These are the people that possess an oracle of Bacchus; this oracle is on the highest range of their mountains. The Bessi are those among the Satræ who interpret the oracles of the temple; a priestess delivers them, as in Delphi, and they are not at all more ambiguous. 112. Xerxes, having traversed the country that has been mentioned, after this passed by the forts of the Pierians, one of which is called Phagres, and the other Pergamus: here he marched close to the very forts, keeping on his right hand Mount Pangæus, which is vast and lofty, and in it are gold and silver mines, which the Pierians and Odomanti, and especially the Satræ, work. 113. Passing by the Pæonians, Doberes, and Pæoplæ, who dwell above Pangæus to the north, he went westward till he arrived at the river Strymon and the city of Eion, of which Boges,

whom I have lately mentioned,[6] being still alive, was governor. The land itself, which is about Mount Pangæus, is called Phillis, extending westward to the river Angites, which falls into the Strymon; and on the south, reaching to the Strymon itself, which the magi propitiated by sacrificing white horses to it. 114. Having used these enchantments to the river, and many others besides, they marched by the Nine Ways of the Edonians to the bridges, and found the banks of the Strymon united by a bridge.[7] But being informed that this place was called the Nine Ways, they buried alive in it so many sons and daughters of the inhabitants. It is a Persian custom to bury people alive; for I have heard that Amestris, wife of Xerxes, having grown old, caused fourteen children of the best families in Persia to be buried alive, to show her gratitude to the god who is said to be beneath the earth.

115. When the army marched from the Strymon, there is a shore toward the sun-set on which it passed by a Grecian city called Argilus; this and the country above it is called Bisaltia; from thence keeping the bay near the temple of Neptune on the left hand, it went through what is called the plain of Soleus; and passing by Stagirus, a Grecian city, arrived at Acanthus; taking with them each of the above nations, and those that dwell round Mount Pangæus, as well as those which I have before enumerated; having those that dwelt near the sea to serve on shipboard, and those above the sea to follow on foot. This road, along which king Xerxes marched his army, the Thracians neither disturb nor sow, but regard it with great veneration even to my time. 116. When he arrived at Acanthus, the Persian enjoined the Acanthians to show them hospitality, and presented them with a Medic dress, and commended them, seeing them ready for the war, and hearing of the excavation *at Mount Athos.*[8] 117. While Xerxes was at Acanthus, it happened that Artachæes, who had superintended the canal, died of disease; he was much esteemed by Xerxes, and was of the race of the Achæmenidæ, and in stature the tallest of the Persians, for he wanted only four fingers of five royal cubits; and he had the loudest voice

[6] Chap. 107. [7] See chap. 24.

[8] See chap. 22. The Acanthians, who bordered on Mount Athos, had probably facilitated the work.

of any man, so that Xerxes, considering his loss very great, had him carried to the grave and buried him with great pomp, and the whole army raised up a mound for his sepulchre. To this Artachæes the Acanthians, in obedience to an oracle, offer sacrifice as to a hero, invoking him by name. King Xerxes therefore, when Artachæes died, considered it a great loss. 118. Those of the Grecians who received the army and entertained Xerxes were reduced to extreme distress, so that they were obliged to abandon their homes; since Antipater, son of Orges, one of the most distinguished citizens, being selected by the Thasians, who received and entertained the army of Xerxes on behalf of the cities on the continent, showed that four hundred talents of silver had been expended on the banquet. 119. In like manner, those who superintended in the other cities gave in their accounts; for the banquet was of the following kind, as being ordered long beforehand, and considered of great importance. In the first place, as soon as they heard the heralds proclaiming it all around, the citizens, having distributed the corn that was in the cities, all made flour and meal for many months; and, in the next place, they fatted cattle, finding the best they could for money, and fed land and water fowl in coops and ponds for the entertainment of the army: moreover, they made gold and silver cups and vessels, and all such things as are placed on a table. But these things were made for the king himself, and those who sat at table with him; for the rest of the army provisions only were required. Whenever the army arrived, a tent was readily pitched, in which Xerxes himself lodged, but the rest of the army remained in the open air. When meal-time came, those who received them had all the trouble; but the guests, when they had been satisfied and passed the night there, on the following day, having torn up the tent and taken all the furniture, went away, leaving nothing, but carrying away every thing. 120. On this occasion, a clever remark was made by Magacreon of Abdera, who advised the Abderites "to go in a body, themselves and their wives, to their own temples, and to seat themselves as suppliants of the gods, beseeching them also for the future to avert one half of the evils that were coming upon them, and to express their hearty thanks for what was passed, that king Xerxes was not accustomed to take food twice every day; for if they had been ordered to prepare a dinner as well as a supper, they, the Abderites, would have been compelled either not to await the arrival of Xerxes, or, if they had awaited him, they must have been worn down the most miserably of all men." They, however, though hard put to it, executed the order imposed on them.

121. At Acanthus Xerxes dismissed the ships from his presence to proceed on their voyage, having given orders to the admirals that the fleet should await his arrival at Therma—at Therma, which is situated on the Thermæan gulf, and from which that gulf derives its name, for he had heard that that was the shortest way. As far as Acanthus the army marched from Doriscus in the following order. Xerxes, having divided the whole land forces into three bodies, ordered one of them to accompany the fleet along the coast; of this division Mardonius and Masistes were commanders. Another of the three divisions of the army marched inland, commanded by Trintantæchmes and Gersis. But the third division, with which Xerxes himself went, marched between the other two, and had for generals Smerdomenes and Megabyzus. 122. The fleet accordingly, when it had been dismissed by Xerxes, and had passed through the canal which was at Athos extending to the bay on which the cities of Assa, Pilorus, Singus, and Sarta are situate, after that, when it had taken troops on board from those cities, sailed with all speed to the Thermæan bay. Doubling Ampelus, the Toronæan foreland, it passed by the following Greek cities, from which it took ships and men, Torone, Galepsus, Sermyla, Mecyberna, and Olynthus; all which country is now called Sithonia. 123. Xerxes's fleet, stretching across from the cape of Ampelus to the cape of Canastræum, which is the most prominent point of all Pallene, thence took ships and men from Potidæa, Aphytis, Neapolis, Æga, Therambus, Scione, Menda, and Sana, for these are the cities that belong to what is now Pallene, but was formerly called Phlegra. Coasting along this country, it sailed to the appointed place, taking with them troops also from the cities near Pallene and bordering on the Thermæan gulf; their names are as follows: Lipaxus, Combrea, Lisæ, Gigonus, Campsa, Smila, and Ænea. The country in which these cities are situate is to the present time called by the name of Crossæa. From Ænea, with which I ended my enumeration of the cities, the course of the fleet was direct to

the Thermæan gulf and the Mygdonian territory; and sailing on, it reached the appointed place, Therma, and Sindus and Chalestra, on the river Axius, which divides the territories of Mygdonia and Bottiæis; on a narrow tract of which, near the sea, stand the cities of Ichnæ and Pella.

124. The naval force encamped there near the river Axius, and the city of Therma, and the intermediate places, awaiting the arrival of the king; but Xerxes and the land army marched from Acanthus, taking the road through the interior, wishing to reach Therma; and he marched through the Pæonian and Crestonian territories toward the river Echidorus, which, beginning from the Crestonians, flows through the Mygdonian territory, and discharges itself into the marsh which is above the river Axius. 125. While he was marching in this direction, lions fell upon his camels that carried provisions; for the lions, coming down by night and leaving their usual haunts, seized nothing else, whether beast of burden or man, but they attacked the camels only; and I wonder what the reason could be that induced the lions to abstain from all the rest, and set upon the camels, a beast which they had never before seen or made trial of. 126. But in those parts lions are numerous, and wild bulls, which have very large horns that are brought into Greece. The boundaries of the lions are the river Nestus, which flows through Abdera, and the Achelous, which flows through Acarnania; for no one would ever see a lion any where eastward of the Nestus, throughout the forepart of Europe, nor to the west of the Achelous, in the rest of the continent, but they breed in the tract between these two rivers. 127. When Xerxes arrived at Therma, he there ordered his army to halt; and his army, when encamped, occupied the following district along the coast; commencing from the city of Therma, and from Mygdonia, to the rivers Lydias and Haliacmon, which divide the territories of Bottiæis and Macedonia, uniting their waters into the same channel. In these countries, then, the barbarians encamped. Of the rivers above mentioned, the Echidorus, which flows from the Crestonians, was the only one that was not sufficient for the army, but failed.

128. Xerxes, seeing from Therma the Thessalonian mountains, Olympus and Ossa, which are of vast size, and having learned that there was a narrow pass between them, through

which the river Peneus runs, and hearing that at that spot there was a road leading to Thessaly, very much wished to sail and see the mouth of the Peneus, because he designed to march by the upper road through the country of the Macedonians, who dwell higher up, to the territory of the Perrhæbi, near the city of Gonnus; for he was informed that this was the safest way. Accordingly, as he wished, so he did. Having gone on board a Sidonian ship, in which he always embarked whenever he wished to do any thing of this kind, he made a signal for all the rest of the fleet to get under weigh, leaving the land forces where they were. When Xerxes arrived, and beheld the mouth of the Peneus, he was struck with great astonishment, and having called his guides, asked if it would be possible to turn the river and conduct it by another channel into the sea. 129. It is said that Thessaly was anciently a lake, since it is inclosed on all sides by lofty mountains; for the side next the east Mount Pelion and Ossa shut in, mingling their bases with each other; and the side toward the north Olympus *shuts in;* and the west, Pindus; and the side toward the midday and the south wind, Othrys: the space in the midst of the above-mentioned mountains is Thessaly, which is hollow. Since, then, several other rivers flow into it, and these five most noted ones, the Peneus, the Apidanus, the Onochonus, the Enipeus, and the Pamisus—these that have been named, accordingly, meeting together in this plain from the mountains that inclose Thessaly, discharge themselves into the sea through one channel, and that a narrow one, having all before mingled their waters into the same stream; but as soon as they have mingled together, from that spot the names of the other rivers merge in that of the Peneus.[9] It is said that formerly, when the pass and outlet did not yet exist, these rivers, and besides them the lake Bœbeis, were not called by the names they now bear, though they flowed not less than they do now, but that by their stream they made all Thessaly a lake. However, the Thessalians themselves say that Neptune made the pass through which the Peneus flows; and their story is probable, for whoever thinks that Neptune shakes the earth, and that rents occasioned by earthquakes are the works of this god, on seeing

[9] Literally, "the river Peneus gaining the victory as to the name, causes the others to be nameless."

this, would say that Neptune formed it, for it appears evident to me that the separation of these mountains is the effect of an earthquake. 130. The guides, when Xerxes asked if there was any other exit for the Peneus to the sea, being accurately acquainted with the country, said, "O king, this river has no other outlet that extends to the sea except this one, for all Thessaly is surrounded by mountains." Xerxes is reported to have said to this, "The Thessalians are prudent men, and therefore they long ago took precautions, and altered their minds, both on other accounts, and because they possessed a country which might be easily subdued and quickly taken; for it would only be necessary to turn the river on to their territory, by forcing it back by a mound at the pass, and diverting it *from the channels* through which it now flows, so that all Thessaly, except the mountains, would be inundated." Xerxes expressed himself thus in reference to the sons of Aleuas,[1] because they, being Thessalians, were the first of the Greeks who gave themselves up to the king, Xerxes supposing that they promised alliance in behalf of the whole nation. Having thus spoken, and viewed the spot, he sailed back to Therma.

131. He remained several days about Pieria, for a third division of his army was employed in felling the trees on the Macedonian range, that the whole army might pass in that direction to the Perrhæbi. In the mean time, the heralds[2] who had been sent to Greece to demand earth returned to Xerxes, some empty, and others bringing earth and water. 132. Of those who gave them were the following: the Thessalians, the Dolopes, the Enienes, the Perrhæbi, the Locrians, the Magnetes, the Melians, the Achæans of Phthiotis, and the Thebans, and all the rest of the Bœotians except the Thespians and Platæans. Against these the Greeks, who engaged in war with the barbarians, made a solemn oath. The oath ran as follows: "Whatever Greeks have given themselves up to the Persian without compulsion, so soon as their affairs are restored to order, that these should be compelled to pay a tithe to the god at Delphi." Such was the oath taken by the Greeks. 133. To Athens and Sparta he did not send heralds to demand earth for the following reasons: on a former occasion, when Darius sent for the same purpose, the former

[1] See chap. 6. [2] See chap. 32.

having thrown those who made the demand into the barathrum,[3] and the latter into a well, bade them carry earth and water to the king from those places; for that reason, Xerxes did not send persons to make the demand. What calamity befell the Athenians, in consequence of their having treated the heralds in this manner, I can not say, except that their territory and city were ravaged; but I do not think that happened in consequence of that crime. 134. On the Lacedæmonians, however, the anger of Talthybius, Agamemnon's herald, alighted; for Talthybius has a temple in Sparta; and there are descendants of Talthybius, called Talthybiadæ, to whom all embassies from Sparta are given as a privilege. After these events, the Spartans were unable, when they sacrificed, to get favorable omens; and this continued for a long time. The Lacedæmonians being grieved, and considering it a great calamity, and having frequently held assemblies, and *at length* made inquiry by public proclamation whether any Lacedæmonian was willing to die for Sparta, Sperthies, son of Aneristus, and Bulis, son of Nicolaus, both Spartans of distinguished birth, and eminent for their wealth, voluntarily offered to give satisfaction to Xerxes for the heralds of Darius who had perished at Sparta. Accordingly, the Spartans sent them to the Medes for the purpose of being put to death. 135. And both the courage of these men deserves admiration, and also the following words on this occasion; for on their way to Susa they came to Hydarnes; but Hydarnes was a Persian by birth, and governor of the maritime people in Asia; he having offered them hospitality, entertained them, and while he was entertaining them, he questioned them as follows, saying, "Men of Lacedæmon, why do you refuse to be friendly with the king? for you may see how well the king knows how to honor brave men, by looking at me and my condition; so also, if you would surrender yourselves to the king, for you are deemed by him to be brave men, each of you would obtain a government in some part of Greece at the hands of the king." To this they answered as follows: "Hydarnes, the advice you hold out to us is not impartial; for you advise us, having tried the one state, but being inexperienced in the other: what it is to be a slave you know perfectly well, but

[3] The barathrum was a deep pit at Athens, into which certain criminals who were sentenced to death were thrown.

you have never tried liberty, whether it is sweet or not; for if you had tried it, you would advise us to fight for it, not with spears, but even with hatchets." Thus they answered Hydarnes. 136. Afterward, when they went up to Susa, and were come into the king's presence, in the first place, when the guards commanded and endeavored to compel them to prostrate themselves and worship the king, they said they would by no means do so, although they were thrust by them on their heads; for that it was not their custom to worship a man, nor had they come for that purpose. When they had fought off this, and on their addressing Xerxes in words to the following effect, "King of the Medes, the Lacedæmonians have sent us in return for the heralds who were killed at Sparta, to make satisfaction for them;" on their saying this, Xerxes answered with magnanimity "that he would not be like the Lacedæmonians, for that they had violated the law of all nations by murdering his heralds; but he would not do the very thing which he blamed in them, nor by killing them in return would relieve the Lacedæmonians from guilt." 137. Thus the wrath of Talthybius, when the Spartans acted in this manner, ceased for the time, although Sperthies and Bulis returned to Sparta. But some time afterward it was again aroused, during the war between the Peloponnesians and Athenians, as the Lacedæmonians say; and this appears to me to have happened in a most extraordinary manner; for that the wrath of Talthybius alighted on the messengers, and did not cease until it was satisfied, justice allowed; but that it should fall on the sons of the men who went up to the king on account of that wrath, on Nicolaus, son of Bulis, and on Aneritus, son of Sperthies, who, sailing in a merchant vessel fully manned, captured some fishermen from Tiryns, makes it clear to me that the occurrence was extraordinary in consequence of that wrath; for they, being sent by the Lacedæmonians as embassadors to Asia, and being betrayed by Sitalces, son of Teres, king of the Thracians, and by Nymphodorus, son of Pytheas of Abdera, were taken near Bisanthe on the Hellespont, and being carried to Attica, were put to death by the Athenians; and with them Aristeas, son of Adimantus, a Corinthian. These things, however, happened many years after the expedition of the king.

138. But I return to my former subject. This expedition

of the king was nominally directed against Athens, but was really sent against all Greece. The Greeks, however, though they had heard of it long beforehand, were not all affected alike; for those who had given earth and water to the Persian felt confident that they should suffer no harm from the barbarian; but those who had refused to give them were in great consternation, since the ships in Greece were not sufficient in number to resist the invader, and many were unwilling to engage in the war, and were much inclined to side with the Medes. 139. And here I feel constrained by necessity to declare my opinion, although it may excite the envy of most men; however, I will not refrain from expressing how the truth appears to me to be. If the Athenians, terrified with the impending danger, had abandoned their country, or, not having abandoned it, but remaining in it, had given themselves up to Xerxes, no other people would have attempted to resist the king at sea. If, then, no one had opposed Xerxes by sea, the following things must have occurred on land. Although many lines of walls had been built by the Peloponnesians across the Isthmus, yet the Lacedæmonians, being abandoned by the allies (not willingly, but by necessity, they being taken by the barbarian city by city), would have been alone; and being left alone, after having displayed noble deeds, would have died nobly. They would either have suffered thus, or, before that, seeing the rest of the Greeks siding with the Medes, would have made terms with Xerxes; and so, in either case, Greece would have become subject to the Persians; for I am unable to discover what would have been the advantage of the walls built across the Isthmus if the king had been master of the sea. Any one, therefore, who should say that the Athenians were the saviors of Greece, would not deviate from the truth; for to whichever side they turned, that must have preponderated. But having chosen that Greece should continue free, they were the people who roused the rest of the Greeks who did not side with the Medes, and who, next to the gods, repulsed the king. Neither did alarming oracles, that came from Delphi, and inspired them with terror, induce them to abandon Greece, but, standing their ground, they had courage to await the invader of their country.

140. For the Athenians, having sent deputies to Delphi, were

anxious to consult the oracle; and after they had performed the usual ceremonies about the temple, when they entered the sanctuary and sat down, the Pythian, whose name was Aristonica, uttered the following warning: "O wretched men, why sit ye here? fly to the ends of the earth, leaving your houses and the lofty summits of your wheel-shaped city; for neither does the head remain firm nor the body, nor the lowest feet nor the hands, nor is aught of the middle left, but they are all fallen to ruin. For fire and fleet Mars, driving the Syrian chariot, destroys it; and he will destroy many other turrets, and not yours alone; and he will deliver many temples of the immortals to devouring fire, which now stand dripping with sweat, shaken with terror; and from the topmost roofs trickles black blood, pronouncing inevitable woe. But go from the sanctuary, and infuse your mind with courage to meet misfortunes." 141. The deputies of the Athenians, having heard this, deemed it a very great calamity; and when they were dejected at the predicted evil, Timon, son of Androbulus, a man reputed at Delphi equally with the best, advised them to take supplicatory branches, and go again and consult the oracle as suppliants. The Athenians yielding to this advice, and saying, "O king, vouchsafe to give us a more favorable answer concerning our country, having regard to these supplicatory branches which we have brought with us; otherwise we will never depart from thy sanctuary, but will remain here till we die." When they had said this, the priestess gave a second answer, in these terms: "Pallas is unable to propitiate Olympian Jove, entreating him with many a prayer and prudent counsel. But to you again I utter this speech, making it like adamant; for when all is taken that the limit of Cecrops contains within it, and the recesses of divine Cithæron, wide-seeing Jupiter gives a wooden wall to the Triton-born goddess, to be alone impregnable, which shall preserve you and your children. Nor do you quietly wait for the cavalry and infantry advancing in multitudes from the continent, but turn your backs and withdraw; you will still be able to face them. O divine Salamis, thou shalt cause the sons of women to perish, whether Ceres is scattered or gathered in." 142. Having written this answer down, for it appeared to them to be of milder import than the former one, they departed for Athens; and when the deputies, on their return, reported it to the people, many different opinions were given by persons endeavoring to discover the meaning of the oracle, and among them the two following most opposed each other. Some of the old men said they thought the god foretold that the Acropolis should be saved; for formerly the Acropolis was defended by a hedge; they therefore, on account of the hedge, conjectured that this was the wooden wall. Others, on the other hand, said that the god alluded to their ships, and therefore advised that, abandoning every thing else, they should get them ready. However, the two last lines uttered by the Pythian perplexed those who said that the wooden wall meant the ships: "O divine Salamis, thou shalt cause the sons of women to perish, whether Ceres is scattered or gathered in." By these words the opinions of those who said that the ships were the wooden wall were disturbed, for the interpreters of oracles took them in this sense, that they should be defeated off Salamis if they prepared for a sea-fight. 143. There was a certain Athenian who had lately risen to eminence, whose name was Themistocles, but he was commonly called the son of Neocles; this man maintained that the interpreters had not rightly understood the whole, saying thus: "If the word that had been uttered really did refer to the Athenians, he did not think that it would have been expressed so mildly, but thus, 'O unhappy Salamis' instead of 'O divine Salamis,' if the inhabitants were about to perish on its shores; therefore whoever understood them rightly would conclude that the oracle was pronounced by the god against their enemies, and not against the Athenians." He advised them, therefore, to make preparations for fighting by sea, since that was the wooden wall. When Themistocles thus declared his opinion, the Athenians considered it preferable to that of the interpreters who dissuaded them from making preparations for a sea-fight, and, in short, *advised them* not to make any resistance at all, but to abandon the Attic territory, and settle in some other. 144. Another opinion of Themistocles had before this opportunely prevailed. When the Athenians, having great riches in the treasury, which came in from the mines of Laureum, were about to share them man by man, to each ten drachmas, then Themistocles persuaded them to refrain from this distribution, and to build two hundred ships with this money, meaning for the war with the Æginetæ; for that war springing up, at this time saved Greece, by compelling the Athenians to apply themselves to maritime affairs. The ships, however, were used for the purpose for which they were built, but were thus very serviceable to Greece. These, therefore, were already built for the Athenians, and it was necessary to construct others besides. And it was resolved, on their consulting after the receipt of the oracle, to await the barbarian who was invading Greece with their whole people on shipboard, in obedience to the god, together with such Greeks as would join them. Such, then, were the oracles delivered to the Athenians.

145. When the Greeks who were better affected toward Greece were assembled together, and consulted with each other, and gave pledges of mutual fidelity, it was thereupon determined, on deliberation, that, before all things, they should reconcile all existing enmities and wars with each other; for there were wars on hand between several others, but the most considerable was that between the Athenians and Æginetæ. After this, being informed that Xerxes was with his army at Sardis, they determined to send spies into Asia, in order to discover the true state of the king's affairs; and to send embassadors to Argos to conclude an alliance against the Persians, and others to Sicily, to Gelon, son of Dinomenes, and to Corcyra, and others to Crete, begging them to come to the assistance of Greece; purposing, if possible, that Greece should be united, and that all should combine in adopting the same plan in dangers which threatened all the Greeks alike; but the power of Gelon was said to be very great, being far superior to that of any other Grecian states. 146. When these things were determined on by them, having reconciled their enmities, they first of all sent three men as spies into Asia; and they having arrived at Sardis, and endeavored to get intelligence of the king's forces, when they were discovered, were examined by the generals of the land-army, and led out to execution, for sentence of death had been passed upon them; but when Xerxes heard of this, disapproving of the decision of the generals, he sent some of his guards, with orders to bring the spies to him if they should find them still alive; and when they found them yet living, and brought them into the king's presence, he thereupon, having inquired for what purpose they came,

commanded the guards to conduct them round, and show them all the infantry and cavalry, and when they should be satisfied with seeing them, to send them away unharmed, to whatever country they should choose. 147. He issued these orders, alleging the following reason, that "if the spies were put to death, the Greeks would neither be informed beforehand of his power, that it was greater than could be described, nor would he do any great harm to his enemies by putting three men to death; whereas, if they returned to Greece, it was his opinion," he said, "that the Greeks, having heard of his power, would, of their own accord, surrender their liberty before the expedition should take place, and so it would not be necessary to have the trouble of marching against them." This opinion of his was like this other one. When Xerxes was at Abydos, he saw certain ships laden with corn from the Pontus sailing through the Hellespont on their way to Ægina and the Peloponnesus. Those who sat near him, having heard that the ships belonged to the enemy, were ready to capture them, and fixing their eyes on the king, watched when he would give the order. But Xerxes asked his attendants where they were sailing. They answered, "To your enemies, sire, carrying corn." He answering, said, "Are not we also sailing to the same place to which these men are, and provided with other things, and with corn? What hurt, then, can they do us by carrying corn thither for us?" The spies, accordingly, having seen the army, and being sent away, returned to Europe.

148. But the Greeks who had engaged in a confederacy against the Persian, after the dispatch of the spies, next sent embassadors to Argos. But the Argives say that what concerned them occurred as follows; that they heard from the very first of the design of the barbarian against Greece, and having heard of it, and learned that the Greeks would endeavor to obtain their assistance against the Persian, they sent persons to consult the oracle of Delphi, and inquire of the god "what course it would be best for them to adopt; for six thousand of their number had recently been slain by the Lacedæmonians, and by Cleomenes, son of Anaxandrides;" for this reason they sent, and the Pythian gave the following answer to their inquiries: "Hated by your neighbors, beloved by the immortal gods, holding your lance at rest, keep

on the watch, and guard your head; the head shall save the body." *They say* that the Pythian gave this answer first, and afterward, when the embassadors came to Argos, they were introduced to the council, and delivered their message; and they answered to what was said that "the Argives were ready to comply, having first made a thirty years' truce with the Lacedæmonians, and provided they might have an equal share of the command of the allied forces; though in justice the whole command belonged to them, yet they would be content with the command over half." 149. This, they say, was the answer of their senate, although the oracle had forbidden them to enter into any alliance with the Grecians; and that they were anxious to make a thirty years' truce, although they feared the oracle, in order that their children might become men during that time; but if a truce was not made, they were apprehensive lest, if in addition to their present calamity, another failure should befall them in the Persian war, they might in future become subject to the Lacedæmonians. Those of the embassadors who came from Sparta gave the following answer to what was said by the council: "that with respect to a truce, it should be referred to the people; but with respect to the command, they were instructed to answer and say that they had two kings, but the Argives only one, and therefore it was not possible to deprive either of their kings of his command, but that there was nothing to hinder the Argive king from having an equal vote with their two." Thus the Argives say that they could not put up with the arrogance of the Spartans, but that they rather chose to be subject to the barbarians than to yield to the Lacedæmonians; and that they ordered the embassadors to quit the territories of the Argives before sunset, otherwise they would treat them as enemies. 150. Such is the account which the Argives themselves give of this affair. But another report is prevalent throughout Greece, that Xerxes sent a herald to Argos before he set out on his expedition against Greece, and it is related that he, on his arrival, said, "Men of Argos, king Xerxes speaks thus to you. We are of opinion that Perses, from whom we are sprung, was son of Perseus, son of Danae, born of Andromeda, daughter of Cepheus. Thus, then, we must be your descendants; it is therefore neither right that we should lead an army against our progenitors, nor that you should assist others and be opposed to us, but should remain quiet by yourselves; and if I succeed according to my wish, I shall esteem none greater than you." It is said that the Argives, when they heard this, considered it a great thing, and at once determined neither to promise any thing nor demand any thing in return; but when the Greeks wished to take them into the confederacy, they then, knowing that the Lacedæmonians would not share the command with them, made the demand in order that they might have a pretext for remaining quiet. 151. Some of the Greeks also say that the following circumstance, which occurred many years after, accords with this: Callias, son of Hipponicus, and those who went up with him as embassadors of the Athenians, happened to be at the Memnonian Susa on some other business; and the Argives at the same time having sent embassadors to Susa, asked Artaxerxes, son of Xerxes, "whether the alliance which they had formed with Xerxes still subsisted, or whether they were considered by him as enemies." King Artaxerxes answered "that it certainly subsisted, and that he considered no city more friendly than Argos." 152. Now whether Xerxes did send a herald to Argos with such a message, and whether embassadors of the Argives, having gone up to Susa, asked Artaxerxes about the alliance, I can not affirm with certainty; nor do I declare any other opinion on the subject than what the Argives themselves say; but this much I know, that if all men were to bring together their own faults into one place, for the purpose of making an exchange with their neighbors, when they had looked closely into their neighbors' faults, each would gladly take back those which they brought with them. Thus the conduct of the Argives was not the most base. But I am bound to relate what is said, though I am not by any means bound to believe every thing; and let this remark apply to the whole history; for even this is reported, that the Argives were the people who invited the Persian to invade Greece, since their war with the Lacedæmonians went on badly, wishing that any thing might happen to them rather than continue in their present troubles. This is sufficient concerning the Argives.

153. Other embassadors went from the allies to Sicily to confer with Gelon, and among them Syagrus on the part of the Lacedæmonians. An ancestor of this Gelon, who was an

inhabitant of Gela, came from the island of Telus, which lies off Triopium; when Gela was founded by the Lindians from Rhodes and by Antiphemus, he was not left behind; and, in course of time, his descendants becoming priests of the infernal deities, continued to be so, Telines, one of their ancestors, having acquired that dignity in the following manner. Some of the inhabitants of Gela, being worsted in a sedition, had fled to Mactorium, a city situated above Gela; these men, then, Telines conducted back again without the assistance of any human force, but with the sacred things to those deities; though whence he got them, or how he became possessed of them, I am unable to say. However, relying on these, he brought back the fugitives on condition that his descendants should be priests of the deities. From what I hear, I am much astonished that Telines should have achieved such an action; for I have ever thought that such actions are not in the reach of every man, but proceed from a brave spirit and manly vigor; whereas, on the contrary, he is reported by the inhabitants of Sicily to have been an effeminate and delicate man. Thus, however, he acquired this dignity. 154. On the death of Cleander, son of Pantares, who reigned seven years over Gela, but was killed by Sabyllus, a citizen of Gela, thereupon Hippocrates, who was brother to Cleander, succeeded to the sovereignty. While Hippocrates held the tyranny, Gelon, who was a descendant of Telines the priest, was with many others, and with Ænesidemus, son of Pataicus, one of the guards of Hippocrates, and soon after was made commander of the whole cavalry on account of his valor; for when Hippocrates besieged the Callipolitæ, the Naxians, the Zanclæans, the Leontines, and, besides, the Syracusans, and divers of the barbarians, Gelon signalized himself in these several wars; and of the cities that I have mentioned, not one, except the Syracusans, escaped servitude at the hands of Hippocrates. But the Corinthians and Corcyræans saved the Syracusans after they had been defeated in battle on the river Elorus, and they saved them, having reconciled them on the following terms, that the Syracusans should give up Camarina to Hippocrates; but Camarina originally belonged to the Syracusans. 155. When Hippocrates, having reigned the same number of years as his brother Cleander, met with his death before Hybla while carrying on the war against the Sicilians, Gelon thereupon, under color of defending the rights of Euclides and Cleander, sons of Hippocrates, the citizens refusing to be any longer subject to them—in fact, when he had defeated the Geloans in battle, possessed himself of the sovereignty, and deposed the sons of Hippocrates. After this success, Gelon, leading back those Syracusans who were called Gamori,[4] and had been expelled by the people, and by their own slaves, called Cyllyrii, leading them back from the city of Casmene to Syracuse, got possession of this also, for the people of the Syracusans gave up the city and themselves to Gelon on his first approach. 156. When he had made himself master of Syracuse, he took less account of the government of Gela, and intrusted it to his brother Hiero; but he strengthened Syracuse, and Syracuse was every thing to him; and it grew up rapidly and flourished; for, first of all, he removed all the Camarinæans to Syracuse, and made them citizens, and destroyed the city of Camarina; and, in the next place, he did with more than half the Geloans the same that he had done with the Camarinæans. Moreover, the Megarians in Sicily, when being besieged they came to terms, the more opulent of them, who had raised the war against him, and, therefore, expected to be put to death, he took to Syracuse and made citizens; but the populace of the Megarians, who had no part in promoting this war, nor expected to suffer any harm, he also took to Syracuse, and sold them for exportation from Sicily. He treated the Eubœans in Sicily in the same manner, and made the same distinction; and he treated them both in this way, from an opinion that a populace is a most disagreeable neighbor. By such means Gelon became a powerful tyrant.

157. At this time, when the embassadors of the Grecians arrived at Syracuse, having come to a conference with him, they spoke as follows: "The Lacedæmonians, the Athenians, and their allies, have sent us to invite you to join with them against the barbarian; for doubtless you have heard that he is marching against Greece, and that a Persian, having thrown a bridge over the Hellespont, and bringing with him all the eastern host out of Asia, is about to invade Greece, holding out as a pretense that he is advancing against Athens, but really designing to reduce all Greece under his own power.

[4] Landholders.

But you have attained to great power, and possess not the least part of Greece, since you rule Sicily; assist, therefore, those who are asserting the liberty of Greece, and join them in maintaining its liberty; for if all Greece is assembled, a large force is collected, and we become able to resist the invaders. But if some of us should betray the common cause, and others refuse to assist, so that the sound part of Greece should be small, then there is great danger that the whole of Greece will fall; for you must not expect that if the Persian should subdue us, having conquered in battle, he will not proceed also against you, but take precautions beforehand; for, by assisting us, you protect yourself. A favorable result is generally wont to attend a well-devised plan." Thus they spoke. 158. Gelon was very vehement, speaking as follows: "Men of Greece, holding arrogant language, you have dared to invite me to come to your assistance against the barbarian; and yet you yourselves, when I formerly besought you to assist me in attacking a barbarian army when a quarrel was on foot between me and the Carthaginians, and when I exhorted you to avenge the death of Doricus,[5] son of Anaxandrides, upon the Ægestæans, and promised that I would join in freeing the ports, from whence great advantages and profits accrued to you, neither for my sake did you come to assist me, nor to avenge the death of Doricus; so that, as far as you are concerned, all this country is subject to barbarians. However, matters turned out well with me, and prospered; and now, when the war has come round and reached you, at length you remember Gelon. But, though I met with disgraceful treatment from you, I shall not imitate your example, but am ready to assist you, furnishing two hundred triremes, twenty thousand heavy-armed troops, two thousand horse, two thousand bowmen, two thousand slingers, and two thousand light-horse; I likewise undertake to supply corn for the whole Grecian army until we have finished the war. But I promise these things on this condition, that I shall be general and leader of the Greeks against the barbarian; on no other condition will I come myself or send others. 159. Syagrus, when he heard this, could not contain himself, but spoke as follows: "Agamemnon, the descendant of Pelops, would indeed groan aloud if he heard that the Spartans had

[5] See B. V. chap. 45, 46.

been deprived of the supreme command by a Gelon and by Syracusans. Never mention this proposition again, that we should give up the command to you; but if you are willing to succor Greece, know that you must be commanded by Lacedæmonians, or, if you will not deign to be commanded, you need not assist us." 160. Upon this, Gelon, when he observed the indignant language of Syagrus, made this last proposal: "Spartan stranger, reproaches uttered against a man are wont to rouse his indignation; yet, though you have used insulting words in your speech, you have not provoked me to be unseemly in return. Nevertheless, since you are so exceedingly anxious for the supreme command, it is reasonable that I also should be more anxious for it than you, since I am leader of a far greater army and many more ships. However, since my proposal is so repugnant to you, I will abate something of my first demand. If, then, you choose to command the army, I will command the fleet; or, if it please you rather to have the command at sea, I will lead the land-forces; and you must either be content with these terms, or return destitute of such allies." 161. Gelon, then, proposed these terms; but the embassador of the Athenians, anticipating that of the Lacedæmonians, answered him in these words: "King of the Syracusans, the Grecians sent us to you, not to ask for a general, but an army. You declare that you will not send an army unless you have the command of Greece, and you are anxious to be made general of it: as long as you required to command all the forces of the Grecians, we Athenians were contented to remain silent, as we knew that the Spartan would be sufficient to answer for us both; but since, being excluded from the whole command, you require to govern the navy, the matter stands thus. Even if the Lacedæmonians should allow you to govern it, we shall not allow it, for that is ours, unless the Lacedæmonians wish to take it themselves. If they, indeed, wish to have the command, we shall not oppose them, but we will never cede to any one else the command of the navy; for in vain should we possess the greatest naval power of the Greeks, if we, being Athenians, should yield the command to the Syracusans, we who are the most ancient nation, and the only people of the Greeks who have never changed their country; from whom also Homer, the epic poet, said, the best man went to

Troy, both for arraying and marshaling an army, so that it is no disgrace to us to speak as we do." 162. To this Gelon answered, "Athenian stranger, you seem to have commanders, but as if you would not have men to be commanded. Since, therefore, you are resolved to concede nothing, but to retain the whole power, you can not be too quick in returning back again, and informing Greece that the spring of the year has been taken from her." The meaning of this saying is, which he wished to intimate, that as the spring is evidently the most valuable season in the year, so of the army of the Grecians, his was the best: Greece, therefore, deprived of his alliance, he compared to a year from which the spring should be taken away.

163. The embassadors of the Greeks, having thus negotiated with Gelon, sailed away; but Gelon, upon this, fearing for the Grecians, that they would not be able to withstand the barbarian, but deeming it an intolerable disgrace that he who was tyrant of Sicily should go to Peloponnesus, and be subject to the Lacedæmonians, gave up all thoughts of that course and adopted another. As soon as he was informed that the Persian had crossed the Hellespont, he dispatched Cadmus, son of Scythes, a Coan, to Delphi, with three penteconters, taking with him much treasure and friendly messages, for the purpose of watching the contest, in what way it would terminate; and if the barbarian should conquer, he was to present him with the treasure, and earth and water for the countries which Gelon ruled over; but if the Greeks *should be victorious*, he was to bring back *the treasure*. 164. This Cadmus, having before these events received from his father the sovereignty of the Coans, firmly established, of his own accord, when no danger threatened him, but from a sense of justice, surrendered the government into the hands of the Coans, and retired into Sicily; there, with the Samians, he possessed and inhabited the city of Zancle, which changed its name to Messana. This Cadmus, therefore, who had in this manner come *to Sicily*, Gelon sent, on account of other proofs which he had of his uprightness; and he, in addition to other instances of uprightness that had been given by him, left this not the least *monument* of them; for having in his possession vast treasures, which Gelon had intrusted to him, when it was in his power to appropriate them, he would not; but

when the Greeks conquered in the sea-fight, and Xerxes had retired, he also returned to Sicily, and took back all the treasures.

165. However, the following account is given by those who inhabit Sicily, that Gelon, notwithstanding that he must be governed by the Lacedæmonians, would have assisted the Greeks, had not Terillus, son of Crinippus, who was tyrant of Himera, being expelled from Himera by Theron, son of Ænesidemus, king of the Agrigentines, at that time brought in an army of three hundred thousand men, consisting of Phœnicians, Libyans, Iberians, Ligyans, Elisycians, Sardinians, and Cyrnians, under the conduct of Amilcar, son of Hanno, king of the Carthaginians. Terillus persuaded him by the hospitality which existed between them, and especially by the zeal of Anaxilaus, son of Critines, who being tyrant of Rhegium, and having given his children as hostages into the hands of Amilcar, induced him to enter Sicily in order to revenge the injury done to his father-in-law; for Anaxilaus had married a daughter of Terillus, whose name was Cydippe. Thus, as Gelon was not able to assist the Greeks, he sent the treasures to Delphi. 166. In addition to this, they say that it happened on the same day that Gelon and Theron conquered Amilcar the Carthaginian in Sicily, and the Greeks conquered the Persian at Salamis. I am informed that Amilcar, who was a Carthaginian by his father and a Syracusan by his mother, and chosen king of Carthage for his virtue, when the engagement took place, and he was defeated in battle, vanished out of sight; for he was seen nowhere on the earth, either alive or dead, though Gelon had search made for him every where. 167. The following story is also related by the Carthaginians themselves, who endeavor to give a probable account that the barbarians fought with the Grecians in Sicily from the morning till late in the evening, for it is said that the conflict lasted so long; and during this time, Amilcar, continuing in the camp, offered sacrifices, and observed the omens, burning whole victims upon a large pile; and when he saw the defeat of his own army, as he happened to be pouring libations on the victims, he threw himself into the flames, and thus, being burned to ashes, disappeared. But whether Amilcar disappeared in such manner as the Phœnicians relate, or in another manner, as the Syracusans, the Carthaginians, in the

first place, offer sacrifices to him, and in the next, have erected monuments to his memory in all the cities inhabited by colonists, and the most considerable one in Carthage itself. So much for the affairs of Sicily.

168. The Corcyræans, having given the following answer to the embassadors, acted as I shall relate; for the same embassadors who went to Sicily invited them to join the league, using the same language to them as they had done to Gelon. They indeed immediately promised to send and give assistance, adding "that they could not look on and see the ruin of Greece, for if it should be overthrown, nothing else would remain for them than to become slaves on the very first day; therefore they would assist to the utmost of their power." Thus speciously they answered; but when they ought to have assisted, with different intentions they manned sixty ships, and having put to sea, after great delays, drew near to the Peloponnesus, and anchored about Pylus and Tænarus of the Lacedæmonian territory; they also carefully watched the war, in what way it would terminate, having no expectation that the Grecians would get the better, but thinking that the Persian, having gained a decided superiority, would become master of all Greece. They therefore acted thus purposely, in order that they might be able to say to the Persian, "O king, when the Greeks invited us to take part in the war, we, who have a considerable force, and were able to supply not the least number of ships, but the greatest number, next to the Athenians, would not oppose you, nor do any thing displeasing to you." By saying this they hoped to get better terms than the rest, which would have been the case, as appears to me; and toward the Greeks their excuse was ready prepared, which indeed they did make use of; for when the Greeks accused them of not having sent assistance, they said "that they had manned sixty ships, but were unable to double Malea by reason of the Etesian winds; and so they could not reach Salamis, and were absent from the sea-fight from no bad motive." In this manner they attempted to elude the charge of the Greeks.

169. The Cretans, when those Greeks who were appointed for that purpose invited them to join the league, acted as follows. Having sent, in the name of the commonwealth, persons to consult the oracle at Delphi, they inquired of the god

whether it would be for their advantage to assist Greece. The Pythian answered, "Fools, you complain of all the woes which Minos in his anger sent you for aiding Menelaus, because they would not assist you in avenging his death at Camicus, and yet you assisted them *in avenging* a woman who was carried off from Sparta by a barbarian." When the Cretans heard this answer reported, they refrained from sending assistance. 170. For it is said that Minos, having come to Sicania, which is now called Sicily, in search of Dædalus, met with a violent death; that after some time the Cretans, at the instigation of a deity, all except the Polichnitæ and the Præsians, went with a large force to Sicania, and during five years besieged the city of Camicus, which in my time the Agrigentines possessed; and at last, not being able either to take it or to continue the siege, because they were oppressed by famine, they abandoned it and went away; and when they were sailing along the coast of Iapygia, a violent storm overtook them, and drove them ashore; and as their ships were broken to pieces, and there appeared no means of their returning to Crete, they thereupon founded the city of Hyria, and settled there, changing their name from Cretans to Messapian Iapygians, and becoming, instead of islanders, inhabitants of the continent. From the city of Hyria they founded other cities, which a long time after the Tarentines endeavoring to destroy, signally failed; so that this was the greatest Grecian slaughter of all that we know of, both of the Tarentines themselves, and of the Rhegians, who, being compelled by Micythus, son of Chœrus, and coming to assist the Tarentines, thus perished to the number of three thousand; but of the Tarentines themselves no number was given. This Micythus was a servant of Anaxilaus, and had been left in charge of Rhegium. He is the same person that was expelled from Rhegium, and who, having settled in Tegea, a city of Arcadia, dedicated the many statues in Olympia. 171. These events relating to the Rhegians and Tarentines are a digression from my history. To Crete, then, destitute of inhabitants, as the Præsians say, other men, and especially the Grecians, went, and settled there; and in the third generation after the death of Minos, the Trojan war took place, in which the Cretans proved themselves not the worst avengers of Menelaus: as a punishment for this, when they returned from Troy, famine and pestilence fell both on themselves and their cattle; so that Crete being a second time depopulated, the Cretans are the third people who, with those that were left, now inhabit it. The Pythian, therefore, putting them in mind of these things, checked them in their desire to assist the Grecians.

172. The Thessalians at first sided with the Mede from necessity, as they showed, in that the intrigues of the Aleuadæ[6] did not please them; for as soon as they were informed that the Persian was about to cross over into Europe, they sent embassadors to the Isthmus; and at the Isthmus deputies from Greece were assembled, chosen from those cities that were better disposed toward Greece. The embassadors of the Thessalians, having come to them, said, "Men of Greece, it is necessary to guard the pass of Olympus, that Thessaly and all Greece may be sheltered from the war. Now we are ready to assist in guarding it, but you must also send a large army; for if you will not send, be assured we shall come to terms with the Persian; for it is not right that we, who are situated so far in advance of the rest of Greece, should perish alone in your defense. If you will not assist us, you can not impose any obligation upon us; for obligation was ever inferior to inability; and we must ourselves endeavor to contrive some means of safety." 173. Thus spoke the Thessalians; and the Grecians thereupon resolved to send an army by sea to Thessaly, to guard the pass; and when the army was assembled, it sailed through the Euripus, aud having arrived at Alus of Achaia, disembarked, and marched to Thessaly, having left the ships there, and arrived at Tempe, at the pass that leads from the lower Macedonia into Thessaly, by the river Peneus, between Mount Olympus and Ossa. There heavy-armed troops of the Grecians, being assembled together to the number of ten thousand, encamped, and to them was added the cavalry of the Thessalians. The Lacedæmonians were commanded by Euænetus, son of Carenus, chosen from among the Polemarchs, though not of the royal race, and the Athenians *were commanded by* Themistocles, son of Neocles. There they remained but a few days; for messengers coming from Alexander, son of Amyntas, a Macedonian, advised them to retire, and not to stay in the pass and be trampled under foot by the invading army, describing the numbers of the army and the

[6] See chap. 6 and 180.

ships. When the messengers gave this advice, as the Grecians conceived the advice to be good, and the Macedonian was evidently well-disposed to them, they determined to follow it; but, in my opinion, it was fear that persuaded them, when they heard that there was another pass into Thessaly and Upper Macedonia, through the country of the Perrhæbi, near the city of Gonnus; by which, indeed, the army of Xerxes did enter. The Grecians, therefore, going down to their ships, went back again to the Isthmus. 174. This expedition into Thessaly took place while the king was about to cross over from Asia into Europe, and was still at Abydos; but the Thessalians, being abandoned by their allies, then readily took part with the Medes, and with no farther hesitation, so much so, that in emergency they proved most useful to the king.

175. The Greeks, when they arrived at the Isthmus, consulted on the message they had received from Alexander, in what way and in what places they should prosecute the war. The opinion which prevailed was, that they should defend the pass at Thermopylæ; for it appeared to be narrower than that into Thessaly, and at the same time nearer to their own territories; for the path by which the Greeks who were taken at Thermopylæ were afterward surprised, they knew nothing of, till, on their arrival at Thermopylæ, they were informed of it by the Trachinians. They accordingly resolved to guard this pass, and not suffer the barbarian to enter Greece; and that the naval force should sail to Artemisium, in the territory of Histiæotis, for these places are near one another, so that they could hear what happened to each other. These spots are thus situated. 176. In the first place, Artemisium is contracted from a wide space of the Thracian sea into a narrow frith, which lies between the island of Sciathus and the continent of Magnesia. From the narrow frith begins the coast of Eubœa, called Artemisium, and in it is a temple of Diana. But the entrance into Greece through Trachis, in the narrowest part, is no more than a half plethrum in width; however, the narrowest part of the country is not in this spot, but before and behind Thermopylæ; for near Alpeni, which is behind, there is only a single carriage-road, and before, by the river Phœnix, near the city of Anthela, is another single carriage-road. On the western side of Thermopylæ is an inaccessible and precipitous mountain, stretching to Mount Œta,

and on the eastern side of the way is the sea and a morass. In this passage there are hot baths, which the inhabitants call Chytri, and above these is an altar to Hercules. A wall had been built in this pass, and formerly there were gates in it. The Phocæans built it through fear, when the Thessalians came from Thesprotia to settle in the Æolian territory which they now possess: apprehending that the Thessalians would attempt to subdue them, the Phocæans took this precaution; at the same time, they diverted the hot water into the entrance, that the place might be broken into clefts, having recourse to every contrivance to prevent the Thessalians from making inroads into their country. Now this old wall had been built a long time, and the greater part of it had already fallen through age; but they determined to rebuild it, and in that place to repel the barbarian from Greece. Very near this road there is a village called Alpeni; from this the Greeks expected to obtain provisions. 177. Accordingly, these situations appeared suitable for the Greeks; for they, having weighed every thing beforehand, and considered that the barbarians would neither be able to use their numbers nor their cavalry, there resolved to await the invader of Greece. As soon as they were informed that the Persian was in Pieria, breaking up from the Isthmus, some of them proceeded by land to Thermopylæ, and others by sea to Artemisium.

178. The Greeks, therefore, being appointed in two divisions, hastened to meet the enemy; but, at the same time, the Delphians, alarmed for themselves and for Greece, consulted the oracle, and the answer given them was, "that they should pray to the winds, for that they would be powerful allies to Greece." The Delphians, having received the oracle, first of all communicated the answer to those Greeks who were zealous to be free; and as they very much dreaded the barbarians, by giving that message they acquired a claim to everlasting gratitude. After that, the Delphians erected an altar to the winds at Thyia, where there is an inclosure consecrated to Thyia, daughter of Cephisus, from whom this district derives its name, and conciliated them with sacrifices; and the Delphians, in obedience to that oracle, to this day propitiate the winds.

179. The naval force of Xerxes, setting out from the city of Therma, advanced with ten of the fastest sailing ships

straight to Scyathus, where were three Grecian ships keeping a look-out, a Trœzenian, an Æginetan, and an Athenian. These, seeing the ships of the barbarians at a distance, betook themselves to flight. 180. The Trœzenian ship, which Praxinus commanded, the barbarians pursued and soon captured; and then, having led the handsomest of the marines to the prow of the ship, they slew him, deeming it a good omen that the first Greek they had taken was also very handsome. The name of the man that was slain was Leon, and perhaps he in some measure reaped the fruits of his name. 181. The Æginetan ship, which Asonides commanded, gave them some trouble, Pytheas, son of Ischenous, being a marine on board, a man who on this day displayed the most consummate valor; who, when the ship was taken, continued fighting until he was entirely cut to pieces. But when, having fallen, he was not dead, but still breathed, the Persians who served on board the ships were very anxious to save him alive, on account of his valor, healing his wounds with myrrh, and binding them with bandages of flaxen cloth; and when they returned to their own camp, they showed him with admiration to the whole army, and treated him well; but the others, whom they took in this ship, they treated as slaves. 182. Thus, then, two of the ships were taken; but the other, which Phormus, an Athenian, commanded, in its flight ran ashore at the mouth of the Peneus, and the barbarians got possession of the ship, but not of the men; for as soon as the Athenians had run the ship aground, they leaped out, and, proceeding through Thessaly, reached Athens. The Greeks who were stationed at Artemisium were informed of this event by signal-fires from Sciathus; and being informed of it, and very much alarmed, they retired from Artemisium to Chalcis, intending to defend the Euripus, and leaving scouts on the heights of Eubœa. 183. Of the ten barbarian ships, three approached the sunken rock called Myrmex, between Sciathus and Magnesia. Then the barbarians, when they had erected on the rock a stone column, which they had brought with them, set out from Therma, now that every obstacle had been removed, and sailed forward with all their ships, having waited eleven days after the king's departure from Therma. Pammon, a Scyrian, pointed out to them this hidden rock, which was almost directly in their course. The barbarians, sailing all day, reached Sepias in Magnesia, and the shore that lies between the city of Casthanæa and the coast of Sepias.

184. As far as this place and Thermopylæ, the army had suffered no loss, and the numbers were at that time, as I find by calculations, of the following amount: of those in ships from Asia, amounting to one thousand two hundred and seven, originally the whole number of the several nations was two hundred forty-one thousand four hundred men, allowing two hundred to each ship; and on these ships thirty Persians, Medes, and Sacæ served as marines, in addition to the native crews of each; this farther number amounts to thirty-six thousand two hundred and ten. To this and the former number I add those that were on the penteconters, supposing eighty men on the average to be on board of each; but, as I have before said,[7] three thousand of these vessels were assembled; therefore the men on board them must have been two hundred and forty thousand. This, then, was the naval force from Asia, the total being five hundred and seventeen thousand six hundred and ten. Of infantry there were seventeen hundred thousand, and of cavalry eighty thousand; to these I add the Arabians who drove camels, and the Libyans who drove chariots, reckoning the number at twenty thousand men. Accordingly, the numbers on board the ships and on the land, added together, make up two millions three hundred and seventeen thousand six hundred and ten. This, then, is the force which, as has been mentioned, was assembled from Asia itself, exclusive of the servants that followed, and the provision ships, and the men that were on board them. 185. But the force brought from Europe must still be added to this whole number that has been summed up; but it is necessary to speak by guess. Now the Grecians from Thrace, and the islands contiguous to Thrace, furnished one hundred and twenty ships; these ships give an amount of twenty-four thousand men. Of land-forces, which were furnished by Thracians, Pæonians, the Eordi, the Bottiæans, the Chalcidian race, Brygi, Pierians, Macedonians, Perrhæbi, Ænianes, Dolopians, Magnesians, and Achæans, together with those who inhabit the maritime parts of Thrace, of these nations I suppose that there were three hundred thousand men, so that these myriads, added to those from Asia, make a total of two millions

[7] Chap. 97.

six hundred forty one thousand six hundred and ten fighting men. 186. I think that the servants who followed them, and with those on board the provision ships and other vessels that sailed with the fleet, were not fewer than the fighting men, but more numerous; but supposing them to be equal in number with the fighting men, they make up the former number of myriads. Thus Xerxes, son of Darius, led five millions two hundred and eighty-three thousand two hundred and twenty men to Sepias and Thermopylæ. 187. This, then, was the number of the whole force of Xerxes. But of women who made bread, and concubines, and eunuchs, no one could mention the number with accuracy; nor of draught-cattle and other beasts of burden; nor of Indian dogs that followed could any one mention the number, they were so many; therefore I am not astonished that the streams of some rivers failed, but rather it is a wonder to me how provisions held out for so many myriads; for I find by calculation, if each man had a chœnix of wheat daily, and no more, one hundred and ten thousand three hundred and forty medimni must have been consumed every day; and I have not reckoned the food for the women, eunuchs, beasts of burden, and dogs. But of so many myriads of men, not one of them, for beauty and stature, was more entitled than Xerxes himself to possess this power.

188. When the fleet, having set out, sailed and reached the shore of Magnesia that lies between the city of Casthanæa and the coast of Sepias, the foremost of the ships took up their station close to land, others behind rode at anchor (the beach not being extensive enough), with their prows toward the sea, and eight deep. Thus they passed the night; but at day-break, after serene and tranquil weather, the sea began to swell, and a heavy storm, with a violent gale from the east, which those who inhabit these parts call a Hellespontine, burst upon them; as many of them, then, as perceived the gale increasing, and who were able to do so from their position, anticipated the storm by hauling their ships on shore, and both they and their ships escaped. But such of the ships as the storm caught at sea it carried away, some to the parts called Ipni, near Pelion, others to the beach; some were dashed on Cape Sepias itself; some were wrecked at Melibœa, and others at Casthanæa. The storm was indeed irresistible. 189. A

story is told that the Athenians invoked Boreas, in obedience to an oracle, another response having come to them "that they should call their son-in-law to their assistance." But Boreas, according to the account of the Greeks, married a woman of Attica, Orithyia, daughter to Erectheus. On account of this marriage, the Athenians, as the report goes, conjecturing that Boreas was their son-in-law, and having stationed their fleet at Chalcis of Eubœa, when they saw the storm increasing, or even before, offered sacrifices to and invoked Boreas and Orithyia, *praying* that they would assist them, and destroy the ships of the barbarians, as they had done before at Mount Athos. Whether, indeed, the north wind in consequence of this fell upon the barbarians as they rode at anchor, I can not undertake to say; however, the Athenians say that Boreas, having assisted them before, then also produced this effect, and on their return they erected a temple to Boreas near the river Ilissus. 190. In this disaster, those who give the lowest account say that not fewer than four hundred ships perished, and innumerable lives, and an infinite quantity of treasure; so that this wreck of the fleet proved a source of great profit to Aminocles, son of Cretinus, a Magnesian, who possessed land about Sepias; he some time afterward picked up many golden cups that had been driven ashore, and many silver ones; he also found treasures belonging to the Persians, and gained an unspeakable quantity of other golden articles. He then, though in other respects unfortunate, became very rich by what he found; for a sad calamity, which occasioned the death of his son,[8] gave him great affliction. 191. The provision ships and other vessels destroyed were beyond number, so that the commanders of the naval force, fearing lest the Thessalians should attack them in their shattered condition, threw up a high rampart from the wrecks; for the storm lasted three days. But at length the magi, having sacrificed victims, and endeavored to charm the winds by incantations, and, moreover, having offered sacrifices to Thetis and the Nereids, laid the storm on the fourth day, or perhaps it abated of its own accord. They sacrificed to Thetis, having heard from the Ionians the story that she had been carried off from this country by Peleus, and that all the coast of Sepias

[8] Παιδοφόνος is by others understood to imply "that he killed his own son." I have followed Baehr.

belonged to her and the other Nereids. Accordingly, the wind was lulled on the fourth day. 192. The scouts on the heights of Eubœa, running down on the second day after the storm first began, acquainted the Greeks with all that had occurred with respect to the wreck of the fleet. They, when they heard it, having offered up vows and poured out libations to Neptune the Deliverer, immediately hastened back to Artemisium, hoping that there would be only some few ships to oppose them. Thus they, coming there a second time, took up their station at Artemisium, and from that time to the present have given to Neptune the surname of the Deliverer.

193. The barbarians, when the wind had lulled and the waves had subsided, having hauled down their ships, sailed along the continent; and having doubled the promontory of Magnesia, stood directly into the bay leading to Pagasæ. There is a spot in this bay of Magnesia where it is said Hercules was abandoned by Jason and his companions when he had been sent from the Argo for water, as they were sailing to Asia in Colchis for the golden fleece; for from thence they purposed to put out to sea after they had taken in water: from this circumstance, the name of Aphetæ was given to the place. In this place, then, the fleet of Xerxes took up its moorings. 194. Fifteen of these ships happened to be driven out to sea some time after the rest, and somehow saw the ships of the Greeks at Artemisium; the barbarians thought that they were their own, and sailing on, fell in among their enemies. They were commanded by Sandoces, son of Thaumasius, governor of Cyme, of Æolia. He, being one of the royal judges, had been formerly condemned by king Darius, who had detected him in the following offense, to be crucified. Sandoces gave an unjust sentence for a bribe; but while he was actually hanging on the cross, Darius, considering with himself, found that the services he had done to the royal family were greater than his faults; Darius, therefore, having discovered this, and perceiving that he himself had acted with more expedition than wisdom, released him. Having thus escaped being put to death by Darius, he survived; but now, sailing down among the Grecians, he was not to escape a second time; for when the Greeks saw them sailing toward them, perceiving the mistake they had committed, they bore down upon them and easily took them. 195. In one of these,

Aridolis, tyrant of the Alabandians, in Caria, was taken; and in another, the Paphian commander, Penthylus, son of Demonous. He brought twelve ships from Paphos; but having lost eleven in the storm that took place off Sepias, he was taken with the one that escaped, as he was sailing to Artemisium. The Grecians, having learned by inquiry what they wished to know respecting the forces of Xerxes, sent these men away bound to the isthmus of the Corinthians.

196. Accordingly, the naval force of the barbarians, with the exception of the fifteen ships which I have mentioned Sandoces commanded, arrived at Aphetæ. But Xerxes and the land-forces, marching through Thessaly and Achaia, had entered on the third day into the territories of the Mælians. In Thessaly he made a match with his own horses for the purpose of trying the Thessalian cavalry, having heard that it was the best of all Greece; and on that occasion the Grecian horses proved very inferior. Of the rivers in Thessaly, the Onochonus alone did not supply a sufficient stream for the army to drink; but of the rivers that flow in Achaia, even the largest of them, the Epidanus, scarcely held out. 197. When Xerxes arrived at Alos in Achaia, the guides, wishing to tell every thing, related to him the tradition of the country concerning the temple of Laphystian Jupiter; how Athamas, son of Æolus, conspiring with Ino, planned the death of Phryxus; and then, how the Achæans, in obedience to an oracle, imposed the following penalty on his descendants. Whoever is the eldest person of this race, having ordered him to be excluded from the prytaneum, they themselves keep watch; the Achæans call the prytaneum Leitum; and if he should enter, he can not possibly go out again except in order to be sacrificed; and how, moreover, many of those who were on the point of being sacrificed, through fear, went away and fled the country; but in process of time having returned back again, if they were taken entering the prytaneum, they related how such an one, being covered with sacred fillets, is sacrificed, and how conducted with great pomp. The descendants of Cytissorus, son of Phryxus, are liable to this punishment; because, when the Achaians, in obedience to an oracle, were about to make an expiation for their country by the sacrifice of Athamas, son of Æolus, Cytissorus, arriving from Aia of Colchis, rescued him, and having done so, drew down the anger of the gods

upon his descendants. Xerxes having heard this, when he came to the grove, both abstained from entering it himself, and commanded all the army to do the same, and he showed the same respect to the dwelling of the descendants of Athamas as he did to the sacred precinct.

198. These things occurred in Thessaly and in Achaia. From these countries Xerxes advanced to Malis, near a bay of the sea in which an ebb and flow takes place every day. About this bay lies a plain country, in one part wide, and in the other very narrow, and around it high and impassable mountains, called the Trachinian rocks, inclose the whole Malian territory. The first city in the bay, as one comes from Achaia, is Anticyra, by which the river Sperchius, flowing from the country of the Ænianes, falls into the sea; and from thence about twenty stades is another river, to which the name of Dyras is given, which, it is said, rose up to assist Hercules when he was burning. From this, at a distance of another twenty stades, is another river, which is called Melas. 199. The city of Trachis is distant five stades from this river Melas, and in this part where Trachis is built is the widest space of all this country from the mountains to the sea, for there are twenty-two thousand plethra of plain. In this mountain, which incloses the Trachinian territory, there is a ravine to the south of Trachis, and through the ravine the river Asopus flows by the base of the mountain. 200. To the south of the Asopus is another river, the Phœnix, not large, which, flowing from these mountains, falls into the Asopus. At the river Phœnix it is the narrowest, for only a single carriage-road has been constructed there. From the river Phœnix it is fifteen stades to Thermopylæ, and between the river Phœnix and Thermopylæ is a village, the name of which is Anthela, by which the Asopus flowing falls into the sea: the country about it is wide, and in it is situated a temple of Ceres Amphictyonis, and there are the seats of the Amphictyons and a temple of Amphictyon himself. 201. King Xerxes, then, encamped in the Trachinian territory of Malis, and the Greeks in the pass. This spot is called by most of the Greeks Thermopylæ, but by the inhabitants and neighbors Pylæ. Both parties, then, encamped in these places. The one was in possession of all the parts toward the north as far as Trachis, and the others of the parts

which stretch toward the south and meridian on this continent.

202. The following were the Greeks who awaited the Persian in this position. Of Spartans, three hundred heavy-armed men; of Tegeans and Mantineans, one thousand, half of each; from Orchomenus in Arcadia, one hundred and twenty; and from the rest of Arcadia, one thousand—there were so many Arcadians; from Corinth, four hundred; from Phlius, two hundred men; and from Mycenæ, eighty. These came from Peloponnesus. From Bœotia, of Thespians seven hundred, and of Thebans four hundred. 203. In addition to these, the Opuntian Locrians, being invited, came with all their forces, and a thousand Phocians; for the Greeks themselves had invited them, representing by their embassadors that "they had arrived as forerunners of the others, and that the rest of the allies might be daily expected; that the sea was protected by them, being guarded by the Athenians, the Æginetæ, and others, who were appointed to the naval service; and that they had nothing to fear, for that it was not a god who invaded Greece, but a man; and that there never was, and never would be, any mortal who had not evil mixed with *his prosperity* from his very birth, and to the greatest of them the greatest *reverses happen;* that it must therefore needs be that he who is marching against us, being a mortal, will be disappointed in his expectation." They, having heard this, marched with assistance to Trachis. 204. These nations had separate generals for their several cities, but the one most admired, and who commanded the whole army, was a Lacedæmonian, Leonidas, son of Anaxandrides, son of Leon, son of Eurycratides, son of Anaxander, son of Eurycates, son of Polydorus, son of Alcamenes, son of Teleclus, son of Archelaus, son of Agesilaus, son of Doryssus, son of Leobotes, son of Echestratus, son of Agis, son of Eurysthenes, son of Aristodemus, son of Aristomachus, son of Cleodæus, son of Hyllus, son of Hercules, who had unexpectedly succeeded to the throne of Sparta. 205. For, as he had two elder brothers, Cleomenes and Dorieus, he was far from any thought of the kingdom. However, Cleomenes having died without male issue, and Dorieus being no longer alive, having ended his days in Sicily,[9] the kingdom thus devolved upon

[9] B. V. chap. 42—45.

Leonidas; both because he was older than Cleombrotus (for he was the youngest son of Anaxandrides), and also because he had married the daughter of Cleomenes. He then marched to Thermopylæ, having chosen the three hundred men allowed by law,[1] and such as had children. On his march he took with him the Thebans, whose numbers I have already reckoned,[2] and whom Leontiades, son of Eurymachus, commanded. For this reason Leonidas was anxious to take with him the Thebans alone of all the Greeks, because they were strongly accused of favoring the Medes: he therefore summoned them to the war, wishing to know whether they would send their forces with him, or would openly renounce the alliance of the Grecians; but they, though otherwise minded, sent assistance. 206. The Spartans sent these troops first with Leonidas, in order that the rest of the allies, seeing them, might take the field and might not go over to the Medes if they heard that they were delaying; but afterward, for the Carnean festival was then an obstacle to them, they purposed, when they had kept the feast, to leave a garrison in Sparta, and to march immediately with their whole strength. The rest of the confederates likewise intended to act in the same manner; for the Olympic games occurred at the same period as these events. As they did not, therefore, suppose that the engagement at Thermopylæ would so soon be decided, they dispatched an advance-guard. Thus, then, they intended to do.

207. The Greeks at Thermopylæ, when the Persian came near the pass, being alarmed, consulted about a retreat; accordingly, it seemed best to the other Peloponnesians to retire to Peloponnesus, and guard the Isthmus; but Leonidas, perceiving the Phocians and Locrians very indignant at this proposition, determined to stay there, and to dispatch messengers to the cities, desiring them to come to their assistance, as being too few to repel the army of the Medes. 208. While they were deliberating on these matters, Xerxes sent a scout on horseback, to see how many they were, and what they were doing; for while he was still in Thessaly, he had heard that a small army had been assembled at that spot, and as to their

[1] For the various methods of rendering τοὺς κατεστεῶτας, see Baehr's note and Cary's Lexicon.

[2] Chap. 202.

leaders, that they were Lacedæmonians, and Leonidas, who was of the race of Hercules. When the horseman rode up to the camp, he reconnoitred, and saw not indeed the whole camp, for it was not possible that they should be seen who were posted within the wall, which, having rebuilt, they were now guarding; but he had a clear view of those on the outside, whose arms were piled in front of the wall. At this time the Lacedæmonians happened to be posted outside; and some of the men he saw performing gymnastic exercises, and others combing their hair. On beholding this he was astonished, and ascertained their number; and having informed himself of every thing accurately, he rode back at his leisure, for no one pursued him, and he met with general contempt. On his return he gave an account to Xerxes of all that he had seen.

209. When Xerxes heard this, he could not comprehend the truth that the Grecians were preparing to be slain and to slay to the utmost of their power; but, as they appeared to behave in a ridiculous manner, he sent for Demaratus, son of Ariston, who was then in the camp; and when he was come into his presence, Xerxes questioned him as to each particular, wishing to understand what the Lacedæmonians were doing. Demaratus said, "You before heard me, when we were setting out against Greece, speak of these men; and when you heard, you treated me with ridicule, though I told you in what way I foresaw these matters would issue; for it is my chief aim, O king, to adhere to the truth in your presence; hear it, therefore, once more. These men have to fight with us for the pass, and are now preparing themselves to do so; for such is their custom, when they are going to hazard their lives, then they dress their heads; but be assured, if you conquer these men, and those that remain in Sparta, there is no other nation in the world that will dare to raise their hand against you, O king; for you are now to engage with the noblest kingdom and city of all among the Greeks, and with the most valiant men." What was said seemed very incredible to Xerxes, and he asked again "how, being so few in number, they could contend with his army." He answered, "O king, deal with me as with a liar if these things do not turn out as I say."

210. By saying this he did not convince Xerxes. He therefore let four days pass, constantly expecting that they would

betake themselves to flight; but on the fifth day, as they had not retreated, but appeared to him to stay through arrogance and rashness, he, being enraged, sent the Medes and Cissians against them, with orders to take them alive, and bring them into his presence. When the Medes bore down impetuously upon the Greeks, many of them fell; others followed to the charge, and were not repulsed, though they suffered greatly; but they made it evident to every one, and not least of all to the king himself, that they were indeed many men, but few soldiers. The engagement lasted through the day. 211. When the Medes were roughly handled, they thereupon retired; and the Persians whom the king called "Immortal," and whom Hydarnes commanded, taking their place, advanced to the attack, thinking that they indeed should easily settle the business; but when they engaged with the Grecians, they succeeded no better than the Medic troops, but just the same, as they fought in a narrow space, and used shorter spears than the Greeks, and were unable to avail themselves of their numbers. The Lacedæmonians fought memorably both in other respects, showing that they knew how to fight with men who knew not, and whenever they turned their backs, they retreated in close order; but the barbarians seeing them retreat, followed with a shout and clamor; then they, being overtaken, wheeled round so as to front the barbarians, and having faced about, overthrew an inconceivable number of the Persians; and then some few of the Spartans themselves fell; so that when the Persians were unable to gain any thing in their attempt on the pass, by attacking in troops and in every possible manner, they retired. 212. It is said that during these onsets of the battle, the king, who witnessed them, thrice sprang from his throne, being alarmed for his army. Thus they strove at that time. On the following day the barbarians fought with no better success; for considering that the Greeks were few in number, and expecting that they were covered with wounds, and would not be able to raise their heads against them any more, they renewed the contest. But the Greeks were marshaled in companies and according to their several nations, and each fought in turn, except only the Phocians; they were stationed at the mountain to guard the pathway. When, therefore, the Persians found nothing different from what they had seen on the preceding day, they retired.

213. While the king was in doubt what course to take in the present state of affairs, Ephialtes, son of Eurydemus, a Malian, obtained an audience[3] of him, expecting that he should receive a great reward from the king, and informed him of the path which leads over the mountain to Thermopylæ, and by that means caused the destruction of those Greeks who were stationed there; but afterward, fearing the Lacedæmonians, he fled to Thessaly; and when he had fled, a price was set on his head by the Pylagori, when the Amphictyons were assembled at Pylæ; but some time after, he went down to Anticyra, and was killed by Athenades, a Trachinian. This Athenades killed him for another reason, which I shall mention in a subsequent part of my history;[4] he was, however, rewarded none the less by the Lacedæmonians. 214. Another account is given, that Onetes, son of Phanagoras, a Carystian, and Corydallus of Anticyra, were the persons who gave this information to the king, and conducted the Persians round the mountain; but to me this is by no means credible; for, in the first place, we may draw that inference from this circumstance, that the Pylagori of the Grecians set a price on the head, not of Onetes and Corydallus, but of Ephialtes the Trachinian, having surely ascertained the exact truth; and, in the next place, we know that Ephialtes fled on that account. Onetes, indeed, though he was not a Malian, might be acquainted with this path, if he had been much conversant with the country; but it was Ephialtes who conducted them round the mountain by the path, and I charge him as the guilty person. 215. Xerxes, since he was pleased with what Ephialtes promised to perform, being exceedingly delighted, immediately dispatched Hydarnes and the troops that Hydarnes commanded; and he started from the camp about the hour of lamp-lighting. The native Malians discovered this pathway, and, having discovered it, conducted the Thessalians by it against the Phocians at the time when the Phocians, having fortified the pass by a wall, were under shelter from an attack. From that time it ap-

[3] Literally, "came to speak with him."

[4] The promised reward is nowhere given in any extant writings of the historian.

peared to have been of no service to the Malians. 216. This path is situated as follows: it begins from the river Asopus, which flows through the cleft; the same name is given both to the mountain and to the path, Anopæa; and this Anopæa extends along the ridge of the mountain, and ends near Alpenus, which is the first city of the Locrians toward the Malians, and by the rock called Melampygus, and by the seats of the Cercopes; and there the path is the narrowest. 217. Along this path, thus situate, the Persians, having crossed the Asopus, marched all night, having on their right the mountains of the Œtæans, and on their left those of the Trachinians: morning appeared, and they were on the summit of the mountain. At this part of the mountain, as I have already mentioned, a thousand heavy-armed Phocians kept guard, to defend their own country, and to secure the pathway; for the lower pass was guarded by those before mentioned; and the Phocians had voluntarily promised Leonidas to guard the path across the mountain. 218. The Phocians discovered them after they had ascended in the following manner; for the Persian ascended without being observed, as the whole mountain was covered with oaks; there was a perfect calm, and, as was likely, a considerable rustling taking place from the leaves strewn under foot, the Phocians sprung up and put on their arms, and immediately the barbarians made their appearance. But when they saw men clad in armor they were astonished; for, expecting to find nothing to oppose them, they fell in with an army; thereupon Hydarnes, fearing lest the Phocians might be Lacedæmonians, asked Ephialtes of what nation the troops were; and being accurately informed, he drew up the Persians for battle. The Phocians, when they were hit by many and thick-falling arrows, fled to the summit of the mountain, supposing that they had come expressly to attack them, and prepared to perish. Such was their determination. But the Persians, with Ephialtes and Hydarnes, took no notice of the Phocians, but marched down the mountain with all speed.

219. To those of the Greeks who were at Thermopylæ, the augur Megistias, having inspected the sacrifices, first made known the death that would befall them in the morning; certain deserters afterward came and brought intelligence of the circuit the Persians were taking; these brought the news while it was yet night; and, thirdly, the scouts running down

from the heights, as soon as day dawned, *brought the same intelligence*. Upon this the Greeks held a consultation, and their opinions were divided; for some would not hear of abandoning their post, and others opposed that view. After this, when the assembly broke up, some of them departed, and being dispersed, betook themselves to their several cities; but others of them prepared to remain there with Leonidas. 220. It is said that Leonidas himself sent them away, being anxious that they should not perish; but that he and the Spartans who were there could not honorably desert the post which they originally came to defend. For my own part, I am rather inclined to think that Leonidas, when he perceived that the allies were averse and unwilling to share the danger with him, bade them withdraw, but that he considered it dishonorable for himself to depart: on the other hand, by remaining there, great renown would be left for him, and the prosperity of Sparta would not be obliterated; for it had been announced to the Spartans by the Pythian, when they consulted the oracle concerning this war, as soon as it commenced, "that either Lacedæmon must be overthrown by the barbarians, or their king perish." This answer she gave in hexameter verses to this effect: "To you, O inhabitants of spacious Lacedæmon, either your vast, glorious city shall be destroyed by men sprung from Perseus, or, if not so, the confines of Lacedæmon mourn a king deceased of the race of Hercules. For neither shall the strength of bulls nor of lions withstand him[5] with force opposed to force, for he has the strength of Jove, and I say he shall not be restrained before he has certainly obtained one of these for his share." I think, therefore, that Leonidas, considering these things, and being desirous to acquire glory for the Spartans alone, sent away the allies, rather than that those who went away differed in opinion, and went away in such an unbecoming manner. 221. The following in no small degree strengthens my conviction[6] on this point; for not only *did he send away* the others, but it is certain that Leonidas also sent away the augur who followed the army, Megistias the Acarnanian, who was said to have been originally descended from Melampus, the same who announced from an inspection of the victims what was about to befall them, in order that he might not perish with them.

[5] The Persian king.

[6] "Is not the least proof to me."

He, however, though dismissed, did not himself depart, but sent away his son, who served with him in the expedition, being his only child. 222. The allies accordingly, that were dismissed, departed, and obeyed Leonidas; but only the Thespians and the Thebans remained with the Lacedæmonians; the Thebans, indeed, remained unwillingly, and against their inclination, for Leonidas detained them, treating them as hostages; but the Thespians willingly, for they refused to go away and abandon Leonidas and those with him, but remained and died with them. Demophilus, son of Diadromas, commanded them.

223. Xerxes, after he had poured out libations at sunrise, having waited a short time, began his attack about the time of full market, for he had been so instructed by Ephialtes; for the descent from the mountain is more direct, and the distance much shorter, than the circuit and ascent. The barbarians, therefore, with Xerxes, advanced; and the Greeks, with Leonidas, marching out as if for certain death, now advanced much farther than before into the wide part of the defile; for the fortification of the wall had protected them, and they on the preceding days, having taken up their position in the narrow part, there fought; but now engaging outside the narrows, great numbers of the barbarians fell; for the officers of the companies from behind, having scourges, flogged every man, constantly urging them forward; in consequence, many of them, falling into the sea, perished, and many more were trampled alive under foot by one another, and no regard was paid to any that perished; for the Greeks, knowing that death awaited them at the hands of those who were going round the mountain, being desperate, and regardless of their own lives, displayed the utmost possible valor against the barbarians. 224. Already were most of their javelins broken, and they had begun to dispatch the Persians with their swords. In this part of the struggle fell Leonidas, fighting valiantly, and with him other eminent Spartans, whose names, seeing they were deserving men, I have ascertained; indeed, I have ascertained the names of the whole three hundred. On the side of the Persians, also, many other eminent men fell on this occasion, and among them two sons of Darius, Abrocomes and Hyperanthes, born to Darius of Phratagune, daughter of Artanes; but Artanes was brother to king

Darius, and son of Hystaspes, son of Arsames. He, when he gave his daughter to Darius, gave him also all his property, as she was his only child. 225. Accordingly, two brothers of Xerxes fell at this spot, fighting for the body of Leonidas, and there was a violent struggle between the Persians and Lacedæmonians, until at last the Greeks rescued it by their valor, and four times repulsed the enemy. Thus the contest continued until those with Ephialtes came up. When the Greeks heard that they were approaching, from this time the battle was altered; for they retreated to the narrow part of the way, and passing beyond the wall, came and took up their position on the rising ground, all in a compact body, with the exception of the Thebans. The rising ground is at the entrance where the stone lion now stands to the memory of Leonidas. On this spot, while they defended themselves with swords, such as had them still remaining, and their hands and teeth, the barbarians overwhelmed them with missiles, some of them attacking them in front, and having thrown down the wall, and others surrounding and attacking them on every side.

226. Though the Lacedæmonians and Thespians behaved in this manner, yet Dieneces, a Spartan, is said to have been the bravest man. They relate that he made the following remark before they engaged with the Medes, having heard a Trachinian say that when the barbarians let fly their arrows, they would obscure the sun by the multitude of their shafts, so great were their numbers; but he, not at all alarmed at this, said, holding in contempt the numbers of the Medes, that "their Trachinian friend told them every thing to their advantage, since if the Medes obscure the sun, they would then have to fight in the shade, and not in the sun." This, and other sayings of the same kind, they relate that Dieneces the Lacedæmonian left as memorials. 227. Next to him, two Lacedæmonian brothers, Alpheus and Maron, sons of Orisiphantus, are said to have distinguished themselves most; and of the Thespians, he obtained the greatest glory whose name was Dithyrambus, son of Harmatides. 228. In honor of the slain, who were buried on the spot where they fell, and of those who died before they who were dismissed by Leonidas went away, the following inscription has been engraved over them: "Four thousand from Peloponnesus once fought on this spot with

three hundred myriads." This inscription was made for all; and for the Spartans in particular: "Stranger, go tell the Lacedæmonians that we lie here, obedient to their commands." This was for the Lacedæmonians; and for the prophet, the following: "This is the monument of the illustrious Megistias, whom once the Medes, having passed the river Sperchius, slew; a prophet who, at the time well knowing the impending fate, would not abandon the leaders of Sparta." The Amphictyons are the persons who honored them with these inscriptions and columns, with the exception of the inscription to the prophet; that of the prophet Megistias, Simonides, son of Leoprepes, caused to be engraved, from personal friendship.

229. It is said that two of these three hundred, Eurytus and Aristodemus, when it was in the power of both, if they had agreed together, either to return alike safe to Sparta, since they had been dismissed from the camp by Leonidas, and were lying at Alpeni desperately afflicted with a disease of the eyes, or, if they would not return, to have died together with the rest—when it was in their power to do either of these, they could not agree; and being divided in opinion, Eurytus, having heard of the circuit made by the Persians, and having called for and put on his arms, ordered his helot to lead him to the combatants; and when he had led him, the man who led him ran away, but he, rushing into the midst of the throng, perished; but Aristodemus, failing in courage, was left behind. Now if it had happened that Aristodemus alone, being sick, had returned to Sparta, or if both had gone home together, in my opinion the Spartans would not have shown any anger against them; but now, since one of them perished, and the other, who had only the same excuse, refused to die, it was necessary for them to be exceedingly angry with Aristodemus. 230. Some say that Aristodemus thus got safe to Sparta, and on such a pretext; but others, that being sent as a messenger from the army, though he might have arrived while the battle was going on, he would not, but having lingered on the road, survived; while his fellow-messenger, arriving in time for the battle, died. 231. Aristodemus, having returned to Lacedæmon, met with insults and infamy. He was declared infamous by being treated as follows: not one of the Spartans would either give him fire or converse with him; and he met with insult, being

called Aristodemus the coward. However, in the battle of Platæa, he removed all the disgrace that attached to him.[7] 232. It is also said that another of the three hundred, whose name was Pantites, having been sent as a messenger to Thessaly, survived; and that he, on his return to Sparta, finding himself held in dishonor, hung himself. 233. The Thebans, whom Leontiades commanded, as long as they were with the Greeks, being constrained by necessity, fought against the king's army; but when they saw the forces of the Persians gaining the upper hand, as the Greeks with Leonidas were hastening to the hill, having separated from them, they held out their hands and went near the barbarians, saying the truest thing they could say, that "they were both on the side of the Medes, and were among the first who gave earth and water to the king, and that they came to Thermopylæ from compulsion, and were guiltless of the blow that had been inflicted on the king." So that, by saying this, they saved their lives; for they had the Thessalians as witnesses to what they said: they were not, however, fortunate in every respect; for when the barbarians seized them as they came up, some they slew, and the greater number of them, by the command of Xerxes, they branded with the royal mark, beginning with the general, Leontiades, whose son, Eurymachus, some time afterward, the Platæans slew, when he was commanding four hundred Thebans, and had got possession of the citadel of the Platæans. 234. Thus the Greeks fought at Thermopylæ. And Xerxes, having sent for Demaratus, questioned him, beginning as follows: "Demaratus, you are an honest man; I judge so from experience; for whatever you said has turned out accordingly. Now tell me how many the rest of the Lacedæmonians may be, and how many of them, or whether all, are such as these in war?" He answered, "O king, the number of all the Lacedæmonians is great, and their cities are many; but I shall inform you of that which you desire to know. In Laconia is Sparta, a city containing about eight thousand men; all these are equal to those who have fought here; the rest of the Lacedæmonians, however, are not equal to these, though brave." To this Xerxes said, "Demaratus, in what way can we conquer these men with the least trouble? come tell me, for you must be acquainted with the course of their counsels,

[7] See B. IX. chap. 71.

since you have been their king." 235. He replied, "O king, since you ask my advice so earnestly, it is right that I should tell you what is best. You should, then, dispatch three hundred ships of your naval force to the Laconian coast. Off that coast there lies an island called Cythera, which Chilon, the wisest man among us, said would be more advantageous to the Spartans if sunk to the bottom of the sea than if it remained above the water, always apprehending that some such thing would come from it as I am going to propose; not that he foresaw the arrival of your fleet, but fearing equally every naval force. Sallying from this island, then, let them alarm the Lacedæmonians; and when they have a war of their own near home, they will no longer give you cause to fear, lest they should succor the rest of Greece, while it is being taken by your land-forces. But when the rest of Greece is subdued, the Laconian territory, being left alone, will be feeble. If you will not act in this manner, you may expect that this will happen. There is in Peloponnesus a narrow isthmus; in this place, all the Peloponnesians being combined against you, expect to meet more violent struggles than the past; whereas, if you do as I advise, both this isthmus and the cities will submit to you without a battle." 236. After him spoke Achæmenes, who was brother of Xerxes, and commander of the naval forces, having been present at the conversation, and fearing lest Xerxes might be induced to adopt that plan: "O king, I perceive you listening to the suggestions of a man who envies your prosperity, or would betray your cause; for the Greeks are commonly of that character; they envy success, and hate superior power. If, therefore, in the present state of our affairs, after four hundred ships have been wrecked, you should detach three hundred more from the fleet to sail round Peloponnesus, our enemies may fight us upon equal terms; but if our fleet is kept together, it becomes invincible, and they will be unable to fight with us at all; moreover, the whole fleet will assist the land-forces, and the land-forces the fleet, by advancing together; but if you separate them, neither will they be useful to you, nor you to them. Having, therefore, ordered your own matters well, resolve to pay no attention to what your enemies are doing, how they will carry on the war, what they will do, or how much their numbers are; for they are able to think about themselves, and we, in like manner, about ourselves; but the Lacedæmonians, if they venture a battle against the Persians, will not cure this one present wound." 237. To this Xerxes answered: "Achæmenes, you appear to me to speak well, and I will act accordingly. But Demaratus said what he thought was best for me, though he is surpassed by you in judgment; for that I will not admit, that Demaratus is not well-disposed to my interests, forming my conclusion from what was before said by him, and from the fact that a citizen envies a fellow-citizen who is prosperous, and hates him in silence; nor, when a citizen asks for advice, will a fellow-citizen suggest what seems to him to be best, unless he has reached a high degree of virtue; such persons, however, are rare. But a friend bears the greatest regard for his friend in prosperity; and, when he asks his advice, gives him the best advice he can. I therefore enjoin all men for the future to abstain from calumny concerning Demaratus, since he is my friend." 238. Xerxes having spoken thus, passed through the dead; and having heard that Leonidas was king and general of the Lacedæmonians, he commanded them to cut off his head, and fix it upon a pole. It is clear to me from many other proofs, and not least of all from this, that king Xerxes was more highly incensed against Leonidas during his life than against any other man, for otherwise he would never have violated the respect due to his dead body, since the Persians, most of all men with whom I am acquainted, are wont to honor men who are brave in war. They, however, to whom the order was given to do this, did it.

239. But I return to that part of my narration where I before left it incomplete. The Lacedæmonians first had information that the king was preparing to invade Greece, and accordingly they sent to the oracle at Delphi, whereupon the answer was given them which I lately mentioned.[8] But they obtained their information in a remarkable manner; for Demaratus, son of Ariston, being in exile among the Medes, as I conjecture, and appearances support my opinion, was not well affected to the Lacedæmonians. However, it is a question whether he acted as he did from a motive of benevolence or by way of exultation; for when Xerxes had determined to invade Greece, Demaratus, who was then at Susa, and had

[8] Chap. 220.

heard of his intention, communicated it to the Lacedæmonians; but he was unable to make it known by any other means, for there was great danger of being detected; he, therefore, had recourse to the following contrivance. Having taken a folding tablet, he scraped off the wax, and then wrote the king's intention on the wood of the tablet; and having done this, he melted the wax again over the writing, in order that the tablet, being carried with nothing written on it, might occasion him no trouble from the guards upon the road. When it arrived at Sparta, the Lacedæmonians were unable to comprehend it, until, as I am informed, Gorgo, daughter of Cleomenes, and wife to Leonidas, made a suggestion, having considered the matter with herself, and bade them scrape off the wax and they would find letters written on the wood. They, having obeyed, found and read the contents, and forwarded them to the rest of the Greeks. These things are reported to have happened in this manner.

BOOK VIII.

URANIA.

THE Greeks who were assigned to the navy were these. The Athenians, who furnished one hundred and twenty-seven ships; but the Platæans, from a spirit of valor and zeal, though inexperienced in the sea-service, assisted the Athenians in manning the ships. The Corinthians furnished forty ships: the Megareans, twenty; the Chalcidians manned twenty, the Athenians having furnished them with ships; the Æginetæ, eighteen; the Sicyonians, twelve; the Lacedæmonians, ten; the Epidaurians, eight; the Eretrians, seven; the Trœzenians, five; the Styreans, two; and the Ceians, two ships and two penteconters; the Opuntian Locrians also came to their assistance with seven penteconters. 2. These, then, were they who were engaged in the war at Artemisium, and I have mentioned how each contributed to the number of the ships. The total of the ships assembled at Artemisium, besides the penteconters, was two hundred and seventy-one. The admiral, who had the chief power, the Spartans supplied, Eurybiades, son of Euryclides, for the allies had refused, "if the Lacedæmonian did not command, to follow Athenian leaders, but *said* they would break up the intended fleet." 3. For from the first there was a talk, even before they sent to Sicily to solicit an alliance, that it would be proper to intrust the navy to the Athenians; but as the allies opposed, the Athenians gave way, deeming it of high importance that Greece should be saved, and knowing that if they should quarrel about the command, Greece would be lost; herein thinking justly; for intestine discord is as much worse than war carried on in concert, as war is than peace. Being, therefore, convinced of this, they did not resist, but yielded as long as they had need of their assistance, as they clearly showed; for when, having repulsed the Persian, they were now contending for his country, they put forward as a pretext the arrogance of Pausanias, and deprived the Lacedæmonians of the chief command; but these things occurred afterward. 4. But at that time, those Greeks who had arrived at Artemisium, when they saw a vast number of ships drawn up at Aphetæ, and all parts full of troops, since the affairs of the barbarian turned out contrary to their expectation, in great consternation deliberated about retiring from Artemisium to the inner parts of Greece. The Eubœans, knowing that they were deliberating on this matter, entreated Eurybiades to remain a short time longer, until they could remove their children and domestics to a place of safety; but finding they could not persuade him, they then went over to the Athenian general, and prevailed on Themistocles, by a bribe of thirty talents, to promise that they would stay and engage the enemy by sea before Eubœa. 5. Themistocles, to retain the Greeks, did as follows. Of this money he gave five talents to Eurybiades, as if, indeed, he gave it from himself; and when he had gained him over, as Adimantus, son of Ocytus, the Corinthian commander, was the only person who resisted, affirming that he would sail away from Artemisium, and not stay, to him Themistocles said with an oath, "You shall not abandon us, for I will make you a greater present than the king of the Medes would send you for abandoning the allies." He at the same time said this, and sent three talents of silver on board the ship of Adimantus. They therefore, being swayed by the present, were gained over, and complied with the wishes of the Eubœans; but Themistocles himself was a considerable gainer, as he secretly kept the rest; but those who took part of this money thought it came from the Athenians on that condition.

6. They accordingly remained in Eubœa, and came to an engagement by sea. It happened in this manner. When the barbarians arrived at Aphetæ, in the afternoon, having been already informed that a few Grecian ships were stationed, and then descrying them at Artemisium, they were eager to attack, in the hope of taking them. However, they did not think it advisable to sail directly upon them for the following reasons, lest the Greeks, seeing them sailing toward them, should betake themselves to flight, and the night should cover their retreat, by which means they would escape; but, according to their saying, they thought that not even the torch-bearer would escape alive. 7. For this purpose, then, they had recourse to the following plan: having detached two hundred ships from the whole fleet, they sent them round, outside Sciathus, that they might not be seen by the enemy sailing round Eubœa, by Caphareus and round Geræstus to the Euripus; that so they might surround them, the one party arriving at the place appointed in that way, and intercepting their retreat, and themselves attacking them in front. Having determined on this, they dispatched the ships appointed for this service, themselves not intending to attack the Greeks that day, nor before the agreed signal should be seen, given by those who sailed round, announcing their arrival. These, then, they sent round, and set about taking the number of the rest of the ships at Aphetæ. 8. At this time, while they were taking the number of their ships, there was in this camp Scyllias of Scyone, the best diver of his time; he, in the shipwreck that happened off Pelion, had saved much of their treasure for the Persians, and had acquired a good deal for himself. This Scyllias had long before entertained the design of deserting to the Greeks, but had had no opportunity of doing so until that time. In what way he at length made his escape to the Grecians I can not certainly affirm, and I wonder whether the account given is true; for it is said that, having plunged into the sea at Aphetæ, he never rose until he reached Arte-

misium, having passed this distance through the sea, as near as can be, eighty stadia. Many other things are related of this man that are very like falsehood, and some that are true. If, however, I may give my opinion of this matter, it is, that he came to Artemisium in a boat. On his arrival, he immediately informed the commanders of the shipwreck, how it had occurred, and of the ships that were sent round to Eubœa. 9. The Greeks, having heard this, held a conference among themselves; and, after much debate, it was resolved that, remaining there and continuing in their station during that day, then, when midnight was passed, they should proceed, and meet the ships that were sailing round. But after this, when no ship sailed against them, having waited for the evening of the day, they sailed of themselves against the barbarians, being desirous to make trial of their manner of fighting, and of breaking through the line. 10. The other soldiers of Xerxes, and the commanders, seeing them sailing toward them with so few ships, attributed their conduct to madness, and, on their part, got their ships under weigh, expecting that they should easily take them; and their expectations were very reasonable, when they saw that the Grecian ships were few, and their own many more in number, and better sailers; taking these things into consideration, they inclosed them in the middle of a circle. Now such of the Ionians as were well-affected to the Greeks, and joined the expedition unwillingly, regarded it as a great calamity when they saw them surrounded, feeling convinced that not one of them would return, so weak did the Grecian forces appear to them to be. But such as were pleased with what was going on, vied with each other how each might be the first to take an Athenian ship, and receive a reward from the king; for throughout the fleet they had the highest opinion of the Athenians. 11. When the signal was given to the Greeks, first of all turning their prows against the barbarians, they contracted their sterns inwardly to the middle; and when the second signal was given, they commenced the attack, though inclosed in a narrow space, and that prow to prow. On this occasion they took thirty ships of the barbarians, and Philaon, son of Chersis, the brother of Gorgus, king of the Salaminians, a man highly esteemed in their army. Lycomedes, son of Æschreus, an Athenian, was the first of the Greeks who took a ship from the enemy, and he received the palm of valor. But night coming on separated the combatants, who in this engagement fought with doubtful success. The Greeks returned to Artemisium, and the barbarians to Aphetæ, having fought with far different success than they expected. In this engagement, Antidorus, a Lemnian, was the only one of the Greeks in the king's service who went over to the Grecians, and on that account the Athenians presented him with lands in Salamis.

12. When night came on, and it was now the middle of summer, heavy rain fell through the whole night, and violent thunder about Pelion; but the dead bodies and pieces of wreck were driven to Aphetæ, and got entangled round the prows of the ships, and impeded the blades of the oars. But the soldiers who were on board, when they heard the thunder, were seized with terror, expecting that they must certainly perish, into such calamities had they fallen; for before they had recovered breath, after the wreck and tempest that had occurred off Pelion, a fierce engagement followed, and after the engagement, impetuous rain and mighty torrents rushing into the sea, and violent thunder. Such was the night to them. 13. But to those who had been appointed to sail round Eubœa, this same night proved so much the more wild, in that it fell upon them while they were in the open sea, and the end was grievous to them; for as they were sailing, the storm and rain overtook them when they were near the Cœla of Eubœa, and being driven by the wind, and not knowing where they were driven, they were dashed upon the rocks. All this was done by the deity, that the Persian might be brought to an equality with the Grecian, or, at least, not be greatly superior. Thus they perished near the Cœla of Eubœa. 14. The barbarians at Aphetæ, when to their great joy day dawned, kept their ships at rest, and were content, after they had suffered so much, to remain quiet for the present; but three and fifty Attic ships came to re-enforce the Greeks, and both these by their arrival gave them additional courage, as did the news that came at the same time, that those of the barbarians who were sailing round Eubœa had all perished in the late storm; therefore, having waited to the same hour, they set sail and attacked the Cilician ships, and,

having destroyed them, as soon as it was night they sailed back to Artemisium.

15. On the third day, the commanders of the barbarians, indignant at being insulted by so few ships, and fearing the displeasure of Xerxes, no longer waited for the Greeks to begin the battle, but, encouraging one another, got under weigh about the middle of the day. It happened that these actions by sea and those by land at Thermopylæ took place on the same days; and the whole struggle for those at sea was for the Euripus, as for those with Leonidas to guard the pass; the one party encouraging each other not to suffer the barbarians to enter Greece, and the other to destroy the Grecian forces, and make themselves masters of the channel. 16. When the barbarians, having formed in line, sailed onward, the Grecians remained still at Artemisium; but the barbarians, having drawn up their ships in the form of a crescent, encircled them as if they would take them, whereupon the Greeks sailed out to meet them, and engaged. In this battle they were nearly equal one to another, for the fleet of Xerxes, by reason of its magnitude and number, impeded itself, as the ships incommoded and ran foul of one another; however, they continued to fight, and would not yield, for they were ashamed to be put to flight by a few ships. Accordingly, many ships of the Grecians perished, and many men, and of the barbarians a much greater number both of ships and men. Having fought in this manner, they separated from each other. 17. In this engagement the Egyptians signalized themselves among the forces of Xerxes, for they both achieved other great actions, and took five Grecian ships, with their crews. On the part of the Greeks, the Athenians signalized themselves on this day, and among the Athenians, Clinias, son of Alcibiades, who at his own expense joined the fleet with two hundred men and a ship of his own.

18. When they had separated, each gladly hastened to their own stations; but the Grecians, when, having left the battle, they had withdrawn, were in possession of the dead and of the wrecks, yet, having been severely handled, and especially the Athenians, the half of whose ships were disabled, they consulted about a retreat to the interior of Greece. 19. But Themistocles having considered with himself that if the Ioni-

ans and Carians could be detached from the barbarian, they would be able to overcome the rest; as the Eubœans were driving their cattle down to the shore, he there assembled the Grecian commanders together, and told them that he thought he had a contrivance by which he hoped to draw off the best of the king's allies. This, then, he so far discovered to them, but in the present state of affairs he told them what they ought to do; every one should kill as many of the Eubœan cattle as he thought fit; for it was better that their own army should have them than the enemy. He also advised them each to direct their own men to kindle fires, and promised that he would choose such a time for their departure that they should all arrive safe in Greece. These things they were pleased to do; and forthwith, having kindled fires, they fell upon the cattle. 20. For the Eubœans, disregarding the oracles of Bacis as importing nothing, had neither carried out any thing to a place of safety, nor collected stores, as if war was approaching, and so had brought their affairs into a precarious state. The oracle of Bacis respecting them was as follows: "Beware of the barbarian-tongued, when he shall cast a byblus-yoke across the sea, remove the bleating goats from Eubœa." As they paid no attention to these verses, in the calamities then present and those that were impending, they fell into the greatest distress. 21. They, then, were acting thus, and in that conjuncture the scout arrived from Trachis; for there was a scout stationed off Artemisium, Polyas of Anticyra, who had been ordered (and he had a well-furnished boat ready), if the fleet should be in difficulty, to make it known to those that were at Thermopylæ; and in like manner Abronychus, son of Lysicles an Athenian, was with Leonidas, ready to carry the tidings to those at Artemisium in a triëconter, if any reverse should happen to the land-forces. This Abronychus then arriving, informed them of what had befallen Leonidas and his army; but they, when they heard it, no longer deferred their departure, but retired each in the order in which they were stationed, the Corinthians first, and the Athenians last.

22. Themistocles, having selected the best sailing ships of the Athenians, went to the places where there was water fit for drinking, and engraved upon the stones inscriptions, which the Ionians, upon arriving next day at Artemisium,

read. The inscriptions were to this effect: "Men of Ionia, you do wrong in fighting against your fathers, and helping to enslave Greece; rather, therefore, come over to us; or, if you can not do that, withdraw your forces from the contest, and entreat the Carians to do the same; but if neither of these things is possible, and you are bound by too strong a necessity to revolt, yet in action, when we are engaged, behave ill on purpose, remembering that you are descended from us, and that the enmity of the barbarian against us originally sprung from you." Themistocles, in my opinion, wrote this with two objects in view; that either, if the inscriptions escaped the notice of the king, he might induce the Ionians to change sides and come over to them; or, if they were reported to him, and made a subject of accusation before Xerxes, they might make the Ionians suspected, and cause them to be excluded from the sea-fights. 23. Themistocles left this inscription, and immediately afterward a certain Histiæan came to the barbarians in a boat, announcing the flight of the Greeks from Artemisium; but they, through distrust, kept the man who brought the news under guard, and dispatched some swift vessels to reconnoitre. When they reported the truth as it was, the whole fleet, as soon as the sun's rays were spread, sailed in a body to Artemisium; and having waited in that place until midday, they then sailed to Histiæa, and on their arrival possessed themselves of the city of the Histiæans, and ravaged all the maritime villages of the Ellopian district, in the territory of Histiæotis.

24. While they were on this coast, Xerxes, having made preparations with respect to the dead, sent a herald to the fleet. And he made the following previous preparations. Of those of his own army who were slain at Thermopylæ, and they were about twenty thousand, of these, having left about one thousand, the remainder, having caused pits to be dug, he buried, throwing leaves over them and heaping up earth, that they might not be seen by those who should come from the fleet. When the herald crossed over to Histiæa, having convened a meeting of the whole encampment, he spoke as follows: "Allies, king Xerxes permits any of you who please to leave his post, and come and see how he fights against those senseless men who hoped to overcome the king's power." 25. After he had made this announcement, nothing was more

scarce than boats, so many were anxious to behold the sight; and, having crossed over, they went through and viewed the dead; and all thought that those that lay there were all Lacedæmonians and Thespians, though they also saw the Helots; however, Xerxes did not deceive those who had crossed over by what he had done with respect to his own dead, for indeed it was ridiculous; of the one party a thousand dead were seen lying; but the others lay all heaped up together, to the number of four thousand. This day they spent in the view, and on the next they returned to Histiæa, to their ships, and those with Xerxes set out on their march. 26. Some few deserters came to them from Arcadia in search of subsistence, and wished to be actively employed: taking these men into the king's presence, the Persians inquired concerning the Greeks, what they were doing. One in particular it was who asked them this question. They answered that they were celebrating the Olympic games, and viewing gymnastic combats and horse-races. He then asked what was the reward proposed to them for which they contended. They mentioned the crown of olive that is given. Upon which Tritantæchmes, son of Artabanus, having uttered a noble sentiment, incurred the charge of cowardice from the king; for, having heard that the prize was a crown, and not riches, he could not remain silent, but spoke as follows before all: "Heavens, Mardonius, against what kind of men have you brought us to fight, who contend, not for wealth, but for glory!" This, then, was said by him.

27. In the mean time, and when the defeat had occurred at Thermopylæ, the Thessalians immediately sent a herald to the Phocians, as they had always[1] entertained a grudge against them, and particularly since their last defeat; for not many years before this expedition of the king, the Thessalians themselves and their allies, having invaded the territories of the Phocians with all their forces, had been worsted by the Phocians and roughly handled; for when the Phocians had been shut up in Mount Parnassus, having with them the Elean prophet Tellias, this Tellias thereupon devised the following stratagem for them. Having smeared over with chalk six hundred of the bravest Phocians, both the men themselves and their armor, he attacked the Thessalians by night, having ordered them to kill every man they should see not covered

[1] See B. VII. chap. 176.

with white. The sentinels of the Thessalians, accordingly, seeing them first, were terrified, supposing it was some strange prodigy, and after the sentinels, the whole army, so that the Phocians got possession of four thousand dead and shields; of these they dedicated one half at Abæ, and the other at Delphi. The tenth of the treasures taken in this battle composed those great statues which stand about the tripod in the front of the temple at Delphi, and others like them were dedicated at Abæ. 28. Thus the Phocians dealt with the infantry of the Thessalians who were besieging them, and they inflicted an irreparable blow on their cavalry when they made an irruption into their territory; for in the entrance which is near Hyampolis, having dug a large pit, they put empty jars in it, and having heaped soil over and made it like the rest of the ground, they waited the attack of the Thessalians; but they, hoping to overwhelm the Phocians, being borne violently on, fell among the jars, whereupon the horses had their legs broken. 29. The Thessalians, bearing a grudge against them for these two things, sent a herald, and made the following announcement: "O Phocians, now at length learn better, and know that you are not equal to us; for both before among the Greeks, as long as that party pleased us, we always proved superior to you; and now, we have so great influence with the barbarian, that it is in our power to deprive you of your country, and, moreover, to reduce you to slavery. We, however, though possessing full power, are not mindful of injuries; therefore, let fifty talents of silver be given us by way of reparation, and we promise you to avert the evils that impend over your country."

30. The Thessalians sent them this message; for the Phocians were the only people of those parts who did not side with the Mede; for no other reason, as I conjecture, than their hatred of the Thessalians; but if the Thessalians had taken part with the Greeks, in my opinion the Phocians would have sided with the Mede. When the Thessalians sent this message, they said they would not give money, and that it was in their power to join the Mede as well as the Thessalians, if they only chose to do so, but that they would not willingly be traitors to Greece. 31. When this answer was brought back, the Thessalians thereupon, being incensed with the Phocians, became guides to the barbarian; and, accord-

ingly, they entered from Trachinia into Doris; for a narrow strip of Doric territory extends that way, about thirty stades in breadth, and situate between the Malian and Phocian territory, and which was anciently Dryopis. This region is the mother country of the Dorians in Peloponnesus. The barbarians, in their passage through, did not ravage this Doric territory; for the inhabitants sided with the Mede, and the Thessalians wished them not to do so. 32. When they entered from the Doric to the Phocian territory, they did not take the Phocians themselves, for some of the Phocians had ascended to the heights of Parnassus; and the summit of Parnassus lying near the city of Neon, which stands apart, is well adapted to receive a multitude; its name is Tithorea; to this, then, they carried their property, and ascended themselves; but the greater number of them had conveyed their effects to the Locrian Ozolæ, to the city of Amphissa, which is situate on the Crisæan plain. But the barbarians overran the whole Phocian territory. 33. For marching this way along the river Cephissus, they ravaged the whole country, and burned down the cities of Drymus, Charadra, Erochus, Tethronium, Amphicæa, Neon, Pedieæ, Triteæ, Elatea, Hyampolis, Parapotamii, and Abæ, where was a rich temple of Apollo, adorned with many treasures and offerings, and there was then, and still is, an oracle there; this temple they plundered and burned; and pursuing some of the Phocians, they took them near the mountains; and they caused the death of some women by having intercourse with them in great numbers. 34. The barbarians, having passed by Parapotamii, arrived at Panopeæ, and from thence their army, being divided, proceeded in two bodies. The largest and most powerful part of the army, marching with Xerxes himself toward Athens, entered Bœotia at the territory of the Orchomenians. But the Bœotians sided with the Mede; Macedonian soldiers, therefore, posted in different places, having been sent by Alexander, saved their cities; and they saved them in order by this means to make it known to Xerxes that the Bœotians favored the cause of the Medes. These barbarians, then, took this route.

35. The rest of them, having guides, proceeded toward the temple of Delphi, keeping Parnassus on their right; and whatever parts of Phocis they came to, they pillaged; for they set fire to the city of the Panopians, and of the Daulians, and

the Æolidæ. They marched this way detached from the rest of the army for this reason, that having plundered the temple at Delphi, they might present the treasures to king Xerxes; but Xerxes, as I am informed, knew every thing that was of value in the temple better than what he had left at home, many persons continually telling him, especially of the offerings of Crœsus, son of Alyattes. 36. The Delphians having heard of this, fell into a great consternation; and being in a state of great terror, consulted the oracle respecting the sacred treasures, whether they should hide them under ground, or transport them to another country. But the god would not suffer them to be moved, saying "that he was able to protect his own." The Delphians, having received this answer, began to think of themselves; accordingly, they sent their children and wives across to Achaia, and the greater part of the men ascended to the tops of Parnassus, and carried their effects into the Corycian cavern, while others withdrew to the Locrian Amphissa. Thus all the Delphians abandoned the city except only sixty men and the prophet. 37. When the barbarians were advanced near, and saw the temple in the distance, then the prophet, whose name was Aceratus, saw the sacred arms, which it was not lawful for any mortal to touch, lying before the temple, having been brought out from within the fane. He therefore went to make known the prodigy to the Delphians who were at hand. But when the barbarians, hastening their march, were near the temple of Minerva Pronæa, prodigies still greater than the former succeeded. And this, indeed, is a great wonder, that warlike instruments should be seen, self-moved, lying before the temple, yet the second prodigies, which succeeded after this, are worthy of admiration beyond all other portents; for when the barbarians had advanced near the temple of Minerva Pronæa, at that moment thunder fell on them from heaven, and two crags, broken away from Parnassus, bore down upon them with a loud crash, and killed many of them, and a loud cry and a war-shout issued from the temple of the Pronæa. 38. All these things being commingled together, a panic struck the barbarians; and the Delphians, having learned that they had fled, came down after them, and slew a great number of them: the survivors fled direct into Bœotia. Those of the barbarians who returned, as I am informed, declared that, besides these, they saw other miraculous things, for that two heavy-armed men, of more than human stature, followed them, slaying and pursuing them. 39. The Delphians say these two were heroes of the country, Phylacus and Autonous, whose precincts are near the temple; that of Phylacus by the road-side, above the temple of the Pronæa, and that of Autonous near the Castalian spring under the Hyampeian summit. The rocks that fell from Parnassus were still preserved in my time, lying in the inclosure of Minerva Pronæa, where they fell when borne among the barbarians. Such, then, was the retreat of these men from the temple.

40. The Grecian fleet from Artemisium, at the request of the Athenians, put in at Salamis. For this reason, the Athenians requested them to direct their course to Salamis, that they might remove their children and wives out of Attica, and, moreover, might consult of what measures were to be taken; for, in the present posture of affairs, they intended to hold a consultation, as they had been disappointed in their expectation; for whereas they expected to find the Peloponnesians with all their forces waiting in Bœotia to receive the barbarian, they found nothing of the kind, but were informed that they were fortifying the isthmus leading into the Peloponnesus, considering it of the greatest importance that it should be saved, and that, keeping guard there, they gave up all the rest. Having been informed of this, they therefore entreated them to direct their course to Salamis. 41. The rest, therefore, held on to Salamis, but the Athenians to their own country; and on their arrival they caused proclamation to be made "that every one should save his children and family by the best means he could;" thereupon the greatest part sent away *their families* to Trœzene, some to Ægina, and others to Salamis. They used all diligence to remove them to a place of safety, both from a desire to obey the oracle, and more particularly for the following reason: the Athenians say that a large serpent used to live in the temple as a guard to the Acropolis; they both say this, and, as if it were really there, they do it honor by placing before it its monthly food: the monthly food consists of a honey-cake; this honey-cake having been in former time always consumed, now remained untouched. When the priestess made this known, the Athenians with more readiness abandoned the city, since even the goddess had forsaken the Acropolis. As soon as every thing had

been deposited in a place of safety, they sailed to the encampment. 42. When those from Artemisium stationed their ships at Salamis, the rest of the naval forces of the Greeks being informed of this, joined them from Trœzene; for they had been ordered to assemble at Pogon, a harbor of the Trœzenians. Many more ships were assembled together than had fought at Artemisium, and from a greater number of cities. The same admiral commanded them as at Artemisium, Eurybiades, son of Euryclides, a Spartan, though he was not of the royal family. The Athenians, however, furnished by far the most and the best sailing ships.

43. The following joined the fleet. From the Peloponnesus, the Lacedæmonians, furnishing sixteen ships; the Corinthians, furnishing the same number as at Artemisium; the Sicyonians furnished fifteen ships; the Epidaurians, ten; the Trœzenians, five; and the Hermionians, three: all these, except the Hermionians, being of Doric and Macednic extraction, having come from Erineum, and Pindus, and last of all from Dryopis. The Hermionians are Dryopians, driven out by Hercules and the Malians from the country now called Doris. These, then, of the Peloponnesians, served in the fleet. 44. The following were from the outer continent: the Athenians, beyond all the rest, alone furnished one hundred and eighty ships; for at Salamis the Platæans did not join their forces to the Athenians, on account of the following circumstance. When the Greeks retired from Artemisium, and were off Chalcis, the Platæans, having landed on the opposite coast in Bœotia, set about carrying away their families; they, therefore, while saving them, were left behind. The Athenians, when the Pelasgians possessed that which is now called Greece, were Pelasgians, and went by the name of Cranai: under the reign of Cecrops they were surnamed Cecropidæ; but when Erectheus succeeded to the government, they changed their name for that of Athenians; and when Ion, son of Xuthus, became their leader, from him they were called Ionians. 45. The Megarenes furnished the same complement as at Artemisium; the Ambraciots assisted with seven ships; and the Leucadians, three: these are of Doric extraction, from Corinth. 46. Of the islanders, the Æginetæ furnished thirty ships; they had also other ships ready manned, but with some they guarded their own country, and with thirty the best sailing

vessels, they fought at Salamis. The Æginetæ are Dorians from Epidaurus, and their island formerly had the name of Œnone. Next to the Æginetæ, the Chalcidians furnished the same twenty as at Artemisium, and the Eretrians the same seven: these are Ionians. Next, the Ceians furnished the same: they are of Ionian extraction, from Athens. The Naxians, four, though they had been sent by their fellow-citizens to join the Medes, like the rest of the islanders; but, disregarding their orders, they went over to the Greeks, at the instigation of Democritus, a man eminent among the citizens, and then commander of a trireme. The Naxians also are Ionians, sprung from Athens. The Styreans furnished the same ships as at Artemisium; the Cythnians, one and a penteconter: both these people are Dryopians. The Seriphians, the Siphnians, and the Malians also joined the fleet, for they only of the islanders refused to give earth and water to the barbarian. 47. All these nations, situate on this side the Thesprotians and the river Acheron, joined the fleet, for the Thesprotians border on the Ampraciots and Leucadians, who joined the fleet from the most distant countries. Of those that dwell beyond them, the Crotoniatæ were the only people who came to assist Greece in this time of danger, with one ship, which Phayllus, who had thrice been victorious in the Pythian games, commanded. The Crotoniatæ are Achæans by extraction. 48. Now the rest joined the fleet, furnishing triremes, but the Malians, Siphnians, and Seriphians penteconters. The Malians, who are by extraction from Lacedæmon, furnished two; the Siphnians and the Seriphians, who are Ionians from Athens, one each; so that the whole number of ships, besides the penteconters, amounted to three hundred and seventy-eight.

49. When the leaders from the above-mentioned cities met together at Salamis, they held a council, *in which* Eurybiades proposed that any one who chose should deliver his opinion where he thought it would be most advantageous to come to an engagement by sea, of all the places of which they were still in possession; for Attica was already given up, and he made this proposition concerning the rest. Most of the opinions of those who spoke coincided that they should sail to the Isthmus and fight before Peloponnesus, alleging this reason, that if they should be conquered by sea while they were at

Salamis, they should be besieged in the island, where no succor could reach them; but if at the Isthmus, they might escape to their own cities.

50. While the commanders from Peloponnesus were debating these matters, an Athenian arrived with intelligence that the barbarian had entered Attica, and was devastating the whole of it by fire; for the army with Xerxes, having taken its route through Bœotia, after having burned the city of the Thespians, who had departed to Peloponnesus, and likewise the city of the Platæans, had arrived at Athens, and was laying waste every part of it. They set fire to Thespia and Platæa, being informed by the Thebans that they were not on the side of the Medes. 51. From the passage over the Hellespont, thence the barbarians began to march, having spent one month there, including the time they were crossing over into Europe; in three months more they were in Attica, when Calliades was archon of the Athenians. They took the city, deserted of inhabitants, but found some few of the Athenians in the temple, with the treasurers of the temple, and some poor people, who, having fortified the Acropolis with planks and stakes, tried to keep off the invaders: they had not withdrawn to Salamis, partly through want of means, and, moreover, they thought they had found out the meaning of the oracle which the Pythian delivered to them, that the wooden wall "should be impregnable," *imagining* that this was the refuge according to the oracle, and not the ships. 52. The Persians, posting themselves on the hill opposite the Acropolis, which the Athenians call the Areopagus, besieged them in the following manner: when they had wrapped tow round their arrows and set fire to it, they shot them at the fence; thereupon those Athenians who were besieged still defended themselves, though driven to the last extremity, and the fence had failed them; nor, when the Pisistratidæ proposed them, would they listen to terms of capitulation, but, still defending themselves, they both contrived other means of defense, and when the barbarians approached the gates they hurled down large round stones, so that Xerxes was for a long time kept in perplexity, not being able to capture them. 53. At length, in the midst of these difficulties, an entrance was discovered by the barbarians; for it was necessary, according to the oracle, that all Attica on the continent should be subdued by the

Persians. In front of the Acropolis, then, but behind the gates and the road up, where neither any one kept guard, nor would ever have expected that any man would ascend that way, there some of them ascended near the temple of Cecrops's daughter Aglauros, although the place was precipitous. When the Athenians saw that they had ascended to the Acropolis, some threw themselves down from the wall and perished, and others took refuge in the recess of the temple; but the Persians who had ascended first turned to the gates, and having opened them, put the suppliants to death; and when all were thrown prostrate, having pillaged the temple, they set fire to the whole Acropolis.

54. Xerxes, having entire possession of Athens, dispatched a messenger on horseback to Susa to announce to Artabanus his present success; and on the second day after the dispatch of the herald, having summoned the exiled Athenians who attended him, he ordered them to offer sacrifices after their own manner, having ascended to the Acropolis; whether he gave this order from having seen a vision in a dream, or a religious scruple came upon him for having set fire to the temple. The exiles of the Athenians performed what was commanded. 55. Why I have recorded these things I will now mention. There is in this Acropolis a shrine of Erectheus, who is said to be earth-born: in this is an olive-tree and a sea, which, as the story goes among the Athenians, Neptune and Minerva, when contending for the country, placed there as testimonies. Now it happened that this olive-tree was burned by the barbarians with the rest of the temple; but on the second day after the burning, the Athenians who were ordered by the king to sacrifice, when they went up to the temple, saw a shoot from the stump sprung up to the height of a cubit. This they affirmed.

56. The Greeks at Salamis, when intelligence was brought them how matters were with respect to the Acropolis of the Athenians, were thrown into such consternation, that some of the generals would not wait until the subject before them was decided on, but rushed to their ships and hoisted sail, as about to hurry away; by such of them as remained it was determined to come to an engagement before the Isthmus. Night came on, and they, being dismissed from the council, went on board their ships. 57. Thereupon Mnesiphilus, an Athenian, inquired of Themistocles, on his return to his ship, what had

been determined on by them; and being informed by him that it was resolved to conduct the ships to the Isthmus, and to come to an engagement before the Peloponnesus, he said, "If they remove the ships from Salamis, you will no longer fight for any country, for they will each betake themselves to their cities; and neither will Eurybiades nor any one else be able to detain them, so that the fleet should not be dispersed; and Greece will perish through want of counsel. But, if there is any possible contrivance, go and endeavor to annul the decree, if by any means you can induce Eurybiades to alter his determination, so as to remain here." 58. The suggestion pleased Themistocles exceedingly; and, without giving any answer, he went to the ship of Eurybiades, and on reaching it, he said that he wished to confer with him on public business. He desired him to come on board his ship, and say what he wished; thereupon Themistocles, seating himself by him, repeated all that he had heard from Mnesiphilus, making it his own, and adding much more, until he prevailed on him, by entreaty, to leave his ship, and assemble the commanders in council. 59. When they were assembled, before Eurybiades brought forward the subject on account of which he had convened the commanders, Themistocles spoke much, as being very earnest; and as he was speaking, the Corinthian general, Adimantus, son of Ocytus, said, "O Themistocles, in the games, those who start before the time are beaten with stripes." But he, excusing himself, answered, "But they who are left behind are not crowned." 60. At that time he answered the Corinthian mildly; but to Eurybiades he said not a word of what he had before mentioned, that if they should remove from Salamis, they would disperse themselves; for when the allies were present, it would be by no means becoming in him to accuse any one; he therefore made use of another argument, speaking as follows: (1.) "It rests now with you to save Greece, if you will listen to me, and, remaining here, give battle, and not attend to those who advise you to remove the fleet to the Isthmus. For hear and compare each opinion. In engaging near the Isthmus, you will fight in the open sea, where it is least advantageous to us who have heavier ships and fewer in number. Besides, you will lose Salamis, and Megara, and Ægina, even if we succeed in other respects; for the land-forces will follow close upon their navy; thus you will yourself lead them to the Peloponnesus, and expose all Greece to danger. (2.) But if you should do what I advise, you will find the following advantages in it. First of all, by engaging in a narrow space with few ships against many, if the probable results of war happen, we shall be much superior; for to fight in a narrow space is advantageous to us, but in a wide space to them. Again, Salamis is preserved, in which our children and wives are deposited. Moreover, there is advantage in the plan I advise, for which, too, you are very anxious: by remaining here, you will fight for the Peloponnesus just as much as at the Isthmus; nor, if you are wise, will you lead them to the Peloponnesus. (3.) But if what I hope should happen, and we conquer with our fleet, neither will the barbarians come to you at the Isthmus, nor will they advance farther than Attica, but will retreat in disorder, and we shall gain, by saving Megara, and Ægina, and Salamis, where it is announced by an oracle we shall be superior to our enemies. To men who determine on what is reasonable, corresponding results are for the most part wont to follow; but to those who do not determine on what is reasonable, the deity is not wont to further human designs." 61. When Themistocles had spoken thus, Adimantus the Corinthian again attacked him, bidding him who had no country be silent, and urging Eurybiades not to go to the vote for a man who had no city; for when Themistocles showed a city, then he would allow him to give his suffrage. He threw out this against him because Athens had been taken, and was in the possession *of the enemy*. Then, at length, Themistocles spoke with much severity of Adimantus and the Corinthians, and showed by his speech that *the Athenians* themselves had a city and a territory greater than they, so long as they had two hundred ships fully manned, for that none of the Greeks could repel their attack. 62. Having intimated this, he transferred his discourse to Eurybiades, saying, with great earnestness, "If you remain here, by remaining you will show yourself a brave man; if not, you will subvert Greece, for the whole success of the war depends on our fleet; therefore yield to my advice; but if you will not do so, we, as we are, will take our families on board and remove to Siris in Italy, which is an ancient possession of ours, and oracles say it is fated to be founded by us; and you, when bereft of such allies, will remember my words." 63. When Themistocles had spoken thus, Eurybiades changed his opinion: in my opinion, he changed his opinion chiefly from a dread of the Athenians, lest they should desert them if he took the fleet to the Isthmus; for if the Athenians deserted them, the rest would no longer be a match for the enemy. He therefore adopted this advice, to stay there and come to a decisive engagement. 64. Thus they at Salamis, having skirmished in words, when Eurybiades had come to a determination, made preparations to come to an engagement there. Day came, and at sunrise an earthquake took place on land and at sea. They determined to pray to the gods, and to invoke the Æacidæ as allies; and as they had determined, so they did; for, having prayed to all the gods, they forthwith, from Salamis, invoked Ajax and Telamon, and sent a ship to Ægina for Æacus and the Æacidæ. 65. Dicæus, son of Theocydes, an Athenian, and an exile at that time esteemed by the Medes, related, that when the Attic territory was being devastated by the land-forces of Xerxes, having been deserted by the Athenians, he happened then to be with Demaratus the Lacedæmonian in the Thriasian plain, and he saw a cloud of dust coming from Eleusis, as if occasioned by about thirty thousand men; they were wondering at the cloud of dust, from whatever it might proceed, and suddenly heard a voice, and the voice appeared to him to be that of the mystic Iacchus. Demaratus was unacquainted with the mysteries of Eleusis, and asked Dicæus what it might be that was uttered; but he said, "O Demaratus, it can not be otherwise than that some great damage will befall the king's army; for this is clear, since Attica is deserted, that what is uttered is supernatural, proceeding from Eleusis to the assistance of the Athenians and the allies; and if it should rush toward the Peloponnesus, there will be danger to the king himself, and his army on the continent; but if it should turn toward the ships at Salamis, the king will be in danger of losing his naval armament. The Athenians celebrate this feast every year to the Mother and the Damsel,[2] and whoever wishes of them and the other Greeks is initiated; and the sound which you hear, they shout in this very festival." To this Demaratus said, "Be silent, and tell this story to no one else; for if these words should be reported to the king, you

[2] Ceres and Proserpine.

would lose your head; and neither should I nor any other human being be able to save you. Keep quiet, therefore, and the gods will take care of the army." He accordingly gave this advice; but from the dust and voice there arose a cloud, and being raised aloft it was borne toward Salamis, to the encampment of the Greeks. Thus they understood that the fleet of Xerxes was about to perish. This account Dicæus, son of Theocydes, gave, calling on Demaratus and others as witnesses.

66. When the men belonging to the fleet of Xerxes, having viewed the Lacedæmonian loss, crossed over from Trachis to Histiæa, they remained there three days, and then sailed through the Euripus, and in three days more arrived off Phalerus. In my opinion, they were not fewer in number when they entered Athens, as well those that came by the continent as those in the ships, than when they arrived at Sepias and at Thermopylæ; for I set off against those that perished by the storm, and at Thermopylæ, and at the sea-fight at Artemisium, the following, who, at that time, did not attend the king: the Malians, Dorians, Locrians, and Bœotians, who attended with all their forces, except the Thespians and Platæans; and, besides, the Carystians, Andrians, Tenians, and all the rest of the islanders, except the five cities whose names I have before mentioned; for the farther the Persian advanced into the interior of Greece, a greater number of nations attended him. 67. When, therefore, all these, except the Parians, arrived at Athens, the Parians, being left behind at Cythnus, watched the war, in what way it would turn out; when, however, the rest arrived at Phalerus, then Xerxes himself went down to the ships, wishing to mix with them, and to learn the opinion of those on board. When he had arrived and taken the first seat, the tyrants and admirals of the several nations, being summoned from their ships, came, and seated themselves according as the king had given precedence to each: first, the Sidonian king; next, the Tyrian; and then the others. When they had seated themselves in due order, Xerxes, having sent Mardonius, asked, in order to make trial of the disposition of each, whether he should come to an engagement by sea. 68. When Mardonius, going round, asked the question, beginning from the Sidonian, all the others gave an opinion to the same effect, advising that battle should

be given, but Artemisia spoke as follows: "Tell the king from me, Mardonius, that I say this. It is right that I, sire, who proved myself by no means a coward in the sea-fight off Eubœa, and performed achievements not inferior to others, should declare my real opinion, *and state* what I think best for your interest. Therefore I say this, abstain from using your ships, nor risk a sea-fight; for these men are so much superior to your men by sea, as men are to women. And why must you run a risk by a naval engagement? Have you not possession of Athens, for the sake of which you undertook this expedition, and have you not the rest of Greece? No one stands in your way; and those who still held out against you have fared as they deserved. (2.) In what way the affairs of your enemies will turn out, I will not say. If you should not hasten to engage in a sea-fight, but keep your fleet here, remaining near land, or even advancing to the Peloponnesus, you will easily effect what you came purposing to do; for the Greeks will not be able to hold out long against you, but you will disperse them, and they will respectively fly to their cities; for neither have they provisions in this island, as I am informed, nor is it probable, if you march your land-forces against the Peloponnesus, that those of them who came from thence will remain quiet, nor will they care to fight by sea for the Athenians. (3.) But if you should hasten forthwith to engage, I fear lest the sea-forces, being worsted, should at the same time bring ruin on the land-forces. Besides, O king, consider this, that the good among men commonly have bad slaves, and the bad ones good; and you, who are the best of all men, have bad slaves, who are said to be in the number of allies, such as the Egyptians, Cyprians, Cilicians, and Pamphylians, who are of no use at all." 69. When she said this to Mardonius, such as were well affected to Artemisia were grieved at her words, thinking she would suffer some harm at the king's hand, because she dissuaded him from giving battle by sea; but those who hated and envied her, as being honored above all the allies, were delighted with her decision, thinking she would be ruined. When, however, the opinions were reported to Xerxes, he was very much pleased with the opinion of Artemisia; and having before thought her an admirable woman, he then praised her much more. However, he gave orders to follow the advice of the majority in this matter, thinking that they had behaved ill at Eubœa on purpose, because he was not present; he now prepared in person to behold them engaging by sea.

70. When they gave the signal for putting to sea, they got the ships under weigh for Salamis, and drew up near it, taking their stations in silence: at that time, however, there was not day enough for them to enter on a naval engagement, for night was coming on; they therefore held themselves in readiness for the next day. But fear and dismay took possession of the Greeks, and not least those from Peloponnesus. They were dismayed, because, being posted at Salamis, they were about to fight for the territory of the Athenians; and if conquered, they would be shut up and besieged in the island, having left their own country defenseless. 71. The land-forces of the barbarians marched that same night against the Peloponnesus, although every possible expedient had been contrived to hinder the barbarians from entering by the main land; for as soon as the Peloponnesians heard that those with Leonidas at Thermopylæ had perished, they flocked together from the cities and stationed themselves at the Isthmus; and Cleombrotus, son of Anaxandrides, and brother of Leonidas, commanded them. Having stationed themselves, therefore, at the Isthmus, and having blocked up the Scironian way, they then, as they determined on consultation, built a wall across the Isthmus. As they were many myriads in number, and every man labored, the work progressed rapidly; for stones, bricks, timber, and baskets full of sand were brought to it, and those who assisted flagged not a moment in their work, either by night or day. 72. Those who assisted at the Isthmus with all their forces were the following of the Greeks; the Lacedæmonians, and all the Arcadians, the Eleans, Corinthians, Sicyonians, Epidaurians, Phliasians, Trœzenians, and Hermionians. These were they who assisted, and were very much alarmed at the dangerous situation of Greece; but the rest of the Peloponnesians did not concern themselves about it; however, the Olympian and Carnian festivals were now past. 73. Seven nations inhabit the Peloponnesus: of these, two, being indigenous, are now seated in the same country in which they originally dwelt, the Arcadians and Cynurians. One nation, the Achæans, never removed from the Peloponnesus, though they did from their own territory, and now occupy

another. The remaining four nations of the seven are foreign, Dorians, Ætolians, Dryopians, and Lemnians. The Dorians have many and celebrated cities; the Ætolians, only Elis; the Dryopians, Hermione and Asine, situate near Cardamyle of Laconia: the Lemnians have all the Paroreatæ. The Cynurians, who are indigenous, are the only people that appear to be Ionians; but they have become Dorians by being governed by the Argives, and through lapse of time, being Orneatæ[3] and neighboring inhabitants. Of these seven nations, the remaining cities, except those I have enumerated, remained neutral; or, if I may speak freely, by remaining neutral, favored the Mede.

74. Those at the Isthmus, then, persevered with such zeal, as having now to contend for their all, and as they did not expect to distinguish themselves by their fleet; meanwhile, those at Salamis, having heard of these things, were alarmed, not fearing so much for themselves as for the Peloponnesus. For some time, one man standing by another began to talk in secret, wondering at the imprudence of Eurybiades, till at last *their discontent* broke out openly, and a council was called, and much was said on the same subject. Some said that they ought to sail for the Peloponnesus, and hazard a battle for that, and not stay and fight for a place already taken by the enemy; but the Athenians, Æginetæ, and Megareans, that they should stay there and defend themselves. 75. Thereupon, Themistocles, when he saw his opinion was overruled by the Peloponnesians, went secretly out of the council; and having gone out, he dispatched a man in a boat to the encampment of the Medes, having instructed him what to say: his name was Sicinnus; and he was a domestic, and preceptor to the children of Themistocles; him, after these events, Themistocles got made a Thespian, when the Thespians augmented the number of their citizens, and gave him a competent fortune. He then, arriving in the boat, spoke as follows to the generals of the barbarians: "The general of the Athenians has sent me unknown to the rest of the Greeks (for he is in the interest of the king, and wishes that your affairs

[3] Baehr takes the word Orneatæ to describe people who were transplanted from a distance, and made to dwell near Argos. One advantage in following his interpretation is, that it obviates the necessity of altering the text.

may prosper rather than those of the Greeks), to inform you that the Greeks, in great consternation, are deliberating on flight, and you have now an opportunity of achieving the most glorious of all enterprises, if you do not suffer them to escape; for they do not agree among themselves, nor will they oppose you; but you will see those who are in your interest, and those who are not, fighting with one another." He, having delivered this message to them, immediately departed. 76. As these tidings appeared to them worthy of credit, in the first place, they landed a considerable number of Persians on the little island of Psyttalea, lying between Salamis and the continent; and, in the next place, when it was midnight, they got their western wing under weigh, drawing it in a circle toward Salamis, and those who were stationed about Ceos and Cynosura got under weigh, and occupied the whole passage as far as Munychia with their ships. And for this reason they got their ships under weigh, that the Greeks might have no way to escape, but being shut up in Salamis, might suffer punishment for the conflicts at Artemisium; and they landed the Persians at the little island of Psyttalea for this reason, that, when an engagement should take place, as they expected most part of the men and wrecks would be driven thither (for that island lay in the strait where the engagement was likely to take place), they might save the one party and destroy the other. But these things they did in silence, that the enemy might not know what was going on. They therefore made these preparations by night, without taking any rest.

77. I am unable to speak against the oracles as not being true, nor wish to impugn the authority of those that speak clearly, when I look on such occurrences as the following. "When they shall bridge with ships the sacred shore of Diana with the golden sword, and sea-girt Cynosura, having with mad hope destroyed beautiful Athens, then divine Vengeance shall quench strong Presumption, son of Insolence, when thinking to subvert all things; for brass shall engage with brass, and Mars shall redden the sea with blood. Then the far-thundering son of Saturn and benign victory shall bring a day of freedom to Greece." *Looking on* such occurrences, and regarding Bacis, who spoke thus clearly, I neither dare myself say any thing in contradiction to oracles, nor allow others to do so.

78. There was great altercation between the generals at Salamis; and they did not yet know that the barbarians had surrounded them with their ships, but they supposed that they were in the same place as they had seen them stationed in during the day. 79. While the generals were disputing, Aristides, son of Lysimachus, crossed over from Ægina: he was an Athenian, but had been banished by ostracism: having heard of his manner of life, I consider him to have been the best and most upright man in Athens. This person, standing at the entrance of the council, called Themistocles out, who was not indeed his friend, but his most bitter enemy; yet, from the greatness of the impending danger, he forgot that, and called him, wishing to confer with him; for he had already heard that those from Peloponnesus were anxious to get the ships under weigh for the Isthmus. When Themistocles came out to him, Aristides spoke as follows: "It is right that we should strive, both on other occasions, and particularly on this, which of us shall do the greatest service to our country. I assure you, that to say little or much to the Peloponnesians about sailing from hence is the same thing; for I, an eye-witness, tell you, now, even if they would, neither the Corinthians, nor Eurybiades himself, will be able to sail away, for we are on all sides inclosed by the enemy. Go in, therefore, and acquaint them with this." 80. He answered as follows: "You both give very useful advice, and have brought good news; for you are come yourself as an eye-witness of what I wished should happen. Know, then, that what has been done by the Medes proceeds from me; for it was necessary, since the Greeks would not willingly come to an engagement, that they should be compelled to it against their will. But do you, since you come bringing good news, announce it to them yourself; for if I tell them, I shall appear to speak from my own invention, and shall not persuade them, as if the barbarians were doing no such thing. But do you go in, and inform them how the case is; and when you have informed them, if they are persuaded, so much the better; but if they attach no credit to what you say, it will be the same to us; for they can no longer escape by flight, if, as you say, we are surrounded on all sides." 81. Aristides, going in, gave this account, saying that he came from Ægina, and with difficulty sailed through

unperceived by those who were stationed round, for that the whole Grecian fleet was surrounded by the ships of Xerxes. He advised them, therefore, to prepare themselves for their defense; and he, having said this, withdrew. A dispute, however, again arose, for the greater part of the generals gave no credit to the report. 82. While they were still in doubt, there arrived a trireme of Tenians that had deserted, which Panætius, son of Sciomenes, commanded, and which brought an account of the whole truth. For that action the name of the Tenians was engraved on the tripod at Delphi, among those who had defeated the barbarian. With this ship that came over at Salamis, and with the Lemnian before, off Artemisium,[4] the Grecian fleet was made up to the full number of three hundred and eighty ships, for before it wanted two of that number.

83. When the account given by the Tenians was credited by the Greeks, they prepared for an engagement. Day dawned, and when they had mustered the marines, Themistocles, above all the others, harangued them most eloquently. His speech was entirely taken up in contrasting better things with worse, exhorting them to choose the best of all those things which depended on the nature and condition of man. Having finished his speech, he ordered them to go on board their ships: they accordingly were going on board, when the trireme from Ægina, which had gone to fetch the Æacidæ, returned; thereupon the Greeks got all their ships under weigh. 84. When they were under weigh, the barbarians immediately fell upon them. Now all the other Greeks began to back water and made for the shore; but Aminias of Pallene, an Athenian, being carried onward, attacked a ship; and his ship becoming entangled with the other, and the crew not being able to clear, the rest thereupon coming to the assistance of Aminias, engaged. Thus the Athenians say the battle commenced; but the Æginetæ affirm that the ship which went to Ægina to fetch the Æacidæ was the first to begin. This is also said, that a phantom of a woman appeared to them, and that on her appearance she cheered them on, so that the whole fleet of the Greeks heard her, after she had first reproached them in these words: "Dastards, how long will you back water?" 85. Opposite the Athenians the Phœnicians were drawn up,

[4] See chap. 11.

for they occupied the wing toward Eleusis and westward; opposite the Lacedæmonians, the Ionians occupied the wing toward the east and the Piræus. Of these, some few behaved ill on purpose, in compliance with the injunctions of Themistocles;[5] but most of them not so. I am able to mention the names of several captains of triremes who took Grecian ships; but I shall make no use of them, except of Theomestor, son of Androdamas, and Phylacus, son of Histiæus, both Samians. I mention these two only for this reason, because Theomestor, on account of this exploit, was made tyrant of Samos by the appointment of the Persians; and Phylacus was inscribed as a benefactor to the king, and a large tract of land was given to him. The benefactors of the king are called in the Persian language Orosangæ. Such was the case with regard to these men. 86. The greater part of the ships were run down at Salamis, some being destroyed by the Athenians, others by the Æginetæ; for as the Greeks fought in good order, in line, but the barbarians were neither properly formed nor did any thing with judgment, such an event as did happen was likely to occur. However, they were and proved themselves to be far braver on this day than off Eubœa, every one exerting himself vigorously, and dreading Xerxes, for each thought that he himself was observed by the king.

87. As regards the rest, of some of them I am unable to say with certainty how each of the barbarians or Greeks fought; but with respect to Artemisia the following incident occurred, by which she obtained still greater credit with the king; for when the king's forces were in great confusion, at that moment the ship of Artemisia was chased by an Attic ship, and she not being able to escape, for before her were other friendly ships, and her own happened to be nearest the enemy, she resolved to do that which succeeded in the attempt; for, being pursued by the Athenian, she bore down upon a friendly ship, manned by Calyndians, and with Damasithymus himself, king of the Calyndians, on board; whether she had any quarrel with him while they were at the Hellespont I am unable to say, or whether she did it on purpose, or whether the ship of the Calyndians happened by chance to be in her way; however, she ran it down, and sunk it, and

[5] See chap. 22.

by good fortune gained a double advantage to herself; for the captain of the Attic ship, when he saw her bearing down on a ship of the barbarians, concluding Artemisia's ship to be either a Grecian, or one that had deserted from the enemy and was assisting them, turned aside and attacked others. 88. In the first place, this was the result to her, that she escaped and did not perish; and, in the next, it fell out that she, having done an injury, in consequence of it became still more in favor with Xerxes; for it is said that Xerxes, looking on, observed her ship making the attack, and that some near him said, "Sire, do you see Artemisia, how well she fights, and has sunk one of the enemy's ships?" Whereupon he asked if it was in truth the exploit of Artemisia: they answered "that they knew the ensign of her ship perfectly well," but they thought that it was an enemy that was sunk; for, as has been mentioned, other things turned out fortunately for her, and this in particular, that no one of the crew of the Calyndian ship was saved so as to accuse her. And it is related that Xerxes said in answer to their remarks, "My men have become women, and my women men." They relate that Xerxes said this.

89. In this battle perished the admiral, Ariabignes, son of Darius, and brother of Xerxes, and many other illustrious men of the Persians and Medes, and the other allies, but only some few of the Greeks; for as they knew how to swim, they whose ships were destroyed, and who did not perish in actual conflict, swam safe to Salamis, whereas many of the barbarians, not knowing how to swim, perished in the sea. When the foremost ships were put to flight, then the greatest numbers were destroyed; for those who were stationed behind, endeavoring to pass on with their ships to the front, that they, too, might give the king some proof of their courage, fell foul of their own flying ships. 90. The following event also occurred in this confusion. Some Phœnicians, whose ships were destroyed, going to the king, accused the Ionians that their ships had perished by their means, for that they had betrayed him. It, however, turned out that the Ionian captains were not put to death, but that these Phœnicians who accused them received the following reward; for while they were yet speaking, a Samothracian ship bore down on an Athenian ship; the Athenian was sunk, and an Æginetan

ship, coming up, sunk the ship of the Samothracians; but the Samothracians being javelin-men, by hurling their javelins, drove the marines from the ship that had sunk them, and boarded and got possession of it. This action saved the Ionians; for when Xerxes saw them perform so great an exploit, he turned round to the Phœnicians, as being above measure grieved, and ready to blame all, and ordered their heads to be struck off, that they who had proved themselves cowards might no more accuse those who were braver. (For whenever Xerxes saw any one of his own men performing a gallant action in the sea-fight, being seated at the foot of the mountain opposite Salamis, which is called Ægaleos, he inquired the name of the person who did it, and his secretaries wrote down the family and country of the captain of the trireme.) Moreover, Ariaramnes, a Persian, who was a friend *to the Ionians*, and happened to be present, contributed to the ruin of the Phœnicians. They accordingly betook themselves to the Phœnicians.[6]

91. The barbarians being turned to flight, and sailing away toward Phalerus, the Æginetæ, waylaying them in the strait, performed actions worthy of record; for the Athenians in the rout ran down both those ships that resisted and those that fled, and the Æginetæ those that sailed away from the battle; so that when any escaped the Athenians, being borne violently on, they fell into the hands of the Æginetæ. 92. At this time there happened to meet together the ship of Themistocles, giving chase to one of the enemy, and that of Polycritus, son of Crius, an Æginetan, bearing down upon a Sidonian ship, the same that had taken the Æginetan ship which was keeping watch off Sciathus, and on board of which sailed Pytheas, son of Ischenous, whom, though covered with wounds, the Persians kept in the ship from admiration of his valor.[7] The Sidonian ship that carried him about was taken with the Persians on board, so that Pytheas, by this means, returned safe to Ægina. But when Polycritus saw the Athenian ship, he knew it, seeing the admiral's ensign; and shouting to Themistocles, he railed at him, upbraiding him with the charge of Medism brought against the Æginetæ.[8] Polycritus, accordingly, as he was attacking the ship, threw out

[6] That is, "the executioners put them to death."

[7] See B. VII. chap. 181.

[8] See B. VI. chap. 49, 50.

these reproaches against Themistocles. But the barbarians, whose ships survived, fled, and arrived at Phalerus under the protection of the land-forces.

93. In this engagement of the Greeks, the Æginitæ obtained the greatest renown, and next, the Athenians; of particular persons, Polycritus of Ægina, and Athenians, Eumenes the Anagyrasian, with Aminias a Pallenian, who gave chase to Artemisia; and if he had known that Artemisia sailed in that ship, he would not have given over the pursuit till he had either taken her or been himself taken, for such had been the order given to the Athenian captains; and, besides, a reward of ten thousand drachmas was offered to whoever should take her alive, for they considered it a great indignity that a woman should make war against Athens. She, however, as has been before mentioned, made her escape, and the others, whose ships survived, lay at Phalerus. 94. The Athenians say that Adimantus, the Corinthian admiral, immediately from the commencement, when the ships engaged, being dismayed and excessively frightened, hoisted sail and fled, and that the Corinthians, seeing their admiral's ship flying, likewise bore away; and when, in their flight, they arrived off the temple of Minerva Sciras, on the coast of Salamis, a light bark fell in with them by the guidance of heaven; that no one appeared to have sent it, and that it came up to the Corinthians, who knew nothing relating to the fleet. From this circumstance they conjectured the circumstance to be divine, for that when those on board the bark neared the ships, they spoke as follows: "Adimantus, having drawn off your ships, you have hurried away in flight, betraying the Greeks; they, however, are victorious as far as they could have desired to conquer their enemies." Having said this, as Adimantus did not credit them, they again spoke as follows: that "they were ready to be taken as hostages, and be put to death if the Greeks were not found to be victorious;" upon which, having put about ship, he and the rest returned to the fleet when the work was done. Such a story is told of them by the Athenians; the Corinthians, however, do not admit its truth, but affirm that they were among the foremost in the engagement, and the rest of Greece bears testimony in their favor. 95. Aristides, son of Lysimachus, an Athenian, of whom I made mention a little before as a most upright man, in this

confusion that took place about Salamis, did as follows: taking with him a considerable number of heavy-armed men, who were stationed along the shore of the Salaminian territory, and were Athenians by race, he landed them on the island of Psyttalea, and they put to the sword all the Persians who were on that little island.

96. When the sea-fight was ended, the Greeks, having hauled on shore at Salamis all the wrecks that still happened to be there, held themselves ready for another battle, expecting the king would still make use of the ships that survived. But a west wind, carrying away many of the wrecks, drove them on the shore of Attica, which is called Colias, so as to fulfill both all the other oracles delivered by Bacis and Musæus concerning this sea-fight, and also that relating to the wrecks which were drifted on this shore, which many years before had been delivered by Lysistratus, an Athenian augur, but had not been understood by any of the Greeks: "The Colian women shall broil their meat with oars."[9] This was to happen after the departure of the king.

97. Xerxes, when he saw the defeat he had sustained, fearing lest some of the Ionians might suggest to the Greeks, or lest they themselves might resolve to sail to the Hellespont for the purpose of breaking up the bridges, and lest he, being shut up in Europe, might be in danger of perishing, meditated flight; but wishing that his intention should not be known either to the Greeks or his own people, he attempted to throw a mound across to Salamis; and he fastened together Phœnician merchantmen, that they might serve instead of a raft and a wall; and he made preparation for war, as if about to fight another battle at sea. All the others who saw him thus occupied were firmly convinced that he had seriously determined to stay and continue the war; but none of these things escaped the notice of Mardonius, who was well acquainted with his design. At the same time that Xerxes was doing this, he dispatched a messenger to the Persians to inform them of the misfortune that had befallen him. 98. There is nothing mortal that reaches its destination more rapidly than these couriers: it has been thus planned by the Persians. They say that as many days as are occupied in the whole journey, so many horses and men are posted at regular inter-

9 Or, "shall shudder at the oars."

vals, a horse and a man being stationed at each day's journey; neither snow, nor rain, nor heat, nor night prevents them from performing their appointed stage as quick as possible. The first courier delivers his orders to the second, the second to the third, and so it passes throughout, being delivered from one to the other, just like the torch-bearing among the Greeks, which they perform in honor of Vulcan. This mode of traveling by horses the Persians call angareïon. 99. The first message that reached Susa, with the news that Xerxes was in possession of Athens, caused so great joy among the Persians who had been left behind, that they strewed all the roads with myrtle, burned perfumes, and gave themselves up to sacrifices and festivity. But the second messenger arriving threw them into such consternation, that they all rent their garments, and uttered unbounded shouts and lamentations, laying the blame on Mardonius. The Persians acted thus, not so much being grieved for the ships, as fearing for Xerxes himself. And this continued with the Persians during all the time that elapsed until Xerxes himself arrived and stopped them *from doing so.*

100. Mardonius, seeing Xerxes much afflicted on account of the sea-fight, and suspecting he was meditating a retreat from Athens, and having thought within himself that he should suffer punishment for having persuaded the king to invade Greece, and that it would be better for him to incur the hazard either of subduing Greece, or ending his life gloriously in attempting great achievements: however, the thought of subduing Greece weighed more with him; having, therefore, considered these things, he thus addressed the king: "Sire, do not grieve, nor think you have suffered any great loss in consequence of what has happened; for the contest with us does not depend on wood alone, but on men and horses. None of those who imagine they have already finished the whole business, will quit their ships and attempt to oppose you, nor will any one from this continent; and they who have opposed us have suffered punishment. If, then, you think fit, let us immediately make an attempt on Peloponnesus; or, if you think right to delay, you may do so; but be not discouraged, for the Greeks have no means of escape from rendering an account of what they have done now and formerly, and from becoming your slaves. By all means, therefore, do this. If, however, you have determined yourself to retire and to with-

draw the army, I have, then, other advice to offer. Do not you, O king, suffer the Persians to be exposed to the derision of the Greeks; for where the Persians fought,[1] your affairs received no damage, nor can you say that we have on any occasion proved cowards; but if the Phœnicians, Egyptians, Cyprians, and Cilicians have shown themselves cowards, this disaster in no respect extends to the Persians. Since, therefore, the Persians are not to blame, yield to my advice. If you have resolved not to stay here, do you return to your own home, and take with you the greatest part of the army; but it is right that I should deliver Greece to you reduced to slavery, having selected three hundred thousand men from the army." 101. Xerxes, having heard this, was rejoiced and delighted, as relieved from troubles, and said to Mardonius that, after deliberation, he would give him an answer as to which of these plans he would adopt. While he was deliberating with his Persian counselors, he thought fit to send for Artemisia to the council, because she was evidently the only person who before understood what ought to have been done. When Artemisia arrived, Xerxes, having ordered his other counselors of the Persians and his guards to withdraw, spoke as follows: "Mardonius advises me to stay here, and make an attempt on the Peloponnesus, saying that the Persians and the land army are not at all to blame for the defeat I have sustained, and wish to give me proof of it. He, therefore, advises me either to do this, or wishes himself, having selected three hundred thousand men from the army, to deliver Greece to me reduced to slavery, and advises me to return to my own home with the rest of the army. Do you, therefore, for you gave me good advice respecting the sea-fight that has taken place, in dissuading me from engaging in it, advise me now, by adopting which measure I shall consult best for my interest." 102. Thus he asked her advice. She answered as follows: "O king, it is difficult for me to say what is best for you who ask my advice. However, in the present state of affairs, it appears to me that you should return home, and leave Mardonius here with the troops he requires, if he wishes it, and promises to effect what he says; for, on the one hand, if he conquers what he says he will, and his plans should succeed, the achievement, sire, will be yours, for your servants

[1] Literally, "among the Persians."

will have accomplished it; but, on the other hand, if things fall out contrary to the expectation of Mardonius, it will be no great misfortune, so long as you survive, and your own affairs are safe at home; for while you survive, and your house, the Greeks will have to hazard frequent struggles for themselves; but of Mardonius, if he should suffer any reverse, no account will be taken; nor, if the Greeks are victorious, will they gain any great victory in destroying your slave; but you, having burned Athens, for which you undertook this expedition, will return home." 103. Xerxes was pleased with her advice, for she happened to say the very things that he designed; for even if all the men and women of the world had advised him to stay, in my opinion, he would not have stayed, so great was his terror. Having commended Artemisia, he sent her to conduct his sons to Ephesus, for some of his natural sons had accompanied him.

104. With the children he sent Hermotimus as guardian, who was by birth a Pedasian, and among the eunuchs second to none in the king's favor. The Pedasians dwell above Halicarnassus; and among these Pedasians the following occurrence takes place: when within a certain time any calamity is about to fall on the different neighbors who dwell round their city, then the priestess of Minerva has a large beard. This has already happened twice to them. 105. Hermotimus, then, was sprung from these Pedasians; and, of all the men we know, revenged himself in the severest manner for an injury he had received; for having been taken by an enemy and sold, he was purchased by one Panionius, a Chian, who gained a livelihood by most infamous practices; for whenever he purchased boys remarkable for beauty, having castrated them, he used to take and sell them at Sardis and Ephesus for large sums; for with the barbarians eunuchs are more valued than others, on account of their perfect fidelity. Panionius, therefore, had castrated many others, as he made his livelihood by this means, and among them this man. Hermotimus, however, was not unfortunate in every respect, for he went to Sardis with other presents to the king, and in process of time was most esteemed by Xerxes of all his eunuchs. 106. When the king was preparing to march his Persian army against Athens, and was at Sardis, at that time having gone down, on some business or other, to the Mysian territory which the Chians

possess, and is called Atarneus, he there met with Panionius. Having recognized him, he addressed many friendly words to him, first recounting to him them any advantages he had acquired by his means, and, secondly, promising him how many benefits he would confer on him in requital if he would bring his family and settle there;[2] so that Panionius, joyfully accepting the proposal, brought his children and wife. But when Hermotimus got him with his whole family in his power, he addressed him as follows: "O thou, who of all mankind hast gained thy livelihood by the most infamous acts, what harm had either I, or any of mine, done to thee, or any of thine, that of a man thou hast made me nothing? Thou didst imagine, surely, that thy machinations would pass unnoticed by the gods, who, following righteous laws, have enticed thee, who hast committed unholy deeds, into my hands, so that thou canst not complain of the punishment I shall inflict on thee." When he had thus upbraided him, his sons being brought into his presence, Panionius was compelled to castrate his own sons, who were four in number; and being compelled, he did it; and after he had finished it, his sons, being compelled, castrated him. Thus the vengeance of Hermotimus[3] overtook Panionius.

107. Xerxes, when he had committed his sons to Artemisia to convey to Ephesus, having sent to Mardonius, bade him choose what forces he would out of the army, and endeavor to make his actions correspond with his words. Thus much was done that day; but in the night, the admirals, by the king's order, took back the ships from Phalerus to the Hellespont as quickly as each was able, in order to guard the bridges for the king to pass over. But when the barbarians were sailing near Zoster, where some small promontories jut out from the main land, they fancied that they were ships, and fled for a considerable distance; but after a while, perceiving that they were not ships, but promontories, they collected together and pursued their voyage. 108. When day came, the Greeks, seeing the land-forces remaining in the same place, supposed that their ships also were at Phalerus; they expected, also, that they would come to an engagement, and prepared to defend themselves; but when they were informed that the ships had departed, they immediately determined to pursue them. How-

[2] At Sardis. [3] Literally, "vengeance and Hermotimus."

ever, they did not get sight of Xerxes's naval force, although they pursued them as far as Andros: on arriving at Andros, therefore, they held a council. Themistocles accordingly gave his opinion "that, shaping their course between the islands, and pursuing the ships, they should sail directly to the Hellespont, and destroy the bridges;" but Eurybiades gave a contrary opinion, saying that "if they destroyed the bridges, they would do the greatest possible harm to Greece; for if the Persian, being shut in, should be compelled to remain in Europe, he would endeavor not to continue inactive; for if he continued inactive, he could neither advance his affairs nor find any means of returning home, but his army must perish by famine; and if he should attack them and apply himself to action, all Europe would probably go over to him, by cities and nations, either through being taken by force or capitulating beforehand; and they would derive sustenance from the annual produce of the Greeks. He thought, however, that the Persian, having been conquered in the sea-fight, would not remain in Europe, and therefore should be permitted to fly, until in his flight he should reach his own country. After that he advised that he should be compelled to fight for his own territories." This opinion the commanders of the other Peloponnesians adhered to.

109. When Themistocles perceived that he could not persuade the majority to sail for the Hellespont, changing his plan, he thus addressed the Athenians (for they were exceedingly annoyed at the escape of the enemy, and were desirous, having consulted among themselves, to sail to the Hellespont, even if the others would not). "I have myself, ere this, witnessed many such instances, and have heard of many more, that men, when driven to necessity after being conquered, have renewed the fight, and repaired their former loss. Since, then, we have met with unexpected success for ourselves and Greece by having repelled such a cloud of men, let us no longer pursue the fugitives; for we have not wrought this deliverance, but the gods and the heroes, who were jealous that one man should reign over both Asia and Europe, and he unholy and wicked; who treated sacred and profane things alike, burning and throwing down the images of the gods; who even scourged the sea, and threw fetters into it—since, then, our affairs are in a prosperous condition, let us remain in

Greece, and take care of ourselves and our families; let every one repair his house, and apply attentively to sowing his ground, after he has thoroughly expelled the barbarian; and at the beginning of the spring let us sail to the Hellespont and Ionia." This he said, wishing to secure favor with the Persian, that, if any misfortune should overtake him from the Athenians, he might have a place of refuge, which eventually came to pass. 110. Themistocles, in saying this, deceived them; and the Athenians were persuaded; for as he had been before considered a wise man, and had now shown himself to be really wise and prudent in counsel, they were ready to yield implicitly to what he said; but after they had been persuaded, Themistocles presently sent off certain persons in a boat, who he was confident would, though put to every torture, keep secret what he had enjoined them to say to the king; and of these his domestic Sicinnus[4] was again one. When they reached the shore of Attica, the rest remained in the boat, and Sicinnus, having gone up to the king, spoke as follows: "Themistocles, son of Neocles, general of the Athenians, the most valiant and wisest of all the allies, has sent me to tell you that Themistocles the Athenian, wishing to serve you, has withheld the Greeks, who wished to pursue your ships, and to destroy the bridges on the Hellespont; now, therefore, retire at your leisure." They, having made this communication, sailed back again.

111. The Greeks, when they had determined neither to pursue the ships of the barbarians any farther, nor to sail to the Hellespont and destroy the passage, invested Andros with intention to destroy it; for the Andrians were the first of the islanders who, when asked for money by Themistocles, refused to give it; but when Themistocles held this language to them, that "the Athenians had come having with them two powerful deities, Persuasion and Necessity, and that therefore they must give money," they answered to this, saying that "the Athenians were with good reason great and prosperous, and were favored by propitious gods; since, however, the Andrians were poor in territory, and had reached the lowest pitch of penury, and two unprofitable goddesses, Poverty and Impossibility, never forsook their island, but ever loved to dwell there—therefore that the Andrians, being in possession

[4] See chap. 75.

of these deities, would not give any money; for that the power of the Athenians would never prove superior to their inability." They then, having made this answer, and refused to give money, were besieged. 112. Themistocles, for he never ceased coveting more wealth, sending threatening messages to the other islands, demanded money by the same persons, using the same language he had used with the Andrians; saying, that unless they gave what was demanded, he would lead the forces of the Greeks against them, and would besiege and destroy them. By saying this he collected large sums from the Carystians and the Parians, who, being informed respecting Andros, that it was besieged for siding with the Mede, and with regard to Themistocles, that he was in the greatest reputation of the generals, alarmed at these things, sent money. Whether any other of the islanders gave it I am unable to say; but I am of opinion that some others did, and not these only. However, the Carystians[5] did not by these means at all defer calamity; though the Parians, having conciliated Themistocles with money, escaped a visit from the army. Themistocles, accordingly, setting out from Andros, obtained money from the islanders unknown to the other generals.

113. The army with Xerxes having stayed a few days after the sea-fight, marched back into Bœotia by the same way, for it appeared to Mardonius both that he should escort the king, and that the season of the year was unfit for military operations; and that it would be better to winter in Thessaly, and to make an attempt on the Peloponnesus early in the spring. When he arrived in Thessaly, Mardonius there selected, first, all the Persians who are called Immortals, except Hydarnes, their general, for he declared he would not leave the king; after these, out of the rest of the Persians, the cuirassiers, and the body of a thousand horse,[6] and the Medes, Sacæ, Bactrians, and Indians, both infantry and cavalry; he chose these whole nations; but from the rest of the allies he selected a few, choosing such as were of a good stature, or by whom he knew some gallant action had been performed. Among them, he chose the greatest part of the Persians who wore necklaces and bracelets; next to them, the Medes; these were not less numerous than the Persians, but were inferior in strength. Thus

[5] See ch. 121. [6] See B. VII. ch. 40, and IX. ch. 62.

the whole together, with the cavalry, made up the number of three hundred thousand. 114. At this time, while Mardonius was selecting his army, and Xerxes was in Thessaly, an oracle came to the Lacedæmonians from Delphi *admonishing them* to demand satisfaction of Xerxes for the death of Leonidas, and to accept whatever should be given by him. Accordingly, the Spartans immediately dispatched a herald as quickly as possible, who, when he overtook the whole army still in Thessaly, having come into the presence of Xerxes, spoke as follows: "King of the Medes, the Lacedæmonians and Heraclidæ of Sparta demand of you satisfaction for blood, because you have slain their king while protecting Greece." But he, laughing, and having waited a considerable time, as Mardonius happened to be standing near him, pointed to him, and said, "This Mardonius, then, shall give them such satisfaction as they deserve." The herald, having accepted the omen, went away.

115. Xerxes, having left Mardonius in Thessaly, himself marched in all haste to the Hellespont, and arrived at the place of crossing in forty-five days, bringing back no part of his army, so to speak. Wherever, and among whatever nation they happened to be marching, they seized and consumed their corn; but if they found no fruit, overcome by hunger, they ate up the herbage that sprung up from the ground, and stripped off the bark of trees and gathered leaves, both from the wild and cultivated, and left nothing; this they did from hunger; but a pestilence and dysentery falling on the army, destroyed them on their march. Such of them as were sick, Xerxes left behind, ordering the cities through which he happened to be passing to take care of and feed them; some in Thessaly, others at Siris of Pæonia, and in Macedonia. Here having left the sacred chariot of Jupiter when he marched against Greece, he did not receive it back as he returned; for the Pæonians, having given it to the Thracians, when Xerxes demanded it back, said that the mares had been stolen, as they were feeding, by the upper Thracians, who dwell round the sources of the Strymon. 116. There the king of the Bisaltæ and of the Crestonian territory, a Thracian, perpetrated a most unnatural deed: he declared that he would not willingly be a slave to Xerxes, but went up to the top of Mount Rhodope, and enjoined his sons not to join the expedition against Greece. They, however, disregarding his pro-

hibition, from a desire to see the war, served in the army with the Persian; but when they all returned safe, being six in number, their father had their eyes put out for this disobedience; and they met with this recompense.

117. The Persians, when in their march from Thrace they arrived at the passage, in great haste crossed over the Hellespont to Abydos in their ships; for they found the rafts no longer stretched across, but broken up by a storm. While detained there, they got more food than on their march, and having filled themselves immoderately, and changed their water, a great part of the army that survived, died; the rest, with Xerxes, reached Sardis. 118. This different account is also given, that when Xerxes, in his retreat from Athens, arrived at Eion on the Strymon, from thence he no longer continued his journey by land, but committed the army to Hydarnes to conduct to the Hellespont, and himself, going on board a Phœnician ship, passed over to Asia; that during this voyage a violent and tempestuous wind from the Strymon overtook him; and then, for the storm increased in violence, the ship being overloaded, so that many of the Persians who accompanied Xerxes were on the deck, thereupon the king becoming alarmed, and calling aloud, asked the pilot if there were any hope of safety for them; and he said, "There is none, sire, unless we get rid of some of those many passengers." It is farther related that Xerxes, having heard this answer, said, "O Persians, now let some among you show his regard for the king, for on you my safety seems to depend." That he spoke thus; and that they, having done homage, leaped into the sea; and that the ship, being lightened, thus got safe to Asia. *It is added* that Xerxes, immediately after he landed, did as follows: he presented the pilot with a golden crown, because he had saved the king's life; but ordered his head to be struck off, because he had occasioned the loss of many Persians. 119. This latter story is told of the return of Xerxes, but appears to me not at all deserving of credit, either in other respects, nor as to this loss of the Persians; for if this speech had been made by the pilot to Xerxes, I should not find one opinion in ten thousand to deny that the king would have acted thus: that he would have sent down into the hold of the ship those who were on deck, since they were Persians, and Persians of high rank, and would have thrown

into the sea a number of rowers, who were Phœnicians, equal to that of the Persians. He, however, as I have before related, proceeding on the march with the rest of the army, returned to Asia. 120. This, also, is a strong proof: it is known that Xerxes reached Abdera on his way back, and made an alliance of friendship with the people, and presented them with a golden cimeter and a gold-embroidered tiara; and as the Abderites themselves say, saying what is by no means credible to me, he there for the first time loosened his girdle in his flight from Athens, as being at length in a place of safety. Abdera is situated nearer to the Hellespont than the Strymon and Eïon, whence they say he embarked on board the ship.

121. Meanwhile the Greeks, finding they were not able to reduce Andros, turned to Carystus, and having ravaged their country, returned to Salamis. In the first place, then, they set apart first-fruits for the gods, and, among other things, three Phœnician triremes; one to be dedicated at the Isthmus, which was there at my time; a second at Sunium, and the third to Ajax, there at Salamis. After that, they divided the booty, and sent the first-fruits to Delphi, from which a statue was made, holding the beak of a ship in its hand, and twelve cubits in height; it stands in the place where is the golden statue of Alexander the Macedonian. 122. The Greeks, having sent first-fruits to Delphi, inquired of the god, in the name of all, if he had received sufficient and acceptable first-fruits. He answered that from the rest of the Greeks he had, but not from the Æginetæ; of them he demanded an offering on account of their superior valor in the sea-fight at Salamis. The Æginetæ, being informed of this, dedicated three golden stars, which are placed on a brazen mast in the corner, very near the bowl of Crœsus.[7] 123. After the division of the booty, the Greeks sailed to the Isthmus for the purpose of conferring the palm of valor upon him among the Greeks who had proved himself most deserving throughout the war. When the generals, having arrived, distributed the ballots at the altar of Neptune, selecting the first and second out of all; thereupon every one gave his vote for himself, each thinking himself the most valiant; but with respect to the second place, the majority concurred in selecting Themistocles. They, there-

[7] See B. I. chap. 51.

fore, had but one vote, whereas Themistocles had a great majority for the second honor. 124. Though the Greeks, out of envy, would not determine this matter, but returned to their several countries without coming to a decision, yet Themistocles was applauded and extolled throughout all Greece as being by far the wisest man of the Greeks; but because, although victorious, he was not honored by those who fought at Salamis, he immediately afterward went to Lacedæmon, hoping to be honored there. The Lacedæmonians received him nobly, and paid him the greatest honors. They gave the prize of valor to Eurybiades, a crown of olive; and of wisdom and dexterity to Themistocles, to him also a crown of olive; and they presented him with the most magnificent chariot in Sparta; and having praised him highly, on his departure, three hundred chosen Spartans, the same that are called knights, escorted him as far as the Tegean boundaries. He is the only man that we know of whom the Spartans escorted on his journey. 125. When he arrived at Athens from Lacedæmon, thereupon Timodemus of Aphidnæ, who was one of Themistocles's enemies, though otherwise a man of no distinction, became mad through envy, reproached Themistocles, alleging against him his journey to Lacedæmon, and that the honors he received from the Lacedæmonians were conferred on account of Athens, and not for his own sake; but he, as Timodemus did not cease to repeat the same thing, said, "The truth is, neither should I, were I a Belbinite, have been thus honored by the Spartans, nor would you, fellow, were you an Athenian." So far, then, this occurred.

126. In the mean time, Artabazus, son of Pharnaces, a man even before of high repute among the Persians, and much more so after the battle of Platæa, having with him sixty thousand men of the army which Mardonius selected, escorted the king as far as the passage; and when the king arrived in Asia, he, marching back, came into the neighborhood of Pallene; but as Mardonius was wintering in Thessaly and Macedonia, as there was nothing as yet to urge him to join the rest of the army, he did not think it right, since he happened to be in the way of the Potidæans who had revolted, to neglect the opportunity of reducing them to slavery; for the Potidæans, as soon as the king had passed by, and the

Persian fleet had fled from Salamis, openly revolted from the barbarians, as also did the other inhabitants of Pallene. 127. Artabazus, therefore, besieged Potidæa; and as he suspected that the Olnythians intended to revolt from the king, he also besieged their city. The Bottiæans then held it, who had been driven from the bay of Therma by the Macedonians. When he had besieged and taken them, having taken them out to a marsh, he slaughtered them, and gave the city to Critobolus of Torone to govern, and to the Chalcidian race: thus the Chalcidians became possessed of Olynthus. 128. Artabazus, having taken this city, applied himself vigorously to the siege of Potidæa; and, as he was earnestly engaged with it, Timoxenus, general of the Scionæans, treated with him for the betrayal of the city; in what way at first I am unable to say, for it is not reported; at last, however, the following plan was adopted. When either Timoxenus had written a letter and wished to send it to Artabazus, or Artabazus to Timoxenus, having rolled it round the butt-end of an arrow, and put the feathers over the letter, they shot the arrow to a spot agreed upon; but Timoxenus was detected in attempting to betray Potidæa; for Artabazus, when endeavoring to shoot to the spot agreed upon, missed the right spot, and wounded one of the Potidæans on the shoulder: a crowd ran round the wounded man, as in usual in time of war; they having immediately drawn out the arrow, when they perceived the letter, carried it to the generals; and an allied force of the other Pallenians was also present. When the generals had read the letter, and discovered the author of the treachery, they determined not to impeach Timoxenus of treason, for the sake of the city of the Scionæans, lest the Scionæans should ever after be accounted traitors. In this manner, then, he was detected. 129. After three months had been spent by Artabazus in the siege, there happened a great ebb of the sea, which lasted for a long time. The barbarians, seeing a passage that might be forded, marched across toward Pallene; and when they had performed two parts of their journey, and three still remained, which they must have passed over to be within Pallene, a strong flood-tide of the sea came on them, such as was never seen before, as the inhabitants say, though floods are frequent. Those, then, that did not know how to swim, perished, and those that did know how, the Potidæans, sailing upon them in boats, put to death. The Potidæans say that the cause of this flux and inundation, and of the Persian disaster, was this, that these very Persians who were destroyed by the sea had committed impieties at the temple of Neptune, and the statue which stands in the suburbs; and in saying this was the cause, they appear to me to speak correctly. The survivors Artabazus led to Thessaly, to join Mardonius. Such, then, was the fate of those troops that had escorted the king.

130. The naval force of Xerxes, that survived when it reached Asia in its flight from Salamis, and had transported the king and his army from the Chersonese to Abydos, wintered at Cyme; and at the first appearance of spring, it assembled early at Samos; and some of the ships had wintered there. Most of the marines were Persians and Medes, and their generals came on board, Mardontes, son of Bagæus, and Artayntes, son of Artachæus; and Ithamitres, nephew *of the latter*, shared the command with them, Artayntes himself having associated him with them. As they had sustained a severe blow, they did not advance farther to the westward, nor did any one compel them; but remaining, they kept watch over Ionia lest it should revolt, having three hundred ships, including those of Ionia. Neither did they expect that the Greeks would come to Ionia, but *thought* they would be content to guard their own territory; inferring this, because they had not pursued them in their flight from Salamis, but had readily retired. By sea, therefore, they despaired of success, but on land they imagined that Mardonius would be decidedly superior. While they were at Samos, they at the same time consulted together whether they could do the enemy any damage, and listened anxiously for news of how the affairs of Mardonius would succeed. 131. The approach of spring, and Mardonius being in Thessaly, aroused the Grecians. Their land-forces were not yet assembled; but their fleet arrived at Ægina, in number one hundred and ten ships. Their leader and admiral was Leotychides, son of Menares, son of Agesilaus, son of Hippocratides, son of Leotychides, son of Anaxilaus, son of Archidamus, son of Anaxandrides, son of Theopompus, son of Nicander, son of Charillus, son of Eunomus, son of Polydectes, son of Prytanis, son of Euryphon, son of Procles, son of Aristodemus, son of Aristomachus, son of

Cleodæus, son of Hyllus, son of Hercules: he was of the second branch of the royal family. All these, except the two mentioned first after Leotychides, were kings of Sparta. Xanthippus, son of Ariphron, commanded the Athenians. 132. When all these ships were assembled at Ægina, embassadors from the Ionians arrived at the encampment of the Greeks, who a short time before had gone to Sparta, and entreated the Lacedæmonians to liberate Ionia; and among them was Herodotus, son of Basilides. These, who were originally seven in number, having conspired together, formed a plan of putting Strattis, the tyrant of Chios, to death; but as they were detected in their plot, one of the accomplices having given information of the attempt, thereupon the rest, being six, withdrew from Chios and went to Sparta, and at the present time to Ægina, beseeching the Greeks to sail down to Ionia; they with difficulty prevailed on them to advance as far as Delos; for all beyond that was dreaded by the Greeks, who were unacquainted with those countries, and thought all parts were full of troops; Samos, they were convinced in their imaginations, was as far distant as the columns of Hercules. Thus it fell out, that at the same time the barbarians dare not sail farther westward than Samos, nor the Greeks, though the Chians besought them, farther eastward than Delos. Thus fear protected the midway between them.

133. The Greeks, then, sailed to Delos, and Mardonius was in winter-quarters about Thessaly. When preparing to set out from thence, he sent a man, a native of Europus, whose name was Mys, to consult the oracles, with orders to go every where, and consult all that it was possible for him to inquire of. What he wished to learn from the oracles when he gave these orders, I am unable to say, for it is not related; I am of opinion, however, that he sent to inquire about the affairs then depending, and not about any others. 134. This Mys clearly appears to have arrived at Lebadea, and having persuaded a native of the place by a bribe, descended into the cave of Trophonius; and arrived also at the oracle of Abæ of the Phocians; moreover, as soon as he arrived at Thebes, he first of all consulted the Ismenian Apollo, and it is there the custom, as in Olympia, to consult the oracle by means of victims; and next, having persuaded some stranger, not a Theban, by money, he caused him to sleep in the temple of Amphiaraus; for none of the

Thebans are permitted to consult there, for the following reason: Amphiaraus, communicating with them by means of oracles, bade them choose whichever they would of these two things, to have him either for their prophet or their ally, abstaining from the other: they chose to have him for their ally: for this reason, therefore, no Theban is allowed to sleep there. 135. The following, to me very strange circumstance, is related by the Theban to have happened: that this Mys, of Europus, in going round to all the oracles, came also to the precinct of the Ptoan Apollo: this temple is called Ptoan, but belongs to the Thebans, and is situate above the lake Copais, at the foot of a mountain, very near the city of Acræphia: that when this man, called Mys, arrived at this temple, three citizens chosen by the public accompanied him, for the purpose of writing down what the oracle should pronounce; and forthwith the priestess gave an answer in a foreign tongue; and that those Thebans who accompanied him stood amazed at hearing a foreign language instead of Greek, and knew not what to do on the present occasion; but that Mys, suddenly snatching from them the tablet which they brought, wrote on it the words spoken by the prophet, and said that he had given an answer in the Carian tongue; and after he had written it down, he departed for Thessaly.

136. Mardonius, having read the answers of the oracles, afterward sent Alexander, son of Amyntas, a Macedonian, as an embassador to Athens, as well because the Persians were related to him (for Bubares, a Persian, had married Alexander's sister Gygæa, daughter of Amyntas, by whom he had the Amyntas in Asia, who took his name from his maternal grandfather; to him Alabanda, a large city of Phrygia, had been given by the king to govern), as because he had been informed that Alexander was a friend and benefactor *of the Athenians;* Mardonius therefore sent him, for in this way he thought he should best be able to gain over the Athenians, having heard that they were a numerous and valiant people; and, besides, he knew that the Athenians had been the principal cause of the late disaster of the Persians at sea. If these were won over, he hoped that he should easily become master at sea, which indeed would have been the case; and on land he imagined that he was much superior: thus he calculated that his power would get the upper hand of the Grecian. Per-

haps, also, the oracles had given him this warning, advising him to make Athens his ally; accordingly, relying on them, he sent.

137. The seventh ancestor of this Alexander was Perdiccas, who obtained the sovereignty of the Macedonians in the following manner. Gauanes, Aëropus, and Perdiccas, three brothers, of the descendants of Temenus, fled from Argos to the Illyrians, and, crossing over from the Illyrians into the upper Macedonia, they arrived at the city of Lebæa; there they entered into the king's service for wages. One of them had the care of his horses, another of his oxen, and the youngest of them, Perdiccas, of the lesser cattle. Formerly even monarchs were poor in wealth, and not only the people, so that the wife of the king used herself to cook their food. Whenever the bread of the hireling lad Perdiccas was baked, it became twice as large as at first; and when this always happened, she told it to her own husband. It immediately occurred to him, when he heard it, that it was a prodigy, and boded something of importance. Having, therefore, summoned the hirelings, he commanded them to depart out of his territories. They answered that they were entitled to receive their wages, and then they would go. Thereupon the king, hearing about wages, as the rays of the sun reached into the house down the chimney, said, being deprived of his senses by the deity, "I give you this as your wages, equal to your services," pointing to the sun. Gauanes and Aëropus, the elder, stood amazed when they heard this; but the lad, for he happened to have a knife, saying thus, "We accept thy offer, O king," traced a circle on the floor of the house round the sun's rays, and having so traced the circle, and having drawn the sun's rays three times on his bosom, departed, and the others with him. 138. They accordingly went away; but one of those who were sitting by him informed the king what the lad had done, and how the youngest of them accepted the offer with some design. He, on hearing this, being in a rage, dispatched after them some horsemen to kill them. In this country is a river, to which the descendants of these men from Argos sacrifice as their deliverer. It, when the Temenidæ had crossed over, swelled to such a height that the horsemen were unable to cross it. They then, coming to another district of Macedonia, settled near the gardens that are said to

have belonged to Midas, son of Gordias, in which wild roses grow, each one having sixty leaves, and surpassing all others in fragrance. In these gardens Silenus was taken, as is related by the Macedonians. Above the gardens is a mountain called Bermion, inaccessible from the cold. Issuing from thence, when they had possessed themselves of this tract, they subdued the rest of Macedonia. 139. From this Perdiccas Alexander was thus descended. Alexander was the son of Amyntas, Amyntas of Alcetes, the father of Alcetes was Aëropus, of him Philip, of Philip, Argæus, and of him, Perdiccas, who acquired the sovereignty. Thus, then, was Alexander, son of Amyntas, descended.

140. When he arrived at Athens, being sent by Mardonius, he spoke as follows: (1.) "Men of Athens, Mardonius says thus: A message has come to me from the king, conceived in these terms: 'I forgive the Athenians all the injuries committed by them against me; therefore, Mardonius, do thus. First, restore to them their territory; and, next, let them choose, in addition to it, another country, whatever they please, and live under their own laws, and rebuild all their temples which I have burned, if they are willing to come to terms with me.' These orders having come to me, I must of necessity execute them, unless you on your part oppose. And now I say this to you. Why are you so mad as to levy war against the king? for neither can you get the better of him, nor can you resist him forever. You are acquainted with the multitude of Xerxes's army, and their achievements; you have heard of the force that is even now with me; so that even if you should get the better of us and conquer (of which, however, you can have no hope, if you think soberly), another much more numerous will come against you. Suffer not yourselves, then, to be deprived of your country, and to be continually running a risk for your existence, by equaling yourselves with the king, but be reconciled to him; and it is in your power to be reconciled honorably, since the king is so disposed. Be free, having contracted an alliance with us, without guile or deceit. (2.) This, O Athenians, Mardonius charged me to say to you; but I, for my own part, will say nothing of the good-will I bear toward you, for you would not learn it for the first time; but I entreat you, listen to Mardonius, for I see that you will not always be able to carry on war against

Xerxes; for if I had seen this power in you, I would never have come to you bringing such a proposal; for the power of the king is more than human, and his arm exceeding long. If, then, you do not immediately come to terms, when they offer such favorable conditions on which they are willing to agree, I greatly fear for you, who of all the allies dwell in the most beaten road, and who must be continually the only people destroyed, since ye possess a territory exposed, as being between both armies. Be persuaded, then, for this is a high honor to you, that the great king, forgiving your offenses alone among all the Greeks, is willing to become your friend." Thus spoke Alexander. 141. But the Lacedæmonians, having been informed that Alexander had arrived at Athens, in order to induce the Athenians to an agreement with the barbarian, and remembering the oracles, how it was fated that they, with the rest of the Dorians, should be driven out of Peloponnesus by the Medes and Athenians, were very much afraid lest the Athenians should make terms with the Persian, and therefore resolved forthwith to send embassadors. It so happened that the introduction of both took place at the same time; for the Athenians had purposely delayed the time, well knowing that the Lacedæmonians would hear that an embassador had come from the barbarian to negotiate a treaty, and that when they did hear of it, they would send embassadors with all speed. They, therefore, designedly so contrived as to show their intentions to the Lacedæmonians. 142. When Alexander had ceased speaking, the embassadors from Sparta, speaking next, said, "The Lacedæmonians have sent us to entreat you not to adopt any new measures with respect to Greece, nor to listen to proposals from the barbarian; for neither would it be by any means just nor honorable either in any others of the Greeks, and least of all in you, for many reasons; for you raised this war against our wish, and the contest arose about your sovereignty; but it now relates to the whole of Greece. Besides, that the Athenians, who are the authors of all these things, should prove the occasion of slavery to Greece, is on no account to be borne; you, who always, and from of old, have been seen to assert the freedom of many nations. We, however, sympathize with you in your difficulties, and that you have already been deprived of two harvests, and that your property has been so long involved in ruin; but, in compensation for this, the Lacedæmonians and the allies promise to support your wives, and all the rest of your families which are useless in war, as long as the war shall continue; therefore let not Alexander the Macedonian persuade you, by glossing over the proposal of Mardonius, for this is what he would naturally do; for, being himself a tyrant, he aids a tyrant's cause. But you should not so act, if indeed you think rightly, because you know that with barbarians there is neither faith nor truth." Thus spoke the embassadors. 143. The Athenians gave the following answer to Alexander: "We ourselves are aware of this, that the power of the Medes is far greater than ours, so there was no need to insult us with that; but, nevertheless, being ardent for liberty, we will defend ourselves in such manner as we are able; but do not you attempt to persuade us to come to terms with the barbarian, for we will not be persuaded. Go, then, and tell Mardonius that the Athenians say, so long as the sun shall continue in the same course as now, we will never make terms with Xerxes; but we will go out to oppose him, trusting in the gods, who fight for us, and in the heroes whose temples and images he, holding them in no reverence, has burned; and do you appear no more in the presence of the Athenians, bringing such proposals, nor, imagining that you do us good service, urge us to do wicked deeds; for we are unwilling that you, who are our guest and friend, should meet with any ungracious treatment at the hands of the Athenians." 144. To Alexander they gave this answer, and to the embassadors from Sparta the following: "That the Lacedæmonians should fear lest we should make terms with the barbarian was very natural; yet, knowing as you do the mind of the Athenians, you appear to entertain an unworthy dread; for there is neither so much gold any where in the world, nor a country so pre-eminent in beauty and fertility, by receiving which we should be willing to side with the Mede and enslave Greece; for there are many and powerful considerations that forbid us to do so, even if we were inclined. First and chief, the images and dwellings of the gods burned and laid in ruins: this we must needs avenge to the utmost of our power, rather than make terms with the man who has perpetrated such deeds. Secondly, the Grecian race being of the same blood and the same language, and the temples of the gods and sacrifices in common, and our similar customs; for the Athenians to become betrayers of these would not be well. Know, therefore, if you did not know it before, that so long as one Athenian is left alive, we will never make terms with Xerxes. Your forethought, however, which you manifest toward us, we admire, in that you provide for us whose property is thus ruined, so as to be willing to support our families; and you have fulfilled the duty of benevolence; we, however, will continue thus in the state we are, without being burdensome to you. Now, since matters stand as they do, send out an army with all possible expedition; for, as we conjecture, the barbarian will in no long time be here to invade our territories, as soon as he shall hear our message that we will do none of the things he required of us; therefore, before he has reached Attica, it is fitting that we go out to meet him in Bœotia." When the Athenians had given this answer, the embassadors returned to Sparta.

BOOK IX.

CALLIOPE.

MARDONIUS, when Alexander, having returned, had made known the answer from the Athenians, set out from Thessaly, and led his army in haste against Athens; and wherever he arrived from time to time, he joined the people to his own forces. The leaders of Thessaly were so far from repenting of what had been before done, that they urged on the Persian much more; and Thorax of Larissa both assisted in escorting Xerxes in his flight, and now openly gave Mardonius a passage into Greece. 2. When the army on its march arrived among the Bœotians, the Thebans endeavored to restrain Mardonius, and advised him, saying that there was no country more convenient to encamp in than that, and dissuaded him from advancing farther, but urged him to take up his station there, and contrive so as to subdue the whole of Greece without a battle; "for that, if the Greeks remained firmly united, as they had done before, it would be difficult even for all mankind to overcome them. But," they continued, "if you will do what we advise, you will without difficulty frustrate all their plans: send money to the most powerful men in the cities, and by sending it you will split Greece into parties, and then, with the assistance of those of your party, you may easily subdue those who are not in your interest." 3. They gave this advice; he, however, was not prevailed on, but a vehement desire of taking Athens a second time was instilled into him; partly by presumption, and partly, he hoped, by signal fires across the islands, to make known to the king while he was at Sardis that he was in possession of Athens. When he arrived in Attica he did not find the Athenians there, but was informed that most of them were at Salamis and on board their ships; he therefore took the deserted city. The capture by the king was ten months before this second invasion by Mardonius.

4. While Mardonius was at Athens, he sent Murychides, a Hellespontine, to Salamis, with the same proposals which Alexander the Macedonian had already conveyed to the Athenians. He sent this second time, although before aware that the disposition of the Athenians was not friendly to him, but expecting they would remit something of their haughtiness, since the whole Attic territory was taken and now in his power. For these reasons he sent Murychides to Salamis. 5. He, on coming before the council, delivered the message of Mardonius, and Lycidas, one of the councilors, gave his opinion, that "it appeared to him to be best to entertain the proposal which Murychides brought to them, and to report it to the people." He delivered this opinion, either because he had received money from Mardonius, or because such was really his opinion; but the Athenians immediately being very indignant, both those belonging to the council and those without, as soon as they were informed of it, surrounded Lycidas, and stoned him to death, but they dismissed Murychides the Hellespontine unharmed. A tumult having taken place at Salamis respecting Lycidas, the Athenian women obtained information of what had happened, whereupon one woman encouraging another, and uniting together, they went of their own accord to the house of Lycidas, and stoned his wife and children. 6. The Athenians had crossed over to Salamis under the following circumstances. As long as they

expected that an army would come from the Peloponnesus to assist them, they remained in Attica; but when they had recourse to delay and extreme tardiness, and Mardonius was advancing and reported to be in Bœotia, then they removed all their effects, and themselves crossed over to Salamis: they also sent embassadors to Lacedæmon, partly to blame the Lacedæmonians because they had allowed the barbarian to invade Attica, and had not gone out with them to meet him in Bœotia, and partly to remind them of what the Persian had promised to give them if they would change sides, and to forewarn them that, unless they assisted the Athenians, they would themselves find some means of escape. 7. At that time the Lacedæmonians were employed in celebrating a festival, and it was the Hyacinthia with them, and they deemed it of the greatest importance to attend to the service of the deity. At the same time they were busied in building the wall at the Isthmus, and it had already received the breast-works.

When the embassadors from the Athenians arrived at Lacedæmon, bringing with them embassadors from Megara and Platæa, they went before the ephori, and spoke as follows: (1.) "The Athenians have sent us to tell you that the king of the Medes, in the first place, offers to restore our country; and, secondly, is willing to make us his allies on fair and equal terms, without fraud or deceit; he is also willing to give us another territory, in addition to our own, whatever we ourselves may choose. We, however, reverencing the Grecian Jupiter, and thinking it disgraceful to betray Greece, have not acceded to, but rejected his offers; though we are unjustly treated and betrayed by the Greeks, and know that it is more for our own interest to come to terms with the Persian than to continue the war, still we will never willingly come to terms with him. (2.) Thus sincerely we have acted toward the Greeks; but you, who were then in the utmost consternation lest we should come to terms with the Persian, when you were clearly assured of our resolution that we will never betray Greece, and because your wall drawn across the Isthmus is now nearly completed, no longer show any regard for the Athenians; for, having agreed to advance with us to meet the Persian in Bœotia, you have betrayed us, and have allowed the barbarian to invade Attica. Hitherto the Athenians are angry with you, for you have not acted in a becoming manner; and now they exhort you to send out forces with us with all expedition, that we may receive the barbarian in Attica; for since we have missed Bœotia, the Thriasian plain in our own territory is the most convenient place to give battle in." 8. When the ephori had heard this message, they put off their answer to the next day, and on the next day to the morrow. This they did for ten days, putting them off from day to day. During this time they proceeded with the wall at the Isthmus, all the Peloponnesians using the utmost diligence; and it was nearly completed. I can give no reason why, when Alexander the Macedonian went to Athens, they took such pains to prevent the Athenians from siding with the Mede, and then took no trouble about it, except that the Isthmus was now fortified, and they thought they had no farther need of the Athenians; whereas, when Alexander arrived in Attica, the wall was not yet built, but they were working at it, being in great dread of the Persians.

9. At length the answer and march of the Spartans happened in the following manner.[1] On the day preceding that on which the last audience was to take place, Chileus of Tegea, who had the greatest influence in Lacedæmon of any stranger, was informed by the ephori of all that the Athenians had said. Chileus, having heard it, spoke to them as follows: "The case is thus, O ephori; if the Athenians are not united with us, but are allied to the barbarian, although a strong wall has been carried across the Isthmus, wide doors leading into the Peloponnesus are open to the Persian; therefore give heed, before the Athenians come to any other determination which may bring ruin on Greece." 10. He, then, gave them this advice; and they, taking his remark into consideration, forthwith, without saying any thing to the embassadors who had come from the cities, while it was still night, sent out five thousand Spartans, appointing seven helots to attend each, and committing the conduct of them to Pausanias, son of Cleombrotus. The command properly belonged to Pleistarchus, son of Leonidas; but he was still a boy, and the former his guardian and cousin; for Cleombrotus, the father of Pausanias, and son to Anaxandrides, was no longer living, but having led back the

[1] Literally, "the following manner of the answer and march took place."

army that had built the wall from the Isthmus, he died shortly afterward. Cleombrotus led back the army from the Isthmus for this reason: as he was sacrificing against the Persians, the sun darkened in the heavens. Pausanias chose as his colleage Euryanax, son of Dorieus, who was a man of the same family. These forces, accordingly, marched from Sparta with Pausanias. 11. The embassadors, when they came, knowing nothing of the march *of the troops*, went to the ephori, being resolved themselves also to depart severally to their own cities; and having come into their presence, they spoke as follows: "You, O Lacedæmonians, remaining here, celebrate the Hyacinthia, and divert yourselves, while you are betraying the allies; but the Athenians, being injured by you, and destitute of allies, will make peace with the Persians on such terms as they can; and having made peace, it is evident that we shall become the king's allies, and shall march with them against whatever country they shall lead us, and then you will learn what the consequence will be to yourselves." When the embassadors had thus spoken, the ephori said with an oath, "that those who had set out against the foreigners were already at Oresteum;" for they call the barbarians foreigners. The embassadors asked what was meant; and on inquiry, learned the whole truth, so that, being much surprised, they followed after them with all possible expedition; and with them, five thousand chosen heavy-armed troops of the neighboring Lacedæmonians did the same. 12. They then hastened toward the Isthmus. But the Argives, as soon as they heard that the troops with Pausanias had left Sparta, sent a herald to Attica, having looked out the best of their couriers, for they had before promised Mardonius to prevent the Spartans from going out. He, when he arrived at Athens, spoke as follows: "Mardonius, the Argives have sent me to inform you that the youth of Lacedæmon are marched out, and that the Argives were unable to prevent them from going out. Under these circumstances, take the best advice you can." He, having spoken thus, went home again.

13. Mardonius, when he heard this, was by no means desirous to stay longer in Attica. Before he heard this, he lingered there, wishing to know from the Athenians what they would do; but he neither ravaged nor injured the Attic territory, being in expectation all along that they would come to terms. But

when he could not persuade them, being informed of the whole truth, he withdrew, before those with Pausanias reached the Isthmus, having first set fire to Athens, and if any part of the walls, or houses, or temples happened to be standing, having thrown down and laid all in ruins. He marched out for the following reasons, because the Attic country was not adapted for cavalry; and, if he should be conquered in an engagement, there was no way to escape except through a narrow pass, so that even a small number of men could intercept them. He determined, therefore, to retire to Thebes, and to fight near a friendly city, and in a country adapted for cavalry. 14. Mardonius accordingly retreated; and while he was yet on his march, another message came in advance that another army had reached Megara, *consisting of* a thousand Lacedæmonians. When he heard this, he deliberated, wishing, if by any means he could, to take these first; therefore, wheeling round, he led his army against Megara; and his cavalry going on before, scoured the Megarian territory. This was the farthest part of Europe, toward the sun-set, to which this Persian army reached. 15. After this, news came to Mardonius that the Greeks were assembled at the Isthmus; he therefore marched back through Decelea; for the Bœotian chiefs had sent for the neighbors of the Asopians, and they conducted him along the way to Sphendale, and from thence to Tanagra; and having passed the night at Tanagra, and on the next day turned toward Scolus, he arrived in the territory of the Thebans. There he cleared the lands of the Thebans, though they sided with the Mede, not out of enmity toward them, but constrained by urgent necessity, wishing to make a fortification for his army, and in case, when he engaged, the result should not be such as he wished, he might have this as a place of refuge. His camp, beginning at Erythræ, passed by Hysiæ and extended to the Platæan territory, stretching to the river Asopus. The wall, however, was not built of this extent, but each front was about ten stades in length.

While the barbarians were employed in this task, Attaginus, son of Phyrnon, a Theban, having made great preparations, invited Mardonius himself and fifty of the most eminent Persians to an entertainment, and they, being invited, came. The feast was held at Thebes. 16. The rest I heard from Thersander, an Orchomenian, a man of high repute at Orchomenus. Thersander said that he also was invited by Attaginus to this feast, and that fifty Thebans were also invited; and that he did not place each person on a separate couch, but a Persian and a Theban on each couch. When supper was over, and they were drinking freely, the Persian who was on the same couch, using the Grecian tongue, asked him of what country he was; he answered that he was an Orchomenian; whereupon the other said, "Since you are a partaker of the same table and of the same cups with me, I wish to leave with you a memorial of my opinion, in order that, being forewarned, you may be able to consider what is best for your own interest. Do you see these Persians feasting here, and the army that we left encamped near the river? Of all these you will see, after the lapse of a short time, only some few surviving." As the Persian said this, he shed abundance of tears; and he himself, being astonished at his words, said to him, "Would it not be right to tell this to Mardonius, and to those Persians who are next to him in authority?" To this he answered, "My friend, that which is fated by the deity to happen, it is impossible for man to avert; for no one will listen to those who say what is worthy of credit; and though many of the Persians are convinced of this, we follow, being bound by necessity. The bitterest grief to which men are liable is this, when one knows much, to have no power to act." This I heard from Thersander the Orchomenian; and this besides, that he immediately told this to several persons before the battle was fought at Platæa.

17. While Mardonius encamped in Bœotia, all the rest furnished troops, and joined in the attack upon Athens, such however of the Greeks who, dwelling in these parts, sided with the Mede; but the Phocians only did not join in the attack, for they took part with the Mede very unwillingly and by necessity. But not many days after his arrival at Thebes, a thousand of his heavy-armed troops arrived; Harmocydes, a man of high repute among the citizens, commanded them. When they also arrived at Thebes, Mardonius, having sent some horsemen, ordered them to encamp by themselves in the plain, and when they had done this the whole cavalry came up. Upon this a rumor spread through the Grecian forces, who were with the Medes, that they were going to dispatch them with their javelins; this same rumor also spread among

the Phocians themselves; werereupon their general, Harmocydes, encouraged them, addressing them as follows: "O Phocians, it is plain that these men are about to deliver us up to certain death, we having been calumniated by the Thessalians, as I conjecture. Now, therefore, it is fitting that every one of you should prove yourselves valiant, for it is better to die doing something, and defending ourselves, than expose ourselves to be destroyed by a most disgraceful death. Let some of these men learn, then, that, being barbarians, they have plotted death against men who are Greeks." 18. Thus he encouraged them; but the cavalry, when they had surrounded them on all sides, rode up as if to destroy them, and brandished their javelins as if about to hurl them; and one here and there did hurl his javelin. They, however, faced them, forming themselves into a circle, and closing their ranks as much as possible, whereupon the cavalry wheeled round and rode away. I am unable to say with certainty whether they came to destroy the Phocians at the request of the Thessalians, and when they saw them prepared to defend themselves, were afraid lest they might receive some wounds, and therefore rode off (because Mardonius had so ordered them), or whether he wished to try whether they had any courage; but when the cavalry had ridden back, Mardonius sent a herald and spoke as follows: "Be of good heart, O Phocians, for you have proved yourselves to be brave men, contrary to what I heard; therefore, sustain this war with resolution, and you shall not surpass me or the king in generosity." Such were the events in regard to the Phocians.

19. The Lacedæmonians, when they arrived at the Isthmus, there encamped; and the rest of the Peloponnesians, who favored the better cause, when they heard of this, and others also who saw the Spartans marching out, thought it would be a disgrace to absent themselves from the expedition of the Lacedæmonians; accordingly, the victims having proved favorable, they all marched out from the Isthmus, and advanced to Eleusis, and, having consulted the victims there also, when they were again favorable, they continued their march, and the Athenians with them, they having crossed over from Salamis, and joined them at Eleusis. When they reached Erythræ in Bœotia, they learned that the barbarians were encamped on the Asopus, and having there-

upon consulted together, they formed themselves opposite, at the foot of Mount Cithæron. 20. Mardonius, when the Greeks did not come down to the plain, sent against them all his cavalry, which Masistius commanded, a man highly esteemed among the Persians (and whom the Greeks call Macistius): he was mounted on a Nisæan horse, that had a golden bit, and was otherwise gorgeously caparisoned. Thereupon, when the cavalry rode up to the Greeks, they charged them in squadrons, and, charging them, did them much mischief, and called them women. 21. By chance the Megarians happened to be stationed in that part which was most exposed, and there the cavalry chiefly made their attack. When, therefore, the cavalry charged, the Megarians, being hard pressed, sent a herald to the Grecian generals; and the herald, when he came into their presence, addressed them as follows: "The Megarians say, We, O confederates, are not able alone to sustain the Persian cavalry, retaining the post in which we were originally stationed: hitherto we have held out against them by our constancy and courage, though hard pressed; but now, unless you will send some others to relieve us, know we must abandon our post." He accordingly delivered this message. Pausanias therefore made a trial of the Greeks, *to see* if any others would volunteer to go to that position, and to relieve the Megarians. When all the others refused, the Athenians undertook to do it, and of the Athenians three hundred chosen men, whom Olympiodorus, son of Lampon, commanded. 22. These were they who undertook *that service*, and who were stationed in front of all the Greeks at Erythræ, having taken with them some archers. After they had fought for some time, the result of the battle was as follows. As the cavalry charged in squadrons, the horse of Masistius, being in advance of the others, was wounded in the flank by an arrow; and, being in pain, he reared and threw Masistius. As he fell, the Athenians immediately attacked him: accordingly, they seized his horse, and killed Masistius as he endeavored to defend himself, though at first they were unable to do so; for he was thus armed: underneath he had a golden cuirass covered with scales, and over the cuirass he wore a purple cloak. By striking against the cuirass they did nothing; until one of them, perceiving what was the matter, pierced him in the eye, so he fell and died. By some means this, while it was going on, escaped the notice of the other horsemen, for they neither saw him when he fell from his horse nor when he was killed; for while a retreat and wheeling round was taking place, they did not notice what had happened; but when they halted, they immediately missed him, as there was no one to marshal them; and as soon as they learned what had happened, all, cheering one another on, pushed their horses to the charge, in order to recover the body. 23. The Athenians, seeing the cavalry no longer advancing in squadrons, but all together, called out for assistance to the rest of the army; and while the whole infantry was coming up to their aid, a sharp struggle took place for the body. Now as long as the three hundred were alone, they were much inferior, and abandoned the body; but when the multitude came up to their assistance, the cavalry no longer maintained their ground, nor did they succeed in recovering the body, but lost many others of their number, besides him. Having, therefore, retired about two stades, they consulted about what ought to be done, and determined, as they were without a commander, to retreat to Mardonius. 24. When the cavalry arrived at the camp, the whole army, and Mardonius most of all, mourned the loss of Masistius, cutting off their own hair, and that of their horses and beasts of burden, and giving themselves up to unbounded lamentations; for the sound reached over all Bœotia, as for the loss of a man who, next to Mardonius, was most esteemed by the Persians and the king. Thus the barbarians, according to their custom, honored Masistius when dead.

25. The Greeks, when they had withstood the attack of the cavalry, and having withstood had repulsed it, were much more encouraged, and first of all, having placed the body on a carriage, they carried it along the line; but the body was worthy of admiration, on account of his stature and beauty; for that reason they did this, and the men, leaving their ranks, came out to view Masistius. After this, they determined to go down toward Platæa, for the Platæan territory appeared to be much more convenient for them to encamp in than the Erythræan, both in other respects, and as it was better supplied with water. To this country, therefore, and to the fountain Gargaphia, which is in this country, they decided that it would be best to remove, and having drawn up their line, there to encamp. Accordingly, having taken up their arms, they

marched by the foot of Mount Cithæron, near Hysiæ, into the Platæan territory; and on arriving there, they formed in line, nation by nation, near the fountain of Gargaphia, and the precinct of the hero Androcrates, on slight elevations and the level plain. 26. There in the distribution of the stations a vehement dispute arose between the Tegeans and the Athenians, for each claimed a right to occupy the other wing,[2] alleging both their recent and former exploits. On the other hand, the Tegeans spoke thus: "We have ever been thought entitled to this station by all the allies, in whatever common expeditions have been undertaken by the Peloponnesians, both anciently and recently, from the time when the Heraclidæ, after the death of Eurystheus, attempted to return to Peloponnesus. We then obtained this honor on the following occasion. When we, in conjunction with the Achæans and Ionians, who were then in Peloponnesus, having marched out to the Isthmus, were posted opposite the invaders, then it is related that Hyllus made proclamation that it would be better not to run the hazard of engaging army with army, but that from the Peloponnesian camp, the man among them whom they judge to be the best, should fight singly with him on certain conditions. The Peloponnesians determined that this should be done; and they took oaths on the following terms: that if Hyllus should conquer the Peloponnesian leader, the Heraclidæ should return to their paternal possessions; but if he should be conquered, the Heraclidæ should depart and lead off their army, and not seek to return into Peloponnesus during the space of a hundred years; and Echemus, son of Aeropus, son of Phegeus, who was our king and general, having volunteered, was chosen out of all the allies, and fought singly and slew Hyllus. From this exploit we obtained among the Peloponnesians of that day both other great privileges, which we continue to enjoy, and that we should always command one wing whenever a common expedition is undertaken. With you, then, O Lacedæmonians, we do not contend, but giving you the choice of whichever wing you wish to command, we concede it to you; but we say that it belongs to us to lead the other, as in former times; and besides this exploit that has been mentioned, we are more entitled to have that station than the Athenians, for many and well-contested battles have been

[2] The Lacedæmonians chose which wing they pleased.

fought by us with you, O men of Sparta, and many with others. It is right, therefore, that we should have one wing rather than the Athenians, for such exploits have not been achieved by them as by us, either in modern or ancient times." Thus they spoke. 27. To this the Athenians answered as follows: "We are aware that this assemblage was made for the purpose of fighting with the barbarian, and not for disputes; but since the Tegean has proposed to mention the former and recent actions that have been achieved by each nation in all times, it is necessary for us to make known to you whence it is our hereditary right, having ever proved ourselves valiant, to hold the first rank rather than the Arcadians. As to the Heraclidæ, whose leader they affirm they slew at the Isthmus; in the first place, these men formerly, when rejected by all the Greeks to whom they came, when flying from slavery at the hands of the Mycenæans, we alone received, and put an end to the insolence of Eurystheus by conquering in battle, in conjunction with them, the people who then possessed Peloponnesus. In the next place, when the Argives who marched with Polynices against Thebes were killed, and lay unburied, we having led an army against the Cadmæans, affirm that we recovered the bodies and buried them in our own territory at Eleusis. We also performed a valiant exploit against the Amazons, who once made an irruption into Attica from the river Thermodon; and in the Trojan war we were inferior to none. But it is of no avail to call these things to mind, for those who were then valiant, the same may now be cowards; and those who were then cowards, may now be brave. Enough, then, of ancient exploits. But if no other achievement had been performed by us, though there were many and gallant ones, if by any others of the Greeks, yet from our exploit at Marathon we are worthy of this honor, and more than this; we, who alone of the Greeks, having fought single-handed with the Persian, and having attempted such a feat, survived, and conquered six-and-forty nations. Do we not, then, from this single action, deserve to hold this post? But as it is not becoming on such an occasion as this to be contending about position, we are ready to submit to you, O Lacedæmonians, wherever it seems most convenient to place us, and against whatsoever nation; for, wheresoever we are stationed, we shall endeavor to prove ourselves brave. Command us, then, as ready to obey." 28. Thus they answered; and the whole army of the Lacedæmonians shouted out that the Athenians were more worthy to occupy the wing than the Arcadians. Accordingly, the Athenians had it, and got the better of the Tegeans.

After this, those of the Greeks who came up later, and those who arrived at first, were drawn up in the following manner. Ten thousand of the Lacedæmonians occupied the right wing; five thousand of these, being Spartans, were attended by thirty-five thousand lightly-armed Helots, seven being assigned to each man. The Spartans chose the Tegeans to stand next themselves, both for honor and valor; of these there were fifteen hundred heavy-armed men; next to them stood five thousand of the Corinthians; and with them they got permission from Pausanias for three hundred Potidæans, who came from Pallene, to stand; next these stood six hundred Arcadians of Orchomenus; next them three thousand Sicyonians; next them were eight hundred Epidaurians; and by the side of these were stationed three thousand of the Trœzenians; and next the Trœzenians two hundred Lepreatæ; next these four hundred of the Mycenæans and Tirynthians; next them one thousand Phliasians; and by the side of them stood three hundred Hermionians; next the Hermionians were stationed six hundred of the Eretrians and Styrians; and next them four hundred Chalcidians; next them five hundred Ambraciots; after them stood eight hundred of the Leucadians and Anactorians; next them two hundred Paleans from Cephallenia; and after them five hundred of the Æginetæ were stationed; and by the side of them were posted three thousand of the Megarians; and next them six hundred Platæans; and last of all, and at the same time first, eight thousand Athenians took their station, occupying the left wing, Aristides, son of Lysimachus, commanding them. 29. These, except the seven assigned to each of the Spartans, were heavy-armed, their total number amounting to thirty-eight thousand seven hundred. All the heavy-armed men assembled to oppose the barbarian were so many. Of the light-armed, the number was as follows: in the Spartans' line thirty-five thousand men, there being seven to each man; every one of these was equipped as for war; and the light-armed of the rest of the Lacedæmonians and other Greeks, about one to each man, amounted to thirty-four thousand five hundred, so that the number of the light-armed fighting men was sixty-nine thousand five hundred. 30. Thus, then, the whole of the Grecian army assembled at Platæa, reckoning heavy-armed and light-armed fighting men, amounted to one hundred and ten thousand, wanting one thousand eight hundred men; and with the Thespians who came up, the full number of one hundred and ten thousand was completed; for the survivors of the Thespians joined the army, to the number of one thousand eight hundred, but they had not heavy armor. These, then, being drawn up in line, encamped on the Asopus.

31. The barbarians, with Mardonius, when they had ceased to mourn for Masistius, having heard that the Greeks were at Platæa, themselves also marched to the Asopus, which flows there; and on their arrival, they were thus drawn up by Mardonius. Opposite the Lacedæmonians he stationed the Persians; and as the Persians far exceeded them in number, they were both drawn up several ranks deep, and extended opposite the Tegeans; and he arrayed them thus: having selected all the most powerful of his forces, he stationed them opposite the Lacedæmonians, and the weaker he arrayed by their side against the Tegeans: this he did by the advice and direction of the Thebans. Next the Persians he ranged the Medes; these fronted the Corinthians, Potidæans, Orchomenians, and Sicyonians. Next the Medes he ranged the Bactrians; these fronted the Epidaurians, Trœzenians, Lepreatæ, Tirynthians, Mycenæans, and Phliasians. Next the Bactrians he stationed the Indians; these fronted the Hermionians, Eretrians, Styrians, and Chalcidians. Next the Indians he ranged the Sacæ; these fronted the Ampraciots, Anactorians, Leucadians, Paleans, and Æginetæ. And next the Sacæ, and opposite to the Athenians, Platæans, and Megarians, he ranged the Bœotians, Locrians, Melians, Thessalians, and the thousand Phocians; for all the Phocians did not side with the Mede, but some of them assisted the cause of the Greeks, being shut up about Parnassus; and sallying from thence, they harassed the army of Mardonius, and the Greeks who were with him. He also ranged the Macedonians, and those that dwelt about Thessaly, against the Athenians. 32. These, the most considerable of the nations that were ranged under Mardonius, have been named, and which were the most distinguished and of most ac-

count; yet there were also mixed with them men of other nations, Phrygians, Thracians, Mysians, Pæonians, Æthiopians, and others; and among them those of the Æthiopians and Egyptians who are called Hermotybians and Calasirians, armed with swords, who are the only Egyptians that are warriors.[3] These, while he was still at Phalerus, he took from on board the ships, they being marines; for the Egyptians were not arrayed with the land-forces that came with Xerxes to Athens. Of barbarians there were three hundred thousand, as has been already shown;[4] but of Greeks who were allies of Mardonius no one knows the number, for they were not reckoned up; but, to make a guess, I conjecture that they were assembled to the number of fifty thousand. These who were thus arrayed were infantry; the cavalry were marshaled apart.

33. When they were all ranged by nations and battalions, thereupon, on the second day, both sides offered sacrifices. For the Greeks, Tisamenus, son of Antiochus, was the person who sacrificed, for he accompanied this army as diviner; him, though an Elean, and by extraction a Clytiad of the Iamidæ, the Lacedæmonians had admitted into the number of their citizens; for when Tisamenus was consulting the oracle at Delphi about offspring, the Pythian answered that he should be victorious in five very great contests. He accordingly, mistaking the answer, applied himself to gymnastic exercises, as if he were to be victorious in gymnastic contests; and having practiced the Pentathlon, he missed winning the Olympic prize by one wrestling match, having contended with Hieronymus of Andros. The Lacedæmonians, having learned that the oracle delivered to Tisamenus referred not to gymnastic but to martial contests, endeavored by offers of money to persuade Tisamenus to become the leader of their wars, in conjunction with their kings of the Heraclidæ; but he, seeing the Spartans very anxious to make him their friend, having discovered this, enhanced his price, acquainting them "that, if they would make him their own citizen, granting him a full participation of all privileges, he would comply, but not on any other terms." The Spartans, when they first heard this, were very indignant, and altogether slighted his prophetic skill; but at last, when great terror of this Persian army was hanging over them, they sent for him and assented; but he,

[3] See B. II. chap. 164.

[4] See B. VIII. chap. 113.

perceiving they had changed their minds, said he would no longer be contented with these things only, but that his brother Hegias must also be made a Spartan on the same terms as himself. 34. In saying this he imitated Melampus, to compare a kingdom with citizenship in his demands; for Melampus also, the women at Argos being smitten with madness, when the Argives would have hired him from Pylus to cure their women of the disease, demanded one half of the kingdom for his recompense; but the Argives not yielding to his terms, but going away, when many more of their women became mad, they at length submitted to what Melampus demanded, and went to present it to him; but he thereupon, seeing them changed, coveted still more, saying that "unless they would give a third part of the kingdom to his brother Bias, he would not do what they wished." The Argives, therefore, being driven to a strait, granted that also. 35. In like manner the Spartans—for they wanted Tisamenus exceedingly—yielded to him entirely, and when the Spartans had thus yielded to him, Tisamenus the Elean, having become a Spartan, accordingly assisted them by his art of divination in gaining five most important battles. These, then, were the only persons of all mankind who were made Spartan citizens. The five battles were as follows: one and the first, this at Platæa; next, that which took place at Tegea, against the Tegeans and Argives; afterward, that at Dipæa, against all the Arcadians except the Mantineans; next, that of the Messenians, near Ithomæ; and the last, that which took place at Tanagra, against the Athenians and Argives: this was the last achieved of the five victories. 36. This Tisamenus, then, the Spartans bringing him, officiated as diviner to the Greeks at Platæa: now the sacrifices were favorable to the Greeks, if they stood on the defensive, but if they crossed the Asopus and began the battle, not so.

37. To Mardonius, who was very desirous to begin the battle, the sacrifices were not propitious; but to him also, if he stood on the defensive, they were favorable; for he too adopted the Grecian sacrifices, having for his diviner Hegesistratus, an Elean, and the most renowned of the Telliadæ. This man, before these events, the Spartans had taken and bound for death, because they had suffered many and atrocious things from him. He being in this sad condition, as being in peril

for his life, and having to suffer many tortures before death, performed a deed beyond belief; for, as he was confined in stocks bound with iron, he got possession of a knife, which had been by some means carried in, and immediately contrived the most resolute deed of all men we know of; for, having considered in what way the rest of his foot would get out, he cut off the broad part of his foot, and having done this, as he was guarded by sentinels, he dug a hole through the wall and escaped to Tegea, traveling by night, and by day hiding himself in the woods and tarrying there. Thus, though the Lacedæmonians searched for him with their whole population, on the third night he arrived at Tegea; but they were struck with great amazement at his daring when they saw half his foot lying on the ground, and were not able to find him. Thus Hegesistratus, having escaped from the Lacedæmonians, fled to Tegea, which was at that time not on friendly terms with the Lacedæmonians, and having been cured of his wounds, and procured a wooden foot, he became an avowed enemy to the Lacedæmonians. However, at last his hatred conceived against the Lacedæmonians did not benefit him, for he was taken by them when acting as diviner at Zacynthus, and put to death. Now the death of Hegesistratus took place after the battle of Platæa; but at that time, on the Asopus, being hired by Mardonius for no small sum, he sacrificed and was very zealous, both from hatred to the Lacedæmonians and from a love of gain.

38. As the victims were not favorable for fighting, either to the Persians themselves, or the Greeks who were with them (for they also had a diviner for themselves, Hippomachus, a Leucadian), and as Greeks were flowing in, and their numbers increasing, Timagenides, son of Herpys, a Theban, advised Mardonius to guard the passes of Mount Cithæron, saying that the Greeks were continually pouring in every day, and that he would intercept great numbers. 39. Eight days had already elapsed since they had been posted opposite each other, when he gave this advice to Mardonius. But he, perceiving that the suggestion was good, as soon as it was night, sent some cavalry to the passes of Cithæron, that lead to Platæa, which the Bœotians call The Three Heads, but the Athenians The Heads of Oak. The horsemen that were sent did not arrive in vain; for, issuing on the plain, they took five hund-

red beasts carrying provisions from Peloponnesus to the army, with the men who attended the beasts of burden. The Persians, having taken this booty, killed them without mercy, sparing neither beast nor man; and when they had had enough of slaughter, they surrounded the rest of them, and drove them off to Mardonius and to the camp. 40. After this action they passed two more days, neither being willing to begin the battle; for the barbarians advanced as far as the Asopus to tempt the Greeks, but neither crossed over. However, the cavalry of Mardonius continually passed on and harassed the Greeks; for the Thebans, being entirely in the interest of the Medes, carried on the war with vigor, and constantly led on even to actual fighting; but after that the Persians and Medes, coming up, gave signal proofs of valor.

41. Accordingly, during the ten days, nothing more than this took place; but when the eleventh day came after the two armies had been encamped opposite each other in Platæa, and the Greeks had become much more numerous, and Mardonius was exceeding vexed at the delay, thereupon Mardonius, son of Gobryas, and Artabazus, son of Pharnaces, who was one of the Persians esteemed by Xerxes, came to a conference; and, on consulting, the following were their opinions: that of Artabazus, "that it was expedient to remove their whole army away as quickly as possible, and march to the walls of Thebes, where a large store of provisions had been laid up for themselves, and forage for their horses; and that, sitting down quietly, they might accomplish their enterprise by doing as follows; for, as they had much coined gold and much uncoined, and much silver and many goblets, they should spare none of these, but distribute them among the Greeks, especially among the principal men of the Greeks in the cities, and they would quickly surrender their liberty, nor run the hazard of an engagement." Thus his opinion was the same as that of the Thebans,[5] since he had more foresight than the other.[6] But the opinion of Mardonius was more violent, pertinacious, and by no means inclined to yielding; "for he thought that their army was far superior to the Grecian, and that they should engage as quickly as possible, and not suffer more to be assembled than were already assembled; and that

[5] See chap. 2. [6] Mardonius

they should dismiss the victims of Hegesistratus, and not do violence to them, but, following the usages of the Persians, to engage." 42. When he thus decided, no one contradicted him, so that his opinion prevailed, for he held the command of the army from the king, and not from Artabazus. Having, therefore, summoned the commanders of battalions, and the generals of the Greeks who were in his service, he asked if they knew any oracle respecting the Persians *which predicted* that they should be destroyed. But when those who were convoked remained silent, some not knowing the oracles, and others knowing indeed, but not deeming it safe to mention them, Mardonius himself said, "Since you either know nothing or dare not speak, I will tell you, as I know perfectly well. There is an oracle *importing* that the Persians arriving in Greece should sack the temple at Delphi, and, after the sacking, all perish. We, therefore, being apprised of this, neither march against that temple, nor intend to sack it, and thus we shall not perish on that account. Let such of you, then, as are well affected to the Persians rejoice on this account, that we shall vanquish the Greeks." Having said this to them, he next gave orders to get all things in readiness, and put them in good order, for that a battle would take place early the next morning. 43. This oracle, which Mardonius said related to the Persians, I know was delivered in reference to the Illyrians, and the army of the Enchelians, and not to the Persians; but the following had been delivered by Bacis in reference to this battle: "The meeting of the Greek and the barbarian-voiced shout on Thermodon and grassy-banked Asopus, in which many of the bow-bearing Medes shall fall, despite of Lachesis and fate, when the destined day shall come." These, and others like these, I know were pronounced by Musæus in reference to the Persians; but the river Thermodon flows between Tanagra and Glisas.

44. After the inquiry respecting the oracles, and the exhortation given by Mardonius, night came on, and they set the watch; but when the night was far advanced, and silence appeared to prevail throughout the camp, and the men were in the most profound sleep, at that time Alexander, son of Amyntas, who was general and king of the Macedonians, having ridden up on horseback to the sentries of the Athenians, desired to confer with their generals. Most of the sentries re-

mained at their post, while some ran to the generals, and, having arrived, told them "that a man had come on horseback from the camp of the Medes, who uttered not a word more, but, naming the generals, said he wished to confer with them."
45. When they heard this, they immediately followed to the outposts, and, on their arrival, Alexander addressed them as follows: "O Athenians, I leave these words with you as a deposit, entreating you to keep them secret, and not tell them to any other than Pausanius, lest you should even ruin me; for I should not utter them were I not extremely concerned for the safety of all Greece; for I am both myself a Grecian originally, and would by no means wish to see Greece enslaved instead of free. I tell you, then, that the victims have not been favorable to Mardonius and his army, or else you would have fought long ago; but now he has determined to dismiss the victims, and to come to an engagement at dawn of day, fearing, as I conjecture, lest you should assemble in greater numbers; therefore be ready; but if Mardonius should defer the engagement, and not undertake it, do you persevere remaining where you are, for in a few days provisions will fail him; and if this war should terminate according to your wishes, it is right that you should bear in mind to effect my freedom, who on behalf of the Greeks have undertaken so hazardous a task, out of zeal for them, wishing to acquaint you with the intention of Mardonius, in order that the barbarians may not fall upon you unexpectedly. I am Alexander the Macedonian." He, having spoken thus, rode back to the camp and his own station.

46. The generals of the Athenians, having gone to the right wing, told Pausanias what they had heard from Alexander; but he, on receiving this intelligence, being in dread of the Persian, spoke thus: "Seeing an engagement will take place in the morning, it is proper that you Athenians should be placed opposite to the Persians, and we opposite to the Bœotians and those Grecians who are now drawn up opposite to you, for this reason; you are acquainted with the Medes, and their manner of fighting, having fought with them at Marathon, whereas we are inexperienced in and unacquainted with those men, for no Spartan has ever made trial of the Medes, but we have made trial of the Bœotians and Thessalians. It is therefore right that you should take up your

arms and come to this wing, and we go to the left." To this the Athenians answered as follows: "To us also from the very first, when we saw the Persians drawn opposite to you, it occurred to mention the very thing which you have now been the first to propose, but we feared that the proposal might not be agreeable to you; since, however, you yourselves have mentioned it, the proposal is both agreeable to us, and we are ready to act accordingly." 47. As this pleased both parties, as soon as morning dawned they changed their stations: the Bæotians having perceived what was done, gave notice to Mardonius; and he, when he heard it, immediately began to alter his order of battle, leading the Persians opposite to the Lacedæmonians; but when Pausanius observed that this was being done, perceiving that he was discovered, he led the Spartans back to the right wing, and Mardonius in like manner toward the left.

48. When they were stationed in their original positions, Mardonius, having sent a herald to the Spartans, spoke as follows: "O Lacedæmonians, you are said to be the bravest by the people in these parts, who admire you exceedingly, because you neither fly from the field of battle nor quit your ranks, but, continuing firm, either kill your adversaries or are killed yourselves. Of all this, however, nothing is true; for even before we engaged, and came to the decision of blows, we have seen you flying and quitting your ranks, leaving the first risk to the Athenians, and ranging yourselves against our slaves; this is by no means the conduct of brave men: we, then, have been very much deceived in you; for whereas we expected, on account of your renown, that you would have sent a herald to challenge us, and that you would be desirous of fighting with the Persians alone, though we were ready to accept these terms, we have found you proposing nothing of the kind, but rather shrinking from us: now, therefore, since you have not begun this proposal, we will begin it; why, then, should not you, on the part of the Greeks, since you are deemed to be the bravest, and we on the part of the barbarians, engage with equal numbers on both sides? If you think the rest ought also to fight, let them fight afterward; but if you do not think so, and that we only are sufficient, we will fight it out; and whichever of us shall obtain the victory, let them be victorious for the whole army." 49. He having spoken thus,

and waited some time, when no one gave him any answer, returned back again, and on his arrival gave Mardonius an account of what had happened; but he, being above measure rejoiced and elated by a cold victory, sent his cavalry to charge the Greeks. When the horsemen rode up they harassed the whole Grecian army, hurling javelins and shooting arrows, since they were mounted archers, and very difficult to be brought to a close engagement; and they disturbed and choked up the fountain of Gargaphia, from which the whole Grecian army obtained water. Near this fountain the Lacedæmonians only were posted, but the fountain was farther off from the rest of the Greeks, according as they severally happened to be stationed; but the Asopus was near. However, being repulsed from the Asopus, they then had recourse to the fountain; for it was impossible for them to get water from the river, by reason of the cavalry and the arrows.

50. When this happened, the generals of the Greeks, as the army was deprived of water and harassed by the cavalry, assembled together to deliberate on these and other matters, going to Pausanias on the right wing; for when these things were so, other circumstances troubled them still more; for they had no longer any provisions, and their attendants, who had been dispatched to the Peloponnesus to get provisions, were shut out by the cavalry, and unable to reach the camp. 51. On consultation, the generals resolved, if the Persians should defer making the attack on that day, to remove to the island. The island is ten stades distant from the Asopus and the fountain of Gargaphia, on which they were then encamped, before the city of the Platæans. Thus it is an island in the midst of the continent; for the river, dividing itself higher up, flows down to the plain from Mount Cithæron, having its streams about three stades separate from each other; and then they unite together, and the name of it is Oëroë; the inhabitants say that she is the daughter of Asopus. To this place they determined to remove, that they might have an abundant supply of water, and the cavalry might not harass them, as when they were directly opposite. They determined to remove when it should be the second watch of the night, in order that the Persians might not see them setting out, and the cavalry might not follow and annoy them. They also resolved, that when they should arrive at this spot which the

Asopian Oëroë encompasses flowing from Cithæron, they would on the same night send away one half of their forces to Cithæron, in order to bring in the attendants who had gone for provisions; for they were shut up in Cithæron. 52. Having taken these resolutions, during the whole of that day they suffered incessant labor by the cavalry pressing on them; but when the day ended, and the cavalry had ceased to attack them, night having come, and it being the hour at which they had agreed to decamp, thereupon the greater part, taking up their arms, marched away, without any intention of going to the place agreed upon; while others, as soon as they were put in motion, gladly fled from the cavalry toward the city of the Platæans; and in their flight they arrived at the temple of Juno: it stands before the city of the Platæans, twenty stades distant from the fountain of Gargaphia; and having arrived there, they stood to their arms before the sacred precinct. 53. They then encamped round the Heræum; and Pausanias, seeing them departing from the camp, ordered the Lacedæmonians also to take up their arms and go in the same direction as the others, supposing they were going to the place which they had agreed to go to; whereupon all the other commanders of troops were ready to obey Pausanias; but Amompharetus, son of Poliades, captain of the band of Pitanetæ, said "he would not fly from the foreigners, nor willingly bring disgrace on Sparta;" and he was astonished at seeing what was being done, because he had not been present at the preceding conference. Pausanias and Euryanax considered it a disgrace that he should not obey them, but still more disgraceful, when he[7] had so resolved, to forsake the band of Pitanetæ, lest, if they should forsake him in order to do what they had agreed on with the rest of the Grecians, Amompharetus himself, being left behind, and those with him, should perish. Considering these things, they kept the Laconian forces unmoved, and endeavored to persuade him that it was not right for him to do as he did.

54. They, then, were expostulating with Amompharetus, who alone of the Lacedæmonians and Tegeans was left behind. But the Athenians did as follows: they kept themselves unmoved where they had been stationed, knowing the dispositions of the Lacedæmonians, who purpose one thing and say

Amompharetus.

another. When, therefore, the army was in motion, they sent one of their horsemen to see whether the Spartans were beginning to depart, or whether they did not intend to depart at all, and to inquire of Pausanias what it was right to do. 55. When the herald came up to the Lacedæmonians, he saw them drawn up in the same spot, and their chiefs engaged in disputes; for when Euryanax and Pausanias urged Amompharetus not to incur danger by remaining *with his men* alone of all the Lacedæmonians, they were by no means able to prevail with him, until they fell into an open quarrel; and the herald of the Athenians having come up, stood by them; and Amompharetus quarreling, took up a stone with both his hands, and laying it down at the feet of Pausanias, said, "With this pebble I give my vote, not to fly from the foreigners;" by foreigners meaning the barbarians. But Pausanias, calling him a madman and out of his senses, then turned to the herald of the Athenians, who was making the inquiry he had been ordered to make, and bade him inform them of the present posture of affairs, and entreated the Athenians to come over to them and act, in relation to the departure, just as they should. 56. He accordingly went back to the Athenians. But when morning found them still disputing with one another, Pausanias, having stayed during all that time, and supposing (as indeed happened) that Amompharetus would not stay behind when the rest of the Lacedæmonians were gone, having given the signal, led all the rest away along the hills; and the Tegeans followed; but the Athenians, drawn up in order of battle, marched by a different way from the Lacedæmonians; for they kept to the rising ground and the base of Cithæron, through fear of the cavalry, but the Athenians took their route toward the plain. 57. But Amompharetus, thinking that Pausanias would on no account dare to forsake them, was very earnest that they should remain there and not abandon their post; but when those with Pausanias had advanced some distance, supposing that they were in real earnest deserting him, he *ordered* his band to take up their arms, and led them slowly toward the main body; which, having marched about ten stades, waited for the band of Amompharetus, halting at the river Moloeis, at a place called Argiopius, where stands a temple of Eleusinian Ceres; and they waited there for this reason, that if Amompharetus and his band should not leave the post in which they had been stationed, but should remain there, they might go back to their assistance. However, those with Amompharetus came up, and the whole of the barbarian's cavalry pressed upon them; for the horsemen did as they were always accustomed to do; but seeing the place empty in which the Greeks had been drawn up on the preceding days, they pushed on continually in advance, and as soon as they overtook them, they pressed them closely.

58. Mardonius, when he was informed that the Grecians had withdrawn under cover of night, and saw the place deserted, having summoned Thorax of Larissa, and his brothers Eurypilus and Thrasydëius, said, "O sons of Aleuas, what will you say now, when you see this ground deserted? For you, their neighbors, said that the Lacedæmonians never fled from battle, but were the first of men in matters of war; these, whom you before saw changing their station, and who now we all see have fled away during the past night. They have clearly shown, when they had to come to the issue of battle with those who are truly the most valiant in the world, that being themselves good for nothing, they have gained distinction among worthless Greeks. And I readily forgave you, who are unacquainted with the Persians, when you extolled them by whom you knew something had been done; but I wondered more at Artabazus, that he should dread the Lacedæmonians, and dreading them, should have advanced a most cowardly opinion, that it was expedient to remove our camp, and retire to the city of the Thebans to be besieged; of this the king shall hereafter hear from me. But these matters will be discussed elsewhere; for the present, we must not suffer them to do what they intended, but they must be pursued until they shall be overtaken, and have given us satisfaction for all the mischief they have done to the Persians." 59. Having spoken thus, he led the Persians at full speed, crossing the Asopus in the track of the Greeks, as if they had betaken themselves to flight; he directed his course only against the Lacedæmonians and Tegeans; for, on account of the hills, he did not discern the Athenians, who had turned into the plain. The rest of the commanders of the barbarian's brigades, seeing the Persians advancing to pursue the Greeks, all immediately took up their standards, and pursued, each as

quick as he could, without observing either rank or order: thus they advanced with a shout and in a throng, as if they were about to overwhelm the Greeks.

60. Pausanias, when the cavalry pressed on him, having dispatched a horseman to the Athenians with this message, spoke as follows: "Men of Athens, when the mighty contest lies before us, whether Greece shall be free or enslaved, we are betrayed by the allies (both we Lacedæmonians and you Athenians), who have fled away during the past night. It is now, therefore, determined what we must henceforth do; for, defending ourselves in the best manner we can, we must support each other. Now, if the cavalry had attacked you first, it would have behooved us and the Tegeans, who with us have not betrayed Greece, to assist you; but now, since the whole body has advanced against us, you ought in justice to come to the succor of that division which is most hardly pressed. If, however, any inability to assist has befallen you, you will confer a favor on us by sending your archers to us. We are aware of your being by far the most zealous in this present war, so as in this instance to listen to our request." 61. When the Athenians heard this, they prepared to assist, and to defend them to the utmost of their power; but as they were already on their way, those of the Greeks who sided with the king, that were arrayed against them, attacked them, so that they were no longer able to render assistance; for the division that pressed upon them harassed them. Thus the Lacedæmonians and Tegeans being left alone, the former with the light-armed men, amounting in number to fifty thousand, and the Tegeans to three thousand (for these last had never separated from the Lacedæmonians), performed sacrifices, purposing to engage with Mardonius and the forces with him. But as the victims were not favorable to them, many of them fell during this interval, and many more were wounded; for the Persians, having made a fence with their osier shields, let fly a number of arrows so incessantly, that the Spartans being hard pressed, and the victims continuing unfavorable, Pausanias, looking toward the temple of Juno of the Platæans, invoked the goddess, praying that they might not be disappointed of their hopes.

62. While he was yet making this invocation, the Tegeans, starting first, advanced against the barbarians; and immedi-

ately after the prayer of Pausanias, the victims became favorable to the Lacedæmonians when they sacrificed. When some time had elapsed, they also advanced against the Persians, and the Persians withstood them, laying aside their bows. First of all a battle took place about the fence of bucklers; and when that was thrown down, an obstinate fight ensued near the temple of Ceres, and for a long time, till at last they came to a close conflict; for the barbarians laying hold of the *enemy's* spears, broke them. And, indeed, in courage and strength, the Persians were not inferior; but, being lightly armed, they were moreover ignorant of military discipline, and not equal to their adversaries in skill; but rushing forward singly, or in tens, or more or fewer in a body, they fell upon the Spartans and perished. 63. In that part where Mardonius happened to be, fighting from a white horse, at the head of a thousand chosen men, the best of the Persians, there they pressed their adversaries most vigorously; for as long as Mardonius survived they held out, and, defending themselves, overthrew many of the Lacedæmonians; but when Mardonius had died, and the troops stationed round him, which were the strongest, had fallen, then the rest turned to flight, and gave way to the Lacedæmonians. Their dress, too, was particularly disadvantageous to them, being destitute of defensive armor; for being light-armed, they had to contend with heavy-armed men. 64. Here satisfaction for the death of Leonidas, according to the oracle, was paid to the Spartans by Mardonius; and Pausanias, son of Cleombrotus, son to Anaxandrides, obtained the most signal victory of all that we know of. (The names of his earlier ancestors have been mentioned in the genealogy of Leonidas;[8] for they were the same.) Mardonius died by the hand of Aïmnestus, a man of distinction at Sparta, who, some time after the Medic affairs, at the head of three hundred men, engaged at Stenyclerus with all the Messenians, there being war; and he himself perished and his three hundred. 65. The Persians at Platæa, when they were put to flight by the Lacedæmonians, fled in disorder to their own camp, and to the wooden fortification which they had made in the Theban territory. It is a wonder to me that, when they fought near the grove of Ceres, not one of the barbarians was seen to enter into the sacred inclosure, or to die in it, but most fell

[8] See B. VII. chap. 204.

round the precinct in unconsecrated ground. I am of opinion, if it is allowable to form an opinion concerning divine things, that the goddess would not receive them, because they had burned her royal temple at Eleusis. Such was the issue of this battle.

66. Artabazus, son of Pharnaces, from the very first had disapproved of Mardonius being left by the king, and at that time, though he strongly dissuaded him, he could not prevail, urging him not to engage. He therefore acted as follows, being displeased with the conduct of Mardonius. Those whom Artabazus commanded (and he had no small force, but to the number of forty thousand men with him), these, as soon as the action commenced, well knowing what the result of the battle would be, he drew up in order and advanced, having ordered them to go where he should lead, whenever they should see him advancing at a quick pace; having given this order, he led his forces as if to join in the engagement; but being in advance of his troops, he discovered the Persians flying; whereupon he no longer led his forces in the same order, but fled with all possible speed; neither toward the wooden fortification nor the walls of Thebes, but to the Phocians, wishing to reach the Hellespont as soon as he could. These, then, took that direction. 67. Although the rest of the Greeks in the king's army behaved themselves ill on purpose, the Bœotians fought with the Athenians for a considerable time; for those Thebans who sided with the Mede displayed no little zeal, fighting and not willingly behaving ill, so that three hundred of them, the first and most valiant, fell there by the hands of the Athenians; but when they also were put to flight, they fled to Thebes, not as the Persians fled, and the whole throng of the other allies, without having fought at all, or performed any thing considerable. 68. And it is manifest to me that on the side of the barbarians all depended on the Persians, since the others, before they engaged with the enemy, fled at once, because they saw the Persians flying. Accordingly, all fled except the rest of the cavalry, and especially the Bœotian: they so far assisted the fugitives, keeping constantly close to them against the enemy, and separating their friends who were flying from the Greeks. 69. The victors, however, followed, pursuing and slaying the soldiers of Xerxes. In the midst of this rout, news came to the rest of the Greeks, who were drawn

up about the Heræum, and were absent from the battle, that a battle had been fought, and Pausanias's party were victorious. When they heard this, without observing any kind of order, the Corinthians took the road that leads by the base of the mountain and the hills direct to the temple of Ceres, and the Megarians and the Phliasians the most level of the roads across the plain. But when the Megarians and Phliasians were near the enemy, the Theban cavalry, seeing them hurrying on without any order, charged them with the horse, which Asopodorus, son of Timander, commanded; and having fallen on them, they threw down and killed six hundred of them, and pursuing the rest, drove them headlong to Mount Cithæron. Thus they perished ingloriously.

70. The Persians and the rest of the throng, when they arrived in their flight at the wooden wall, mounted the towers before the Lacedæmonians came up, and having mounted it, defended the wall in the best way they could; so that when the Lacedæmonians arrived, a vigorous battle took place before the walls; for, so long as the Athenians were absent, the barbarians defended themselves, and had much the advantage over the Lacedæmonians, as they were not skilled in attacking fortifications; but when the Athenians came up, then a vehement fight at the walls took place, and continued for a long time. But at length the Athenians, by their valor and constancy, surmounted the wall, and made a breach; there, at length, the Greeks poured in. The Tegeans entered first within the wall; and these were they who plundered the tent of Mardonius, and among other things took away the manger for the horses, all of brass, and well worth seeing: this manger of Mardonius the Tegeans placed in the temple of the Alean Minerva; but all the other things they took, they carried to the same place as the rest of the Greeks. The barbarians, when the wall had fallen, no longer kept in close order, nor did any one think of valor; but they were in a state of consternation, as so many myriads of men were inclosed within a small space; and the Greeks had such an easy opportunity of slaughtering them, that of an army of three hundred thousand men, except the forty thousand with which Artabazus fled, not three thousand survived. Of Lacedæmonians from Sparta, all that died in the engagement were ninety-one; of Tegeans, sixteen; and of Athenians, fifty-two.

71. Of the barbarians, the infantry of the Persians and the cavalry of the Sacæ most distinguished themselves, and Mardonius is said to have shown himself the bravest man. Of the Greeks, though the Tegeans and Athenians showed great bravery, the Lacedæmonians exceeded in valor. I can prove this in no other way (for all these conquered those opposed to them) except that they were engaged with the strongest part of the enemy's army, and conquered them; and, in my opinion, Aristodemus proved himself by far the bravest; he, being the only one of the three hundred saved from Thermopylæ, was held in disgrace and dishonor. After him, Posidonius, Philocyon, and Amompharetus the Spartan, most distinguished themselves. However, when it was debated which of them had been the bravest, the Spartans who were present decided that Aristodemus, evidently wishing to die on account of the disgrace attached to him, and acting like a madman, and leaving the ranks, had performed great deeds; but that Posidonius, not wishing to die, had shown himself a brave man, and, therefore, that he was the better. Perhaps, however, they may have said this through envy. All these that I have mentioned, except Aristodemus, of those that died in this battle, were honored; but Aristodemus, wishing to die on account of the before-mentioned guilt, was not honored. 72. These, then, were they who acquired the greatest renown at Platæa; for Callicratides died out of the battle, who came to the army the handsomest man of the Greeks of that day, not only of the Lacedæmonians themselves, but also of the other Greeks; he, when Pausanias was sacrificing, was wounded in the side by an arrow; and then they fought, but he being carried off, regretted his death, and said to Arimnestus, a Platæan, that he did not grieve at dying for Greece, but at not having used his arm, and at not having performed any deed worthy of himself, though he desired to perform it. 73. Of the Athenians, Sophanes, son of Eutychides, of the borough of Decelea, is said to have acquired great renown; of the Deceleans, who had once performed an action that was beneficial for all future time, as the Athenians themselves say; for in ancient time, when the Tyndaridæ entered the Attic territory with a numerous army in search of Helen, and drove out the people, not knowing where Helen had been carried to, then they say that the Deceleans, but some say that Decelus himself, being indig-

nant at the insolence of Theseus, and alarmed for the whole country of the Athenians, discovered the whole matter to them, and conducted them to Aphidnæ, which Titucus, a native of the place, delivered up to the Tyndaridæ. In consequence of that action, the Deceleans in Sparta continue to enjoy immunity from tribute and precedence up to the present time, so that in the war that occurred many years after these events between the Athenians and Peloponnesians, when the Lacedæmonians ravaged the rest of Attica, they abstained from Decelea. 74. Of this borough was Sophanes, and having at that time distinguished himself above all the Athenians, he has two different accounts given of him: one, that he carried an iron anchor fastened by a brass chain from the girdle of his cuirass, which, when he approached the enemy, he used to throw out, in order that the enemy, rushing from their ranks, might not be able to move him from his position; and when the flight of his adversaries took place, he determined to take up the anchor and so pursue. Thus this account is given. But the other account, varying from that before given, relates, that on his shield, which constantly turned round and was never at rest, he wore an anchor as a device, and not one of iron fastened from his cuirass. 75. There is also another splendid feat done by Sophanes, for that when the Athenians invested Ægina, he challenged and slew Eurybates of Argos, who had been victor in the pentathlum. But some time after these events it befell this Sophanes, who proved himself a brave man, as he was commanding the Athenians jointly with Leagrus, son of Glaucon, to die at the hands of the Edoni at Datus, as he was fighting for the gold mines.

76. When the barbarians were overthrown by the Greeks at Platæa, thereupon a woman came voluntarily over to them, who, when she learned that the Persians had perished, and that the Greeks were victorious, being a concubine of Pharandates, son of Theaspes, a Persian, having decked herself and her attendants in much gold, and in the richest attire she had, alighted from her carriage, and advanced toward the Lacedæmonians, who were still employed in slaughter, and when she observed that Pausanias directed every thing, having before become acquainted with his name and country, since she had often heard of them, she knew it must be Pausanias, and embracing his knees, spoke as follows: "King of Sparta, de-

liver me, your suppliant, from captive servitude; for you have thus far benefited me by destroying these men, who pay no regard either to gods or heroes. I am by birth a Coan, daughter to Hegetorides, son of Antagoras. The Persians, having taken me away by force at Cos, kept me." He answered as follows: "Lady, be of good heart, both as a suppliant, and, moreover, if you have spoken the truth, and are indeed the daughter of Hegetorides the Coan, who is the best friend I have of all who dwell in those parts." Having thus spoken, he committed her to the care of the ephori, who were present, and afterward sent her to Ægina, where she herself wished to go. 77. Presently after the arrival of the lady, the Mantineans came up when all was over, and, finding they were come too late for the engagement, they considered it a great calamity, and confessed that they deserved to be punished; but being informed that the Medes with Artabazus had fled, they wished to pursue them as far as Thessaly, but the Lacedæmonians dissuaded them from pursuing the fugitives. They, therefore, having returned to their own country, banished the generals of their army from the land. After the Mantineans came the Eleans; and the Eleans, in the same manner as the Mantineans, considering it a calamity, marched away; and they also, on their return home, banished their generals. Such were the events relating to the Mantineans and Eleans.

78. In the camp of the Æginetæ at Platæa was Lampon, son of Pytheas, one of the most eminent of the Æginetæ: he, having a most iniquitous proposal *to make*, went to Pausanias, and, having come into his presence, spoke with earnestness as follows: "Son of Cleombrotus, a superhuman feat has been achieved by you, both on account of its greatness and splendor; and God has granted to you, by delivering Greece, to acquire the greatest renown of all the Greeks whom we know of; but do you complete what remains to be done after this, in order that still greater fame may attend you, and henceforth every barbarian may beware of attempting to do wicked deeds against the Greeks; for when Leonidas died at Thermopylæ, Mardonius and Xerxes, having cut off his head, fixed it on a pole. By requiting him in the same manner, you will have praise first from all the Spartans, and then from the rest of the Greeks; for by impaling Mardonius, you will avenge your uncle Leonidas." He spoke thus,

thinking to gratify *Pausanias.* 79. But he answered as follows: "Æginetan friend, I admire your good intentions and your foresight, but you have failed to form a right judgment; for, having highly extolled me, my country, and my achievement, you have thrown all down again to nothing by advising me to insult a dead body, and saying that if I do so I shall increase my fame, which is more fit for barbarians to do than Greeks, and which we abhor even in them; I can not, therefore, in this matter please the Æginetæ, nor those to whom such things would be pleasing; it is sufficient for me to please the Spartans, by doing and speaking what is right. As for Leonidas, whose death you exhort me to avenge, I affirm that he has been amply avenged; both he and all the others who fell at Thermopylæ have been avenged by the countless deaths of these men. However, do not you hereafter come to me with such a proposal, nor give such advice; and be thankful that you escape unpunished." He, having received this answer, went away.

80. Pausanias, having made proclamation that no one should touch the body, commanded the helots to bring together all the treasures. They, accordingly, dispersing themselves through the camp, found tents decked with gold and silver, and couches gilt, and plated and golden bowls, and cups and other drinking vessels; they also found sacks on the wagons in which were discovered gold and silver caldrons; and from the bodies that lay dead they stripped bracelets, necklaces, and cimeters of gold; but no account at all was taken of the variegated apparel. Here the helots stole a great deal and sold it to the Æginetæ, and they also produced a great deal, such of it as they could not conceal; so that the great wealth of the Æginetæ hence had its beginning, for that they purchased gold from the helots as if it had been brass. 81. Having collected the treasures together, and taken from them a tithe for the god at Delphi, from which the golden tripod was dedicated which stands on the three-headed brazen serpent, close to the altar, and having taken out *a tithe* for the god at Olympia, from which they dedicated the brazen Jupiter, ten cubits high, and *a tithe* to the god at the Isthmus, from which was made the brazen Neptune, seven cubits high; having taken out these, they divided the rest, and each took the share they were entitled to, as well the concubines of the Persians

as the gold, silver, and other treasures, and beasts of burden. Now what choice presents were given to those who most distinguished themselves at Platæa is mentioned by no one, yet I am of opinion that such presents were given to them; but for Pausanias ten of every thing was selected and given him—women, horses, talents, camels, and all other treasures in like manner. 82. It is said also that the following occurred: that Xerxes, flying from Greece, left all his own equipage to Mardonius; Pausanias, therefore, seeing Mardonius's equipage furnished with gold, silver, and various-colored hangings, ordered the bakers and cooks to prepare a supper in the same manner as for Mardonius; and when they being ordered had so done, that Pausanias thereupon, seeing gold and silver couches handsomely carved, and gold and silver tables, and magnificent preparations for the supper, being astonished at the profusion set before him, in derision ordered his own attendants to prepare a Laconian supper, and that when the repast was spread the difference was great, and Pausanias, laughing, sent for the generals of the Greeks, and when they had assembled, Pausanias, pointing to each preparation for supper, said, "Men of Greece, I have called you together for this reason, to show you the folly of the leader of the Medes, who, having such fare as this, has come to us, who have such poor fare, to take it from us." It is related that Pausanias said this to the generals of the Greeks. 83. A considerable time after these events, many of the Platæans found chests of gold and silver, and other precious things; and still later than this, the following also was discovered, when the bodies were bared of flesh—for the Platæans brought together the bones to one place—there was found a skull without any seam, consisting of one bone; there was also discovered a jaw, and the upper jaw had teeth growing in a piece, all in one bone, both the front teeth and the grinders; there was likewise discovered the skeleton of a man five cubits high.

84. The next day after, the body of Mardonius had disappeared; by whom *removed* I am unable to say for certain. I have indeed heard of many men and of various nations who are said to have buried Mardonius, and I know that several have received large presents from Artontes, son of Mardonius, for so doing; yet who of them it was that carried off and buried the body of Mardonius I am unable to ascertain

with certainty; however, Dionysiophanes, an Ephesian, is commonly reported to have buried Mardonius. Thus, then, he was buried. 85. But the Greeks, when they had divided the booty at Platæa, buried their own dead, each nation separately. The Lacedæmonians made three graves; there, then, they buried the young officers,[9] among whom were Posidonius, Amompharetus, Phylocion, and Callicrates; accordingly, in one of the graves the young officers were laid; in another, the rest of the Spartans; and in the third, the helots: thus they buried *their dead*. The Tegeans *buried* all theirs together in a separate spot, and the Athenians theirs in one place, as also did the Megareans and Phliasians those that had been destroyed by the cavalry. Of all these, therefore, the sepulchres were full, but of all the others whose sepulchres are seen in Platæa, they, as I am informed, being ashamed of their absence from the battle, severally threw up empty mounds, for the sake of future generations. For instance, there is a sepulchre there called that of the Æginetans, which, I hear, Cleades, son of Autodicus, a Platæan, who was their friend, threw up ten years after these events, at the request of the Æginetans.

86. When the Greeks had buried their dead in Platæa, they immediately determined, on consultation, to march against Thebes, and to demand the surrender of those who had sided with the Medes, and among the first of them Timegenides and Attaginus, who were the chief leaders, and if they should not give them up, *they resolved* not to depart from the city before they had taken it. When they had determined on this, they thereupon, in the eleventh day after the engagement, arrived and besieged the Thebans, requiring them to give up the men, and when the Thebans refused to give them up, they both ravaged the country and attacked the walls. 87. As they did not cease damaging them, on the twentieth day Timegenides spoke thus to the Thebans: "Men of Thebes, since the Greeks have so resolved that they will not give over besieging us until either they have taken Thebes or you have delivered us up to them, let not the Bœotian territory suffer any more on our account. But if, being desirous of money,

[9] Ἰρένες were those who had attained their second year from boyhood, and now held a command. The MSS. read ἱρέας, "those who held sacred offices."

they demand us as a pretense, let us give them money from the public treasury; for we sided with the Mede by general consent, and not of ourselves alone. If, however, they carry on the siege really because they want us, we will present ourselves before them to plead our cause." He appeared to speak well and to the purpose; and the Thebans immediately sent a herald to Pausanias, expressing their willingness to surrender the men. 88. When they had agreed on these terms, Attaginus escaped from the city, and his sons, who were brought before him, Pausanias acquitted from the charge, saying that boys could have no part in the guilt of siding with the Mede. As to the others whom the Thebans delivered up, they thought that they should be admitted to plead their cause, and, moreover, trusted to repel the charge by bribery; but he, as soon as he had them in his power, suspecting this very thing, dismissed the whole army of the allies, and conducting the men to Corinth, put them to death. Such were the events at Platæa and Thebes.

89. In the mean time, Artabazus, son of Pharnaces, flying from Platæa, was already at a considerable distance, and on his arrival among them, the Thessalians invited him to an entertainment, and asked him news of the rest of the army, knowing nothing of what had happened in Platæa. But Artabazus, being aware that if he should tell the whole truth respecting the conflicts, both he and his army would be in danger of destruction, for he thought that every one would attack him when informed of what had happened; considering this, he told nothing to the Phocians, and to the Thessalians he spoke as follows: "I, O men of Thessaly, as you see, am hastening my march to Thrace with the utmost expedition, and am using all possible diligence, having been sent on certain business with these forces from the army. Mardonius himself and his army may be expected following close on my heels. Entertain him also, and do him all the good offices you can; for you will never have cause to repent of doing so." Having said this, he marched his army with all speed through Thessaly and Macedonia direct toward Thrace, making all the haste he could, and cutting across by the inland road. At last he reached Byzantium, having left many of his men behind, partly cut off by the Thracians on the march, and partly having to contend with hunger and fatigue. From Byzan-

tium he crossed over in boats. Thus, then, he returned to Asia.

90. On the same day on which the defeat at Platæa occurred, another happened to take place in Mycale in Ionia; for while the Greeks[1] were stationed at Delos, those who had gone there on shipboard with Leotychides the Lacedæmonian, there came to them as embassadors from Samos, Lampon, son of Thrasycleus, Athenagoras, son of Archestratides, and Hegesistratus, son of Aristagoras, being sent by the Samians, unknown to the Persians and the tyrant Theomestor, son of Androdamas, whom the Persians had made tyrant of Samos. When they came to the generals, Hegesistratus used many and various arguments, and that, "if only the Ionians should see them, they would revolt from the Persians, and that the barbarians would not withstand them; or if they should withstand them, the Greeks would not find any other such booty." Invoking, too, their common gods, he besought them to deliver Grecian men from servitude, and to repel the barbarian; and he said "that this would be easy for them to do, for that their ships sailed badly, and were not fit to fight with them; and, if they suspected at all that they were leading them on deceitfully, they were themselves ready to go on board their ships as hostages." 91. As the Samian stranger was earnest in his entreaties, Leotychides, either wishing to hear for the sake of the presage, or by chance, the deity so directing it, asked, "O Samian friend, what is your name?" He answered, "Hegesistratus;" upon which he, interrupting the rest of his discourse, if Hegesistratus intended to add more, said, "I accept[2] the Hegesistratus, my Samian friend; only do you take care that before you sail away, both you yourself and those who are with you pledge your faith that the Samians will be zealous allies to us." 92. He at the same time said this, and added the deed; for the Samians immediately pledged their faith and made oath of confederacy with the Greeks; and having done this, the others sailed home, but he ordered Hegesistratus to sail with the fleet, regarding his name as an omen. The Greeks, therefore, having tarried that day, on the next sacrificed auspiciously, Deiphonus, son of Evenius, of Apollonia in the Ionian gulf, acting as diviner.

[1] See B. VIII. chap. 131, 132.

[2] Hegesistratus means "leader of an army."

93. The following incident befell his father, Evenius. There are in this Apollonia sheep sacred to the sun, which by day feed near the river that flows from Mount Lacmon through the Apollonian territory into the sea, near the port of Oricus; but by night, chosen men, the most eminent of the citizens for wealth and birth, keep watch over them, each for a year; for the Apollonians set a high value upon these sheep, in consequence of some oracle. They are folded in a cavern at a distance from the city. There, then, on a time, Evenius, being chosen, kept watch, and one night, when he had fallen asleep during his watch, wolves entered the cave and destroyed about sixty of the sheep. He, when he discovered what had happened, kept silence, and mentioned it to no one, purposing to buy others, and put them in their place. This occurrence, however, did not escape the notice of the Apollonians; but as soon as they discovered it, having brought him to trial, they gave sentence that, for having fallen asleep during his watch, he should be deprived of sight. When they had blinded Evenius, from that time forward neither did their sheep bring forth, nor did the land yield its usual fruit. An admonition was given them at Dodona and Delphi, when they inquired of the prophets the cause of the present calamities: they told them "that they had unjustly deprived Evenius, the keeper of the sacred sheep, of his sight; for that they themselves had sent the wolves, and would not cease avenging him until they should give such satisfaction for what they had done as he himself should choose, and think sufficient; and when they had done this, the gods themselves would give such a present to Evenius, that most men would pronounce him happy from possessing it." 94. This answer was delivered to them; and the Apollonians, having kept it secret, deputed some of their citizens to negotiate the matter; and they negotiated it for them in the following manner. When Evenius was seated on a bench, they went and sat down by him, and conversed on different subjects, till at length they began to commiserate his misfortune; and having in this way artfully led him on, they asked "what reparation he would choose, if the Apollonians were willing to give him satisfaction for what they had done." He, not having heard of the oracle, made his choice, saying, "If any one would give him the lands of certain citizens," naming those who he knew had the two best estates in Apol-

Ionia; "and besides these a house," which he knew was the handsomest in the city; "if put in possession of these," he said, "he would thenceforth forego his anger, and this reparation would content him." He accordingly spoke thus; and those who sat by him, immediately taking hold of his answer, said, "The Apollonians make you this reparation for the loss of your eyes, in obedience to an oracle they have received." He thereupon was very indignant, on hearing the whole truth, as having been deceived; but the Apollonians, having bought them from the owners, gave him what he chose; and immediately after this, he had the gift of divination implanted in him, so that he became celebrated.

95. Deiphonus, who was the son of this Evenius, the Corinthians having brought him, officiated as diviner to the army. Yet I have heard this also, that Deiphonus, having assumed the name of Evenius's son, let out his services for hire throughout Greece, though he was not really the son of Evenius. 96. When, therefore, the sacrifices were favorable to the Greeks, they got their ships under weigh from Delos for Samos; and when they were off Calami of the Ionian territory, having taken up their station there near the temple of Juno on that coast, they made ready for an engagement. But the Persians, being informed that they were sailing toward them, on their part also got the other ships under weigh for the continent, and permitted those of the Phœnicians to sail home; for, on consultation, they determined not to come to an engagement by sea, because they thought they were not equal. They therefore sailed away to the continent, that they might be under the protection of their land-forces that were at Mycale, which, by the order of Xerxes, had been left behind by the rest of the army, and guarded Ionia; their number was sixty thousand; Tigranes commanded them, who surpassed the Persians in beauty and stature. Under the protection of this army the commanders of the navy resolved, having fled, to draw their ships on shore, and to throw up a rampart, as a defense for the ships, and a place of refuge for themselves. 97. Having taken this resolution, they got under weigh; and having passed by the temple of the Eumenides in Mycale, they came to the Gæson and Scolopois, where is a temple of Eleusinian Ceres, which Philistus, son of Pasicles, built, who accompanied Neleus, son of Codrus, for the purpose of found-

ing Miletus: there they drew their ships on shore, and threw up a rampart of stone and wood, having cut down the fruit-trees, and around the rampart they drove in sharp stakes. They made preparations to sustain a siege and to gain a victory, both one and the other, for they made their preparations deliberately.

98. The Greeks, when they learned that the barbarians had gone to the continent, were vexed that they had escaped, and were in doubt what to do, whether they should return home, or sail to the Hellespont; at length they determined to do neither of these, but to sail to the continent; having, therefore, prepared for a sea-fight both boarding-ladders, and all other things that were necessary, they sailed to Mycale. When they were near the camp, and no one was seen ready to meet them, but they beheld the ships drawn up within the fortification, and a numerous land-force disposed along the beach, thereupon Leotychides, advancing first in a ship, and nearing the beach as much as possible, made proclamation by a herald to the Ionians, saying "Men of Ionia, as many of you as hear me, attend to what I say, for the Persians will understand nothing of the advice I give you. When we engage, it behooves every one first of all to remember Liberty; and next the watch-word, Hebe; and let him who does not hear this, learn it from those who do hear." The meaning of this proceeding was the same as that of Themistocles at Artemisium; for either these words, being concealed from the barbarians, would induce the Ionians to revolt, or if they should be reported to the barbarians, would make them distrustful of the Greeks. 99. Leotychides, having made this suggestion, the Grecians in the next place did as follows: putting their ships to shore, they landed on the beach, and drew up in order of battle. But the Persians, when they saw the Greeks preparing themselves for action, and *knew* that they had admonished the Ionians, in the first place suspecting that the Samians favored the Greeks, took away their arms; for when the Athenian captives, whom, being left in Attica, the forces of Xerxes had taken, arrived in the ships of the barbarians, having ransomed them all, they sent them back to Athens, furnishing them with provisions for the voyage: on this account they were under no slight suspicion, having redeemed five hundred of the enemies of Xerxes. In the next place,

the passes that lead to the heights of Mycale they appointed the Milesians to guard, because forsooth they were best acquainted with the country, but they did it for this purpose, that they might be at a distance from the army. Those of the Ionians, then, who they suspected might attempt something new if they had the power, the Persians took such precautions against; and they themselves brought their bucklers together, to serve as a rampart.

100. When, therefore, the Greeks were prepared, they advanced toward the barbarians; and as they were marching, a rumor flew through the whole army, and a herald's staff was seen lying on the beach: the rumor that spread among them was this, that the Greeks had fought and conquered the army of Mardonius in Bœotia. Thus the interposition of heaven is manifest by many plain signs; since on this same day on which the defeat at Platæa took place, and when that at Mycale was just about to happen, a rumor reached the Greeks in this latter place, so that the army was inspired with much greater courage, and was more eager to meet danger. 101. There was also this other coincidence, namely, that there was a temple of Eleusinian Ceres near both the engagements; for at Platæa, as I have already said, the battle took place near the temple of Ceres; and at Mycale it was about to happen in like manner. The rumor that a victory had been obtained by the Greeks under Pausanias turned out to be correct; for the battle of Platæa was fought while it was yet early in the day, and that of Mycale toward evening; and that both happened on the same day of the same month, not long afterward became manifest on inquiry. Before the rumor reached them, great alarm prevailed among them, not so much for themselves as for the Greeks, lest Greece should stumble in the contest with Mardonius. When, however, this report flew among them, they advanced with greater readiness and alacrity. Accordingly, the Greeks and the barbarians hastened to the battle, as both the islands and the Hellespont were held out as the reward of victory.

102. The Athenians, and those who were drawn up next them, forming about half the army, had to advance along the shore over level ground; but the Lacedæmonians, and those drawn up near them, along a ravine and some hills: so that while the Lacedæmonians were making a circuit, those in the

other wing were already engaged. Now, so long as the bucklers of the Persians remained standing, they defended themselves strenuously, and had not the worst of the battle; but when the Athenians and those next them, having mutually encouraged one another, in order that the victory might belong to them, and not the Lacedæmonians, applied with more vigor to the battle, then the face of affairs immediately changed; for, having broke through the bucklers, they fell in a body on the Persians; and they having sustained their attack and defended themselves for a considerable time, at last fled to the fortification. The Athenians, Corinthians, Sicyonians, and Trœzenians, for thus they were drawn up in order, following close upon them, rushed into the fortification at the same time. When, therefore, the fortification was taken, the barbarians no longer thought of resisting, but all except the Persians betook themselves to flight; they, in small detachments, fought with the Greeks who were continually rushing within the fortification; and of the Persian generals, two made their escape, and two died. Artayntes and Ithramitres, commanders of the naval forces, escaped; but Mardontes and Tigranes, general of the land army, died fighting. 103. While the Persians were still fighting, the Lacedæmonians and those with them came up and assisted in accomplishing the rest. Of the Greeks themselves many fell on this occasion, both others, and especially the Sicyonians, and their general Perilaus. The Samians, who were in the camp of the Medes, and had been deprived of their arms, as soon as they saw the battle turning, did all they could, wishing to help the Greeks; and the rest of the Ionians, seeing the Samians lead the way, thereupon revolted from the Persians and attacked the barbarians. 104. The Milesians had been appointed to guard the passes for the Persians, in order for their safety, to the end that, if that should befall them which did befall them, they might, having guides, get safe to the heights of Mycale. The Milesians accordingly had been appointed to this service for this reason, and in order that, by being present in the army, they might not form any new design. They, however, did every thing contrary to what was ordered, both guiding them in their flight by other ways which led to the enemy, and at last themselves became most hostile in slaying them. Thus Ionia revolted a second time[3] from the Persians. 105. In this battle, of the Greeks the Athenians most distinguished themselves; and of the Athenians, Hermolycus, son of Euthynus, who had practiced in the pancratium. It befell this Hermolycus after these events, when there was war between the Athenians and the Carystians, to die fighting at Cyrnus of the Carystian territory, and to be buried at Geræstus. After the Athenians, the Corinthians, Trœzenians, and Sicyonians distinguished themselves. 106. When the Grecians had killed most of the barbarians, some fighting and others flying, they burned the ships and the whole fortification, having first brought out all the booty on the beach; and they found several chests of money; and having burned the fortification and the ships, they sailed away. The Greeks, having arrived at Samos, consulted about transplanting the Ionians, and in what part of Greece, of which they themselves were masters, it would be best to settle them, *intending* to leave Ionia to the barbarians; for it was clearly impossible for them to protect and guard the Ionians forever, and if they did not protect them, they had no hope that the Ionians would escape unpunished by the Persians. Upon this it seemed expedient to the men of rank among the Peloponnesians to remove the marts of the Grecian nations that had sided with the Medes, and give their territory to the Ionians to inhabit; but it did not appear at all expedient to the Athenians that the Ionians should be removed, or that the Peloponnesians should give advice respecting their colonies. However, as they opposed, the Peloponnesians readily gave way; and accordingly they took into the alliance the Samians, Chians, Lesbians, and other islanders, who were then serving with the Greeks, binding them by pledges and oaths that they would remain firm and not revolt. When they had bound them by oaths, they set sail to destroy the bridges, for they expected to find them still stretched across; accordingly, they sailed to the Hellespont.

107. The barbarians who fled, and were shut up in the heights of Mycale, not many in number, got safe to Sardis. But as they were marching, on their way, Masistes, son of Darius, having been present at the defeat, uttered many hard words to the general Artayntes; saying, among other things,

[3] The Ionians were first subjugated by Harpagus (i. 164, &c.), afterward revolted (v. 28), and were again reduced (vi. 32).

that he was more cowardly than a woman for having commanded the army in such a manner, and that he deserved the most extreme punishment for having brought mischief on the king's house. Now, among the Persians, to be called more cowardly than a woman is the greatest affront; he, therefore, when he heard a good deal, being exceedingly indignant, drew his cimeter upon Masistes; but Xenagoras, son of Praxilaus, a Halicarnassian, who stood behind Artayntes, perceiving him rushing forward, seized him round the middle, and having lifted him up, threw him on the ground; and in the mean while the guards of Masistes came to his assistance. Xenagoras did this, thereby laying an obligation both on Masistes himself and on Xerxes, by saving his brother; and for this action Xenagoras received the government of all Cilicia as the gift of the king. While they were marching on the road, nothing more than this occurred, but they arrived at Sardis. At Sardis the king happened to be from the time when he fled thither from Athens, after his failure in the sea-fight.

108. While he was at Sardis he fell in love with the wife of Masistes, who was also there; but when she could not be moved by sending to solicit her, and he did not offer violence, out of regard for his brother Masistes (and this same circumstance restrained the woman, for she well knew that she would not meet with violence); thereupon Xerxes, being shut out from any other resource, brought about the marriage of his son Darius with the daughter of this woman and Masistes, thinking that he should get possession of her if he did thus. Having, therefore, concluded the marriage and performed the usual ceremonies, he departed for Susa. When he arrived there, he introduced the wife of Darius into his own house; and then his passion for the wife of Masistes ceased; and having changed his inclinations, he fell in love, and succeeded, with the wife of Darius, the daughter of Masistes: the name of this woman was Artaynte. 109. In course of time the matter was discovered in the following manner. Amestris, the wife of Xerxes, having woven a large, various-colored, and beautiful mantle, presented it to Xerxes, and he, being delighted, put it on, and went to Artaynte. Being pleased also with her, he bid her ask whatever she pleased as a reward for the favors she had granted him, for that she should have whatever she

asked. Thereupon, for it was fated that misfortune should befall the whole family by her means, she said to Xerxes, "Will you give me whatever I shall ask of you?" He, imagining she would ask for any thing rather than what she did, promised and swore; and she, when he had sworn, boldly asked for the mantle. Xerxes used every expedient, not wishing to give it; for no other reason than that he was afraid of Amestris, lest, having before suspected what was going on, he should thus be detected; he therefore offered her cities, and a vast quantity of gold, and an army, which no one but herself should command; but an army is a common Persian gift. However, as he could not persuade her, he gave her the mantle; and she, being overjoyed with the present, wore it, and prided herself in it; and Amestris was informed that she had it. 110. Having learned what had been done, she was not angry with the woman herself; but believing that her mother was the cause, and that she had done this, she planned the destruction of the wife of Masistes. Having, therefore, watched the time when her husband Xerxes should give the royal feast (this feast is prepared once a year, on the day on which the king was born; and the name of this feast is, in the Persian language, "tycta," and in the Grecian language, "perfect;" and then only the king washes his head with soap, and makes presents to the Persians), Amestris then, having watched that day, asked Xerxes to give her the wife of Masistes. He considered it a dreadful and cruel thing first of all to give up the wife of his brother, and next, one who was innocent of what had taken place; for he understood why she made this request. 111. At last, however, as she persisted, and being constrained by custom, for it is not allowed for any petitioner to be denied when the royal feast is spread, he therefore very reluctantly granted her request; and having delivered the woman to her, he did as follows. He bade her do what she pleased, and then, having sent for his brother, spoke thus: "Masistes, you are the son of Darius, and my brother, and, moreover, you are also a brave man. Cohabit, then, no longer with the wife you now have; and instead of her I will give you my own daughter. Cohabit with her; but the wife whom you now have, as it does not seem well to me, no longer retain." Masistes, astonished at what was said, answered, "Sire, what mischievous language do you hold to me, bidding me *put away* a wife, by whom I have three young sons, and daughters, of whom you have married one to your own son, and this wife too is very much to my mind; you bid me put away her and marry your own daughter? I, however, O king, though I deem it a great honor to be thought worthy of your daughter, will do neither of these things, and do not you use force in your desire to accomplish this end. Some other man, not inferior to me, will be found for your daughter, but let me cohabit with my own wife." Such was the answer he gave; but Xerxes in a rage replied, "Masistes, you have thus done for yourself; for neither will I give you my daughter in marriage, nor shall you any longer cohabit with your present one, that so you may learn to accept what is offered." He, when he heard this, withdrew, having said this much: "Sire, you have not yet taken away my life." 112. In the intermediate time, while Xerxes was in conference with his brother, Amestris, having sent for the body-guards of Xerxes, mutilated the wife of Masistes: having cut off her breasts, she threw them to the dogs, and also her nose, ears, and lips, and then, having cut out her tongue, she sent her home thus mutilated. 113. Masistes, who had not yet heard any thing of this, but suspecting some evil had befallen him, rushed home in great haste, and seeing his wife utterly destroyed, he thereupon consulted with his sons, and set out with them and some others for Bactria, designing to induce the Bactrian district to revolt, and to do the king all the mischief he could, which, in my opinion, would have happened, if he had been beforehand in going up to the Bactrians and Sacæ, for they were attached to him, and he was governor of the Bactrians; but Xerxes, being informed of his intentions, sent an army after him, and slew him and his sons and his forces upon the way. Such were the circumstances respecting the amour of Xerxes and the death of Masistes.

114. The Greeks having set out from Mycale toward the Hellespont, being overtaken by a storm, anchored near Lectis, and from thence they went to Abydos, and found the bridges broken in pieces, which they expected to find stretched across, and for this reason chiefly they came to the Hellespont. Upon this the Peloponnesians with Leotychides determined to sail back to Greece, but the Athenians and their

commander Xanthippus *resolved* to stay there and make an attempt on the Chersonesus. The former, therefore, sailed away, but the Athenians, having crossed over from Abydos to Chersonesus, besieged Sestos. 115. To this Sestos, as being the strongest fortress in these parts, when they heard that the Greeks were arrived in the Hellespont, there came together men from other neighboring places, and among others Œobazus, a Persian from Cardia, who had had all the materials of the bridges conveyed thither. Native Æolians occupied it, and there were with them Persians, and a great body of other allies. 116. Xerxes's viceroy Artayctes ruled over this district, a Persian wicked and impious, who had even deceived the king on his march to Athens by secretly taking away from Elæus the treasures of Protesilaus, son of Iphiclus; for in Elæus of the Chersonesus is a sepulchre of Protesilaus and a precinct around it, where were great treasures, both gold and silver vessels, and brass, and robes, and other offerings, which Artayctes plundered by permission of the king. By speaking as follows he deceived Xerxes: "Sire, there is here the habitation of a certain Grecian, who, having carried arms in your territories, met with a just punishment and perished. Give me this man's house, that every one may learn not to carry arms against your territory." By saying this he would easily persuade Xerxes to give him the man's house, as he had no suspicion of his intentions. He said that Protesilaus had carried arms against the king's territory, thinking thus: the Persians consider that all Asia belongs to them and the reigning monarch. When, however, the treasures were granted, he carried them away from Elæus to Sestos, and sowed part of the precinct and pastured it, and whenever he went to Elæus, he used to lie with women in the sanctuary. At this time he was besieged by the Athenians, neither being prepared for a siege nor expecting the Greeks, so that they fell upon him somewhat unawares. 117. But when autumn came on, as they were engaged in the siege, and the Athenians were impatient at being absent from their own country, and not able to take the fortification, they besought their leaders to take them back; they, however, refused, until either they should take the place, or the people of Athens should recall them; accordingly, they acquiesced in the present state of things.

118. In the mean while, those who were within the fortification were reduced to the last extremity, so that they boiled and ate the cords of their beds; and when they had these no longer, then the Persians, and Artayctes, and Œobazus made their escape by night, descending by the back of the fortification, where it was most deserted by the enemy. When it was day, the Chersonesians from the towers made known to the Athenians what had happened, and opened the gates; and the greater part of them went in pursuit, but some took possession of the city. 119. As Œobazus was fleeing into Thrace, the Aspinthian Thracians seized him, and sacrificed him to Plistorus, a god of the country, according to their custom; but those who were with him they slaughtered in another manner. Those with Artayctes, who had taken to flight the last, when they were overtaken a little above Ægos-Potami, having defended themselves for a considerable time, some were killed, and others taken alive, and the Greeks, having put them in bonds, conveyed them to Sestos; and with them *they took* Artayctes bound, himself and his son. 120. It is related by the Chersonitæ that the following prodigy occurred to one of the guards as he was broiling salt fish; the salt fish lying on the fire leaped and quivered like fish just caught; and the persons who stood around were amazed; but Artayctes, when he saw the prodigy, having called the man who was broiling the salt fish, said, "Athenian friend, be not afraid of this prodigy, for it has not appeared to you; but Protesilaus, who is in Elæus, intimates to me, that, though dead and salted, he has power from the gods to avenge himself on the person that has injured him. Now, therefore, I wish to make him reparation, and instead of the riches which I took out of his temple, to repay one hundred talents to the god; and for myself and my children, I will pay one hundred talents to the Athenians if I survive." By offering this, he did not persuade the general, Xanthippus; for the Elæans, wishing to avenge Protesilaus, begged that he might be put to death, and the mind of the general himself inclined that way. Having, therefore, conducted him to that part of the shore where Xerxes bridged over the pass, or, as others say, to a hill above the city of Madytus, they nailed him to a plank and hoisted him aloft, and his son they stoned before the eyes of Artayctes. 121. Having done these things, they sailed back to Greece, taking

with them other treasures and the materials of the bridges, in order to dedicate them in the temples; and during this year nothing more was done.

122. Artembares, the grandfather of this Artayctes who was hoisted aloft, was the person who originated a remark which the Persians adopted and conveyed to Cyrus, in these terms: "Since Jupiter has given the sovereign power to the Persians, and among men to you, O Cyrus, by overthrowing Astyages; as we possess a small territory, and that rugged, come, let us remove from this, and take possession of another, better. There are many near our confines, and many at a distance. By possessing one of these, we shall be more admired by most men; and it is right that those who bear rule should do so; and when shall we have a better opportunity than when we have the command of many nations, and of all Asia?" Cyrus having heard these words, and not admiring the proposal, bade them do so; but when he bade them, he warned them to prepare henceforward not to rule, but to be ruled over; for that delicate men spring from delicate countries, for that it is not given to the same land to produce excellent fruits and men valiant in war. So that the Persians, perceiving their error, withdrew and yielded to the opinion of Cyrus; and they chose rather to live in a barren country and to command, than to cultivate fertile plains and be the slaves of others.

INDEX.

THE END.

CPSIA information can be obtained
at www.ICGtesting.com
Printed in the USA
LVHW100557210323
742065LV00002B/82

9 783382 127671